IMPECCABLE CREDENTIALS

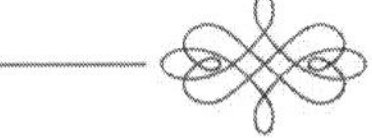

By

Patricia E. Walker

ISBN-13: 978-1546744993
ISBN-10: 1546744991

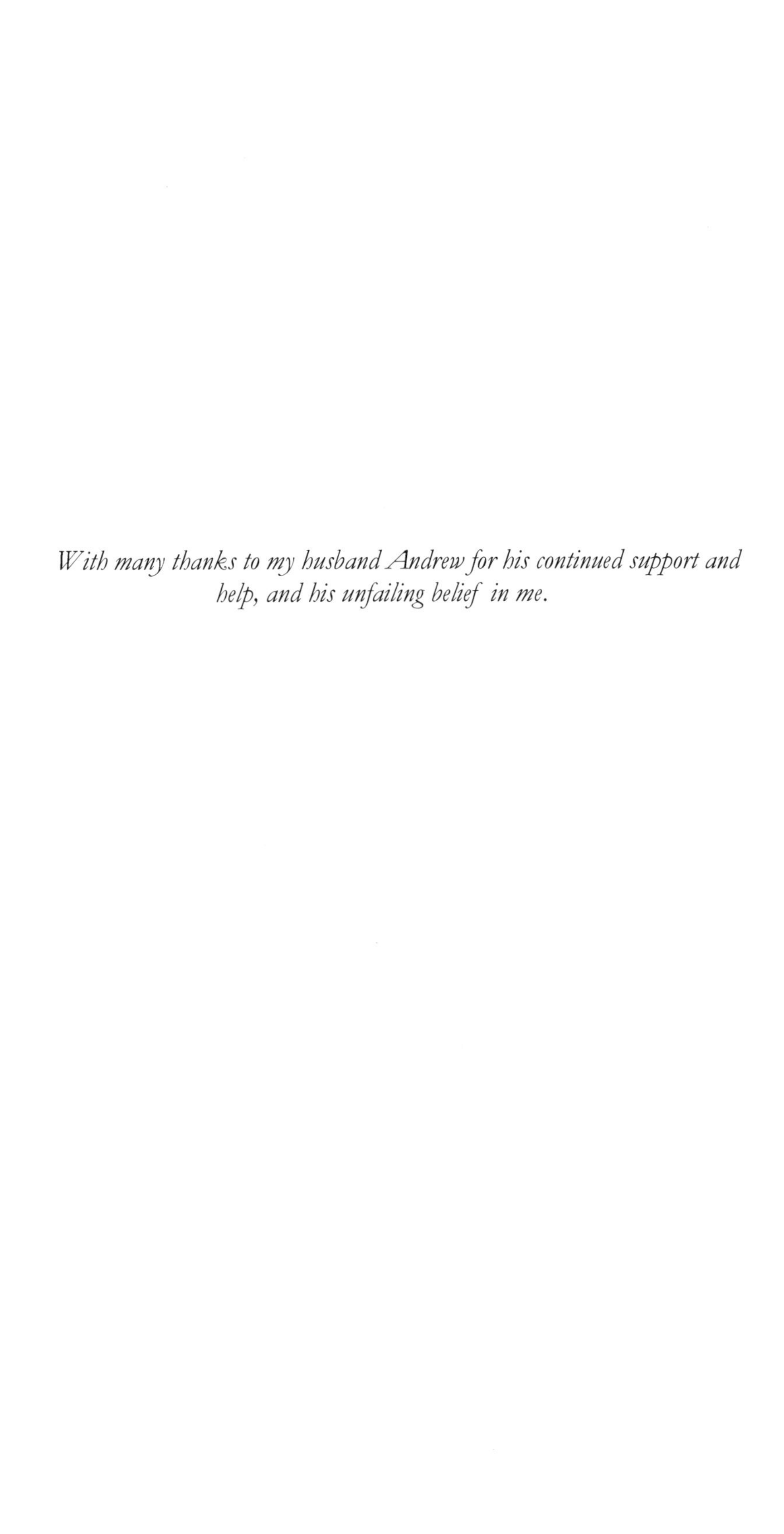

With many thanks to my husband Andrew for his continued support and help, and his unfailing belief in me.

CONTENTS

This is a work of fiction. Names, characters, businesses, organizations, places, events and incidents either are the product of the author's imagination or are used fictitiously. Any resemblance to actual persons, living or dead, events, or locales is entirely coincidental.

Chapter One

February, 1899

Apart from a few days spent with his half-sister and her family in London on his arrival in England, since disembarking at Southampton two months previously on the RMS *Marie Louise* from New York, Anthony Ambrose Mortimer Mawdsley-Dart had been established in the family home, Childon Manor in Kent, having taken up the title of seventh Viscount Childon on the death of his maternal grandfather in October. His half-sister, Beatrice, with whom he had always enjoyed a close relationship despite the thousands of miles which often separated them, had written to him begging him to come to London and stay with them for several weeks, if not longer, declaring that the few days he had spent in Mount Street upon setting foot in England had been far from long enough, adding that Childon Manor must be as inhospitable as the moon with all the workmen busily employed renovating the place. He had needed no further prompting and instantly packed his bags and caught the first available train to London, arriving in Mount Street to a riotous welcome from his niece and nephews.

His mother, who had died three years earlier in New York aged fifty-six from appendicitis, had been the Honourable Letitia Mawdsley, only child of Anthony Mortimer David Mawdsley, sixth Viscount Childon, whose first marriage to Vernon Maxwell Philip Carr, seventh Viscount Vilcary, had produced one daughter, Beatrice, but due to her husband contracting pneumonia barely two years into the marriage, his death had left her a very young and distraught widow. It had not been an arranged marriage but a love match, and therefore upon his death she had felt unable to bear the emptiness of their house in Brook Street with its happy, if all too brief, memories, so, taking her daughter into Kent, she had taken up residence with her parents, remaining quietly there for almost six years, becoming almost reclusive in her grief and going no further than Tunbridge Wells or Canterbury.

Attending the funeral of a lifelong friend who had died in childbirth had been what had taken her back to London after so long away, and had also brought about that meeting with her future second husband, the forty-five year old bachelor American press magnate from New York, Ambrose Wilson Washington Dart, a man who had not only brought her back to life, but had fallen in love with her the moment he had first set eyes on her. Having travelled to London to transact business in company with his lawyer, they had, on the advice of a friend, put up at The Clarendon where that quiet American's eye had spotted the twenty-seven year old Viscountess Vilcary, who also had rooms there. It was inevitable they would meet, and after several brief encounters in the foyer, accompanied with a polite 'Good morning,' or, 'Terrible weather, isn't it?' he had invited her to join him for dinner and she had accepted, admitting years later to her son that she had no idea why she had done so, but for whatever reason she knew she liked him and felt comfortable with him; that was all it had taken, and before she realised it had fallen deeply in love with him; their marriage followed within months.

They had wanted to take Beatrice to America with them but her health, which had caused concern since babyhood, had been regarded by their doctor as most unwise, deeming it better to leave her in Kent with her grandparents until she was older. It had been a tearful and painful farewell but the birth of their son, Anthony Ambrose Mortimer Mawdsley-Dart within twelve months of their marriage in New York, had rendered her separation from Beatrice less distressing. Regular visits back and forth across the Atlantic together with exchanging letters and photographs, had lessened the pain but Beatrice, who, at ten years of age, having outgrown the various ailments which had frequently attacked her, had finally accompanied her mother to New York. Sadly, she had never really settled down in America even though she had grown to love her step-brother and step-father and they her, Ambrose treating her as though she was in fact his own daughter, but she had missed the life she had known in England as well as her grandparents and, at the age of thirteen, she had sailed back home. But she had never forgotten her half-brother, whom she loved very much, sending him presents and, when he was older, letters, to which he had happily responded.

Between the penthouse apartment in New York and the cattle ranch in Montana, Anthony had enjoyed his young life in America. His father may have spared no expense in the private tuition he had arranged for his son, but he had not kept him tied to his own or his mother's apron strings any more than he had shielded him from the harsh realities of life. Anthony was by nature quick and eager to learn, with an industrious and diligent turn of mind, and, at a very early age, had shown a genuine interest in the newspaper business, wanting to learn all he could. He had therefore needed no persuading by his father to understand all about running a newspaper, perfectly happy and contented to act as runner, and when, which was all too often the case, he could not be found, his parents, having looked for him all over, would more often than not find him working with the typesetters as they set their compositors ready for printing, or, which was by no means unusual, had gone out with a reporter armed with a notepad and pencil.

Having inherited his love of the outdoors and all its activities from his father, Anthony had also enjoyed the time he had spent at The Straight Dart ranch in Montana, his energy and aptitude to learn new things finding a natural outlet in that wild and beautiful country. His father's friend, Malpasso Smith, a man whose past was as varied as his loyalty to Ambrose Dart was absolute, had, in between regaling Anthony with exciting stories of the wild west, taught him how to lasso and rope cattle for branding and, on one occasion, had even allowed him to join him on a cattle drive. But his father, who had no doubt as to his son's competency or his abilities to administer either The Straight Dart ranch or the newspaper empire he would eventually inherit, was nevertheless very conscious of the fact that one day he would succeed to his maternal grandfather's title, there being no other male heir, and had therefore sent him to England when he was thirteen to be educated at Harrow and Cambridge, in true Mawdsley tradition.

For the duration of his time at these establishments of learning he had spent the holidays in Kent with his grandparents and half-sister, except during the long vacation when he had sailed to New York to be with his parents. Over the years, he had gradually lost his American accent, only a faint trace still discernible at certain times, but no amount of instruction from his tutors had managed to prevent him from pronouncing certain words in a typically American way or using words and phrases no one this side of the Atlantic had ever heard before. He was proud of his half American roots; imbuing him with the pioneer spirit which had seen that vast continent crossed and inhabited through hard work and a sheer determination not to be beaten by nature or man, instilling in him the belief that nothing was impossible as well as an openness to change and embracing new ideas. But the blood of his English lineage dating back centuries also ran strongly through his veins; his respect for tradition and all that his ancestry stood for as inherent as they were ingrained, and since neither of these widely differing cultures could be separated any more than he could denounce either one of them, they had contentedly co-existed, forging his personality.

Since leaving Cambridge at the age of twenty-three six years ago, he had experienced the grief of losing his maternal grandmother, his paternal grandparents having died long before he was born, quickly followed by the anxiety of his father's first heart attack, which had seen him unhesitatingly taking the reins in his own capable hands. His father's second heart attack four years ago, and the loss of his beloved mother one year later had been extremely painful, then, more recently, his father's death following a third and fatal heart attack and a few short months after, the death of his maternal grandfather. All of this had meant crisscrossing the Atlantic as well as the vast interior of America to Montana, the place his father had really called home, and where he had eventually been buried alongside the woman who had captured his heart in London nearly thirty years ago.

Had it not have been for a late pregnancy which had ended in a miscarriage, his sister would certainly have set sail for America to attend her mother's funeral, but Beatrice was able, some months later, to book a passage to New York to spend a little time with the man who had been as unstinting in his love to his step-daughter as he had to his son. The news of Ambrose Dart's death, reaching her by cable from Anthony several months after her return home, had saddened and distressed her, her grief intensified as she was unable to attend his burial service due to her daughter succumbing to a most severe attack of influenza and bronchitis, and as her brother had been unable to attend their grandfather's obsequies in Kent, they had not seen one another for over twelve months.

Affairs had naturally kept Anthony in America, resulting in over three months' delay in coming to England to deal with his new responsibilities as Viscount Childon, only to discover, much to his surprise, that his maternal grandfather's estates had not been in such good order of late as he had thought, requiring a great deal of work and financial outlay to set things to rights, and although he begrudged neither it had meant leaving his American business affairs in the hands of others during his absence.

He knew it was neither practical nor convenient to juggle both his inheritances in the air at the same time, but even though he was a man who thought and acted decisively he was not one to make important decisions rashly, and so he was perfectly content to keep things as they were for the time being, or, at least, until he had time to consider matters more deeply. For now, he was fairly settled in England for the foreseeable future, and since the exterior of Childon Manor was presently under scaffolding and the interior virtually uninhabitable, he was quite happy to stay in Mount Street, a circumstance which not only pleased his sister, but his brother-in-law as well.

Of no more than medium height with a slightly thickening waistline and pale blue eyes which looked tolerantly upon the world from out of a cheerfully round face, Sir Thomas Shipton looked every inch the good-natured and placid man he was, but like his brother-in-law he was shrewd and perceptive, whose business acumen had turned his father's moderately profitable banking business into one of the most prosperous and successful in the City, earning for himself a reputation for being honest and entirely trustworthy. Having, over the years, met no one for whom he felt in the least degree inclined to marry, he had come to believe, like his family and friends, that he would remain a bachelor all his days, a circumstance he had by no means contemplated with dismay, but then, when he had least expected it, he had met the Honourable Beatrice Carr, a lady no less than twelve years his junior. If no one questioned his integrity in business they certainly questioned his wisdom in marrying a lady so much younger than himself, but having taken one look at the beautiful creature whose eyes had met his across that crowded ballroom, he could no more have stopped himself from falling in love with her than he could prevent night following day, and since the lady clearly reciprocated his feelings he had asked her to marry him without a moment's hesitation or regret. If there were those who had prophesied disaster at such a marriage, not because the lady was ineligible or because any scandal attached to her, but that such an age gap, as so many before, could not possibly prosper, then they were doomed to disappointment. At forty-eight years of age, entering his eleventh year of marriage and the father of two sons and a mischievous imp of a daughter, Sir Thomas Shipton was still very much in love with his wife, and if he had any regrets at all it was simply that he had not met Beatrice sooner, and what made it even more wonderful was that she felt precisely the same. He knew his feelings for her would never change, in fact, he was more in love with her than ever, so much so that he was more than ready to indulge her, but this evening, much to her disappointment, he considerably preferred to attend a political dinner at The Mansion House instead of accompanying his wife to the opera, not that he could not have made his excuses had he wanted to, and was not at all surprised when she cajoled her brother into escorting her.

Like his brother-in-law, Anthony, except for musical works by his favourite composers, was not really an opera enthusiast, but since he had not seen much of Beatrice over the last twelve months or so, he was perfectly happy to keep her company. His sister, who loved him dearly, looked affectionately at him now as he checked his white bow tie in the drawing-room mirror, at a loss to understand why he had not yet found himself a wife. Apart from them both having inherited the Mawdsley nose, which was slightly aquiline, his being more prominent than his sister's, they were not alike. He was tall and loose-limbed with broad shoulders, his skin burned brown from constant exposure to the elements, unlike Beatrice, who took after their mother in being slim and quite petite with a fair complexion, but where she had her mother's thick blonde hair his was jet black like his father's, brushed back off a broad forehead with dark grey eyes which held a great deal of humour as well as forbearance, perfectly concealing his shrewd business mind. He had an even temper and a keen sense of humour and was capable of seeing another point of view other than his own, but his generous mouth, like his square chin with the deep cleft, both clean-shaven, held a determination which told the onlooker that he was perfectly capable of making up his own mind and, once he had, nothing would change it. He was as comfortable wearing white tie and tails as he was smart daytime wear or the workmanlike jeans and check shirt he wore whenever he stayed at the ranch in Montana, and Beatrice, looking at him now, would have been hard put to say which suited him the most. He could not be called handsome precisely, which she was the first to acknowledge, nevertheless, there was something very attractive about him, which made his bachelorhood hard to fathom.

"You know, Tony," Beatrice shook her head, her blue eyes widening, "I can't for the life of me understand why you are not married!"

"Can't you, Bea?" he asked, turning to face her, raising an amused eyebrow.

"No," she shook her head, "I can't," totally ignoring her husband's advice not to plague him. "You have money and a title and not at all bad looking. I really I don't understand it!"

"Why, *thank you* Bea!" he said with exaggerated gratitude, his eyes alight with amusement.

"I'm serious Tony," she nodded.

"Yes, I can see you are," he said genially.

She sighed. "Surely there must have been someone for whom you felt *something*!"

"I never said there hadn't." He shook his head, his eyes brimful with laughter. "In fact," he told her irrepressibly, "there have been any number of women for whom I've *definitely* felt something."

"I daresay!" she said reprovingly, pursing her pretty lips. "But you know perfectly well what I mean!"

"Yes, Bea," he laughed, kissing her forehead, "I do."

"Well?" she urged hopefully.

"Well, what?" he asked innocently, picking up his white gloves.

"*Tony…!*"

"Bea," he said resignedly, "I know you most probably have any number of young women in your eye lined up and ready to parade in front of me, but I beg you won't. I am quite capable of finding myself a wife, and, also," he smiled, showing an excellent set of strong white teeth, "when I meet the woman I want to marry I shall know her instantly, without help from anyone. Shall we?" he suggested, thwarting any further attempts on her part to discuss it further, draping her fur-lined cape around her slim shoulders.

"Oh, very well." She smiled up at him, allowing him to pull her arm irresistibly through his before escorting her outside to the carriage, which, like the road and the pavements, was already white over with snow.

Considering the opera being performed at Covent Garden was supposed to be one of her favourites, or so she had told her brother when she had persuaded him to escort her this evening, she had not, as he had thought, devoted her full attention to the performance, but had spent the whole of the first act glancing periodically across at one of the boxes on the opposite side of the auditorium within her direct line of vision. The latecomers had not taken their seats until ten minutes after the curtain had gone up and although their occupancy had been quite unobtrusive, causing not the least disturbance to anyone around them, it had nevertheless caught her ladyship's attention, but once secured she could not refrain from continually viewing the box's inhabitants more closely through her opera glasses. The lights may be down, but there was enough illumination from the stage for her to see that the lady, who was sitting bolt upright in her seat staring blindly down at the stage, did not seem to be enjoying the performance in the least, in fact, she looked decidedly unhappy, and unless Beatrice was very much mistaken she had a pretty shrewd idea why.

When the lights eventually went up and the curtain fell on the first act, which, for some inexplicable reason, seemed longer than she remembered, Beatrice again raised her glasses to her eyes to glance once more across at the box, a circumstance which made her brother lean towards her saying, in an amusing under voice, "You know Bea, to say you were mad on coming here tonight and coerced me into escorting you because of it, I swear you've paid more attention to that box over there than the performance!" nodding his head in that direction. "What's the attraction?"

"That poor child!" she sighed.

Taking the glasses from her, he looked across at the box which had occupied his sister's attention to see for himself what had held her interest. He found himself looking at a young woman of no more than twenty years of age dressed in the very height of fashion, with her dark blonde hair simply but elegantly arranged, forming a perfect frame for her exquisitely beautiful but rather pale face. She had a narrow forehead and a straight little nose beneath which was the most kissable mouth he had ever seen and, from this distance, he would say her eyes were of a deep blue, large and expressive, perhaps a little too large, for which he accurately deduced their distinctly sombre look to be responsible. He gained the impression that under different circumstances or, perhaps, in different company, her elfin face could become quite animated, but apart from his natural curiosity to know what had brought about such an air of despondency, somewhere deep inside him he instinctively knew that at long last he had found the woman for whom he had unconsciously been searching his whole life. Her companion, a man he judged to be in his mid-forties, was of no more than medium height, thick-set with a tendency to corpulence and a pink fleshy face out of which bulged a pair of pale blue eyes. His sandy coloured hair was brushed back from a rather prominent forehead with thick bushy side whiskers that met into a moustache over his thick loose lips, which were now compressed into a thin uncompromising line.

"Who are they?" Tony enquired, handing the glasses back to his sister, wondering if perhaps she was his daughter.

"Sir Braden and Lady Collett," Beatrice replied unhappily. "She was, before her marriage," she informed him, "Eleanor Tatton. Her mother Amelia was some years older than me, but we were nevertheless very good friends until her death three years ago."

He stared at her in astonishment. "Are you seriously telling me that that lovely creature is his *wife*?" he demanded.

"I don't wonder you stare!" She nodded. "Oh, Tony!" she cried. "I feel so dreadfully sorry for that poor child! What on earth induced Tatton to permit such a despicable marriage, I can't imagine!"

Neither could Tony. "Tatton?" he repeated, his forehead creased in thought. "Never heard of him!" He shook his head. "At least, I can't remember hearing his name or running across him. Who is he?" he invited, casting another glance across the auditorium.

"Sir Miles Tatton," Beatrice explained, "is a most respectable man and comes from a very good family. He has a place in Suffolk, or somewhere that way," she shook her head, not at all sure on this point, "but for most of the time he lives in Bruton Street. He is now seldom to be seen in society and rarely receives visitors, although when Amelia was alive they entertained regularly. They had two children, a boy and a girl. Eleanor," indicating the young woman across the way with a nod of her head, "is five years younger than her brother, Reginald."

"Go on," Tony encouraged.

"Well, Amelia rather had hopes of marrying Eleanor to Frisby Sykes, you wouldn't know him," Beatrice shook her head, "his father is quite something in the City, but from one cause or another it never came off. I don't think Eleanor was too upset over it because from what she let fall to me," she confided, "quite innocently you understand, she was not at all keen on Frisby; not that he is not respectable, he is I promise you, in fact," she informed him, "I have always gained the impression that he is a little, well… what shall I say?" She shrugged. "A little too old for his years. In the end, he married Mary Pittaway, Giles Pittaway's youngest daughter. You wouldn't know him either," she shook her head, "but quite a rich man; acquired his wealth in rubber. As for Reginald," she told him, "he was always a little wild. I learned from Amelia that when he was at Eton he was always in some scrape or another and then, when he went up to Oxford, he fell in with a set his father most strongly disapproved of. Then, when he left there, Sir Miles, who has connections in the government, got him a post in the Home Office but, unfortunately, it didn't come to anything. It seemed he much preferred to spend his time pursuing other interests such as gaming and… well," she coughed delicately, twisting her bracelet around her wrist, "I think you know what I mean!"

"Yes, Bea," Tony smiled, "I think I know what you mean."

"Anyway," she sighed, "he cost his father a pretty penny; his gambling debts I understand were quite enormous. Tatton, or so rumour had it," she explained, "ended up being all to pieces."

"You mean broke!" he said straightforwardly.

"Yes," she nodded. "That is," she sighed, shaking her head, "until he married that poor child to that dreadful man."

Tony glanced across at the box then back at his sister. "He looks old enough to be her father!" he observed bluntly.

"Twenty-five years older if you want the truth!" Beatrice scorned. "That child only turned twenty less than six months ago."

"What do you know about him?" he asked, indicating Sir Braden Collett with a nod of his head.

"Well, we are not intimately acquainted with him, you understand. In fact, apart from his own close circle of friends he does not associate with many, except those members of his clubs with whom I believe he plays cards. He *does* have a temper," she conceded, "and certainly does nothing to make himself agreeable, indeed," she nodded, "he can be quite insufferable when he chooses, and has more than once upset people, but I know nothing to his detriment, I only wish I did," she said truthfully. "I admit he is nothing like his father, a most pleasant and charming man, and his mother was the most adorable and beautiful creature with the sweetest nature, but Braden, sadly, does not take after either. He is, of course, rich as well as bearing an old and respected name and a keen patron of the arts as well as contributing most generously to charitable causes." She cast a sidelong glance at her brother's suddenly stern profile. "I assure you Tony, he is received everywhere; no door is closed to him."

"But?" he pressed.

"There *is* no 'but'!" she said a little regretfully. "I only wish there were."

"But you don't like him, do you?" Tony said perceptively.

"No," Beatrice shook her head, her voice a little hollow, "I don't. Oh, I don't know why," she cried, dropping her hands helplessly onto her lap, "but I just don't! There is something about him, although what I don't know, that makes me rather uneasy."

"He clearly makes his wife uneasy," he remarked, taking another look at the opposite box through the glasses, the object of his scrutiny receiving a quiet word in her ear, "she looks far from happy. In fact," he said candidly, "I'd say she was afraid of him."

"Yes," Beatrice acknowledged, "I think so too."

Tony nodded. "So, tell me," he asked interestedly, "what happened to Reginald?"

"Well," she breathed conspiratorially, leaning her head a little towards him, "Sir Miles eventually packed him off to Ceylon."

"Ceylon?" he echoed.

"Yes," she confirmed. "Sir Miles's brother has a tea plantation there or something like that. That was, oh let me think," screwing up her face, "yes, that would be about thirteen or fourteen months ago."

"So, what you are saying," Tony summarised, "is that by packing his son off to try to instil some responsibility into his head and hoping he will learn economy and restraint, as well as marrying his daughter to that man Collett," indicating him with a nod of his head, "the Tatton coffers are now full to bursting?"

"Something like that, yes!" she confirmed.

Tony leaned back in his seat, crossing one long leg over the other, his eyes fixed on the box almost directly opposite their own. "Tell me," he smiled, "how well do you know Eleanor Collett?"

"Very well indeed. In fact," she told him, "until her marriage she was a regular visitor to Mount Street."

"And since her marriage?" he prompted.

"Unfortunately," Beatrice sighed, "I'm sad to say that I hardly ever see her; alone that is, unless I happen to run across her in Bond Street or somewhere like that, and then she is not really alone, her maid always seeming to be with her, although," she pointed out, a little perplexed, "this woman she has in tow now is not the one she had before she married. Mary, who always looked after her, was dismissed, but why I don't know. And that's *another* thing!" She nodded vigorously at her brother. "Who takes their maid with them when they go shopping? Why, it's unheard of nowadays!" She saw the frown crease his forehead but continued as though there had been no pause. "She has not accepted one invitation I have sent out to her," she told him, her voice reflecting her concern, "at least," she hastily corrected herself, "she *has* attended the odd evening gathering I have got together, but her husband is always with her when she does come, so I have no opportunity to speak privately with her, but she has never once accepted an invitation to partake of luncheon with me in Mount Street or to accompany me on a shopping expedition as she always used to. But that's not all, Tony," she confided, her lovely eyes clouding a little.

"Go on," he encouraged, his eyes straying towards that other box.

"Well, the thing is," she explained, "one will see her at the theatre or some such thing virtually every evening for about two weeks in a row, though not without *him*, of course," she disparaged, "and even, though only on the odd occasion, they open their doors in Cavendish Square, then no one sets eyes on her for about a week or more until she ventures out again for another week or so, then afterwards keeps to the house; and so it goes on. It's quite inexplicable. In fact," she nodded, "I am surprised to see her here this evening because this is the first time for nearly two weeks she has been seen in public."

Tony's eyes narrowed and his lips pursed but he said, quite evenly, "Cavendish Square! Why, as I recall that's only a few blocks away from Mount Street."

"You know, Tony," she smiled, "it is a good thing I am familiar with these American sayings and descriptions of yours, but yes," she nodded, "Cavendish Square is only the other side of Oxford Street; not too far away at all!"

"Have you called in Cavendish Square at all to try to speak to her?" Tony asked, his eyes still on that other box.

"Oh yes," Beatrice assured him, "many times, but on each occasion I am informed by Peterson, Collett's butler, who," she told him firmly, "looks more like a prizefighter than a respectable butler, that she is unwell and not receiving visitors or has gone out-of-town to stay with friends. Yes," she nodded, a thought just occurring to her, "and that's something else! Mitchell had been butler to Braden's father for many years, but certainly not old enough to be pensioned off or anything like that! It seems to me," she pointed out candidly, "that Collett has brought in all new staff, but why he should do so I cannot tell!"

"Does she ever visit her father at all?" Tony asked, glancing sideways at his sister.

"I don't know," she shook her head, "she could well do, but as I say I don't see her privately any more to speak to and, as I told you, Tatton is seldom to be seen in public, and if I go to Bruton Street and ask him it could be, well," she shrugged helplessly, "a little embarrassing."

"You know, Bea," Tony said quietly, "I've taken a dislike to our friend Sir Braden Collett!"

"Well, you are not the first," she declared, "nor, I expect, shall you be the last!"

Tony nodded. "Tell me, Bea," he asked conversationally, "could you, do you think, effect an introduction, say," he suggested, "during the next interval?"

She eyed him closely, wondering what was going through his mind. "Why?" she asked warily.

He shrugged a careless shoulder. "Oh, simply that I'd like to meet Sir Braden and Lady Collett." He saw the doubt on her face and grinned. "You know Bea, I thought you would want me to get to know my fellow nobles and peers and suchlike now that I am Viscount Childon!"

"No," she said slowly, shaking her head after considering a moment, "that's not the reason." She saw him raise an innocent eyebrow and suddenly recalled his remark earlier that evening, her eyes widening to their fullest extent as enlightenment dawned. "Do not tell me that she is…?"

"The second act, Bea." Tony smiled, placing a finger against his lips, as the lights began to dim and the curtain slowly rise. She threw him a warning look which told him she would like nothing more than to box his ears, to which he grinned, whispering, "The next interval, Bea." Since she knew him well enough to be certain that he would forge a meeting himself if she did not, she reluctantly nodded her head, not at all sure whether to be glad or sorry that the beginning of the second act had prevented her from pursuing it further, little realising that his attention, like her own in the first, would be solely taken up with the box on the other side of the auditorium.

Chapter Two

The aria which was being passionately sung by Georgio Carlucci and Lucia Camolitto, two matchless Italians whose names not only guaranteed opera houses all over the world would be packed to capacity but also a marked increase in the price of a ticket, held their audience spellbound as their voices reverberated around the auditorium with unparalleled superiority. From the uppermost seats down to the stalls not a jewel bedecked soul stirred, every eye fixed quite mesmerised on the stage; apart from two pairs, the one belonging to a young woman and the other to a gentleman, both sitting on opposite sides of the auditorium, total strangers to one another yet both completely oblivious to the sublime performance being played out on stage below them.

So lost in admiration was she that Beatrice failed to notice her brother pick up the opera glasses resting on top of the balustrade to their box and raise them to his eyes to grant him a closer look at the young woman in the one opposite, noting that although she was facing towards the stage her eyes were gazing far beyond the performers at nothing in particular. Encircling her right gloved wrist was a diamond bracelet with matching drops in her ears, and around her neck was a single row of perfectly cut diamonds and sapphires, which she unconsciously fingered with her left hand, her mind completely lost in thought. It was then that he saw her husband lean towards her and whisper something in her ear to which she quickly turned her head towards him, then, after leaning back in his chair she returned her gaze back to the stage, but within seconds Collett slowly reached out his left hand to cover her right one resting on top of the balustrade to their box, forcing it down out of sight onto her lap. Tony saw her bite down on her bottom lip as she turned a fearful face towards her husband, the fingers of her left hand instantly releasing the necklace; her infinitesimal shaking of the head in mute pleading for him to stop going quite unheeded, or, indeed, noticed by the audience whose attention was firmly fixed on the stage.

Tony's fingers gripped the glasses, his anger mounting as he watched helplessly her lovely eyes close on a shaft of pain which her husband was clearly inflicting by squeezing that delicate hand and wrist tighter, his bulbous blue eyes glinting with a look which filled Tony with sickening disgust. He had no idea what had brought about this unexpected act of brutality, but he felt certain it was not the first, in fact it merely proved what he had thought when Bea had told him about her periodic disappearances from society. That any woman should have to suffer such cruelty was despicable, but that this lovely creature, who, when he had least expected it, unlocked the door to his heart from the moment he had seen her through the opera glasses, should have to endure such treatment, filled him with a fury he rarely experienced. It would give him tremendous satisfaction to take men like Sir Braden Collett and beat the hell out of them, but the Royal Opera House Covent Garden was not the place. All the same, he could not just sit calmly by and do nothing, and so, with characteristic decisiveness, he rose unobtrusively to his feet, dropping the glasses onto his chair before quietly leaving the box.

The sight of this tall and rather imposing man strolling leisurely along the curve of the corridor as the muted waves of music and song filtered on the air, could not help catching the ushers' attention, but as they were by far too used to seeing gentlemen step out of their boxes to enjoy a cigarette or cigar, having become bored with the performance, or paying a visit to another box whose sole occupant happened to be a lady, they merely touched their hats in acknowledgement. As Tony approached the midpoint of the curve in the corridor he came upon a marble-topped table placed against the wall immediately opposite the central box just as the sound of rapturous applause broke out, signifying the aria had just finished, but as he knew this was not the end of the second act and no one would be leaving their boxes yet, he calmly pulled out one of the chairs and sat down. Retrieving a small notepad and pen from his inside pocket he scribbled a few lines and after tearing off the sheet he returned the notepad and pen to his pocket, then, folding the sheet in half, he rose to his feet and continued to walk leisurely along the corridor until he came to Sir Braden Collett's box. Catching sight of an usher standing against the wall with his gloved hands behind his back, Tony inclined his head slightly which immediately brought that sharp-eyed young man to his side, receiving the note and his instructions without a blink, tucking the coin Tony handed him into his jacket pocket without a glance. Anyone leaving the boxes on this side of the auditorium to go downstairs to the foyer would have to turn left for the stairs, so walking past the door to Sir Braden Collett's box a little way, Tony positioned himself behind a conveniently placed pillar just to the right, totally concealed to a departing occupant. He did not have long to wait before the door to the box opened and the usher stepped out accompanied by Sir Braden Collett, demanding to know, in a deep and belligerent voice, who had delivered the note he was thrusting into the young man's face.

"I don't know who the gentleman was, sir," he shrugged.

"Damn you!" Collett barked. "You must know!"

"No, sir," the usher shook his head, "I have no idea who delivered it."

From his concealed vantage point behind the pillar, Tony heard Collett let out several exasperated expletives followed by an angry warning that it had better not be some damned jest, then, pushing the young man out of the way, he strode off towards the stairs. The usher, standing back on his heels with his hands dug into his trouser pockets, whistled silently to himself as he watched Collett disappear from his view, then, turning his head to the left, nodded to Tony that all was clear, pocketing the extra coin tossed at him.

Eleanor, enormously relieved that her husband had unexpectedly been called away, even if only for a few moments, nevertheless dreaded his return, gently rubbed her wrist from where his strong fingers had twisted it with such excruciating agony, the bracelet having dug into her soft skin through her glove where he had deliberately pressed it down. Upon hearing the door open and close behind her she felt her stomach lurch, hoping Braden would have been gone a little longer, but taking a deep breath she turned round, almost jumping out of her skin when she saw, not Braden's cruel blue eyes looking at her with that febrile glint she feared, as she had fully expected, but a pair of dark grey ones, warm and smiling and quite unknown to her, and for one bemused moment she thought that in her wretchedness her imagination had conjured up a knight-errant in this tall dark stranger who was taking his seat beside her.

"Forgive me if I startled you," Tony said softly, seeing that she was far more beautiful than he had at first thought.

"Who… who are you?" she whispered fearfully, her eyes darting towards the door.

"A friend," he told her quietly, noting that not even the use of face powder had managed to hide the dark circles under her eyes.

"A friend?" she shook her head. "You mean, you know my husband?"

"No," Tony shook his head, "I don't know your husband."

"I don't understand. I… I don't know you!" Eleanor cried, uneasily.

"*That,*" Tony said firmly, "is a circumstance I fully intend to rectify."

"Sir!" she cried, her eyes darting once more towards the door. "If this is some jest I beg you end it now!"

"It is no jest," he assured her softly.

"Oh, please," Eleanor urged frantically, "you *must* leave." Tony slowly shook his head, his heart wrung as he saw her growing alarm. "I have no idea who you are or what you are doing here," she cried desperately, "but my husband could return at any moment; he must not find you here!"

"I am afraid it will be a little longer than a moment before he returns." Her eyes widened at this. "It will, unless I've figured it all wrong," Tony smiled, "be at least half an hour before he resumes his seat. He is, as we speak," he told her with no little satisfaction, "on his way to a destination some four or five blocks away to meet some imaginary person who has a most urgent need to speak to him."

Eleanor felt a sudden bubble of hysterical laughter building up inside her, but although she managed to clamp down on the irresistible urge to give in to it she could do nothing to prevent the tears of relief mingled with apprehension which had steadily been welling up at the back of her eyes from falling unheeded down her cheeks. Through a blurry mist she saw Tony lean forward, and for one heart-stopping moment wondered what he was going to do and automatically cowered in her seat.

"It's all right," Tony said softly, conscious of wanting to inflict the direst punishment on the man who had instilled so much fear into her, "I am not going to hurt you."

For reasons Eleanor could not explain she intuitively knew he would not and that there was no need to fear this man. Even so, when his gloved finger lightly touched her cheek she instinctively drew in her breath and pressed her stiffening body against the back of the chair, her hands gripping its arms, but as that gentle finger slowly began to wipe away her tears she gradually began to relax, conscious of an alien yet delicious tingling sensation coursing through her as she did so.

"There," Tony smiled, "that's better. Such beautiful eyes as yours," he told her truthfully, "should not be marred by tears." Unused to such gentleness or consideration Eleanor looked a little uncertainly at him, her bewilderment clearly reflected in those large blue eyes. "You have no need to fear me," he assured her gently, "I promise you."

Her eyes darted fearfully towards the door. "You... you mean *you* sent that note?" she managed huskily. He nodded. "It... it was nothing but a ruse?" she breathed faintly.

Tony nodded again. "I am ashamed to say that I could think of nothing better on the spur-of-the-moment," he told her ruefully, his eyes twinkling, "so I found myself forced into adopting the only tactic available to me. It is a very old trick," he smiled, "but it never fails!"

"But... but why?" Eleanor shook her head, feeling somewhat bewildered.

"You know," Tony told her conversationally, "these opera glasses," indicating the pair resting on the edge of the balustrade with a nod of his head, "are far more powerful than one would suppose." She looked a little apprehensively at them, then back at him. "It is amazing what one can see through their lenses." He may have spoken lightly but the meaningful look in his eyes was unmistakable, leaving her in no doubt that he had seen what had happened. "In that box directly opposite," he told her helpfully, nodding his head in that direction, "you will see my sister; a lady whom you know well."

She glanced in the direction Tony was indicating, her bottom lip trembling as she recognised the sole occupant. "Beatrice!" she cried on a sob, turning back to face him. He nodded. "Then... then you are her brother from America?" she gasped. "Anthony! Viscount Childon!"

"'Fraid so," Tony smiled, inclining his head.

"But why are you here now?" she asked breathlessly, unable to refrain from casting another scared look at the door.

"It's all right," Tony assured her softly, "he won't return just yet. As for what I am doing here," he smiled, "it's no mystery." After indicating the opera glasses again, he told her about how his sister had drawn his attention to her and what he had seen during the beginning of the second act. "So, you see," he pointed out softly, "it is quite useless to try to make me believe he has not hurt you, or has never done so!"

Eleanor turned her head away to hide fresh tears, her shoulders trembling from the combined effects of fear and tension, but under no circumstances could she even so much as let him suspect the truth so, taking a deep breath, she turned and faced him, her eyes wide and frightened. "I… I don't know what it is you think you saw, sir," she whispered, "but…" darting a quick look at the boxes on either side, relieved that the occupants of both had not been disturbed or distracted by their whispered conversation, she turned and faced him, "but I assure you, you have it quite wrong."

"Why did your husband hurt you?" he asked gently, totally ignoring her denial.

"He… he didn't," she shook her head, showing him a travesty of a smile, "however it may have appeared to you, I… I assure you, you are mistaken."

The only response Tony made to this was to lean forward and take hold of her hand, gently removing the bracelet from her wrist and carefully pulling down her long white evening glove until the vivid red patch, clearly visible in the shaft of light which filtered into the box from the corridor through the glass at the top of the door, which would bruise overnight, and the bracelet's indentation, were glaringly exposed. "Do you still say he has not hurt you?" he asked softly.

Eleanor pulled her hand away and began to hurriedly pull on her glove and fasten her bracelet, her breasts heaving and her eyes, dilated with fear, darting once again to the door of the box. "I… I promise you, sir," she cried breathlessly, "it is not how it seems," conscious of that alien sensation resurging in the pit of her stomach.

"It is precisely how it seems," Tony said unequivocally, resisting the impulse to take her in his arms, "and you and I both know it is not the first time he has subjected you to such despicable treatment."

Eleanor shook her head, her emotions in danger of spilling over. "Please, will you leave now," she sobbed, "I assure you I am in no need of assistance."

"I wish I could believe that," Tony told her quietly, "but I can't, neither can I just walk away from you and leave you to a brute of a man who deserves to be horsewhipped for what he does to you."

"You are most kind, sir," Eleanor said in a stifled voice, "but indeed, my husband treats me just as he ought."

"I know you are afraid," Tony acknowledged, covering her hand with his, aware that the curtain was coming down on the second act, "but apart from the fact that I have a deep-rooted dislike of bullies and men who beat up their wives in particular, I would very much like to get to know you better."

"No, it is impossible!" She shook her head as rapturous applause broke out, trying to banish the agreeable thought of becoming better acquainted with this man.

"*Nothing* is impossible," Tony smiled, feeling the small slim hand convulse beneath his fingers.

"*Please*," Eleanor begged, "do not say anything more, I beg of you!"

"Very well," Tony nodded, "it shall be as you wish, for now, but you will be seeing a lot more of me, I promise you."

Eleanor shook her head, her voice barely audible, "My husband will not…"

"Allow it," Tony cocked his head.

Eleanor nodded. "Please," she urged, casting a pleading glance at him, "you *must* leave now; indeed, you must."

Tony could see in her eyes that she trusted him, but her fear was such that it overrode everything else. "You have no need to either fear me," he reiterated, "or fear for me." He smiled disarmingly. "And my name, by the way, is Tony; not 'sir' or 'Your Lordship', or even 'my lord'."

She was just about to say something when the door to the box opened, the unexpectedness of it making her jump out of her skin, but upon seeing the familiar figure of Beatrice, she let out a sob of pure relief.

"Ah, Bea!" Tony smiled, releasing the small trembling hand as he rose to greet his sister. "I am glad you have joined us. I have already made Eleanor's acquaintance!"

Beatrice's eyes looked troubled, but just as she was about to say something Eleanor sprung to her feet and rushed towards her, crying. "Oh, Beatrice! It is so good to see you again!"

Like everyone else, Beatrice's attention had been on the performance and not on what her brother was doing, but when the curtain rose and the lights went up to find he was not beside her as she had thought but across the other side of the auditorium sitting next to Eleanor with no sign of her husband, she immediately feared the worst. She had not heard Tony leave their box and he had not told her he was doing so, and she could not begin to understand what was going on or where Collett had disappeared to, but one thing she did know, and that was Eleanor's husband would most certainly not have left his wife alone with another man voluntarily. The thought that Tony had knocked him out could not help but obtrude, but as Beatrice made her way to the other side of the auditorium she told herself that she was being ridiculous and that her brother, no matter how strong a dislike he had taken to someone, had far more sense than to do something so drastic in the middle of an opera at Covent Garden.

In her haste to reach Braden Collett's box to discover precisely what was happening, it seemed that all her acquaintance had decided to wander the corridors at the same time to stretch their legs, encountering so many of them en-route that she thought she would never get there, but when she eventually opened the door, fully expecting to find Braden Collett lying stretched out on the floor unconscious, she was not at all certain whether to be glad or sorry he was not. Tony had been rather insistent on forging an introduction during this interval and although she could not see the wisdom of it, because nothing would convince her that he had not taken quite a liking to Eleanor, she had agreed to do so, but what could have possibly induced him to make his own introduction at some point during the second act, had her somewhat at a loss.

Clearly, something had happened whilst her concentration had been on the performance, but just as she was about to question her brother Eleanor sprang up out of her seat and almost ran towards her, but since Beatrice was as kind as she was generous and had never once intended to either repulse the child or blame her for keeping her distance, as it was blatantly obvious it was not her fault, she opened her arms and held Eleanor tight against her. Over that blonde head brother and sister's eyes met, and Beatrice, reading Tony's silent warning correctly, decided to leave asking questions until later, but she could not prevent herself from asking where Sir Braden was.

"He got called out, Bea," Tony told her, "but I expect him to return at any moment."

"Called out?" Beatrice questioned. "What do you mean?"

"Just that," Tony nodded, the tone of his voice stemming any more questions.

"Oh, Beatrice!" sobbed Eleanor, easing herself a little away from her, raising watery blue eyes to her compassionate face. "I am so happy to see you! Please forgive me."

"Oh, my dear child!" Beatrice soothed. "There is nothing to forgive, I promise you. I can't tell you how worried I have been over you!"

"I am afraid," Tony broke in quietly, "that this will all have to keep until tomorrow."

"Tomorrow?" Beatrice queried.

"Listen, Bea," Tony emphasised, "Collett must not find me here, but you are to wait with Eleanor until he returns." She raised a surprised eyebrow at this, but kept silent. "I don't want him to know anything about me just yet, but when he returns he will obviously want to know what you are doing here. You must simply say that you spotted Eleanor from your box and came over to speak to her, and this is *most* important Bea," he stressed, "you are to invite Eleanor to Mount Street tomorrow for luncheon or anything you please, but you are *not* to take no for an answer!"

"But I can't," Eleanor cried, turning round in Beatrice's arms and casting frightened eyes at him.

"Yes, you can," Tony said firmly, "indeed you *must*. For one thing," he smiled, "there's a great deal I want to talk to you about."

"No! Truly I cannot!" Eleanor shook her head.

"My dear," Beatrice said soothingly, "if Tony thinks it is for the best, then indeed you can be assured it is so."

As this seemed to calm her a little, Tony smiled comfortingly at her, then, looking at his sister, said firmly, "Under no circumstances are you to allow Collett to dissuade Eleanor from visiting you; throw a fit of the vapours or have a temper tantrum if need be," he smiled, "but she *must* come to Mount Street tomorrow," stressing, "*and alone.*"

"Very well," Beatrice nodded, "I shall certainly do my best to persuade him."

Tony then turned to Eleanor, his eyes warm and tender as they looked down at her, taking hold of her hands in both of his, saying gently, "I know you are afraid, but you must try to be very brave; will you do that for me?" he coaxed.

Eleanor may have dreamt of a knight-errant coming to her rescue, but of course such things never happened outside the covers of a novel, but now it appeared that this was precisely what was happening, but in her fear she was not at all certain whether to feel relief or not, but nodding her head she managed to utter a frightened and breathless,

"Yes," not daring to think what he could possibly do to alleviate her unbearable situation, but then, how could he do anything when she dared not tell him?

"Good girl." Tony smiled, then, looking at Bea said, "Collett will be here any minute, so I'd better be moseying along."

"Yes, of course," Beatrice nodded.

Beatrice had no objection to entertaining her young friend in Mount Street tomorrow or at any time, but she was quite at a loss to account for Tony's insistence that she somehow or other persuade Braden into permitting his wife to come to see her. Clearly, her brother had his reasons which he was not about to impart in front of Eleanor, but Beatrice was quite convinced that something had happened to bring about this unprecedented state of affairs, and had to contain her impatience as best she could until they were alone. She could not rid her mind of what he had said earlier this evening any more than she could the idea that in Eleanor Collett Tony had finally met the woman for him, but unless she had grossly misread the case, having closely watched the two of them together, then she would say that he was heading for trouble; Braden Collett was not the type of man to relinquish his wife to another. Unfortunately, there had been no time to ply Tony with questions, especially the one about whether he was responsible for their absent host's sudden departure, but since it was clear that Eleanor was not in any fit state to tell her anything and certainly not what had become of her husband, Beatrice sat down in her brother's vacated chair and anxiously awaited Collett's return.

She was, of course, delighted to have a little time alone with Eleanor, a young woman who had been like a daughter to her and whose mamma had been her dearest friend, but seeing her now, sitting nervously on the edge of her seat and constantly darting fearful eyes towards the door, it was extremely difficult to engage her in conversation. Perhaps tomorrow when she visited in Mount Street, providing of course Collett did not forbid it, she would be feeling a little more comfortable when, hopefully, she would open her mind a little, if not to herself, then to Tony. The child was clearly afraid of her husband, and although Beatrice had no idea that he subjected her to such brutal treatment as her brother had witnessed, there was clearly something terribly wrong. Collett was certainly not the man to whom she would have given Eleanor in marriage and neither would her mamma had she been alive and, not for the first time, Beatrice found herself wondering why Sir Miles had sanctioned such a match. The reason could, of course, have been money, in fact the more she thought about it the more likely it seemed, especially when she considered Reginald's gambling debts, but to virtually sell his daughter to a man over twenty years her senior for no other reason than to try to reclaim some of the money he had lost in settling his son's debts, was, in her opinion at least, nothing short of mercenary. Her close friendship with Amelia naturally did not give her the right to speak to Sir Miles about it or to question his dealings regarding his son and daughter, not that she would expect him to discuss his family's affairs with her or anyone come to that but, surely, he could see that since her marriage Eleanor was very far from being the happy young woman she had once been.

Beatrice may not be prone to fanciful assumptions or flights of fantasy, but even so she found she had to continually berate herself for being over imaginative when her mind recurrently conjured up all manner of reasons to account for Eleanor's behaviour over the last twelve months. To say her periodic absences from society or the need to take a maid with her whenever she went out shopping was a little unusual was a gross understatement, but since Beatrice could not come up with anything feasible to account for either, she was left with only speculation. It was true what she had told Tony in that she knew nothing to Collett's detriment, but she was as convinced as anyone could be that he was solely responsible for Eleanor's obvious fear as well as for keeping her distance from all her friends and acquaintances, and Tom, who had no more liking for Collett than she did, had found himself in complete agreement with her, and as she sat with Eleanor waiting for her husband to return she was more certain than ever that Collett had a hold of some kind over her, forcing her to do as he wanted.

As it was patently clear from Eleanor's breathless and frightened "Yes" and "No's" to her various comments that nothing would be gleaned from her tonight, Beatrice maintained a flow of artless chatter for the few minutes left to them before Collett returned. It was just when she was on the point of telling Eleanor that she had no need to be afraid when the door was suddenly thrust unceremoniously open and Sir Braden Collett walked in, his cheeks suffused with angry colour, turning his face a deeper shade of pink than usual, and his chest heaving from his hurried and wasted visit to *'The Music Stand'* public house where he had angrily discovered his errand had been nothing but a trick. One swift glance at Eleanor's face was more than enough to prove Beatrice's suspicions correct; she went as white as her dress and her eyes widened in apprehension as she shot a scared glance up at him, but whatever blistering retort was on his lips the sight of an unexpected visitor, especially one whom he knew had a fondness for his wife, held him silent, his bulbous blue eyes narrowing as they looked from one to the other.

"Oh, Braden!" Eleanor cried unsteadily, not giving him time to say anything. "You… you know Beatrice; Lady Shipton!"

He looked down at his wife, her face a picture of innocence, and although he doubted very much whether she had instigated such a trick, he would nevertheless have a word or two to say to her upon their return home. Anger, frustration, and an urgent wish to know who had played such a hoax on him, rendered him speechless for a moment or two, and Beatrice, raising her hand, gained the very strong impression that had she not have been here then he would most probably have taken his anger out on Eleanor, but it was with admirable restraint that he said, with cool politeness, "Yes, of course," bowing over her hand. "How do you do?" offering neither apologies nor reasons for his absence.

"I do hope I am not intruding," Beatrice smiled up at him, "but you see," she explained, "I happened to catch sight of you," pointing in the general direction of her box, "and I just could not resist calling upon you." Then, turning to Eleanor, said, with a casualness she was very far from feeling, "I cannot tell you how pleased I am to see you here this evening, my dear; it has been some little time since you have been out."

"Yes," Eleanor managed, conscious of her husband's eyes upon her. "I… I have regrettably found it necessary to remain indoors; influenza."

"Influenza!" Beatrice cried innocently, not believing such a tale for one moment. "But how very dreadful for you!"

"Yes," Eleanor breathed, casting a glance up at her husband from under her lashes. "It… it was a most severe attack; was it not, Braden?"

"Yes," he confirmed stiffly, "most severe."

"Well," Beatrice nodded at Eleanor, "I can see you still look a little pulled, but it is good to see you up and about again." Then, bearing in mind Tony's strategy, said, with a smoothness which completely belied how tense she had suddenly become under Collett's hard and penetrating stare, "In fact," she smiled, incorporating him it its beam, "it is most fortunate that you are here at this precise moment because you see, my dear," she said in the tone of a conspirator, leaning forward a little in her seat and covering Eleanor's cold hand with her own, "I really *do* need a second opinion about a new dress I had delivered this morning for me to wear tomorrow evening at the Kirkmichaels' wedding anniversary party. It is useless to ask Sir Thomas because men," smiling up at Collett and waving her furled fan at him in the manner of a mother chastising her child, "have *positively* no idea about such things, but you, my dear Eleanor, have always had such good taste and I have relied so much upon your opinion in the past that I feel sure I may do so again. Now, do not," she nodded, "I beg of you, say you cannot come to Mount Street tomorrow because I will not take 'no' for an answer. Besides," she smiled, "it has been an age since you and I had a comfortable gossip together." Then, looking up at Collett, she saw the frown furrowing his forehead, but deliberately misinterpreting this, she took a deep breath and said, "Yes, I know you are most concerned for her health my dear Collett, but indeed, it will do her good to step out a little. Now *do*, I beg of you," she pleaded, "spare her to me tomorrow." She saw him hesitate and pressed home her advantage. "I shall take the greatest care of her, I promise you, indeed, I will even send my own carriage for her, even though we are only a step or two away."

"You are most kind, Lady Shipton," Collett managed, glancing down at his wife, "but I am afraid it is a little too soon for her to be going out and about, indeed," he nodded, "I should not have permitted her to come here this evening, but she would insist on seeing Carlucci."

"Now, *please*," Beatrice begged, rising to her feet, "do not say 'no'!"

"At the risk of offending you, Lady Shipton," Collett said firmly, "I really must. As you yourself remarked a moment or two ago, she still looks rather pulled."

Bitterly regretting that idle comment, Beatrice realised it was going to be no easy matter to persuade him, and from the stubborn look which had descended onto his face she could see that she may have to resort to that temper tantrum or fit of the vapours as Tony had humorously suggested after all. She looked down into Eleanor's upturned face, her expression a nice mix of hope and dread, but since Beatrice knew it was pointless seeking either her opinion or her acceptance, at least in her husband's company that was, she tried again to sway him. She was not usually at a loss for words or social conversation and being a most popular and charming hostess it was seldom her invitations were refused, but from the look on Collett's face it was clear that she was going to have to resort to more forceful tactics if she wanted Eleanor to visit her tomorrow. "Well, yes," she said thoughtfully, looking down at Eleanor, "she *does* look a little pulled, but you know Collett," she smiled disarmingly, laying a gloved hand on his arm, "I am sure you will agree that a little fresh air is all that is needed to put the colour back into her cheeks. Now," she nodded, "have I not already promised to take the greatest care of her? I will, I assure you."

He was by no means happy to let his wife go jaunting about town without either his own or Eliza's escort and certainly not to the home of one with whom she had long been on very close terms, but to refuse could well give rise to suspicions which he could well do without, but since it was clear that Beatrice Shipton was not going to take 'no' for an answer, he reluctantly granted his permission, adding that it would not be in the least necessary for her to send her own carriage as he would make sure his wife arrived in Mount Street in their own. "I shall look forward to seeing you tomorrow then, my dear." Beatrice smiled down at Eleanor, kissing her cheek. Then, as if a thought had just occurred to her she said, at her most animated, incorporating Collett in her sparkling glance, "Oh, but *do* tell me Sir Thomas and I shall see you at the Kirkmichaels' tomorrow evening!"

Eleanor opened her mouth to speak, but giving her no time to respond Collett informed Beatrice politely, "We have certainly accepted the invitation."

From her vantage point she could just make out Tony sitting right at the very back of the box out of Collett's view, and feeling extremely proud, if a little mentally exhausted from her efforts, she bent down to kiss Eleanor's cheek once more, reiterating how much she looked forward to welcoming her tomorrow in Mount Street as well as seeing her at the Kirkmichaels', then, straightening up, she gave her hand to Collett, who, after raising it briefly to his lips, bowed his head, saying that it was a pleasure to see her again.

By the time Beatrice entered her box the curtain had just gone up on the last act, but conscious of Collett's eyes cast in her direction she merely nodded her head, which Tony understood to mean she had managed to get Eleanor to Mount Street tomorrow. His sister however, consumed with curiosity as to what was going on and just how he had managed to get rid of Collett, sat with only half her mind on the remainder of the performance, barely able to contain her impatience to fire questions at him.

Within ten minutes of Beatrice's return, Tony saw Collett rise to his feet and assist his wife out of her chair, placing her cape around her shoulders before taking hold of her arm and leaving their box. Beatrice too had seen their early departure and could scarcely refrain from saying something, but instead had to wait with what patience she could until they finally stepped up into their carriage about forty-five minutes later; the door hardly closed upon them before she plied her brother with questions.

Upon hearing Tony describe what he had witnessed at the beginning of the second act she was genuinely shocked, looking at her brother as though she could not believe her ears. She may not like Sir Braden Collett, but the very thought that a man of his standing, in fact any man for that matter, could commit such a brutal act was something she would never have thought possible, and could not refrain from asking Tony if he was sure he had seen right. "Do not forget," she reminded him, "the lights were down."

"I know what I saw, Bea," Tony told her unequivocally. "I saw too the marks on her wrist, and she did not get those by merely resting her arm on the balustrade!"

But no matter how shocked and appalled Beatrice was, she could not prevent the chuckle which escaped her lips upon hearing how he had tricked Collett so he could get him out of the way for half an hour or so, but all humour aside she was not at all certain whether to applaud such a clever manoeuvre or not. She could not argue against her brother's assertions in that Eleanor was afraid of her husband, she had seen that for herself, but since she could see that Tony was determined to involve himself in something which she instinctively knew would end in trouble, she nevertheless felt it behoved her to warn him against doing anything which could only make that poor child's situation infinitely worse than it already was.

"So, what are you saying, Bea?" Tony asked. "That I just turn a blind eye and leave her to that brute of a bully?"

"No, of course I am not!" She shook her head.

"What then?" Tony asked, seeing the troubled look which had descended onto her pretty face. "Listen Bea," he said seriously, "unless I am very much mistaken, and I know I am not," he added firmly, "I'd say he makes a habit of beating her; what else could possibly account for her regular disappearances?"

She eyed him, aghast. "You can't mean he has done this before?" she cried, horrified.

"Too right he has!" he bit out. "A man just doesn't take it into his head one night to start physically abusing his wife for the first time in the middle of an opera!"

"No," Beatrice acknowledged sickeningly, having given it some thought, "he does not. Oh, Tony," she cried, "that poor, *poor* child! What she must suffer at his hands! I only hope that he does not prevent her from coming to see me tomorrow after all!" She saw the grimness around his mouth and hesitated before asking tentatively, "Tony, about Eleanor; how… how taken with her are you?"

Tony turned his head sideways to look at her, but she knew the answer before he opened his mouth. "Very taken, Bea," he told her earnestly, taking her hand a giving it a squeeze.

"So, what you said earlier this evening," she said quietly, "about knowing the right woman when you…"

"Exactly so, Bea," he broke in. "Exactly so!"

"But you hardly know her!" she pointed out reasonably.

"Tom hardly knew you, but that did not stop him from falling in love with you the moment he laid eyes on you," Tony reminded her.

"Yes, but…" she began.

"And just like Tom with you," he smiled, "I fully intend to get to know Eleanor better."

Beatrice said no more, but by the time they were eventually set down in Mount Street her thoughts were in turmoil. She may not like Collett, but at no time had she ever thought he was the type of man to treat his wife in such a way and the horror of discovering that he was in fact perfectly capable of perpetrating such brutality, and apparently not for the first time, left her rather sickened and bemused. Then, on top of this, it seemed her brother had set his heart as well as his mind on Eleanor Collett, and whilst under different circumstances she would not be displeased at such a match, considering the child was already married she failed to see how he could possibly get to know her better, especially when it seemed her husband always ensured she was never alone. Even if Tony had not been irresistibly drawn to Eleanor, Beatrice knew that his own sense of decency would not have altered his attitude towards Collett's treatment of her, but her brother's determination to put a stop to what he deemed not only unacceptable but totally objectionable, concerned her. At no time could she advocate such treatment, in fact it was something to be condemned by everyone, but considering that Collett seldom, if ever, allowed Eleanor out alone, Beatrice failed to see what her brother could possibly do.

Chapter Three

At no time did Sir Braden Collett like being made a fool of and now was no exception, and by the time he returned to his box at Covent Garden his temper, unpredictable at the best of times, had grown to fever pitch and was in need of venting, but upon setting eyes on his wife entertaining a woman he knew full well was an old friend of her mother, he had to somehow curb the blistering words which rose to his tongue. He had, of course, heard of Beatrice Shipton's brother and how he had recently inherited his grandfather's title and dignities, but so far their paths had never crossed, and as he was unaware of his visit to England and that he was presently residing with his sister and brother-in-law in Mount Street, much less that he was watching interestedly from a box opposite, he had no idea that it was he who had played that trick on him. He wondered if it was Beatrice Shipton, but as it was something he could not openly charge her with he had no choice but to receive her with as much politeness as he could, his mind rampant with suspicion.

He by no means liked the idea of his wife jaunting about without either himself or Eliza to accompany her, and as for paying a morning call on a woman she had always looked upon with affection as well as a friend of her late mother into the bargain, most certainly not. Having endeavoured to keep Eleanor as far away from Beatrice Shipton as possible unless, of course, he was with her, leaving her alone with this woman was clearly asking for trouble, but since Beatrice Shipton had virtually made it impossible for him to say no without giving grave offence, it had been with the utmost reluctance he had agreed to the visit. He was far from happy with it, especially as his wife may, under her gentle coaxing, be inclined to confide in her as to the reason for her frequent absences from society because he could not fool himself into thinking that this astute woman had not drawn her own conclusions. It would be perfectly natural for her to enquire of Eleanor if all were well, voicing her concerns to her, and even, perhaps, looking upon herself as standing in place of her mother thereby urging her to unburden herself and this, as he well knew, would not do at all.

Sir Braden Collett, having come into the title following his father's fatal heart attack seven years ago, had, almost from the day he was born, been perfectly aware of the fact that he could not only trace his lineage back for centuries but also claim to being related to half the noble houses in England, ensured everyone else was aware of it as well. Unlike his late father, he was a proud and unpleasant man with a reputation for being argumentative and one, moreover, who made no effort to be polite or conciliating, doing nothing whatever to make himself agreeable, but his name and wealth would always ensure every door was open to him and no hostess would ever dream of offending him by failing to send him a card of invitation. He may not be the darling of society or the most popular member of his social circle, but his name and reputation were alike unsullied by either scandal or gossip, in fact no underhand dealings attached to his name, and no hostess who saw him grace her house in response to her invitation could be anything other than both gratified and honoured. He was a well-educated and cultured man, and one who certainly liked his benevolence to be seen; a patron of the arts and a regular contributor to charitable causes, he could often be seen at the opera or the ballet or at a gallery exhibiting the paintings of an up-and-coming young artist whose work he admired and to whom he had given his sponsorship. He was also a man with a taste for rich living and all the fine things in life which his wealth could more than adequately provide, including attending race meetings, quite often in the company of the Prince of Wales, and playing cards at his club for very high stakes, at which he was extremely skilled, with a reputation for being meticulous in all matters of play, enjoying the convivial companionship of his fellow members in an atmosphere which suited him very well.

But this man of impeccable credentials and unsullied reputation, who could proudly claim friendship with his future king, was known among his close circle of intimates as one who took no small gratification from betting heavily at the illegally convened cock and dog fights he often attended as well as bareknuckle bouts, and as he was by nature a violent and aggressive man he was by no means sickened or disgusted by a particularly gruesome display. Society may know him to be a most disagreeable man who could take an exception to a casual remark or deliberately pick a quarrel for no reason they could see other than it suited his mood, but they did not know of how he regularly bullied and beat his wife or of those visits he frequently made to a certain establishment where he found a more gratifying outlet for his aggressive tendencies. None of these hidden pastimes, however, had as yet come to polite society's attention, much less to the ears of the ladies who sent out cards of invitation to him, and whilst such despicable and illegal pursuits such as witnessing a vicious contest between two equally matched dogs or other evenly paired species would shock and outrage should they come to notice, they would not, like his other and more covert pursuits, ostracise and condemn him.

Apart from his close circle of intimates, all of whom were like-minded spirits who looked upon his activities as well as their own as amusing rather than shocking, Sir Braden Collett was by no means popular, but even so his name would always make him acceptable as well as received and he for one had no intention of jeopardising that, which could well be the case if he allowed his wife to go out and about without either himself or Eliza to go with her.

He had, of course, run across Eleanor Tatton at any number of social gatherings, but from the outset she had made it perfectly clear that she wanted none of him. His friends, all of whom knew of his aspirations in that direction, could not quite understand what it was he saw in her because although she was undeniably beautiful she was not, as they well knew, in his usual style, and had they been asked to give their opinion they would have strongly advised him to forget her, especially as she appeared none too eager for his company. But there was something about this shy and reserved eighteen-year-old young woman that had strongly appealed to him and her tendency to shrink away from him only served to strengthen his attraction to her. He knew perfectly well that she tried to avoid him whenever she could, the sight of dread in her eyes whenever he approached her or attempted to solicit her hand for the next dance, instead of discouraging him merely served to increase his desire to become better acquainted with her.

Sir Miles Tatton, who had not the least wish to see his daughter married to a man for whom she held neither liking nor affection, especially as he himself could not claim to being overly fond of Sir Braden Collett, had therefore known no compunction in refusing the two requests he had made to pay his addresses to his daughter. Sir Braden Collett, not the most patient of men, had somehow managed to put a curb on his impatience, believing that it was only a matter of time before Sir Miles capitulated, but just when he had begun to think that nothing would influence Tatton into acceding to his requests to permit him to marry his daughter, Reginald Tatton had, quite unwittingly, brought about the means whereby his father had found himself with no choice but to accept the painful inevitable regarding his daughter.

It would be an exaggeration to say that it had been the marriage of the season, but it certainly ranked as one of the most prominent on the social calendar, St. George's Hanover Square being more than respectably filled, even if those honoured with an invitation were still astonished at the connection. Sir Miles Tatton may have played his part in the marriage ceremony with becoming dignity, but it could not be said that he was the happiest father they had ever seen give his daughter away and, as for Eleanor, she looked positively downcast.

Having learned of the marriage upon her return from New York Beatrice had stared aghast at her husband, but since he had not been honoured with an invitation and he was not, he was glad to say, a crony of Collett's any more than he was on intimate terms with Sir Miles, he could no more enlighten her as to the reason for the match any more than he could for her father's sanctioning it in the first place. But the Shiptons were not the only ones who questioned it. Of course, Collett's wealth could be at the root of it, especially when one considered Reginald Tatton's gambling debts, but there was no denying that for a father to marry his daughter, who was just turned nineteen for goodness' sake, to a man old enough to be her father and one, moreover, whose disagreeable temperament had more than once brought him into conflict with his peers, was not only mercenary but hardly likely to appeal to a young bride who was as shy and reserved as Eleanor Tatton.

But over the ensuing twelve months, speculation as to the reason for the marriage naturally began to die down, especially when other and by far more scandalous indiscretions came to society's notice, but there were those, like Beatrice Shipton and her husband, who had by no means banished Eleanor from their minds. Nothing would convince them that she had married Collett out of choice or that it was a happy marriage, but since any private contact with her dearest friend's daughter had ceased and any attempt to visit in Cavendish Square had proved fruitless, Eleanor's periodic disappearances from society as well as her never being allowed out-of-doors unaccompanied, continued to give Beatrice and her husband cause for grave concern.

It seemed that the only one who was happy with the marriage was Collett himself; in fact, he could not be more delighted, even though his wife's natural instincts were to shy away from him. In Eleanor Tatton he had found a woman who suited him very well; her fear of him, coupled with her shyness, a trait which, before her marriage, had caused one romantically minded young man to fall hopelessly in love with her, met his needs perfectly. He could not claim to being in love with her, in fact he had never been in love in his life and doubted he ever would be, but since there was no way he could avoid marriage if he wished to prevent his cousin Hubert from stepping into his shoes, he had decided he would rather his wife be Eleanor Tatton than anyone else.

Eleanor may accord him all the respect due to him as her husband, but he knew that lying behind the polite façade she could not bear him to come near her let alone touch her, but since it was this very repugnance and dread which had attracted him to her in the first place, his more intimate moments with his wife, accompanied as they were by not a fraction of participation from her or the smallest sign of enjoyment, provided him with far more excitement and pleasure than they did her. She may not encourage his advances, much less want them, but she had never once repulsed them which, when he considered how he had from the very beginning made it clear, not only by word but by deed, what he expected of her, it was hardly surprising that she had come to accept it as her duty to respond to any demands he made of her as and when it suited him as well as instilling into her the imprudence of disobeying him or plying him with questions. Subjecting her to more than one painful experience, whilst affording him no small amount of gratification, was primarily to instil into her the wisdom of saying or doing nothing which ran counter to his wishes, ensuring his visits to a certain discreet house to enable him to satisfy his needs in a way he could not exact from his wife, meant she remained in complete ignorance of his preferences as well as his extramarital activities.

This man of impeccable credentials then, had, in this quiet and shy young woman, who longed to break free from a marriage she had never wanted with a man she hated and feared, the ideal wife who catered to his needs; dutiful, subservient and, above all, afraid of him. He may know no compunction in bullying and beating her into submission, in fact he took no small degree of pleasure from it, but he did not want to alert her to that side of his nature he knew full well she would never understand, not only that, but it was something he much preferred to keep secret. His visits to *'Mother Discipline's'* discreet establishment, which had for long enjoyed his patronage, had continued, but they had, regrettably, brought about a circumstance which rendered his wife something of a threat. Unfortunately, it had meant that Mitchell too, who had been in his father's service for many years, had to be dealt with in the only way which would permanently eliminate the very real risk he had posed and, however regrettable, it had certainly been expedient; his replacement being one who was every inch the prizefighter Beatrice had described him to Tony. Mary too, had found herself dismissed and replaced by Eliza Boon, a woman who knew precisely how to deal with reluctant young women who would not do as they were told; she had not acquired her soubriquet *'Mother Discipline'* for nothing! As each of these unscrupulous individuals, whose past careers were anything but commendable, had no more wish to come to the notice of the authorities than their noble employer, they were more than prepared to adopt the role of gaoler to a young woman who could bring all to ruin if left unchecked.

Sir Braden Collett, who experienced no qualms about implementing such unprincipled measures any more than he did in subjecting his wife to unspeakable brutality, had no doubt whatsoever that these two most capable individuals between them would ensure that Eleanor was constantly kept in check, eliminating any risk of her letting something fall, either wittingly or unwittingly. So far, his strategies had worked, his wife, far too terrified to do anything other than what she was told, giving him no real cause for concern, but now, with Beatrice Shipton attempting to re-enter her life, he saw that far more stringent methods would have to be adopted, especially when he considered what was at stake. Under no circumstances could he allow the events of that never to be forgotten night, which his wife had unfortunately witnessed, to come to public notice.

He could not prove that Beatrice Shipton had engineered that hoax which had cunningly been played on him, but considering the several visits she had paid in Cavendish Square to see Eleanor as well as her efforts to try to get her alone when they ran across her at some function or other, he could not entirely acquit her of instigating it. After all, had she not seen them from her box directly opposite? Despite accepting the odd invitation to a little gathering in Mount Street, which he knew had been more for Eleanor's sake than his own, he could not claim friendship with her, but he knew enough to realise that she could be dangerous and by allowing Eleanor time alone in her company could only increase that danger. But his position had been most awkward. To have openly questioned her, much less accused her, of bringing about his brief removal from their box at Covent Garden by a cunningly contrived ruse to enable her to have a private word with Eleanor, would have immediately raised suspicions in her mind and, whilst he had reluctantly granted his wife permission to visit her tomorrow, short of adamantly refusing, running the risk of grossly offending, there had been little else he could have done. In all honesty, he could not see Eleanor confiding in her if, for no other reason, than she would be far too frightened, but he had seen enough of Beatrice Shipton to feel confident enough to say that she could be quite persuasive, and should Eleanor succumb to her gentle coaxing then there was every chance that Beatrice Shipton could well take his wife's confidences to the authorities and, in an effort to obviate this risk, he had therefore determined that Eliza would accompany her tomorrow. Had he but known that a man of equal resource and determination as himself was waiting just in the wings to thwart his devious scheming and to put an end to the brutal treatment he handed out to his wife, he would not have left the opera house in such a positive frame of mind.

Eleanor was not entirely surprised to find herself being escorted out of Covent Garden Opera House well before the performance had ended; just one glance at those protruding blue eyes with that warning glint she feared had been enough to tell her that a most unpleasant time awaited her. All too familiar with her husband's temper and, worse, the bullying which accompanied it, she inwardly quaked, and no sooner was their carriage door closed upon them than she felt his strong fingers encircle her right wrist, still extremely tender from his earlier infliction.

"You know, my dear," Collett said softly, exerting pressure on her already stinging skin, her long white gloves affording no protection from this further assault, "should I discover that you had a hand in playing that trick upon me this evening, I shall take it very ill."

"Braden," she said earnestly, shaking her head, "I *swear* I know nothing!" biting her bottom lip as his fingers squeezed tighter.

"It was not, I hope," he said ominously, "a cleverly contrived ruse between you and Beatrice Shipton."

"No," she cried, tears stinging her eyes as those strong fingers relentlessly gripped her wrist, their pressure causing the diamonds of her bracelet to embed themselves into her skin. "How… how could it be when I have not…" she winced, "spoken to her… for some time?"

"Do not lie to me, Eleanor," he warned. "You know I do not like it when you keep things from me."

"I am not lying!" she cried, her attempts to break away from his painful grip quite ineffectual. "I *swear* I have no idea who sent that note!"

He turned to look at her, the light from the street lamps entering the carriage emphasising the gleam in his protruding eyes, her whole body trembling at what it signified. "Do not provoke me, my dear," he warned softly, leaning towards her, his face only inches from her own. "You must *not* provoke me."

"I'm not!" Eleanor cried frantically. "You *must* believe me, Braden!" She shook her head. "I have no idea who…"

"Do not take me for a fool, Eleanor," Collett advised menacingly.

"I'm not!" she cried, wincing as he raised her hand and shook it like a rag doll. "I swear I don't know anything about that note!"

As they had by now arrived in Cavendish Square he released her hand, but not before warning her that they would discuss it later, the very thought of which made her feel sick, and just one look at Eliza Boon waiting for her on the first landing as they entered the house did nothing to lessen Eleanor's fear or dispel the nausea growing inside her.

Eliza Boon, who, before being forced into retiring early from a very lucrative business at the age of fifty-five due to two most unfortunate circumstances, had been better known as *'Mother Discipline'*, a not undeserving epithet to which the girls she had presided over could adequately testify. Over a long and successful, if dubious, career of ensuring that those with somewhat out of the ordinary tastes were entertained to their satisfaction, she had neither shrunk nor hesitated from using aggressive, even violent, means to induce her recruits, who dared not go against her if they knew what was good for them, to comply with any request made of them. Early on in her career she had discovered that there was more money to be made from catering to the somewhat unusual needs of those like her current employer, a most openhanded man who had been a regular visitor to her establishment, than to the requirements of those who sought nothing either irregular or specific, and had therefore soon acquired a reputation for being able to provide who or whatever took one's fancy with no questions asked.

Being one who did not concern herself with ethics, or anything else if it came to that, she could always be relied upon to supply or do whatever the client required, providing of course the price was right, and when events beyond her control necessitated a hasty exit from her profitable place of business she had, however unfortunate, looked upon it as expedient. It had been a pity that Sir Braden Collett had allowed his temper to get the better of him that night which had come about as a direct result of the unfortunate death of one her girls a month or so before. Both had been regrettable incidents, but like Sir Braden she was keen to prevent either from leaking out; not only because society would look far from favourably upon the kind of activities which had brought them about in the first place but, again like Sir Braden, she knew that whilst the death of a prostitute would most probably not raise much of an energetic enquiry by the police, the same could not be said of the death of Sir Philip Dunscumbe. Just because they had so far found neither a motive nor the perpetrator responsible for the brutal death of such a prominent Member of Parliament it did not mean they had given up the investigation altogether, but should they ever suspect that his death was due to the result of questions he had meant to raise in the House after he had learned of the accidental death of one of her girls which had involved his brother Dennis, which, in turn, had led him to Sir Braden, it would not take them long to visit her premises, which would, as she knew very well, be closed down with herself in the dock and Collett hanging from the end of a rope. She had never even so much as considered retiring from her very profitable business, but that discreet visit from Sir Braden, within a few hours of the vicious but fatal attack he had inflicted on Sir Philip Dunscumbe, had rendered it essential.

Peterson, whose fortunes had taken a downward turn after he had accidentally killed his opponent in the ring, had gone from collecting money with menaces for the more unsavoury usurers which abounded, to acting as sentinel for Eliza Boon, a woman who had, over the years, often found agreeable company for him. Being a man who had neither qualms nor a ticklish stomach over what he was asked to do, he had known no hesitation in accompanying Sir Braden to Cavendish Square to surreptitiously dispose of the body lying on his study floor as Eliza had instructed. It was unfortunate that Lady Collett had returned home earlier than expected due to the concert she had attended at the Royal Albert Hall finishing before the time shown on the programme and witnessed her husband in the throes of committing such a brutal attack, but like Sir Braden Eliza Boon knew that under no circumstances could Lady Collett be allowed to tell anyone what she had seen.

Even though Eliza had been most reluctant to put the shutters up before she was ready, necessity had rendered it advisable, and since Sir Braden Collett had assured her he would make it worth her while she had readily acquiesced in his request to take up the role of his wife's warder by taking up permanent residence in Cavendish Square. Having acquired a small fortune over the years, her ill-gotten gains had increased considerably upon the sale of her business to a rival, a man who had for some time had his eye on *'Mother Discipline's'* lucrative concern, and since he had been willing to take the girls under his wing as well she had happily walked away from her house of ill repute without a backward glance.

No one setting eyes on this neatly dressed and rather respectable-looking woman would ever have guessed that beneath her demeanour of righteousness was an amoral as well as a dissipated woman who, prior to her early retirement, had led a far from virtuous past. At no time had she been reluctant to bully and coerce her girls into doing whatever she wanted them to do to please either herself or her clientele due, in the main, to the simple fact that she was, like Sir Braden, a domineering bully by nature and just one look at Eleanor Collett had been more than enough to tell her that in this quiet and shy young woman her expertise, or the threat of it, would soon kill any inclination she may have of telling anyone what she had seen.

Eliza, having made her way to the first landing as soon as she knew they had returned, waited with narrowed and watchful eyes as Eleanor climbed the stairs, her fears growing with every lagging step and, not for the first time, thought about making a dash for the front door to try to escape, but as always Peterson was there to prevent her. Physically she was no match for the man who not only towered above her but was far too powerfully built for her to even try to push him out of the way and however disheartening the idea had, yet again, to be abandoned, as her inevitable failure would most probably result in her being locked in her room again.

Eliza Boon, whose tastes, as Sir Braden knew very well, ran in only one direction, had, from the moment she first laid eyes on the young and vulnerable Lady Collett, been irresistibly drawn to her, but realised that were she to lay a finger on his wife other than as a means of restraint, it would go very ill with her. Sir Braden may have no compunction in beating his wife himself and taking immeasurable pleasure from it, but he would not allow anyone else to do so. Collett, as Eliza needed no reminding, was, for all his generosity, a violent and brutal man who would know no hesitation in punishing her for such audacity should she ever make any kind of sexual approach to his wife and should she dangle his crime over his head, then she could easily suffer the same fate as Sir Philip Dunscumbe and Mitchell. Setting aside the fact that she had been brought here specifically to guard Sir Braden's wife as well as threaten her about being foolish enough to tell all she knew and not to attempt to indulge her own inclinations, it could not be denied that it afforded her no little gratification to bully and frighten her.

Upon Eleanor reaching the first landing Eliza's hand took hold of her arm in a firm grip before walking beside her to her room, giving her no opportunity to run away, almost thrusting her through the door before quickly following her inside, instructing her sharply to get undressed, turning the key in the lock as she did so. Relieving Eleanor of her jewellery, she then told her to turn around so she could unfasten her gown, those hideously tactile fingers on the soft skin of her back making Eleanor shiver, wishing, and not for the first time, that there was some way she could escape this unbearable life she was enduring. She hated Braden to touch her as much as she did this dreadful woman because despite her inexperience she had not misread the look in those usually hard brown eyes when they looked at her to know the thoughts which went around in Eliza Boon's head and this, as much as being kept a virtual prisoner and brutally handled by her husband, instilled her with fear and dread.

"Now," Eliza instructed briskly, turning back the coverlet, "into bed with you. Sir Braden will be here directly, and you know how he hates being kept waiting."

Yes, she did: and the thought made Eleanor tremble, her eyes dilating with fear and apprehension as they darted towards the interconnecting door which led to his dressing room, nervously waiting for it to open to admit the man she hated and feared, only vaguely aware of Eliza putting her clothes and jewellery away before she turned the key in the lock and left her. In her agitated state of mind, it seemed no time at all before Eleanor saw the mahogany door open and instinctively she cowered back against the pillows, her trembling fingers clutching the edge of the quilt and drawing it up to her neck as though it were her only lifeline and protection. Just one look at that pink and fleshy face with the protruding blue eyes which glistened feverishly made her fear the worst, her heart beating so fast she felt sick, hoping he would do no more than reprimand her and then leave her. With every slow and determined step he took her unease increased, and when he stood for a moment or two with his hands thrust into the pockets of his dressing gown looking thoughtfully down at her upturned face, she thought she was going to faint from pure fright. Removing his hands from his pockets he seated himself on the edge of the bed, his thick warm fingers easily prising her hands away from the quilt to hold them in a firm grip against his chest, the soft coverlet falling away down to her waist, exposing her heaving breasts beneath the delicate material of her nightgown. "So, my dear," he said softly, "do you still say you have no idea who played that prank on me this evening?"

Eleanor was not fooled by that deceptively gentle tone, and nervously licking her suddenly dry lips managed a quivering, "No," shaking her head. "I *swear* I know nothing about it."

His eyes narrowed and his expression was such that she swallowed anxiously, feeling the increased pressure of his fingers on her own. "A circumstance I find difficult to believe," he told her doubtfully, his eyes sweeping over her, "especially as I found Beatrice Shipton installed in my place upon my return."

"It… it must have been coincidence." She winced as those fingers increased their painful grip.

"Coincidence!" he echoed, raising a bushy eyebrow. "Oh, a little more than that I think," he replied with disturbing smoothness, sliding his fingers down to her wrists and giving them a sharp squeeze. She drew in her breath as the pain shot through her, shaking her head in mute denial. "Do not lie to me, Eleanor," he warned quietly, "you know you do not like it when I get angry."

"P-please, Br-Braden!" she cried. "I don't know anything about that note. I promise you I don't!" Another painful twist of her wrists brought a cry from deep within her throat, but instead of making him stop it only served to increase the pressure of his fingers. "Oh, *please!*" she choked. "You *must* believe me!"

He did, implicitly. He had no need to hear her denials to know that she was telling him the truth; for one thing she was far too frightened of him to do anything which could possibly bring retribution down on her head and, for another, considering he had deliberately kept her away from her friends and acquaintances for the last ten months or so as well as making sure she never went out alone, there really had been no opportunity for her to apply to anyone to help her do any such thing. Whoever had sent that note it was certainly not his wife, and whilst he had every intention of discovering its author, if for no other reason than to let them know he was not a man to take kindly to such tricks, right now he had no wish to bring to a premature end something that was affording him no small amount of excitement. "If I thought for one moment," he told her ominously, giving her wrists one final twist before releasing them, "that you had a hand in that charade, I should be extremely angry. You know that, don't you?"

Eleanor nodded, thankful that he had at last freed her hands from the painful confinement of his, unfortunately her relief was only short-lived as she saw him lean towards her until his face was only inches away from her own, his left hand coming up to encircle her throat.

"So," he mused, "you hope to visit Beatrice Shipton tomorrow, do you?"

Her heart was beating so fast she felt sick, and her breath, by now coming in quick short gasps, made it only possible for her to say faintly, "If… if you don't mind, Br-Braden."

His eyes narrowed slightly. "And if I *did* mind?" he enquired, raising an eyebrow, gently pressing his fingers into the softness of her throat. "Are you saying you would disobey me?"

"No," she shook her head, "of course I would not," her body tensing as those fingers tightened slightly.

"I am glad to hear you say so," he said smoothly, "because you know, my dear," he smiled, "I should not like it were you to do so."

"You know I would never…" she swallowed nervously, "do anything you would not like."

"I am relieved to hear it," he said softly, his fingers pressing tighter around her throat, "because were you ever to do so," he told her, his voice deepening, "I should not like it at all, in fact," he nodded, "I should take it very ill."

"I promise I would not," she managed, her head beginning to throb.

A low-voiced laugh escaped Collett's lips at this, causing Eleanor's stomach to lurch in dread, holding her breath as he lowered his head to allow his mouth to seize her own in a brutal and suffocating kiss which she dared not repulse. She could feel the rapid beating of his heart next to her own and the growing excitement emanating from him, such ominous signs being more than enough to tell her he was not going to merely take her to task about that note, on the contrary this mockery of a kiss was just a foretaste of what was to come, and mentally she braced herself for what her whole mind and body cried out against. To her overwrought nerves, it seemed he would never release her, but gradually he freed her bruised mouth from the repugnant confinement of his; his eyes glistening as they searched her face, those fingers around her neck beginning to caress instead of hurt. "Of course you may visit Beatrice Shipton, my dear," he assured her. "Have I not already promised her the pleasure of your company tomorrow?" Eleanor nodded, hardly able to breathe. "How unforgivably rude it would be in me to disappoint her by reneging on my promise."

"Th-thank you, Br-Braden," Eleanor managed, feeling almost choked.

He eased himself a little further away from her, his eyes travelling down from her pale and frightened face to her breasts, heaving from mingled fright and relief, then back to her face, his thick lips parting into a smile which made her inwardly shiver. "You *shall* visit in Mount Street tomorrow, my dear," he assured her, *"but,"* he emphasised, "Eliza will go with you." She threw him a surprised look. "You *surely* did not think I would let you go alone, did you?" he raised an enquiring eyebrow, his thick repellent fingers sliding her nightdress off her shoulder. "No, no my dear," he said softly, "I think not," lowering his head to run his lips over the soft silken sheen of her skin.

"B-but don't you think it will create a v-very odd a-appearance?" Eleanor dared to ask, her entire body trembling from the combined effects of dread and relief. Dread, because she knew he was going to make love to her, and relief because her visit to tomorrow, although that hateful woman would be with her, he was not, as she had thought, going to forbid it.

"Odd?" Collett queried, raising his head to look up at her. "What could possibly be odd about a husband's concern for his wife? Having only just recovered from a most severe attack of the influenza," he said ominously, "what could be more natural than to have your maid accompany you to satisfy my *very* genuine anxiety lest you should unexpectedly suffer a relapse?" Without giving her time to respond he warned quietly, "You will take Eliza with you, or you will *not* go at all," to which she could do no more than nod. "You must know, my dear," he breathed heavily, his fingers repulsively stroking her skin, "that I cannot possibly allow you to tell anyone, least of all Beatrice Shipton, what you saw that night." The look in his eyes made her inwardly cry out. "You would not do that, would you, my dear?" he asked softly. Eleanor shook her head. "I thought not," he said a little thickly. She drew in her breath and bit down hard on her bottom lip, her small hands clenching into fists at her sides as his lips began to pave a repugnant path from her throat down to her breast, his teeth sinking sharply into its soft fullness. She felt the tears sting her eyes at such a vile and distasteful onslaught, and when he at last released her and straightened up so he could look at her, her heart thudded painfully.

She had of course read about the death of Sir Philip Dunscumbe in the newspapers, but even though they had gone into quite a lot of detail about the police investigations and their failure to even come up with a motive for such a brutal crime let alone finding a culprit, no write-up had so much as intimated at the questions he was intending to raise in the House which could possibly have provided a reason for his death. She had no idea why her husband had found it necessary to murder him, and since he had made it clear that he had no intention of furnishing her with a reason when she had dared to ask him and he had forbidden her to mention it if she knew what was good for her, she had no idea that it was in any way connected to a house of questionable activities where her husband had been a frequent visitor.

Braden may never have subjected her to, or even demanded of her, such practices as he did of those with whom he had associated within the secure confines of *'Mother Discipline's'*, but it could not be said that his lovemaking was either considerate or tender, in fact it was extremely insensitive and abhorrent, calculated only to please himself. As Eleanor at no time liked the feel of his hands and lips on her body, upon hearing him thickly mutter, "Do you not think, my dear," taking hold of her hands and pulling her towards him, "that it is time you thanked me nicely for allowing you to visit your friend tomorrow?" She devoutly prayed to God to let her die this instant, deeming it far preferable to being subjected to this nightmare of a life for another a minute, unaware that the man she had hysterically likened to a knight-errant earlier in the evening was about to come to her rescue.

Chapter Four

Sir Thomas, having returned home a bare five minutes before his wife and brother-in-law were set down at the front door, hardly had time to take the stopper off the whisky decanter before Beatrice entered the study, leaving Tony to follow leisurely behind. Having reluctantly allowed herself to be persuaded by her brother to say nothing of this evening's events until he himself had spoken to Tom, even though she was bursting to mention it to him, she refrained from doing so, containing her eagerness to tell him everything until he joined her upstairs later. Kissing him affectionately on the cheek, she enquired how his evening had fared at the Mansion House after which she laughingly told him that since it was obvious the two of them wanted to talk she would leave them to their whisky and cigars, fondly kissing her brother as he held open the door for her with a recommendation not to keep Tom up all night.

"Here," Tom grinned, handing him a glass of whisky, "you look as though you need it."

"Thanks, I do," Tony said with feeling.

"I take it from your pained expression that you didn't enjoy the opera!" Tom observed amusingly, easing himself into a leather chair by the fire. "Told you, you wouldn't," he nodded as Tony sat down opposite him, crossing one long leg over the other. "Should have come to the Mansion House with me."

"Perhaps," Tony shrugged, taking out a cigarette from the gold case he had pulled out of the inner pocket of his evening coat.

"You're not saying you actually *enjoyed* it, are you?" Tom asked, his eyes widening, knowing his brother-in-law had no real love for opera.

"No," Tony shook his head, "I'm not saying that."

"But you're not sorry you went," Tom commented perceptively.

"No, I'm not sorry I went," Tony confirmed quietly.

"So," Tom wanted to know, wondering who had caught Tony's eye, "who was there tonight; anyone in particular?"

"According to Bea," Tony smiled, lighting his cigarette, having a pretty shrewd idea what was going through Tom's mind, "the world and his wife."

Tom laughed. "You know, I believe that's the only reason she goes to these things."

"Knowing Bea," Tony smiled, "I think you're right."

"So, who *was* there?" Tom asked interestedly, eyeing his brother-in-law through a cloud of cigar smoke. "Anyone you know?"

"No," Tony shook his head, "no one I know – *yet.*"

Tom raised an amusing eyebrow, recognising the gleam which had entered those dark grey eyes. "But someone you intend to know, is that it?"

"Something like that!" Tony smiled, inhaling on his cigarette.

"She's beautiful, of course!" Tom said knowingly.

"Exquisitely so!" Tony confirmed, the gleam in his eyes more pronounced.

"And this delectable creature," Tom enquired, "do I know her?"

"According to Bea," Tony nodded, taking a drink of whisky, "you both know her very well."

"And, of course," Tom commented humorously, "you persuaded Bea to effect an introduction!"

"Well," Tony admitted, somewhat ruefully, "that would have been a little difficult, not to say embarrassing."

Tom eyed his brother-in-law closely, saying suspiciously, "Why do I get the feeling the lady has a husband?" The look in Tony's eyes as he held Tom's was more than enough to tell him that whoever the lady was, she had not only made quite an impact on his brother-in-law, but that she most definitely had a husband. Suddenly his shoulders shook as he pictured the scene, appreciating the incongruousness of it. "I see what you mean," he acknowledged, "the lady's husband would, of course, have rendered the situation just a little awkward."

A smile played at the corner of Tony's mouth at this and were the circumstances different he would have fully appreciated the humour of it, but taking a few moments to savour his whisky said, a little soberly, "As it happened, I did get to meet the lady, at the beginning of the second act, *out* of her husband's company." Tom raised a surprised eyebrow at this, but said nothing. "The lady," Tony inclined his head, "as you have rightly deduced, is not only the most exquisite creature I have ever seen and one I fully intend to become better acquainted with, but one who has the unenviable misfortune of being married to a man who is not only wholly undeserving of her but a bully into the bargain."

An arrested expression entered Tom's eyes at this, asking warily, "Who is this lady?"

"You know, Tom," Tony told him conversationally, as though the question had not been asked, "I have always known that I would know the only woman for me the moment I laid eyes on her; well, as you have rightly concluded," he inclined his head, "I laid eyes on her tonight at Covent Garden."

"Well?" Tom pressed.

Tony held his brother-in-law's look unflinchingly. "Eleanor Collett!"

Tom may have been shaken out of his habitual placidity, but it was nevertheless several moments before he could find his voice to reply to this. Having fallen in love with the Honourable Beatrice Carr upon first setting eyes on her, he could not criticise Tony for doing the same with Eleanor Collett because he was as sure as a man could be that this is what he had done. He could not blame him, after all Eleanor was quite a taking a little thing and certainly deserved better than Sir Braden Collett, a man who, he felt sure, could be relied upon to be rather severe in his dealings with her. Even now he could not, for the life of him, understand why Sir Miles Tatton had sanctioned the marriage in the first place because although Tom was not one of Collett's cronies, indeed, apart from an acknowledgement in passing or a polite social exchange when he and Eleanor had accepted their invitation to a gathering in Mount Street, they had nothing whatever to do with one another, but he knew enough of him to know that there was a ring of truth in Tony's comment about him being a bully. Like Beatrice, Tom could no more explain Eleanor's periodic disappearances from public life than he could her father's reasons for agreeing to the match, but of one thing he had no doubt, and that was Sir Braden would by no means welcome another man's attentions to his wife. Tom liked Tony, they got along extremely well, indeed, he knew of no finer or more decent man, and although he accepted without question that his brother-in-law was no inexperienced youth, he had never yet known him do anything which could be construed as even remotely ungentlemanly, much less embarking on something which could lead to jeopardising a lady's reputation by deliberately seeking her out. But this business of Eleanor Collett could quite easily lead to trouble. "*Eleanor*!" he managed at last. "Good God!" he cried, sitting forward in his seat when he had finally recovered his voice, not at all sure whether it was her being seen in public for the first time in over two weeks or the fact that of all the women to choose from his brother-in-law had to set his heart on a lady who was not only married, but married to Sir Braden Collett of all people, which surprised him the most. "You can't be serious!"

"Sure I'm serious," Tony told him unequivocally. "Not only am I determined to get to know to her better, for reasons which you of all people, having fallen in love with Bea at first sight," he reminded him, "should understand, but I am equally determined to get her away from that bully of a husband."

"Yes but…"

"No 'buts', Tom." Tony shook his head. "My mind is quite made up; as for my heart," he shrugged, "it could no more forget her than it could leave her in the hands of a man who is nothing but a brute."

"But Tony," Tom pointed out reasonably, "you don't know for certain that Collett *is* a brute! I own," he admitted, "I can't claim a liking for the man, and whilst I admit he has a temper and can be quite objectionable when he's a mind as well as being quite wrong for Eleanor, you can't possibly know…"

"I *do* know, Tom," Tony broke in firmly, a steely look entering those dark grey eyes. "I know him for the bullying thug he is, and had you been there this evening and saw what I did with my own eyes, you would have been left in no doubt."

Tom, who was beginning to feel just a little uneasy, hardly dared to ask, "And just what *did* you see?" It was true that he had never liked Collett, an argumentative and difficult man at the best of times and one who, on more than one occasion, had given offence for no other reason than it suited his mood, but nothing quite prepared him for Tony's revelation. Tom knew his brother-in-law as being a man not given over to mendacity any more than he was to exaggeration and, certainly, not one to succumb to deceit for his own ends, on the contrary he was open and honest and totally straightforward, but whilst at any other time he would have found Tony's old-fashioned trick of getting rid of Collett for a short time amusing, so shocked was he at what he heard that it was several moments before he could find his voice to exclaim, "Good God!" sitting bolt upright, looking rather taken aback at his brother-in-law. "You don't mean it!"

"I'm afraid I do," Tony grimaced. "Not very edifying, is it?"

"Edifying!" Tom repeated, disgustedly. "Why, it's the most diabolical thing I've ever heard! I would never have believed it, not even of him!" his usual calm deserting him, taking a much-needed drink. "For God's sake, Tony!" he exclaimed. "This is a man who goes to the races with the Prince of Wales!"

"He may well," Tony shrugged, "but I know what I saw, Tom," he told him unequivocally, "and if you went to the opera more often you would know that those glasses are far more powerful than you suppose, but I did not need opera glasses to see the marks on her wrists."

"Damn it, Tony!" Tom cried. "I'm not doubting your word, it's just that it takes some getting used to!" Discovering something of this nature had understandably come as a severe shock, but as he had himself witnessed Collett's outbursts of temper on more than one occasion, Tony's disclosure went a long way to explaining Eleanor's behaviour. "Dear God!" he cried with revulsion. "That poor child!"

"Collett may well associate with the Prince of Wales," Tony conceded, "but it does not alter the fact that he is a vicious bully who treats his wife in a way I would not treat a dog!"

"The man deserves to be horsewhipped!" Tom exclaimed vehemently.

"My sentiments exactly!" Tony said with feeling, refilling their glasses. "Especially when I consider that he makes a habit of it!"

"But *why* in God's name," Tom exclaimed, taking his glass, "does he do it?"

"Because he enjoys it," Tony stated in a hard voice, resuming his seat. "I saw the look in his eyes as he twisted her wrist," he explained in response to Tom's horrified stare, "and he did it for no other reason than he took pleasure from it." Swallowing a generous mouthful of whisky, he went on, "I think it's these beatings which make it necessary for her to remain indoors every now and then for a spell; after all," he nodded, his mouth grim, "Collett would not want it known that he beats his wife, and you must admit," pointing his glass at Tom, "that bruises do not disappear overnight. In fact," he told him, "according to Bea, she put her recent absence down to a severe attack of influenza!"

"I admit," Tom acknowledged, sickened at the thought, "that we have often wondered what could possibly account for her frequent absences, but we never suspected anything like this!" He shook his head. "But Tatton," he cried at a loss, "surely he must know something like this is going on!"

"I couldn't say," Tony shook his head. "From what Bea told me she has no idea whether Eleanor sees her father or not, but given the circumstances I should think it most unlikely or, if she does," he acknowledged, "it must only be infrequently. He may have sold his daughter into marriage to a man for reasons I can only guess at, but he would have to be blind not to recognise the truth."

"What Tatton was thinking of to permit such a marriage," Tom shook his head, quite at a loss, "beats me! Why," he exclaimed disgustedly, "Collett's old enough to be her father!"

"Bea thinks the reason could well have something to do with Reginald's gambling debts," Tony offered.

"That wouldn't surprise me." Tom nodded. "From all I hear it cost Tatton a fortune to settle them before packing him off to Ceylon." He inhaled on his cigar, then, looking straight across at Tony, said forcefully, "Damn it Tony, for a man to sell his daughter into marriage, because that's exactly what it was and to a man like Collett of all people, is nothing short of mercenary!"

"I agree." Tony inclined his head, inhaling on his cigarette.

"I tell you, Tony," Tom said seriously, "Collett is not the man I would give my daughter to in marriage, no matter how straitened my circumstances!"

"No, neither would I," Tony agreed.

Tom swallowed a generous mouthful of whisky. "Even before you told me all of this, I for one, Bea too, would be happy to see Eleanor out of that marriage, which," he pointed his glass at Tony, "I am convinced was not of her choosing."

"So am I," Tony said firmly, a hard light entering those dark grey eyes, "and I saw enough tonight to tell me just what it must be like for her; which is why I am determined to get her away from him as quickly as possible; no matter what it takes."

Tom eyed his brother-in-law thoughtfully, saying at length, "That may not be so easy, Tony. Don't misunderstand me," he said earnestly, "I abhor men like Collett, but considering how he makes sure she is never alone, although why that is I have never understood and never will, and she never seems to be at home when Bea calls," he shook his head, "I can't see how it can possibly be done."

"Well, a way must be found, and soon," Tony said determinedly, throwing the end of his cigarette onto the fire. "So," he cocked his head, "what do you know about Collett?"

"What is it you want to me to tell you?"

"What Bea didn't."

"Well, that's not much more, I'm afraid," Tom sighed. "We are not friends, you understand," he nodded. "Apart from a bow in passing our paths seldom cross, I'm glad to say. The invitations Bea sends to Cavendish Square are for Eleanor's sake and not for the pleasure of *his* company!" he assured him.

"But you must know or, at least, hear things Bea does not," Tony said reasonably.

"Well, yes," Tom acknowledged, "I suppose I do, but I assure you, Tony," he stressed, "apart from his uncertain temper and his frequent rudeness, there is nothing known against him. As Bea has no doubt told you, he is a most upright citizen; a patron of the arts and one who can be seen regularly at the opera or the ballet as well as being a generous donator to charitable causes." Pausing only to inhale on his cigar, he continued, "He is a member of *'The Stephenson Club'* where he regularly plays cards – no," he shook his head, when he saw Tony raise an eyebrow, "he does not cheat, he is far too skilled a player for that, which accounts for him rising a winner nine times out of ten. He is meticulous in all matters of play and pay, even his most severest critic acknowledges that." He shrugged. "Apart from fellow club members he does not appear to associate with any but his close circle of intimates, none of whom," he said, somewhat relieved, "I am fully acquainted with. I assure you, Tony," he nodded, "whether we like him or not, Collett is a most respectable and law-abiding citizen; in fact, a man of impeccable credentials."

"Sure," Tony grimaced, "a man who beats his wife for the sheer hell of it is a real nice guy!" He took a mouthful of whisky, his forehead creased in thought and, upon being asked what was on his mind, said thoughtfully, "I was thinking, surely a man like Collett, who takes pleasure from brutality, would need more of an outlet for it than inflicting pain on his wife."

"Very probably," Tom agreed, not pretending to misunderstand him, "but if Collett does indulge his inclinations outside the matrimonial home to satisfy a need he can't exact from his wife," catching the hard look which entered Tony's eyes at this, "then it's hardly likely such activities will become common knowledge. As for his intimates," he shrugged, finishing the remainder of his whisky, "they may know or, even, participate themselves, but I have heard nothing to suggest this, which is hardly surprising."

"No," Tony said harshly, "men like Collett have a way of hiding their true nature behind a cloak of respectability, and any suggestion to the contrary will be met with outrage and denial, but he has to be stopped, Tom."

"I agree," Tom nodded, "but whilst I admit you played a blinder tonight in getting rid of him for a short time, has it occurred to you that he may well vent his anger over being made a fool of on Eleanor?"

Tony's eyes clouded. "Yes," he nodded, "it has, but something tells me he won't."

"Oh," Tom raised an enquiring eyebrow, "and what makes you so sure of that? If he's the type of man we take him to be, what's to prevent him?"

"The fact that he is allowing Eleanor to come here tomorrow to see Bea." He saw the look of scepticism on Tom's face, and sighed, "Yes, I know I'm gambling an awful lot on that, but think Tom," he advised, "the last thing he wants is his wife to come here tomorrow with marks on her; he's no fool, he knows that Bea would notice them, and the last thing he wants is for her to question the reason for them."

Tom considered a moment, watching a curl of cigar smoke waft up into the air. "Yes," he conceded at length, "I think you're right, but if Eleanor does come tomorrow, and I say *if*," he emphasised, "because there is every possibility Collett could well change his mind and prevent her, just what do you hope to gain from it?"

"Her trust," Tony said simply.

"You want her to confide in you, is that it?" Tom commented, a little doubtfully.

"Something like that," Tony sighed.

"Tony, don't you think you're hoping for a little too much?" Tom suggested steadily. "Don't forget," he reminded him reasonably, "she's been married to Collett for over twelve months, and if we are right in that he has been ill-treating her all this time, the chances are pretty good that her faith in men is not very high."

"I realise that," Tony conceded, "but her reaction to me tonight was not one of fear," he pointed out, "which leads me to hope that she *will* trust me."

"Tony, I have a fairly shrewd idea what's in your mind," Tom told him, not unsympathetically, "not that I blame you for falling for Eleanor; she's quite a taking little thing, but Collett won't give her up without a fight, and I'd say he can fight pretty dirty. Not only that," he warned him, "but Collett has powerful friends in high places and he won't hesitate to use them to help him get rid of you if he thinks you're becoming something of a nuisance."

"So, what are you saying Tom?" Tony asked, raising a questioning eyebrow. "I just forget all about it and turn my back?"

"No," Tom told him unequivocally, "that's not what I'm saying and you know it's not," he nodded. "However much we may deplore Collett's treatment of her, we have to consider the consequences to Eleanor should we attempt any intervention on her behalf." He saw the frown which had descended onto Tony's forehead, but even though he expected nothing less from a man of his integrity, Tom felt it incumbent upon him to point out one or two pertinent facts, facts which, in his anger and disgust over what he had seen tonight, not to mention his feelings for Eleanor, he had momentarily lost sight of. "We have known one another a long time Tony, and you don't need me to tell you what I think of you. I fully agree that men like Collett should be strung up, but you know as well as I do that what takes place between a man and his wife, however despicable, remains there and I have no doubt that this holds true in America too. Don't misunderstand me, Tony," he stressed, "no one would be happier than Bea if Eleanor could be taken out of that marriage, the same goes for me, but anything you attempt to bring it about must work the first time; because you know as well as I do that should it fail then the consequences to Eleanor would be severe. Collett will make sure of that!" After finishing off his whisky he pointed his empty glass at him, nodding, "Not only that, but it will leave Eleanor exposed to innuendo and gossip, and Collett," he reminded him, "will not take kindly to that, but if you think for one moment that such an action would induce him into granting her a divorce, you are quite wrong."

Tony, who had listened to his brother-in-law in contemplative silence, could not argue against such reasoning; every word he had spoken was no less than the truth, but the mere thought of the woman who had entered his life only a short time ago and who had quite unexpectedly taken such a hold of his heart being subjected to such brutality, made him determined to do all he could to remove her from a life which he knew must be intolerable. When he had written that note it had been with the sole intention of ridding Eleanor of her husband's company for just long enough for him to speak to her, but as he slowly climbed the stairs a good three-quarters of an hour after his brother-in-law had retired, his instincts, which had so far never let him down, were telling him that there was more to this business than he yet knew. As far as removing Eleanor from her home and husband was concerned, he could not deny that such an action would have catastrophic consequences in themselves, leaving her dangerously exposed to vicious tittle-tattle and idle speculation, but he could no more ignore her unbearable situation than he could his feelings for her.

If he was right about Collett taking pleasurable satisfaction from his violent behaviour towards Eleanor as well as seeking a far more gratifying outlet for it outside the marriage, then he could only guess as to whether Sir Miles Tatton knew of it or not, but as it appeared the two men did not associate with one another any more than was necessary, it was entirely possible that he did not know the full extent of either his son-in-law's indulgences or the ill-treatment he handed out to his daughter. Even so, for a father to consider for so much as a moment giving his daughter in marriage to a man who was twice her age and one, moreover, to a man like Collett, whose disagreeable manner was well-known, was beyond his comprehension. Tony knew Tom was right when he said that there was every possibility Collett may, for whatever reason, change his mind about allowing Eleanor to visit Bea tomorrow after all, and having seen enough this evening to know precisely the kind of man he was dealing with, Tony knew that Eleanor would not dare to come here without his permission. Should she not do so, then he could only hope that Collett, having told Bea he had accepted the Kirkmichaels' invitation for tomorrow evening on behalf of them both, they would attend after all, when, with any luck, the opportunity to speak to her alone would present itself.

But more worrying than anything else right now was Collett's reaction to the trick he had played on him this evening. A man of his temperament and aggressive tendencies would not take kindly to being made a fool of by a ruse, and from what Bea had told him he had been far from pleased upon returning to his box to find her there with his wife, especially as her presence followed hard upon the heels of him discovering he had been tricked. Tony could not discount Tom's comment about him taking his anger out on Eleanor. It was more than probable, and by the time he had reached the first landing he was beginning to have serious doubts about his earlier confidence in that, due to her coming here tomorrow, Collett would not run the risk of hurting her and leaving any tell-tale marks. The last thing Tony had wanted when he had offered Eleanor a brief respite from his company at Covent Garden was to place her in jeopardy, but now, as he unconsciously turned to walk slowly up the next flight of stairs, he could not rid his mind that this could well be what he had done. He could not bear the thought that his actions this evening could well be responsible for any pain and indignities her husband may choose to inflict upon her in a fit of anger, but just as unbearable was the thought of her being subjected to any sexual demands he made of her, and were it at all possible he would go to Cavendish Square right now and forcibly remove her. The knowledge that he could not do so only served to increase his frustration and uneasiness, and by the time he reached the second landing his thoughts were very far from elevating, but just as he was about to walk across the highly polished floorboards towards his room he heard an urgently whispered, "*Uncle Tony, Uncle Tony!*" coming from the floor above. Immediately the frown disappeared and a smile lit up his face as he saw his eldest nephew kneeling on the floor with his head pushed against the rails and two small hands stretching up to hold the banister.

"Toby! *Now*, what's all this?" he asked amusingly when he was halfway up the next flight of stairs leading to the upper landing which housed the nursery quarters.

"I thought you were never coming upstairs!" Toby cried, standing up. "I've been waiting for *ages and ages*!" he told him, coming up to him and tucking one small hand in his.

"Do you know what time it is?" Tony asked quietly.

"No," Toby shook his head, "but that doesn't matter."

"No," Tony smiled indulgently, "I don't suppose it does when you are eight years old."

"I want to show you something," Toby told him excitedly, his face lighting up.

"And what is it you want to show me at this time of night?" Tony asked leniently, who loved his niece and nephews as much as they did him.

"It's hidden in the drawer beside my bed," Toby told him conspiratorially.

"What is?" Tony laughed, unable to resist the urgent tugging of Toby's hand to follow him.

"You'll see," he smiled, revealing a lost front tooth.

Creeping stealthily into the room where his younger brother was fast asleep, Toby pulled Tony towards a small chest of drawers that separated the two beds and covered in a multitude of paraphernalia which both boys regarded as sacrosanct, and after instructing his uncle to sit down on the edge of his bed, he carefully opened the top drawer of the chest to pull out a glass jar three-quarters full of water in which a newt suddenly darted to life at the unexpected sight of light. "I got it off Johnnie Webster today at school," he confided in a whisper. "I swapped it for my catapult. Isn't it *super*, Uncle Tony?" he cried excitedly, sitting comfortably down beside him and generously handing him the jar so he could have a closer look.

"Now *that's* what I call a newt!" Tony said approvingly, his eyes alight with amusement.

"I knew you'd like it! Mummy doesn't know I have it yet," Toby confessed, pleased it had met with his uncle's approval. "Daddy does though, and he thinks it's super too, but Nanny Susan says I ought to get rid of it."

"Does she?" Tony asked sympathetically.

"Yes," Toby said seriously, "she thinks it's dirty and full of germs," he told him.

"Well," Tony suggested, "why not keep it a few days and see how you feel?"

This suggestion having found immediate favour, Toby then said, somewhat scornfully, "Alice thinks it's beastly. How stupid! *Sisters!"* he disparaged. "I *do* think girls are silly, don't you, Uncle Tony?"

"I expect I did when I was your age," Tony smiled, handing him his jar back, "but you won't," he told him, ruffling his thick dark hair, "when you get older."

Toby gave this due consideration, his face creased in thought, saying at length, "Do you mean that I shall actually *like* girls, Uncle Tony?" shuddering at the thought.

"Yes," Tony told him, not quite able to hide the laughter in his voice, "very much so!"

"Ugh!" Toby screwed up his face.

Tony laughed. "Don't worry, it won't be as bad as you think."

"Is that you, Uncle Tony?" came a sleepy voice from the opposite bed.

"Yes it's…" he began.

"I've just been showing him my newt," Toby cut in, placing his jar carefully back inside the drawer. "He thinks it's super too; don't you, Uncle Tony?"

"Yes, I think it's *super*," he confirmed amusingly, "but if you two don't…"

"Are you going to tell us a story, Uncle Tony?" Patrick asked hopefully, a dark curly head emerging from under the covers.

"I think it's a little late for stories," Tony pointed out, the serious note in his voice not very convincing.

"Oh *please*, Uncle Tony," Patrick begged on a yawn. "Tell us the one about that general surrounded by Indians in a place called 'Little Something'. I like that one."

"I daresay you do," Tony said on a quiver, "but if you two don't go back to sleep I shall be in the doghouse!"

"What's the doghouse?" Patrick yawned again, rubbing his eyes as he sat up in bed.

"Never you mind," Tony told him as sternly as he could.

"Uncle Tony," Toby said anxiously as he climbed into bed, "you won't tell Mummy, will you?"

"Do you mean about the newt or being up so late?" his lips twitched, pulling the covers over him.

"Both," Toby replied impishly.

"No," Tony shook his head, "I won't tell Mummy, providing you go to sleep… both of you," incorporating Patrick in this far from stern warning.

"But, *Uncle Tony…?*" they cried in unison.

"*Sleep*!" he warned, ruffling their heads. "Or I shall lasso the pair of you and tie you up!" this dreadful prospect making his nephews laugh.

Chapter Five

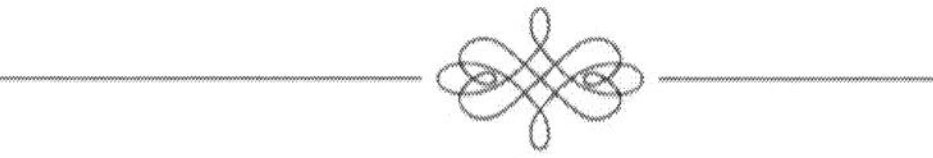

Beatrice, having had to contain her impatience as best she could until her husband joined her upstairs to speak to him about what had occurred at Covent Garden, had poured the whole story into his ears together with her concerns almost before he had closed the bedroom door behind him, ending by stating that no matter how much she loved her brother she wished he would pause and think before going headlong into something which could well end up the worse for him. "Because whilst I have nothing against Eleanor," she told him truthfully, "indeed, I love her dearly," she assured him, "in fact," she said firmly, "nothing would make me happier than to see her removed from that marriage, and under different circumstances she would be ideal for Tony, but I cannot help feeling that something dreadful is going to happen. I mean," she asked helplessly of her husband, "what *does* he think he can possibly do?"

Tom, who loved his wife very much, knew from experience that it was useless to try to interrupt her when she was in the middle of explaining something, and therefore waited in good humoured silence until she had finished before telling her, though not all, of what had passed between himself and Tony in the study. "You know, Bea," he said quietly, sliding into bed beside her, "you don't need me to tell you what I think of Tony; a finer man I have never known…"

"Yes, but…" she began.

"Listen Bea," Tom said gently, taking hold of her agitated hands, "I know Tony well enough to say that even if he had not fallen in love with Eleanor upon first setting eyes on her because that is precisely what he has done, his reaction to what occurred this evening would be exactly the same, and whilst I would not go so far as to say he would consider intervening if his affections were not engaged, he would still regard such behaviour as not only contemptible, but downright despicable." He kissed her cheek. "You know it's true," he smiled.

"Yes," she sighed, "I know."

"I have no more idea than you how he intends to set about freeing her from a most intolerable marriage or, for that matter," he nodded, "what he hopes Eleanor will tell him tomorrow, providing Collett does not change his mind about her coming here that is, but you know as well as I do that once Tony has made up his mind to something it takes a deal of changing."

"Yes," she sighed again, "I know." A slight frown suddenly creased her forehead and upon being asked what she was thinking, turned to face Tom, saying, "It's just that when I was teasing him a little before we left for the opera about marriage, he told me that he needed no help in choosing the right woman, in fact," she nodded, "he said he would know her the moment he laid eyes on her."

"Well," Tom smiled, "it looks very much as though he laid eyes on her tonight."

"Yes, but," she shrugged helplessly, "it all seems to have happened so very quickly."

"As I recall," Tom reminded her affectionately, "it happened that quickly for me too." Giving her no opportunity to reply to this, he folded her in his arms and kissed her, and since she was only too happy to respond, blissfully shelved the worry of her brother and Eleanor until tomorrow.

Like her husband, Beatrice might be a little at a loss to know how her brother intended to help Eleanor without incurring her husband's wrath and therefore bringing further mistreatment down upon her, let alone finding a way of ever marrying her, but she was even more at a loss when she looked through the drawing-room window the following morning upon hearing a carriage pull up to see Eleanor being set down in Mount Street and the startling discovery that she was not alone. "Good gracious!" she cried. "I don't believe it!"

"What don't you believe?" Tony asked, his voice a nice mix of curiosity and amusement as he came to stand beside her.

"Eleanor!" Beatrice breathed, turning to face him. "She's got that *dreadful* woman with her!" She shook her head, bewildered. "But *what on earth* makes Collett think she needs her?" She saw the frown descend onto Tony's forehead, just catching the barely audible curse which left his lips. "Oh, Tony!" she cried, laying a hand on his arm. "You do not think that she intends to remain with us throughout, do you?"

"That's precisely what I think," he said grimly, looking through the window just in time to catch sight of Eliza Boon as she said something in Eleanor's ear.

"But I…"

"Listen Bea," Tony said urgently, "there's not much time. I don't want that woman to know I'm here because I get the feeling she reports Eleanor's movements to Collett as well as who she meets."

"But why?" she cried, bemused.

"I can't answer that yet," he shook his head.

"Yes, but…"

Forestalling the words which were about to leave her lips, Tony gripped her arm. "Look Bea," he nodded, "that woman must not see me; so, this is what I want you to do…"

"But Tony I…" she began when he had finished giving her his instructions.

"You *must,* Bea," he said. "Offer any excuse you like, but you must get Eleanor to go up to your room, and alone. I need to speak to her."

"But to what purpose?" Beatrice asked, shaking her head. "What do you think she can possibly tell you? Do not forget," she reminded him, unconsciously echoing her husband's thoughts, "she does not know you well enough and may not trust you!"

"Please, Bea," Tony smiled, giving her hand a squeeze, "it's important."

"Oh, very well," she sighed, "I'll try."

"Thanks Bea," he smiled, kissing her forehead.

"Do not thank me yet," she warned, "because I would not put it beyond that dreadful woman to go upstairs with her!"

She did not, but it did not escape Beatrice's notice that she kept a very close eye on Eleanor, which was having a most adverse effect upon her, so much so that her contribution to any topic of conversation initiated was somewhat inattentive, her rather vague replies suggesting that her mind was elsewhere. Beatrice had tried with all the adroitness at her command to dislodge Eliza Boon from Eleanor's side, but not all her efforts would move her, and since nothing short of ordering her out of the room, something which, from the nervous look which descended onto her young friend's face, would clearly have distressed her, she had no choice but to accept her presence and the reason for it with what dignity she could muster. Eleanor may well be pleased to see Beatrice again, but unlike the previous evening her greeting was very far removed from the impulsive one she had given her hostess upon entering Sir Braden's box at Covent Garden, and Beatrice, who was never usually at a loss in any social situation, was beginning to find her virtually one-sided conversations something of a strain. She may have a well-earned reputation for being a most charming and hospitable hostess as well as being an essential guest at any gathering, but despite her liveliness and entertaining conversation she was nevertheless a very astute woman, and it did not take her long to see that, despite Eleanor's subdued behaviour, the look in her eyes clearly suggested that she longed to be alone with her. It also did not take Beatrice long to acknowledge that Tony could well be right after all in that this odious woman, who seemed more like a gaoler than a maid, did in fact report the child's conduct and conversations to Collett.

Eleanor did indeed long to be alone with her friend, but she knew that had she insisted on visiting in Mount Street alone Braden would have forbidden it altogether, becoming instantly suspicious, and since it had been some considerable time since she had seen Beatrice out of her husband's company she had been left with no choice but to let Eliza Boon come with her. Unfortunately, it was impossible for Eleanor to explain to Beatrice the reason for this, any more than she could tell her how restricted and suffocated she felt in this woman's presence, or that she dreaded returning to Cavendish Square and her husband to find herself being interrogated as to exactly what had passed between them. She was not at all certain whether to be glad or sorry that Beatrice's brother was not here as she had thought, especially having gained the impression last night that he would be, but the sight of her gaoler sitting stiffly upright just a little away from where she sat beside Beatrice on the sofa, keeping her under close observation, forced her to admit that it was perhaps as well he was not.

Even though she had not been fully concentrating on the performance last night it had nevertheless made a welcome change to escape from the suffocating and unbearable confines of Cavendish Square, so much so that she hated the thought of having to return there, especially when she knew what would await her. Braden did not take kindly to being made a fool of and although she had not expected him to be called out halfway through the performance the truth was that to suddenly find herself free of his company for only a few minutes was an immeasurable relief, especially after that unprovoked assault on her wrist. That his removal had been deliberately contrived to allow his place to be taken by a man she had never set eyes on before had quite startled her, but even before he had made his identity known to her she had known straightaway that she liked him and had no need to fear him, but more than this was the feeling, as compelling as it was surprising, of not only having known him all her life but also that in this tall dark stranger she had found the other half of herself.

Somewhere on the periphery of her consciousness Eleanor heard Beatrice telling her about the dress she had had made purposely for her to wear at the Kirkmichaels' wedding anniversary party this evening, but although she responded suitably and told her that it was really quite beautiful her voice as well as her admiration sounded forced even in her own ears. Beatrice, having had the forethought to bring it downstairs in readiness before Eleanor arrived just in case Collett took it into his head to come with her, especially when she remembered that it was the reason she had put forward to account for the visit, could not help feeling a little disappointed over Eleanor's unenthusiastic response, but only a moment's thought was enough to tell her that the child must be finding it difficult to rouse interest in anything with that hateful woman in constant attendance.

If it had been at all possible for Eleanor to have read Beatrice's mind she would have fully agreed with her, but no matter how much she delighted in visiting her friend so conscious was she of Eliza Boon sitting some little way from them, closely watching her and storing up everything which passed between them to tell her husband, that it was almost impossible to be relaxed and sociable. She hoped Beatrice would not hold it against her or think ill of her because of it, she did not think so, Beatrice was nothing if not kind and understanding, but although her whole body cried out with the need to fling herself into Beatrice's arms and confide the whole to her, she knew she could not. It was not only because she was afraid of what Braden would do to her should he ever discover it, but she had to think of her father; one word from her to anyone about the burden she was carrying, not to mention her husband's brutal treatment of her, would be enough for Braden to bring her father to ruin. Braden had extracted a heavy penalty from her last night, not only because he needed to vent his anger over the trick played on him but also as a reward for allowing her to come here today. It had been a long time after Braden had left her before Eleanor finally fell asleep, and then for only a short time, to lie inertly back against the pillows to watch the dawn begin to break over the rooftops through a slight gap in the curtains with a numb detachment not even the brief emergence of a watery sun, striving to lighten the snow leaden sky, could motivate her out of. Last night, no more than at any other time when he forced himself upon her, did her unresponsive reaction to the degradation he imposed on her either create comment or deter him, but even now she could still feel his repellent kisses on her skin, making her inwardly shudder.

From the very first moment she had married Braden Collett her life had been unbearable, not simply because he deemed it his right to force himself upon her whenever he chose or his regular beatings, but ever since that fateful evening when she had returned home earlier than expected to find her husband had committed cold-blooded murder in his own study, it had been intolerable. It had been bad enough before being subjected to his bullying obliging her to remain in her room for a day or two, sometimes even a week, to give the bruises time to fade, but ever since the horrifying incident she had witnessed that night, his mistreatment had become more frequent, but worse than this was being kept constantly under surveillance and never being allowed out-of-doors on her own in case she took it into her head to report what she had seen. Since her husband had not seen fit to enlighten her as to the background of Peterson and Eliza Boon, she could only hazard a guess as to how he knew them, but that he did so and well had been obvious from the moment they had entered the house. Between these two detestable and frightening individuals as well as her husband, Eleanor not only felt trapped and helpless but contaminated, and knew she could no longer bear this abhorrent existence which passed as her life, and after a little over twelve months into her marriage she could all too easily understand what it was she had always feared in him.

She dreaded every day dawning; knowing that she would be watched and spied upon, denied any privacy and stripped of her freedom, even Mary being taken from her. Last night, resting limply back against the pillows as she numbly watched the dawn slowly break over the snow-covered rooftops, it was with a sickening thud of her heart that she realised there was no escape from what passed as her life; death, it seemed, was the only thing which would free her, the mere thought bringing the tears to her eyes. It was just as they were on the point of falling freely down her cheeks that her mind, without any warning, conjured up the tall dark figure of a man who, in a despairing moment of hysteria earlier in the evening, she had hailed as her knight-errant; a man she had instinctively recognised as the one she had been unconsciously seeking her whole life and whose gentle touch, even when she was at her most wretched, made her draw in her breath with anticipation. But now, in the cold light of day in Beatrice's drawing-room with Eliza Boon closely watching her and no sign of the man she had stupidly believed liked her and wanted to help, Eleanor was reluctantly forced to acknowledge that she had foolishly allowed her dreams to get the better of her, and it was with a painful sinking of her heart that she felt every vestige of hope disappear.

"I can't imagine what I was thinking of!" Beatrice's voice broke into her not very edifying thoughts. "I am certain I would forget my head if it was not attached to my shoulders! You do not mind, do you, my dear?"

Since Eleanor had not been altogether concentrating she shook her head, a little bewildered, her eyes somewhat blank as they focused on Beatrice, still holding the dress of rustling pink taffeta over her two arms. "I'm sorry, Beatrice," she smiled absently, "I was not fully attending."

As this had not escaped Beatrice's notice, which she had no hesitation in attributing to Eliza Boon's presence, she merely laughed and shook her head, then, with an excellent attempt at appearing totally scatter-brained, confessed, "I do that all the time, my dear, as Tom has told me often," falsely maligning her innocent husband; consoling her conscience with the knowledge that it was all in a very good cause. "It is merely that I have stupidly left the cape to this dress in my room and I do so want your excellent opinion. I wondered if you would be so kind as to run up and fetch it for me?" this oversight proving a very useful excuse. "You know which room it is, don't you?"

"Yes," Eleanor smiled, "of course."

"Oh, wait a moment," Beatrice called after her as though she had just remembered something, needing to offer a reason to account for Eleanor being gone for far longer than it would ordinarily take her to retrieve the cape off the bed to give Tony time to speak to her without this hateful woman becoming suspicious, "let me think a moment," her face bearing all the signs of forgetfulness, "I think… yes, I am perfectly sure I left it lying on the bed, but…" screwing up her face, "or did I leave it in the dressing room?" she pondered. "Oh, of course, how silly of me," she giggled, "I remember now," she nodded contritely at Eleanor, so very conscious of those sharp brown eyes looking keenly from one to the other, "I took it up to Nanny." She giggled again. "Do not tell Tom, will you my dear, because he will only accuse me of being totally empty-headed again, but you see," she offered, with all the air of one participating in some childish game, "there was a slight missing of some stitches on the hem. I really should have sent it back to the dressmakers, indeed, had I told Tom he would have insisted I return it to have them attend to it, but I do particularly want to wear it tonight at the Kirkmichaels' and had I returned it I doubt it would be ready for this evening and Nanny, you know," she nodded happily, "is a most excellent needlewoman."

"I'll find it," Eleanor smiled faintly, hurrying out of the room as she spoke, leaving Beatrice to do what she could to avert suspicion in the mind of Eliza Boon by adopting the mien of one who was not only totally forgetful, but frivolous into the bargain.

At no time could it be said that Beatrice ever looked upon herself as being too proud or high and mighty to converse with servants, considering them as far beneath her, on the contrary every member of her domestic household liked her very much, knowing her to be a kind and generous mistress who never failed to thank and reward them for any service they performed for her, in fact she knew all their troubles and life histories by heart, having a genuine concern for their welfare, but it took every ounce of resolution she possessed to converse with a woman she was totally convinced was up to no good as well as spying on Eleanor for her husband. If it were not essential to divert Eliza Boon's mind and to keep her from wondering what Eleanor was doing upstairs, she most certainly would not have done so.

Had Eleanor not have been so taken up with her own thoughts she would have questioned Beatrice's comments about her husband, a man whom she knew loved and adored his wife, as it was she climbed the stairs in a mood of complete and utter wretchedness, dreading the thought that she would soon be returning to Cavendish Square.

Tony may have every faith in Beatrice doing everything she could to get Eleanor up to her room on some pretext or other without her guard becoming suspicious and therefore taking it into her head to accompany her, but nevertheless he did not expect to see Eleanor for some little time as it could well take Beatrice a while before she could forge the right opening to engineer such a move. Having only had time to quickly glance at the newspaper before sitting down to breakfast, he took a moment to retrieve it from the study to read upstairs while waiting for Eleanor, having caught sight of a lengthy article on the second page reporting on the progress of a story which had caught his interest when Bill had cabled it to him in New York about ten months previously when it first broke. It was not only his own newspapers *'The Daily Bulletin'* and its sister newspaper *'The London Chronicler'* which had covered the story, but every newspaper in Fleet Street had run lengthy pieces on it, and in fact still were. The brutal murder of Sir Philip Dunscumbe MP had been front-page news for weeks following the discovery of his body early one morning by a man on his way to work, having washed up a few miles downriver at Greenwich, but whilst the police had identified the cause of death as being the result of a savage beating to the head, they had been unable to come up with a motive to account for such a vicious crime. Having ruled out larceny as the reason for his death since his watch and signet ring, in fact everything he had on his person, including his wallet, had not been removed, it seemed that, despite a most thorough investigation over the ensuing months, the reason for such a brutal act continued to elude them.

Such a savage attack indicated that his murder had not been premeditated, but rather a spur-of-the-moment thing, unless, of course that was how the murderer wanted it to appear. Due to the gradual deterioration of the body after being in the water for three days it had not been possible to arrive at a precise time of death, but tracking back from when Sir Philip Dunscumbe had last been seen until his body was discovered, the police had calculated that his death had occurred at some point within the last four days. As the methodical search of the entire area around the waterfront at Greenwich to try to find evidence to suggest his murder had taken place in the vicinity had drawn a blank, the search had eventually been extended to cover a broader field, but as this had proved just as unsuccessful and all those in the locality interviewed by Superintendent Dawson of Scotland Yard had seen or heard nothing and all the deceased's colleagues and acquaintances could shed no light on the affair, discovering the exact location of his brutal death was proving just as much of a problem to the police as a lack of motive. But regardless of the question marks raised as to the reason let alone the scene of his murder, much less the time, the fact remained that irrespective of where the murder was in fact committed, hurling the body into the river would inevitably have to be carried out at night to reduce the risk of being seen due to there being fewer people about than during the day. From the very first moment this story had come to Tony's notice, he had been somewhat surprised to learn that not even so much as one bystander witnessed it, or, at the very least, saw something they considered suspicious or a little out of the ordinary, after all throwing a body into the Thames, even at night, no matter how disguised, would be no simple undertaking.

Since arriving in England Tony had paid several visits to the offices of *'The Daily Bulletin'* and *'The London Chronicler'* in Fleet Street, both publications being the reason his father had come to London to personally oversee the finalising of their acquisition when he had met his mother. Their dual editor, Bill Pitman, a fellow New Yorker as well as a newspaperman of unparalleled experience, who had cabled the story to him in New York when it first broke, had been quite unable to shed any further light on the death of so prominent a man as Sir Philip Dunscumbe than had originally been reported when Tony had questioned him about it. That initial visit a little over three weeks ago, had been the first time he had seen Bill in a quite a long time, a man his father had always had the utmost faith and trust in, and knew that nothing much got past this shrewd American reporter whose nose for a story had prompted more than one competitive newspaper to try to tempt him to work for them. Like his father, Tony had great faith in Bill and knew he could rely upon him totally, knowing that between this astute and experienced editor and his English lawyers, his business interests this side of the Atlantic were in good hands.

Bill, a seasoned reporter who had climbed the ladder in Ambrose Dart's newspaper business, had more than justified the decision to send him to London just over five years ago as chief editor of *'The London Chronicler'* and *'The Daily Bulletin',* and Tony, who had taken to Bill and his sense of humour the moment his father had introduced him to him when he had been nothing more than a scrubby schoolboy, had soon forged a firm friendship with him, so much so that it had not been long before he was tagging along with him when he had gone out to cover a story. This friendship had grown and strengthened over the years, in fact Tony had learned as much about the newspaper business from him as he had from his father, and now, as he waited for Eleanor, he could not resist the smile which came to his lips upon recalling that morning a few weeks ago when he had put his head round the door. "Hello, Bill. Long time no see."

"God damn, Tony!" the legs of Bill's chair scraping on the floor as he hurriedly rose to his feet, shaking him vigorously by the hand before wrapping his arms around him and slapping him on the shoulder. "Where in the name of all that's wonderful have you sprung from?"

"I'm pleased to see you too, Bill," he had smiled.

"Son of a…!" Bill had grinned. "Or should I call you 'my lord' or 'Your Lordship' now that you are Viscount Childon?"

"You should know better than to ask that, Bill," Tony had laughed.

The sound of footsteps hurrying across the polished floorboards of the first landing broke into Tony's thoughts, and rising to his feet he dropped the newspaper onto the chair just as the bedroom door opened and Eleanor stepped inside, her eyes widening in surprise at the unexpected sight of him, something between a cry and a sob leaving her parted lips. Despite her skilful use of powder, something she would never wear ordinarily, her face was rather pale and a little drawn, and in the daylight the dark circles under her eyes looked more pronounced than they had under the dimmed lights of Covent Garden Opera House, a circumstance which did not escape Tony's notice any more than it had his sister's, but Eleanor, upon seeing that warm and tender smile and the reassuring look in those dark grey eyes, a slight tinge of colour stole into her cheeks. "*You*!" she cried faintly, hardly daring to believe her eyes; her heart reacting somewhat erratically at the sight of him.

"I'm sorry if I startled you," Tony smiled, shortening the distance between them, "as well as for resorting to such a subterfuge, but you see," he explained, "it was the only way I could get to speak to you alone; I had not expected that woman to come with you."

Eleanor shook her head, bewildered. "I… I don't understand!"

"There's nothing *to* understand," Tony told her calmly, closing the door behind her before taking hold of her hands, cold and trembling in his warm ones. "Don't you remember?" he asked gently. "I told you last night that I would see you today."

Eleanor had a long way to look up into his face, her head not quite reaching his shoulders, but although her eyes were fearful they did not shy away from the warmth in his, a warmth that not only served to banish the doubts which had attacked her during the night, but filled her with such a sense of happiness that for one brief and wonderful moment she was almost able to dismiss Braden and Eliza Boon from her mind. For some reason Eleanor could not explain, this man, who had been a total stranger to her until last night, had, when she least expected it, taken a hold of her heart, indeed, she had been conscious of it almost from the moment he had entered their box, and inexperienced though she was unless her feminine instincts had got it terribly wrong, the look in his eyes as they held her own was more than enough to tell her that she had definitely taken a hold of his. It was the same look she had seen last night; a look which made her want to melt into him, but try as she did she could not ignore that warning voice cautioning her as to the imprudence of being here alone with him. The very thought of that dreadful woman deciding to come upstairs after her and reporting her suspicions back to her husband had the immediate effect of intensifying the fear in her eyes and her hands to convulse in his.

"It's all right," Tony told her gently, needing no explanation to account for such a reaction, reassuringly squeezing her hands in a firm warm clasp, "you are quite safe here, I promise you."

Torn between immense relief to know that her doubts about him had been wrong and fear of Eliza Boon who could, despite Beatrice's efforts to keep her downstairs, decide to come after her, she darted a quick look towards the door, saying hurriedly, "I…I came to get to Beatrice's cape."

"So, that's how she managed it, is it?" Tony smiled, indicating the delicious confection lying on the bed with a slight inclination of his head.

"But I don't understand," she shook her head, "why are you here? What is it you want?"

"To talk to you," Tony told her quietly, "and I can't do that in front of someone who looks more like a gaoler than a lady's maid." Her eyes flew to his at this, revealing more than she knew to the man who knew beyond doubt that he had at last found the woman with whom he wanted to spend the rest of his life.

"T-talk to m-me," Eleanor faltered. "W-what about?"

"Partly about what happened last night," Tony told her gently, "and, also…"

"Last night!" Eleanor repeated guardedly, evading his eyes. "I'm afraid I don't know what you mean!" she shrugged unconvincingly.

"Eleanor," Tony said softly, "I know you are afraid of your husband and why, but I suspect there is something else you are afraid of. Why is it you are never allowed out alone and why has the woman who passes herself off as your maid come with you today?" She shook her head in mute denial. "Why won't you tell me?" he asked gently, his thumbs beginning to rhythmically stroke her wrists, but light though his touch was her skin was still very sore, causing her to bite down on her bottom lip on a sharp intake of breath, tensing as she saw his eyes narrow, but before she could pull her hands out of his hold he eased back the stiffened coffee coloured silk of her sleeves to expose her skin, hearing him draw in an angry breath when he saw the additional bruising. "He did this to you when you arrived home last night, didn't he?" he urged, clamping down on his anger, mentally promising himself the pleasure of bringing this bully to book. "Was it because of the trick I played on him?"

"No," she shook her head, quickly pulling her hands out of his slackened clasp, "Braden would never… he… he treats me…"

"'Just as he ought' was the phrase you used last night," Tony pointed out quietly, "but you forget," he reminded her, "I saw an example of him treating you 'just as he ought'."

"It… it was not how it appeared," Eleanor hastily assured him, hurriedly brushing past him to pick up the cape from where it was laid out on top of the big four-poster, her heart giving a sickening thud and her fingers stilling as she caught sight of the newspaper lying on the chair beside the bed, still opened at the page Tony had been reading, its headline and photograph of Sir Philip Dunscumbe staring horrifyingly up at her. For one awful moment she thought she was going to faint, but managing to overcome it she picked up the beautiful creation of rose pink taffeta in her nervous hands, turning an extremely white face to Tony.

"It was precisely how it appeared," he said gently, seeing the colour drain from her face.

"No," she cried anxiously, clasping the cape to her, her fingers trembling so much that she almost dropped it, "no, it was not. Oh, *please*," she begged, "do not ask anything more."

"What is it?" Tony asked concerned, taking a step nearer to her. "You have gone dreadfully pale. Aren't you feeling well?"

"Yes," she smiled, "I am quite well, thank you. It is merely a headache."

"I really think you should sit down for a moment," he told her solicitously, picking up the newspaper and putting it onto the bed so she could sit down. "No, truly!" Eleanor replied rather agitated, unable to prevent herself from casting another glance at the newspaper Tony had just dropped onto the bed, failing to notice his slightly narrowed eyes as he saw her almost horror-struck reaction to the article which seemed to draw her attention against her own volition, "I really must be going."

"I'm sorry," Tony apologised, "that article has clearly upset you. Had I known you knew Sir Philip I would certainly not have left the newspaper open at that page," he said quietly, wondering if this was the reason for the effect it had on her.

"Knew him?" Eleanor repeated, her distressed state of mind rendering her voice a little shrill. "No," she shook her head, "no, I… I did not know him. What makes you think I did?"

"I'm sorry," Tony apologised, "it's just that you seem to be very much upset by the article."

Realising that she had allowed her nerves to overcome her and that, if she was not careful, he could so easily prise the truth out her, she forced a smile, saying as calmly as she could, "Well, it… it was a particularly dreadful thing to happen to him."

"Yes, it was," he agreed slowly.

"I… I really must go now," she shook her head, averting her eyes from his.

"What is it?" Tony asked softly. "Why won't you let me help you?"

"You are most kind," Eleanor shook her head, "but I assure you I am in no need of help."

"I wish I could believe that," he said quietly.

"You can," she nodded.

"How can I help you if you do not confide in me?" Tony asked gently, noticing the scared glance she could not help casting towards the bed where that article was staring chillingly up at her.

"You cannot help me," she exclaimed, shaking her head, tears glistening in her eyes.

"Don't you trust me?" he wanted to know.

"Please," Eleanor urged, "do not… oh, I really must go!" she told him almost frantically, clutching the cape to her breast as she turned towards the door. "I… I must not linger."

As it was patently obvious she was afraid her attendant would come upstairs after her to see what she was doing, it merely proved to Tony that her fears went far deeper than he had originally thought, but even though he needed her to tell him the truth in order for him to help her, she was by far too nervous and on edge now to say anything further, let alone confide in him, and as he did not want to aggravate her distress, he did not press her further, so asked instead if he would see her at the Kirkmichaels' party that evening.

"I… I think so," she said more calmly.

"I hope so," he smiled, "I shall certainly look for you."

Eleanor shook her head, her eyes wide with alarm. "No, no, you must not! Oh, please, do not!" she cried. "You… you *must not* seek me out."

"Why not?" Tony asked, smiling warmly down at her.

"Because you must not, that's all!" so very conscious of how, if things were different, she would very much like him to seek her out. "You must not because… oh, just because you *must* not!" she said fervently.

"Huh, huh," Tony shook his head, "not good enough."

"Oh, please," she begged, laying an impulsive hand on his arm, her eyes wide and pleading as they looked up into his face, "*promise* me you will not!"

"Sorry," he shook his head again, covering her cold hand with his warm one, "no can do."

"You *must*," Eleanor almost sobbed. "If you feel anything for me at all," she told him fervently, "and I believe you do, you will not come near me or try to seek me out," then, without giving him time to respond, she blindly headed for the door.

"Eleanor," Tony forestalled her as she was about to turn the handle, his voice deep and compelling, "you know I cannot do that. I can no more stand by and watch you suffer at the hands of a brutish bully who deserves to be horsewhipped for what he does to you, any more than I can explain or ignore my feelings for you."

"Tony I…" Shaking her head, then, as if thinking better of what she had been about to say, Eleanor opened the door and hurried out of the room, leaving its occupant in no doubt that not only were his feelings entirely reciprocated, but that it was imperative he removed her from her husband's vicinity as soon as possible; a sadistic bully who would ultimately destroy her.

Beatrice had, of course, seen Eliza Boon when she had come across her in town accompanying Eleanor on a shopping trip, but even though she had suspected that this sharp-eyed woman was in attendance more to keep a close eye on her than anything else, although why this should be Beatrice had no idea, it was not until now that she was finally able to confirm this suspicion in her own mind. She had no difficulty in understanding why Eleanor was a little afraid of this Eliza Boon because nothing would convince her to the contrary. Beatrice could only speculate as to why Collett had dismissed Mary and set this odious woman in her place because she would lay her life that Eleanor had had no say in the matter. Beatrice may have no liking for entertaining a woman she was quite certain spied on the child, but if distracting her for just long enough to give Tony enough time to speak to Eleanor then she was quite willing to do it, even so, she could not pretend to being anything other than relieved when Eleanor eventually returned to the drawing-room as honesty compelled her to admit that taking part in what had been a virtually one-sided conversation had taxed even her abilities.

Eleanor, who was totally convinced she had been gone for hours when in fact it had only been just a little over fifteen minutes, cast an anxious glance at Eliza Boon, but since she could detect no tell-tale signs in that forbidding face to suggest she had come under suspicion or that she had read more into her heightened colour other than the result of running up and down several flights of stairs, she was thankfully able to breathe more easily. Had Eliza Boon realised that Beatrice had deliberately given her the impression that she was nothing but a featherheaded woman with nothing on her mind but frivolity and that she had cleverly contrived Eleanor's errand to fetch her cape, she would not have been so confident in the belief that there was nothing to worry about, as it was she felt it reasonably safe to relax her vigilance of the prisoner for just long enough to admire her surroundings a little, especially a painting on the opposite wall in her direct line of vision, at which point Beatrice gave Eleanor a discreet, if not conspiratorial, wink, causing the flush in Eleanor's cheeks to deepen.

As far as Beatrice was concerned it was such a relief to see some colour back in her cheeks because whilst she did not believe for one moment that Eleanor had been suffering from the influenza as she had claimed, there was no denying that her life must be rather restricted and far from enjoyable to say the least. Like her brother, Beatrice knew Eleanor was frightened of her husband and, if she was not mistaken, of this woman sitting guard over her as well, and whilst Beatrice failed to see what Tony could possibly do to either ease Eleanor's unhappy situation or get her away from Collett, at no time did she doubt that he would give both a very good try. When Tony had told her last night, and in this very room, that he would know the only woman for him as soon as he saw her, Beatrice had not the least idea that this would turn out to be the case within so short a time of him saying it, in fact she would go so far as to say that neither did Tony. Like her husband, Beatrice knew her brother well enough to say that once his mind was finally made up nothing would change it, and since he had set this very determined organ as well as his heart on Eleanor Collett, not that Beatrice could blame him for that because she really was the most adorable creature, he could no more stop loving her than he could leave her to a husband whose treatment of her was such that her life must be nothing short of unbearable. Considering Eleanor's obvious nervous tension, Beatrice doubted very much whether anything of importance had been discussed in so short a time, in fact it would not surprise her to learn that it had taken that long for Tony to assuage Eleanor's anxiety, even so, unless Beatrice had misread the situation, and she was certain she had not, then from what she had briefly witnessed last night she would say that Eleanor was by no means indifferent to her brother.

Despite Eleanor's evident fear of her husband and that woman he had foisted onto her, Tony had no difficulty in arriving at the same conclusion because although her initial reaction upon finding him waiting for her was one of total surprise before being quickly supplanted by fear at the prospect of being discovered, he had not missed that all too brief look which had entered her eyes telling him that she was very far from indifferent to him. He could only guess as to why Sir Miles Tatton had approved the marriage of his daughter to a man like Collett, whose violent temper and aggressive manner were not only public knowledge but hardly likely to render him a suitable husband, especially for one of Eleanor's shy and gentle nature. Nevertheless, for one brief and joyous moment, Tony had caught a glimpse of the real Eleanor Collett hiding behind the fear, longing to break free: shy, certainly, but a young woman who was vitally and passionately alive and one, moreover, who had clearly given her heart to him, and that was the woman he longed to know as well as determined to liberate from a man whose brutal treatment would eventually annihilate her.

Chapter Six

"Oh, Tony!" Beatrice cried when Tony joined her downstairs within minutes of Eleanor's departure about twenty minutes later, "that poor child; she is so afraid!"

"She's more than afraid, Bea," he said firmly, "she is terrified, and not only of Collett."

"*That* woman!" she said bitterly.

"Yes, that woman certainly, but there's something else," he said thoughtfully.

"Something else?" she repeated, raising a surprised eyebrow. "What?"

"I don't know," Tony said slowly, glancing pensively down at the folded newspaper he had brought downstairs with him and was now absently tapping against the palm of his left hand. "And yet…" a thought suddenly occurring to him, which, no matter how fanciful, he could not dismiss. "Tell me, Bea," he asked curiously, "how long has Eleanor been married to Collett?"

"Too long if you must know!" she told him forthrightly.

"I'm serious, Bea," he told her earnestly.

"And so am I!" Beatrice nodded. "Oh, all right," she conceded in answer to the look on his face. "Now, let me think," screwing up her face in an effort of memory, "when was it? Oh, yes, just a little over twelve months. Yes, that's right," she remembered, "it was while I was in New York visiting your father. She had only just turned nineteen when she married him," she sighed regretfully. "She celebrated her twentieth birthday just a few months ago. Why?"

Tony looked at her for several moments, his forehead creased in thought, asking at length, "When did you and Tom first notice that she was no longer alone when she ventured out?"

"Why?" she wondered.

"Please, Bea," he urged.

Beatrice sighed. "Well, I can't be certain," she shrugged helplessly, "but I would say about nine or ten months ago."

"Are you sure about that, Bea?" Tony asked urgently. "It's very important."

"Well, as sure as I can be." She shook her head.

He thought for a moment, his frown deepening. "Is that about the time Collett dismissed his butler and Eleanor's maid?"

"Yes," Beatrice said slowly after giving it some thought, "now you come to mention it, it was about then."

Tony looked steadily across at her, his lips compressed as he thought for a moment. "What happened to them, do you know?" he urged.

"No," Beatrice shrugged, "I have no idea."

"How long had Mary been with Eleanor?" he asked.

She thought a moment, saying at length, "A long time; five years, at least."

"Can you recall her surname?"

Beatrice's brow puckered in thought. "Stanley, I think," she said at length. "Yes, that's it," she nodded, "Mary Stanley."

"Do you know anything about her?" Tony asked. "Where she came from?"

"No," Beatrice shook her head rather helplessly, "I'm afraid I don't. All I know," she sighed, "is that she had been with Eleanor for quite a long time."

Tony nodded. "This new man of Collett's," he queried, "you said, I think, he looks more like a prizefighter than a butler."

"Yes," she said with feeling, "he does. He's no more a butler than I am!" she disparaged. "And as for this woman who came with Eleanor," she scorned, "if she's attended on a lady before then I'll eat my hat! In fact," she added firmly, "if you want to know what I really think I would say she looks more like a prison warder than a lady's maid!"

"Yes, so do I, in fact," Tony nodded, "I think that is why Collett brought her in to replace this Mary."

"What are you thinking, Tony?" Beatrice asked worriedly, her eyes keenly searching his face.

It was some little time before he answered this question, mainly because he could well be way off course in his thinking, but try as he did he could not dismiss Eleanor's reaction to that piece in the newspaper about Sir Philip Dunscumbe from his mind. It was, of course, a most tragic incident and one which all decent people would feel repugnance over, even more so when one remembered that to date the police had made no arrest for such a vicious crime, but her response to that article had been more than just natural shock and outrage, in fact, Tony would go so far as to say it had hit her like a body blow. If Bea was right when she said that Eleanor's escorted outings, even down to a shopping trip, had commenced around the time of Sir Philip's brutal death, then all the signs pointed to the fact that, even if Eleanor never knew him, she certainly knew something about his untimely and violent death, and although Tony easily acquitted her of any wrongdoing if his brief summing up was correct, then it certainly went some way to answering the many questions he had. Eleanor's fear of her husband was easily explained; he was a bully who enjoyed inflicting pain, but Tony had suspected from the very first that there was more to her fear than Collett's regular beatings and if the idea going around in his head, brought about as a direct result of her disproportionate reaction to that article was true, then Tony could quite well understand Collett's dread in allowing her out of the house unaccompanied. There was no doubting the fact that Eleanor was terrified, and not only of her husband and that woman who passed as her maid and, most probably, of the man who had taken the place of Collett's butler because from what Bea had told him Mitchell had been butler in his father's time and not yet of an age to be pensioned off. Tony could only guess at Collett's reasons for dismissing two members of his household staff and replacing them with individuals, one of whom unquestionably bore the distinct appearance of being a gaoler, but for him to take such drastic measures could surely only mean that something untoward had occurred which he knew could not be hidden from them or, which was more than likely, he could not trust them to keep it to themselves. Tony had no way of knowing whether Collett and Sir Philip Dunscumbe knew one another, but what if they did? Or, which could well be the case, their paths had crossed for some reason resulting in an altercation of some kind. Tony knew nothing about Sir Philip Dunscumbe, but he certainly knew enough about Sir Braden Collett and his aggressive temperament to say with a certainty that he was not the kind of man to let an action or comment pass unchallenged. At the moment Tony was unable to say that the two men had ever met, much less argued to the point where Collett had lost his head and killed him, but whilst this theory may seem utterly preposterous that instinct which had never yet failed him, told him that somewhere along the way Collett was deeply involved in Sir Philip Dunscumbe's death and that Eleanor, how Tony could not say precisely at this moment, had either witnessed it or stumbled upon something which could seriously damage her husband. For some reason or other which he could not put his finger on, he was firmly convinced that Collett was inextricably linked with Sir Philip's death, but although there were numerous pieces of the jigsaw surrounding such a vicious crime missing, Tony was in no doubt that they all fitted in with Sir Braden Collett. Surely Eleanor being kept so close and her disproportionate reaction to that newspaper article, proved it. Tony sighed, raising his eyes to look at his sister, his forehead deeply creased. "If I were I to tell you that, Bea," he told her quietly, "you would think it too fantastical."

Her pretty eyes narrowed at this. "Is… is it serious, Tony?"

"If I am right," he sighed, "yes Bea, it is."

"I see," she said slowly. She took a step nearer to him, laying a hand on his arm, asking, "Can't you tell me, Tony?"

He patted her hand and shook his head. "Not yet, Bea. It's not that I don't trust you, I do," he smiled, "but I could well be wrong in what I'm thinking, and until I have settled it in my own mind, I would much rather not say anything."

Beatrice nodded. "Very well, but what about Eleanor? Did you manage to say very much to her?"

Tony shook his head. "No, she was far too terrified in case that woman decided to take it into her head to follow her upstairs."

"Hateful creature!" Beatrice cried, her eyes sparkling. "I expect that even now she is pouring everything which passed between us into Collett's ears!" Her face flushed.

"Very probably," Tony ground out, going on to tell her about those fresh bruises on her wrists.

"Oh Tony!" she cried, horrified. "You don't mean it?"

"I'm afraid I do," he bit out, "but I blame myself. If I had not…"

"You must not say that, Tony," Beatrice said earnestly, gripping his arm, "you must not even think it. You did what you thought was right, which," she said firmly, "it was."

"It's no use, Bea," Tony smiled, shaking his head, "I should have known that he would take his anger out on her." He grimaced. "I was counting on the fact that knowing she was coming here today to see you he would not hurt her in case you spotted anything. God!" he cried in self-recrimination, raking a hand through his hair. "To think that I am the cause of such a brutal act!"

"You must not blame yourself, Tony," Beatrice soothed. "If Collett is the kind of man we take him for then nothing anyone can say or do is going to stop him from inflicting such brutality on her whenever it pleases him."

It may not be what Tony wanted to hear but he knew it was true, even so, it did not make him feel any better, but when he saw Eleanor later that evening at the Kirkmichaels' anniversary party he was given every reason to believe that she had, for today at least, been spared any more ill-treatment.

The Kirkmichaels' twenty-fifth wedding anniversary party was every inch the squeeze Tom had predicted it would be, so much so that by the time they entered the ballroom of the Park Grove Hotel in Park Lane which Lady Kirkmichael had hired for the occasion, he threw such a meaningful glance at his brother-in-law that it was all Tony could do to stop himself from bursting out laughing. Beatrice, looking extremely beautiful in the pink creation which she had had made specially for tonight, was affectionately told by her doting husband in a whispered aside that he doubted this evening would be remembered for anything other than being a dreadful crush, but it was worth it just to have her on his arm, to which she blushingly thanked him.

Having learned from Beatrice that Tony was for the time being in England, it was not surprising that the eyes of all her friends and acquaintances from the moment they entered the flower bedecked ballroom, tried to catch sight of her brother from America, waiting eagerly for her to introduce the new Viscount Childon to them. "Not that I expect you to remember the half of them," she smiled up at him as she guided him around the room, with Tom sauntering behind, "but they are all of them dying to meet you."

"Really!" Tony raised a surprised eyebrow, a gleam of pure

amusement in his eyes. "They all seem very much alive to me, Bea," he said without a tremor, causing his sister to admonishingly tap his hand and his brother-in-law to burst out laughing. Tony had no need to be told that there were any number of expectant mammas here tonight with their daughters all hoping that they would not only catch his eye but hold his attention long enough to raise hopes in eager breasts, a man whom they knew to be a most eligible bachelor, but although it was with the utmost good humour that he allowed Beatrice to introduce him to them as well as any number of heavily jewelled ladies and their husbands or escorts, his good manners and winning smile gave no one the least cause to suspect that there was really only one person he wanted to see here tonight, discreetly surveying the room to see if he could catch sight of her. "Have you seen them, Bea?" he asked quietly, as he walked leisurely beside her to meet yet another awe-inspiring mamma.

"Yes," she smiled, nodding to an acquaintance several feet away, "I believe they are already here. Ah, Augusta!" she cried. "I don't believe you have met my brother…"

"How many more, Bea?" Tony asked amusingly, several minutes later, leaving her friend nodding agreeably as they walked away from her.

"You know, Tony," Beatrice smiled, not without a touch of pride in her strategy, nodding her head to another acquaintance, "you may be very clever and everything, but if you don't want Collett to suspect that you are singling out his wife, which he will if I introduce you to them and no one else, then I am afraid this procession around the room is very necessary."

Over her head, Tony's laughing eyes met his brother-in-law's, but said, quite seriously, "You know Bea," raising her hand to his lips, "if you were not my sister, I'd marry you myself!"

"As if I would have you!" she hunched a shoulder, her eyes looking fondly up at him.

"Well," Tom nodded, "at least they're here because I don't mind saying I wondered whether they would be."

Over the heads of a sea of people, including numerous high headdresses, Tony's height enabled him to easily pick out Sir Braden Collett standing beside a pilaster somewhat dubiously decorated with what was clearly intended to represent vines, talking with a man Tom immediately identified as Sir Wilfred Moore, an eminent physician in Harley Street, whilst Eleanor, seated on the very edge of a chair next to him, was looking somewhat nervously down at her feet.

Experience had taught Eleanor that accepting an invitation was one thing, but keeping it was quite another as Braden could, for no apparent reason, decide not to honour it at the last minute without offering her any apologies or explanations. She had meant what she said to Tony in that he must not seek her out, not only because Braden would take great exception to it, but the secret he was forcing her to carry in agonising silence had long since become an impossible burden; a burden that she could easily divest herself of, especially to Beatrice's brother, a man who had not only made his feelings for her perfectly clear but also that he wanted to help her. In Tony's company, she could so easily succumb to his persuasions and tell him what was worrying her and whilst it would be a tremendous relief to relieve herself of what was nothing short of a lead weight on her shoulders, to do so would bring retribution down on her head the like of which made her tremble. But worse than this was the irreparable harm Braden could do her father should he ever discover that his wife had divulged his secret, knowing no compunction in exposing her father's momentary transgression at a time when he had been at his weakest, then, of course, there was the very real possibility that her husband could, who was not without powerful friends, do untold damage to Tony's reputation or, even, do him physical harm. But despite all the dreadful ramifications which could result from any confidences she shared, the woman inside her very much wanted to see Tony again. Even though she knew nothing could possibly result from becoming better acquainted with him, she could not prevent the thrill of sheer excitement running through her at the prospect of seeing him this evening, this wonderful sensation, which she had never experienced before, intensified by the fact that he fully intended to disregard all her entreaties for him to keep his distance. Prior to her marriage, she had met any number of young men who had made it quite clear that they would like to get to know her better, and whilst she liked them very well and was not averse to enjoying their company at some dance or party, not one of them had made her pulse race or her heart skip a beat as Tony did by doing nothing more than smiling at her or looking at her in just such a way. She knew she should not be feeling like this, not only because she was not free to receive the attentions of another man but also because their acquaintanceship was of less than twenty-four hours' duration. Her practical mind, pointing out several rather unpleasant and inescapable facts, none of which her heart, suddenly behaving rather strangely, was taking any notice of, nevertheless left her feeling somewhat undecided whether she wanted him to attend the Kirkimichaels' party tonight or not. Common sense told her that as far as she was concerned it should make no difference either way, and even though she knew this was true it did not prevent her from taking more than her usual care in her appearance, hoping that Braden would not disappoint her at the eleventh hour by telling her that he had sent their apologies.

Like Beatrice, Eleanor had an eye for colour and style, and certainly approved of the bustle being replaced by just a small pad which, thanks to the new S-bend corset, allowed the back of the gown to gradually peter out from tightly gathered pleats at the small of the back into soft folds to the floor. Braden, who, regardless of her hatred and fear of him and his treatment of her, nevertheless liked to see her well turned out, begrudged not a penny of the clothing allowance he made her and even though she would far rather go about in rags than accept one penny from him, should she ever dare sling his money back in his face he would be more than capable of choosing her clothes himself or, dreadful thought, that hateful woman doing it for her. Rather than suffer that added humiliation, far better to accept his financial offering and select own clothes and create her own style than having it done for her, at least it was an independence denied her in everything else.

But the soft folds of aquamarine silk of the elongated skirt which floated behind her as she walked and the rustle of taffeta in a deeper shade of the same colour which made up the dress with its low décolleté, threaded all round with a narrow trimming of white chiffon gradually widening out until it reached the shoulders where it draped from the top of the back to combine with the back fall of silk, went a long way to helping her forget the intolerable life she was enduring. As she studied the results of her efforts in the mirror, Eliza having thankfully left her, Eleanor was by no means disappointed with what she saw, in fact the reflection looking back at her reminded her of the carefree young woman she had once been, before her father had found himself coerced into consenting to her marriage with a man she could not bear being near, a man who, whether she liked it or not, dictated her very existence.

Braden, deeming no tap in the least necessary before entering his wife's room, opened the interconnecting door, and Eleanor, having fully expected him to tell her at the last minute that they would not be attending the Kirkmichaels' party after all, silently let out her pent-up breath to see him dressed in evening clothes and holding his white gloves in his hand. Resting a hand on his proffered arm, she accompanied him down the stairs and into the waiting carriage, her heart skipping a little beat at the thought of seeing Tony again – and Beatrice and Tom, of course!

With so much going around in her head as well as a ballroom full of people, it was hardly surprising that she had failed to notice Beatrice's arrival in company with her husband and brother, and it was not until Eleanor raised her eyes from the reflective contemplation of her delicate silk slippers to glance around her, did she see them approach. Had Sir Braden Collett been paying as much attention to his wife as he usually did instead of his conversation with Sir Wilfred Moore, he would have instantly recognised that glow in her eyes and the colour which had crept into her cheeks for what they really were, but it was not until he heard Beatrice greet Eleanor that he turned round, by which time his errant wife had had enough time to school her somewhat revealing response at the sight of Tony.

Waiting until Tom had briefly nodded his acknowledgement to both men and Sir Wilfred, spying an acquaintance, had walked away, Beatrice cried, "Ah, Collett!" forcing a smile to her lips. "I was just telling Eleanor how much I enjoyed her visit this morning. Thank you for sparing her to me," the words choking her behind the smile, but felt it incumbent on her to do all she could to obviate the risk of him subjecting Eleanor to any mistreatment, "I know how concerned you were for her." Having inclined his head in polite acknowledgement of this, she smiled, "I don't believe you have met my brother, Viscount Childon."

Tony, who stood head and shoulders above most men in the room and Braden Collett especially, looked down at the red face and protruding blue eyes with an innocence which totally belied what he knew as being the truth about this man, but to his sister's profound relief he betrayed none of the repugnance she knew he felt for Collett by slightly inclining his head, saying politely, "Collett."

"Childon," he nodded, clearing his throat before saying, "I don't believe you have met my wife, Eleanor," indicating her presence by a wave of one white-gloved hand.

"No," Tony replied calmly, having no difficulty whatsoever in easing his conscience with this blatant lie, "I have not yet had that pleasure." Then, turning to Eleanor, who was sitting bolt upright in her seat looking from one to the other hardly daring to breathe, automatically raised her gloved hand which he took in his and raised briefly to his lips. "It is a pleasure to make your acquaintance, Lady Collett," he smiled. "I have heard my sister speak of you, and can only apologise for being away from Mount Street when you called this morning."

Eleanor smiled and nodded, managing faintly, "How do you do," fully conscious of those dark grey eyes upon her, not to mention her husband's bulbous blue ones. "I am sorry to have missed you."

Apart from a few polite exchanges, nothing which either man could take the least exception to, Tony and Collett made no effort to enter into any lengthy discussion; the former because his overriding inclination, far from wanting to converse with him, was to knock him senseless and the latter, not only because he did not hold with Americans, or half-Americans for that matter, taking possession of a title, even more so when it took precedence over his own, but because he saw no need to do so. Beatrice, presaging an uneasy lull descending which could easily create a scene, especially when she considered that Collett could take offence to the slightest thing, gently squeezed Tom's arm with her hand as it rested lightly upon it, signifying he said something.

Interpreting the gesture perfectly, Tom, who had not the least thing in common with Collett, turned to Eleanor, enquiring if she were now fully recovered from her recent indisposition, whereupon he immediately felt another squeeze on his arm, signifying this to mean he had said the wrong thing, especially as none of them believed for one moment that Eleanor had succumbed to the influenza.

Eleanor, uncomfortably aware of four pairs of eyes looking attentively down at her, particularly those bulbous blue ones, smiled, saying in her gentle way, "Oh, yes, thank you. I am quite recovered."

Tom, who would never be brought to believe that this lovely young woman had married Collett of her own free will, felt it incumbent upon him to try to make amends for such a *faux pas* and the possibility that he could, however unwittingly, have exposed her to even more ill-treatment upon her return home, said, as cheerfully as he could under that distinctly hard stare from her husband, that he was certainly pleased to hear she had fully recovered and how good it was to see her here this evening, then, after glancing around him, turned back to Eleanor, smiling, "Dreadful squeeze though, don't you think?"

"Yes," Eleanor smiled faintly, having every sympathy for him, "it is, but I believe Lady Kirkmichael has many friends and acquaintances."

"Well," Beatrice nodded, feeling the danger point had passed sufficiently to inaugurate some topic of conversation, smiled, "I have always said that Sally certainly knows precisely how to entertain her guests, although," she sighed, turning her head to scan the room for a moment, "with all those flowers one can hardly see the orchestra!"

"Tell me, Lady Collett," Tony raised an enquiring eyebrow, her reaction to him a few minutes earlier not lost on him, "do you like dancing?"

As this question took her completely by surprise she swallowed nervously, her body stiffening a little as she found herself torn between her fear of her husband and the wonderful exhilaration of wanting to dance with Tony, but so very conscious was she of Braden's eye upon her that she could only manage a faint, "Well…yes, I do actually."

"In that case," Tony smiled, doing her pulse rate no good at all, "I wonder if you would honour me with the next dance? With your permission, Collett," inclining his head in her husband's direction.

Beatrice, who had not expected this but realised now that she should have done, held her breath and, like Tom and Eleanor, waited apprehensively for Braden's reply, only Tony it seemed unperturbed by his request.

Sir Braden Collett, who by no means liked the idea of relinquishing his wife to a man whose sister he firmly believed could prove a threat if given half the chance, was just on the point of refusing when only a moment's thought sufficed to tell him that he was most probably exaggerating the danger. Not only was Eleanor too terrified to say anything, but should Beatrice Shipton ever suspect that something was wrong, although according to Eliza there was nothing to fear from this frivolous and empty-headed woman, then Childon, once having returned to America, would be in no position to either interfere in his affairs or to take his suspicions to the authorities.

A slight inclination of the head was the only answer Collett vouchsafed to this, whereupon Eleanor, who was not at all sure whether to feel relief or not at her husband's consent, felt her gloved hand irresistibly taken in Tony's as he assisted her to her feet, her legs in imminent danger of collapsing under her.

"You… you really should not have… done that," Eleanor said nervously as she walked away on Tony's arm.

"Why not?" Tony asked gently, warmly covering her hand as it rested lightly on his left arm with his right one. "What does he think I can do to you in the middle of a crowded ballroom and in full view of him?" he smiled, leading her onto the floor. When she made no answer to this, he took her completely by surprise by saying, "You do not surely expect me to believe that he is jealous? Were it any other man but him, who we both know treats you shamefully, I could well understand it, especially when his wife is as beautiful as you; particularly so this evening."

"Please, do not…" she began, a little flustered, her skin tingling as his gloved hand came to rest lightly on her back.

"Pay you compliments?" he supplied, raising a questioning eyebrow. "I'm not," he told her firmly, "it's the plain unvarnished truth, and you know it. Compliments are given because they are generally expected, not only by the one who receives them, but by the one who offers them. When you get to know me better," he smiled down at her, "and you will," he nodded, "I promise you, you will know that I do not give empty or insincere praises."

Deciding it was perhaps better to leave this unanswered, not only because her suddenly wayward heart leapt at the words as well as the look in his eyes, but she was so very conscious of her husband watching them, said instead, "It's… it's not that," she faltered, "it's because Braden thinks I will…"

"Will what?" Tony urged softly.

"Nothing," Eleanor shook her head, allowing him to guide her smoothly around the floor in time to the music, mentally warning herself about being careful not to let something slip again.

"Why won't you tell me what's making you so afraid?" Tony asked gently.

"I'm not," she assured him, not very convincingly. "You have it quite wrong!"

"Huh, huh," he shook his head, "you know I have not."

"Yes," Eleanor said a little breathlessly, "you have; quite wrong."

"It's no use, Eleanor," Tony smiled tenderly.

"Oh please, Tony," she begged, "you must not ask me anything or seek me out again."

"Why mustn't I?" he asked reasonably.

"Because… oh, just because you must not…" she said anxiously.

"So you keep saying," Tony said conversationally, "but you have not yet given me a reason."

"Promise me you will not do so again," Eleanor pleaded.

"You know," Tony teased, "this way you have of half answering a question could be construed by some as being somewhat provocative." She raised her head at this, her eyes widening, but upon seeing the amusement in his, her lips broke into a smile. "*That's* better!" he rallied.

"I was beginning to wonder what I had to do to make you smile."

"Oh, Tony!" she cried, between tears and laughter. "Please, do not."

"Do not what?" he asked gently, his hold tightening a little.

"Do not make me like you!" the words leaving her lips before she could stop them.

"I'm not making you do anything Ellie," Tony told her softly. "You decided for yourself last night that you liked me, *in fact*," he emphasised, "you decided you more than liked me."

"W-what did you c-call me?" she faltered a little breathlessly, looking up at him, trying to ignore the fact that he had spoken no less than the truth.

"Ellie. Don't you like it?" he smiled.

She nodded, saying a little huskily, "Yes, I do. It's just that, well… no one has ever called me that before."

"Haven't they?" Tony smiled, his eyes looking down into her slightly flushed face with such warmth that the colour in her cheeks instantly deepened. She shook her head. "Well, I can't say I'm sorry," he confessed, "because you see, I like being the only one who calls you that." As this warmly delivered admission corresponded with the change of direction the Viennese waltz required now and then, she completely forgot to do so and soon found herself being firmly but gently turned, her body being drawn closer into his to avoid contact with another couple whose concentration, unlike her own, was on the continual rotating movement of the dance. "You know," he warned tenderly, "if you blush any more I shall have your husband tapping me on the shoulder inviting me to step outside."

Her head shot up at this, but although Tony could see fear in those beautiful blue eyes there was also a mischievous sparkle combined with a light he had no difficulty in defining, and he was honest enough to admit that had they been anywhere but here he would have known no hesitation in kissing her.

"Why are you doing this, Tony?" she asked breathlessly, trying to ignore the meaning of what he was saying and the excitement his nearness as well as his words evoked inside her.

"Doing what?" he smiled.

If only he would not look at her in just that way it would be so much easier, but the truth was that even though she was never once out of view of her husband's watchful eye she liked the way Tony looked at her, liked the feel of his arms around her and to hear words she never thought she would. "Why are you seeking me out?"

"Because for one thing," he told her earnestly, his voice deep and compelling, "I am fully determined to get you away from that bullying brute of a man who passes as your husband and, for another, I love you."

"*L-love* me!" Eleanor cried when she could find her voice, almost stumbling.

Tony nodded, holding her tighter, then, lowering his head, said in a deep voice, "I knew the moment I saw you that I had at last found the woman with whom I wanted to share my life. You knew it too about me," he said firmly, forestalling the denial on her lips. "I love you Ellie; that's all I know. *That,*" he stressed, "and the indisputable fact that you feel precisely the same about me!"

She looked frantically around her, not entirely certain whether she wanted the dance to end or not. "B-but you can't!" she cried on a breathless sob.

"Why can't I?" he wanted to know, his eyes smiling down into her upturned face in such a way that she was left in no doubt he was telling the truth or that she did indeed feel precisely the same about him.

"B-because… well, I'm married for one thing and, also, well, you… you don't know me for another!" she faltered.

"I know all I need to, and as for the rest," Tony said softly, "I shall have the rest of my life to find out."

"The rest of your life!" she echoed, astonished. "W-what do you mean?"

"I told you a moment or two ago that you will come to know me better; don't you remember?" he asked quietly.

"Yes, but… oh, Tony!" she cried. "What …?"

"Oh, haven't I told you?" Tony smiled, raising an enquiring eyebrow. "I intend to marry you, Eleanor Collett!"

Chapter Seven

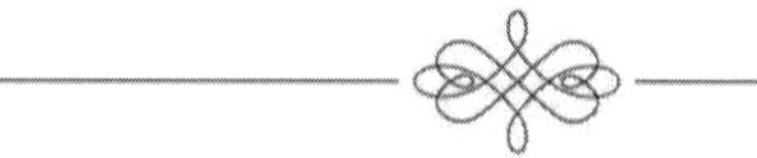

Eliza Boon, far from happy in allowing Eleanor to visit her friend even though she would remain with her throughout, knew there was every possibility that Lady Shipton could well take exception or, indeed, gross offence, to a maid being present during what was undoubtedly intended as a private get-together, and could quite well order her out of the room to wait in the hall or even in the kitchen, in which case she would have no choice but to leave the two women alone. Despite Eliza's earnest representations to Sir Braden on this point, bearing in mind what was at stake, he had, for some obscure reason, permitted it, but luckily the excuse she had glibly put forward to account for her presence, faintly endorsed by a nervous Eleanor, was politely accepted, but there was no denying that Lady Shipton was certainly taken aback.

Eliza, having summed up Lady Beatrice Shipton and concluded she was nothing but an empty-headed woman bent on nothing but gaiety and frivolity, had seen nothing amiss or contrived in her attempts to get Eleanor upstairs, and therefore decided that there was no need for her to either question it or go up with her. In Eliza's candid opinion it was not surprising that Eleanor returned to the drawing-room just a little flushed and out of breath having hurried up and down several flights of stairs to retrieve the cape, never for one moment suspecting the real reason for her heightened colour. Fortunately for Eliza Boon's peace of mind, however, she remained in complete ignorance of the fact that Beatrice, who had arrived at a fairly accurate assessment of her true function within the household in Cavendish Square, had deliberately adopted every appearance of being one who was totally self-centred and given over to frivolity to enable her to manoeuvre Eleanor upstairs so that Tony could have a private word with her, an individual Eliza had no idea even existed, much less that he had resolved to come to the aid of her prisoner. This blissful unawareness, together with the conversation she had paid close attention to between the two women, which had not touched upon anything remotely incriminating, more than satisfied her, and so it was with the utmost conviction that Eliza was confidently able to report favourably to Sir Braden Collett about what had occurred in Mount Street that morning.

Since Eliza had as much to lose as himself if the truth ever leaked out, Collett, having listened with keen interest to her account of what had taken place in Mount Street upon her return to Cavendish Square with Eleanor, had no reason to doubt her word in that nothing occurred to give them cause for concern. Of course, he could not entirely rule out the possibility that Eleanor would not at some point feel the need to unburden herself to someone, which was why he had her continually watched, but he was astute enough to realise that prohibiting the visit could well have created the kind of suspicion in Beatrice Shipton's mind which he was trying desperately hard to avoid. He was not saying that it would not cross Eleanor's mind to try to shake off Eliza so she could confide in Beatrice Shipton, but considering that she was too scared of what he would do to her as well as what he could do to her father, he doubted very much that she would take such a drastic step. It was as well that her fear of the consequences revolved solely around what he would do to her and her father should she ever decide to divulge what she knew, never once pausing to think that such a disclosure would have catastrophic consequences for himself; a circumstance he was fully determined not to alert her to as this knowledge could quite well be all she needed to give her the courage to inform against him. As it was it had not occurred to Eleanor what such a confession would mean to himself, firmly believing that she and her father would be the ones to bear the brunt of any retribution directly resulting from it, but the truth was he would be given no opportunity to do anything because such news, whether imparted unwittingly or deliberately, even in the fullest confidence, especially to someone like Beatrice Shipton, would inevitably come to the notice of the authorities and, once that happened, it would not take them long to pay him a visit. Although Collett knew his rank and standing in society would demand he be treated with courtesy, even respect, throughout what would be the ignominy of a visit to Scotland Yard for questioning followed by a very public trial, they would not prevent him from dangling at the end of a rope. Compared to Eleanor's father succumbing to temptation in what had been a passing moment of weakness brought about by shock and despair, however damaging to Sir Miles Tatton's reputation, it would be nothing when placed beside cold-blooded murder!

Useless for Collett to tell the police he had not meant to kill Sir Philip Dunscumbe, that it had occurred on the spur-of-the-moment when in the throes of an ungovernable rage exacerbated by the onset of panic if for no other reason than they would inevitably ask him why, if such was the case, he had not contacted the police instead of disposing of the body by hurling into the Thames. The truth was that Collett could not go to the police now any more than he ever could as such an admission would not only mean he would be exposed as a murderer but also as a man who indulged his out of the ordinary sexual tastes in an establishment where, less than a couple of months before he bludgeoned Sir Philip to death, he had been present when the unfortunate death of Annie Myers had taken place. It had been a most regrettable tragedy brought about through Sir Philip's brother, Dennis Dunscumbe, a man who, upon learning that she would not comply to a certain demand he had made of her, had allowed his temper to get the better of him by hitting her far more forcefully than he had intended, resulting in her losing her balance and striking her head on the solid brass bedstead, killing her instantly.

No more than Eliza did Collett want the police to learn of what had happened to Annie Myers, any more than he wanted them to know that he had done his best to help cover up the dreadful events of that night to save his own as well as his friend's reputation and ensuring Eliza's premises were safe from investigation by the police, but Dennis, much to their surprise, had unexpectedly threatened to ruin everything. Setting aside his unusual proclivities and somewhat hasty temper, Dennis Dunscumbe was nevertheless an honest man who, having tried unsuccessfully to dismiss such an awful incident from his mind, had found himself unable to live with the thought that he had been the one responsible for bringing about the death of a girl, irrespective of her profession, and had announced his intention of reporting the matter to the police. Reasoning and persuasion had failed to change his mind, so too had coercion and, Eliza Boon, taking matters into her own capable hands and deciding only one course was open to them, had instructed Peterson to pay him a discreet visit at his home in Hertford Street, ensuring Dennis Dunscumbe was no longer in any position to say anything. Such drastic measures were unfortunate, of course, and, naturally, his death was to be regretted, but given all the factors there had really been no other option because had Dennis Dunscumbe gone to the police the results of his confession would have been disastrous.

Collett may have had no hand in the death of Annie Myers any more than he had in Dennis Dunscumbe's, but the fact remained that he had certainly been a party to them as well as helping cover up the one and totally denying any knowledge of the other, and it was not until the authorities had arrived at a verdict of suicide in the case of Dennis Dunscumbe as well as nothing being mentioned or anything coming to light about Annie Myers, had Collett been able to breathe more easily. That was, until Sir Philip had paid him that visit!

Of course, it was too late now for Collett to regret his actions with regards to Sir Philip Dunscumbe, but when unexpectedly faced with him on his doorstep that night and the accusations he had charged him with about the death of his brother and the events which had brought it about, followed by him stating his intention of reporting it to the police as well as raising questions in the House about such establishments, Collett had momentarily lost his head and viciously attacked him with the heavy brass poker. Panic and an overwhelming sense of self-preservation to prevent denunciation had driven everything from his mind, even to wondering how Sir Philip had come by such intelligence in the first place. Only after the deed was finally done did such a vital question present itself, leaving Collett to conclude that Dennis must at some point have confided in his brother.

If only the concert at the Royal Albert Hall had not finished ahead of the time scheduled on the programme, then Eleanor would not have arrived home earlier than expected and seen with her own horrified eyes the sight of Sir Philip's dead body lying in a rapidly spreading pool of blood on the study floor with her husband still holding the weapon he had used in his hand, and his shirt and waistcoat splattered with blood; the shocked gasp which had left her lips at the ghastly sight in front of her soon giving way to hysterical screams. Being a man who did not perform well in a crisis Collett's brutal slaying of Sir Philip had stemmed from fear and alarm, and what followed from sheer panic, intensified even more by his wife's attempts to run from the room to call for help and, to prevent her reaching the door, he had hurriedly grabbed hold of her and clamped a thick hand over her mouth, his eyes glistening as he warned her to be quiet. Sobs of pure fright had left her throat the moment he had taken his hand away and, for one awful moment, Collett fully expected Mitchell to tap on the door asking if anything was amiss, and therefore to obviate this risk Collett had given her a stunning blow to the face with his fist which immediately rendered her unconscious. Pausing only to catch his breath, he opened the door to cast a nervous glance into the hall, relieved to see no one in sight, then, picking Eleanor up in his arms, he quickly locked the study door and carried her up the stairs to her room, knowing perfectly well that she would be insensible for some considerable time, and after dropping her unceremoniously onto the bed he quickly left the room without a backward glance, locking the door behind him.

When he eventually returned to the hall he was considerably out of breath; but of Mitchell there was still no sign, to which his relief in knowing that this diligent man had not heard either his wife's screams or any of the recent commotion, was only exceeded by the knowledge that Mary, Eleanor's maid, would not be back for several days, having had to return home due to the sudden illness of her mother. Collett may not be overly squeamish when it came to witnessing something brutal such as two men beating one another until they could no longer see out of bloody and swollen eyes or a vicious dog fight where one or the other had to be put out of its suffering due to severe injuries, even the abuse he meted out to his wife, but to actually take a life by means of his own hand was something quite different, and the shock of realising what he had done took its inevitable toll. It was close on half an hour before he could either move or think, sitting in a wing chair by the fire with a decanter in one hand and a glass in the other, staring with horrified eyes down at the body he had ferociously killed, but it was not until the clock on the mantelpiece chimed the half hour that he was finally able to rouse himself out of the inertia which had held him in its grip. Under no circumstances could he allow Mitchell to see the body, much less the blood on the carpet, and since he could not enlist his help in disposing of either or any of the other servants come to that, there seemed to be only one course of action open to him and, with the desperate determination of a frightened man, quickly put on his hat and coat and left his study, locking the door behind him before letting himself out of the house, calling up a hackney to take him to a quiet and outwardly respectable address in Bloomsbury.

Any gentleman wishing to visit the premises of *'Mother Discipline'* was bound by two requirements; the first, and by far the most important, they would only be admitted on the personal recommendation of a regular patron, and the second that entry and egress were alike via the back door. No carriage or hackney setting down a gentleman outside her front door had ever been witnessed by neighbours or passers-by and none of her girls had ever been seen to set foot beyond it unless respectably dressed, thereby leading no one to suspect the kind of house she kept or what went on behind the shuttered windows. It was, therefore, in a mood of considerable annoyance that Eliza Boon had seen Collett enter the house by the front door in Peterson's wake, but one look at his blotched and anxious face was enough to tell her that something rather untoward had occurred, but nothing quite prepared her for the story that he had poured into her ears accounting for his unexpected visit. Her quick and agile brain had swiftly assimilated the facts and recognised the danger Sir Philip Dunscumbe's death posed, not only for Sir Braden but for herself and her profitable little business, but as Collett appeared to be momentarily at a loss as to how to remedy a situation which had been unexpectedly thrust upon him, it was with characteristic decisiveness that she instructed Peterson to return to Cavendish Square with him and see what he could do to dispose of the body. Fortunately, she had no clients in that night and so assured Collett that she would follow later, but she needed time to make various arrangements with the girls, to which he nodded, wiping his damp forehead with a handkerchief.

Peterson, utterly devoted to Eliza Boon and her interests, whose varied career had encompassed everything from prizefighting and collecting money with menaces to enticing men from incoming merchant ships with their pockets full of pay to a cosy little place where they could be assured of pleasurable entertainment, only to knock them senseless *en route* and steal their hard-earned wages, saw nothing to either concern or alarm him in being asked to dispose of a body. His whole life having comprised violence and illicit dealings meant that he was not only untroubled by his conscience but also not overly squeamish in whatever anyone asked him to do; and disposing of one more body was of no more concern to him than when Eliza had asked him to dispose of the dead body of Annie Myers. He may stand no more than five feet nine inches, but his appearance bore more than adequate testimony to the aggressive and violent life he had led; boasting a massive pair of shoulders and a huge barrel of a chest with biceps which bulged beneath the sleeves of his shirt. To a man of his physique, lifting and carrying the dead weight body of a man who had stood head and shoulders above him would pose no more problem than when he had carried Annie's slim and lifeless body down the dimly lit back streets to throw her ignominiously into the cellar of an empty house whose floors had gone and awaiting demolition without feelings or remorse, in fact he had looked upon disposing of her body in the same inconsequential way as he had dealt with Dennis Dunscumbe. His weather-beaten and slightly pitted face, battered and badly scarred around the pale blue eyes, displaying a broken nose which had at some point been inexpertly set, exhibited no signs of emotion upon hearing what had happened or that he was to get rid of yet another body, on the contrary he accompanied Eliza's client to Cavendish Square in her own carriage, completely devoid of thought or feeling at what she had asked him to do. Sir Braden Collett, although immensely relieved to be able to shelve the responsibility of disposing of Sir Philip's body onto the shoulders of a man who knew neither qualms nor misgivings, could only hope that his diligent butler would not suddenly remember his duties and emerge from his downstairs domain just as Peterson was arriving or, God forbid, on the point of carrying Sir Philip's body out of the house!

Having opened the door to Sir Philip Dunscumbe and ushered him into Sir Braden's study, Mitchell had made his way back to his own quarters to read the newspaper until Sir Braden rang the bell for him to show the visitor out. Not having anticipated falling asleep, Mitchell had opened his eyes almost two hours later to the horrifying discovery that he had inadvertently done so, hastening up the back stairs fearing the worst, only to discover that no reply came from his tap on the study door. Taking a deep breath, he turned the handle only to find that Sir Braden had locked the door, something he always did when he was not at home, but as he had not mentioned anything about leaving the house once Sir Philip had left, Mitchell could only assume that his employer had personally let his guest out of the house then took the decision to go out himself. He knew that Lady Collett should have returned home by now, the concert at the Royal Albert Hall being a late matinée, but as he had not heard her ring the bell he could only assume that she had let herself in or, which was more than likely, Sir Braden had been on the watch for her and opened the door himself, in either case, he could only suppose that she was in her room. Not wanting to disturb her to enquire if she knew the whereabouts of her husband, Mitchell decided against it, besides which, if Sir Braden had not gone out and was in fact with her, the chances were that he would be taken to task for not making himself available when wanted, and knowing his employer's uncertain temper from painful experience if he was going to be given a dressing-down, then he would far rather it be in the morning when, hopefully, after a good night's sleep and several glasses of something fortifying, he would be in a better frame of mind to a receive it. Nevertheless, it was out of character for Sir Braden to let something like dereliction of duty to pass without saying anything; Mitchell's experience of his employer leaving him in no doubt that he would have fully expected him to act upon the misdemeanour straightaway either by ringing the bell or setting up a shout for him. That he had done neither was inexplicable, but no doubt he would feel the full lash of his tongue in the morning.

Sir Braden, fully aware that every member of his domestic household from Mitchell down stood in considerable fear of him, knew that because of this no explanation would be required to account for his sudden absence, but he could not deny to feeling no small measure of relief upon seeing no sign of Mitchell when he stepped inside the hall with Peterson following behind him. Upon unlocking the door to his study and setting eyes on Sir Philip's body stretched out on the floor with the blood congealing on his head and a pool of it on the carpet, Sir Braden experienced a momentary feeling of nausea, but the man beside him, impervious to such sights, set briskly to work. The carpet, which he could not risk being seen by Mitchell or one of the maids, much less order it to be cleaned, was therefore rolled up with Sir Philip's body inside it without a blink from the man whose task it was to dispose of it.

Sir Braden, who by no means liked the idea of finding himself in the position whereby he was totally dependent upon others, was reluctantly forced to face up to the fact that this was one occasion when he could not deal with something himself, comforted only by the thought that he had no need to fear either Peterson or Eliza informing against him as they had as much to lose as himself. Nevertheless, he could not say he was sorry to see Peterson eventually haul the body into Eliza's carriage wrapped in the soiled carpet, unutterable relief engulfing him when he saw no one in the hall or any curious passer-by. Collett knew Peterson was a man of few words, but following a brief consultation with him it was mutually agreed that the only safe place to dispose of Sir Philip's body was by throwing it into the Thames, because when it did finally wash up it would be some miles distant, eliminating any possibility of the police connecting it to a residence in Cavendish Square.

Unused to such physical or mental exertion, Sir Braden felt extremely exhausted after the events of the last few hours, but by the time he had consumed several glasses of brandy he was slowly able to see his way and, as far as he could see, his main problem was Mitchell, easily discounting his wife on the grounds of her being too used to his methods of dealing with her and therefore she would do as he ordered without question. Once she knew that he would ruin her father's reputation if she did not keep silent and Mary had been dismissed and replaced with Eliza to make sure of it, he envisaged no difficulties with regards to Eleanor, but when Eliza arrived in Cavendish Square over two hours later, whilst she had no wish for the events of this evening or anything to do with Annie Myers and Dennis Dunscumbe to come to light, she was far from convinced that Sir Braden's measures for dealing with Mitchell and Lady Collett were the right ones. As far as Mitchell was concerned, she placed very little store in him keeping his mouth shut because for a man to find himself suddenly dismissed after many years of long and faithful service on nothing but a trumped-up charge and expect him to go quietly was really asking for too much. If her experience of human nature was anything to go by, it was reasonably safe to say that he would feel very much aggrieved and therefore could well harbour thoughts of paying back Sir Braden for being treated in such a way, and upon reading of Sir Philip's murder in the newspapers he could quite well see this as the means of doing precisely that. Eliza was no fool, she realised perfectly well that just because Mitchell had shown Sir Philip into Sir Braden's study it did not mean that he killed him, but Mitchell would know, or, at least, suspect that Sir Braden was most probably the last man to see Sir Philip alive and he would have to be stupid not to realise the damage this information could do to his former employer. What better revenge then than to report this to the police! If nothing else, it would certainly see Sir Braden being questioned, and even if such enquiries did not lead them back to the death of Annie Myers and Dennis Dunscumbe, they would, at the very least, seriously embarrass Sir Braden. No! To let Mitchell leave was madness. It was far too great a risk and, as she told Sir Braden, if he had any sense he would see that in letting Peterson dispose of Mitchell it would mean that she would not spend goodness only knew how many years in gaol as an accessory to or even conspiring or soliciting to commit murder, and he and Peterson would not be facing the gallows for perpetrating it! It was certainly something for Sir Braden to ponder on, but it only took him a matter of moments to see that Eliza had spoken no less than the truth. Mitchell may have carried out his duties satisfactorily, but he had never really accorded him the same respect as he had his father and therefore Sir Braden instinctively knew that to dismiss him would be to open himself up to all manner of repercussions because he could not fool himself into thinking that Mitchell would accept such treatment tamely, and because he had no more wish than Eliza to face the Queen's Bench he nodded a tacit agreement to her sensible suggestion.

With regards to Lady Collett, Eliza had no objection to taking on the role as her gaoler, after all it was in her own interests that no tales leaked out, but being a practical as well as a shrewd woman she knew that it would mean taking up residence in Cavendish Square, and although she was by no means averse to this it did mean that arrangements would have to be made about her lucrative business. She had never thought about retirement, in fact there was no reason why she should, especially as she was making money faster than she could spend it, but in view of the unprecedented events over the last month or so she considered that the illicit venture she conducted within the outward respectability of her smart town house in Bloomsbury, was no longer viable. The death of Annie Myers was to be regretted, of course, not only because she had been a most popular young woman with her clients, but should questions ever be raised about her, especially when Eliza considered that the gentleman she had been with that night was none other than Sir Philip Dunscumbe's brother, a regular visitor to her discreet establishment, then it could make things rather uncomfortable, and since she had acquired a reputation for discretion she wanted no police officer calling at her premises. But Sir Braden's promise that he would more than make it worth her while if she and Peterson came to Cavendish Square in place of Mitchell and Mary had resolved the issue, and since she had long been aware that Reggie Wragge would like nothing more than to get his hands on her business, she decided to make her long-standing rival an offer he could not refuse. However, before taking this final step Eliza felt it behoved her to point out to Sir Braden that there was another course open to him to solve the problem of his wife because although it was not beyond her capabilities to instil the fear of death into her, it could not be argued that keeping a constant watch on Lady Collett could well end up being a lifetime's job, especially as doing away with her would only create difficulties; the less bodies, the better!

Sir Braden Collett could not deny that Eliza was right when she had said that rather than keep his wife constantly guarded by one or the other of them and putting a period to her existence was far too dangerous, it would surely be far more practical and certainly far safer, if he had his wife committed to an institution for the insane, eliminating at a stroke any risk of her saying anything to anyone and, if she did, who would believe the cries and allegations of a woman locked up in a cell for insanity? It was an idea not without its merits especially as the servants had already grown accustomed to being told that Lady Collett was not feeling well and resting in her room, but whilst this would avert any risk of her saying anything it would most probably create as many problems as it solved, because despite her shyness his wife could boast a wide circle of friends and was very well liked and there were those, the Shiptons for a start, who would find it difficult to believe that she had suddenly succumbed to a mental disorder necessitating having her placed in an asylum. Eliza Boon, seeing that Sir Braden was not overly fond of her suggestion for dealing with his wife, accepted his decision easily enough, convinced that in time he would finally be brought round to her way of thinking.

Peterson meanwhile, having returned to Cavendish Square after accomplishing his nefarious errand, no more than shrugged an indifferent shoulder when informed by Eliza that she needed him to carry out one more job. Upon discovering that he was to dispose of the man whose position he would assume to cut down the risk of him blabbing to all and sundry, he gave no more thought to it than he had to any of the other tasks asked of him. Having listened to Eliza callously telling him that neither she nor Sir Braden cared how he achieved it so long as Mitchell was no longer around to talk, he merely nodded his head before settling himself down for the night in Sir Braden's study with a totally clear conscience. However, Eliza, having given the question of disposing of Mitchell a little more thought, concluded that his death was far too important to leave to Peterson to deal with in any haphazard way he saw fit, and therefore following a consultation with Sir Braden she put forward an idea which was as brilliant as it was guaranteed to eliminate any repercussions rebounding on themselves.

Certain decisions having been satisfactorily arrived at, not only the domestic household but Eleanor as well, awoke the following morning to the startling discovery that Mitchell had been dismissed on a charge of stealing and Mary, having returned to Cavendish Square earlier than expected, had found herself discharged on the grounds of having taken a longer leave of absence than had been agreed. Mary, shocked and bemused, had strenuously argued against the allegations Sir Braden had charged her with, vehemently defending herself, but upon discovering that he was neither listening nor interested she made her exit without so much as a reference or even being allowed to speak to Her Ladyship.

To open her eyes to an extremely painful jawbone and the terrifying recollection of what had occurred the night before was bad enough, but upon being informed of the dismissal of two people, both of whom had been replaced with individuals quite unknown to her, Eleanor was instantly seized with intense panic, but her dash to the door of her bedroom and her screams for help were summarily dealt with by the woman who was to form a major part of her life. The very thought of knowing that her husband had committed murder and in his own study then rid himself of two people to ensure his protection, one of whom was very dear to her, was more than Eleanor could bear. Her innate sense of right and wrong cried out at such an outrage, but this, like her questions as to why he had done such a wicked thing and her demand to know what had happened to Mary and Mitchell, were quickly silenced with the ominous warning that if she did not desist from questioning the events of last night or do as she was told then not only would her father suffer public condemnation for his offence, but she would find herself committed to an asylum for the mentally insane. Sir Braden, now fully restored to calm and self-possession after the fear which had engulfed him the night before, forestalled any cries of horror which fell from her lips by stressing that he had no doubt his friend Sir Wilfred Moore would know no hesitation in taking pity on a distraught husband whose wife was not only beginning to act irrationally but suffering delusions as well, by signing the committal papers and having them countersigned by a medical colleague in order for her to be restrained by admitting her to an institution.

Their installation of fear about what would result should she ever be foolish enough to impart what she had seen had been enough to subdue her, but even though Eleanor resented never being allowed out of the house without either her husband or that odious woman accompanying her, the very thought of what would happen to her as well as her father was enough to quell any idea she may have had of telling the truth, as had any notion of attempting anything in the way of escape. Peterson, a man she had come to hate and fear as much as her husband and Eliza Boon, was never far away, always hovering by the front door, watching and spying and waiting only for her to try to make a move to escape. More than once he had caught her looking longingly out into the square from the side windows in the hall or the drawing-room only to find herself locked in her room to prevent her making a run for the door. If all this were not bad enough, she was repeatedly subjected to her husband's ill-treatment, partly because it was his nature to bully and browbeat but also to make sure she did as he and Eliza told her, necessitating her keeping to her room due to the extent and severity of her injuries. Were it not for the threat hanging over her father, Eleanor would rather tell all she knew than endure this unbearable existence another minute, but as she was given no opportunity to do so it seemed that death would be her only release; that was until her unexpected encounter with Beatrice's brother at Covent Garden Opera House.

Sir Braden, satisfied with Eliza's evaluation about the visit his wife had paid Beatrice Shipton in Mount Street as well as being blissfully unaware of the role her brother was about to play in his life, had seen no reason why they should not honour the invitation to the Kirkmichaels' anniversary ball that evening. Of course, he was still somewhat ruffled over the trick which had humiliatingly been played on him at Covent Garden, and whilst he discounted any skulduggery on his wife's part and his partners in crime had no reason to adopt such a ruse, he was left with only Beatrice Shipton as a possible suspect, but as it was not something he could either charge her with or openly question her about he nevertheless felt it incumbent upon him to keep a closer eye on her, especially as it seemed she was quite determined to re-establish herself with his wife.

As his acquaintanceship with Sir Thomas Shipton was scant, in fact they were on no more than polite nodding terms, apart from being a most successful banker and a man of unquestionable integrity, Sir Braden knew hardly anything about him, and although he and Eleanor had attended one or two gatherings in Mount Street he could not claim to being on anything like friendly terms with the Shiptons. To be honest he had seen enough of Beatrice Shipton, and not only at Covent Garden, to more than adequately bear out Eliza's opinion of her in that she was nothing but a scatter-brained woman who thought of nothing but herself, and whilst it would afford him tremendous satisfaction to sever even the light ties which existed between them, the fact remained that he was very suspicious of not only her intentions but her innocent behaviour the other night. Considering the lengths to which he and his two conspirators had gone to make sure that nothing leaked out about their involvement in recent events, he failed to see how getting rid of him at Covent Garden could have anything to do with them, and upon hearing them swear they knew nothing about it, not that he needed them to swear at all, he was utterly convinced that it had been merely a trick. Even so, he by no means liked the idea of being taken for a fool, and if it was the last thing he ever did he would discover the prankster responsible and take no small gratification from letting them know that he was not the man to be treated with such ridicule. As he was still unaware of Tony's presence at the opera and what he had observed through those glasses, it never entered Sir Braden's head to so much as consider him, and even upon being introduced to him at the Park Grove Hotel no suspicion crept into his mind that he was looking at the man responsible for his hurried exit.

Viscount Childon may take precedence in rank to himself, but apart from the fact that Sir Braden had no liking for Colonials coming here and taking up titles he believed should most definitely not be held by those who were not born here and most certainly not entitled to, and through the maternal line at that, he had taken an instant dislike to Lady

Shipton's brother and, for both these reasons, it would have given him immense satisfaction to have ignored him, but he could not deny that it had been purely for courtesy's sake that he had not. In Viscount Childon he had detected a man who had neither regard nor respect for the honour his title bestowed upon him much less what it signified, in fact he bore all the appearance typical of those the other side of the Atlantic who had either married into English aristocracy or had fallen lucky by having a title thrust upon them through family circumstances, and he felt sure that it meant nothing more to him than what it could offer him, such as requesting the honour of his wife's hand for the next dance. Childon's father may have made his fortune in the newspaper business, although Sir Braden had no doubt it had its roots in cheating at cards or shooting a man for his goldmine or something equally as scurrilous, but he would have this man know that his wife, indeed the very fabric of the world he had unexpectedly been catapulted into, was not his for abusing and had it not been for the fact that a refusal to permit it would have been a gross insult to one whose rank demanded respect as well as bringing his own conduct into question, he had, with cold politeness, granted his impertinent request.

Had Sir Braden the least idea that his estimation of Tony ran extremely wide of the mark and that he was the very man who had brought about his hasty departure from Covent Garden, he would not so easily have dismissed him as being quite so inconsequential. It was perhaps as well for Sir Braden's peace of mind that he remained in complete ignorance of what Tony had seen last night and that he had already had the pleasure of making Lady Collett's acquaintance as well as having not the slightest inkling that this man was not only determined to bring him to account for his treatment of his wife, but was beginning to piece together what he was strenuously trying to hide. Had he known what was in Tony's mind or have been privileged to have seen him the following morning, he would not have been either so contemptuous of him or so complacent.

Beatrice, who had not failed to notice the look on Eleanor's face as she glided around the floor in Tony's arms, glanced significantly up at her husband who, like his wife, had also seen the transformation which had come over her and although he could not deny that they were more than ideally suited, for the life of him he could see nothing coming from it. As they had by now stepped a little away from Sir Braden, Tom, casting a quick glance in his direction, was left in no doubt from the look on his face that he was by no means pleased to see his wife clearly enjoying the company of another man, and although he could well understand Tony's determination to remove Eleanor from a marriage which could not be anything other than intolerable, unless his brother-in-law could perform a miracle he failed to see how he could possibly bring it about. Tony may have made no attempt to ask for her hand again, but even though Tom had seen him lead one or two young women out onto the floor as well as his sister as good manners demanded, his eyes always seemed to forge a path to where Eleanor was sitting beside Braden. Having fallen in love with Beatrice across a crowded ballroom himself and read the response in her eyes as he had stood looking at her, Tom was easily able to interpret the unspoken messages which passed between Tony and Eleanor and although not by a word or gesture did she give herself away to her husband, it came as no surprise to Tom, when, just over an hour later, he saw them take their leave of their hostess.

It had taken every ounce of self-restraint Tony possessed not to ask for her hand for another dance as well as making no attempt to approach her as he saw her leave on her husband's arm, but no matter difficult such feats proved to be, he took comfort from knowing that Eleanor Collett, despite her fear of her husband, felt precisely the same about him. His liaisons to date had been extremely pleasurable, in fact he would have been more than human had he not enjoyed the company of those women with whom he had spent such an agreeable time, but although they had filled a very natural need in his life he had never once even considered marriage and as it appeared they too had no desire to see his ring on their finger, or a ring from any man for that matter, both parties had enjoyed the relationship for as long as it had lasted, eventually going their separate ways with no regrets or recriminations. He had spoken no less than the truth to Beatrice when he had told her that he would know the woman for him as soon as he set eyes on her, and from the moment he had seen Eleanor through those opera glasses he had known instinctively that he had at last found the woman with whom he wanted to spend the rest of his life. He had no regrets about his past amorous interludes nor was he ashamed of them, but Eleanor had, at a stroke, rendered them entirely meaningless, so much so that he wanted nothing more than to place his ring on her finger and to love and protect her for the rest of his life.

Right now, Tony had no more idea than Tom as to how he was going to engineer her removal from a man who was not only totally undeserving of her but deserved to be thrashed for his treatment of her, but if his suspicions about Sir Braden Collett and Sir Philip Dunscumbe were correct, then not only would this bring a murderer to justice but also provide the means to release Eleanor from an unbearable marriage. But when Tony opened his mind to Tom later that evening when they were alone, his brother-in-law, although aghast at the thought of a man, even one as disagreeable as Sir Braden Collett, was quite capable of committing such a heinous crime as murder, he nevertheless had to admit that, however objectionable, it certainly explained Eleanor's constant supervision.

"I don't pretend to have all the answers, Tom," Tony shook his head, "in fact I could be way off line, but if I am right, then you must admit it goes a long way to explaining a lot."

"Yes, it does," Tom nodded, taking a drink of whisky, "but assuming Collett did murder Sir Phillip," he queried, pointing his glass at him, "why are you so sure it took place in Cavendish Square."

"If I am right about Collett murdering Sir Philip," Tony nodded, "although for the life of me I can't figure out why he should especially as the police investigations have never tied the two men together, but when I think of Eleanor's reaction to that piece in the newspaper, which went far beyond a natural revulsion at such a vicious crime, in addition to her fear of Collett as well as never being allowed out on her own and the time from when her constant supervision began, my gut feeling is telling me Collett *did* murder Sir Philip and if I am right it had to be in Cavendish Square. Had the murder taken place elsewhere, then I fail to see the need to keep Eleanor so close."

"But are you seriously suggesting that Collett actually *murdered* Sir Philip in front of her!" Tom exclaimed, shocked.

"I don't know, Tom," Tony shook his head, "but knowing something of his treatment of her it would not surprise me, but I have to say," he acknowledged, "I think it most unlikely. It could well be that she walked into such a dreadful scene quite by chance or, even," he shrugged, "found some evidence which had somehow been overlooked. Whichever way it was," he told him, "she's frightened to death."

"And no wonder!" Tom said with feeling. "Good God, Tony!" he cried, appalled. "It's iniquitous what they're doing to her!" inhaling on his cigar.

"It sure is!" Tony agreed grimly.

"But what I don't understand is," Tom shook his head, bewildered, "who *are* these people he's brought in?"

Tony shrugged. "I have no idea, but I know *one* thing for sure," he said firmly, "whoever they are, they are no more domestic staff than I am."

"Well," Tom inclined his head, "I won't argue with that. To think that Bea had to resort to such a subterfuge in her own home because of this woman is beyond everything!" to which Tony nodded his agreement. "But Mitchell," Tom queried, his brow creasing, "I mean, he'd been with the family for years! It would have been no easy matter dismissing him!"

"No, it wouldn't," Tony agreed, "but what beats me is why this Mitchell guy has not come forward."

"How do you mean?" Tom cocked his head.

"If I am right, then it's logical to assume that Mitchell let Sir Philip into the house. I can't say what time this would have been, but surely once he read the stories in the newspapers about Sir Philip's murder and the time frame in which the police put on his death, then it goes against all logic to think he did not put two and two together."

"So, are you saying they killed him too?" Tom asked, aghast.

Tony shrugged. "I don't know, Tom. All I *do* know is that at no point have the police found it necessary to interview Collett, which would most certainly have been the case if Mitchell had told them about Sir Philip's visit to Cavendish Square. The fact they have not done so leads me to believe that Mitchell has said nothing. Whether this is because he has been paid handsomely to turn a blind eye or because he is no position to say anything, is anyone's guess, but it's *my* guess that Collett could not afford to have him around and run the risk of being blackmailed. If Mitchell *was* murdered," he nodded, "then I think it's safe to say that it would not have been Collett who carried it out."

Tom could not argue against this sound reasoning, but it appeared the more they dug the worse it seemed, but in view of what Tony had said he could not help questioning him about Mary.

"The same goes for her," Tony shrugged. "Bea tells me Mary had always looked after Eleanor and Collett would not be fool enough to keep her on, it would be far too risky. I'm not saying she has been murdered," he nodded, "purely because her position within the household did not encompass the same tasks as Mitchell's and therefore she would mostly be confined to Eleanor's rooms upstairs. It could simply be that Collett knew she was not around at the time, but in view of what Eleanor saw or stumbled upon she had to be dismissed so he could bring this woman in whose job I am quite convinced is to watch her!"

A frown descended onto Tom's forehead, as he said thoughtfully, "You know Tony, everything you say makes perfect sense as well as supporting Eleanor's behaviour, but do you think you will be able to prove any of this? What I mean is," he nodded, "if you are right, and I believe you are, Collett seems to have left nothing to chance."

"No, he hasn't," Tony replied grimly, "but apart from the fact that I don't like to think of Collett getting away with murder, there's Eleanor to think of. How much longer she can bear such treatment I don't know; not long I should have thought," he shook his head, swallowing a generous mouthful of whisky. "I just hope that Bill can come up with something!"

Tom wholeheartedly agreed with this as he did with not telling Bea too much because like her brother she was open and honest and although he loved and trusted her there could come a moment when she accidentally let something slip, and the chances were very good it would filter back to Collett. Should that happen, not only would he have grounds for legal action, but it would make Eleanor's life even more intolerable.

"Just one thing, Tony," he smiled ruefully, before he said goodnight, "I know I am not as young as I used to be, or as slim," patting his thickening girth, "but I'm still pretty useful with my fives, if you should ever need me for anything."

"Thanks Tom," Tony laughed, slapping him on the shoulder, "but I hope it won't come to that," accurately reading his brother-in-law's expression to mean that it would be a pity if he was not permitted to have just one touch at Collett.

Chapter Eight

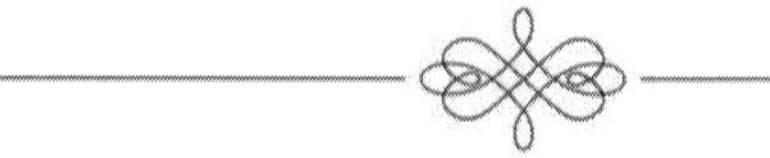

Upon seeing Tony stroll into his office just after ten o'clock the next morning following his casual tap on the glass door, Bill Pitman, a thin and wiry man in his late fifties, raised an amusing eyebrow as he sat back in his seat, resting his hands on the padded leather arms. Having known Tony ever since he was a boy when he had not only haunted the printing room bombarding the men with questions as well as getting round every one of his father's reporters by persuading them into letting him tag along when they were going out to cover a story, himself included, neither man stood on ceremony with the other. He knew Tony to be an intelligent and clever man and one, moreover, who had a real feel for the newspaper business as well as being blessed with a fair and open mind and a keen sense of humour and therefore no inducement offered him, and there had been many, would entice Bill away from a man to whom, like his father, he had an inflexible loyalty. Bill knew Tony had loved and adored his mother, but he also knew of the deep and genuine love which had existed between Ambrose Dart and his son, so much so that, even now, it seemed indissoluble and, looking up at the man whose father he had respected and admired and who had been inordinately proud of his only son, grinned. "Tony! I hadn't expected to see you this morning. What is it?" He cocked his head. "Got nowhere else to go? Or are you looking to take my job?"

"I may just do that, Bill!" Tony smiled, removing his hat and overcoat and hanging them on the stand.

Bill laughed at this. "It would serve you right if I *did* go over to the '*The Times*' or '*The Telegraph*'."

"You won't." Tony shook his head, his eyes alight with amusement, dropping his gloves onto the desk before holding out his hands to the fire.

"Oh," Bill queried, raising another amusing eyebrow, "what makes you so sure of that?"

"You would have done it by now," Tony smiled, "besides, I doubt they have ever met anyone from the Bronx before; they would never understand half of what you were saying," easing himself into the chair on the opposite side of Bill's desk.

"Wise guy, huh!" Bill nodded. "Well, let me tell *you* something." He pointed a finger at him, not quite able to hide the affection he had for Ambrose Dart's son. "Your old man didn't send me here to pretty up the place," he nodded again, "he knew brains when he saw 'em," tapping his head with a bony forefinger, to which Tony burst out laughing. "Yeah, sure," Bill shrugged, "laugh, but you'd be surprised how much Cockney slang I've learned since I've been here!"

"I don't doubt it," Tony grinned, "but I think *'The Times'* and *'The Telegraph'* would prefer just plain English; which lets *you* out!"

"Cor blimey, Guvna!" Bill mimicked. "*H'are you sayin' that H'I cannot speak propa H'English?"* Once again Tony's sense of the ridiculous got the better of him at this and burst out laughing, to which Bill managed, *"H'I think 'The Times' h'and 'The Telegraph' would be h'ever so h'impressed."* Bill may have lost the rough edges to his accent during the five years he had been here, but nothing could disguise the distinctive twang of the Bronx, especially in his pronunciation of certain words.

"Sure they would!" Tony laughed. "Until you forgot yourself. But it won't do, Bill," he shook his head, "you'll never pass for an Englishman. Is that real coffee I smell?" he asked, twisting round in his seat to see a freshly made pot behind him.

"Sure is," Bill grinned. "Help yourself."

"Thanks, I will," leaving his seat to walk over to the table, pouring out two cups. "How'd you come by this?" briefly raising the pot in his hand, laughing when Bill tapped his nose with a knowing forefinger. "Okay, I'll skip that one," and handed Bill his coffee.

"Must protect my sources, Tony," he grinned. "Besides, you know what they say; *'Ask no questions and you'll be told no lies.'*"

"I always wondered where you got your information from, Bill," he nodded, sitting down and making himself comfortable. "You clearly know some pretty unsavoury individuals."

"Not *'unsavoury'* Tony!" Bill cried in mock horror, a gleam of pure amusement lurking at the back of his eyes. "I prefer to call it *'being in the know'*."

"You were clearly born to be hanged, Bill!" Tony laughed.

"Sure," he grinned, "but not without taking my notebook with me! So," he nodded, sitting back in his seat, "what *does* bring you to Fleet Street? Not that I'm not pleased to see you," he assured him.

Taking a moment to savour his coffee, the one thing he missed in England, Tony looked straight across at Bill, saying at length, "The Dunscumbe case."

Bill nodded. "I had a feeling it was." He eyed Tony thoughtfully for a moment, asking suspiciously, "What is it about this case that's got to you? And don't say nothing," he warned, "because you forget," he pointed a finger at him, "I *know* you. You've had an interest in this ever since I cabled the story to you in New York."

"Yes," Tony nodded, "I know, but since then my interest has moved on from the professional to the personal."

Removing his eye shade with slow deliberation, Bill eyed Tony narrowly. "In less than a week?" he asked suspiciously, running a hand through his thinning grey hair. "What's happened since I saw you a few days ago, that you now know and I and Scotland Yard don't?" The eyes narrowed even more. "Have you got an angle on this, Tony?"

"No," Tony shook his head, "not an angle precisely."

"Come on Tony, give," his hand beckoned. "What's on your mind?"

"Tell me, Bill," Tony asked thoughtfully, taking out his cigarette case, "what do you know about this case that has not been reported?"

"So," Bill mused confidently, "you *have* got an angle!" lighting a huge cigar which he fished out of the pocket of his waistcoat.

"Perhaps," Tony replied carelessly, which did not fool Bill in the least.

"Come on, Tony," he encouraged, "out with it."

Tony lit his cigarette, eyeing Bill thoughtfully. "Tell me what you know first."

Bill may have been tied to a desk for the last eight or nine years, but the reporter in him smelled a scoop when one came under his nose, and the look in Tony's eyes did nothing to dispel this. "Why do I get the feeling I smell something big?" he said slowly, eyeing Tony through a cloud of cigar smoke.

"If I am right," Tony nodded, "it'll be the biggest thing to hit Fleet Street since I don't know when; so, come on Bill," he urged, "let's have it."

"Okay," Bill shrugged at length, knowing it was useless to argue when Tony had made up his mind to something, "we'll play it your way – for now, but what you expect me to tell you that I haven't already, I don't know." Taking only long enough to swallow a mouthful of coffee, he sat back in his seat, rolling his cigar between his thin fingers. "Like I told you," he explained, "on the afternoon of Friday April twenty-nine last year Dunscumbe left his rooms at Westminster and was not seen again until his body washed up at Greenwich three days later."

"What time did he leave his rooms?" Tony enquired.

"According to what his personal and private secretary told the police," Bill shrugged, "about half past three. As there was nothing in his diary to indicate Dunscumbe had an appointment and he had made no mention that he may have to go somewhere, his secretary was rather surprised to see him go out, especially as there was a debate in the House that night which Dunscumbe apparently had every intention of attending. When he asked where he was going Dunscumbe didn't say, just said that he would be back presently." After inhaling on his cigar, Bill went on, "When Dunscumbe had not returned to his office several hours later, Hallerton, that's his secretary," he nodded, "thought he may have gone straight to the House, but when he looked for him there, there was no sign of him. As it was a debate on a topic which was apparently very close to Dunscumbe's heart, Hallerton became rather concerned so he decided to call at Sir Philip's home in Curzon Street to see if he was there, only to be told by his butler that he had not seen him since he had left home that morning."

"Did anyone report he had disappeared to the police?" Tony enquired. "Or was it simply a case of nothing being done until his body washed up?"

"Apparently, when he put in no appearance in the House that night," Bill explained, "or the next day either, his absence was in fact remarked upon by the Prime Minister himself."

"Lord Salisbury!" Tony exclaimed.

"The very same," Bill grimaced. "Ordinarily the absence of a Member of Parliament in the House would not create much attention, but although Salisbury is a rather reserved and distant man he and Dunscumbe went way back, in fact," he told him, "they were old buddies and were due to meet for lunch, but when Dunscumbe did not attend that debate or show up next day Salisbury began to ask Hallerton some questions, none of which he could answer." Bill saw the frown which had descended onto Tony's forehead through a haze of cigar smoke, saying, "Of course, Salisbury did not want to start a hue and cry, especially at that stage, just in case Dunscumbe's disappearance was nothing very serious," he shrugged, "but Dunscumbe's butler reported it to the local cops and they called in Scotland Yard."

Tony nodded rather absently, asking at length, "Did the police manage to track his movements prior to his body showing up?"

"Huh huh," Bill shook his head, "from the moment he left Westminster it seems he just disappeared from off the face of the earth."

"This Superintendent Dawson at Scotland Yard; what do you know of him?" Tony queried.

"I've run across him a few times. He's a good cop," Bill inclined his head, "and not one to jump to conclusions, but he does have the tendency to go with his gut feelings as well as being known for treading on a few toes." Tony raised an enquiring eyebrow at this. "Dawson's a guy who says what he thinks," Bill told him. "I like him; I think you will too; he's definitely your kind of guy!" Bill nodded. "From what I hear though there are those at The Yard who don't much care for him telling it like it is or the way he sticks to tried and trusted methods instead of moving with the times; but he gets the job done."

"I understand he dismissed the motive for Sir Philip's murder as larceny because nothing had apparently been taken from the body. You were a crime reporter Bill," Tony nodded, "how many instances can you bring to mind where a dead body had not been stripped of its belongings?"

Bill shook his head. "Not one. Dunscumbe was quite a rich man by all accounts," he pointed out, "but when the police searched his body before it was eventually taken away they found that the six one pound notes in his wallet and about ten shillings in change in his coat pocket were still there; as was his gold watch and chain and the signet ring he always wore on the little finger of his right hand. Of course," he shrugged, "Dawson did take in to account that due to the body being in the Thames for several days some of his personal effects could easily have washed out of his pockets, but the upshot was that most of his belongings were still on him, which means," he pointed out, "that Dawson's right; whoever killed him had another reason for doing so."

"This man who found the body, who was he?" Tony asked curiously.

"George Wilkins," Bill answered. "A coal man. Fifty years of age and lived in Duck Lane with his wife and five children. Honest; trustworthy. Nothing known against him."

Tony nodded. "So," he pondered, "if the motive for Sir Philip's murder was not larceny; what was it, personal or political?"

"Dawson questioned everyone who knew him most thoroughly," Bill emphasised, "parliamentary colleagues as well as friends and all his domestic staff and not one of them could shed any light on it."

"What do we know about him as a politician?" Tony questioned.

"Well," Bill shrugged, "according to my sources inside Westminster he was very well respected; a good conservative of long-standing, stood for a constituency somewhere in the Midlands, but in spite of his friendship with Salisbury he was never a member of the Cabinet. He was known to straddle the fence nine times out of ten, except when it came to his hobby-horse."

"Which was?" Tony raised a questioning eyebrow.

Bill sighed. "Look Tony, what is all this?"

"Just humour me, Bill," Tony smiled, "for a while longer."

"Damn it, Tony!" he cried, frustrated. "If you're on to something I…"

"Don't worry, Bill," he assured him, "you'll get the scoop."

"What scoop?" Bill asked curiously, inhaling hard on his cigar.

"Not yet, Bill," Tony shook his head. "What hobby-horse?"

Bill sighed. "Very well, if you *must* have it!"

"I must," Tony nodded.

"Abuse and cruelty in any form to animals or people, children in particular," he explained. "It seems the debate in the House that night was about the number of scientific experiments being carried out on live animals; something he was very keen to stop or, at least, restrict."

"And his personal life?"

"From what I can figure out," Bill told him, "he didn't have one. Strange huh!" He shrugged upon seeing Tony raise an eyebrow in surprise. "Especially when you think the guy was almost fifty, but that's how it was. Dunscumbe had no family. Apparently, he never married and, as far as I can tell, there's never been any scandal attached to his name through womanising or anything else." He nodded meaningfully.

"Apart from visiting his club two or three times a week, *'The Barrington Club'* just around the corner from Piccadilly, he lived a very quiet life. Sorry, Tony," he sighed when he saw the frown descend onto his forehead, "but there it is!" He shrugged. "If you were hoping for skeletons in the closet to account for his murder, then I'm afraid you're out of luck."

"No brothers or sisters?" Tony shrugged an enquiry.

"There *was* a brother," Bill nodded, "Dennis. He lived in Hertford Street, but I'm afraid he's dead. Committed suicide."

Tony's eyes narrowed at this. "When?" he asked sharply.

"Eleven, twelve months ago," Bill shrugged.

"Are you sure of this, Bill?"

"Sure I'm sure! I can get the cuttings out if you want," he offered.

"No," Tony shook his head, "that won't be necessary. Eleven or twelve months ago, you say?" Bill nodded then sat in exasperated silence while Tony seemed to turn something over in his mind. "How he did take his own life?"

"Put a Derringer to his temple and pulled the trigger, which, by the way," Bill nodded, "was lying on the floor just inches from his hand when his body was later discovered."

Tony thought a moment, then, after looking a little doubtfully at Bill, asked at length, "I don't suppose it's any use asking if the gun was ever tested for fingerprints?" In response to Bill's raised eyebrow, Tony smiled. "Okay, I know it's not an accepted form of identification – yet, but it's been recognised by the courts in British India for a while now and I was just wondering if…" He shrugged.

"Then don't," Bill told him. "In case you've forgotten," he reminded him, "this is England; and things don't move so fast here."

"I know but…"

"Sure, it'll come," Bill pointed his cigar at him, "and soon; but," he shrugged, "right now it's figured as being just a bit too dicey."

Tony sighed, then asked, "Who found him?"

"His man the next morning," Bill told him.

"Was there a note?"

"No," Bill shook his head, "at least," he corrected himself, "none was found."

"Odd," Tony mused, "people who commit suicide normally leave a note."

"They may well," Bill sighed, inhaling on his cigar, "but if Dunscumbe wrote one it was never found."

Watching the smoke curl up from his cigarette, Tony's brow creased in thought as he seemed to ponder something, asking at length, "I take it Scotland Yard was not called in?"

"Huh huh," Bill shook his head. "There was no evidence to suggest suspicious circumstances so it was dealt with by the local cops at Vine Street."

"What was the reason for his suicide, do you know?"

"The official verdict," Bill informed him patiently, "was that he had taken his own life while the balance of his mind was disturbed."

"And the unofficial verdict?" Tony cocked his head.

Bill pursed his lips. "*No* unofficial verdict, Tony." He shook his head.

Tony raised a sceptical eyebrow at this. "There's always an '*unofficial* verdict', Bill," he smiled.

Bill sighed, nodding, "Okay, you win. The rumour was, and that's *all* it was," he emphasised, "was that Dennis Dunscumbe, who had always been a little wild, was involved with a set his brother most strongly disapproved of."

"Who was this set?" Tony asked curiously.

"Dewey Tarkington, for one," Bill replied, "the Honourable Sidney Dyton for another, and Sir Braden Collett, to mention but three."

"*Collett!*" Tony repeated in an odd voice, causing Bill to eye him anxiously.

"Do you know him?" Bill asked suspiciously.

"I've met him," Tony nodded significantly.

"I get the feeling you don't like him," Bill commented shrewdly.

"I don't," Tony shook his head, a hard note in his voice, "but never mind that now," he dismissed. "Tell me what you know about the others."

Bill sighed. "Not much, I'm afraid," he shook his head, "although I can tell you that Dyton went through a pretty public divorce three years ago; apparently it was his wife who brought an action against *him,* the reason on the petition being mental cruelty, but the word was," he nodded, "she had him followed thinking he was having an affair, which he was, but not with another woman, if you take my meaning," he said knowingly, "so, instead of infidelity, which would have meant everything coming out in court, the reason was tactfully changed to mental cruelty." Tony nodded, and Bill went on, "As for Tarkington, he certainly enjoys rich living, which he can well afford. He goes to the races regularly and enjoys playing cards; especially poker, in fact," he pointed his cigar at him, "he's known for being a high roller, winning most of the time. Although he's been married for some years there are no children and he's seldom seen out with his wife, but again the word is," he nodded, "that he doesn't just like his eggs sunny-side up! Of course, it's all pretty much under wraps, as it is with Dyton. Their reputations would be ruined if any of it got out."

"Anything else?"

"Not that I know of," Bill shrugged.

"So," Tony mused, "*these* are the men Dennis Dunscumbe was involved with. What do you know about him?"

"If it's the full low-down you want, I haven't got it," Bill shook his head, "but I *can* tell you that he was a good few years younger than his brother," he shrugged, "although from their behaviour you'd never think they were related. Sir Philip was a quiet and rather reserved man, a respectable pillar of society whereas Dennis was known to be a little wild who frequently spent more than he could afford. Apparently, he enjoyed playing cards and going to the races; usually losing rather heavily."

"Women?" Tony raised an eyebrow.

"You bet! And the word was," Bill nodded, "he had a habit of slapping 'em around too!"

"Did he?" Tony said slowly, stubbing his cigarette. "Now, *that's* interesting."

"Okay, Tony," Bill said, goaded, "I've played it your way, now you play it mine! Either you spill the beans or nothing doing. I'm zipped! Capisce?" He nodded. "So, come on, Tony," he pressed, "give."

"Okay, Bill," Tony smiled, "I will, but hold on to that cigar of yours because if I am right, and I'm certain I am, I'll give you a story that will set Fleet Street alight!"

The faded brown eyes lit up at this and, leaning forward in his seat, his cigar clenched firmly between his teeth, Bill listened to Tony's account of what he had seen take place at Covent Garden between Sir Braden Collett and his wife and his later meetings with Eleanor followed by his carefully thought-out theory without interruption, but although the reporter in him was unable to either dismiss or ignore it, his logic argued against it as too fantastical. "Have I got this right?" Bill pointed his cigar at him. "You're actually saying that you believe Collett *murdered* Sir Philip Dunscumbe?"

"That's precisely what I'm saying, Bill," Tony said firmly.

Bill thought for a moment, chewing on his cigar. "No," he said at length, "I don't buy it, Tony. Even if he did know Sir Philip, and I say *if*," he nodded, "because there is nothing to tie the two men together, what possible motive could he have had? You've *heard* of 'motive'," he asked with heavy irony, raising a questioning eyebrow.

"What's the matter, Bill," Tony smiled, "ulcers playing up?"

"Never mind my ulcers!" he dismissed impatiently. "What about a motive?"

"Oh, I've got a motive," Tony soothed, "or, at least, I do *now*."

"Oh, you do *now*!" Bill replied ironically. "Well that's a relief because for a minute there I thought you were going to do without one!"

"You worry too much, Bill," Tony told him good humouredly.

"You pay me to worry, remember?" Bill nodded. "And worrying over whether you have a motive only makes me worry more!"

"Is this your subtle way of asking me for a raise?" Tony asked amusingly.

"You couldn't afford it!" Bill retorted, not quite able to suppress the smile hovering on his lips. "Now," he pointed his cigar at him, "tell me about this motive you have suddenly come up with to account for Collett murdering Sir Philip?"

"Well, actually," Tony confessed, "it's you who have come up with it." Bill looked rather closely at him. "Look, Bill," he nodded, "I admit I was struggling to figure out what could possibly have been the reason for Collett murdering Sir Philip Dunscumbe, but as soon as you mentioned his brother I knew that was it."

"You did, did you?" Tony nodded and Bill sighed. "But you still don't know for certain that Collett knew either brother!" Bill pointed out reasonably.

"Collett knew Dennis, Bill," he said firmly, "*that* is a fact."

"No, Tony," Bill shook his head, pointing his finger at him, "*that* is not a fact."

"Come on, Bill," Tony nodded, "you and I know that these rumours nearly always have some basis in fact. It's just that they're covered up for the sake of respectability! You said that yourself only minutes back about Dyton and Tarkington!"

"Okay," Bill sighed, "let's say Collett knew Dennis Dunscumbe, but it doesn't prove squat about him knowing Sir Philip!"

"So, what are you saying Bill?" Tony broke in. "You don't trust your sources? You said yourself that Dennis Dunscumbe was involved with a set his brother did not approve of, which included Collett," he reminded him in answer to Bill's irritable sigh. "What if Sir Philip blamed Collett for his brother's suicide and decided to charge him with his suspicions?"

"Okay, okay," Bill cried, raising his arms in exasperated capitulation, "let's say he knew the guy, but that does not *prove* Collett killed Sir Philip!"

"No," Tony conceded, "but it certainly opens the door to investigate that possibility."

"Okay, Tony," Bill sighed, "let's see if I've got this straight. You're saying that Sir Philip, by means unspecified," he pointed out sceptically, "was put on to Collett and then decided to charge him as being in some way responsible for his brother taking his own life. Things got out of hand and Collett whacks him over the head, when he realises he's killed him he throws the body into the river – oh, I was forgetting," he amended, upon seeing the look on Tony's face, "he brings someone in to do it for him, this guy you say is now acting as his butler. Lady Collett either witnesses the murder or stumbles onto something which means they have to keep her quiet so this shady dame is brought in to keep guard over her and the real maid and butler are fired!"

Tony nodded. "You see how it all fits together, Bill."

"The way *you* have it, yeah," he told him.

"So, what are you saying, Bill?" Tony asked. "That I have twisted the facts to suit my personal feelings?"

"No, God damn it!" he cried. "That's not what I'm saying and you know it," he told him irritably. "I know you too well for that. I've been in this game a long time, Tony," he nodded, pointing his cigar at him, "and I know a story when I see one, and unless I'm reading this all wrong that's precisely what I think you've got, but you don't need me to tell you that this could well turn out to be dynamite, and therefore we must be certain of our facts. For one thing," he nodded, inhaling hard on his cigar, "Lady Collett's behaviour may well fall in with what you say, but we don't know if she saw or stumbled upon anything!" he pointed out reasonably.

"Damn right she did!" Tony said unequivocally. "Apart from the fact that she's terrified of something other than her husband, why else is she never allowed out on her own? Why has she been watched over and guarded ever since Sir Philip's death? And why has Collett found it necessary to get rid of two members of his staff; one of whom had been with the family for years, if nothing was amiss?"

"Okay," Bill conceded, "Lady Collett is terrified of something other than her husband and he has rid himself of two members of staff, but you don't know for certain that it's because of Sir Philip's murder!" he pointed out. "Lady Collett may well be afraid of her husband as well as never being allowed out alone and then reacted to a piece she saw in a newspaper, but it's not enough, Tony," he shook his head. "Her reaction could easily be slammed by even a halfway decent lawyer!"

"I know I'm right, Bill," Tony told him firmly. "Call it a gut feeling if you like," he nodded, "but whilst I admit I have not worked out the ins and outs of it, any more than I can hazard a guess as to where Collett found this butler guy and the woman who passes as a maid from yet, I'd stake my life on it!"

"Well," Bill admitted, inclining his head, "I've had a few of those in my time, but gut feeling or not," he warned, "unless Lady Collett comes forward, which I can't see her doing and, even if she did, you know as well as I do that she can't give evidence incriminating to her husband; proving it is going to be one hell of a long shot! But hey, don't get me wrong, Tony!" he raised a hand. "I'm sold; I think you've got something, but if we're going to run with this we've got to think it through. For one thing," he pointed out, "right now it's impossible to say how she could possibly have seen the murder, especially as it's not likely her husband would do it in front of her and, for another," he nodded, "even a rookie cop would be bound to question your motives!"

"Okay," Tony conceded, "I hold my hands up to the fact that I'm far from indifferent where Lady Collett is concerned, but my feelings for her do not alter anything." Bill raised a slightly sceptical eyebrow. "Okay," Tony agreed, "I admit that I have no proof of Collett's complicity in murder, but it's there all right; all we have to do is find it. Look Bill," he nodded, "Sir Philip Dunscumbe was brutally murdered by several severe blows to the head and his body thrown into the Thames where it washes ashore at Greenwich three days later; now, according to the police," he reminded him, "they made a thorough search of the surrounding area in case evidence came to light suggesting that the murder occurred within the vicinity, but unless whoever killed him scrubbed the sidewalk or wherever it was clean before they made a run for it, there was no sign of *any* evidence. Supposing he *was* murdered in the neighbourhood," Tony raised a questioning eyebrow, "what could possibly have taken him there? Don't forget," he pointed out, "he was going to the House later that evening for the debate, but there would be no way he could get to Greenwich, deal with whatever business took him there *and* back to Westminster in time. No, Bill," he shook his head, "whatever Sir Philip's business was it was most certainly not in Greenwich and nor was he murdered there, both were somewhere much closer to home and, unless I miss my guess, I'd say in Cavendish Square."

"Are you saying that Sir Philip Dunscumbe was *actually* murdered in Collett's house?" Bill asked incredulously, eyeing Tony in disbelief.

"That's exactly what I'm saying," Tony said emphatically. "Where else could it have been?"

"A hundred places!" Bill replied firmly.

"No, Bill," Tony shook his head, "it *had* to be in Cavendish Square."

"Why had it?" Bill demanded reasonably.

"If I am right about Sir Philip approaching Collett regarding his brother's death," Tony nodded, "where else could that conversation have taken place other than in Cavendish Square? Don't forget," he reminded him, "Sir Philip's butler would have known if Collett had paid a call in Curzon Street, but since the police never questioned him on this point, it could only be because Collett had never visited Sir Philip at his home and was, to all intents and purposes, not acquainted with him. I can't say how it came about, Bill," he shook his head, "perhaps Sir Philip had been turning things over in his mind or someone had tipped him off or, even," he shrugged, "it could be that Dennis confided certain things to him, but however it was something *must* have happened to take Sir Philip out of his rooms at Westminster that day even though there was nothing in his diary as far as his secretary could see to show he had arranged to see Collett, had there been the police would have questioned him, but not only that," he pointed out, "how else could Lady Collett have witnessed it or, if not witnessed it, then stumbled upon something to alert her to the fact?" Tony asked reasonably. "No, Bill," he shook his head, "it *had* to be Cavendish Square and, I believe," he told him firmly, "that if we could only discover the reason for Dennis Dunscumbe's suicide the answers to the rest will fall into place."

"I can't argue against your reasoning," Bill told him, after thinking it over for a moment or two, "it makes perfect sense, but surely Collett would not be stupid enough to commit murder in his own home! Why, the guy would have to be crazy!"

"I agree," Tony surprised him by saying, "but suppose it wasn't planned; suppose it was a spur-of-the-moment thing upon finding Sir Philip unexpectedly on his doorstep accusing him of all manner of things! Look Bill," he said practically, "if, as we suspect, Collett knew Dennis Dunscumbe, then it's reasonable to suppose that he knew the circumstances surrounding his suicide. As I see it," he reasoned, "the two deaths *must* be linked, it goes against all logic to believe otherwise. How?" he shrugged. "I can't say, but it certainly leaves three questions which need answering: what did Collett know of Dennis Dunscumbe's death? Did he have anything to gain by it? And what's become of Mitchell and Mary?" He saw Bill purse his lips. "Look Bill," Tony nodded, "it stands to reason that Mitchell let Sir Philip into the house so why he has not come forward?"

"Has it occurred to you that he could have moved away?" Bill suggested. "People do, you know."

"Where to, Bill?" Tony smiled. "The moon! Which is where he would have to have been all this time not to read the newspapers!"

"Okay," Bill shrugged, "so he's not moved away, which leaves us with either, one," raising his forefinger, "he's been done in or," raising another finger, "two, he's been paid to keep quiet!"

"He could, yes," Tony said sceptically, "but I doubt it. We have to find him Bill or, as I suspect," he nodded significantly, "what's happened to him. The same goes for Mary Stanley."

"You don't think…?" Bill began.

"No," Tony shook his head, "I don't. I can't say for certain when she was dismissed; perhaps around the same time as Mitchell," he shrugged, "but I fail to see what reason they could possibly have had for murdering her. Her position in the household was such that she would be mostly upstairs away from visitors coming and going so she would have no way of knowing who called at the house that night. As for stumbling on any evidence," he shook his head, "I think it most unlikely especially when one considers her duties were solely to look after Lady Collett and not to carry out domestic work in the rest of the house. It's my guess Collett knew Mary posed no threat, in which case," he nodded, "her dismissal could only have been to get her out of the way so he could bring this Eliza Boon woman in, after all he couldn't have her asking questions or telling anyone that her mistress was being kept a virtual prisoner. Even so," he nodded, "we need to find her."

Bill, chewing his cigar, nodded his head, before suggesting, "About what Collett had to gain; money, do you think? That's usually reason enough!"

"It could be," Tony sighed, pouring out some coffee, "but I'm not so sure. Collett is wealthy certainly, but as for Dennis Dunscumbe you said yourself he often spent more than he could afford."

"Okay, I'll see what I can dig up." A frown suddenly creased Bill's forehead and, upon being asked what he was thinking, said, "What beats me, Tony," taking his refilled coffee cup from him, "is this business of disposing of the body! That would be some job. Dicey too! If Collett is our guy, and it looks very much like it, surely, he would need help in getting rid of it! And, why throw it in the river?"

"You bet he'd need help!" Tony said firmly. "And I doubt if Collett had a hand in it. It would have to be someone known to Collett, most probably this guy he's foisting off as a butler. As for throwing the body into the river, where else could they have disposed of it where it would not have been found almost straightaway?" he asked reasonably. "They knew the current would take it downstream, the further away the body was found the better it would be for them. In fact, I'd say his body was probably hurled into the Thames…" pausing only long enough to walk over to where a map of London was pinned to the wall, "…about… here," pointing to the area around Waterloo Bridge. "That would be a convenient offloading point from Cavendish Square."

Coming to stand beside him, Bill looked closely at the map, saying at length, "What makes you think they threw the body into the river at Waterloo Bridge? Why not here?" pointing at the map. "The Embankment? Or… even here?" pointing his finger at Westminster Bridge.

"Huh huh," Tony shook his head, "to get to the Embankment would mean taking a more public route; just look at where they'd have to travel; along Regent Street, Piccadilly Circus and Charing Cross and, to Westminster Bridge more or less the same, and whilst I admit," he nodded, "that Westminster Bridge is nearer there would be far too many people about. No, Bill," he said firmly, "it would have been far too risky. Besides," he pointed out, "anything could have happened; they couldn't risk being stopped and," he nodded again, "what if they met with an accident? Huh huh," he shook his head, "Waterloo Bridge would mean a far quieter and much less frequented route."

"It's the hell of a distance to carry a body; I mean," Bill shrugged, "even though they would have to wrap it in something they could not carry it through the streets, in which case they would have had to use Collett's own carriage or hire a hackney."

"If *I* was going to dispose of a body, Bill," Tony nodded, "I wouldn't risk using my own carriage for the simple reason that it would alert the staff and, to hire one, would be equally dangerous; it would be running the hell of a risk because no hackney driver would fail to see something being carried out of the house and into the vehicle which looked suspiciously like a body and not ask questions."

"So," Bill mused, resuming his seat, "you think it could be someone this new butler guy knew who did the driving?"

"Either that," Tony inclined his head, "or he drove the vehicle himself, but as I have already said," he shrugged, "I don't have all the answers and those I *do* have stand a very good chance of being shot to pieces!" Taking a moment to swallow a mouthful of coffee, he looked directly at Bill, saying firmly, "All I *do* know for certain is that Lady Collett is absolutely terrified, and not only of her husband and that woman, who seems permanently attached to her side, and her reaction to the piece she saw in the newspaper yesterday morning, which went far beyond what one would expect, as well as the fact that during the last ten months or so she has been constantly watched and accompanied wherever she goes, tells *me* that it's all connected with the murder of Sir Philip Dunscumbe and his brother's supposed suicide."

"If we're right about all of this, Tony," Bill pointed his cigar at him, "and I believe we are, it'll do more than set Fleet Street alight!"

"What was it *'The New York Times'* printed on its front page a couple of years ago, Bill?" Tony raised a questioning eyebrow; *'All the news that's fit to print'*." Bill nodded, and Tony smiled. "Well, I know damn well this story is not fit to print as it now stands, were we to do so all hell would break loose, but with your help I intend to make sure it *is* fit to print."

"Okay," he nodded. "Do you want me to put someone on to this?"

Tony shook his head, a martial light entering in his eyes. "No Bill; this is *my* pigeon."

"Okay," Bill nodded, "you're the boss, but just don't make it too personal," he warned, "that's not objective reporting!" Tony nodded, whereupon Bill asked, "What is it you want *me* to do?"

"I need a pair of eyes, Bill," Tony told him, finishing off his coffee.

"You want Collett followed, is that it?" Upon receiving a confirming nod, he warned, "Well, that could be dangerous. I can't say I've ever come across Collett but I know enough to tell you that he is not without friends, which I am sure you already know," he nodded significantly, "but if we're to prove anything that's only way to do it."

"I can keep my eyes on Lady Collett," Tony smiled, "Bea will help there, but it could prove awkward if Collett saw me everywhere he went."

Bill nodded before saying thoughtfully, "Jerry Taylor is your man."

"Do I know him?"

"No," Bill shook his head, "he's not on the payroll. Ex-cop, turned private dick a couple of years ago."

"Retired?" Tony queried.

"No. He'd a reputation for being insubordinate; questioned the sense of his orders one time too many apparently, so he should suit you," Bill grinned, "so, rather than wait to be booted out, he quit. I can vouch for him, Tony. He's as good a man as any to have in your corner. He'll do what you want."

"Okay, Bill," Tony nodded, rising to his feet, "Jerry Taylor it is. Can you get him here this afternoon?"

"I'll try," Bill nodded, standing up. "I have the number for Mount Street so I'll ring you."

"Thanks Bill," Tony smiled easing himself into his overcoat. "Just one thing, Bill." He raised a questioning eyebrow. "Dunscumbe's suicide; was it the right or left temple?"

Bill thought a moment, rubbing his forehead with the cigar still held between his two fingers. "The right; yeah, the right; definitely!" An arrested expression entered his eyes at this. "Are you saying you think it was murder made to look like suicide?"

"It's possible, Bill," Tony said realistically, putting on his hat.

"Yeah," Bill agreed, "if you're right about the rest of it, it is. *Son of a…!*"

Tony smiled at this unfinished expletive, saying, "See what you can do about finding out whether Dunscumbe was right or left-handed."

"Sure," he nodded, "you got it, Tony."

"Thanks, Bill. Oh," Tony cocked his head, "about Mary Stanley; see if you can trace her and, as for Mitchell; although I can't say for certain whether he was married or not, see if you can find out if someone has reported a husband or male relative missing over the last ten or eleven months as well as seeing if the police have discovered a body which has not yet been identified."

"So, you *do* think he's been done in?" Bill raised an eyebrow.

"The more I think about it, Bill," Tony replied realistically, "the more convinced of it I am, especially as he has not come forward with any information."

"What are you going to do now?" Bill asked.

"I think it's time I paid a look in at Westminster," Tony grinned, pulling on his gloves. "I get the feeling Hallerton's been holding out."

"Yeah, I think he knows more than he's said." Bill nodded, a huge grin suddenly crossing his face. "So, you're going to see if your title carries more weight than the power of the press within such hallowed portals!"

"Something like that," Tony smiled, heading for the door.

"Tony," Bill forestalled him, not quite able to hide the soft spot he had always had for Ambrose Dart's son, "you may be a viscount, but *God damn it* you're a newspaperman at heart!"

Tony laughed, his liking and affection for this tough as old boots reporter evident in his eyes. "So long, Bill," waving a careless hand before quietly closing the door behind him.

Chapter Nine

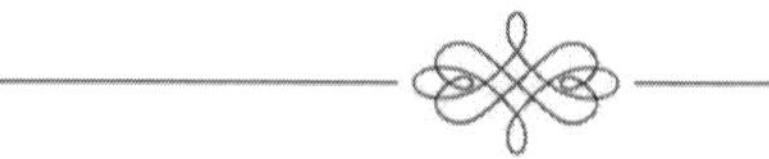

Even though Eleanor could feel the anger emanating from her husband as they made their way back to Cavendish Square from The Park Grove Hotel, she could not help reliving those precious moments she had spent with Tony as he guided her round the floor in his arms. She could no more have prevented the colour from flooding her cheeks when she saw him approach her than she could her heart from pounding in her breast, and although she had instinctively known he would not betray their two previous encounters, no less than Beatrice and Tom had she held her breath when Tony asked Braden's permission to dance with her. She had not expected him to do so but she supposed she ought to have done, and although she had been extremely fearful of the consequences resulting from such a perfectly natural request, she had also been breathlessly hopeful as she waited nervously for Braden to either permit or refuse it. She had sensed Braden's wariness and Tony's antipathy beneath their politely exchanged courtesies, and it would not have surprised her if Braden had refused his consent; after all, it would not have been the first time he had disregarded his surroundings as well as his company to either challenge or argue a point, but for whatever reason she had found herself being led onto the floor with her hand resting on Tony's arm.

Given her dislike and fear of Braden, Eleanor had not expected her own marriage to be as happy as the one her parents had enjoyed, in fact she had envisaged anything but a rosy future resulting from their union, but at no time had she so much as suspected anything remotely resembling what would turn out to be the abhorrent truth. From the very beginning her experiences with Braden, who had made no effort whatsoever to ease his young bride's natural apprehension, were not only so far removed from those her mother had enjoyed, but had profoundly shocked her; his natural tendency for physical violence, habitually leading to his sexual aggression, had left her stunned and traumatised in disbelief. His brutal handling of her, far from instilling her with a desire to respond to the assault he called lovemaking, which he regularly inflicted on her, or awakening any feelings of love, had merely served to intensify her fear of him, and since that never to be forgotten evening when she had walked into what had become a never-ending nightmare and the beginning of her virtual imprisonment, even more so. Prior to her visit to Covent Garden, she would have said that Braden had killed any natural feelings she had as a woman, but that unexpected encounter with Beatrice's brother, and in the most unlikely of circumstances, had proved to her that she was very much alive, and far from destroying her intrinsic need to love and be loved it had risen from the ashes of her despair into a wonderful awakening.

For a young woman who had, for just over a year, been subjected to physical as well as mental agonies by a husband who, for some perverse reason, enjoyed bullying and hurting her, to find herself in the arms of a man whose feelings and behaviour towards her were very different, took her a little time to accustom herself to. She had no doubt that were it at all possible for her to confide in someone they would strenuously recommend caution, and not to read too much into the words and actions of a man who was quite unknown to her. Not only that, but it was quite possible that in her distressed state of mind she could so easily read more into Tony's kindness towards her than what was in fact true, and that it was perfectly natural for her to compare him to her husband, thereby mistaking her feelings as well as misinterpreting his intentions.

Eleanor may be inexperienced when it came to the arts of flirtation and seduction, but unless her instincts had grossly misled her she knew beyond doubt that she had not mistaken her own feelings or her heart, and that Tony, far from merely indulging in a flirtation to while away the time until he returned to America, felt the same about her. She had known the moment she had set eyes on him last night at Covent Garden that she liked him, and in spite of her fear she had been most conscious of the fact that somewhere deep inside her, for reasons which were really quite inexplicable, not only had she been irresistibly drawn to him but she felt he was the other half of herself as well as knowing that should he leave her life as unexpectedly as he had entered it, she would feel quite bereft. She knew Tom and Beatrice had fallen in love at first sight, but that surely was a rare occurrence as such things only happened between the covers of a novel and not in real life. But Eleanor's heart, despite the cautious warnings of her mind, not yet cowed into total submission, had known the truth of it from the very beginning; its assertion reinforced this morning when she had seen Tony in Mount Street, but as she had moved round the floor in his arms that assertion had turned into complete and utter conviction.

Despite her anxiety in knowing that her husband had been closely watching her throughout the whole time she had glided round the floor in Tony's arms as well as the possible repercussions which would follow hard on its heels, the fact remained that after only a very few minutes the thought of her disapproving husband as well as both these ills had been lost sight of as she heard Tony tell her he loved her and, "Oh, haven't I told you? I intend to marry you, Eleanor Collett!" She had not needed to see the look in his eyes to know he meant it; she had felt it emanate from him as he held her in his arms, heard it in every word he had uttered and even though she knew it could never be, just knowing he loved her filled her with such a warm sense of wellbeing that for once the thought of what payment Braden would extract from her had been relegated to the back of her mind.

Tony may not have asked her to dance again, but Eleanor had not missed those looks he had cast in her direction any more than she had misinterpreted the messages they conveyed, unfortunately though neither had her husband, and so when, just a little over an hour later, like Tom, she had not been at all surprised to hear him whisper in her ear that it was time they were leaving. In some strange way she had felt, still did in fact, a little like Cinderella, who, after the most wonderful time at the ball and falling madly in love with the Prince, was now on her way home to her wicked stepmother to face the consequences of an evening she would never forget, but although the memories of being held in the arms of the man who had told her he loved her and wanted to marry her would live with her forever, she could not fool herself into believing that Braden would permit her to visit in Mount Street again, thereby running the risk of coming into contact with Beatrice Shipton's brother. Somehow Eleanor had managed not to look in Tony's direction as Braden escorted her out of the ballroom and into the foyer, but she had felt his eyes upon her and although she had wanted to run to him, to plead with him to keep her safe and protect her from her husband, she knew she could not, the same as she knew that the chances of seeing him again, and certainly alone, were remote. Being all too familiar with that look in Braden's eyes it had come as no surprise when, after folding her cape around her shoulders before escorting her out of the Park

Grove Hotel into their waiting carriage, to feel his fingers painfully gripping her arm and, sensing the anger inside him, knew she would be made to suffer for her all too brief a moment of happiness in the arms of the man she would not be allowed to see again.

Sir Braden Collett may not love Eleanor any more than she loved him, but she was his wife and she would be made to mind him better in the future. He could not deny that she had comported herself throughout the entire evening in a manner which befitted Lady Collett, but he had seen those looks which had passed between her and Lord Childon and the sparkle in her eyes when he had returned her to his side, but under no circumstances would he permit this brief attachment to continue. It was clear that Eleanor had taken to Beatrice Shipton's brother and, unless he had grossly erred, it was just as clear that Childon had taken to her, but he was not prepared to allow his wife to indulge in an affair, not that he really expected her to, but any further association with this man could well bring all to ruin because the chances were that under his influence she could well divulge all she knew and Childon, however much Sir Braden had taken him in instant dislike, was in a prime position to investigate matters he much preferred never to see the light of day. Sitting beside Eleanor in the carriage in ominous silence, his anger steadily mounting, exacerbated by a slight touch of uneasiness he could not quite dispel, he could not rid his mind of the possibility that she could so easily, in her excitement, have let something slip which Childon had picked up on and, at all costs, he had to discover precisely what they had said to one another. He had no doubt of being able to persuade her into telling him the truth, but even if she had said nothing it certainly behoved him to keep a stricter guard over his wife than he had so far.

Collett may have marked Childon down as a Colonial who had yet to know his place among his betters, if not in title then certainly in manners, but he had not struck him as being a man either lacking in intelligence or slow on the uptake and he would be a fool to dismiss him out of hand and, left unchecked, he could be dangerous, and with his newspapers behind him even more so. Collett could not fool himself into thinking that Childon could be so easily silenced liked Sir Philip Dunscumbe and his brother or Mitchell, and so to attempt anything in the way of disposing of him would not only be rather difficult but extremely reckless because whatever Collett may personally think of him, the fact remained that Lord Childon, apart from bearing all the hallmarks of being a man who would not be so easily caught napping, another unexplained death could well be just one too many! Far better then, and evidently more sensible, to concentrate his efforts on his wife; by ensuring she was no longer in a position whereby she could be tempted into disclosing what she had seen that night by a man who palpably liked her, would be much better than running the risk of allowing her to be in his company. Before Beatrice Shipton's brother came on the scene, Collett had been reasonably confident of Eleanor saying nothing to anyone, and with Eliza and Peterson to help keep her in check there had been no real cause for concern, but now it seemed that her continued silence could no longer be relied upon. He knew perfectly well that his wife had not been totally cowed into submission, and that behind her subdued compliance to his wishes was a hint of independence which could prompt her into doing him irreparable harm, but since keeping Eleanor locked in her room for the rest of her life was really quite impractical, it seemed that short of having her committed, sending her to stay in the country on the grounds of a slight nervous disorder, was the only way his own protection could be assured.

Of course, Collett realised only too well that her disappearance would occasion some remark, and unless he was very much mistaken the Shiptons would figure large among those who would question her being sent into the country, but due to her withdrawing from society for days, even weeks on end when he had rendered her unfit to be seen, putting forward reasons of lengthy spells of migraine brought about through agitation of the nerves, he had no doubt that her unexpected and somewhat sudden succumbing to some slight mental disorder, requiring complete rest, would not be so surprising. He had seen enough of Childon to be in little or no doubt that he for one would not believe it, but although Collett fully expected him to make a nuisance of himself about Eleanor's disappearance, he did not think he would go to such lengths whereby he acquired a name for himself by letting it be known that he was chasing after another man's wife. Not only that, but he did not expect him to remain in England forever and, once he was safely on the other side of the Atlantic Ocean, there would be nothing whatever he could do about it and, furthermore, he doubted very much whether Childon's feelings, based on no more than twenty minutes in Eleanor's company, would survive the initial surprise of her continued absence. With this end in view then, Sir Braden entered his house in Cavendish Square, a nervous Eleanor hanging on his arm, in the full expectation of ridding himself of possible difficulties before many days were out, especially as he had dismissed the man he had regarded as a threat on very practical grounds, little realising that far from forgetting Eleanor,

Childon was busy formulating plans of his own.

It was almost midday by the time Tony left Bill's office, and as he was unaware of the schemes Sir Braden Collett was evolving regarding the permanent removal of his wife from his company and society in general, he strolled along Fleet Street and into The Strand towards Whitehall in a positive frame of mind, the reassuring and familiar sight of Big Ben coming into view long before he came up to Westminster Bridge. Making his way into the imposing building of the Houses of Parliament through the impressive St. Stephen's entrance, he leisurely made his way along St. Stephen's Hall, which, although not deserted, was frequented only by a small number of people, towards the Central Lobby. This was not the first visit Tony had made here, several times in the past he had accompanied his grandfather, but now, as then, he could not fail being filled with awe by what he saw; this mother of Parliaments, magnificent and inspiring, never failing to move him. Upon entering the large octagonal hall with its central chandelier and sculptures of past Prime Ministers strategically placed around the lobby, he removed his hat and took a moment to look about him. It was while he was admiring his surroundings anew that an usher approached him, easily forging a path through the large number of people who had come to see their Member of Parliament. Upon discovering the reason for Tony's visit, the usher shook his head and pursed his lips, before informing him somewhat dispassionately that he was not aware Mr. Hallerton had any appointments today and since there was nothing on his list to suggest that he was expecting a visitor, it would, perhaps, be better if he contacted him to arrange a meeting. Having fully expected something like this, Tony smiled down at the man who was looking apologetically if immovably up at him, politely enquiring if he could ask Mr. Hallerton if he would be good enough to spare him a few moments due to the urgency of the matter he had come to discuss. The lips pursed again, and Tony, reluctant to fall back on his title, realised he had no choice, so pulling out his wallet he retrieved a calling card which he handed to him; the neatly printed legend immediately having the desired effect. "I *beg* Your Lordship's pardon!" He inclined his head. "I did not realise… if Your Lordship would be good enough to wait here a moment I will see if Mr. Hallerton is receiving."

"Thank you," Tony nodded, managing to suppress the twitch at the corner of his mouth.

After watching him walk away, Tony turned to admire the mural above the arched entrance while he waited for the usher to return, but within seconds he heard a familiar voice behind him exclaim, "Tony! I thought it was you."

Upon turning round Tony found himself looking down into the face of Lady Randolph Churchill who, at the age of forty-five, could still claim to being an exquisitely beautiful woman. Having supported and even campaigned on behalf of her late husband, Lord Randolph Churchill, who had died some four years previously, she had since transferred that tireless energy and single-mindedness to her son, Winston, whose military reports in *'The Daily Graphic'* and *'The Morning Post'* Tony had read with interest. Immaculately dressed in royal blue velvet with a white fur Russian Cossack-style hat adorned with a peacock's feather and a matching muff, he could well understand why she was known as one of the most beautiful women of the age, but as he bowed over the slender white hand she extended he saw not the elegant and sophisticated aristocrat she had become but Jennie Jerome, the girl from Brooklyn, whose father, Leonard, a wealthy and successful businessman, had known his father. "Lady Randolph!" he smiled. "This is a most unexpected pleasure," raising her hand it to his lips.

"For me too," she smiled. "It has been quite some time since I saw you last. You know, Tony," she nodded, "as I was standing over there watching you, I thought how very like your mother you are, but that, I think," she said mischievously, "is because you have the Mawdsley nose, but now, close up, I see that you are very much your father's son."

"Thank you." Tony inclined his head, his eyes alight with amusement.

"I do believe," she said confidentially, an impish gleam suddenly entering her eyes, "I have made a social solecism by failing to address you as my lord or Lord Childon?"

"If you have," he laughed, "then I am perfectly happy to overlook it."

"I am so glad," she smiled.

"How is Winston?" Tony asked, remembering her son well even though Winston had been junior to him at Harrow. "I hear good things of him."

"He is very well," Lady Randolph informed him. "Although," she confessed, "he does seem to be up and doing faster than I can sometimes keep pace with him!" Tony laughed. "But tell me," she enquired, "what are you doing here? Are you, I wonder," she raised an eyebrow, "considering entering this hallowed structure with a view to furthering a political ambition? Or am I being impertinent?"

"Not at all," Tony assured her amusingly; "it is merely a private matter that brings me here," to which she nodded her head. He smiled, "And you? Or am *I* being impertinent?"

Lady Randolph smiled up at him. "I have been invited to luncheon."

"Ah!" he smiled. "And who, may I ask, is the fortunate host?"

"Arthur Balfour," she told him. "You must know he was a political colleague of Randolph's."

"Ah, yes," Tony nodded.

"Tell me," she smiled, "have you been in England long?"

"A couple of months," he told her. "Unfortunately, due to my father's death and affairs back in the States I was not able to come any sooner, and regrettably missed my grandfather's funeral."

She nodded. "Yes, of course. So, are you making a long stay in England?" she enquired.

"I'm not sure," Tony told her, "that very much depends on circumstances."

"Well," she smiled mischievously up at him, "I shall not be inquisitive and ask what they are even though I am dying to know, but I take it you are staying with your sister in Mount Street?"

"Yes, for the foreseeable future," Tony smiled. "I am afraid that Childon Manor is presently under siege by an army of workmen."

"Yes," she nodded, "I can see just how uncomfortable that would be. You know," she told him, "I never see your sister without being conscious of how very like your mother she is." She paused, saying gently, "I miss her very much you know, your father too."

"Thank you." He inclined his head. "So do we."

She nodded, then smiled. "Ah, I see Arthur approaching. I shall leave you now, but please," she begged, laying a hand on his arm, "do give my regards to Beatrice. It seems an age since I saw her last."

"I shall certainly do so," Tony smiled, raising her hand to his lips before she strolled away on Arthur Balfour's arm.

A tactful little cough a discreet distance to his left brought Tony's head round to find the usher had now returned. "Begging your pardon, my lord," he inclined his head, "but Mr. Hallerton will see you now; if you would care to follow me."

"Thank you," Tony nodded, waiting only long enough until Lady Randolph had disappeared from his sight, memories of the many kindnesses she had shown him, extending far beyond the promise she had made to his parents to keep an eye on him, bringing a fond smile to his lips.

Having followed the usher down a corridor leading off the Central Lobby, he then veered right into another, where, about halfway along, the usher tapped lightly on a door, whereupon he was instantly told to enter. "Lord Childon, sir," the usher said dispassionately, inclining his head, stepping aside for Tony to enter.

"Thank you, Southern," Hallerton nodded. "Lord Childon!" he exclaimed when Southern had closed the door behind him, holding out his hand. "I had not expected the pleasure."

"It is good of you to see me. I am sorry if my visit has inconvenienced you," Tony smiled, shaking his hand, "but I am afraid there has been no time for me to make an appointment."

"I see," Hallerton nodded, indicating the chair on the opposite side of his desk. "I am, of course, privileged, my lord," he told him, resuming his seat, "but whilst I am happy to assist you in any way I can, I must confess to being somewhat at a loss to know what possible matter could be of such urgency to bring you here." He was a man in his mid to late forties, of no more than medium height and thin build whose sparse head of light brown hair and receding forehead emphasised an already rather unprepossessing appearance. His face, pale and slightly drawn with a permanently harassed expression, bore adequate testimony to a lifetime of political administration, and his black horn-rimmed spectacles, which he had a habit of removing from his nose every few minutes to wipe with a handkerchief, only served to make him look older than he really was.

"I would like to talk to you about Sir Philip Dunscumbe's death," Tony told him without preamble.

"Sir Philip!" Hallerton echoed in disbelief, removing his glasses and vigorously wiping them with the handkerchief he had pulled out of his pocket. "I am afraid I do not understand!" he cried. "Were you by any chance a friend of his, my lord."

"No," Tony shook his head, "I never knew him."

"Never knew him! Then, why… I mean," Hallerton faltered, "what is your interest in his death? Are you saying that you are assisting the police with their enquiries?" he asked, surprised.

"Something like that," Tony smiled, pulling out a card from his wallet and handing it to Hallerton.

"'*The London Chronicler*' and '*The Daily Bulletin*'" he read out loud, looking at Tony rather nonplussed. "Are you saying, my lord," he asked, somewhat bemused, "that you *work* for these newspapers?"

Tony's lips twitched at this. "In a manner of speaking," he nodded. "You see, Mr. Hallerton, I own them, and my reporters have been covering the story of Sir Philip's murder from the beginning."

"Oh, I see," he nodded comprehendingly, handing Tony the card back. "So," he shrugged an enquiry, "are you saying that new evidence has come to light?"

"I'm afraid I'm not at liberty to discuss that," Tony apologised. "What I can tell you, however, is that I am not here to malign Sir Philip, but to try to ascertain the circumstances leading up to his death and to bring the murderer to justice."

Removing his spectacles to give them another vigorous wipe, Hallerton shook his head. "Dreadful business! Dreadful! Well," he sighed, putting on his spectacles, "I shall, of course, be only too pleased to do whatever I can, but really," he shrugged, "I fail to see what else I can say that I have not already told the police."

"How long had you been Sir Philip's private secretary?" Tony enquired.

"Oh, many years, my lord," he replied. "It would have been, let me see, yes," he nodded, "ten years had he not…" his voice failing.

Tony nodded sympathetically. "So, it is fair to say that you knew him well?"

"I think I can safely say that I knew him better than most," Hallerton conceded, "but Sir Philip, you understand," he nodded, "was a most reserved man. Oh, do not misunderstand me, my lord," he hastily pointed out, "he was not at all standoffish, on the contrary he could always find a moment to pass the time of day, indeed, he was all consideration."

"But I am right in thinking that you knew very little about his private life?" Tony stated reasonably.

Eyeing Tony thoughtfully for a moment or two, Hallerton cleared his throat, saying awkwardly, "I have no wish to be disobliging, my lord, but really," he coughed, "I fail to see how that has anything to do with…"

"Mr. Hallerton," Tony broke in unceremoniously, "I have already told you that I am not here to malign Sir Philip Dunscumbe, but the fact remains he was brutally murdered and his body thrown into the Thames. So far," he told him, "the police, having ruled out larceny because all his possessions were still on the body when it was found, have no motive for his death, and since I do not believe it was a case of mistaken identity the reason must have its roots in either his private or public life, and if there is anything you can tell me to help bring the murderer to justice, I would strongly advise you to do so."

Hallerton heaved a deep sigh, but taking a moment or two to answer, he removed his spectacles from his nose and absently wiped them on his handkerchief. "Your observations are quite just, my lord," he conceded, returning the spectacles to his nose, "and, God knows," he shrugged, "I would dearly like to see the perpetrator brought to justice, but I am afraid I cannot tell you anything about his personal life," he shook his head, "other than what I have already in that he was a very private man, really quite reserved, but I can *assure* you," he stressed, "that I know nothing whatever to his detriment, what I mean is," he said awkwardly, "there was no scandal attached to his name in any way." Clearing his throat, he looked from Tony down to his entwined fingers resting on his desk and back again, saying, not just a little uncomfortably, "As you know, Sir Philip never married, but there was no… well, no… lady or… well," he coughed delicately, "you know…"

"Yes," Tony nodded, "I know."

Extremely relieved to have scaled this most delicate hurdle, Hallerton went on, "As far as his political life was concerned, he was most assiduous as well as punctilious in dealing with all matters which crossed his desk and, I must say, he was very highly respected. The Prime Minister himself had a great regard for him."

"So I understand," Tony nodded. "Tell me, how did Sir Philip take his brother's death?"

"His brother's death!" Hallerton repeated, shocked, opening his eyes to their fullest extent.

"Yes," Tony nodded.

"But I… I don't understand, my lord!" He shook his head. "You… you are not, *surely*, suggesting that his suicide was in any way connected with…?"

"I am not suggesting anything, Mr. Hallerton," Tony told him, not wishing to alert him to his own theories. "So," he repeated firmly, "how *did* Sir Philip take his brother's death?"

Hallerton sighed, then, as if realising his visitor was not going to be put off, said resignedly, "Well, he never spoke of it, but then," he sighed again, "Sir Philip was not the kind of man to... well, what shall I say?" He shrugged. "Let his feelings show or discuss anything of a personal nature. I offered my condolences naturally," he told him, "but apart from thanking me he never mentioned it. I do believe, however," he said hesitantly, "that they had had their differences over time; Dennis Dunscumbe being a little, well... what shall I say? A little more outgoing than his brother, but for all that," he nodded, "I gained the impression that it hit Sir Philip rather hard."

"Tell me, Mr. Hallerton," Tony enquired, "getting back to the day you last saw him, were you surprised when Sir Philip came out of his room," indicating the door a little to his left with a slight inclination of his head, "and told you he was going out without any prior appointment?"

"Oh, yes," Hallerton said firmly, "most surprised. You see, my lord," he explained, "it was most unlike him, especially as he had every intention of attending the debate that evening in the House."

"I understand it was a debate on a topic which was very close to his heart," Tony raised an enquiring eyebrow.

"Oh, yes," Hallerton confirmed, "very much so, which is why," he offered, "when he had not returned I went to the House to see if he had gone straight there, but there was no sign of him, no sign at all."

"You told the police," Tony reminded him, "that upon your enquiries at his home in Curzon Street his domestic staff had not seen him since he left that morning."

"That's right," Hallerton nodded. "Indeed, I was at a loss!"

"Yet you did not contact the police either that night or the following morning when he still put in no appearance," Tony pointed out. "Why was that?"

Hallerton swallowed, removing his glasses to give them a wipe. "I realise how that appears, my lord," he admitted, "but indeed the Prime Minister did not want anything done rashly in case there was a perfectly reasonable explanation to account for his disappearance."

"I see," Tony nodded. "Tell me, Mr. Hallerton," he enquired, "did anything unusual happen that day?"

"Unusual?" he repeated.

"Yes, or anything out of the ordinary?"

"No," Hallerton shook his head, "I can't recall anything happening of an unusual nature."

"I see you have the telephone system installed," Tony pointed out, indicating the instrument on Hallerton's desk, "so I assume you would know if Sir Philip received any…"

"No," Hallerton intervened, shaking his head, "I would have known. You see, I took all his calls except those that rang directly to his private telephone," inclining his head towards the door to the other room, "and he received none because I can hear when the telephone next door rings."

Tony nodded. "What about his correspondence? Did you always open his letters?"

"Oh, yes," Hallerton assured him, "always… that is," he hastily corrected himself, "unless anything was specifically marked 'private and confidential' or 'personal'."

"I see," Tony smiled briefly. "Did anything marked 'private and confidential' or 'personal' arrive in his mail that day?"

"Yes," Hallerton said with more animation than Tony would have thought possible, "there *was* a private letter in his correspondence."

"And what time did the mail arrive that morning?" Tony asked.

"It was almost an hour late," Hallerton replied. "I remember it distinctly," he nodded in response to Tony's raised eyebrow, "because the usher who handed me Sir Philip's letters told me that there had been a delay of some kind at the central postal receiving office."

"So, what time *did* it arrive?" Tony queried.

"It came about eleven o'clock, but for some reason," Hallerton shook his head, "Sir Philip did not read any of the letters I put in front of him until about three o'clock that afternoon."

"How do you know that?" Tony asked sharply.

"Well, my lord," Hallerton sighed, "when I went in about that time to raise a matter with him, I could see they were still where I had left them in his pending tray on the small side desk. They had not been touched. In fact, my lord," he informed him, "Sir Philip was just opening the envelope marked 'personal' when I went in."

"Did he tell you who the letter was from or give any indication as to its content?" Tony asked.

"No," Hallerton shook his head, "but it was not long after, half past three precisely," he said firmly, "when he came out of his room dressed in his hat and coat telling me he was going out."

"And he didn't tell you where he was going or who he was going to see?"

"No," Hallerton sighed. "Although…" he began.

"Although?" Tony urged.

Looking across at Tony, Hallerton absently removed his spectacles and slowly wiped them with his handkerchief, "Well, it's just that… well, this letter," he sighed, "from the handwriting on the envelope I gained the impression it was from a woman."

"A constituent?" Tony raised an eyebrow, discounting a clandestine assignation as Sir Philip, according to Bill, was not known to be a man who embarked on affairs.

"I do not think so, my lord," Hallerton shrugged, replacing his spectacles on his nose. "You see," he explained, "although the postmark was somewhat smudged, I could see it had been posted in London and not from his constituency."

"What happened to this letter?" Tony queried. "According to the police, all Sir Philip's possessions were still on the body, which means that he either must have left the letter here or…"

"He did, my lord," Hallerton broke in a little nervously, "in fact, he threw it onto the fire before he left."

"Threw it onto the fire!" Tony repeated, unable to dispel the thought that this letter could well hold the key to Sir Philip's murder.

"Yes," Hallerton replied gravely. "You see," he explained, "it was about twenty minutes after Sir Philip had left when I had occasion to enter his room, and I saw that a sheet of paper had only partly burned with the charred remains of an envelope lying underneath it. Sir Philip had not torn the sheet into pieces or screwed it up but threw it onto the fire flat with the address end nearest to the front gridiron. The fire, you see," he told him, "had not been replenished with coal as the room was quite warm, so by the time Sir Philip threw the letter onto the fire it had burned down a little so the top end of the letter, which had not been destroyed by the fire, had dropped to the front of the fireplace." He swallowed, looking a little guilty. "You see," he cleared his throat, "that letter was the only one I had not opened, all the other envelopes I had put into my wastepaper basket, so I knew it was the one marked as 'personal' which he had burned and so I could not help but wonder if that letter was the reason for Sir Philip leaving so suddenly so I… well, I…"

"You read the address," Tony supplied, not at all shocked by this.

Hallerton nodded. "Yes, I am afraid I did."

"And it was?" Tony urged.

Clearing his throat again Hallerton said, "Thirty-six, Fisher Street, Holborn."

"Anything else?" Tony questioned. "A name perhaps or even the first few lines of the letter?"

"No, nothing," Hallerton shook his head.

"I take it," Tony raised an eyebrow, "that you did not acquaint Lord Salisbury to the fact that this letter could well account for Sir Philip's disappearance or even," he shrugged an enquiry, "upon learning of his death, visit this address to try to find out whether it was his destination that afternoon?"

Hallerton shook his head. "No, I did not," swallowing a little uncomfortably, "although," he admitted, "the thought did cross my mind about visiting the address but," he sighed, shrugging his narrow shoulders, "I decided not to. As for acquainting Lord Salisbury," he sighed, "no I did not. I thought…"

"Best leave well alone!" Tony supplied meaningfully, eyeing Hallerton eloquently. "I take it that you threw it back onto the fire after you had read the address," Tony sighed.

"I am afraid I did, yes," Hallerton confirmed.

"But you did not tell the police about the letter, did you?" Tony pointed out. Upon receiving a shake of the head, he asked, "Why not?"

Hallerton sighed, shrugging his narrow shoulders. "The shock of learning what had happened to Sir Philip was… well," he sighed again, "it drove everything from my mind and, well…" he shrugged, "by the time I remembered it was several days later."

"Yet you still did not report it," Tony accused. "Did it not occur to you that this letter could be an important piece of evidence which could shed light on Sir Philip's death or, at the very least, bear even the slightest connection to him going out almost as soon as he had read it?" A helpless shrug of the shoulders was the only response he received to this and Tony, firmly of the belief that not only was this letter the reason for Sir Philip leaving his rooms so unexpectedly, but also had Hallerton come forward with the information at the time then the chances were that Sir Braden Collett would, if not taken into custody, then at least be questioned, and Eleanor spared all manner of abuse.

"I take it you will now have to report this to the police," Hallerton said anxiously.

"Yes, I am afraid so," Tony concurred, refraining from telling him that it would not be until his own investigations had uncovered the evidence to prove his suspicions.

As it was apparent that Hallerton could tell him nothing more Tony thanked him for his time and left, at a loss to understand how a man of his intelligence had failed to report something as significant as that letter or, if nothing else, tried to discover its author. Having been Sir Philip's personal and private secretary for ten years Hallerton would, surely, despite his earnest assurances to the contrary, have come to know the man he had served well enough to realise that the letter was not from a woman who had her claws into him and threatening to either expose or blackmail him for some reason. Whilst Tony could well understand Hallerton's reluctance to question Sir Philip as to the letter's author and content, the fact remained that he had allowed a vital clue to Sir Philip's murder go unquestioned. Tony easily acquitted him of harbouring any ulterior motive and, he supposed, in Hallerton's defence, it could be argued that he could well have deliberately refrained from mentioning it in the misguided belief that he was protecting Sir Philip from posthumous adverse criticism or possible scandal but, at the very least, he was guilty of withholding evidence which could so easily have brought this matter to a conclusion long since.

Even though Tony was firmly convinced that Sir Philip's death was directly connected with that of his brother, until he had worked it out in his own mind as to just how they fitted in with one another, apart from enquiring as to Sir Philip's reaction upon learning of the death of his brother, he had deliberately avoided disclosing his own view to Hallerton in that he believed the two deaths were somehow connected as well as his suspicions about Sir Braden Collett. The chances were that Hallerton was not acquainted with Sir Braden Collett, but it went against all reasoning that he had not heard of him and it could well be that once the seed of doubt had been sown in Hallerton's mind about the question mark hanging over Dennis Dunscumbe's death, he may feel it behoved him, perhaps even look upon it as atonement for his failure to act upon that letter, especially considering his obvious loyalty to Sir Philip, to seek out Collett and mention it to him direct or confide the suspicion to someone else who could so easily approach Collett with it. In either case it would not only impede Tony's chances of arriving at the truth but would put Collett, who was by no means stupid, on his guard, and the last thing Tony wanted at this stage was to alert Collett, who had so far managed to cover his tracks, to the fact that he had come under suspicion because he would not put it beyond him to vent his anger on Eleanor, irrespective of whether he believed her to have said anything or not. At all costs, Tony had to do all he could to protect her from the repercussions ensuing from his own investigations, because even though Eleanor had not breathed one word to him Collett could be relied upon to convince himself that she had and therefore subject her to even worse treatment than he had thus far.

The temperature, which had dropped considerably during the night, had rendered the roads and pavements treacherous, but even though it had warmed up during the course of the morning, by the time Tony emerged from Westminster into the cold grey atmosphere outside the temperature had dropped again, so much so that every hackney he saw was either occupied or pulling up for a passenger not wishing to risk walking in such hazardous conditions, and it was not until he had almost reached The Strand that he came upon an empty vehicle. Having instructed the driver of his direction he hurriedly climbed inside whereupon he pulled out his watch to see that it wanted only a couple of minutes to half past two, but even though he was eager to reach Mount Street in case Bill telephoned about Jerry Taylor, he was just as eager to arrive at his first destination. The last thing Tony wanted was to make things difficult for Eleanor by arousing suspicion in her husband's mind and leaving her a prey to his maltreatment, but try as he did he could not dispel the uneasy feeling which had steadily been creeping upon him ever since last night. Tony had come across men like Collett before, bullying thugs who took a perverse delight in tormenting those weaker than themselves and, unless he had misread the signs, the look on Collett's face when he had escorted Eleanor out of The Park Grove Hotel had been more than enough to cause Tony grave concern and as he sat anxiously forward in his seat, his concern for Eleanor uppermost in his mind, it seemed to take a very long time before the driver eventually pulled up outside Collett's house in Cavendish Square.

Instructing the driver to wait Tony quickly mounted the three shallow steps and pulled on the wire, stepping back to look up at the upper windows while he waited, but no sign of life could be evinced from any of the windows. He had no idea which room Eleanor occupied, but unless his instincts had grossly misled him about the expression on Collett's face boding no good for her, he could not see him allowing her to look through the window to draw someone's attention to her plight. It was just as Tony was about to give the pull another vigorous tug when the door opened to reveal the man he had no hesitation in recognising as being every inch the prizefighter, or rather ex-prizefighter, Beatrice had described him, but whilst Tony was neither a violent nor an aggressive man he found himself looking forward to trading blows with this so-called butler.

"May H'I 'elp you, sir?" Peterson enquired, the slow deliberation with which he spoke clearly denoting a painstaking attempt to adopt a tone and accent which were totally unnatural to him.

"Is Lady Collett at home?" Tony asked with a politeness he was very far from feeling.

"H'I very much regret, sir," he told him, "that Lady Collett h'is away from 'ome."

"When do you expect her to return?" Tony enquired, his attempts to peer over Peterson's shoulder into the hall thwarted as he blocked his view.

"May H'I ask who h'is enquirin'?" He inclined his head again.

"Lord Childon," Tony replied, handing him his card.

"H'I see," Peterson nodded, glancing down at it. "H'and may H'I enquire, my lord, wot h'is your business with 'Er Ladyship?"

It was on the tip of Tony's tongue to tell him that it was no concern of his, in fact he was experiencing extreme difficulty in preventing himself from sending this dubious individual sprawling, but whilst this would afford him tremendous satisfaction it could well make things extremely difficult for Eleanor and it was therefore not without an effort that he said, as inconsequentially as he could, "I am here on my sister's behalf; Lady Shipton. When do you expect Lady Collett to return?"

"'Er Ladyship," Peterson informed him, "'as gone into the country, my lord, visitin' friends, h'and H'I could not say 'ow long she will be gone."

"Gone into the country!" Tony exclaimed, astonished.

"Yes, my lord," Peterson inclined his head. "She left h'early this mornin'."

"Where into the country?" Tony demanded, extremely concerned for Eleanor's safety, attempting yet again to peer into the hall.

"H'I h'am h'afraid H'I h'am not h'at liberty to inform you, my lord," he told him, preparing to close the door.

"One moment," Tony forestalled him, placing a restraining hand on the door. "Who are these friends? Has Sir Braden gone with her?"

"H'it h'is not for me to say, my lord," Peterson inclined his head, signifying he had nothing more to say. "Gud morning, my lord," closing the door firmly in Tony's face.

Tony had no doubt that he could more than adequately deal with this obnoxious individual and force his way into the house to see for himself if Eleanor had in fact gone into the country, not that he believed it for one moment, but such an action would merely advertise his involvement as well as his intentions which would not serve his purpose in the least, as well as placing Eleanor in a most awkward position. Anger, frustration and an ever-growing anxiety for the safety and wellbeing of the woman whose life had come to mean more to him than his own raged inside him as he descended the steps, his curt instructions to the waiting hackney driver signifying just how worried he was, but as time was of the essence he stepped briskly up into the vehicle without a backward glance, missing the weak but frantic hand attempting to move the blind at the first-floor window to try to attract his attention.

Upon reaching Mount Street Tony once again told the driver to wait and, taking the three shallow steps in one, he quickly let himself into the house with his key, calling to Beatrice as soon as he had closed the door behind him. She knew perfectly well that he had confided in Tom and although her husband had only told her a fraction of what had passed between them, knowing of Tony's feelings as well as his concerns for Eleanor, not to mention how difficult it was to dissuade him from doing something once he had made up his mind, Beatrice had waited anxiously for him to return home. She knew he had gone to see Bill but she had not expected him to be out this long and as the minutes had relentlessly ticked by the disturbing thought that he had approached Braden Collett to charge him with his dealings assailed her, rendering it impossible for her to either relax or feel easy, but the relief upon seeing her brother in one piece was short-lived. Walking into the hall from the drawing-room where she had attempted several times to sit and work on her embroidery, upon seeing the crease which furrowed his forehead her alarms immediately resurfaced. "Tony!" she cried, coming up to him. "I have been so worried. Where on earth have you been?"

"In a moment, Bea," he told her, removing his hat and gloves, before taking hold of her arm and walking her back into the drawing-room.

Seeing he had not removed his overcoat, she asked nervously, "Are you going out again?"

"Yes," he nodded, "but first, has Bill rung?"

"No," she shook her head, still marvelling at such wonderful inventions as the telephone and electricity. "Are you expecting a call from him?"

"Yes," he told her.

"But Tony…" she began.

"It's all right, Bea," Tony smiled, "don't worry yourself over me," giving her hands a reassuring squeeze before going on to give her a brief outline of what had happened since he had left the house earlier.

"Gone into the country!" she exclaimed, more shocked over Eleanor than anything else. "I don't believe it!"

"No," he shook his head, "neither do I."

"But what could have happened to the child?" she cried anxiously, wringing her hands. "What have they done to her? She mentioned nothing to me about going into the country!"

"She's no more gone into the country to visit friends than you have!" Tony ground out. "It's my guess they have her held in the house," a hard light entering his eyes.

"Oh, Tony!" Beatrice shook her head, anxiously laying a hand on his arm. "I am so afraid for her. We have to get her away from there!"

"I intend to," Tony promised her grimly. "But you were right about that butler guy," he bit out, "he's no more a butler than I am!"

She was just about to say something when the telephone rang and Tony, after comfortingly patting her hand, left her while he went to answer it, but although her mind was busy conjuring up all manner of dreadful things, she nevertheless heard Tony say, "Okay, Bill, I'm on my way."

Walking into the hall to see him putting on his hat and gloves, she said anxiously, "Tony, I have no idea what you are going to do and although I know you would much rather not tell me anything just yet, even though you have discussed things with Tom, you will be careful, won't you?"

"Sure I will," Tony smiled, kissing her cheek before hurriedly leaving the house.

Through the narrow side window next to the front door Beatrice watched him run down the steps and shout, "Fleet Street!" up at the driver of the waiting hackney, but it was not until she had seen him drive away that she returned to the drawing-room, her mind so taken up with what was happening to Eleanor as well as what could happen to her brother, that she was quite unable to think of anything else.

Chapter Ten

Jerry Taylor may have acquired the reputation at Bow Street of being insubordinate, but Bill had told Tony no less than the truth when he said that he was as good a man as any to have in your corner. A sensible and no-nonsense type of man in his early fifties, Jerry Taylor had joined the Metropolitan Police Force at the age of thirty-one upon leaving the army after thirteen years due to him striking an officer he had discovered forcing his attentions upon a girl young enough to have been his daughter. The commanding officer and senior ranks, eager to have no dishonourable conduct attached to the regiment or to that of the officer's character, had therefore decided a court-martial would be in no one's interests as it would inevitably lead to the truth being made known about the officer whose name would be ruined in the event. Corporal Gerald Elisha Taylor of the 1st Battalion Lord Leas Regiment of Foot therefore, was honourably discharged, the recommendation cited by the commander-in-chief as 'being to well-deserved reward for long and meritorious service and good conduct in the service of his Queen and Country.'

Jerry may have had cause to be grateful for receiving an honourable discharge ensuring no questions would be asked on his return home to England and therefore impeding his chances of gaining civilian employment, but he certainly had no regrets about his actions. Being an honest and upright man himself whose ideas of right and wrong were deeply embedded in his consciousness, he had no time for those who either took advantage of their position or those who got away with wrongdoing simply because of who they were, and had he been asked if he would do it again he would have replied with a definite yes. Having married Janie Marsh, the coal merchant's daughter who had lived two streets away when he was eighteen and she sixteen, she had accompanied him to India with his regiment upon him joining the army and, after twenty-nine years of happily married life, he had four sons and one daughter resulting from their union. It had been the thought of his own daughter that had brought about that fit of anger resulting in him striking the officer he had seen taking advantage of his rank and abusing a young woman who had been in no position to either fight back or refuse; experiencing no regrets in having taken the law into his own hands.

Nor did he experience any regrets about his attitude towards questioning the orders he had sometimes been given by senior officers at Bow Street; orders which, in his opinion, were neither sound nor practical but, on the contrary, issued without much thought being given to the consequences resulting from them either on the one having to carry them out or for the situation they were in fact supposed to deal with. He had been neither smug nor conceited when they had turned out to be every bit the waste of time he had claimed, but the 'I told you so' look on his face had sorely tried his senior officers' patience, leading them to question both his loyalty and commitment to not only the job but themselves. Being a man who possessed a sharp mind as well as one who had a natural aptitude for working things out, he had long since come to the logical conclusion that he could do far better than those who gave the orders, and therefore upon casting off his police uniform of his own volition seven years ago, he had set himself up as a private detective, and now, with the help of all his four sons, he could boast quite a flourishing little business.

He had first met Bill Pitman when he had worked on a case which one of Bill's reporters had covered for both *'The London Chronicler'* and *'The Daily Bulletin'* and since he had come into possession of certain information pertinent to the case he had gone along to Fleet Street to offer his help. That had been the first of many instances they had worked together, and since both were upholders of law and order as well as being plain-speaking men, despite the difference in language, they had got along extremely well from the start. It had been with the utmost faith and confidence in Jerry that Bill had suggested him for the job Tony had in mind because not only could he find someone who did not wish to be found or ferret out information no one else seemed able to do, he was more than capable of taking care of himself should it ever come to making a fight of it, apart from which, he still had friends in the Metropolitan Police who were perfectly willing to help out, unofficially of course, as and when required.

When Tony arrived back at the office it was clear that Bill had already acquainted Jerry with the job in hand and it was also clear from the manner they adopted towards one another that a good friendship had long since been established between them, leaving Tony in no doubt that it was Jerry Taylor to whom Bill owed his thanks for his knowledge of Cockney slang. Tony found himself looking at a man of fifty-two years of age who stood no more than medium height, but he had a solid, muscular physique which told him that this Jerry Taylor would have no difficulty should any exertion be required during one of his investigations and that he could more than adequately take care of himself. He had a head of thick sandy hair, parted down the middle, the sides being brushed back off a broad forehead, beneath which he had a pair of thick bushy eyebrows which flew upwards at the ends and keen pale blue eyes which Tony guessed missed very little. His face, slightly rounded and weather-beaten from years of exposure to the elements, not only boasted a thick handlebar moustache but character and determination as well, and Tony, shaking the huge paw held out to him, took an instant liking to him.

"I take it Bill has already filled you in," Tony enquired.

"Yes, my lord, he has and I…"

"I will make a deal with you," Tony smiled, his eyes laughing as they caught Bill's knowing ones, "I won't call you Mr. Taylor if you don't call me 'my lord'."

Having taken immediate stock of Tony and liked what he saw, this pact met with Jerry's full approval, saying cheerfully, "That'll do me just fine, Guvna! Providin' o' course," he nodded, "you're sure."

"Quite sure, Jerry," Tony laughed, pouring himself a cup of coffee. "I have had my fill of being called 'my lord' for one day."

"Hallerton?" Bill grinned, raising a questioning eyebrow as Tony took a seat.

"After almost every sentence," Tony grinned. "But you were right, Bill," he nodded, "it certainly got me past the front door."

"So," Bill mused, "the title took precedence over the power of the press, did it?"

"'Fraid so," Tony grinned, "although," he inclined his head, "putting the two together they certainly got Hallerton talking."

"Did he say much?" Bill asked, fishing out a cigar from his waistcoat pocket.

"More than I bargained for," Tony nodded, lighting a cigarette, going on to recount what had passed between himself and Hallerton as well as the outcome of his visit to Cavendish Square.

Having followed the Dunscumbe case with keen interest, Jerry had long since arrived at the conclusion that there was far more to it than met the eye and fully agreed with Tony and Bill that Sir Philip Dunscumbe's death, following hard on the heels of that of his brother, albeit a recorded suicide, was too much of a coincidence to be ignored. He could find no fault with Tony's reckoning to account for his reasons for suspecting Sir Braden Collett as being the perpetrator of Sir Philip's death, in fact far from being implausible, given all the factors, including Lady Collett's behaviour and constant supervision and the time from when it all began, it not only fitted snugly into place but made perfect sense.

"Tell me, Jerry," Tony asked, "have you ever seen Sir Braden Collett? Would you know him if you saw him?"

The look which descended onto Jerry's face told its own tale. "Hm!" he snorted. "Just about I would! Came into Bow Street one night arguin' the toss about somethin' or other. Seen 'im a few other times since, too. I'd say 'e could be a nasty piece o' work!"

"You're not wrong there, Jerry!" Tony nodded. "Which is why I want him watched day and night. If I am right, and I know I am," he said firmly, "he not only murdered Sir Philip Dunscumbe but knows a great deal about his brother's death as well. Right now," he nodded, "he thinks he's safe, especially with his wife kept prisoner and too terrified to say anything, but sooner or later he's bound to give himself away."

"But what if he doesn't?" Bill asked, inhaling on his cigar.

"Then I shall just have to give him a nudge," Tony told him calmly.

"But what about Lady Collett?" Bill demanded. "Are you really saying he has her locked in the house?"

"I'd lay any money on it that far from having gone into the country to stay with friends she has not stepped foot outside the house since last night," Tony said firmly, "and that Collett has no intention of letting her do so again if he can prevent it. That guy Peterson who passes as his butler," he nodded, "made damn sure I wouldn't see anything by keeping himself well within the door."

Jerry, who had no liking for men of Collett's stamp any more than Tony and Bill, much less to knowing that wrongdoers escaped the law, gave it as his opinion that the sooner Lady Collett was out of there and in a place of safety the better, not only because she was at risk of being subjected to all manner of abuse, something which he most certainly did not hold with, but if they were to prove Collett guilty of murder they stood a far better chance of doing so without having his wife to worry about.

"I agree," Tony said with feeling, "and the sooner the better. Something wrong, Jerry?" he asked upon seeing the frown which had suddenly appeared on his forehead.

"Peterson?" Jerry mused, rubbing his chin thoughtfully. "You know, Guv," he nodded at length, "I seem to know that name. Ringin' a bell, like. What's 'e look like?" He cocked his head at Tony.

"About five-nine," Tony shrugged, "well built; muscular. His face is rather scarred around the eyes and it looks as though he has suffered a broken nose at some time or other, but my guess is that he was a…"

"Gawd love us!" Jerry exclaimed, breaking in unceremoniously. "I thought 'e'd cocked up 'is toes I don't know 'ow many years back!"

"Do you know him, Jerry?" Tony asked urgently.

"Ah," Jerry nodded, "just about I do, Guv; not in the way of my duties as officer of the law, mind," he told him in answer to the look on Tony's face. "A bruiser 'e was," he enlightened him, "a good'un too as I remember. Jim Peterson's 'is name. 'Ad the most punishin' left you've ever seen."

"What happened to him?" Tony asked.

"'Is last fight it was," Jerry told him, "at Turn'am Green against Billy Boy McGraw. O' course," he nodded, "McGraw 'ad the footwork, no question. As light on 'is pins as you could ever wish for," he nodded, "but 'e 'ad short jabs like; didn't 'ave Peterson's length nor," he nodded, "a punch to do 'im any 'arm."

"So, what happened?" Bill asked, chewing his cigar.

"McGraw 'ad been strugglin' right from the off. Then, in the third it was," Jerry told him reminiscently, "McGraw was on the ropes, almost to pieces 'e was when Peterson delivered a left to the 'ed which seen 'im fall to the floor like a sack of potatoes. Nothin' they could do," he sighed, "dead on the instant 'e was. Nothin' to do but put 'im to bed with a shovel!"

"You mean he killed his man!" Bill almost choked.

"Ah," Jerry nodded, "an unlucky punch it was. To be fair," he sighed, "not Peterson's fault, an' though no charges were brought, 'e never stepped foot inside the ring again."

"When was this?" Tony asked, stubbing his cigarette.

"Oh, ten or twelve years now, Guv," Jerry told him.

"And you say he's not come to the notice of the police at all since," Tony remarked.

"Not a whiff of 'im," Jerry assured him.

"So," Tony pondered, "what has he been doing all this time? A man who fought for a purse in the ring then accidentally killed his opponent would not be forgotten in a hurry and, surely, easily recognisable." Then, looking at Jerry, said, "See what you can dig up on this Peterson guy since he left the ring and, also, see what you can discover about this woman who calls herself Eliza Boon," giving him a description of her. "I get the feeling those two go way back," to which Jerry nodded. "I want Collett watched day and night, Jerry," Tony told him, "and this Eliza Boon and Peterson; where they go, you go too!" He thought a moment, then, turning to Bill, said, "Bill, about Mary Stanley and Mitchell…"

"I'm on it." He raised a hand. "You'll know as soon as I do."

"Thanks Bill," Tony smiled.

A brief consultation then followed between the three men, concluding with Jerry explaining the procedure he and his sons would work to in keeping an eye on the inhabitants of Cavendish Square and how he would maintain contact and report their findings through Bill. Tony, who could find no fault with any of it, said considerately, "Jerry, I know I have no need to say this, but Lady Collett is my main consideration; she must be yours too. If, during your observations, something arises, her safety must come first."

"Don't you worry," Jerry assured him, putting on his thick overcoat, "we'll make sure 'ers safe."

"Thanks, Jerry," Tony smiled, rising to his feet and shaking his hand. "You know," he laughed, "I get the feeling you're going to be worth your weight in gold!"

"And *I* get the feeling," Jerry grinned, donning his hat, "that you'd 'ave made a pretty good Peeler!"

"Well," Bill cocked his head when Jerry had left, "what do you think of him?"

"He's okay, Bill," Tony nodded. "He may be *persona non grata* with the Metropolitan Police but he's certainly *persona grata* with me!"

"So," Bill commented, "it seems you were right about Hallerton holding out. Do you think he was telling the truth about why he did not tell the police about that letter?"

"Yes," Tony threw over his shoulder, pouring out two fresh cups of coffee. "He was genuinely upset about Sir Philip's death, but whilst I accept that the initial shock would have temporarily relegated everything else to the back of his mind, I am sure the reason he did not report it after he remembered it was because he may have had an idea that the letter threatened blackmail or something equally as scurrilous and therefore did not want to open up a possible can of worms just in case and smear Sir Philip's reputation."

"But Sir Philip was not known for having affairs," Bill pointed out.

"Well," Tony sighed, "either Hallerton knew something no one else did about Sir Philip or perhaps he thought it could have had something to do with his brother since it appears that he was by no means averse to the female sex, thereby casting a slur on the memory of a man he had served for ten years and to whom he had been extremely loyal."

Bill nodded. "Do you think you will learn much from whoever lives at that address in Holborn?"

"Perhaps," Tony shrugged. "Of course, there's every chance that the writer of the letter no longer lives there, in which case it will mean back tracking to come up with a name and their new address, but I am absolutely convinced that that letter not only holds the key to all of this but it was why Sir Philip left his rooms so unexpectedly."

"And Lady Collett?" Bill said carefully. "Do you really believe that Collett's holding her prisoner?"

"Damn right I believe it, Bill!" Tony said unequivocally, going on to tell him about the previous evening at the Kirkmichaels' anniversary party. "At no point," he told him firmly, "did she mention anything to either me or to Bea that she was going to stay with friends in the country!"

"I know Collett has kept her closely guarded, but what do you think has prompted him into taking this new step of keeping her to the house?" Bill asked, inhaling on his cigar.

"He's worried, Bill," Tony nodded. "He knows the friendship which existed between Lady Collett's mother and Bea and that my sister has always had a fondness for her, which is why he has done everything possible to keep them apart, unless, of course, he's with her or that woman he passes off as her maid. Over the last ten months or so he has kept her away from all her friends and acquaintances just in case she says something either accidentally or deliberately, which could expose him for what he is. So far," he shrugged, "Lady Collett has said nothing, but although she is afraid of him I gain the impression that he has threatened her with something other than a beating if she talks, but he's no fool, Bill," he acknowledged, "nor is he blind; he could not have failed to have seen her reaction to me last night and that, if he is not careful, I could persuade her into telling me what is worrying her and therefore I pose a very real threat to his peace of mind."

"Are you saying you hope he'll come after you?" Bill asked, not at all certain whether this would be a good thing or not, watching Tony through a cloud of cigar smoke.

"He's sure welcome to try," Tony told him firmly, "but he won't." He shook his head. "Like I say, he's no fool, but right now he's got nothing to go on but pure guesswork. He may look upon me as a threat," he nodded, "but as things stand now he's on a pretty sticky wicket. He doesn't know for certain if I suspect anything let alone *know* anything, and until he does he won't do anything which could possibly incriminate him." A deep frown creased his forehead. "I get the feeling he'll work on Lady Collett until he's satisfied she's said nothing to either me or to Bea, which is why," he said purposefully, "I've got to get her out of there as soon as possible."

Although Bill wholeheartedly agreed, like Tom, he failed to see how Tony could do it. If Collett was the kind of man they believed him to be, he was hardly likely to stand aside while Tony removed his wife from under his nose without doing anything to prevent it and even though Tony knew this as well as anyone, Bill nevertheless felt it incumbent upon him to reinforce the fact. "I don't like men like Collett any more than you," he pointed his cigar at him, "but in the eyes of the law she's his wife, which means he can treat her in any way he chooses."

"I know that," Tony bit out, "but God damn Bill that don't make it right!"

"I'm not saying it does," he acknowledged, "but if she's kept closely guarded how are you going to get inside to remove her, since she's not allowed to step one foot out of the house on her own?"

While Tony sat in grim silence considering this, Bill, who knew perfectly well that it was pointless trying to change Tony's mind once he had decided on something, believed it would be well to divert his thoughts into less emotive channels by saying, "By the way, I've managed to find out that Dennis Dunscumbe was left-handed."

Tony raised his eyes from the thoughtful contemplation of the cigarette he was holding between his fingers at this. "Was he?" he said slowly.

"Which means," Bill nodded, "it looks as though you were right in that he was in fact murdered after all."

"And whoever killed him made it look as though he had committed suicide," Tony supplied, sitting up in his chair.

"And there's more," Bill told him, handing him several sheets of official-looking paper which he had fished out of his desk drawer. "Have a look at those!"

"*Good God*, Bill!" Tony exclaimed after casting his eyes over them. "Where the hell did you get these from?"

"Like I said before," Bill shrugged, tapping his nose with a forefinger, "must protect my sources."

"I wasn't born yesterday, Bill!" Tony reminded him. "It had to be a police officer who pulled these!" The look on Bill's face told him he had hit the nail on the head. "Damn it, Bill!" Tony cried. "Do you have any idea what you could get for tampering with police evidence?"

"I haven't tampered with police evidence," Bill told him truthfully, "just borrowed it."

"I'm sure a jury will appreciate the distinction!" Tony said with awful irony.

"Stop worrying and just read them," Bill recommended. "They'll be returned tonight without anyone being the wiser."

Tony threw him a sceptical look. "I suppose it's useless to ask who it was you got to take these for you?"

"Just a cop I know who owes me one," Bill told him, relighting his cigar.

Tony looked up from the papers in his hand. "He must owe you big time!"

"Never mind that!" Bill dismissed. "Just read those statements and tell me what's wrong with them."

"Okay, Bill," Tony shrugged after reading them, "I give up. What *is* wrong with them?"

"And I thought you were a wise guy!" pointing his cigar at him. "*Nothing*," Bill shrugged, as though it was of no importance, "except that here we have two guys who knew Dennis Dunscumbe; Brown, his manservant, who had been with him from way back and who found him dead and his brother who formally identified the body, and yet neither of them even questioned the fact that the bullet had entered the right temple and not the left, which would have been the case if he had really committed suicide! *Two guys*," he emphasised, holding up two fingers, "who would know that Dunscumbe was left-handed!"

"God damn!" Tony exclaimed, almost to himself.

"Too right God damn!" Bill cried with feeling.

"But hold on a minute, Bill," Tony held up a hand, "are you saying that you asked whoever it was to let you see these?"

"Huh, huh," Bill shook his head.

"So why…?"

"Hey!" Bill dismissed. "He's a rookie cop and hungry to get on! So," he hunched a shoulder, "I helped him out one time!" In response to Tony's raised eyebrow he said, "After I found out that Dunscumbe was left-handed I just sent a runner with a note to Vine Street police station to see if he had anything he could tell me. He didn't, but he brought these round to me not above a half an hour before you got back from seeing Hallerton, just paying me back by showing me something he thought might help. He doesn't know anything more than that guy Dawson."

"Then why…?"

Bill spread his hands. "Because Brown and Sir Philip were two guys who knew Dennis Dunscumbe better than most. He just thought that I might find something in their statements to help with the case."

"Come on, Bill," Tony urged, "if this rookie cop doesn't know anything, who told you about Dennis Dunscumbe being left-handed?"

"Like I say?" Bill shrugged.

"To hell with your protecting your sources!" Tony dismissed. "This is me you're talking to Bill," he reminded him.

"Okay, okay," Bill raised his hands in surrender, "if you must have it,

I got it from Dewey Tarkington's man." Upon seeing the look which crossed Tony's face he cried, exasperated, "Well how the hell do you think I know so much about him and Dyton? They don't volunteer information about themselves!"

Tony sighed, raking a hand a through his hair. "Damn it, Bill! I suppose you're going to tell me that he owes you one too!"

"Too right he does!" Ignoring the look Tony threw him at him, Bill shrugged. "I turned a blind eye to something about Tarkington once by not printing it, pretty juicy stuff too," he nodded.

"In return for what?" Tony raised an enquiring eyebrow.

"In return for feeding me information about who and whatever as and when," he hunched a shoulder.

Leaning back in his chair and clapping a hand to his face, Tony said, not without a touch of amusement, "I was right about you Bill, you were surely born to be hanged!"

Bill grinned. "And I was right when I told your old man once that he ought to take your pants down and give your backside a dusting!" To which Tony burst out laughing. "Yeah, very funny," Bill waved a hand at him, "but what about those statements? Why did two guys who knew Dennis Dunscumbe was left-handed never even mention it to the cops?"

Tony thought a moment. "Did we print anything about which side the bullet entered his head?"

"No?"

"Did the other dailies?" Tony asked.

"No," Bill shook his head, "like us they just reported that he had committed suicide by shooting himself. The police never released that information. Why?"

"Well," Tony sighed, "it's just that I fail to see what motive either of them could have had for not mentioning it to the police other than the shock of it driving it out of their minds. Sir Philip, who was his own brother for God's sake," he nodded, "would surely not have deliberately withheld information from the police which could have helped in their investigations to uncover the truth and," Tony reminded him, "let us not forget that Sir Philip is now dead, which," he pointed out, "came about as a result of receiving that letter and his own subsequent enquiries which must surely exonerate him of holding any ulterior motives!"

Bill digested this for a moment or two. "You could be right, but what about this Brown guy?"

"I take it he was investigated?"

"Sure!" Bill confirmed. "Came up clean."

"Well," Tony sighed after thinking it over, "I can't see him having anything to gain from withholding such information, and as for being in league with Collett and his crew," he nodded, "I should think it most unlikely, especially when one considers that he had been in service to Dennis Dunscumbe for a long time. What's he doing now?" Tony shrugged. "Any ideas?"

"Got another job I expect," Bill shook his head. "Dunscumbe's house in Hertford Street is up for let, has been ever since his death; no takers." Tony nodded and Bill, after inhaling on his cigar, asked, "But why was Dennis Dunscumbe killed? Blackmail, do you think?"

Tony thought a moment, then, looking straight at Bill said, "Not in the way you mean, Bill. Whoever killed him," he nodded, "had to be right-handed, but why shoot a left-handed man in the right temple? It doesn't make sense, unless, of course," he shrugged, "whoever pulled the trigger didn't know he was left-handed. If we are right in that Collett knew Dennis Dunscumbe, and I am convinced he did and, right again in that he had a hand in arranging his death," he said thoughtfully, "or, at the very least, knew of it, then he was pretty careless in briefing whoever did kill him."

"But surely they would be bound to know that at some point it would be questioned?" Bill put in.

"Unless, of course," Tony grimaced, "Dennis Dunscumbe was ambidextrous!"

Bill shook his head. "Huh huh; nothing doing there. It could have been a spur-of-the-moment thing?" he shrugged helpfully.

"Perhaps," Tony nodded absently. "But why kill him at all?" He thought for a moment, saying at length, "Unless, of course, he knew something and was going to talk or," he nodded, "perhaps threatened to in the hope of getting hush money."

"It's possible," Bill sighed, "but what *did* he know and, more importantly," he nodded, "who was it he had a hold over? Collett?"

"Possibly, but if not Collett," Tony replied thoughtfully, "then someone both men knew. Whatever it was Dennis Dunscumbe knew, assuming he did, it must have been pretty damaging stuff."

"'Assuming he did'," Bill repeated, "suggests you're not entirely sure that was the reason he was killed."

"The truth is, Bill," Tony confessed, "I'm not sure of anything, except that Dennis Dunscumbe was cold-bloodedly killed to ensure his silence."

"If it was Collett who killed him then…"

"No, Bill," Tony shook his head, having giving it more thought, "Collett may have arranged it or, if not that, then heavily involved in it, but he would not have pulled the trigger himself."

"How do you know?" Bill demanded. "Strikes me he's a guy who will go to any lengths to protect himself."

"He may well," Tony agreed, "but like I say, he's no fool; on the contrary," he assured him, "he's astute and extremely careful." He pulled out his watch to see that it wanted only a few minutes to five o'clock. "Well," he sighed, returning the watch to his pocket and rising to his feet, "there's nothing more we can do now. Time I was moseying along. Oh, and Bill," he reminded him, shrugging himself into his overcoat, "make sure you *do* return these tonight!" indicating the police statements with a wave of his hand.

Except for Tom and Beatrice no one knew Tony better than Bill and just one look at those dark grey eyes was enough to tell him that he was planning something and, unless he was way off course, which he doubted, he would lay his life he was working out how to get Lady Collett away from Cavendish Square. Bill could not really blame him for this because even though he had never been married, much less felt the way about some woman as Tony obviously did about Lady Collett, his work being his whole life, he nevertheless had had his moments and fully sympathised with Tony's need to shield her, but his words of caution to Tony before he left, although good humouredly received, were clearly not being attended to.

Chapter Eleven

During the short drive from Park Lane to Cavendish Square total silence reigned inside the Collett carriage, not that Eleanor needed Braden to say anything to tell her how angry he was, she could feel it emanating from him like a powerful force and so ominously foreboding was it that she trembled. She knew that he had by no means liked the idea of her dancing with another man, especially Beatrice's brother, not because he loved her and was jealous but because he was afraid she would say something, but so attuned was she to the man sitting threateningly silent beside her that she knew he would not rest until she told him what had passed between her and Tony. She dreaded the thought of returning to Cavendish Square; to Eliza Boon and Peterson, guarding her as if she were a criminal, but most of all she was afraid of her husband, a man who exercised no restraint in his dealings with her. She managed to stifle the sob which caught in her throat at the thought of what awaited her, her whole body violently trembling and, were it at all possible, she would have opened the door of the carriage and jumped out irrespective of the weather or whether she was injured by another vehicle or not, but even this preference to what she knew would soon follow was unhappily denied her as Braden always took the precaution of having the door on her side of the carriage locked from the outside.

Even though the thought of what was to come terrified her, somewhere deep inside her Eleanor knew she had no regrets about either her feelings for Tony or the exhilarating sensation of being held in his arms and hearing those wonderful words, 'I love you.' Instinctively she knew she would never see him again, Braden would see to that, but at least she could take some comfort from knowing that for just once in her life she had felt loved and wanted, and although it was going to be all she would ever have to carry her through the remainder of her life, at least no one, not even Braden, could take away those few precious moments she had spent in Tony's arms.

As usual Eliza Boon was waiting for her at the top of the stairs; cold, cruel and totally unfeeling and, below in the hall, was Peterson, a man who would stand his post by the front door until she was safely in Eliza's custody. Any idea of flight was useless as it seemed that Braden had considered every eventuality which could give rise to her doing so, and it was with a rather lagging step and a fast-sinking heart that she entered her room with an ever-watchful Eliza beside her. While those hideously tactile fingers removed the necklace from around her neck Eleanor pulled the bracelet off her wrist and removed the diamonds from her ears without even looking at the woman she hated and feared, but no sooner had she dropped these precious gems into Eliza's outstretched hand and pulled off her gloves than the inter-connecting door opened and Braden walked in. It seemed he had paused only long enough to remove his black evening jacket, his white waistcoat hanging open and the two top buttons of his shirt unfastened with his white bow-tie hanging loosely around his neck, and Eleanor, taking one look at his fleshy red face almost contorted with rage, knew the moment she had dreaded had arrived.

Unless specifically ordered to remain, Eliza immediately left her when Braden entered her room, but just as she was about to leave she saw the slight shake of his head and so stepped a little way back from Eleanor, standing stiffly upright and folding her hands in front of her. With soft, almost menacing, treads, Braden walked slowly towards Eleanor, his bulbous blue eyes glistening with a look which made her take an instinctive step backwards, but Eliza, standing right behind her, impeded her retreat and Braden, reaching out a hefty hand, took Eleanor's chin between his fingers and thumb and raised it, forcing her to look up into his ever-darkening face. "What do you think, Eliza?" he asked at length, raising a questioning eyebrow as he briefly glanced at her. "Beatrice Shipton's brother is over here from America. Come to take up his grandfather's title. Isn't that right, my dear?" he said softly, looking down into his wife's terrified face and squeezing her chin. "Staying in Mount Street, too," he said ominously. "And guess who visited Mount Street this morning?" he asked menacingly.

"Her Ladyship, Sir Braden," Eliza nodded, her lips thinning.

"Yes, Her Ladyship," he repeated dangerously.

"I… I never saw him." Eleanor shook her head. "I… I did not know he was…"

"Did not know," he mocked, cruelly. "And I suppose you did not know that he would be accompanying his sister and her husband to the Kirkmichaels' party this evening or that he would ask you to dance! You know, my dear," he told her with deceptive calm, "you are very beautiful, but not very clever. I am neither a fool nor blind," he informed her ominously.

"Please," Eleanor urged, "I did not…"

Ignoring this, Collett glanced at Eliza, his eyes glinting feverishly. "Our little songbird sang tonight, Eliza, and guess who to!" he raised an eyebrow.

"Lady Shipton's brother," she supplied in a hard and unfeeling voice.

"*No!*" Eleanor cried frantically. "I swear I said nothing!"

"Do you believe that, Eliza?" Collett asked, raising another questioning eyebrow.

"No, Sir Braden," she said firmly, "I don't."

"No," he said softly, "neither do I."

"*Please!*" Eleanor begged, fear etched into every inch of her face. "I swear I said nothing!"

"Tell me what you said," he told her, the gentleness of his voice not fooling her in the least, "and I won't hurt you."

"He… he was telling me about A-America!" she managed.

"*America!*" he echoed. "Do you believe that, Eliza?" he asked.

"No, Sir Braden," she shook her head, "I think she told him something."

"You see, my dear," Collett said softly, his face only inches away from her own, "Eliza does not believe you either. Now, tell me," he warned, "what did you say to him?" Eleanor shook her head, her throat too dry to speak. *"Tell me,"* he demanded, fast losing what frail hold he had on his temper.

"Nothing," she managed, "I swear it!"

"You were dancing with Childon for close on twenty minutes," he pointed out, "and you expect me to believe that you talked of nothing but America?"

"It's true," she told him weakly. "I… I promise."

"I see," he nodded releasing her chin, then, as if making to walk away from her, he suddenly turned and struck her a heavy blow with the back of his right hand across the right side of her face which sent her sprawling to the floor, the diamond in the centre of his heavy gold signet ring on his little finger cutting her cheek. "Tell me what you said to him," he ordered, bending down to grab hold of her arm, pulling her roughly to her feet before giving her another forceful blow on the right cheek with the back of his hand. "*Tell me,*" he panted, painfully gripping her right arm as he raised his right hand to deliver a smack with tremendous force against Eleanor's left cheek, giving her no time to recover by quickly following it up with a further vicious smack.

"I… I…" she could get no further, feeling stunned and her head throbbing painfully, the blood trickling down her face from the small cut on her cheek.

"What do you think, Eliza," he demanded, his eyes glinting, "do you believe our little songbird had no song to sing tonight?"

"No," Eliza shook her head, "I don't. I've told you before, Sir Braden," she nodded, "we've been too lenient with her."

"Yes," he nodded, his eyes glistening, "you're right, but the time for leniency is over."

"*No*!" Eleanor choked, her eyes dilating with fear as she felt the fingers of his left hand dig into her right shoulder, shrinking in terror as his right hand clenched into a fist, which, before she could even try to evade it, hit her full in the face, sending her reeling backwards to fall in a crumpled heap at Eliza's feet, but Braden, having lost all control of his temper, bent down and grabbed hold of her by the soft chiffon that made up the neckline of her dress and pulled her up off the floor as though she were a rag doll, the soft material ripping in his hands, giving her another forceful punch in the face. "Tell me," he demanded, ruthlessly shaking her by the shoulders, but Eleanor, who was beyond all speech, merely shook her head, whereupon he once again violently punched her in the face before throwing her back down onto the floor with such force that she struck her head on the corner of the dressing table, immediately rendering her unconscious and totally oblivious to the vicious kick in her ribs.

Several hours later, still wearing her evening dress, Eleanor opened her eyes to the painful discovery that she could not fully open her right eye, and the left one, although partly open, was swollen and her vision blurred, and her lips, when she tenderly touched them with her trembling fingers, were sore and puffy. Although she was unable to open her eyes to their fullest extent it did not prevent the tears from escaping the half-closed lids, and gently wiping her right cheek she discovered traces of blood from the cut caused by Braden's ring. Much too hurt and bruised to get up, she continued to lie inert on the floor, and it was not until she heard the little French ormolu clock on the mantelpiece which had belonged to her mother strike four o'clock, did she have any idea what time it was. After what seemed an aeon of time, she half crawled and half dragged herself to the big four-poster, her trembling fingers gripping the quilt to try to heave herself up onto the bed, but every movement was an excruciating agony and her head swam so much she felt sick and, after several painful but futile attempts, she eventually gave up any idea of trying to get onto the bed, but remained motionless on the floor.

She did not think she would be able to sleep, especially as she felt icily cold, the fire having burned down some hours ago, but shock and fear had taken a heavy toll and, to her surprise, she did not wake until the daylight filtered in through a slight gap in the curtain several hours later. By now her right eye was firmly closed, and she knew from experience it would take several days, perhaps even a week, before the bruising eased sufficiently to allow her eyelid to open properly, and her face, which had by now become quite inflamed, was too tender to allow her even to touch it. Movement of any kind was extremely painful, but bit by bit she managed to raise her head only to find that the room swam violently around her, and was only too thankful to sink back onto the floor. Somewhere on the periphery of her consciousness she was vaguely aware of movement in the adjacent dressing room, but so stiff and bruised was she that for once she could find no strength to try to move to escape her husband and not even when she heard him open the door and walk over to her, could she rouse any energy to evade him. Through her left eye, Eleanor dimly saw him look down at her, his face exhibiting neither remorse nor guilt as he looked almost dispassionately at her; his lips pursed and his eyes devoid of any warmth or feeling.

"Well?" he demanded. "Have you come to your senses yet? Are you going to tell me what you said to Childon?"

Her mouth felt extremely dry and her lips were by far too swollen for her to speak with any clarity, but since he fully expected her to answer him, she slurred, "I… said… nothing."

"In that case," he told her firmly, pulling her roughly up onto her feet by her dishevelled hair, "you will remain locked in this room until you tell me, no matter how long!"

"I ..." she began inaudibly.

"Tell me what you said to him," he told her with barely concealed anger, thrusting her head back by painfully tugging her hair, "and I shall release you." Eleanor shook her head in denial, words too much of an effort, to which he responded by angrily striking her across the right cheek with the back of his right hand, the force of it causing Eleanor to fall backwards onto the floor, lying as if dead at his feet. Bending down he wrathfully pulled her to her feet by the front of her ripped and torn dress, asking her again to tell him what she had said to Childon about what she had seen that night, but a shake of the head was all she could manage, to which he responded by gripping Eleanor's exposed shoulder and punching her in her already swollen face. "Very well, then," he bit out, throwing her back onto the floor and kicking her in her already painful ribs with a booted foot, "you will remain here until you tell me," venting his anger by kicking her again before stepping over her, leaving her where he had left her without a backward glance.

Beaten, bruised and with only a blurry vision of the patterned carpet, she remained motionless where Braden had left her, unable to move any part of her body without it being excruciatingly painful, but as the minutes turned into hours with her flitting in and out of consciousness, she had no idea how long she had been lying cold and shivering on the floor. She had no way of knowing whether Eliza Boon had looked in on her or not, but since Eleanor could not bear her to touch her she would far rather remain where she was on the floor than have her do so, even though she longed to lie in bed and wrap herself up and get warm. At one point, she thought she heard the little French clock chime two o'clock, but she was not certain, any more than she was when she thought she heard a vehicle pull up outside and the clanging of the bell. Everything seemed vague and remote, even the voices which appeared to be coming from just below her window had a faraway sound to them, although they seemed familiar. She tried to concentrate, but her head hurt so much and she was beginning to feel rather sick, but gradually the sound of voices wafting up from what, in her disoriented condition, seemed the general direction of the front steps, began to penetrate more into her confused brain and, for one insanely wonderful moment, she thought it was Tony and tried to cry out, but no words left her lips, tears stinging her eyes at the thought he was here and she could not make him hear her. Desperate to gain his attention she tried to crawl her way along the floor to the window, but she felt so weak that even to move was an agony, but fighting off the nausea which swept over her she very slowly began to inch her way along the floor to the window, but even though she managed to reach it trying to get to her knees was such an effort. She tried to cry out again but no sound left her lips, then somehow finding the strength she stretched herself up and raised her left hand until the tips of her fingers found the side of the blind, feebly trying to hit the window pane with the flat of her hand, but her ineffectual and frantic attempts proved fruitless, collapsing unconscious to the floor as the hackney drove away.

Eliza Boon, upon being informed of Tony's visit by Peterson, hurried up the stairs to Eleanor's room, unlocking the door with more haste than usual, but one look at her prisoner lying unconscious on the floor was enough to tell her that she was safe enough. She knew perfectly well that Eleanor hated her and could not bear her to touch her, but the fact remained that Eliza Boon was irresistibly drawn to this young woman and she was honest enough to admit to herself that had she been anyone other than Sir Braden's wife, one of her girls for instance, she would have known no compunction in bullying her into doing what she wanted. Unfortunately, she *was* Sir Braden's wife but, more importantly, the circumstances in which they presently found themselves were such that there was more at stake than her own feelings, but these apart, she was by nature self-serving and cruel and one, moreover, who, like her noble employer, took no small amount of pleasure from either inflicting pain or witnessing it being carried out, and not for the first time she had therefore watched Sir Braden beat his wife without lifting a finger to stop him. As far as she was concerned this brother of Lady Shipton's could cause all manner of trouble, and since she had as much to lose as Sir Braden the further away from this family Eleanor was kept the better because she for one had no intention of facing the Queen's Bench resulting in a lengthy prison sentence for her involvement in recent events simply because Sir Braden's wife was unfortunately blessed with a conscience.

This latest idea of Sir Braden's about sending Eleanor into the country was all very well, but it still presented the problem of someone keeping permanent guard over her and whilst Eliza Boon had no objection to continuing her role as gaoler so long as she was handsomely paid, it did not alter the fact that the risk of her talking remained. She knew perfectly well that to do away with Eleanor would be asking for trouble, for one thing too many people would be bound to ask some rather pertinent questions, not the least being Sir Miles Tatton, but not only that they already had four deaths on their hands without having another! No one may be overly interested in the death of a girl who had earned her living in a way society heartily condemned, but whilst they had up to now been fortunate in getting away with covering it up, murdering Sir Philip Dunscumbe and his brother as well as Mitchell, thanks to Peterson and the carefully contrived way it had been brought it about, the chances were they would not be so lucky in arranging a similar fate for Lady Collett, especially now that Lady Shipton's brother, a man Eliza instinctively knew meant trouble, had arrived on the scene. It seemed to her that the only sure way of keeping Eleanor permanently silent was for Sir Braden to have her committed as soon as possible, and although the Shiptons could be relied upon to question the sudden institutionalising of Lady Collett, not to mention her father, the fact remained that as her husband Sir Braden had rights over his wife which were not only indisputable but took precedence over those naturally held by her father. Eliza felt sure that should Sir Miles, out of concern for his daughter, decide to question his son-in-law about his decision to have her locked away, he would, after only a little reminder from Sir Braden about his social solecism, soon be brought to see that any allegation he put forward could only render his own position even more untenable than it was. As for the rest of society, including the Shiptons, who would dare question either the ethics or the motives of Sir Wilfred Moore? A man who was not only an eminent physician but a most respectable pillar of society into the bargain. Eliza was firmly resolved therefore to speak to Sir Braden when he returned and felt sure such a logical solution would meet with his full approval because although he had argued against the idea of having Eleanor committed when she had mentioned it to him right at the very beginning, surely now, with the unwelcome advent of Beatrice Shipton's brother, he would be brought to see that it was not only expedient but imperative.

As it was out of the question to call for a doctor to tend to Eleanor's injuries any more than it had on the previous occasions when her husband had brutally beaten her, Eliza Boon, having no doubt that they would heal themselves in time as they had before, made no effort to try to get her onto the bed and pull the covers over her or try to make her even remotely comfortable. Apart from drawing back the curtains she made no effort to help her and, like Sir Braden, left her lying on the floor, walking out of the room without a backward glance.

For the next few hours Eleanor slipped in and out of consciousness, but in her concussed condition she had no idea what time it was or how long she had lain inert on the floor. She vaguely heard the little French clock chime six o'clock, all she knew for certain was that she was shivering with cold, and her body, stiff and badly bruised, rendered even the slightest movement unbearably painful, but through the blurry mist of her left eye she could just make out the shadows of the furniture from the light of the street lamp outside her window. She tried to move her head, but the throbbing was so acute, bringing with it an overwhelming sense of nausea that she refrained from attempting it again, deciding that it was not worth the effort. Her right eye, swollen and badly bruised, was now completely closed and the sore puffiness of her lips too tender even for her tongue to try to moisten them, and she could not even manage to cry out for the water she desperately needed. Suddenly she saw the light go on in Braden's dressing room and somewhere on the periphery of her consciousness she heard voices, but before she could even make out whose they were, the door opened and Braden walked in with Eliza Boon following closely behind. Eleanor closed her eyes and feigned unconsciousness, deeming this preferable to being subjected to any more of her husband's brutality, and as he switched her light on Eliza walked over to the window, unconcernedly walking round Eleanor's lifeless body, and pulled down the blind and drew the thick heavy curtains across the window.

"How long has she been like this?" Sir Braden asked curtly, not even bothering to ask how she had managed to move herself from the side of the bed where he had left her over to the window.

"Since this morning," Eliza replied dismissively.

He thought a moment as he looked dispassionately down at his wife lying unconscious on the floor just feet away from him before demanding, "Does she know that Childon came here today?"

"How could she?" Eliza shrugged.

"Has she said anything?" he enquired, totally unsympathetic to his wife's serious condition.

"No," she said firmly, "not a word."

"Damn it, Eliza!" he said irritably. "I have to know what she said to Childon last night!"

"I know, Sir Braden," she nodded, "but I don't think you'll get much out of her right now. Best leave her until the morning."

"This Childon tyke could be dangerous," he warned her.

"He'll be less of a danger when *she's* dealt with," Eliza assured him, nodding her head towards Eleanor. "When she's out of the way and he's gone back to America, there will be nothing he can do."

Eleanor felt Braden's tread on the carpet as he approached her, nudging her painful ribs with the toe of his shoe. "Mm," he nodded, "she will come round eventually."

"About what I said earlier, Sir Braden," Eliza reminded him, "you must agree it's the only thing we *can* do. It's not safe to have her leave the house any more, even with one of us going with her. She knows too much. She'll bring us to ruin if you don't do it. We can't risk Childon coming here again!"

Another nudge in Eleanor's ribs, which again yielded no response from his apparently unconscious wife, Sir Braden stepped away from her, eyeing Eliza Boon thoughtfully. "You're right. It's too great a risk keeping her constantly watched. I'll see Wilfred Moore tomorrow; he can have the committal papers drawn up."

"What will you tell him?" she asked, sharply eyeing Sir Braden.

"That my wife has, for some considerable time, been behaving in a manner that is causing me grave concern. She has become delusional; thinks she can fly or some such thing!" He grimaced cruelly. "Why," he raised an amusing eyebrow at Eliza, "she even tried to prove it by attempting to do precisely that down the stairs only last night; hence her present condition."

"Yes," Eliza said thoughtfully, experiencing no more twinges of conscience than Sir Braden, "but do you think he'll believe you? After all," she pointed out practically, "he is bound to ask why you did not consult him about Lady Collett's condition well before now."

"Because my wife adamantly refused to acknowledge she was ill," he told her. "He will believe me, never fear," he said firmly, "besides, he will only have to question the servants to verify what I tell him. Thanks to the tale we have spun them that she is suffering from nervous disorders which accounts for you being here to keep a constant watch on her, they will be able to confirm what I say with a clear conscience. No," he shook his head, "once Moore has spoken to them as well as seeing how distraught and concerned I am about my wife's worsening condition, he will not hesitate to take the necessary steps."

"But of what Sir Miles?" Eliza cocked her head.

Something resembling a sneer twisted Collett's lips at this. "Sir

Miles," he told her firmly, "will say and do *nothing,* not if he knows what's good for him!"

After nodding her head approvingly, Eliza asked, "Do you want me to stay with her?"

He thought for a moment or two, saying at length, "No, there's no need for that. She's not going anywhere tonight."

"Very good, Sir Braden," Eliza nodded. "I take it you're going to your club?"

"Yes," he confirmed, "but I should not be back late." Glancing at the clock he then pulled out his watch to compare the times. "Half past six. I should be back about eleven."

"Very good, Sir Braden," she nodded, then, casting one last look down at Eleanor's lifeless body, she followed him out of the room, switching the light off as she went.

Eleanor, upon discovering that Braden was going to have her committed to an asylum after all as he threatened he would if she did not do as she was told terrified her, tears stinging her already swollen and painful eyes at the mere thought of being locked away for the rest of her life because she could not fool herself into thinking that she would ever be let out. Once inside one of those dreadful places she would never be released, and Braden, determined to keep his secret at all costs, would ensure she never would be and with such a highly respected and eminent physician such as Sir Wilfred Moore at his back, no one would dare question it. Somehow, she had to get out of here. If she could make it to Beatrice in Mount Street she knew she would be safe, but even though she could hardly move she could not allow them to shut her away forever; she was not mad, she just knew too much, and Braden and Eliza Boon as well as that hateful Peterson, would give her no chance to say anything.

Through the narrow gap at the bottom of the door leading to Braden's dressing room Eleanor could see there was no light showing, and as Braden had told Eliza that there was no need for her to stay and keep watch over her and he had left for his club, this was the only opportunity she would have to escape. The door to her room was always kept locked whenever she was alone within its confines, but Eleanor had not heard the key turn in the lock of the door to the dressing room which separated her bedroom from Braden's, which meant that they had either forgotten to do so or they thought there was no danger, but if she could make it into Braden's bedroom she could hopefully open the door which would take her onto the landing. What came after that she would leave to fate, but one thing she did know, she could not leave through the front door, which meant that somehow she would have to make her way down the back stairs which led to the kitchen quarters and the basement corridor where, hopefully, she could leave the house by way of the basement steps leading on to the square, keeping her fingers crossed that the servants would be far too occupied to either notice or hear anything.

Slowly Eleanor raised her pounding head, nausea combined with dizziness sweeping over her, but as this was not the time to give in to either she raised it a little higher to try to peer through the darkened room towards the dressing room door. Inch by painful inch, she crawled across the carpeted floor on her stomach, hardly daring to raise her head, every movement an excruciating agony, feeling so weak that several times she had to stop, but very gradually she managed to reach the connecting door, pausing to catch her breath and relax her aching body before proceeding further. When, after a moment or two, the nausea and giddiness had receded a little, she eventually raised her right arm to try to turn the handle, but it was much too high up to reach, but panic and fear came to her rescue and, from somewhere, she found the strength to get to her knees, enabling her to take hold of the handle, pressing it down as hard as she could until the door slid silently open. Again, that feeling of nausea swept over her and her head throbbed painfully and, for one awful moment, she thought she was going to lose consciousness, but even to linger for so much as a second to ease her racked and battered body could mean the end to her attempted flight. But her spirits were soon uplifted when, to her relief, having crawled little by little on her elbows through the dressing room, somehow or other managing to pull open the door to Braden's bedroom, she could just make out a dim ray of light filtering into it from the landing. Clearly, he had not closed the door behind him when he had left, but as this was not the time to question the reason for such an oversight, she took a deep breath and, like a trapped animal in fear of its life, crawled slowly across the bedroom floor, edging nearer and nearer to her only means of gaining access to the first landing.

As she had only partial use of her left eye and the right was totally closed her vision was very much impaired, seeing everything through a kind of blurry mist, but with a determination that had its roots in terror and alarm, she feverishly tried to clasp the bottom edge of the door to pull it towards her, only to find herself clutching at the air. Eventually though, her fingers managed to clasp the edge of the door to pull it towards her to create a gap wide enough for her to slip through, but the effort had taken a lot out of her, causing her to drop her head, exhausted, onto her bruised and sore forearms. Taking a moment to regain enough strength, she slowly emerged onto the first landing, heaving a tremendous sigh of relief when she heard no one moving about, then, after taking a deep breath, she crawled painfully out of the darkened bedroom and onto the dimly lit landing, edging her way towards the rear alcove where a door concealed the disused back stairs.

Since Eleanor could not stand up let alone walk, she eyed the door with a sinking heart, having no idea how she was going to manage to open it, but again fear drove her on and, very slowly, she stretched up an unsteady hand to take hold of the handle, but her fingers, almost stiff from the cold, failed to take a firm grip. Tears of frustration and unbearable tension stung her eyes as she sank dejectedly to the floor, dreading the thought of what would happen to her if someone caught her, but just as she was about to heave herself up to try again she heard a door opening and closing downstairs and the all too familiar footsteps of Eliza Boon crossing the hall. In her agitated state of mind Eleanor could not tell in which direction Eliza Boon was heading, but the fear of her coming up the stairs and discovering her desperate efforts to escape made Eleanor feel sick, a sob of pure fright leaving her dry and swollen lips. Like a snared animal awaiting its fate, her eyes dilating with fear as she knelt inert and petrified on the floor, her whole body shivering from the combined effects of pain and intense cold, Eleanor stared with terrified eyes towards the stairs for the sight of her gaoler, but when, somewhere on the periphery of her numbed consciousness, she heard a door at the rear of the hall open and close, relief and desperation came to her aid by galvanising her into frantic action. Eliza Boon may have shut herself away in the privacy of her sitting room, but there was no telling how long for, and Eleanor, in fear of her life as well as the woman who would stop at nothing to prevent her escaping, tried again to open the door only to find, to her horror, that her cold and trembling fingers, failing to take a firm grip, slid down its smooth surface, her failure to reach the relative safety of the back stairs intensifying her fear. Time and again she tried frantically to take a secure hold and depress the handle while at the same keeping a frightened but constant watch on the stairs, but after what seemed an agonisingly long time she finally managed to get a grip and press down with her all the strength she could muster. Without even waiting to catch her breath, she pulled the door open just wide enough to allow her access to the back stairs, crawling inch by inch across the small square landing until she reached the top step.

Looking anxiously down the two flights of steep and narrow stone stairs with no idea how she was going to negotiate them, tears of frustration and pure terror began to roll unheeded down her cheeks, but in her desperate need to escape Eleanor managed to pull herself together to work out the best way of descent. In the end, she had no choice but to take hold of the narrow iron rail and sit her way down each step at a time, but her descent was agonisingly slow and painful, rendered infinitely worse due to the dizziness which engulfed her, but in her hurry to reach the basement corridor before Eliza Boon discovered she was not in her room she had no time to stop to either catch her breath or ease her aching body. So close was she to reaching the narrow passageway which led to freedom that Eleanor could not bear the thought of being discovered now and, with a resolution born out of desperation, she continued her descent of the stairs, reaching the first landing in a state of near exhaustion. Pain cut through her like a knife and for several minutes she was quite unable to move, but again fear put life into her tortured body, not daring to think what would happen to her if Eliza Boon came upon her now she had managed to come this far. Half crawling and half dragging herself towards the top of the next flight of stairs which would lead her to the passageway and the door that gave access to the basement steps at the front of the house, Eleanor began the step by step descent, her cold and stiff fingers gripping the equally cold iron rail as though it were a lifeline until she eventually negotiated the last step, but it was a few minutes before she recovered her breath sufficiently to set her mind to covering the short distance to the basement entrance door.

Down the passageway to her right she could hear the low murmur of voices coming from the huge kitchens and the sound of pots and pans being put away, glad to know that she did not have to pass it, but as any one of the servants could emerge from the kitchens into the corridor at any time and see her she yet again found the strength to crawl the short distance on the cold stone floor to the basement door. Even though it was only a matter of a few feet it seemed more like a mile, having to rest on her hands and knees beside a small table where a lamp was always kept for the boot boy or one of the servants who needed to gain access to the front of the premises at night, but having managed to recover her breath she inched her way to the door only to find to her dismay that not only was the handle beyond reach, but bolted top and bottom. For one in her weak and feeble condition reaching up to take hold of the handle was a daunting task, but worse than this was having to try to stand up and reach the bolt at the top of the door, but refusing to give in, especially having come this far, she first drew back the bottom bolt which, to her immense relief, slid noiselessly out of its holder, then, with a superhuman effort, Eleanor somehow managed to get to her feet, stretching up to pull back the top bolt, almost crying out as pain shot through her. She would have liked to take a moment to catch her breath and ease the pain darting through her head and body, but knew she dared not linger especially as one of the servants could step into the corridor, so grabbing hold of the handle she pulled with all her strength only to find that the solid block of oak refused to respond to her ineffectual pulling. As she leaned heavily against the door, frightened, beaten and totally exhausted, she felt the dizziness begin to sweep over her, gradually at first and then like a tidal wave while everything suddenly started to move in front of her eyes until disappearing altogether until she knew no more, collapsing unconscious onto the cold stone floor.

The sound of breaking crockery followed by a sharply worded rebuke to the effect that if someone or other had their minds on what they were doing it would never have happened promptly followed by a tearful assurance that she had not meant to drop the plates, gradually penetrated through the layers of stupor which held Eleanor too weak to move. It was some little time before she realised the voices were coming from the kitchen, and opening her left eye to its fullest extent to peer hazily down the passageway in that direction, she was just able to make out a sliver of light from under the gap of the securely closed kitchen door. In her confused state of mind, it was impossible to calculate how long she had been unconscious, but as her presence in this cold and cheerless kitchen corridor had so far gone unnoticed it must only have been for a few minutes, were it otherwise she would by now be locked in her room with Eliza Boon keeping a very watchful eye on her. The very thought of this woman not only discovering her escape attempt, but touching her so she could get her back to her room roused Eleanor from the inertia which enveloped her. Little by little she managed to get to her feet, the buzzing in her ears combined with an overwhelming nausea rendering it necessary for her to pause a moment before trying to open the door again, but eventually she straightened up and reaching out two cold and trembling hands for the handle, tugged with every ounce of strength she possessed to pull it towards her. At first it seemed as if it was not going to budge, but very slowly it began to slide open, tears of relief and achievement mingling with fear running down her cheeks as she gave it one last jerk to prise a gap just wide enough for her to slip through, totally unprepared for the icy gust of air which came in.

The dramatic drop in temperature having brought a heavy fall of snow during the last two hours or so had, over the last thirty minutes, eased considerably, but the light flurry which met her eyes felt like pin pricks on her already frozen skin, her ripped and torn dress, a garment far from suitable for such conditions, affording her no protection. In her frantic attempts to escape she had given no thought to the weather or that she was hardly dressed for these icily cold temperatures; the evening slippers she was still wearing providing no safeguard from the freezing slush within the basement area or on the steps leading up to the pavement. Barely able to see, overwhelming nausea swamping her and her whole face and body battered and bruised and scarcely capable of taking one more step, she had no idea how she was going to manage to climb the half dozen or so steps, but fear of being discovered, especially by Eliza Boon, was more than enough for her to summon up every ounce of strength she had left. Leaning heavily on the snow-covered rail Eleanor half heaved and half dragged herself up the steps to the gate, finding just enough strength to pull it open and slip through onto the pavement, tears of hopelessness and panic building up at the back of her eyes when she realised she would never make it to Mount Street. Unable to go any farther, completely exhausted and shivering from mingled shock and cold, her legs incapable of taking her weight any longer, she finally gave herself up to the dark chasm which was fast coming up to meet her, surprised but totally beyond caring when, instead of collapsing onto the cold wet flagstones, her shattered body was ably caught in two strong arms which lifted her effortlessly up to hold her close against a firm and solid one.

Chapter Twelve

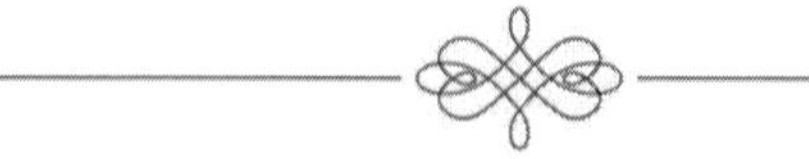

Tony's determination to rescue Eleanor from the clutches of a man whose temper would one day carry him too far in his treatment of her was such that by the time he arrived back in Mount Street he was firmly resolved in getting her out of the house by any means available and, if possible, tonight. He had not needed Bill's words of caution, or Tom's for that matter, to know that Braden Collett would not let him just walk into the house and take her, but he could no more leave her there than he could stop breathing. If he was right about Collett murdering Sir Philip, and he was absolutely convinced he was, whose battered skull had been the direct result of Collett's frenzied attack, then Eleanor had to be removed from her husband's vicinity without loss of time.

Tony fully agreed with Jerry that it would be far better to get Eleanor out of the house to a place of safety so that their investigations could go ahead without worrying over any repercussions rebounding on her, and although Tony had no doubt that he could deal with both Collett and Peterson without too much difficulty he would much rather gain access to the house as unobtrusively as he could. Collett may suspect him of having a hand in his wife's disappearance, but since that so-called butler of his had already told him she had gone into the country to stay with friends, no matter how convinced Collett was that she had sought sanctuary in Mount Street, Tony could not see him making enquiries there about his wife any more than he would approach Sir Miles Tatton, in whose care Tony fully intended to place her once he had removed her from Cavendish Square; to do so would not only take a lot of explaining, but would be acutely embarrassing. Until Tony had managed to get hold of the evidence to prove Collett guilty of murder he wanted his part in this affair to remain undisclosed because no matter what suspicions Collett held about his involvement in Eleanor's disappearance, he could neither openly charge him with them nor make enquiries. Tony's main aim then was to gain access to the house without anyone being aware of it and knew that his best chance would be when Collett had gone out for the evening, when, under the cover of darkness, hopefully entry could be made by way of the basement area and, if good luck was with him, it may well be tonight and because he wanted to be on hand when the opportunity presented itself, he was fully resolved in joining Jerry on his vigil later.

Beatrice was certainly taken aback to learn that her brother would not be joining them for dinner and that a sandwich and a cup of coffee was all he needed, but upon learning what he had in mind, despite her apprehension, she sent word to the kitchen for a tray to be prepared. She fully agreed that Eleanor had to be removed from Cavendish Square and brought here for her own safety until Tony could place her under her father's protection, but she could not help being fearful when she thought of the danger her brother would be exposed to, and even if he managed it without anyone being the wiser, Sir Braden was astute enough to put two and two together and come here looking for her.

She failed to share Tony's view in that whilst Collett may suspect him of having a hand in his wife's disappearance, it was extremely unlikely that he would visit Mount Street to enquire after her much less want it known, which is what would happen if he began setting about making enquiries. Beatrice remained unconvinced of this because although she had no doubt that should Braden Collett come looking for Eleanor here she was more than capable of denying any knowledge of having seen her since last night at the Park Grove Hotel as well as preventing him from searching the house to make sure of it, she knew him well enough to feel confident that he could quite well report her disappearance to the police. Upon receiving a definite, "That's the one thing he won't do, Bea," she looked closely up at her brother, asking suspiciously, "Why, what's to prevent him?"

Tony may have confided his concerns to Tom, but he had not wanted his sister to know anything at this stage. It was not only because he had no wish to alarm her, but she was by nature open and sincere, and it could well be that should she ever run into Collett at some function or other that innate honesty could inadvertently alert him to their suspicions as well the investigations taking place about his involvement in Sir Philip's murder and his brother's so-called suicide, but now, in view of the way things seemed to be turning out, Tony deemed it prudent to take her into his confidence. Not unnaturally she was utterly shocked and appalled; the enormity of it taking several stunned moments for her to take it all in, but if nothing else it certainly explained why Eleanor was constantly watched and accompanied wherever she went. "But are you saying that poor child witnessed such a horrific act?" she cried.

"Either that," Tony nodded, helping himself to another scalding cup of coffee, "or she stumbled upon something to alert her to the truth. In either event, she knows enough to see Collett hang!"

Not at all certain which aspect of the matter horrified and sickened her the most, Beatrice sank into the nearest chair, shaking her head, bewildered. "But why should Collett want to murder Sir Philip?" she asked, bemused.

"I'm still figuring that one out," Tony nodded, "but that he did so I am quite convinced!" he told her firmly.

"But why do you think Sir Philip's brother was murdered and that Collett had something to do with? I mean," she shrugged, "according to the newspapers he committed suicide!"

"Dennis Dunscumbe apparently shot himself in the right temple, now, according to Bill," Tony told her, "Dunscumbe was left hand-handed. Now, why would a left-handed man shoot himself in the right temple?" he asked reasonably. "He wouldn't," he said firmly.

"I know I don't like Collett," she confessed, "but even if he did kill Sir Philip, there is nothing to say he had anything to do with his brother's death!"

"It goes against all logic to think otherwise, Bea," Tony nodded. "Sir Philip's brutal murder, coming within just over a month of his brother's supposed suicide, was not committed for no reason!" He shook his head firmly. "I doubt we shall ever know the precise content of that letter Sir Philip received," he said realistically, "but that it was what took him out of his rooms that day, I am certain."

"Are you really going to that address tomorrow?" she asked, somewhat concerned.

"Too right I am!" Tony replied firmly. "Whoever wrote that letter clearly knows something about Dennis Dunscumbe," he nodded, "and I fully intend to find out what."

Beatrice thought this over for a moment or two, asking at length, "But what makes you think she will tell you anything? At least, I assume it's a woman," she shrugged.

"According to Hallerton he thought it looked like a woman's handwriting and, unless I miss my guess," Tony told her, "if what Bill tells me is true, and I've never yet known Bill be wrong, Dennis Dunscumbe was something of a ladies' man, therefore," he nodded, "I think we can safely say that it was most definitely a woman who wrote that letter to his brother."

"But this Eliza Boon woman who's always with Eleanor and that horrible man who passes as a butler," she demanded, "who are they? I mean," she shook her head, "where did Collett find them?"

"That's something I hope Jerry will be able to discover," Tony replied, pushing his tray away and rising to his feet.

"But this Jerry," she queried, "I mean, is he…?"

"He's okay, Bea," Tony assured her. "He's worked with Bill before. Don't worry," he shook his head, "Jerry's a first-rate guy."

"Oh, Tony!" she cried, springing anxiously to her feet and laying a hand on his arm. "You will take care, won't you?"

"I thought I told you not to worry over me," he smiled, kissing her forehead.

"Yes, I know you have," she nodded, "but if Collett is guilty of all we believe, he could be dangerous! Then there's this hateful little man, Peterson!"

"I don't intend to go storming in through the front door," Tony grinned, walking into the hall and shrugging himself into his thick overcoat, "because whilst I would like nothing better than to send them both sprawling, it wouldn't answer the purpose. Tell Tom," he told her, putting on his hat and gloves, "that I'll fill him in when I get back; although when that will be I'm not sure! Oh, I almost forgot," he smiled, "I met Lady Randolph today; she sends her regards," opening the front door as he spoke.

"Lady Randolph!" she cried.

"I'll tell you later, Bea. Must go!"

By now the snow, which had come down heavily over the last two hours, had eased into a light flurry, but the air, which was icily cold, stung his exposed face, and after raising his overcoat collar he descended the steps and, turning left, walked along Mount Street until he turned left again into Davies Street which, on a raw cold evening such as this, was practically deserted. Crossing over Brook Street he walked on until he came on to Oxford Street, but although there were any number of pedestrians and hackney carriages plying their trade, it was by no means the busy thoroughfare it usually was. Crossing over to the other side he walked on until he came to Hollis Street and, turning into it, walked straight on until he came to Cavendish Square when, instead of traversing this exclusive location, he strode through the gardens to the far end, spotting Jerry huddled between two snow laden bushes with an unrestricted view of Collett's imposing house.

"Thought you might like some company," Tony smiled, pulling out Tom's hip flask from his pocket which he had filled before leaving Mount Street. "Here," he grinned, "take a pull of this; you look as though you need it."

"Ah," Jerry nodded, "it's a parky night, sure enough!" swallowing some of the fiery liquid before handing the flask back to Tony.

"I'm sorry to have to bring you out on such a dirty night, Jerry," Tony apologised.

"Think nothin' of it," Jerry blew on his gloved hands, "I've been out in worse."

"Anything happening?" Tony asked, directing a glance across at Collett's house.

"Collett went out, about three-quarters of an 'our back," Jerry informed him. "Called up an 'ackney just down there on the corner of Oxford Street," nodding in that direction. "But 'e won't go anywhere that we won't know of," he told him firmly, "my eldest is on 'is tail at this very minute."

"I see what you mean by a family business!" Tony smiled.

"Oh, ah!" Jerry grinned. "Me and my four sons," he said proudly. "'Ere's my youngest now, Arthur," he nodded as he saw him emerge from behind a row of snow-laden bushes the other side of the path to where he was keeping watch, and Jerry, after briefly introducing the two men, disparagingly told Tony, "That cove who calls 'imself a butler, slipped 'is moorings not five minutes after Collett."

"Where has he gone, do you know?" Tony asked, handing the flask to Arthur who was blowing on his gloved hands.

"Came this way 'e did, Guv," Jerry told him, "so I followed 'im to see were 'e was 'eadin' and saw 'im myself skulk inside *'The Old Bush'* several streets away down there on the left," jerking his head in that direction. "They serve a nice drop of brown ale in there," he informed him, "so I expect 'e'll in be in there for a spell."

Tony nodded before asking, "Have you seen anything of that woman who passes herself off as a maid?"

"No, Guv," Jerry shook his head, taking another pull of whisky from the flask Arthur handed him, "not a sign, although," he told Tony, handing him his flask back, "a light came on in that room on the first floor about an 'our or so ago. On for about fifteen minutes it was, then it went off. Not long after Collett came out, followed by that gravedigger minutes later. Since then there's been no sight nor sound of anythin'!"

Tony could only hazard a guess as to whether the room Jerry had indicated was Eleanor's or not, but as far as he could see it was going to be now or never in trying to get Eleanor out of the house. With Collett and Peterson out of the way he estimated that apart from this woman who called herself Eliza Boon and possibly one or two domestic servants, there should really be no one to give them too much trouble. "Tell me, Jerry," he asked amusingly, glancing down at him, "how are your scruples?"

Jerry returned the look without a blink. "Oh, very flexible they are, Guv," he assured him, "especially when it comes to dealin' with rogues like these!"

"That's what I was hoping you'd say," Tony grinned.

Jerry eyed him knowingly, a twinkle lurking at the back of his pale blue eyes. "Is it now?" he mused, pushing his hat back off his forehead a little. "Are you thinkin' what I think you're thinkin'?" he asked, not unhopefully.

"I am!" Tony said firmly.

"Well now," Jerry pondered, rubbing his chin with his gloved hand, "it's a good job I came prepared, ain't it!"

"You're a man after my own heart, Jerry!" Tony laughed, pulling out his watch. "It's just gone half past seven; we'll give it a few minutes, then we'll make our…"

The slight creaking sound which wafted on the still night air made him break off what he was saying and look up, hardly able to believe his eyes when he saw who had emerged from the basement steps of twenty-nine Cavendish Square onto the pavement. Without waiting for Jerry and Arthur Tony ran towards Collett's house, reaching Eleanor just in time to catch her as she collapsed into his arms, a low-voiced curse leaving his lips, but as it was by far too dangerous to linger right outside the house he carried her quickly back to the shelter of the bushes in the Square's garden. In the light given off from the many street lamps erected around the square, Tony had no difficulty in seeing just how badly beaten she was and the anger which raged inside him at the sight of her was such that had Braden Collett suddenly appeared before him he would have returned the compliment in full. As Eleanor was still wearing the same dress as she had the night before, it was clear Collett had brutally assaulted her the moment they had returned home and that she had been in this condition ever since. Badly beaten and bruised and most probably feeling the effects from the onset of hypothermia and concussion, he had to get her back to Mount Street as quickly as possible, but first he had to wrap something warm around her, so handing his precious charge into Jerry's care, he hurriedly removed his overcoat and put it around her frozen body then, after unbuttoning his coat and waistcoat, took her back in his arms and held her close against him, instructing Arthur to call up a hackney and to have it pull up on the other side of the Square out of sight of Collett's house.

"Gawd love us!" Jerry cried. "'Er ain't dead, is 'er, Guv?" he asked concerned, looking down into the bruised and cut face with horror.

"No, she's not dead," Tony bit out, "but her husband will be when I've finished with him!"

"I don't know what 'e deserves for doin' this!" Jerry exclaimed. "E's given 'er a right old goin' over! Why, it's downright wicked!"

"Well *I* certainly know what he deserves," Tony bit out, shielding Eleanor as best he could from the cold and snow, "and I aim to make sure he gets it!"

From the look on Tony's face Jerry did not doubt it, in fact he would go so far as to say that it would go ill with Collett should Tony ever come up with him and he for one would do nothing to prevent it, but as he anxiously stood beside Tony waiting for his son to return with a hackney nothing could hide his concerns for the woman lying unconscious in Tony's arms because from the looks of it she was in a pretty bad way and urgently in need of medical attention. Her face had taken a terrible beating, and left to Jerry he would have no hesitation in stringing Collett up for such a despicable crime, in truth, it would give him tremendous satisfaction to whip him at the cart's tail. He did not hold with such things as this because no matter which way you looked at it there was no excuse for beating up a woman, not only that, but she was no bigger than a morsel and if Collett could do something like this to his own wife without so much as batting an eyelid, then he would not think twice about battering a man over the head and dumping his body into the Thames.

Tony, whose thoughts ran along parallel lines to Jerry's, was totally impervious to the weather as he held Eleanor tightly against him so she could take some benefit from his body's warmth, but as he looked down into her swollen and beaten face with that cut on her cheek and distended lips, he vowed to pay Collett back for such a brutal and unconscionable act of violence. After what seemed hours but was in fact only a few minutes, it was to Tony's relief when he saw the hackney approaching them with Arthur leaning forward and pointing a directing finger, such a welcome sight immediately relegating all thoughts of retribution to the back of his mind for now; the important thing was to get Eleanor to the safety of Mount Street so she could receive the attentions of a doctor. Taking Eleanor's lifeless body off Tony while he settled himself inside the hackney, Jerry then carefully handed her up into his arms, then, stepping back from the vehicle, slapped the door and watched as it disappeared from sight before returning to his vantage point with his son, filled with a renewed vigour for the task in hand, because although he always applied the same commitment to any job, he was firmly determined to bring this man Collett to book, if only for the brutal treatment he had handed out to his wife.

Tony meanwhile, anxious to get Eleanor to the warmth and safety of Mount Street, gently brushed her tangled and bloodstained hair off her face, his fingers coming in to contact with the gash on her head which was more than enough to tell him that the force of Braden Collett's fist must have caused her to fall backwards and strike her head on something, resulting in the concussion. Her face had clearly been subjected to more than one punch as well as several ruthless smacks, most probably with the back of Collett's hand, to inflict such severe injuries and swelling as well as accounting for the cut which Tony put down to a heavy ring, almost certainly Collett's signet ring, which had clearly drawn blood. Unless Tony missed his guess, he would say she had been lying on the floor unattended and without warmth or any covering over her where Braden must have left her after his brutal assault last night until she had tried to escape, accounting for the onset of hypothermia.

Eleanor may not have admitted it, but Tony knew this was not the first time Collett had subjected her to his bullying. Why else would it have been necessary for her to feign illness or allege to have been staying with friends to account for her frequent absences from society if it were not so? Besides, he had witnessed Collett's brutality himself! Tony could only hazard a guess as to how severe her injuries had been before resulting from his previous attacks, but if her present condition was anything to go by, then Collett certainly exercised his right to treat his wife in any way he saw fit, apart from which, he clearly enjoyed it, as the look in his eyes when he had hurt her at Covent Garden amply testified. For women like Eleanor, constantly subjected to a husband's tyranny, who looked upon his wife as his personal property and therefore felt himself at liberty to treat her in any way which suited his mood, they had no recourse to the law, but had to suffer in silence the torment all too frequently handed out to them. Usually with no money of their own but entirely dependent upon their husband, especially as, for the most part at least, any assets a wife took into the marriage became her husband's, she could neither leave to live independently nor return to her family as they would neither welcome what they considered a disgraced daughter nor accept the stigma which attached to either divorce or separation.

Eleanor, who knew this as well as anyone, must have felt desperate indeed to try to escape, and although Tony could not blame her he was firmly convinced that something other than this beating must have influenced her to make the attempt. The very fact that she was still wearing the same dress she had worn at the Kirkmichaels' anniversary party last night was more than enough to tell him that Collett must have been extremely worried about what they had said to one another and had tried to beat it out of her and, if he needed any further confirmation of this, then Peterson's announcement that she had gone into the country to visit friends was surely it. Tony knew that in Eleanor's concussed condition she would most probably have flitted in and out of consciousness for most of the day and wondered if, during a brief emergence from unconsciousness, she had overheard something which had rendered it necessary for her to try to get away. In her desperate efforts to leave the house he felt sure that in her confused state of mind she had no idea where she was going or that she would not get very far, not only because she had no strength to do so, but the flimsy dress and slippers she had on meant she would not have survived many minutes in these freezing temperatures.

Like his brother-in-law and Jerry, Tony despised men like Collett who took advantage of rights which they should really be ashamed to adopt or condone, and he looked forward to pitting his wits against a brutish bully of a man and bringing him to justice for murder and, if it were in his power at all, also for the vicious treatment of his wife. As this was unfortunately out of the question Tony was firmly resolved therefore, before handing Collett over to the police, of dealing with him personally for what was nothing short of a crime.

The roads, which had become quite treacherous, made the short drive from Cavendish Square a rather slow one, but when the corner of Mount Street came into Tony's view, he briskly called out the number of the house before manoeuvring Eleanor into a better position for him to lift her out of the vehicle. The movement roused her and, half opening her left eye, she saw through a hazy mist the outline of a man she could not quite identify, and for one horrifying moment she thought it was Braden taking her to an asylum and, in her distressed state of mind, a terrified cry left her dry and swollen lips, struggling to free her aching body.

"It's all right," Tony soothed gently, stroking her hair, "it's Tony. I have you quite safe, my darling."

She knew his voice and immediately her body, beginning to feel the benefit of his warmth and wrapped in his overcoat as Tony held her close against him, relaxed, her left eye closing of its own volition as she slipped back into unconsciousness.

Beatrice, who had been on tenterhooks from the moment Tony had left the house until Tom arrived home almost an hour later to pour her concerns into his ears, was slightly soothed by his calm assurances that Tony knew precisely what he was doing and that he was more than capable of taking care of himself. Tom had no more liking for murderers going free of the law than Tony, let alone allowing such treatment as Eleanor was regularly subjected to going unanswered, and he could only hope that Beatrice was right in that Tony's investigations had progressed to the point where he was going to follow up the lead that letter had presented to try to help him in bringing Collett to book. Tony had certainly got things moving, but even if this woman could shed some light on the matter, Tom doubted very much whether she would be prepared to come forward and testify because it was reasonably safe to assume that she must hold some rather damaging information, in which case she would most probably be far too scared to give evidence in open court and, it could even be that she may not be very forthcoming when Tony visited her tomorrow. Collett may have committed murder, whether intentionally or not was yet to be seen, but the fact remained that he had so far covered his tracks very well, including terrifying his wife into silence, but Tom felt sure that Tony did not need him to tell him that unless this woman came forward, then the chances of bringing Collett to account for his crimes seemed rather remote, especially as Eleanor's evidence would really count for nothing. Deep down Tom was hoping that he could be of help to Tony, even though he prudently refrained from telling Beatrice of his eagerly offered pugilistic services to her brother should the need arise. Although he believed that it was far better not telling her, he nevertheless felt it incumbent upon him to remind her of the need for caution because like her brother she was open and honest and deceit and dissimulation were abhorrent to her, but if Tony's suspicions were correct, and from what he could see of it they were, then it was paramount that Beatrice say or do nothing which could possibly alert Collett to the fact that they were on to him.

Beatrice was just on the point of agreeing to this when the sudden and imperative kicking on the front door made her jump and, for one awful moment, she wondered if something had happened to Tony, but nothing quite prepared her for seeing her brother stride into the hall carrying Eleanor's lifeless body in his arms. Not by a word or gesture did Bennett, who had been butler in the Shipton household for many years, give the slightest indication as to his feelings about such goings-on, on the contrary his impassive demeanour was such that he could have given the onlooker every reason to suppose that this was a regular occurrence and, accordingly, closed the door quietly behind Tony before calmly waiting for any instructions he may be given. Upon being asked by Sir Thomas to send for Doctor Little, he merely inclined his head saying that he would instruct the boot boy to take a message immediately, seeing as how that medical practitioner was not connected to the telephone.

"Good God, Tony!" Tom cried, coming up to him and looking down into Eleanor's beaten face. "You don't mean…?"

"I'm afraid I do," Tony bit out. "I'll explain later, now though, I need you to wait for the doctor and Bea," he nodded, "I shall need you to come upstairs with me!" before taking them two at a time.

Husband and wife exchanged concerned glances, but without waiting for anything Beatrice followed her brother up the stairs, overtaking him on the first landing to show him into the guest room which was always ready and prepared. Throwing back the covers so that Tony could lay Eleanor down on the bed, Beatrice immediately rang the pull to summon her own personal maid Sarah to come to her in order that they could tend to Eleanor, then, after putting a light to the fire and drawing the curtains, she joined Tony who was sitting on the bed beside Eleanor, her two cold hands held firmly in his, looking anxiously down at her lifeless body. "Dear God!" Beatrice cried. "What *has* he done to her?"

In the light from the central chandelier Tony, having removed his overcoat from around Eleanor and thrown it unceremoniously onto a chair, could now see the true extent of her injuries for the first time and, what he saw, filled him with so much fury that he wanted nothing more than to return to Cavendish Square and beat the hell out of Sir Braden Collett. But managing to clamp down on this overwhelming impulse, he leaned forward and gently moved a strand of hair off Eleanor's face, his eyes softening perceptibly as he looked down at her, trying not to think what would have happened had he and Jerry not have been on hand. Beatrice, who knew precisely what her brother would like to do to Collett, and would not blame him in the least if he did, told him softly that she needed to get Eleanor ready for Doctor Little's arrival, but although her brother nodded his head he was very reluctant to leave her side, let alone leave the room while she and Sarah prepared her for the doctor's examination. Tony knew he had to leave, but so disinclined was he to do so that it was not until Sarah entered the room that he gave in to his sister's perfectly natural request, but he could not prevent himself from casting one last glance at Eleanor before he left her to the care of his sister and Sarah.

Sarah, who had been with Beatrice long before she had married Sir Thomas Shipton, was a plump and rosy-cheeked woman in her mid-fifties with a cheerful and happy disposition, and one who could proudly boast of having received more than one offer of marriage. Unfortunately however, none of these claimants to her hand had been what she called 'husband material' and no matter how taken she had been with them all it seemed had an ever-roving eye, and therefore she had decided to turn down any chance of having a home of her own, much preferring to spend the rest of her days in the service of one who was as kind as she was generous rather than go through a lifetime of worrying over what her husband was up to behind her back. If anyone were to ask her if she had any regrets, she would have responded with a categorical no, because no matter which way she looked at it she considered herself to be far better off than she would have been tied to a man she was forever wondering who he was with, and although she did not think any the less of them for something they could not seem to help, she had nevertheless decided instead to devote herself entirely to Beatrice.

Beatrice, who had often teased her about her past romances, was genuinely sorry that not one of them had led to marriage because not only would Sarah have made a good wife but an extremely good mother, and although nothing would please Beatrice more than to learn that this warm-hearted woman was going to take a walk down the aisle, she was honest enough to admit that she would miss her very much should she ever do so. She knew perfectly well that Sarah was only too happy to perform any task she asked of her, and whilst it was totally against Beatrice's nature to take advantage of one whose position automatically meant that she made herself available at any time day or night, she knew that her devotee was the only one she could turn to in this present extremity.

Sarah, upon setting eyes on the young woman lying as one dead on the bed, let out a shocked cry, covering her rosy cheeks with two plump hands, demanding to know what had happened to the poor child, but Beatrice's calm voice, telling her that she would explain everything later, but now she needed her to get a clean nightdress, a bowl of hot water and towels, as well as a number of other essential items including a cup of hot, strong, sweet tea, had the effect of settling her nerves, and disappeared on the instant to bring these necessary commodities.

Tony, having reluctantly left the room, made his way downstairs to the study where he found Tom, a glass of whisky in one hand and a cigar in the other, sitting beside the fireplace with a deep frown creasing his forehead. After helping himself to a drink and lighting a cigarette, Tony stood in front of the fireplace, one hand resting on the mantelshelf and one well shod foot on the fender, staring broodingly down into the fire. "What kind of a man does that, Tom?" he asked at length, raising his eyes to his brother-in-law's face. "What kind of a man beats his wife to within an inch of her life and then calmly walks away and leaves her?"

Tom sighed and shook his head. "I'm damned if I know, Tony, and that's the truth!"

Tony straightened up, taking a much-needed drink, his face echoing his anger and anxiety, saying, "I'm sorry to involve you and Bea in this, but there was nowhere else I could take her."

Tom waved a hand. "You did right to bring her here. In fact," he told him firmly, "even if Sir Miles *had* returned to town, I would have been extremely offended, not to say deeply hurt, had you not done so. This is your home too, Tony," he reminded him unequivocally. "Do not forget that."

Tony, deeply touched, eyed him gratefully. "There's no need to tell me that, Tom," he smiled, "I know. It's just that this could turn out nasty."

Tom rose to his feet and, laying a hand on Tony's shoulder, said seriously, "Nasty or not, Eleanor remains here."

"Thanks, Tom." Tony gripped his hand.

"I meant what I said last night, Tony," Tom nodded, "if there is anything I can do to help bring that brute of a man to justice, I'm with you."

"I know," Tony nodded. "Thanks Tom, but…"

He got no further as the door opened and Bennett walked in to inform them that Doctor Little had arrived, whereupon Tom briefly excused himself to speak to the man who had been their personal physician and friend for a good many years. He was back in a matter of minutes, telling Tony that he had no need to worry over Little's discretion, but some explanation would be due to him because there was no getting away from it that the minute he laid eyes on Eleanor he would know instantly how she had come by her injuries. Tony nodded and, waiting only until he had finished his drink, he furnished Tom with all the events of the day, culminating in finding Eleanor and bringing her here.

Not at all sure which aspect of the whole thing shocked and appalled him the most, Tom was unable to do anything more than shake his head in disbelief, but after the initial shock had worn off he told Tony that whilst he realised Little would have to be told something, he did not mind admitting that he was momentarily at a loss to know what to say to him because under no circumstances could they tell him the whole truth as to do so would mean running the risk of alerting Collett to the fact that they were on to him for murder as well as offering his wife sanctuary. Tony fully agreed to this as well as to Tom's firmly held opinion that something must have occurred other than that beating to induce Eleanor to escape and that it was a very good thing it was he who had come upon her and not Collett or that man who passed as a butler.

Meanwhile, Beatrice and Sarah between them carefully removed Eleanor's clothing, shocked to see the bruising around her ribs, and after exchanging knowing looks followed by freely expressing their feelings as well as what they would like to do to her husband, they gently cleaned her bruised and swollen face and body before easing her into the nightdress, their patient regaining consciousness for long enough to allow Beatrice to gently raise her in order for her to swallow some of the hot tea. As it was patently clear from the congealed blood in her hair that Eleanor had somehow or other gashed her head, Beatrice had no wish to cause her any further discomfort by using a comb to try to untangle the thick blonde tresses, so quickly going in search of the soft brush she used for Alice which she kept in her room, she gently ran this through the entangled curls. Eleanor did not regain consciousness again, but she was nevertheless extremely agitated over something, as the incoherent words which intermittently left her lips testified, but by the time Doctor Little was eventually shown into the guest bedroom, she was at least looking a little less harrowing than she had earlier in her torn and stained dress and her face smeared in blood.

For Tony and his brother-in-law, it seemed a very long time before Doctor Little joined them in the study, although in fact it was little more than half an hour, but it was clear from the expression on his rather angular face that he knew precisely how the patient had come by her injuries. It was seldom he was called upon to treat a woman in this condition as neither party to the assault were any too eager to advertise the results of such conduct and, on the odd occasion he had been consulted, the reason to account for her injuries had covered a wide field, but it was something he totally deplored and if only those who made the law included such a vicious felony a criminal offence, he would prosecute the perpetrator with the utmost vigour.

Beatrice, who had deemed it prudent to leave any explanations to her husband and Tony in case she put her foot in it, although it would have given her tremendous satisfaction to lay the blame where it fully belonged, had dexterously evaded Doctor Little's probing questions, to which he had attributed this to her very natural distress upon seeing the injuries sustained by a woman she had told him was a very dear friend. But the name of this very dear friend had not been divulged, and although he could hazard a very good guess as to why he refrained from pressing her, and hoped instead that Tom would be able to tell him more than Beatrice. As it happened, it was from Tony he received most of his answers, firmly endorsed by Tom, who reconciled his conscience with the fact that he had no wish to see Collett let off the hook for murder which could well be the case if he truthfully answered the questions raised by his friend and physician about Collett's callous usage of his wife, even though he deserved the direst punishment for that alone. Doctor Little, upon discovering that the patient's husband, whose identity had deliberately been kept from him, was under investigation by Tony's newspapers and it was imperative that this most terrible incident was not made public knowledge in case it impeded not only their own enquiries but also those of the police, Doctor Little nodded his head as he carefully turned over in his mind all Tom and his brother-in-law had told him. As a medical practitioner he told Tom, gratefully accepting the whisky and soda he handed him, he believed that, although the law did not acknowledge such a gross offence, he was very much inclined to advise the patient lying as one dead upstairs to take out a private prosecution to which he would fully support her, but in view of what Tony had told him he would, as a personal favour to an old friend and for the sake of the woman whose injuries were severe as well as having no wish to be the cause of further distress, refrain from doing so. "But," he nodded to both men, "only on the condition that you return the favour by ensuring that the man responsible, whoever he is, for that young woman's injuries, will, at some point, be brought to account!"

Upon receiving their assurance that he would, Doctor Little finished off his whisky and soda and bid them both goodnight, to which Tom told Tony upon his return to the study after seeing his friend out that he had not dared to hope they would brush through it as well as they had. "But he is right, Tony," he said firmly, refilling their glasses, "that brute has to be brought to account for that child's condition!"

"He will be," Tony said determinedly, taking his glass, "because I'm going to make damn sure of it!"

Just one look at his brother-in-law's face was enough to tell Tom that he meant it, especially as they had since learned that Eleanor had sustained a cracked rib and heavy bruising to both sides of her body resulting from several forceful kicks. Tom, who fully shared Tony's outrage, told him that whilst he had no doubt he was right in that Collett would not come looking for her here in view of Peterson telling him she had gone into the country, apart from which Collett would not want it known that his wife had disappeared any more than how he had inflicted such severe injuries upon her, Tom was rather hoping he would not because he doubted he would be able to keep his hands off him! "Because I tell you, Tony," he told him with more anger than Tony had ever yet heard from him, "when I think of what that child has suffered at his hands he deserves to have a sample of his own medicine!"

"I agree," Tony nodded, finishing off his drink, "and I fully intend to make sure he does, but I tell you now, Tom," he said firmly, "*that* pleasure will be mine!"

Beatrice, having left Sarah to sit with their patient, entered the study palpably upset, saying that the thought of that dear child lying upstairs in a such a dreadful condition was more than she could bear, upon which she burst into tears. Tom, putting his arms around her, assured her Doctor Little had every confidence that with care and rest Eleanor would fully recover. "I daresay," she sniffed, "but it's downright wicked what Collett's done to her!" Then, after vigorously blowing her nose, she told Tony that she dreaded to think what would have happened to Eleanor had he not have been on hand to help her and, as for him asking her if she minded him bringing her here, she had never heard such nonsense! "You were quite right to bring her here," she declared roundly, "*and,*" she added firmly, standing on tiptoe to kiss his cheek, "I fully intend to make sure she remains here; because no matter *what*," she told them both determinedly, "there is no way I am allowing her to return to that brute of a man, come what may!"

"Thanks, Bea," Tony smiled, giving her a hug. "But tell me, how did you leave her?"

"Well," she sighed, "she is more comfortable now and Doctor Little said that it would take time for the cracked rib to heal, possibly two or three weeks, perhaps longer; as for her being cold and shivering he advised keeping her as warm as possible and plenty of hot drinks. He said it was as well you wrapped her in your coat before she became too exposed to the weather, especially as it seems she had lain for such a long time in a cold room without any cover over her. He has applied arnica to the bruises which will help reduce the swelling as well as the discolouring and something or other to the cut on her face and her head injury, as well as leaving a sleeping draught in case she becomes restless, but apart from opening her eyes for long enough for me to get her to drink the tea, she is still unconscious," she told him, concerned. "Also, she seems rather agitated about something; she keeps trying to speak, but the words are so incoherent that neither Sarah nor I can make out what she is saying."

"Thanks, Bea," Tony hugged her again, "I'll go up to her now."

"Well, Sarah is with her and…"

Upon discovering that Tony intended to stay with Eleanor all night instead of just sitting with her for a little while as she had thought, Beatrice was immediately torn between being touched by his love and concern and a natural disinclination considering they were not married, but Tom, reading the thoughts going around in her head with unerring accuracy, having managed to suppress the smile which twitched at the corner of his mouth, said that he thought it was a good idea, especially if Eleanor awoke during the night to find herself in a strange room with someone she did not know.

"*Well!*" Beatrice cried when Tony had left.

"Well what?" Tom laughed, taking her in his arms.

"They're not…"

"Married?" he smiled, to which she nodded. "What difference does that make?" he laughed. "He loves her, Bea, and, unless I have misjudged your brother all these years, I somehow cannot see him taking advantage of her!"

"I know he would not," she said firmly, "it's just that if Eleanor awakes during the night and needs something…"

"I know," Tom soothed, holding her closer, "but he came close to losing her tonight, let us not forget that," to which she nodded, resting her head comfortably against his shoulder.

Tony was very much aware of how close he had come to losing Eleanor because if he had not come upon her when he did she would not have survived very long in such freezing temperatures. He could only imagine how she had managed to drag herself out of her room and down the stairs to the basement area without being seen, especially in her condition as every movement must have been excruciatingly painful, which only served to convince him that something other than that brutal beating must have occurred to induce her to attempt such a brave but dangerous feat.

Rising to her feet on his entrance, Sarah told him that even though Eleanor was now a little more comfortable she still seemed very agitated about something, but was unable to make out what she was saying as her words were quite unintelligible, to which Tony nodded and thanked her, saying that he would now sit with her. Sarah, who had her own ideas of what should happen to men who did this kind of thing, was not quite able to refrain from keeping them to herself, pausing as Tony opened the door for her and, looking up at him, gave vent to her feelings in a fierce whisper, to which he fully agreed.

Walking softly over to the bed, Tony stood for several moments looking down at Eleanor's beaten face, watching helplessly as she moved her head fretfully from side to side trying to formulate words which made no sense with such a look of grim determination on his face that no one privileged to have seen it would be in any doubt that he fully intended to make Collett pay for such a brutal act. Taking off his jacket and hanging it over the back of the chair, he gently sat down on the edge of the bed, his face softening as he tenderly brushed a wayward strand of hair off Eleanor's forehead before changing the damp compress for a fresh one, the coolness of it and the touch of his fingers having the effect of momentarily stilling her, enabling him to moisten her dry lips. The agony of seeing her lying here, knowing there was nothing he could do other than keep her warm and safe, tore through him like a knife, wishing there was something he could do to hasten her recovery; his only solace being that he had found her when he did and that she had not fallen into the hands of Collett or one of his cohorts. It was just as he was about to stand up that she began moving her head restlessly from side to side, and her attempts to speak, although just as incoherent as before, made him lower his head to try to make out what it was she was trying to say. "I… .am… asy… no…." Putting his ear as near to her lips as possible, he listened again. "Not… mad… as… y… asyl… no!" Again and again, she repeated the jumbled mass of broken words and, after several minutes, Tony managed to discern enough to explain the reason for her escape, but just as he was about to move away from her she suddenly opened her left eye to its fullest extent, his face a misty blur, calling out his name.

"I'm here," Tony told her soothingly. "I have you quite safe, my darling," he assured her gently. "Quite safe."

"Don't… leave… me!" Eleanor cried faintly, pulling her right hand from under the covers to urgently grip his.

"I won't," he said softly, taking hold of her hand in his two strong ones and raising it to his lips. "I am going to be right here with you throughout the night."

"Promise," she whispered.

"I promise, my darling," Tony vowed. "Now, you must rest," he told her softly. He watched her close her left eye, but only when she fell asleep did he gently put her hand back under the covers, then, rising to his feet, stood looking down at her for several moments, his expression one of extreme concern, before making himself comfortable in the wing chair beside the bed to begin his nightly vigil of the woman who, despite only having entered his life a mere forty-eight hours ago, had come to mean more to him than life itself.

Chapter Thirteen

It could not be said that the domestic staff in Cavendish Square had any more liking for Peterson than they had for Eliza Boon, but since their feelings and opinions went for nothing they had no choice but to accept these two latest members to their number with as good a grace as possible. Like Tony, they very much doubted whether Peterson had ever been a butler in his life before, in fact they would take their dying oath that his past career had been every bit as eventful as his face suggested and, as for that woman who was now looking after the mistress, she was so far removed from what she purported to be that they regularly speculated about her credentials for such a post as well as conjecturing where Sir Braden had found two of the most unpleasant individuals they had ever had the misfortune to encounter. This baffling question was unfortunately destined to remain unanswered, but gossip below stairs was rife and, even now, almost eleven months on, they still found it hard to believe that Mitchell, who had been in service here for as long as most of them could remember, had, without any warning, been dismissed on charges of theft and that Mary, Lady Collett's maid, had also been discharged on equally suspect grounds.

It was not for them to question Sir Braden, but the fact remained they were totally at a loss to account for Mitchell's dismissal because no matter how hard they tried they failed to see how their noble employer could have believed for one tiny instant that a man who had given loyal service to the family for many years had suddenly taken it into his head to pilfer. However, by the time Sir Braden had called them all together the morning after the supposed theft to inform them of the changes made to his household staff, Mitchell, or so Sir Braden had led them to believe, had already made his exit earlier that morning having been ordered to vacate the premises forthwith, so there had unfortunately been no opportunity for any one of them to ply him with questions, unlike Mary, who, having gone upstairs to collect her belongings and denied admittance to Her Ladyship's room, had poured forth her tearful grievances into their ears in the safety of the kitchen. It all seemed very odd, especially as Sir Braden had not seen fit to call in the police and have Mitchell arrested, but since they could rely upon Sir Braden to dismiss them without a reference if they showed any curiosity, and to secure other employment without one was well-nigh impossible, they kept their thoughts to themselves, but it could not be argued that something mighty peculiar was going on at twenty-nine Cavendish Square.

As for Her Ladyship, it was not for them to give the lie to Sir Braden about her nervous disorder, all they knew was that no one would ever think it to look at her, especially with that sweet and beautiful face and always a kind word for every one of them. A real lady was the mistress, too good for Sir Braden if anyone were to ask them, but it seemed that since the arrival of Mitchell and Mary's replacements they seldom laid eyes on her and, when they did, they were given no chance to do more than pass a harmless pleasantry or to raise a domestic matter with her as that hard-nosed woman who looked after her ensured that they were given no opportunity to do so.

Mrs. Timms, who had been cook in the Collett household long before Sir Braden had come into the title, no more believed him when he told them about Mitchell any more than she did when he advised about Her Ladyship's delicate nervous condition, this being the reason he had brought in Eliza Boon, a woman he had told them who had long experience in dealing with ladies in his wife's unfortunate state of health. She may well, although Mrs. Timms seriously doubted whether anyone with a face on her that would turn milk sour could have anything but a most adverse effect on her patients, but one thing she did know and that was at no time did she believe the tales Eliza Boon put about in that Her Ladyship had had another mental relapse and was obliged to remain quiet in her room, any more than she did upon learning that she had suffered another delusional attack and had managed to hurt herself, making it necessary for her to keep to her room for days on end. It seemed to Mrs. Timms that Her Ladyship's mental disorder, not that she believed it for one moment, had come upon her quite suddenly about ten months or so back, in fact unless she was mistaken, and she was sure she wasn't, it all started about the same time Mitchell and Mary had unexpectedly been dismissed; yes, and now she came to think of it, it was the very day after her youngest had made her a grandma again!

In between these so-called nervous lapses, which apparently attacked her from time to time, Her Ladyship appeared to be her usual self, still venturing out, but not it seemed without Sir Braden or that hateful woman accompanying her, but in spite of being assured by Ellen, the upstairs parlour maid, that, at least according to what Eliza Boon had told her, it was merely to ensure that if Her Ladyship was suddenly taken ill there would be someone with her to convey her safely home, Mrs. Timms for one still had doubts about Her Ladyship's condition. Even before this supposed nervous disorder had come upon the mistress, who, from the very beginning of her marriage, had from time to time found it necessary to remain secluded in her room on the grounds that she had a migraine or something equally as incapacitating, Mrs. Timms had often gained the impression that Sir Braden, whose temper brooked no argument, subjected her to rather harsh treatment because no one would convince her that those dark circles under Her Ladyship's eyes or the bruises she had tried to hide with cleverly applied face powder had just appeared for no reason!

Mrs. Timms had deliberated several times whether to go and see Lady Shipton, a woman whom she knew held a fondness for the mistress, but each time she had decided against it, not because she did not have Her Ladyship's interests at heart, but it could so easily make bad infinitely worse, even so, this did not prevent Mrs. Timms from thinking that something was not quite right. Of course, not being a doctor she had no understanding of these nervous disorders, that went without saying, but nothing would persuade her into believing that Her Ladyship was suffering from any kind of mental illness at all, in fact it was her opinion there was nothing wrong with the mistress that being out of a marriage to a man who had a most violent temper would not cure.

Mrs. Timms, a no-nonsense and forthright woman, had more than once found it necessary to keep her tongue because nothing would convince her that Mitchell had helped himself any more than she believed the tales about the mistress, but upon being told first thing this morning that Her Ladyship had suffered another relapse during the night, making it necessary for her to keep to her room, her fears grew. In fact, so troubled in her mind was she about Her Ladyship that as she prepared Eliza Boon's dinner tray ready for Ellen to take up to her, it was all this plain-speaking woman could do to stop herself from taking the tray upstairs personally to Eliza Boon and giving her a piece of her mind as well as demanding to see the mistress.

Since Sir Braden had not deemed it necessary for her to stay with

Eleanor in view of her being unconscious, Eliza had waited only until he had left the house and Peterson had gone to *'The Old Bush'* to refresh himself before requesting her dinner to be brought up to her in the sitting room that Sir Braden had turned over to her. She knew perfectly well that neither she nor Peterson had found favour with the rest of the servants, Mrs. Timms especially, as well as the gossip and speculation which ran rife in the kitchen and the servants' quarters. However, since Eliza was not here to curry favour with them but to do all she could to prevent herself from facing a lengthy prison sentence and Peterson and Sir Braden from dangling at the end of a rope, she had no more to do with them other than what was necessary to further their cause.

Eliza may find herself drawn to Lady Collett but she was perfectly willing to put this to one side to ensure her own self-protection, and therefore she had not turned a hair when Sir Braden had given her a thorough beating and left her for dead on the floor. Despite Eleanor's fear, Eliza had not failed to notice the subtle change in her when she had returned home on her husband's arm last night, and knew perfectly well that someone other than Sir Braden was the reason for it, and whilst she could not say for certain that Lady Collett had told Lady Shipton's brother anything, the chances were very good that at some point she would, especially when Eliza considered the visit he had made this afternoon. According to Peterson, he had told him he had come on his sister's behalf… well, perhaps he had, but the fact remained he posed a threat, and therefore the sooner Sir Braden approached Sir Wilfred Moore about having his wife committed the better because there was no denying that the longer she resided in Cavendish Square the greater the risk would become. It came as no surprise to Eliza that Sir Braden had finally been brought round to her way of thinking because as she had told him at the outset it was impractical to keep his wife shut up in her room indefinitely, and even though the servants may not talk outside the house she was not fool enough to believe that they did not gossip among themselves.

Once Lady Collett was securely locked away then there would be nothing to prevent her from setting up in business again because there was no reason that Eliza could see to keep either herself or Peterson here any longer. Her ill-gotten gains had accumulated to quite a nice little sum over the years and with what she had received from selling her business, together with what Sir Braden had paid her, she could, if she wished, retire, but since there would be time enough to consider this once Lady Collett was safely out of the way Eliza shelved the question of her future for now, deciding it was time she checked on her prisoner.

As she climbed the stairs she was conscious of no remorse or regrets in being instrumental in having a young woman committed to an asylum any more than she was about any of her actions so far, on the contrary she regarded them with a practicality that bordered on complete detachment. She had no intention of being imprisoned and if all that stood in the way of this was having a woman put away to guarantee her silence, then she was more than prepared to do it.

Upon reaching the first landing she heard the clock in the hall strike half past nine, reasonably certain that Eleanor would most probably have regained consciousness by now and, hopefully, come to her senses by realising how futile it was to stubbornly refuse to tell them what they wanted to know. Had Eliza the least idea that Eleanor had managed to escape and was in fact at this very moment safely tucked away in Mount Street she would not have been so complacent. As it was, she unlocked the bedroom door without the least suspicion that the room was empty. As she had given instructions that no one was to enter the room as Her Ladyship was resting and not to be disturbed and she would see to her every need, the atmosphere was icily cold, the fire having long since died out as well as being in total darkness, but without even glancing to where Eleanor had been left lying on the floor, taking it for granted she was still there, Eliza unconcernedly switched on the light, a shocked gasp leaving her lips upon turning round to see there was no sign of her.

For several stunned moments she could do no more than stare at the spot where they had left Eleanor lying unconscious, unable to think where she could be, but gradually Eliza pulled herself together, reasoning that she could not have gone very far in the condition she was in, but a quick look under the bed and in the two huge wardrobes standing against the far wall evincing no sign of her, Eliza stared around the room as though one in a daze, until her eye fell upon the connecting door to Sir Braden's dressing room standing ajar. She could have sworn they had closed it behind them earlier when they left, in fact she was sure of it, and hurrying into the dressing room in the hope Eleanor was there, possibly hiding in one or other of the huge wardrobes or cupboards, Eliza's thorough search failed to find her and so too, to her dismay, did her equally thorough search of Sir Braden's bedroom.

It was while Eliza was casting a last glance around Sir Braden's bedroom, her fingers pressed to her temples in complete bemusement, that she caught sight of the bedroom door which gave access to the first landing standing open. She could not remember whether Sir Braden had closed it behind him or not, but try as she did she could not quite quell the sickening thought that somehow or other Eleanor had managed to get out, but only a little further thought was enough to tell Eliza that Eleanor could not have gone far in her condition and so she must surely be in the house somewhere. Eliza doubted very much whether Eleanor could have made it up the next flight of stairs leading to the second floor or even down the stairs to the hall to try to escape by way of the front door, but as this was something Eliza could not take for granted, she hurried back downstairs to check that it was securely locked. After seeing for herself that it was and Eleanor could not possibly have left the house by this way, Eliza decided to make a search of the ground floor, only to discover that her prisoner was not hiding in any one of the rooms, which meant she must somehow or other have managed to reach the second landing. As most of the rooms on this floor were guest rooms it could well be that Eleanor had sought refuge in one of them in the misguided belief that no one would think to look for her in any one of these impressive though seldom used apartments, and Eliza, having raced back up the stairs to the first landing, was just about to put her foot on the first step leading to the upper floor when a slight draught behind her made her pause and turn. It was then, to her horror, that she saw the discreetly tucked away door in the alcove leading to the disused back stairs standing open and, in that instant, she knew, with a sickening thud of her heart, that it could only have been her prisoner who had opened it.

At first Eliza wondered if Eleanor had only gone as far as the kitchens to seek sanctuary with Mrs. Timms, which would not be at all surprising considering the good relations which existed between them, but if this was in fact what Eleanor had done, then Eliza knew that Mrs. Timms would not need to have her young mistress's condition explained. Eliza neither liked nor trusted this forthright woman, but she had recognised at the outset that Mrs. Timms was by no means stupid and she would not fail to recognise Eleanor's bruises for what they really were, but as Eliza leaned over the iron balustrade to peer down the well of the stairs she knew that wherever Eleanor had gone it was certainly not to Mrs. Timms as only the basement door standing open could account for the cold draught of air which came up to meet her. As this stairway was no longer used due to Sir Braden's father having made several structural changes to the interior of the house, the servants now had to use the stairway situated at the other end of the kitchens which would lead them into the main part of the house via the rear of the hall, so none of them would see the basement door was open. Eliza had been resident in Cavendish Square long enough to know that today was the boot boy's monthly day off and as Peterson would know better than to leave it standing open it left only one other person, so unless her prisoner had feigned unconsciousness when she and Sir Braden had left her earlier, Eliza knew that it had to be Eleanor and no one else.

She could not even begin to think how Eleanor had managed to make her way to the basement area of the premises in the condition she was in and it briefly crossed Eliza's mind whether Eleanor, in an intermittent period of consciousness, had rung for one of the maids to help her. However, the more Eliza considered this possibility the more convinced she became that Eleanor had done no such thing, but had in fact somehow or other managed to make it all the way down to the basement on her own and, in view of this, Eliza decided against making enquiries in the kitchen which would not only draw the servants' attention to the fact that Her Ladyship had gone missing, meaning some pretty pertinent questions would be asked, but it could well set up a hue and cry for nothing. Upon reflection, Eliza decided it would be better to wait until Sir Braden returned so she could speak to him. Nevertheless, she could not discount the very real possibility that Eleanor, having miraculously made her way to the basement only to find she could get no further, was, even now, lying comatose in the basement passage or at the foot of the area steps and, needing no further prompting, Eliza sped down the two flights of stairs to the basement passageway. Except for a fine layer of snow which had gathered on the cold stone floor in and around the arc of the half-opened basement door, through which a flurry of snow was still coming in, the cold and dimly lit corridor evinced no sign of Eliza's escapee. It was certainly vexing, but undeterred she hurried along the passageway to the door, but no sooner had she pulled it further open to peer into the darkness to see if her prisoner was lying huddled outside or, failing this, any discernible footprints in the fresh covering of snow, she saw Peterson stumble in through the gate and ungainly descend the basement steps.

Unaware that he and Eliza, like Sir Braden, were under surveillance, much less the stirring events that had dramatically been played out in his absence, Peterson staggered unconcernedly down the basement steps just a little the worse for wear, paying no heed to the gate standing ajar, but the unexpected sight of the basement door standing wide open and Eliza Boon peering into the darkness, made him stop dead in his tracks. Upon setting eyes on him she unceremoniously took hold of his arm and virtually dragged him inside, the force of it almost causing him to fall over, telling him in a fierce whisper that the prisoner had somehow managed to escape, urgently demanding if he had seen her.

"Ain't sin a soul," he shook his head, shutting the door before taking off his hat and coat and shaking them out, hanging them on a hook in the narrow passageway. "Yer shua 'ers gawn?" he asked.

"Of course, I'm sure," she bit out. "I thought she was unconscious, but she couldn't have been." Her eyes narrowed into hard slits. "The cunning thing must have only been pretending. She must have heard everything. That's why she's made a bolt for it."

Peterson rubbed his chin thoughtfully. He knew it was imperative that their prisoner was found, but his potations as well as the cold had given him an appetite and he was in much need of his supper, but since Eliza deemed this as totally irrelevant when compared with the dangers which threatened them if Eleanor was not found and returned to Cavendish Square, she told him rather sharply that this was not the time to be thinking of food.

He may not possess the sharpest of minds but he knew danger when he smelled it, and whatever remnants of his liquid refreshment still lingered Eliza's startling announcement had the effect of sobering him up. Peterson knew as well as anyone that Lady Collett was armed with damaging information and although he had no hand in killing Annie Myers or Sir Philip Dunscumbe he *had* disposed of their bodies, but there was no way he could wriggle out of murdering his brother Dennis or Mitchell. Like Eliza, Peterson had no qualms about doing whatever was asked of him, but that innate sense of self-preservation had started him thinking. It was one thing to do something when no one knew about it but quite another when someone did, and although Lady Collett only held one piece of the jigsaw once she divulged that her husband had murdered Sir Philip it would not take the police long to put two and two together and come knocking on his door. He had no wish to climb the scaffold any more than the next man, but unless they found Lady Collett and got her safely back here to Cavendish Square double-quick, then the chances of that happening were more than odds on, but where to start looking for her had him in a puzzle.

Eliza, easily discounting the idea of Eleanor having tried to make it to Bruton Street as her father was out-of-town at the moment and the house closed up, had a pretty shrewd idea where Eleanor was, but for the life of her she had no idea how she had got from here to Mount Street in the condition she was in because although she had managed to leave her room and make her way down the back stairs and out of the house, it must have taken rather a lot out of her, then there was the weather to contend with. Eliza doubted very much whether Eleanor would have even considered the icy conditions in her desperate efforts to escape much less taking the time to retrieve a coat or something warm from one of her wardrobes, which meant that by the time she arrived on Lady Shipton's doorstep, because nothing would convince Eliza that she had not taken refuge there, she would have been practically frozen.

Of course, there was always the possibility that in her weakened condition and dazed state of mind she may not have made it to Mount Street, which meant she was either hiding somewhere outside or someone had offered her assistance and taken her to the nearest hospital, but only a moment's thought was enough to tell Eliza that this was most unlikely. Lady Collett was a familiar figure in society and should anyone have come to her aid they would surely have brought her home rather than take her to a hospital and, even if they had, they would have surely been apprised of such an eventuality by now. As Eliza had no idea that Lady Shipton's brother had involved himself in their affairs as well as investigating what they were desperately trying to avoid being made public, not to mention having the house and its members watched, he never so much as entered her head. Even so, like Peterson, she knew trouble when she smelled it and although it was logical to assume that Eleanor would be in no fit condition to tell anyone anything for a day or two at least, Eliza could not fool herself into thinking that Lady Shipton would not at some point get the truth out of Eleanor as well as wanting to know how she came to be so badly beaten up. Once she discovered all of this then nothing would keep them from facing the Queen's Bench; the first thing then was to find her, and Peterson, needing no urging, put on his hat and coat and hurriedly left the house to go and look for her, his hope of finding her and getting her back here before Sir Braden returned just as fervent as Eliza's.

Just as Jerry had rightly predicted, Peterson did not leave *'The Old Bush'* until almost an hour and a half after he had seen Tony drive away with Lady Collett in the hackney, shrewdly suspecting that his slow and unsteady walk back to Cavendish Square had more to do with how much he had imbibed rather than the treacherous weather conditions. Watching closely as Peterson slouched across the road Jerry then saw him disappear down the basement steps, leaning heavily on the rail, only to emerge again and step through the gate ten minutes later, pausing for a moment to look right and left as if undecided which way to go before glancing across at the Square's garden. Jerry, letting out a low-voiced curse, stepped silently back into the shadows with Arthur immediately behind him as he saw Peterson walk over to the garden which, due to the snow being reflected back from the light of the lamps, was dangerously illuminated, to stand by the gate peering in front of him in case Lady Collett was hiding behind one of the snow laden bushes. The slightest movement would be enough to alert Peterson to their presence and since they dared not even so much as raise their heads to see what he was doing, they waited with bated breath as they heard his heavy tread crunching on the snow-covered path, coming to a halt within a couple of feet of where they were hiding behind the bushes. Had Peterson not been focusing his attention solely on scanning the garden for a glimpse of Lady Collett in his direct line of vision, or had his vision not have been quite so blurred thanks to what had clearly been a heavy session at *'The Old Bush'*, he would have seen their footprints on the path where they had crossed over to this side of the garden which had not been totally obliterated by the fresh fall of snow, and Jerry, nudging his son and nodding his head to this effect, could only hope that Peterson would not chance to look down. He did not, but it seemed the devil of a long time before he finally turned round to make his way back to the gate, veering to the right down Cavendish Square towards Oxford Street, and Arthur, after a brief discussion with his father, began to follow him at a discreet distance.

Jerry, removing his hat and wiping his forehead, knew it had been a rather hair-raising few minutes, but having seen the light go on in the upstairs bedroom not half an hour before, it certainly confirmed his belief that they had discovered Lady Collett's disappearance and that Peterson was now looking for her. Jerry, taking himself to task for failing to anticipate such an eventuality as Peterson looking for her in the gardens, nevertheless took consolation from knowing that whatever heart-stopping moments he and Arthur had experienced, it was nothing to what Peterson and that Eliza Boon woman must clearly be feeling. Jerry could well imagine their panic in knowing that their prisoner, because the poor soul had certainly been nothing less, had escaped, and did not envy them having to tell Sir Braden the bad news. Whether Lady Collett had witnessed her husband commit cold-blooded murder or merely stumbled onto something which alerted her to the truth, the fact remained she knew enough to make her dangerous. Were it otherwise they would not have found it necessary to keep her so closely guarded. No more than Tony could Jerry be sure at this precise moment which way it was, but he for one had no regrets about helping her get away especially when he thought of the beating she had received, which he knew was not the first. Apart from Peterson's nocturnal comings and goings no one else had arrived or departed since Tony had left for Mount Street, and Jerry, having seen his son disappear from his sight in Peterson's wake, resumed the rest of his watch behind the bushes for the next few hours until his two other sons took over the remainder of the surveillance.

Sir Braden meanwhile, completely indifferent to the fact that he had left his wife lying on the floor as though dead following his brutal attack, was enjoying a well-dressed dinner washed down with several glasses of the finest wine in the company of a few convivial friends at his club followed by three glasses of the best French cognac and a Havana cigar over several games of cards, without the least suspicion of the stirring events taking place in Cavendish Square. He gave no more thought to the injuries he had inflicted upon Eleanor any more than he ever did and, as far as approaching Sir Wilfred Moore about having her committed was concerned, he regarded it as essential rather than something to feel regret over. Confident that he would very soon be rid of the risk his wife posed as well as knowing that Beatrice Shipton's brother would not linger any longer than necessary in England, together with rising from the card table a considerable winner, Sir Braden Collett arrived back in Cavendish Square just before fifteen past eleven o'clock in a tolerably tranquil frame of mind. Totally unaware that his movements had not only been followed but would subsequently be reported to the man who, had he but known it, had Eleanor safe in his care as well as taking on the mantle of his nemesis, he would not have entered his house in such a positive frame of mind.

Eliza, having searched the house again from top to bottom with no sign of Eleanor while Peterson was out looking for her, found it virtually impossible to just sit still in her sitting room and do nothing but await events, particularly as she had the very strong feeling that Sir Braden, despite his horror of a hue and cry being set up, would accuse her of not trying hard enough to find his wife, and had therefore decided to venture downstairs to the kitchen after all in the hope of gleaning something of Eleanor. Ellen, who held the privileged position of upstairs parlour maid, was just putting on her hat and coat to go out to meet her young man for half an hour when Eliza entered the kitchen, but upon hearing the reason for her unexpected foray downstairs Ellen could not help looking a little surprised, her hands stilling in the act of pulling on her gloves. Ellen, who had no more liking for Eliza Boon than Mrs. Timms did, showed her just enough respect to keep Sir Braden from taking her to task, but when Eliza repeated the question, a little more sharply this time, Ellen eyed her resentfully, saying that as she had herself told her only this morning that the mistress was poorly and would remain in her room fòr the rest of the day she had not laid eyes on her and knew nothing at all about Her Ladyship missing an earring.

Eliza, annoyed at finding herself in this position, bit back the retort on her lips, quickly amending her query by saying that it was not today Her Ladyship had lost the earring but yesterday, whereupon Ellen shrugged, promising she would search for it tomorrow, hurrying out of the kitchen on the words. Mrs. Timms, eyeing Eliza Boon closely, neither liked nor trusted her and made no effort to hide the fact and, unlike Ellen, was not fooled by such a harmless query, but Eliza, who would not put it past Mrs. Timms to hide her mistress, had no choice but to accept her word in that, like Ellen, she had not laid eyes on Lady Collett today and nor could she shed any light on the missing earring. Eliza, making her way back upstairs to the sitting room, had long since arrived at the conclusion that Mrs. Timms was definitely Eleanor's most stalwart partisan in Cavendish Square, and despite her assurances that she had not laid eyes on Her Ladyship the nagging doubt at the back of Eliza's mind that she had somehow assisted in her escape, persisted. She was in no doubt that Eleanor was at this very moment in Mount Street, but unless she had miraculously grown wings and flew there it would have been impossible for her to have either walked or called up a hackney herself which meant that someone must have done it for her, and that someone could well have been Mrs. Timms. Of course, it did not answer the question as to why, if Mrs. Timms had assisted her mistress, she had left the door to the basement steps standing open unless, of course, it was a deliberate tactic to avert suspicion, but however it was, the fact remained that Eleanor was now at large armed with damaging information. When Eliza had sent Peterson out to look for her it had been merely to satisfy Sir Braden that they had done everything possible to find her and not with any real hope that Peterson would do so, but as she waited anxiously in her sitting room for him to return to tell her what she already knew she could not help feeling a little apprehensive at the thought of informing Sir Braden that his wife had managed to escape.

With no sign of Lady Collett hiding anywhere within the immediate vicinity of Cavendish Square, Peterson decided to see if she had gone to Bruton Street because even though Eliza had discounted this possibility on the grounds of her father being currently out-of-town, she may, in her confused state of mind, have tried to make her way there, and hurriedly made off in that direction. To his disappointment, Sir Miles Tatton's town house was in total darkness and the windows shuttered, with no sign of Lady Collett either hovering outside or huddled on the step, but as it was as much in his and Eliza's interests as well as Sir Braden's to find Lady Collett before she could start talking, Peterson crossed over Berkeley Square until he came to Mount Street. Totally impervious to the biting cold, he walked down this deserted thoroughfare until he came to Sir Thomas Shipton's house and, after pondering the problem for several moments, at least as far as he was able, he decided to take up a position immediately opposite. As he was not as adept as Jerry and his sons in carrying out a surveillance without being seen, it was perhaps fortunate for Peterson that no one was close by to witness his intense interest in the house just across the way where Eliza was sure Lady Collett had taken refuge. She may be in no condition to say anything for quite some time, but he had not needed Eliza to tell him that once she did then everything they were striving for would all be for nothing and, were it at all possible, he would have gained access to the house there and then and removed Lady Collett from her sanctuary. This feat would certainly not be beyond him, but apart from the fact that Eliza had told him to merely spy out the land in Mount Street should he fail to come across her anywhere else, he had no idea which room she would be in and he felt quite sure that she would not be left alone. He had no doubt at all that he could cope with any number of combatants, but he would much rather deal with it quietly than embark on a bout of fisticuffs which would in all probably bring the law down on him so, instead, he stood for some little time with his hands dug deep into his pockets watching the house across the street.

Not only had Beatrice given Eleanor's predicament a lot of thought, but she was also fully conscious of the fact that Eleanor had nothing but the clothes she had on when Tony had found her. Since the poor child could not possibly wear even the undergarments again, being completely ruined, and it was just as impossible for either herself or one of the maids to go to Cavendish Square to collect some of her clothes, she decided to sort out one or two things from her own wardrobe which would hopefully suffice until other arrangements could be made, so leaving Tom to work on some papers in his study, she made her way upstairs to their bedroom. Due to a slight gap where the curtains did not quite meet in the middle the light from the street lamps flooded into the room, but just as she was about to pull them together before switching on the light the sight of a man standing on the opposite side of the street with his cap pulled low over his forehead and his hands thrust into his pockets looking in their direction, caught her attention. At first, she had no idea who it could be or why anyone would be standing about in a deserted street on such a dreadful night, but upon seeing him raise his head to enable him to look up at the upper windows she had no difficulty in recognising Peterson, Sir Braden Collett's supposed butler. She did not think he could see her, but so surprised was she that she instinctively gripped the edge of the curtain with suddenly nervous fingers before quickly stepping back in case he caught sight of her. The fact that he was here could only mean they had discovered Eleanor's disappearance and, for one awful moment, Beatrice wondered if he was going to try to gain entrance to the house and remove her, but only a moment's thought told her she was being ridiculous because even though they may believe Eleanor was here in Mount Street it was hardly likely that one or the other of them would break down the door to prove their suspicions, even so, she felt she ought to tell Tony. Slowly edging away from the window, she managed to reach the bedroom door, hardly daring to open it for fear that she would be seen in the light entering the room from the landing, but taking a deep breath she darted through it to hurry across to the guest room.

As Tony's presence seemed to soothe Eleanor, she gradually became less fretful and soon closed her eyes and went back to sleep; her last recollections being the words of endearment which had left his lips and the warm reassurance of his hands as they had held her cold one. Making himself comfortable in the armchair he had pulled up beside the bed, he looked at the bruised and swollen face of the woman he loved, not daring to think what would have happened had he and Jerry not come upon her. Tony had managed to glean enough from her incoherent mutterings to understand why she had risked everything in trying to escape and although he had a pretty shrewd notion that she had it in mind to come here to Bea, he doubted it had occurred to her that in her condition and the severe weather, she would never make it. He could only marvel at how she had managed to get as far as she had and dreaded to think what would have happened if she had run into Peterson or Collett instead of himself but, if nothing else, it was some comfort to him that not all her husband's bullying, although instilling fear into her, had totally browbeaten her into submission.

Beatrice's quiet entrance made him look up and in answer to her beckoning he rose to his feet, taking one look at Eleanor before he joined his sister on the landing. Upon hearing that Peterson was standing on the pavement across the street watching the house, Tony followed her into the big front bedroom she shared with Tom to stand unseen by the window, gently easing the thick brocade curtains apart to enable him to look down into the street.

"So," Tony mused, "they've discovered she's gone, have they!"

"Oh, Tony!" Beatrice cried, laying a hand on his arm. "Do you think he will try to gain admittance to the house and demand we give Eleanor up?"

"No," Tony shook his head, reassuringly patting her hand, "that's the one thing he won't do. It's my guess this Eliza Boon woman has merely instructed him to see if he can find her; they won't risk doing anything more than that until they have informed Collett she has disappeared."

"Yes, but…"

"Listen Bea," Tony told her calmly, "they may have a pretty shrewd idea that this is where she is, but they don't know for certain and, even if they did," he pointed out reasonably, "there's nothing they can do about it, especially having told me this afternoon that Eleanor has gone into the country to stay with friends."

"Well," Beatrice said determinedly, "even if they *do* know, just let them try to remove her; that's all!"

"*That's* my girl!" Tony grinned down at her. "I knew I could rely on you."

"I mean it, Tony," she nodded firmly. "What they have done to that poor child is nothing short of criminal, and *nothing* would induce me to hand her back to them. In fact," she added determinedly, "she is *never* going back there again!"

"Too right she's not!" Tony ground out. "Especially after what I have discovered tonight."

Beatrice looked sharply up at his suddenly stern profile, asking warily, "What have you discovered?"

"The reason for her escape," the harshness around his mouth not lost on his sister. "You know how she was trying to say something, but you could not make out what it was," she nodded, "well, I managed to piece it together." She looked an enquiry, holding her breath. "It seems our friend Collett," he ground out, "is going to have her committed to an asylum."

"Ah, no!" Beatrice cried, putting her fingers to her mouth, her eyes staring up at him in disbelief. "You don't mean it?"

"I *do* mean it," Tony said grimly.

"Oh, Tony!" Beatrice cried, shaking her head. "That's *iniquitous!*"

"It sure is," he agreed, "and it's my guess he's threatened her with it before."

"Oh, no wonder she's terrified!" Beatrice breathed. "What she must have suffered at his hands!"

"Yeah, a real nice guy is Collett!" Tony scathed.

"No wonder she tried to get away!" Beatrice shook her head. "I don't know what he deserves for such wickedness!" she exclaimed.

"Well I surely do!" he told her firmly, moving away from the window when he saw Peterson leave his post and walk away. "And I'm going to make sure he gets it! He's mighty fond of beating up on defenceless women well, he's going to find out what it's like to tackle someone his own size before much longer!"

"Oh, Tony," she exclaimed fretfully, "it's all my fault. I should have realised what…!"

"You're not to blame yourself, Bea," he told her firmly.

"Yes, but," she shrugged helplessly, "if only I had insisted on seeing Eleanor when I called upon her in Cavendish Square and not just accepted what they said, I may have…"

Tony shook his head. "You weren't to know." He smiled comfortingly down at her, taking hold of her agitated hands.

"No," she sighed, "but whilst I knew something was dreadfully wrong I never for one moment suspected what was really happening to Eleanor!"

"No one did," Tony reminded her, "but from now on," he told her determinedly, "no one is going to hurt her again; not Collett; not Peterson or that woman who calls herself a maid: *no one!*"

"Oh, but how I would love to see Collett's reaction when they tell him she has gone!" Beatrice cried, following Tony out of the room.

She would not have been disappointed. To say that Sir Braden Collett reeled at the news was a gross understatement, in fact his reaction was everything Beatrice hoped it would be. Incredulity, shock and overwhelming fear held him speechless for several minutes, his lips forming words which refused to come out, his face purple with rage as he turned his bulging pale blue eyes from Peterson to Eliza Boon, neither of whom could offer him any explanation to account for his wife's escape. Pushing them unceremoniously aside, he hurried up the stairs to Eleanor's room but, unfortunately, he was unable to glean anything more from the scene than Eliza had and, upon turning round to see that she had followed him, spluttered, "How could you have let this happen?"

"You told me there was no need for me to stay with her," she reminded him sharply, not liking the way he was turning the blame onto her. "Like you, I thought she was unconscious."

"Well, clearly she wasn't!" he bit out. "She must have only been pretending and heard everything we said about having her put away; deciding to make her escape while she could!"

"We have searched everywhere for her," Eliza told him again. "Peterson has even been to Bruton Street in case she went there."

"No," Collett shook his head, his eyes glinting, "she would not have gone there with her father being away." He eyed Eliza thoughtfully, saying at length, "She's in Mount Street; I'd stake my life on it!"

"I'm sure of it," she nodded, "that's I why I told Peterson to check there, but even though he saw nothing out of the ordinary I'm convinced that's where she is, but I can't see how she managed it; not in the condition she was in."

"It makes no difference how she got there," he bit out, "that's where she is right enough!"

"But, how *could* she? She could barely stand!" Eliza exclaimed. "She could not have walked from here to Mount Street. Besides," she pointed out, "someone surely would have seen her and brought her back here."

"Or maybe she didn't have to walk," he mused at length, having given it some thought.

"You mean a hackney?" she said sharply, her hard eyes narrowing. He nodded. "I've thought of that," she told him, "but she could not have called one up herself let alone pay the fare; perhaps one of the servants helped her?"

Collett shook his head. "No, they wouldn't *dare!*"

Having given it some thought Eliza had to admit he was right; she did not think that even Mrs. Timms would dare do anything to cross Sir Braden. "Who then?" she asked urgently.

"Childon," Collett nodded, his voice ominously quiet.

"Childon?" Eliza repeated. "You mean Beatrice Shipton's brother?"

"Yes," he said slowly, thinking it through as he went along. "What if," he looked down at her, "they arranged it between them last night?"

Eliza lips pursed at this, but having thought it over she shook her head. "No," she said firmly, "there would not have been enough time. Besides," she pointed out practically, "you said yourself they were in sight of you all night, and why should they even discuss Lady Collett's escape let alone arrange it when they had only just met?"

"Suppose it was not the first time they had met?" he said suggestively, his bulbous blue eyes searching her thin and pale face.

"*Not the first time*!" Eliza echoed, shocked. "If not last night, then when?" she demanded, gasping in disbelief as enlightenment suddenly dawned. "You don't seriously believe they met in Mount Street yesterday morning?"

Collett thought for a moment. Suppose; only suppose, they *had* met yesterday morning when Eleanor had visited in Mount Street? After all, she *was* out of sight of Eliza's watchful eyes for at least fifteen minutes and who was to say that Childon had not seen her then? Collett's eyes narrowed as he looked down at Eliza and although he easily acquitted her of lying about what had taken place, after all she had just as much to lose as he did, it was just the kind of thing Beatrice Shipton could well have arranged, but why? Why should she arrange a secret meeting with her brother and Eleanor upstairs if they had never met before? To deliberately go to the lengths of contriving a ruse about some cape or other to get his wife out of the room could only mean they *had* met before, but where? Of course, Covent Garden! It was Childon who had tricked him into leaving his box! But why? Collett had no recollection of seeing him sitting in the box on the opposite side of the auditorium with his sister, but he must have been there, but why had he played that trick on him? Why had he felt the need to get him out of the way? To speak to Eleanor certainly, but there had to be more to it than that. He could not deny that his wife was rather a taking little thing, in fact she was exceedingly beautiful, but surely no man, not even one like Childon with his Colonial 'care for nobody' attitude, would do such a thing merely to gain an introduction to a woman he had taken a fancy to and one who was attending the opera in company with her husband? Why then? Why had he tricked him? Collett cast his mind back, and then it came to him. Beatrice Shipton admitted herself that she had seen them in the box opposite before the beginning of the second act and she must have pointed Eleanor out to her brother who, no doubt through their opera glasses, had not only decided he liked what he saw and wanted to get to know Eleanor better, but had also witnessed his treatment of her and elected to put a stop to it. Yes, that must have been it!

Were it not for the seriousness of the matter Collett could almost have laughed at such gung-ho cowboy tactics, but the fact remained that through Childon's meddlesome interference he stood on the brink of exposure and a walk to the scaffold because it was stretching optimism too far to expect Eleanor to keep her mouth shut. Collett knew that she would be in no fit condition to say anything to anybody for a few days, but once her injuries began to heal it was only to be expected that Beatrice Shipton and her brother would want to know how she had come by them, not that they could be in any doubt and, once they knew that, it was only a short step to discovering about Sir Philip Dunscumbe, and Collett felt reasonably sure that it would not take Childon long to find out about what happened to Annie Myers resulting in Dennis Dunscumbe's supposed suicide as well as Mitchell's carefully contrived death. It was useless to fool himself into believing that Eleanor would not say anything, she would, particularly when he considered that Childon appeared to have taken quite a liking to Eleanor and, when faced with his gentle coaxing, it went against all reasoning to suppose she would not respond to him especially when Collett recalled the look on her face when she had danced with him last night; a look he had never seen on his wife's face before.

No, Eleanor was no more indifferent to Childon than he was to her, but this did not necessarily mean they had arranged an escape between them and, this being so, how did Eleanor manage to get to Mount Street? Ordinarily it was only a short step from Cavendish Square, but for one in her condition, not to mention the freezing temperatures and the treacherous state of the roads and pavements, it would have been virtually impossible, in fact Collett failed to see how she could have made it. She must have had help, there was no way she could have managed it on her own and that help had to come from Childon and no other! He began to wonder whether a secret assignation had been made between the two of them which would have made it necessary for Eleanor to sneak out of the house to meet Childon, probably in the Square's garden, but no sooner had this thought occurred to him than he discounted it if, for no other reason than she knew it would be impossible for her to leave the house with Peterson and Eliza on constant watch. No, the more Collett thought about it the more reasonable it seemed that Eleanor must have feigned unconsciousness and overheard them discussing his intention of contacting Sir Wilfred Moore tomorrow about having her committed as well as hearing him announcing to Eliza that he was visiting his club and that there was no need for her to stay with her, Eleanor had simply taken the chance when it presented itself. In view of this there was no way Childon could have known what she was going to do which left the question as to how did he just happen to be in Cavendish Square at the precise moment Eleanor was making her escape?

Nothing would convince him that Eleanor was not now safely ensconced in Mount Street and that Childon had seen her safely there, but as he had discarded all the possible reasons to account for him being on hand at the right moment, Collett was left with only one conclusion and that was Childon must have been lingering outside the house, probably hidden in the Square's garden, either in the vain hope of catching sight of her or for some other motive which momentarily escaped him. "No," he said slowly, looking down at Eliza, "she's in Mount Street right enough and Childon helped her there, and it's only a matter of time before she starts talking!"

Eliza, who had been thinking along the same lines as Collett, knew that sooner or later their absconded prisoner would talk, and since she had no more wish than he did to face the Queen's Bench a way had to be found of preventing Eleanor from bringing all to ruin. "Yes," Eliza nodded, her thin face screwed up in thought, "she will. It's a pity though," she criticised subtly, "that you instructed Peterson to inform callers that she went into the country this morning to visit friends because it means we can't go there enquiring for her."

Collett looked annoyed at this, but biting down the blistering accusation that had she looked in on his wife sooner than she did she could well have prevented this from happening, but since he needed Eliza's help too much he said, in a more moderate tone than he ordinarily would have, "Well, since we can't go there openly we shall have to try to get her out. Where's Peterson?" he asked abruptly.

"No," Eliza shook her head, laying a restraining hand on Collett's arm, her agile brain having rapidly assessed the situation, "that's not the answer, Sir Braden."

"Then what is?" he demanded, the thought of what could possibly be the outcome of tonight's fiasco, especially if Eleanor disclosed what she saw that night, rendering him somewhat tetchy.

Eliza eyed him narrowly for a moment, beginning to see that she was gaining the ascendancy, particularly as recent events had shown her that despite his violent temper and aggressive behaviour he was not, when under severe duress or panic, capable of either thinking coherently or working out a means of extricating himself from his difficulties. It seemed then, that once again it was to fall to her to rid themselves of a problem, and although it would take no little thought to bring it off right, it was most certainly not beyond her capabilities. Immoral and self-serving she may be, but no one could say of Eliza Boon that she was not capable of great cunning and inventiveness when the occasion demanded and, as she made her way to her room some little time later, having left Sir Braden with the brandy decanter to fret and fume over this evening's events, so confident was she of coming up with a plan to stop Eleanor from talking once and for all that at no point did she even think it remotely doubtful.

It was seldom, if ever, anyone had managed to pull the wool over her eyes, but however reluctant she was to admit it this was precisely what Beatrice Shipton had done by her cleverly contrived ruse in getting Eleanor out of the room. Bearing in mind the affection this woman obviously had for Eleanor, it was reasonably safe to assume that she would make sure her young friend was not left on her own for very long, especially in the condition she was in, which meant that gaining access to her was going to prove extremely difficult, if not impossible, particularly as both she and Peterson were known to her. It could well be that Lady Shipton had even called in a doctor to tend Eleanor, but this did not worry Eliza unduly because although any medical practitioner worth his salt would recognise at a glance how she had come by her injuries, Eliza felt it reasonably safe to say that, apart from Eleanor being in no fit state to answer any questions for the time being much less name her assailant, it was extremely doubtful whether Beatrice Shipton or her brother would divulge the perpetrator of such an assault on Eleanor's behalf. If Eliza's summing up of the crisis they faced was correct, and she was sure it was, then it was a realistically foregone conclusion that the inhabitants of Mount Street would much prefer to mull things over before they said anything to a doctor or, indeed, anyone, about Eleanor's injuries and how she had sustained them and, certainly, not until they had discussed it with her.

This brother of Beatrice Shipton's may well be familiar with the events surrounding Sir Philip Dunscumbe's murder, after all his newspapers had covered the story along with all the rest but, even so, Eliza felt reasonably confident that he had no idea it was Sir Braden who had inflicted those fatal injuries or the events leading up to them. A wife may not be able to give evidence incriminating to her husband, but the fact remained that once Eleanor recovered sufficiently it was only a matter of time, perhaps days, before she succumbed to the joint coaxing of Beatrice Shipton and her brother and, once that happened, it would not be long before the whole story came out. The moment it did, there would be nothing either she or Collett could do to stave off the inevitable because Eliza could not fool herself into believing that Childon would not trace events back to Annie Myers and Dennis Dunscumbe, he would and, having linked everything together, no court of law would need Lady Collett's testimony, especially when Eliza considered that Sir Braden had a most unfortunate tendency to lose his head in a crisis. In fact, she felt it relatively safe to say that Sir Braden, when faced with relentless questioning, would soon lose what common sense he had thereby eventually condemning himself out of his own mouth, and taking her and Peterson with him. Far better then, to lock the stable door before the horse bolted, but whilst Eliza admitted that gaining access to the stable in the first place momentarily eluded her, at no point did it even so much as cross her mind that she would not.

Chapter Fourteen

Despite Sir Braden's efforts, fully supported by Eliza Boon, to keep the lid on his wife's escape for as long as possible by informing the staff that Her Ladyship had, regrettably, suffered another relapse during the night and was not to be disturbed under any circumstances, Mrs. Timms, unlike the rest of the servants, was not fooled for one moment. Apart from the fact that she neither liked nor trusted Eliza Boon, so concerned was she over her mistress that nothing would disabuse her mind that something rather havey-cavey was going on especially when she considered that tale last night about a missing earring, and although she had no idea what this could possibly be, she felt convinced that something was not right and decided the time had come to put her concerns to Lady Shipton, a woman whom she knew had a particular fondness for her young mistress. Mrs. Timms was neither fanciful nor prone to indulging her imagination, but this business about Lady Collett's so-called mental disorder had played on her mind for some little time, and realising that she could not just sit back another minute and do nothing she decided to pay a visit in Mount Street immediately after breakfast was out of the way. Not wanting to entrust her concerns to Ellen or any of the other servants for fear of it getting back to Sir Braden, she therefore kept her own counsel when asked by Susan the second parlour maid why she was putting her hat and coat on. "Just an errand, dearie," she nodded briskly, pulling on her gloves. "I'll be back in the shake of a lamb's tail!"

Since it was not Susan's place, or any of the servants for that matter, to question Cook, she merely nodded and carried on with her jobs, but Pearl, who needed no excuse to break off from her scullery duties, looked up from her task in scrubbing the floor to ask, "But wot'll I do if the Masta wonts sumut'?"

"The same as you always do," Mrs. Timms told her firmly, "nothin'. Ellen'll see to all that. Now, don't you be dawdlin'; when you finish scrubbin' that floor there's the silver to clean."

"Yes, Missis Timms," Pearl replied dutifully.

"And don't you be thinkin' that because my back's turned you can shirk off with that lazy good for nothin' Albert, my girl!" she warned darkly.

Upon hearing Mrs. Timms mention the boot-boy-cum-general-factotum Pearl's eyes lit up, but quickly bending her head over her scrubbing-brush said, mournfully, "No, Missis Timms."

"Just see you don't," Mrs. Timms warned, picking up her bag before heading for the basement area door, hoping that Lady Shipton would not have stepped out before she arrived in Mount Street. She supposed she ought to have written her a note first requesting to see her, but as her concerns, especially after what she had learned yesterday about Lady Collett having succumbed to a nervous attack the night before which had made it necessary for her to keep to her room and then to be told this morning that she had suffered yet another attack during the night, had increased to the point where she was utterly convinced something was seriously wrong, she consoled her conscience by telling herself that observing the proprieties would not help her young mistress and, in this determined frame of mind, proceeded on her way to Mount Street.

Having handed his vigil over to Sarah so he could bathe and shave and change his clothes, Tony eventually arrived downstairs a little after eight o'clock looking remarkably wide awake. Beatrice, convinced that he could not have had much sleep despite his assurances that he had had all he needed, looked doubtfully at him, but since it was obvious he had not minded in the least spending the night in an armchair by Eleanor's bedside, she did not press the point.

Beatrice was not altogether surprised to learn that their patient had spent a somewhat fretful night, Eleanor's sleep being disturbed by recurring attacks of delirium which had seen her restlessly moving her head from side to side on the pillow with a jumbled mass of words incoherently leaving her lips, clearly the effects of the concussion. As for Eleanor's physical injuries, which were severe, although it would be a while before she would be able to open her eyes properly as well as the swelling to her lips subsiding, Tony assured his sister that they would heal in time. Beatrice, having to quickly search for her handkerchief, vigorously blew her nose, telling her brother in no uncertain terms that if Collett was not called to account for Eleanor's injuries if not his other crimes, then it would be a gross miscarriage of justice, to which he fervently agreed.

"I'll go up to her now," she said a little unsteadily, pouring a cup of tea to take upstairs to her patient who, she felt sure, would welcome a hot drink, providing of course, she was awake.

"She was asleep when I left her," Tony told her gently, "but if she is awake, then a hot drink will most certainly do her good."

"Yes," Beatrice nodded, then, her lovely eyes mistily looking up at him, cried, "Oh, Tony!" putting the cup and saucer down. "How could anyone be so cruel and wicked to do such a dreadful thing?" Whereupon she fell into tears.

"I'm damned if *I* know, Bea," Tony told her frankly, holding her in his arms as she gave vent to her emotions, "and that's the truth."

"She… she will get well, won't she?" she asked hopefully when her crying had abated.

"Yes," he promised her, "but it will take time and plenty of rest."

"Well," Beatrice nodded, easing herself out of his arms, "she can be certain of both here."

"You're a treasure, Bea," he smiled down at her.

She gave a wobbly little laugh, before saying, "I… I'd better not let Eleanor see me like this."

"It doesn't matter if she does," Tony said gently, kissing the top of her head, "she already knows you have a heart," upon which she picked up the cup and saucer and hurriedly left the breakfast room.

No one looking at Tony as he sat down to a substantial breakfast several minutes later would have had the least guess that he had hardly closed his eyes all night. Eleanor had indeed been extremely fretful and not all his soothing had calmed her, but eventually she had fallen into a light sleep which, unfortunately, had soon been disturbed by a nightmare, causing several frightened cries to leave her swollen lips. In one swift movement, he was sitting beside her on the bed holding her shivering body close against him, gently soothing her fears until gradually she became more calm, resting her throbbing head against his comforting shoulder, content to remain warm and protected against him until she finally fell asleep.

He was neither a violent nor an aggressive man, but as he had held that pain-racked body in his arms the vow he had made earlier to repay Sir Braden Collett in kind for such despicable brutality was renewed with vigour. Were it at all possible he would have no compunction in seeking out Collett right now, but there was more at stake than his own feelings, and although it went very much against the grain with him to allow such brutality to pass Tony realised that should he confront Collett about the vicious treatment of his wife it could well jeopardise everything he was striving for in bringing him to justice for cold-blooded murder. Be that as it may, however, Tony was fully determined that, at some point, he would mete out to Collett what he had so cruelly and callously meted out to his wife, but before he could go any further with these thoughts, the sound of voices in the hall intruded on his consciousness.

Mrs. Timms, having made short work of Bennett's insistence that Lady Shipton was not receiving, strongly recommended that he tell Her Ladyship that she wanted to speak to her on a private matter which, she nodded, was urgent and, begging pardon she was sure, but she was not leaving here until she had. Bennett, recognising a forthright and strong-minded woman when he met one, knew she meant precisely that so, inclining his head, said he would inform Her Ladyship if she would care to wait. Nodding her head, Mrs. Timms, clutching her bag in front of her ample proportions, watched as he majestically climbed the stairs, experiencing neither qualms nor regrets in intruding on Lady Shipton when her own young mistress was in urgent need of help, which she would take her dying oath she was, and spent the next few minutes rehearsing what she would say, but upon setting eyes on the sylph-like figure tripping lightly down the stairs towards her some minutes later, so far removed from what she had imagined Lady Shipton to be, she felt momentarily at a loss for words.

"Mrs. Timms?" Beatrice smiled, holding out her hand. "Forgive me if I have kept you waiting."

"I'm sorry, m'lady," she bobbed a curtsy, "I did not mean to intrude, but…"

"It's quite all right," Beatrice smiled. "I understand you wish to speak to me on an urgent matter?"

"Yes, m'lady," Mrs. Timms bobbed another curtsy, "I do. Beggin' your pardon, I'm sure, m'lady."

"In that case," Beatrice smiled, "why don't we make ourselves comfortable in here?" indicating the drawing-room with a sweep of her hand, giving Mrs. Timms no opportunity to decline the invitation by gently shepherding her into this spacious and comfortable apartment.

Upon being informed by Bennett that a Mrs. Timms had arrived on the doorstep wanting to speak to her urgently on a private matter and refused to leave the premises until she did so, Beatrice hesitated before agreeing to see her especially as she had never before heard of this woman, but for some reason she could neither explain nor understand she had the very strong feeling it was in some way connected with Eleanor and therefore agreed to see her, but not before requesting Bennett to ask His Lordship to join her in the drawing-room in a few minutes. One look at Mrs. Timms was enough to inform Beatrice of her calling and, like Bennett, recognised the strong-minded and plain-speaking woman behind the politeness, but although she could only hazard a guess as to what she wanted to discuss with her she nevertheless deemed it prudent to conduct what she believed was going to be a somewhat sensitive matter in private. "Please, do sit down," she invited. Waiting only until Mrs. Timms had settled her ample proportions in an armchair, Beatrice smiled, saying encouragingly, "Now, tell me, what is it that has brought you here, and in such dreadful weather?"

"I'm sure I beg your pardon, m'lady," Mrs. Timms nodded, "but…" breaking off immediately as the door opened and Tony walked in.

"Oh, Tony!" Beatrice smiled. "Please, allow me to introduce Mrs. Timms to you. Mrs. Timms," she invited, "I would like you to meet my brother, Viscount Childon."

"How do you, Mrs. Timms," Tony smiled, holding out his hand to her. "No," he shook his head, "please, do not get up."

"Thankin' you kindly, m'lord." She bobbed a curtsy as she took his hand before resuming her seat.

"Tony," Beatrice told him, when he took his seat beside her on the sofa, "Mrs. Timms has paid us a visit to discuss a private matter." Then, looking across at her visitor, said, "Mrs. Timms, you may speak quite freely in front of my brother, I promise you."

After glancing from one to the other and liking what she saw, said, "Thankin' you kindly, m'lady," she nodded. "I don't know what you must be thinkin' about me comin' 'ere like this, m'lady, but I want you to know," Mrs. Timms assured them, "that I'm not one for tellin' tales out of school, so to speak. I'd like that understood!"

"No, of course, not!" Beatrice agreed soothingly. "But clearly you are upset over something which, I believe, you think I can help you with."

"That's why I'm 'ere, m'lady. I'm sure I beg your pardon for the intrusion," Mrs. Timms apologised, "but… well, I wouldn't be 'ere now except that… well, the thing is, m'lady, I know you 'ave a fondness for 'Er Ladyship."

"Her Ladyship?" Beatrice enquired, knowing instinctively to whom she referred.

"Lady Collett, m'lady," Mrs. Timms nodded. "I'm cook for Sir Braden, you see," whereupon she burst into tears.

Waiting until she had retrieved a handkerchief from her bag and vigorously blown her nose, Beatrice asked gently, "Has something happened to Lady Collett?"

"As to that, m'lady," Mrs. Timms nodded, giving her nose another brisk blow, "I don't know, but what I *do* know, is that I'm terribly afraid for 'er." Giving her eyes a quick wipe, she looked from one to the other saying, "I've thought many a time about comin' to see you, m'lady," she admitted, "so worried I've been an' that's the truth, but then I thought no because I could well make bad worse."

"Bad worse?" Beatrice repeated, faintly.

"Yes, m'lady," she nodded again.

"May I ask, Mrs. Timms," Tony intervened calmly, "has something happened to make you change your mind about coming here now?"

"*Indeed* there 'as, m'lord!" She sniffed into her handkerchief. "Not that I believe it or ever 'ave, no matter what they say," she told him forcefully, "no, nor will I, not if I live forever I won't!

"Believe what, Mrs. Timms?" Tony pressed gently.

She sniffed again, but pulling herself together, said, "They say 'Er Ladyship suffers from mental disorders, m'lord."

"Who says she does?" he asked, leaning forward a little.

"Sir Braden, m'lord," she told him, "an' *that woman!*" she disparaged. "Although if she's ever nursed anyone in 'er life before you can call me a 'nodcock'!"

"'That woman'?" Tony enquired, knowing perfectly well who she meant.

"Yes, m'lord," she confirmed. "Calls 'erself Eliza Boon. *I'd Eliza Boon 'er* given 'alf the chance!" she said fiercely. "*What*!" she scorned. "'Er nurse anyone with a face that looks like a butcher's saw! I wish I may see it!"

"Mental disorders!" Beatrice repeated in a strangled voice, glancing at her brother, this statement reinforcing what he had gleaned from Eleanor's ramblings last night.

"I don't wonder you stare, m'lady," Mrs. Timms told her, having recourse to her handkerchief. "Well," she repeated firmly, "I don't believe it, *no*," she said emphatically, "not even when they tell us that 'Er Ladyship 'as 'ad a relapse, like yesterday and then again this mornin' an' 'as to be kept to 'er room with no one but Sir Braden an' that 'ard-nosed woman allowed anywhere near 'er!"

Beatrice saw Tony's mouth harden, but when he spoke his voice was perfectly controlled. "Is that what Sir Braden told you this morning, Mrs. Timms?"

"Yes," she nodded, "it was, m'lord, and that Eliza Boon woman was with 'im. Called us all up to the drawin'-room 'e did, early it was, told us that 'Er Ladyship 'ad 'ad another relapse an' she was to be kept quiet; no one, not even Ellen, that's the upstairs parlour maid, m'lady," she digressed, looking at Beatrice, "was to go anywhere near 'er. An' it's not the first time, m'lord, that we've been told 'Er Ladyship 'as 'ad a relapse." She shook her head, wiping her eyes. "Well, I don't know about mental disorders, m'lord," she told him frankly, wiping her eyes again, "an' that's the truth, but I don't believe it; no, nor when they say that dear sweet creature 'as delusions. 'Urts 'erself they tell us, don't know what she's doing when she 'as a relapse. That's why she's never allowed out alone in case she's taken poorly, m'lord, or," she said doubtfully, "that's what we're told."

Beatrice felt Tony stiffen but not by a word or gesture did he betray himself; his voice perfectly calm. "Why don't you believe them when they tell you about Lady Collett's mental disorder?"

"Because I *don't*," Mrs. Timms told him firmly. "'Sides," she wanted to know, "if 'Er Ladyship is as ill as they say, then why 'aven't they taken 'er to a doctor or called in Sir Braden's own doctor, Sir Wilfred Moore? I'll tell you why, m'lord," she told him vigorously, "because she's not ill, that's why!"

"But why should Sir Braden lie about it?" Tony asked calmly, more convinced than ever that it was all tied up with Sir Philip Dunscumbe.

Mrs. Timms sniffed. "As to that, my lord, I don't know," she said candidly. "Sir Braden," she inclined her head meaningfully, "meanin' no disrespect I'm sure," not very convincing on this point, "not bein' the kind o' man you'd question, so to speak, but that somethin' is goin' on

I'm sure, an' nothin' an' no one," she told him defiantly, "will make me think different. When I think of that dear sweet child," dabbing her eyes at the recollection, "always a smile an' a kind word she 'as, at least," she amended, "she did, until that nasty piece o' work who calls 'erself Eliza Boon came along! *Now*," she nodded vigorously, "not one of us ever sees 'Er Ladyship alone; you can trust that Boon woman for that! Every mornin' m'lady," she looked at Beatrice, "when I went up to see 'er about the day's menu," she shook her head, "always 'ad a cup o' tea with me she did; askin' me about me family an'…" then, recollecting herself, she leaned forward in her seat, looking back at Beatrice and saying earnestly, "I came 'ere today m'lady because I know you 'ave a fondness for my mistress an' to ask if there's *anythin'* you can do to 'elp 'er!"

Before Beatrice could open her mouth, Tony said calmly, "There is no need for you to worry over Lady Collett, I assure you."

"Indeed, m'lord, I *do* worry, an' that's the truth," she told him honestly. "When I think of *that woman* bein' left in charge of the mistress, who looks more like a prison warder than a nurse, not that I think for one minute that's what she is, it makes me turn cold! An' as for that man Peterson," she scorned, "I doubt 'e's ever been a butler in 'is life!"

"I assure you, Mrs. Timms," Tony smiled, "no harm will come to Lady Collett, you have my word on that." Before she could respond to this he asked, "But tell me, what do you know of this Eliza Boon and Peterson?"

"That's just it, m'lord," she said firmly, vigorously nodding her head, "nothin! There they were one mornin' out o' nowhere an' there they still are!"

"But what happened to Mitchell and Lady Collett's maid, Mary?" Beatrice enquired.

"Hm!" Mrs. Timms snorted. "Dismissed!"

"Dismissed?" Beatrice repeated. "Why?"

"As to that, m'lady," Mrs. Timms nodded, "your guess is as good as mine. Meanin' no offence," she told her, "but accordin' to Sir Braden, 'avin' called us all up to 'is study one mornin', yes," she said disgustedly, "even before Pearl could get the fire goin' in the kitchen, that from now on Peterson would be butler in Mitchell's place because Mitchell 'ad been ordered to leave as 'e'd been caught stealin'. Well," she nodded, leaning forward a little, "you could 'ave knocked me down with a feather, m'lady, an' that's the truth! 'Onest as the day's long was Mitchell, been with the family well before Sir Braden's father took ill an' passed on."

"And Mary?" Beatrice enquired.

"Well, m'lady," Mrs. Timms took a deep breath, "'er ma," she explained, as though she was talking to an old friend, having taken quite a liking to Beatrice and her brother, "'ad been taken ill, all of a sudden it was," she nodded. "Well, Mary was right worried about 'er so 'Er Ladyship, when she knew, said it would be all right for 'er to go an' spend a few days with 'er, 'til she was better like, sayin' that she would do very well with Ellen, well," she said, almost conspiratorially, leaning a little more forward, "off goes Mary to see 'er ma never suspicionin' that when she gets back she'd be let go."

"Are you saying that Lady Collett dismissed Mary?" Beatrice asked, surprised.

"No, m'lady," Mrs. Timms shook her head, "not 'Er Ladyship, Sir Braden. 'E told 'er," she nodded, "that she'd taken a longer leave of absence than 'Er Ladyship 'ad granted 'er. Well, very upset Mary was," she assured them, "'specially as Sir Braden took no notice of 'er an' accusin' 'er of lyin' an' takin' advantage. Well, Mary was cryin' to us in the kitchen before she left like you've never seen, sayin' that she'd not even been allowed to speak to 'Er Ladyship an' she who 'ad been with 'er before she married Sir Braden!"

"And Mitchell," Tony asked, "did he say anything to you before he left?"

"No, m'lord," Mrs. Timms shook her head, "we didn't see 'im. In fact, 'e'd left the 'ouse well before Sir Braden told us 'e'd been caught stealin' an' would no longer be employed."

Tony thought a moment, asking at length, "So, Mitchell and Mary were both dismissed by Sir Braden on the very same day?"

"Yes," Mrs. Timms confirmed, "an' quite a shock it was too, m'lord, I can tell you! But it just so 'appened, m'lord," she told him, "that none of us expected Mary back so soon; 'Er Ladyship 'avin' told 'er to take as long as needed, but came back early because 'er ma got well quicker than thought."

"And Peterson and Eliza Boon were already established in the house when Sir Braden informed you of this?" Tony queried.

"Yes, m'lord, they were, an' been so ever since!" she snorted.

"Mrs. Timms," Tony smiled, "can you, do you think, remember

when this was?"

"Yes, m'lord, I can," she smiled, her bosom swelling, "it was on the Saturday mornin' 'e dismissed them, the thirtieth April last year it was."

"That's very precise," he smiled. "What makes you so certain of the date?"

"Because, m'lord," she nodded, "the day before, Friday the twenty-ninth, my youngest went an' 'ad 'er third an' it was that same night that 'Er Ladyship attended a concert at the Royal Albert 'All. I remember it most particler m'lord because we were all surprised that Sir Braden allowed 'er to go on 'er own, well," she corrected herself, "she was not alone as such, a friend of 'ers went with 'er, *but*," she said firmly, "I *can* tell you that 'Er Ladyship returned 'ome earlier than expected, the concert, m'lord, 'avin' finished earlier than they thought."

"Do you know if Sir Braden received any visitors that night at all?" Tony asked, his smile having a most beneficial effect on Mrs. Timms.

"No, m'lord," she shook her, "I don't. You see," she explained, almost apologetically, "that night I went to visit my youngest, 'er 'avin' just gone an' 'ad 'er third like I say. I didn't get back until about eleven o'clock."

"Forgive me, Mrs. Timms," Tony smiled, "but if you did not arrive back until late how do you know that Lady Collett returned home early due to the performance finishing sooner than expected?"

Not at all put out by this, Mrs. Timms said, "Ellen, m'lord, upstairs parlour maid. A good girl," she told him firmly, "but don't miss much, if you take my meanin'. Anyway," she nodded, "she was just comin' back, sneaked out when my back was turned to meet that young man who works for Mr. Titley at the stables round the corner," she told Beatrice indulgently, "only a few minutes after seven o'clock it was, when she sees 'Er Ladyship pull up outside."

Tony nodded, then asked, "Did you see Mitchell at all when you returned to Cavendish Square?"

"I *did* see 'im yes," she confirmed, "but not to speak to mind. You see," she told him in answer to his raised eyebrow, "'e was asleep in 'is pantry with the newspaper lyin' on 'is stomach an' 'avin' no wish to disturb 'im I made my way to my room."

"And the following morning you learned of his dismissal?" Tony confirmed.

"That's it, m'lord, yes," she sighed. "A terrible shock it was, too."

"Tell me, Mrs. Timms," Tony raised a questioning eyebrow, "do you know where Mitchell and Mary are now?"

"Well, as for Mitchell, m'lord, no I don't. You see," she informed him, "'e never married an' 'ad no family to speak of… well, I say that," she nodded, "'e did 'ave a widowed sister, lived Bromley way but passed on, or so I 'eard, over a year back, so when I 'eard Sir Braden say 'e'd been dismissed, I couldn't for the life of me think where 'e'd go because 'is 'ome 'ad always been Cavendish Square. As for Mary," she shrugged, "I imagine 'er went back 'ome to 'er ma because Sir Braden, from what Mary told me, never even gave 'er a reference!"

"And where does she live, do you know?" Tony smiled.

"Well," Mrs. Timms pondered, considering the matter, "I seem to recall it bein' Dagenam way, m'lord, but if it's an address you're wantin'," she shook her head regretfully, "I can't oblige."

"No," Tony smiled, shaking his head. "You have been most helpful. Thank you, Mrs. Timms."

"It's a pleasure an' no mistake," she smiled, having taken a real liking to her hostess's brother, "but if you *could* see your way clear to 'elping 'Er Ladyship," heaving herself out of her chair.

"Mrs. Timms," Tony smiled, rising to his feet, "it is clear you have Lady Collett's best interests at heart."

"*I do, indeed,* m'lord," she said vehemently. "I only wish there was somethin' I could do to 'elp 'er!"

"You already have," Tony said quietly. Then, after casting a brief glance at Beatrice, he looked down at Mrs. Timms, saying, "I take it you have told no one of your feelings and concerns or that you have come here today?"

"No, m'lord," she told him unequivocally. "I'm not sayin' there's not talk in the servants' quarters and the kitchen because there is, which is natural," she nodded, "an' I'm not sayin' I 'aven't questioned things with them, because I 'ave, but I've *never once* said a word to any one of them about 'ow I really feel. As for tellin' them I've come 'ere today, I take my dyin' oath I've not said a word nor will."

"And I am not doubting your word," Tony assured her, smiling down at her. "You see, Mrs. Timms," he informed her, "when I told you that you need have no fears for Lady Collett, I meant it. Like you, I do not believe for one moment that she is suffering from mental or nervous disorders, and neither does my sister, and whilst I cannot at this moment give you reasons or explanations, I must ask you to believe me as well as trust me."

"I do," she nodded firmly. "I saw at the outset you were a decent man, beggin' your pardon m'lord an' meanin' no offence."

"None taken," he smiled. "Lady Collett is certainly most fortunate to have you looking out for her."

"Well," Mrs. Timms sighed, "I always will. A real lady is Lady Collett, if you take my meanin'?" He nodded. "Well, if you say I'm not to worry, then I won't because I can see you mean what you say."

"I do," Tony said firmly.

"In that case," she nodded, "it's time I was takin' my leave," pulling on her gloves.

"Mrs. Timms," Beatrice smiled, laying a hand on her arm, "thank you for coming; you did right."

"Well, m'lady," she sighed, "I beg your pardon, I'm sure if I've put you out but…"

"Not at all," Beatrice smiled. "Indeed, I am truly grateful and honoured that you felt you could repose your trust in me."

"That's very kind of you, m'lady," Mrs. Timms sniffed, "I'm sure." Then, not wishing to embarrass herself, said briskly, "Well, I'd best be on my way."

"Thank you again, Mrs. Timms," Tony smiled, taking her hand in his. "You have been most helpful."

"Well, I'm glad of that m'lord," she nodded as he opened the drawing-room door for her to pass through.

"If you will wait a moment," he smiled, "I'll call up a hackney for you."

"That's very thoughtful of you I'm sure, m'lord," she nodded, "but best not. If they see me turnin' up in an 'ackney they'll put two an' two together an' come up with five. 'Sides," she told him, "it's not snowin' now an' I've not far to go."

"If you are sure," he nodded.

"Quite sure, m'lord," she assured him, "it's only a step, an' after all it's not as though I've got to walk through the front door ruinin' the carpets. I don't think Sir Braden would like 'avin' another one taken up," she said conversationally.

At this Tony looked searchingly down at her, asking sharply, "Sir Braden had a carpet taken up! When was this?"

"Oh, some time ago now," Mrs. Timms shrugged. "In fact," she told him, "I forgot all about it, but now I come to think of it, it was Ellen who noticed it that day 'e called us all upstairs to 'is study to tell us about Mary an' Mitchell."

"Mrs. Timms," Tony told her, taking hold of her gloved hand and warmly clasping it, "you will never know how *very* grateful to you I am."

"Oh," she blushed, lowering her eyes, "much obliged I'm sure, m'lord!"

Chapter Fifteen

Eleanor, opening a heavy lidded and rather blurry left eye to discover that her surroundings were quite unfamiliar to her was, for the moment at least, far too disoriented to think where she could possibly be; all she knew was that this was not her room in Cavendish Square. Somewhere on the periphery of her consciousness she sensed she was not alone and, slightly turning her head on the pillow, had a somewhat hazy vision of a rosy-cheeked woman sitting on a chair just to the right of the bed with her head bent over some sewing. To her recollection, she had never seen her attendant before and wondered who she was, but as her head was throbbing painfully and it was too much of an effort to think, she easily gave up on this far too strenuous a mental exercise and closed her eyes, sleep claiming her almost immediately.

But the images her dreams relentlessly conjured up as well as Braden's last haunting words about having her put into an institution, Eleanor's sleep was unfortunately rendered hideous; causing her to cry out and move her head fretfully from side to side on the pillow in a desperate attempt to banish them, but quite unexpectedly another voice, soothing and gentle, gradually overrode them, having the effect of rousing her. "There dearie, you've had a bad dream, that's all." For one panic-stricken moment the dreadful suspicion crossed Eleanor's mind that despite the luxury of her surroundings she was in a private room in some institution or other and this woman was a private nurse Braden had hired to take care of her, but worse than this was the horrifying thought that Tony had not come to her rescue after all and that her last words to him before she had fallen asleep had, in fact, been nothing but a delusional dream and, in her panic, made a desperate attempt to get up, only to find herself being gently eased back against the pillows.

"It's all right, dearie," Sarah smiled warmly down at her. "No one's going to hurt you here."

"I… I'm not m-mad!" Eleanor managed desperately.

"No, of course you're not, dearie, the *very* idea!" Sarah soothed, wishing, and not for the first time, she had that husband of hers here right now; she would give him what for for beating his wife! "You just lie there quietly and I'll let Her Ladyship know you're awake. Ever so worried we've all been over you, dearie," she nodded. "Her Ladyship will be *ever* so pleased; came to see you not above an hour ago, because although she managed to get you to swallow some hot tea you were just a little unsettled and, as for His Lordship… well," she nodded, "sat up with you all night he did!"

Eleanor, confused and dazed, could do no more than look bewilderingly up at the cheerful face smiling reassuringly down at her, but just as Sarah was about to pull the tug for a maid to inform Beatrice that their patient was awake, the door softly opened and Tony walked in. For one unnerving moment Eleanor thought that in her bemusement she had conjured him up and therefore fully expected him to disappear, but when, after several minutes, he was still in her blurry line of vision quietly talking to her attendant with no sign of his tall and reassuring figure vanishing in front of her eyes, she felt the tears sting them as she realised he was no figment of her imagination after all. Something between a choke and a sob of relief escaped her parted lips and, after he had closed the door behind her unknown chaperon and come up to the bed, she cried faintly, "Tony!"

"Good morning," he smiled, sitting gently down on the edge of the bed and taking hold of the hand she had pulled out from under the covers to touch him to make sure he was real.

"Tony!" she managed weakly, her fingers moving in his. "Is… is it *really* you?" taking comfort from the warmth of his hand.

"Yes, my darling," he said tenderly, "it's *really* me."

"Oh!" she breathed, relieved. "I… I thought I was dreaming."

"I am no dream," he assured her, his eyes smiling warmly down at her. "I am very real, I promise you."

"Oh, Tony!" she managed, huskily. "I… I am so *glad* to see you."

"Now *that*," he smiled, "is what I like to hear because I am certainly glad to see *you*!" he told her in a deep voice, kissing her fingers.

"Y-you are?" she asked hesitantly, her heart skipping a beat upon hearing this, realising that she must look rather dreadful, especially as this had been a most violent attack and no one other than Braden and Eliza had ever seen her looking like this.

"You must know I am," he assured her in the same deep voice.

Although her bruises had become more pronounced overnight, they were not as prominent as they would have been had Doctor Little not applied the arnica, nevertheless, her right eye was appallingly blackened and swollen and completely closed whilst the left, although partly open, was rather distended and badly discoloured. The cut incurred by Collett's ring, still reddened and inflamed, was clearly visible beneath the dark bluish-purple bruises on her right cheek, but even though the left one was badly bruised and swollen it was obvious that her right side had taken the brunt of his punches as well as the forceful blows across the face with the back of his right hand, not even her lips, puffy and slit at the right corner, escaping such despicable treatment.

"Even though I…" she faltered, turning her head a little away from him. "Oh, I must look an *awful* fright!" she said wretchedly.

"Oh, *awful*!" Tony agreed, his voice a caress. "So much so," he said lovingly, placing a forefinger lightly under her chin and gently turning her head round for her to face him, "that I can hardly bear to look at you," the love in his eyes filling her with a warm sense of well-being. "As for poor Bea," he sighed, sadly shaking his head, "she is quite overcome every time she sees you!"

"Beatrice?" Eleanor managed, her fingers moving in his. "You… you mean I am in Mount Street?"

"Mm," he nodded, "I brought you here last night. You collapsed in my arms, don't you remember?" he asked gently, kissing her hand.

Her forehead puckered a little in an effort of memory, the events of the previous evening somewhat disjointed. "I…I remember leaving the house," she told him slowly, trying to work it out, "but it… it was *so cold*," she recalled.

"Do you remember anything after that?" he asked softly, gently removing a strand of hair from her forehead, biting down his anger when he thought of Collett's vicious and brutal handling of his wife.

"No," she shook her head, "nothing until I opened my eyes to find I was in your arms and I… I began to feel warm again." Her hand trembled in his and fresh tears stung her eyes as she called to mind with agonising clarity her initial assumption. "I… I thought at first it was… that he was taking me to…"

"Is that why you escaped," Tony asked gently, wanting nothing more than to take her in his arms and hold her close, "because he not only beat you, he threatened to have you confined?" He believed it a pretty safe bet to say that it was not the first time Collett had threatened to do this, but unless he was very much mistaken, which he doubted, Tony suspected that last night he did more than threaten otherwise she would not have made such a drastic attempt to escape and certainly not in the condition she was in. She nodded, the recollection still harrowing. "Did he do this to you because he wanted to know if you had said anything to me about what you either saw or stumbled upon that night?" he asked softly.

Eleanor stared up at him, her fingers convulsing in his, instinctively knowing that he knew the truth. "You… you *know*?" she breathed, hardly above a whisper.

"About Sir Philip? Yes," he nodded, "pretty much," comfortingly squeezing her hand.

"B-but how?" she managed.

He thought a moment. "Well," he sighed at length, "to begin with, it seemed a little strange to me when Bea told me that you were never seen out without your husband or that woman who came here with you, even down to a shopping trip. Then," he told her gently, "there was your reaction to that piece you saw in the newspaper, which went far beyond a natural aversion at such a horrific crime," he felt her hand tremble in his and gently tightened his reassuring hold. "It was obvious to me that you were afraid of that woman who passes as your maid, not to mention your husband, and not merely because he subjects you to such unforgivable treatment as this," nodding meaningfully at her beaten and bruised face, "but as soon as I learned from Bea that your constant supervision started around the time of Sir Philip's death and Collett's dismissal of Mitchell and Mary," kissing the hand which suddenly convulsed in his, "it didn't take much figuring out."

"But…" she choked, "how could you possibly have…?"

"Put it all together?" he raised an eyebrow. She nodded. "I'm a newspaperman, remember?" he smiled, "or hasn't Bea told you?"

Eleanor thought a moment, saying at length, "Yes, I… I do seem to remember now; your father's newspapers?" He nodded. "Oh," she cried, quite ashamed, turning her head a little away, "what must you think of me?"

"You know what I think of you," he told her warmly, proving the point by gently turning her head and tenderly kissing her forehead. "I love you."

She shook her head, managing, "But how *can* you, when you know that I have withheld the truth all this time and…?"

"Very easily," he told her lovingly. "You must not blame yourself; you were hardly in a position to say or do anything. As for last night," he said warmly, "you were very brave, my darling. It took a lot of courage to do what you did, but," he shook his head a little, giving her hand a squeeze, "although I understand why, where were you going? Were you trying to make it here, to Bea?"

"Yes," she said in a stifled little voice, "but I… I could not go any farther and, later, when I opened my eyes I… I thought that Braden had found me and was taking me to…"

"Did you really think I would allow that to happen?" he asked in a deep voice, carefully wiping away the stray tear which fell from out the corner of her eye. "No, my darling," he told her lovingly, "you must know I would not."

Her fingers moved in his and, looking up at him through a blurry mist, managed unsteadily, "But I… I don't understand."

"There's nothing *to* understand," he smiled. "All that matters is that you are quite safe. I shall tell you everything, my darling," he promised, "but not now. *Now*," he told her, kissing the hand he was still holding, "you need to rest."

It was only to be expected that the horrors of the last twenty-four hours and more would take their emotional toll eventually, but Tony's comforting presence combined with his assurances that he had her safe were more than enough to open the floodgates to her pent-up emotions, especially when she realised how close she had come to being shut away for the rest of her life, and that stray tear, which Tony had gently wiped away with his forefinger, soon became an unceasing flow, running freely down her swollen face. Whenever Eleanor looked back on this moment she would never be entirely certain whether she reached up to Tony or he took her in his arms and gently raised her of his own accord, but as he held her close against him at no point did it occur to her to question the rights and wrongs of it, his much-needed strength offering her emotions, which had been steadily building up inside her for a long time, a natural release. Gradually, hazy recollections began to filter into her mind of him doing exactly the same thing at some point during the night and now, like then, she not only felt very safe but knew there was nowhere else she would rather be.

Tony held her battered and bruised body as tightly as he dared, but as he felt her shuddering in his arms as she gave vent to her emotions he instinctively drew her closer to him. He could well imagine her fear upon opening her eyes this morning to finding herself in unfamiliar surroundings with a totally unknown woman keeping watch over her especially knowing that Collett had threatened to have her committed, and as Tony soothingly allayed her fears he promised himself the pleasure of coming up against this man, a man who apparently knew no compunction in treating his wife to such despicable cruelty whenever it suited him. "It's all right, my darling," he soothed, tenderly stroking her hair, "I have you quite safe."

"Oh, Tony!" she cried, her words muffled against his shoulder. "I have been so afraid!"

"I know," he said gently, feeling her stir in his arms, "but there is no need to be afraid any more."

"I am not afraid when I am with you," she told him truthfully, her aching body momentarily forgotten as she eased herself a little away from him to look up into his face, but her fear of Braden was such that she could not dismiss him. "But what if Braden…?" she urged, not quite able to hide her panic.

"Having been told by that so-called butler of his that you had gone into the country yesterday morning to visit friends," Tony told her, kissing her forehead, "he cannot now come here enquiring after you. What is it?" he asked gently, in answer to the look on her face.

"It *was* you who came to the house!" she cried tearfully. "I… I didn't imagine it! Oh, Tony!" she exclaimed, "I… I tried to call to you but I… I could not. I was too weak and…"

An agonised groan left his lips at this and, holding her close against him said, with barely suppressed vehemence, "I should have kicked the door down there and then and not waited until last night! Had I have done so," he admitted, not able to forgive himself, "I could have spared you so much!"

"You… you mean you came to Cavendish Square last night to rescue me!" Eleanor cried, raising her head from his shoulder to look up at him.

He felt her tremble in his arms, though not with fear, and had circumstances been different he would have known no hesitation in kissing her, but clamping down on this irresistible impulse, he smiled, saying urgently, "Did you really think I was going to leave you in that house another day?" He shook his head. "Huh, huh. I was quite determined to get you out of there come what may."

"Oh, but you... you could have been hurt and..." she breathed, laying her hand against his cheek.

Taking her hand to kiss its soft palm he smiled down at her, a smile which made her heart somersault. "There was no chance of that," he assured her. "Besides," he told her, "I had Jerry with me."

"Jerry?" she queried.

"Mm," he nodded, "a very good friend of mine. A very useful guy is Jerry," he told her, "but I'll tell you all about him later, when you have rested." She was just about to say something when he forestalled her, saying earnestly, "My darling, it took a lot of courage to do what you did last night, and I can only thank God I was there, but now," he told her, "you must try to sleep."

"But there is so much I have to tell you," she stressed.

"And so you shall," he promised softly against her forehead, "but not now," gently easing her back against the pillows. "Now, I want you to rest or I shall have Sarah taking me to task," he pulled a face in mock dread.

"Sarah? You mean the woman who was here just now?" she queried.

"Mm," he nodded. "You need not be afraid of her," he assured her gently.

"I'm not," she told him truthfully. "She has been so kind."

"She's also a particular friend of mine," he smiled. "She's been with Bea forever and, between them," he told her, "they looked after you last night when I brought you here before the doctor came to tend you!"

Swallowing the lump in her throat, quite overcome by everything, she said huskily, "I... I don't know what to say. Everyone has been so kind and... oh, Tony I..." gripping his arm, "I could not have endured any..."

"Ssh," he soothed, "you won't have to endure anything again; I have you quite safe, my darling. No one is going to hurt you ever again," he promised. "There is no need to be afraid."

Eleanor may have been a little calmer when he rose to his feet to take his leave of her a few minutes later, but he nevertheless deemed it wiser not to tell her he had to go out, it could well be that once she knew he was not in the house she would neither sleep nor rest, particularly as he could see the dread etched into every inch of her bruised and swollen face, clearly reflected in her partially opened left eye, and although he gently soothed her fears he knew it would be some time before they would be entirely laid to rest. However, the news that Mrs. Timms had called earlier that morning, a woman Eleanor knew as being as kind as she was trustworthy, went a long way to lifting her spirits, and by the time Tony left her she was more relaxed and inclined to sleep.

Having allayed her parting fears that there was no likelihood that Peterson or Eliza Boon, acting on Collett's instructions, would try to remove her, possibly by stealth, from the safety of Mount Street, Tony left her in a calmer frame of mind, but as he descended the stairs he could not fool himself into thinking that they would not attempt something, if not today, then soon, as the information Eleanor held could do them untold damage. They would know her injuries were such that it would be a while before she was able to say anything, and even though a wife's testimony would not be admissible in court if her evidence was in any way incriminating to her husband, they knew that once she did reveal all she knew, especially to a man who was in a perfect position to investigate her allegations, there would be no stopping the scandal that followed as well as a most public trial which would in all probability see Sir Braden Collett being found guilty of murder and hanged. Of course, without the evidence to prove Collett guilty of murder it meant there was some way to go before he received his just desserts, which meant that sifting out the facts would see Tony being away from Mount Street a lot of the time, leaving his sister and Eleanor exposed to whatever stratagems Collett and the others may employ to try to gain admittance to the house. At all costs Tony had to ensure their safety during both his and Tom's absence, and therefore he was resolved on arranging some protection for them; determined to speak to Jerry on this point.

Tony knew as surely as though he had witnessed it that Collett, whether premeditated or on the spur-of-the-moment, had murdered Sir Philip and, if Mrs. Timms was right about that carpet, and Tony believed she was, then Collett had killed him in his own study and Eleanor, having returned home earlier than expected, had either walked straight in on it or accidentally stumbled onto something which had alerted her to the truth. As far as Peterson and Eliza Boon were concerned, although Tony could only hazard a guess as to the full extent of their crimes that they were guilty, if nothing else, of complicity in that murder, he felt certain. Until Eleanor was in a fit condition to tell him everything, he could only speculate as to the exact sequence of events, but he was firmly convinced that it was Peterson who had disposed of Sir Philip's body by throwing it into the Thames and, unless Tony's instincts were at fault, more than likely rolled up in that carpet which, unfortunately, had so far not come to light, but considering Sir Philip's head injuries it would unquestionably have been heavily bloodstained. Under no circumstances could Collett allow Mitchell to see such damning evidence any more than he could trust him to keep silent by not telling the police about letting Sir Philip into the house that night once the cry went up about his death; these two factors alone would be more than enough to condemn him.

As far as the household staff was concerned, Collett's uncertain temper would be more than enough to discourage any one of them posing questions, but Mitchell, whose position within the household was more privileged, could easily have led to him asking about the carpet and this, coupled with the fact that he had answered the door to Sir Philip, would have been more than sufficient to make him dangerous. Tony could only speculate whether Mitchell had inadvertently stumbled upon events, especially as he had not been summoned to show Sir Philip out of the house or whether Collett had taken the initiative by ridding himself of Mitchell before he could put two and two together thereby averting disaster, but that he had been swiftly disposed of to ensure his silence Tony was totally convinced.

According to Mrs. Timms, Peterson and Eliza Boon were already installed in Cavendish Square when Collett had summoned them upstairs to tell them about Mitchell and Mary and, unless Tony missed his guess, he would say that at some point after killing Sir Philip and silencing Eleanor, no doubt by hitting her senseless, Collett must have left the house to seek them out. Tony had seen enough of these two individuals to say that they were not only devious but entirely unscrupulous as well as not turning squeamish over carrying out whatever task they deemed necessary in order to serve their own ends, but unless he had misread the signs he would lay any odds that their past careers would not take too much, if any, scrutiny. Peterson certainly corroborated Jerry's knowledge of him; bearing all the hallmarks of being a bruiser in his day and Tony felt sure he still put those formidable fists to use. As for Eliza Boon, he fully agreed with Mrs. Timms when she had said that she doubted she had ever nursed anyone in her life before, in fact he had gained the very strong impression that her attendances at a bedside had nothing whatever to do with administering to the sick and, unless he had figured it wrong, he would go so far as to say that Eleanor's overseer was nothing short of a 'madam'. If he was right when he had remarked to Tom that Collett could well satisfy his aggressive inclinations outside the matrimonial home by visiting certain establishments which catered for such out of the ordinary tastes, then it would easily explain how he had come to know Peterson and Eliza Boon. If Tony's thinking was right about her past profession in that she had kept a house whose sole aim was to satisfy the needs of those in a way which could not be accommodated anywhere else, then it was fairly certain that Collett had come to know Eliza Boon from visiting her premises; as for Peterson, it could well be that he had been employed by her, most probably to keep the girls as well as the clients in check. Out of necessity, discretion was the watchword for these establishments, but for the kind of premises which Tony felt certain Eliza Boon had run, secrecy rather than discretion was the order of the day, where only a personal recommendation would get you through the door. Tony felt sure that these establishments were not so anonymous that they had escaped either the interest or the notice of the police; perhaps Jerry could help out there?

As for Dennis Dunscumbe's death, whilst Tony acquitted Collett of pulling the trigger himself, if for no other reason than he seemed a man mighty prone to protecting himself and his reputation, Tony felt certain that it had been most cunningly arranged, but it went against all logic to believe that he was not a party to it. That there was a link between the brutal murder of Sir Philip Dunscumbe and the supposed suicide of his brother could not be argued, but what that link was remained unclear, but under no circumstances could they be looked upon as unconnected. According to Bill, Dennis Dunscumbe had acquired something of a reputation for being somewhat aggressive in his treatment of women as well as associating with men his brother had most strongly disapproved of, and if Tony's own thinking was right about Collett's extramarital activities then it could well be that he had perhaps introduced Dennis Dunscumbe to Eliza Boon's establishment. But even supposing he had done it did not automatically mean that the reason for his supposed suicide had anything to do with his visits there, but the fact remained Peterson and Eliza Boon did keep cropping up, and whilst Tony accepted that he only caught a brief glimpse of her as she alighted from the carriage when she had accompanied Eleanor to see Bea, he had recognised the sharp-eyed astuteness straightaway.

If Eliza Boon had been in that line of business as Tony believed, then it was a foregone conclusion that she was no fool; running a house for specific activities without her neighbours being any the wiser would take some doing and, unless he was very much mistaken, she would know precisely how to keep her girls in check. As things stood at the moment he had no proof whatsoever that Dennis Dunscumbe's death was in any way connected with Eliza Boon, all the same whoever had planned his death had done so with calculated precision and whilst Tony was not saying she had pulled the trigger herself, she was certainly capable of formulating such a scheme. Presuming Eliza Boon *was* the architect of Dennis Dunscumbe's murder, then by not taking into account the essential fact that he was left-handed she had made a fatal mistake, but from what Tony had been privileged to see of her he doubted whether she would have made such a gross error; the chances were that whoever she had instructed to put a pistol to Dennis Dunscumbe's head had, for whatever reason, forgotten this most essential fact. The more Tony considered it the more certain he was in his own mind that Dennis Dunscumbe's death was undoubtedly due to his association with Collett and their surreptitious visits to her establishment, but whilst Tony may not as yet be able to work out what had occurred to deem his murder expedient, he felt sure that Eliza Boon was behind it and that Collett, most probably to save his own skin and reputation, had condoned it, and unless Tony missed his mark that Peterson had most certainly been the one to carry it out.

Of course, all of this was pure conjecture and, as Tony knew very well, without evidence to prove it he could no more run with the story than he could put it to Scotland Yard, but hopefully his visit to Holborn later today would not only provide the missing pieces of the puzzle but would turn his theories into fact, and if Jerry could dig up something on Peterson and Eliza Boon, all the better.

Peterson's return to Cavendish Square following his search for Lady Collett and his not very discreet observations in Mount Street with Jerry's son Arthur bringing up the rear a few minutes later, Jerry waited another half an hour before handing over his vigil to his second son, Edward, deciding to make his way to *'The Prince Albert'* public house before going home. Jerry may well be *persona non grata* with the hierarchy in the Metropolitan Police but to the men with whom he had walked the beat he was as good a man as any to have in your corner, in fact better and, as far as they were concerned, he had more gumption in his little finger than all the inspectors and such like put together. It was not to be expected that his down-to-earth approach as well as regularly questioning the sense of his orders would go down well with his senior officers, in fact both had more than once brought him into conflict with them, resulting in him dispensing with his uniform for civilian attire well before his retirement. As far as these high-ranking officers were concerned, especially at Bow Street Police Station, none of whom would forget his insubordination in a hurry, their thoughts were very far from magnanimous, but his many cronies, who still looked upon him as one of their own, were not unwilling to give him information to assist his private investigations over as nice a drop of ale as you would ever find at their local watering hole.

'The Prince Albert' public house, a three-storey red bricked building situated halfway down on the right-hand side of Percival Street, was as cosy a pub as you would ever find, and Sam Nelson, who could proudly boast of being its landlord for more years than he cared to remember, could also claim to seeing his bar and comfy little snug filled most nights. Being located just two streets away from Bow Street he was regularly accustomed to serving those officers of the law who patronised his establishment after the end of a tiring duty, but if there were those who considered his establishment as being a little too close to a police station for their liking, he was not deprived of their custom. He was himself an honest and upright man who ran a reputable pub and one, moreover, who had never been known to be tempted into taking part in whatever illicit venture was sometimes put to him and so he could serve a peeler with a clear conscience and, certainly, with no objection, providing they paid for what they wanted like everyone else. As for those who were not quite so upstanding, it was nothing to do with him how they made a living as long as no underhand dealings or women attempting to ply their trade were ever conducted inside his premises, but since his more law-abiding customers paid no heed to those whose careers would not stand too much, if any, scrutiny, no unpleasant occurrences took place.

Despite the dreadful weather Sam was having a busy night and when Jerry entered his premises just a few minutes before eleven o'clock his tall imposing figure was easily discernible at the far end of the counter, serving pints as fast as his muscular arms could pull them, but by the time Jerry had manoeuvred his way through the rowdy throng the crowd at the bar had thinned out sufficiently for Sam to take a minute to wipe the counter, catching sight of his old crony as he did so. After cocking his head in acknowledgement, Sam pulled him a pint and put it in front of him, then, after taking a much-needed drink from his own glass which he retrieved from under the counter, he leaned on his right elbow and, after wiping the froth off his thick handlebar moustache with the back of the other, looked quickly all around him before saying in a conspiratorial under voice, "Best be cerful, Jerry; there's bin an inspecta in 'ere."

"In 'ere?" Jerry repeated surprised, taking a pull of his ale. "I ain't never known 'em come in 'ere before!"

"Well," Sam nodded, "there's bin one in tonight," he told him. "An' none of 'em ain't no friends o' yourn!"

"Is 'e still 'ere, or 'as 'e gone?" Jerry asked, stretching back his head to look towards the closed door of the snug, knowing that Sam had spoken no less than the truth when he said that none of the senior officers at Bow Street were any friends of his.

"I ain't sin 'im go," Sam told him, 'but 'old on a bit," nodding his head to Jim who stood at the other end of the bar pulling pints.

Jim Drake, a wiry little man whose grizzled hair and wrinkled face had been a familiar sight at *'The Prince Albert'* almost as long as Sam, pushed the pint he had just pulled towards a customer before wiping his hands on his apron and, with his bowlegged gait, walked up to Sam, cocking his head at Jerry. Upon being asked if he had seen the Inspector leave he nodded. "'E's gawn."

"Are yer sure o' that, Jim?" Sam asked.

"Sin 'im wi' me own eyes not five minutes back," he nodded, then, after a few words with Jerry, returned to his post at the far end of the counter.

Jerry, remaining at the bar only long enough to have a word in Sam's ear, walked away towards the snug, this cosy little room rendered all the more inviting on such a bitterly cold night by a roaring fire burning in the grate. After being cheerfully greeted by three of his old police pals, enjoying Sam's best brown ale, he was laughingly told about Inspector Jenks. "Anotha minute," Sergeant McLeary told him, "an' you'd 'ave run slap bang into the 'stick'."

Jerry, all too familiar with this customary but affectionate term for senior officers who carried a walking stick when on duty, stepped up to the counter calling for another round. "What did 'e want?" he cocked his head. "'E ain't never been in 'ere before; come to think of it," he mused, "I ain't never known a 'stick' come in 'ere before!"

"Nothin' to do with you, me old mucker!" Constable Jack Evans told him, a cheerful Yorkshireman who readily made room on the leather seat beside him for Jerry. "Seems 'Old Smiley' 'ere," indicating a dour looking man on the opposite side of the fireplace, "forgot to do somethin'."

Jerry, looking round at Constable Herbert Jones, cocked an eyebrow. "You know, Bert," he nodded, "I ain't never seen you with a smile on your face yet!"

Bert, after taking a generous mouthful of Sam's best ale, eyed his old crony, saying glumly, "Wot's ter smile about?"

"Well, it could be worse," Sergeant Liam McLeary grinned, "yer missus ain't run off with the lodger yet!"

"I dunno why not," Constable Jack Evans laughed, "with a face like that I'm surprised 'er ain't run off with 'im already!"

This good-natured banter lasted for several minutes, and Bert, too used to their teasing about his habitually glum expression, neither took offence nor felt fired with the need to try to be cheerful but, on the contrary, continued to drink his ale with unruffled equanimity, whereupon Jerry settled himself down to a most enjoyable, if not very profitable, hour or more.

Chapter Sixteen

Unaware of Tony's involvement in his affairs and the conclusions drawn from his investigations to date, Sir Braden Collett was not only secure in the belief that no one knew the truth about Sir Philip Dunscumbe's murder except Eleanor, much less the other three deaths on their hands, but also that not one member of his domestic household would dare to either question him or flout his orders. As it was imperative to keep Eleanor's escape to themselves and the reason for it as long as they possibly could or, at least, until they had her safely back in Cavendish Square until further arrangements could be made, it was with his customary authority that he informed them of Her Ladyship's unfortunate relapse following hard on the heels of the one she had suffered the previous evening. As expected this was fully endorsed by Eliza Boon who, with her habitual sharpness, added the instruction that no one but herself would tend to all Lady Collett's needs and no one was to enter her room as complete quiet and rest were necessary to ensure her speedy recovery. Like Sir Braden, Eliza knew it was absolutely vital that they say or do nothing which could possibly alert the servants to Eleanor's flight, but as she watched them file out of the drawing-room to resume their duties, she was by no means certain that Mrs. Timms was as convinced as the others appeared to be about Her Ladyship's condition. It had more than once crossed Eliza's mind to strongly recommend Sir Braden to rid himself of this woman, not only because she was Eleanor's most devoted partisan and more than capable of trying to see the mistress for herself to make sure that what they had told her was in fact true, but from the look on her face as she made her way back to the kitchen Eliza Boon had the very strong feeling that Mrs. Timms could very well spell trouble if they were not careful. However, just a very little thought was enough to persuade Eliza that this was not the answer, not only because to dismiss her could well create talk once it became known that Sir Braden had discharged yet another well-established member of staff but, like Mitchell, Mrs. Timms posed the very real danger of pouring her grievances as well as her concerns into the ears of those who could make things extremely awkward; the Shiptons for instance. Far better then, for her to remain here where a close eye could be kept on her, in the meantime though the far more important question of getting Eleanor back to Cavendish Square before she confided everything to Lady Shipton or her brother took precedence over everything else. Had Eliza the least idea that Mrs. Timms, whose doubts ran far deeper than even she suspected as well as being firmly of the unshakeable belief that something most peculiar was going on, was actually planning to visit Lady Shipton in Mount Street that very morning, not only would Eliza not have dismissed dealing with Mrs. Timms so casually, but would have seen that it was just as imperative to deal with her as it was Eleanor.

Like Sir Braden, Eliza Boon had seen that lingering hint of independence behind Eleanor's frightened blue eyes and knew perfectly well that in spite of her fear and subservience she had not been totally cowed into submission, were it otherwise she would never have effected such a dramatic escape. After having lain awake for some considerable time pondering the crisis which Eleanor's flight posed and the difficulties any disclosure she made would present them with, Eliza had desperately sought for a way of getting Eleanor away from Mount Street, but by the time she eventually closed her eyes several hours later without a blink or twinge of conscience, she believed she had arrived at the very thing that would serve the purpose admirably.

Sir Braden, who had mulled over Eliza's proposed plan to get Eleanor back to Cavendish Square before she could start talking from the moment Eliza had outlined it to him first thing, foresaw any number of things going wrong with it, and no sooner had the servants filed out of the drawing-room he tetchily pointed these out to her. It took time and patience to instil into his anxious mind that since they could not go to Mount Street to get her out without the Shiptons either refusing them admittance and preventing them from doing so or calling in the police, both of which would set up a hue and cry especially after Peterson had announced she had gone into the country to stay with friends, then getting Eleanor to remove herself of her own accord was the best and by far the safest way. Collett remained unconvinced, demanding to know what was to stop her from throwing in her lot with the Shiptons and showing them the letter.

"She won't," Eliza told him firmly. "She loves her father too much to see his name brought into disrepute. She will do as she's told," she nodded. "Make no mistake about it," she added confidently, "she will be back here by tonight because she knows if she is not, then her father will suffer for it!" Her thin lips parted into the faintest semblance of a smile. "Rest assured, Sir Braden," she nodded, "she will do what we want her to because she will be too afraid of the consequences to her father if she doesn't!"

Some doubts still lingered in his mind, but since he could not come up with anything better than Eliza's plan any more than he could argue against her reasoning in that although the Shiptons would be bound to know they had had a hand in Eleanor's decision to leave their protection whilst their backs were turned, once they had her back in Cavendish Square there would be nothing they could do about it, he shut himself up in his study to begin composing the letter which would see his wife surreptitiously leaving Mount Street of her own volition. Eliza may be devious and unscrupulous but she had not failed him yet and he had no reason to suppose that now would be any different, but no matter how much faith he had in her he was honest enough to admit that he could not so readily dismiss Lord Childon. Collett could, of course, only speculate as to how much Childon knew if, in fact, he knew anything at all, which was doubtful, but the truth was for some reason Collett could not quite explain, this man, who had clearly taken quite a liking to Eleanor, could cause all manner of difficulties given half the chance. Nevertheless, Eliza's calm logic did go a long way to settling his nerves and he could only hope that by this time tomorrow his errant wife would be back here just as Eliza predicted she would be.

Eliza, having put Sir Braden's mind at rest or, at least, as far as it was possible for her to do under the circumstances, let herself out of the house via the front door an hour and a half later to hurriedly make her way to the corner of Oxford Street where she hoped she would not have too long to wait for an available hackney. As none of the domestic staff were under observation, Harry, Jerry's third son, standing solitary guard in Cavendish Square gardens until one of his brothers joined him, had no more than noted the hurried emergence of Mrs. Timms from the basement steps in his notebook some time before, but upon seeing the woman who fitted Tony's description as being one of the three people they were keeping under close surveillance unexpectedly leave the house by way of the front door, threw him into a quandary. Whether her errand was innocent or not their instructions were to follow any one of the prime suspects, but since Harry had no way of knowing if one of the other two would take it into their heads to go out as well, he was a little undecided whether to stand his post in case or follow the woman he could see heading towards Oxford Street. It was just as he was debating the issue when he heard his elder brother Edward come up behind him followed seconds later by his youngest one Arthur, and waiting only long enough to fill them in on what had taken place during his watch, he left them to oversee things here while he left the gardens to hurry after Eliza Boon.

Little realising that she was under observation, Eliza Boon emerged from Hollis Street into Oxford Street where she was fortunate enough to come upon an approaching hackney and, after flagging it down, she briefly instructed the driver to take her to an address in Bloomsbury, whereupon she quickly climbed into the antiquated vehicle. Sitting comfortably back against the squabs to look unconcernedly out onto the busy streets, clutching her bag with Sir Braden's letter tucked safely inside, she was not only supremely confident in her strategy for dealing with Lady Collett but also in knowing that Reggie Wragge would have no objection to her making use of Molly for a few hours, a young woman whom she knew as being more than capable of carrying out the job she had in mind.

Being fortunate enough to flag down a vehicle which came into view just as Eliza Boon's pulled away, Harry, having told the driver to follow the vehicle in front, sat anxiously forward in his seat as he tried to keep the hackney which conveyed his quarry, now several vehicles ahead of him, in his sights, was unfortunately not to go any farther in his pursuit than the corner of Tottenham Court Road due to a woman slipping on the icy cobbles as she tried to dash across the road in between the press of vehicles passing in both directions. This not only meant the end of his chase but caused the driver of his hackney to make a desperate attempt to pull up his snorting horse to prevent him from colliding into the one immediately in front. Waiting only for the vehicle to come to a shuddering halt, Harry hastily thrust a coin at the driver before jumping down onto the pavement to run along Oxford Street in the hope of picking up another vehicle, but unfortunately the accident had brought virtually all the traffic to a standstill and all he was able to do was make a note of Eliza Boon's hackney carriage number before the vehicle was lost from view. Eliza Boon, totally unaware of the incident and the pandemonium it had inevitably created behind her as well as the frustrated young man who was left standing powerless on the pavement staring exasperated at her retreating hackney, knowing there was nothing he could do but hopefully trace the driver and his fare's destination from the vehicle's hire number, continued her journey in blissful ignorance.

It could not be denied that number fifty-one Periton Place, an elegant four-storey Georgian house of Bath stone standing on the corner of Marlborough Square, looked every inch as dignified and respectable as its neighbours. No one who chanced to look up at the gleaming sash windows with their cream blinds drawn halfway down and the heavy velvet curtains draped gracefully behind would think it anything other than a modest and well-run household, a camouflage which Eliza Boon had insisted upon and, after paying off the hackney, she noted with approval that Reggie Wragge had maintained the façade, not that she had expected anything different, indeed, to do otherwise would do such a profitable little business no good at all. Unlike herself, Reggie Wragge, having a most desirable and impressive residence in Belgravia where he resided in luxurious and single state, did not live on the premises, but being the astute businessman he was she knew he spent a couple of hours here every morning to go over the books and to ensure there were no problems, and so the thought that she may have a wasted journey never so much as crossed her mind. Treading purposefully up the three stone steps to the highly polished black door, shining in the weak rays of the morning sun which was trying desperately hard to break through a leaden sky, she firmly hit the knocker against the brass plate with her thin gloved fingers, hardly having time to look around her before the door was opened by a middle-aged man of spare build and unprepossessing features. With complete detachment, he asked her name and business, then, as if satisfied with what she told him, he opened the door wider to allow her to step inside. Although she found herself in familiar surroundings it was all so very different to how she remembered it, but no matter where her keen eyes rested she could not help noticing that everywhere was still expensively and tastefully decorated and furnished. As business was never conducted during the day or the girls allowed to wander around the rooms in various stages of undress, the interior of fifty-one Periton Place bore all the signs of being a respectable home and not an establishment where some not very respectable activities took place.

Hardly had Reggie Wragge's live-in general factotum, whose duties covered a multitude of tasks including that of overseer in his employer's absence during the hours of darkness when the rooms were all being used to entertain those gentlemen who favoured the particular entertainment on offer, asked her to wait a moment than he returned inviting her to step this way. As he clearly had no idea that he was addressing the former and renowned *'Mother Discipline'*, he merely inclined his head as he ushered her into a rear drawing-room before closing the door quietly behind him.

Reggie Wragge, far from being the flamboyant fly-by-night his name suggested, was in fact a hard-headed businessman who had his fingers in more than one financial pie, and if some of those pies were not entirely above board it could not be said that he was either a crook or a fraudster. His legitimate dealings, which had earned him an unimpeachable reputation in the City, were kept completely separate to his rather more illegal enterprises such as fifty-one Periton Place and, whilst he had no wish for this or any of his other somewhat suspect undertakings to become public knowledge, his dealings, whether legitimate or otherwise, were all professionally conducted. No one looking at this tall, rather angular and well-dressed man, whose whole bearing exuded money and respectability, would have had the least guess that he presided over a number of establishments specialising in activities which were very far from respectable, but since all those who came into lawful contact with him knew him for an honest businessman whose undertakings were well within the law, it never so much as crossed their minds that he was anything other than what he purported to be. He was neither an immoral nor an unscrupulous man but he had an uncanny instinct when it came to business, and if there were those whose tendencies veered from the acceptable or the usual then so be it. He saw no reason why they should not have their unorthodox proclivities accommodated, especially as they were more than willing to pay to indulge them as well as for complete secrecy about patronising his establishments. To his way of thinking morality never entered into it, as far as he was concerned it was simply business and if a client asked him to provide something or someone in order for him to be entertained in a certain way to gratify his needs he regarded it as being no different to supplying any other service or commodity; on the contrary it was purely a case of supply and demand.

He had no regrets about taking this enterprise off Eliza's hands even though he knew perfectly well that she had made him pay through the nose for it, but if he were honest he could not understand why, after his many offers, all of which she had turned down, she had suddenly decided to sell it to him. He had known without even looking at her books that it was a profitable business which was why he had had his eye on it for a long time, but no amount of cajoling had persuaded her to sell it and so it had come as something of a surprise when she had unexpectedly approached him. However, as he was a man who never allowed personal feelings to interfere with matters of business, he had accepted the figure she had demanded as well as her stipulation that all the girls remain, and since the girls were partly the reason for its success, he had accepted the deal she had put before him; delving no deeper into the reason she offered for selling than that of retiring early.

Fifty-one Periton Place, or *'Mother Discipline's'* to the initiated, was not just known among its patrons for discretion but also for the excellent entertainment provided, for which there were no boundaries or limits. There were still none, but whilst Reggie Wragge had no qualms about supplying anything or anyone the client deemed necessary to fulfil his particular needs, unlike Eliza, he was purely a businessman and not a participator. It was hard to imagine that this sharp featured woman had been quite something to look at in her day, in fact her name and reputation still went before her in that dark and shaded world she had adorned for such long a time, indeed, he was often asked about her. She had not acquired the soubriquet *'Mother Discipline'* for nothing! She had known to a nicety, still did in fact, precisely how to please and to what degree and, although she had not actively involved herself with her clients for a long time, she had never hesitated to use her particular disciplinary skills on the girls should they prove a little reluctant to accommodate a client whose request was more unusual than normal.

But whilst there were those who would strongly condemn him as being a man totally devoid of any social or personal morality should they ever discover his illicit dealings, no one could ever say of Reggie Wragge that he had either colluded in or committed cold-blooded murder. As far as Annie Myers was concerned Eliza had led him to believe that she had simply decided to leave Periton Place for pastures new and, as for Dennis Dunscumbe, his suicide had nothing whatever to do with fifty-one Periton Place, and since she had told the girls the same thing they had no more idea of the truth than he did, and so there had been no reason for him to either doubt or question what Eliza had told him. As it was, he had no idea that the woman sitting calmly opposite knew very well that Annie Myers, far from leaving her establishment, had in fact died on the premises as a direct result of her refusal to accommodate the very man whose reported suicide had shocked society, and that her dead body had been unceremoniously thrown into a derelict building only streets away, let alone having arranged Dennis Dunscumbe's death and being heavily involved in covering up and instrumental in others.

Eliza may not go so far as to say that she had sold him her business under false pretences, but she knew as well as anyone who had ever had dealings with Reggie Wragge that he was scrupulously honest in his undertakings and that if she had told him the real reason why she wanted to sell her flourishing concern he would not have taken her up on her offer. She had no intention of alerting him to her participation in covering up the death of Annie Myers or that she had engineered Dennis Dunscumbe's so-called suicide, to do so would not only be foolhardy but extremely dangerous and she certainly had no intention of telling him that the reason she wanted Molly was to ensure her own safety and protection as well as that of a man who Reggie knew very well had been a regular visitor here.

Leaning back in his leather chair, a huge cigar held loosely between his long bony fingers, Reggie eyed Eliza closely, his alert blue eyes narrowing. He had not expected to see her today, in fact he had not expected to set eyes on her again, and whilst it had been pleasant enough talking over old times, he could not help wondering what it was that had motivated her into coming to see him. "I can't deny it's been good to see you again," he acknowledged, "but you're not here for a trip down memory lane, Eliza." He nodded knowingly. "What is it that really brings you here?"

She shrugged her thin shoulders. "A favour."

He looked thoughtfully at her through a cloud of cigar smoke. "A favour?" he repeated slowly, raising a questioning eyebrow. She nodded. "I see," he said thoughtfully. "You're not by chance thinking of setting up in business again, are you?"

"No," Eliza shook her head, "what makes you think I might be?"

"Oh, no reason," Reggie Wragge shrugged, "except it did cross my mind that you might have come to regret selling the business and looking to buy it back."

"And if I were," Eliza asked, her eyes narrowing, "are you saying you would refuse?"

"Let us just say," he nodded, "that I would give your offer the same careful thought that I would give to any prospective buyer's offer."

"I take that to mean 'no'," she nodded, "so, it's just as well I'm not. Now," she said briskly, having no more time to waste, "about that favour. I'm prepared to pay anything you ask, within reason that is," she pointed out firmly.

"I see," he nodded. "And for what are you prepared to pay 'anything within reason'?" he raised a questioning eyebrow.

"Not for what," Eliza told him, "for who."

Reggie Wragge took time to answer this by inhaling on his cigar, his eyes never leaving her face. "I don't trade in human beings, Eliza," he told her quietly.

She raised a sceptical eyebrow at this. "*You* say that!" she cried, astonished, glancing sardonically at her surroundings. "*You*, who run…"

"A brothel?" he supplied. "Oh, I know it may seem a strange thing for me to say," he admitted, "but it's true."

"Just what *are* you trying to say, Reggie?" Eliza demanded, leaning forward in her chair.

"You ran a good business Eliza," he told her at length, "were it otherwise I would not have touched it, but you kept the girls here out of fear and by holding threats over their heads, but now," he nodded, "they are here because they want to be. I pay them a wage, more than they could earn in any shop, office or factory; they receive benefits and holidays and are free to leave whenever they wish." Again she looked sceptical. "The girls work hard Eliza, you of all people should know that. They do things most women would shrink from doing, but they do whatever the client asks of them and, should they not wish to, then I don't force them; in return I make sure they are well looked after. I'm a businessman, Eliza," he told her firmly, "not a pimp or a slave trader, and this," indicating his surroundings with a wave of his hand, "is no different to any of my other businesses, and therefore I treat the girls here in exactly the same way as those who work for me in a factory turning out machinery parts or whatever else. It's not good business practice to mistreat your workforce, Eliza."

"Are you saying that I mistreated the girls?" she asked angrily. When he made no answer she rose hastily to her feet, demanding, "Very well then, let's ask them; get them in here to tell me to my face that I…"

"Let us just say," he cut in quietly, "that you were a trifle heavy-handed."

A blistering condemnation of his business practices were on the tip of her tongue but as she needed Molly's help too much she bit them back, saying instead, "Very well," she scoffed, "you look after the girls, but I didn't come here for a lecture but a favour."

"I'm sorry if you thought I was giving you a lecture," Reggie Wragge said quietly, "I wasn't. I'm just pointing out to you that the girls are my employees and not my personal property to either buy or sell or hire out." He leaned forward on his elbows, "But you haven't yet told me who the girl is you have in mind."

"Molly Clark," she replied promptly.

"Molly?" he repeated at length, stubbing his cigar in the large glass ashtray. Like Sir Braden, Reggie Wragge knew Eliza was by nature bullying and cruel as well as where her true inclinations lay and that she had not failed to use her harrying tactics on any one of the girls who had taken her fancy, Molly Clark especially, but although he was not above doing business with Eliza he could claim no liking for her.

"I take it she's still here?" she wanted to know, eyeing him sharply.

"Yes, she's still here and," he nodded, straightening up, "*still* as popular."

Like Reggie Wragge Eliza had a shrewd business head on her shoulders and whilst she fully expected him to put quite a price on hiring out Molly, she was not going to be cheated into paying an astronomical sum, especially for a girl who had once been one of *'Mother Discipline's Daughters'*. "Well?" she demanded.

Reggie Wragge thought a moment. "What's so special about Molly?" he asked curiously, leaning back in his chair.

"Do you need to ask?" Eliza shrugged.

"She's beautiful, yes," he inclined his head in acknowledgement, "and, of course, I know that you have or, shall I say," he raised an eyebrow, "*did* have a liking for her but…?"

"How much?" she broke in unceremoniously, opening her bag.

He pursed his lips. "You can't have been attending, Eliza," he admonished quietly. "I distinctly remember saying that I don't hire out the girls."

"And I thought you were a businessman!" she bit out disparagingly.

"That's right, Eliza," Reggie Wragge nodded, "a businessman; not a merchant in human beings."

"What's the matter, Reggie?" she demanded, not accustomed to being questioned or dismissed so casually. "Afraid I am going to steal her from you?"

"You know something, Eliza," he told her candidly, "I really don't think you could."

"Well?" she demanded, obliged to bite down another blistering retort. It would do no good to set his back up, but so very conscious was she that time was running out that her temper, born out of urgency, was beginning to get rather frayed.

"Why do you want her?" he enquired.

"*That,*" she told him firmly, her eyes narrowing, "is *my* business, not yours."

"That's where you're wrong, Eliza," he told her quietly, rising to his feet, "it is very much *my* business."

"Are you refusing?" she demanded sharply.

"No," he shook his head, "not refusing, merely protecting my interests; Molly's too. Something *you* of all people," he nodded significantly, "should understand."

"What do you mean?" she asked sharply.

"The thing is, Eliza," Reggie Wragge sighed, "I have a certain reputation; a reputation I am in no hurry to see jeopardised. In fact," he nodded, "I have no intention of that happening."

"What's that to me?" she wanted to know.

"Well," Reggie Wragge inclined his head, coming to stand in front of her, "until you tell me what it is you want Molly for, which," he shrugged, "could quite well be illegal for all I know, I am rather reluctant to…"

"It's not illegal," Eliza broke in heatedly. "Do you think I'm stupid?"

"No," he shook his head, "you're far from being stupid, Eliza, but surely you must see that from my point of view I…"

"Very well," she bit out, having no more time to argue. "I only want Molly for a few hours; to deliver a letter, that's all."

"Deliver a letter?" he repeated. "To whom?"

"Does it matter?" she shrugged, not having expected him to be so reluctant to do her a favour. "All you need know is that it's all above aboard," she lied glibly. "Damn you, Reggie!" she said angrily, when he made no immediate effort to answer. "Do you think I'd let something happen to Molly?" Reggie Wragge eyed her closely. "I'm known to the household," which was as far as she was prepared to commit herself, "which is why I can't go anywhere near it, but it's important Her Ladyship gets the letter. All I want is Molly to tell a white lie so they won't know it's from me and to ensure that it's handed to her unopened."

"Her Ladyship?" he repeated.

"It's all right," Eliza assured him, far from pleased at having to either explain or justify herself, "it's not what you think," adding a little mendaciously, "I don't have designs on her."

"Very well," he conceded at length, after thinking it over, "you can ask Molly yourself, but," he warned, "if she's no mind for it I'll not force her and," he warned again, "neither will you."

She knew enough of Reggie Wragge to know that he was a man who could not be pushed any more than he could be browbeaten with threats or bullying, and although it went very much against the grain with her to conciliate there really was nothing else for her to do but accept his ultimatum. Waiting in the rear drawing-room which had once been her office-cum-private room with what patience she could muster, she tried not to think what would happen should Molly refuse to help her, which could well be the case considering the bad terms on which they had parted. Even so, she was looking forward to seeing Molly again for her own sake, but it was clear from the moment Molly entered the room that she was by no means as eager to see *'Mother Discipline'* as she apparently was to see her.

"Molly!" Eliza cried, walking towards her. "It's good to see you again. I've missed you," she smiled, her cold eyes softening at the sight of so beautiful a young woman.

"Reggie told me you wanted to see me," Molly told her, not very encouragingly.

Ignoring this, Eliza brushed the soft cheek with the back of her forefinger, saying, with a softness not usually heard from her, "I have missed you so much," rather surprised when Molly turned her head away. "You had not used to turn away from me," she chastised gently.

"You had not used to give me the choice," Molly flashed back, her hazel eyes reflecting the unpleasant memories she had of this woman.

"Are you saying you did not enjoy the times we spent together?" Eliza asked softly, laying the palm of her hand against the soft skin of

Molly's face.

"That's exactly what I'm saying," Molly told her firmly, taking several steps away from her, unable to bear the touch of those horridly tactile fingers, desperately trying to shut out the unwanted images which suddenly flashed into her mind.

Eliza's cold eyes snapped together, but her voice was perfectly calm, not unhopeful of picking up where they had left off. "Then why didn't you say?"

"To have my back laid open like some of the other girls!" Molly bit out.

"I would never have done that to you," Eliza told her earnestly, the very thought of harming this lovely creature too horrendous to contemplate.

"You certainly threatened it often enough," Molly reminded her.

"But I never did," Eliza said softly.

"No," Molly shook her head, "you never did, but you would have done had I not let you…"

"Was it so very bad?" Eliza coaxed, raising a finger to stroke the luscious soft brown hair. "I don't think so."

"Well, you wouldn't, would you?" Molly pointed out. "After all, you aimed to please yourself rather than the girl you were with."

"But there was never anyone like you, Molly," Eliza told her truthfully.

"It's over, Eliza," Molly said firmly, "and I have no intention of resuming it. Now," she said determinedly, "what is it you want me to do?"

Far too experienced to press the point, realising that she could kill any hopes she may have in attaching Molly again, Eliza smiled, saying calmly, "I don't want you for a special client if that's what you are thinking, I promise you. I merely want you to deliver a letter."

When Reggie had told her that Eliza Boon was in his room and wished to see her, Molly's stomach lurched, distasteful recollections of what it had meant to be one of *'Mother Discipline's Daughters'* springing involuntarily to mind, but upon him telling her the reason for Eliza's visit as well as being given his assurances that she did not have to do it, by the time Molly entered the rear drawing-room she felt more relaxed.

However, the sight of the woman she had feared and hated brought everything back, and when Eliza had begun touching her she was quite repulsed by it.

"Well," Eliza urged, when she had come to the end of her explanations and instructions, "will you do it?" Upon receiving no immediate response, Eliza smiled, saying coaxingly, "Won't you do a favour for an old friend? I was good to you, Molly," she reminded her softly.

Compared to her treatment of the other girls she was, but even so Molly was by no means happy to put herself in a position whereby Eliza could take further advantage of her. "I don't know," she shook her head. "I don't want to get into any trouble."

"You won't," Eliza promised her gently. "Providing you follow my instructions everything will be all right. I promise you," she smiled, "you will be back here safe and sound by this afternoon." Seeing some further reassurances were clearly called for, she lied gently, "I swear to you Molly, I would never involve you in something which could get you into any trouble."

Eliza could, when the occasion demanded, be very persuasive, and since she considered this occasion to be vital to her own protection as well as Sir Braden's and Peterson's, she was more than prepared to lie or do whatever was necessary to further this end. Despite having told Molly she had missed her, the truth was that over the last ten or eleven months she had not given much, if any, thought to her at all, but upon setting eyes on her again after all this time she realised that she would not be averse to enjoying her company again. Be that as it may, however, before Eliza could resume storming the citadel to try to bring this about, there was the far more important task of preventing Lady Collett from talking and since she could not go to Mount Street herself to forcibly remove her any more than Peterson could, all Eliza's hopes were now pinned on Molly Clark to do it for her. Eliza did not think that Molly, despite her reluctance, would fail her, she hoped not because whilst Eliza had every confidence in her own abilities to come up with ideas, she had to acknowledge that this was one crisis to which she could find no feasible alternative to the strategy she was now desperately trying to bring to fruition, and it was with devastating effect that her persuasive tongue went to work.

Like the rest of the girls, Molly knew just how deceitful and dangerous Eliza Boon was and, if she needed further confirmation of this, all she had to do was bring to mind the treatment she had meted out to get them to do as she wanted. Molly may have no idea about what had happened to Annie Myers that night and the ruthless and dispassionate way Eliza had dealt with her lifeless body with the help of that hateful Peterson, the same as she had no idea about Eliza's involvement in the death of Dennis Dunscumbe and the others, but had she discovered any of it, it would not have surprised her. No one had been more pleased than Molly to learn that Eliza had sold her business to Reggie Wragge and had made no attempt to take her away with her, but the truth was Reggie treated them with courtesy and respect which Eliza never had, and it was the agreed opinion of all the girls that they were well rid of her. Molly knew as well as anyone that the business conducted within the walls of fifty-one Periton Place was against the law, even immoral, but since Reggie had taken over somehow it seemed eminently more respectable.

Eliza did not need to have Molly tell her this any more than she needed reminding that at no time could her handling of the girls be called motherly, in fact her harsh treatment had not only ensured they did as she told them but afforded her a perverse kind of gratification; a gratification only half satisfied in her dealings with Lady Collett. Eliza may have been in Molly's company for little more than ten minutes, but she was not so blind nor so insensible that she could not see that Molly had a loyalty to Reggie she never had for her and, unless she was very much mistaken, she was sure the rest of the girls felt the same. Nevertheless, she was not here to score points in a favourite person contest but to try to save herself and Sir Braden as well as Peterson from facing the Queen's Bench, and if this meant adopting dirty tactics, then so be it. There was far too much at stake for her to be complacent or to give Molly the opportunity of refusing, particularly as Eliza knew that should the truth ever come out nothing would prevent her from serving a prison sentence or Sir Braden and Peterson from climbing the scaffold because although she personally had not committed murder she had, in the eyes of the law, certainly incited it by having someone else do it for her.

So far, Reggie Wragge had shown just how proficient he was in ensuring that the reins of his legitimate business interests never became entangled with the more illegitimate ones, in fact so skilled was he in this that no one who ran across him at a Mansion House dinner or society party would have the least guess that he ran several very successful bawdyhouses. It was not in Eliza's interests to give the game away, but this matter of Lady Collett was of far too much importance to pay no heed to and it was therefore in that smoothly ominous voice Molly remembered so well that Eliza pointed out what could happen to Reggie if his more dubious interests were ever made known in certain quarters. The threat worked as Eliza knew it would, and Molly, turning a pale and horrified face towards her, cried, "You wouldn't!"

"Of course I wouldn't," Eliza soothed, patting the soft cheek, "but you must see how very awkward it would be for Reggie if someone did?"

Molly was not fooled, but she liked Reggie, all the girls did. He was fair and generous and treated them in a way Eliza had never done and it would be grossly unfair if he was made to suffer simply because she refused to deliver a letter, nevertheless, it was very much against her better judgement that she allowed herself to be persuaded.

Chapter Seventeen

By the time Tony walked into Bill's office a few minutes after eleven o'clock, Jerry, who was looking remarkably refreshed and wide awake considering he had imbibed several glasses of Sam's best brown ale with his old police pals until well after closing time, had already been comfortably established in Bill's warm domain for close on three-quarters of an hour, during the course of which he had put Bill in the picture about the previous evening's unprecedented events. Bill was by no means surprised to learn that Tony had turned up in Cavendish Square last night with the full intention of gaining access to Collett's house to remove Lady Collett, but upon discovering that she had managed to leave the premises under her own steam and in the most appalling physical condition shocked him, so much so that it was several moments before he could find his voice to say anything, in fact he had still not quite recovered from Jerry's disclosure when Tony eventually strolled into his office. Just one look at Tony's face was more than enough to tell Bill that even though Lady Collett was now safely installed in Mount Street he was by no means through with her husband, and by the time Tony had finished telling them about what had happened once he had got Eleanor safely to Mount Street and what he had discerned from her fretful utterances, Bill was left in no doubt. "God damn!" he exclaimed, fishing out a cigar from his waistcoat pocket. "Collett's some guy!"

"He sure is!" Tony agreed with feeling, then, turning to Jerry, he asked about Collett's whereabouts last night, to which Jerry told him that he went no farther than *'The Stephenson Club'*, arriving back home about quarter past eleven.

"An' there 'e stayed!" Jerry nodded.

"No one else left the house?" Tony enquired.

"No Guv," Jerry shook his head. "Once that butler cove got back from searchin' all over for Lady Collett, there weren't a sign of any a one!" going on to tell them about what he had gleaned from his cronies at *'The Prince Albert'*.

"Are you sure about that, Jerry?" Tony urged. "That the police having nothing on Peterson!"

"Not a thing," Jerry asserted. "Whatever 'e's been doin' since 'e left the ring it's either all been above board or 'e ain't never been caught."

"He may have a clean sheet, Jerry," Tony nodded, "but I'd lay my life it's not because he's been law-abiding! What about this woman who calls herself Eliza Boon?" He cocked his head. "Anything on her?"

"Not a thing. Pity," Jerry shook his head, 'because I thought we'd be lucky with 'er."

"So did I," Tony agreed, "especially as I've a pretty good idea what her profession is or," he corrected himself, "was and, if I am right, and I know I am, I find it hard to believe that she's been able to carry out her business without coming to someone's notice. Keep digging on those two, Jerry." Then, looking at Bill, asked, "Any luck your end, Bill?"

Bill, who had been leaning forward on his elbows, eased himself up into a sitting position and removed the cigar from his mouth. "Not your day, Tony," he sighed. "As far as Mary Stanley goes I've come up with zilch, but I've got someone still looking into that, but you may have to speak to Lady Collett about her," he nodded. "As far as unidentified bodies go," he told him, "only two have not been accounted for in the Greater London area, one of them being a young woman. As for the man," he shrugged, "he was found in Stepney six months ago, but apart from being much too young for our guy his body was later identified by a brother."

"What!" Tony exclaimed. "Are you sure Bill?"

"Sure I'm sure!" he shrugged. "Sorry, Tony," he hunched a shoulder, "but I can't pull stiffs out of the air!"

"Damn it, Bill!" Tony exclaimed. "I know you can't, but surely to God if Mitchell's been murdered, which I'm convinced he has been, then where the devil have they left his body? And, if he's alive, he can't just have disappeared!"

Bill waved a hand. "If he's not dead, seems that just was he has done."

Tony strode over to the window and stared down into the busy street below for several moments, a deep frown creasing his forehead, but just as he was about to say something the sound of voices coming from the secretary's office next door wafted through, followed within seconds by the sudden opening of the door. "I'm sorry, Mr. Pitman," a harassed middle-aged woman hastily apologised, "but this young man insists…"

"'Arry!" Jerry exclaimed, heaving himself out of his chair as he caught sight of his son. "What d'you think you're doin'? You should be…"

"Sorry," Harry shook his head, "but I 'ad to come."

Having dismissed his secretary, Bill looked indulgently at the young man and asked, "What is it, son?"

Harry, looking apprehensively at each man in turn, promptly whisked off his cap before falteringly favouring his audience with how he had followed Eliza Boon then unfortunately lost sight of her at the corner of Tottenham Court Road. His father, pursing his lips, was just on the point of raking him down when Harry informed them, having by now got his breath back, "I got the 'ackney's number; 7205, driven by an Arthur Price. I managed to speak to 'im not fifteen minutes back; 'e told me that the fare 'e picked up at the corner of 'Ollis Street and Oxford Street asked 'im to take 'er to an address in Bloomsbury."

"Bloomsbury!" Jerry repeated.

Harry nodded. "Periton Place, number fifty-one."

The three men exchanged glances and Jerry, scratching his head bewilderingly, shrugged, "Now, what's the likes of 'er doin' in Bloomsbury?"

"Tell me Harry," Tony cocked his head, "has Sir Braden or Peterson left the house at all this morning?"

"No, sir," Harry shook his head, "that is, not while I was there they 'adn't, but they cud 'ave done since I 'anded over my watch. The only other person was a woman who left by the basement steps, a rather stout lady, Sir, but as you only wanted those three followed I just made a note of what time she left."

Tony smiled. "It's all right, Harry. That was Mrs. Timms, Sir Braden's cook. She came to Mount Street to see my sister regarding her concerns for Lady Collett. You will find," he nodded, "that she is very much our friend and, if I am not mistaken, she will not be backward in offering help should we need it. By the way, Bill," Tony nodded, "about

Mary Stanley, Harry's just reminded me of it; Mrs. Timms told me that she comes from the Dagenham area and her mother still lives there."

"You got it, Tony!" Bill nodded.

"'Who's watchin' the 'ouse now?" Jerry demanded of his son.

"Arthur and Edward," Harry told him. "Sam's due to start 'is watch in a couple of 'ours."

"Well," Jerry instructed him, "you get back there; I'll be along directly an'…"

"One moment, Jerry," Tony broke in. "I am afraid I am going to have to take Harry away from his surveillance," noting that, like his father, Harry was sturdily built and looked very well able to take care of himself as well as being more than capable of taking on all-comers.

"What d'you 'ave in mind?" Jerry asked.

"It's no use pretending Collett does not know we have his wife safely in Mount Street," Tony explained. "He does, that's why Peterson stood watch for some time on the opposite side of the street, but Collett knows too that once her injuries begin to heal it's only a matter of time before she starts talking. At all costs he must prevent this from happening, and it's my guess he will take a crack at removing her. Unfortunately," he sighed, "I can only speculate what he will attempt in the way of this and when, but since I can't always be on hand any more than my brother-in-law can I need someone inside the house to protect Lady Collect and my sister."

"Do you really think he will try something?" Bill asked.

"I think it's a pretty safe bet, Bill," Tony nodded. "So, Jerry," he smiled, "if you can spare Harry to me for however long it takes, I should be obliged."

Harry, receiving his father's go-ahead, could not believe his good fortune in being given such a cushy number, especially in such bitterly cold weather as this. "Bill, ring my sister and tell her to expect Harry, and Harry," Tony smiled across at him, "I'll give you a note to hand to my sister."

"Yes, sir," he nodded.

While Bill rang Beatrice and Tony scribbled a brief note for her, Jerry, who had no qualms about his son's abilities to carry out such an important job, took him to one side in order to prime him for the task in hand, to which that young man nodded and shook his head where necessary.

"I'm sorry if I have messed up your arrangements by taking Harry away from his duties, Jerry," Tony smiled when Harry had left, "but I cannot leave my sister and Lady Collett unattended." Jerry, after dismissing this as all part of the job he had hired them to do, said it was a pity Harry had lost sight of his quarry, to which Tony told him to put it out of his mind. "It couldn't be helped, but it's thanks to his quick thinking that we know her destination."

"Bloomsbury!" Jerry pondered. "Why Bloomsbury? What could 'ave took 'er there?" He scratched his head. "Of course," he shrugged, though not very convincingly, "it could be all innocent."

"No, Jerry," Tony shook his head, "if she found it necessary to visit that address in Bloomsbury this morning, then she had a very good reason for doing so, but what that reason is," he pulled a face, "I know no more than you except that I am certain it's something to do with Dennis Dunscumbe and his brother." He paused a moment as he turned something over in his mind, then, looking down at Bill, cocked his head, "Bill, about this young woman whose body has not been identified, where was she found, and when?"

Placing his cigar between his teeth, Bill leaned forward to rummage through some papers on his desk until pulling out a torn off sheet on which his secretary had noted down the information earlier, not having paid too much attention to it since his enquiries were about Collett's butler and not a woman. "Well, God damn!" he cried, taking the cigar out of his mouth and looking up at Tony. "Bloomsbury; eight months back give or take!"

"Bloomsbury!" Tony repeated. "Are you sure, Bill?"

"You bet!" he nodded.

"Good God!" Jerry exclaimed, looking from Tony to Bill. "There's got to be a connection!"

"Yes, there has," Tony said, almost to himself, his brain racing. Then, turning to Bill asked, "Do you have a description of the dead woman, Bill?"

"Not to speak of," he nodded, glancing at the information his secretary had hurriedly written down. "Apparently she was no pretty sight by the time she was found, which," he sighed, "was at least a couple of months after her body had been left there."

"Where was it left precisely?" Tony urged.

"Somewhere called Heron Street," Bill told him, after scanning his notes.

"That's only a few streets away from this Periton Place!" Jerry told them. "As I remember it was a row of derelict 'ouses; some of 'em," he nodded, "the floors 'ad gone."

"Jerry's right, Tony," Bill said, "there *has* to be a connection. It's much too near to this house where the maid dame went."

Tony, having taken a turn about the room, came back to stand in front of Bill's desk, his forehead creased in thought. "Give me everything you've got on this girl, Bill."

"Okay," Bill sighed, "but it's not much. According to the autopsy her death resulted from a severe blow to the back of the head, but from the decomposed condition of the body it was not possible to say whether it was an accident or not, but it was definitely moved and thrown down into the cellar through a collapsed floor in one of the houses in Heron Street."

"Who found her?" Tony urged.

"A couple of Council officials who had gone there to see about the demolition work. From the looks of it," Bill told him, perusing the notes in his hand, "she was quite young, early twenties apparently, about five-five, slim with blonde hair. That's it, Tony."

"And no one has reported a young woman fitting that description as missing?" Tony raised an enquiring eyebrow.

"Huh huh," Bill shrugged.

"So," Tony mused, after giving it some thought, "we have Eliza Boon visiting a house in Bloomsbury where, only a block or two away, the body of a young woman was found eight months ago give or take, which means her death occurred about ten or eleven months back; she has not been reported as missing and no identification has ever been made."

"That's about the size of it!" Bill nodded, inhaling on his cigar.

"And what does all of this suggest to you, Bill?" Tony raised an eyebrow.

"She was a hooker," he said simply.

"Yes," Tony agreed, "and I'd stake my life she worked for Eliza Boon at this house in Periton Place."

"Well," Bill sighed, "I pretty much figured this Eliza Boon dame was kind of involved in something like that."

"I'd stake my life she was," Tony said firmly, "and I'd also stake my life that this young woman's death is somehow tied up with that of Sir Philip Dunscumbe and his brother."

"Now *that's* what I call close to 'ome," Jerry nodded, "but can we prove it, Guv?"

"Jerry's got a point, Tony," Bill nodded. "I admit everything points that way, but we're going on nothing but guesswork."

"Are we?" Tony raised an eyebrow. "I don't think so. Okay," he conceded when he saw the frown crease Bill's forehead, "I admit that I don't have all the answers, but let's have a look at what we *do* have, which is three unexplained deaths for a start, and all within a couple of months of one another, not to mention Mitchell's disappearance and the dismissal of Mary Stanley! No, Bill," he shook his head, "I may not at the moment be able to put the pieces in the right order, but it's definitely not guesswork, and whatever else those deaths might be they are not coincidence, far from it! Dennis Dunscumbe apparently shot himself in the right temple, now," he nodded, "why would a left-handed man do that? He wouldn't! And, what possible reason could he have had for doing so? It can't have been money," he shook his head, "he was far too used to living on what little he had to suddenly let it worry him to the point where he could not face it any longer. No," he said firmly, "his death was not suicide but murder, and whoever committed it made the fatal error of shooting him right-handed. My guess is that it was this Peterson guy who pulled the trigger, but I doubt very much whether he planned it, in fact," he nodded, "I'd say it was this Eliza Boon woman and that Collett was a party to it. I admit I have only seen her once and that briefly, but what I saw was enough to tell me that she is not only determined but extremely resourceful and, however much it goes against the grain with me to say it, I am rather surprised a woman like that could have made such a monumental error as not knowing Dennis Dunscumbe was left-handed; either that," he shrugged, "or Peterson forgot it once he arrived in Hertford Street."

"I know I've asked this before," Bill threw over his shoulder as he poured out three cups of much-needed coffee, "but why plan his murder at all?"

"It could only have been to stop him from talking," Tony said firmly.

"About what?" Bill hunched a shoulder.

"About what happened to that poor girl whose body was found dumped like a piece of garbage!" Tony replied harshly.

"You really think he had something to do with it?" Bill questioned.

"Damn right I do!" Tony said firmly. "Look, we know that he was mixed up with a set his brother apparently disapproved of, one of whom was Sir Braden Collett, who just happens to have Peterson and Eliza Boon living in his house don't forget, looking after his wife or," he corrected himself, somewhat severely, "to keep guard over her, a woman who, only this very morning, visits this house in Bloomsbury! Now, unless I've suddenly lost the brain I was born with," he told them, "I'd say it looks very much as though this Eliza Boon kept a certain type of establishment, not the usual kind," he nodded meaningfully, "but one that caters for men like Collett and Dennis Dunscumbe whose natural tendencies veer very much towards brutality, fifty-one Periton Place unless I'm mistaken, and that this young woman whose body was found only blocks away was one of her girls. I'd lay any money on it that both Collett and Dennis Dunscumbe were regular visitors and that, at some point, something happened to this girl in which they were both involved, and although I know I'm only guessing here," he nodded, "I'd say it was Dennis Dunscumbe rather than Collett. I'm not saying he deliberately murdered her," he inclined his head, "but let us suppose things just got a little out of hand and, before he realised what had happened, he discovered she was dead. Let us again suppose that Collett and Eliza Boon helped cover it up to prevent a scandal and that Peterson disposed of the body, but Dunscumbe, despite his habit of slapping women around, started to feel remorseful and was going to tell the police or, perhaps, his brother, something which they could not risk."

"An' Sir Philip?" Jerry enquired, who had no fault to find with Tony's summing up.

"I can't say whether it was his brother who confided in him about what had happened or this woman who wrote to him at his rooms in Westminster who put him on to the truth," Tony admitted, "but one or the other of them *must* have done," he said firmly, "but I'm absolutely certain that this letter was the reason he not only left his rooms that afternoon, but took him to Collett's house where he confronted him, and it's thanks to Mrs. Timms," he told them, "that I am now firmly convinced that is where Sir Philip met his death," going on to give them a brief outline of what had passed between himself and Mrs. Timms earlier that morning in Mount Street. "I am only surmising here I know," he confessed, "but I'd say Collett, when faced with Sir Philip on his doorstep and his accusations, lost his head and killed him. Why else would he have had the carpet in his study taken up? It could only be because it was heavily bloodstained, in fact," he nodded, "I'd say that Sir Philip's body was actually rolled up in the soiled carpet when it was eventually disposed of."

"And Lady Collett, returning home earlier than expected from the concert, either walks in and witnesses it or stumbles on to something which alerted her to it!" Bill concluded.

"Precisely!" Tony nodded.

"And Mitchell?" Bill cocked his head. "Do you still believe he suffered the same fate as Sir Philip?"

"Too right I do, Bill!" Tony said firmly. "I may only be able to speculate on what kind of guy Mitchell was, but one thing I *can* say for certain and that is he would have to have been blind as well as stupid not to put two and two together and come up with the truth. As for Collett, well," he shrugged, "we know he's mighty prone to protecting his interests and so we can be pretty sure he would have recognised the threat Mitchell posed and, if Collett's track record is anything to go by, he would have taken steps to deal with it. Even if he did buy Mitchell off he would always be wondering if that was the end of it or just the start of paying Mitchell for his silence, something Collett could not risk, so instead he had Mitchell put permanently out of the way and, unless I've figured it all wrong," he nodded, "by this Peterson guy who I am absolutely convinced not only disposed of Sir Philip's body by throwing it into the Thames, but also hurling the body of that young woman into what was left of one of those derelict houses. I can't say for certain whether the idea of getting rid of Mitchell was Collett's idea or Eliza Boon's, but either way Mitchell posed a threat they dared not ignore. As for Mary," he sighed, "dismissing her could only have been to bring this Eliza Boon woman in to keep guard over Lady Collett." After taking a generous mouthful of coffee, Tony raised a questioning eyebrow at Bill. "Do you still say it's guesswork, Bill?"

"No," he shook his head, "in fact, it all fits like a glove, even down to the date, but proving it," he sighed, "is going be some job especially as Lady Collett is no good to us when it comes to giving evidence."

"I know," Tony acknowledged, "which is why I am hoping I shall find out more when I visit this address in Holborn this afternoon."

"I guess it's already occurred to you," Bill told him, "that it stands a pretty good chance that the woman who wrote the letter to Sir Philip worked for this Boon dame, assuming that is," he nodded, "this Hallerton guy is right and the letter *was* from a woman. If not," he shrugged, "then I guess we're back at…"

"It was from a woman, Bill," Tony broke in firmly, "make no mistake. Apart from the fact that Hallerton was pretty certain it was a woman's handwriting my gut feeling is telling me it was, on that I'd stake my life, in which case," he nodded, "she must have seen something or, at the very least, overheard something, which is why she wrote to Sir Philip."

"Well," Bill sighed again, "if what we've come up with so far *is* the truth, and I believe it is, then I'd say it *was* a woman, but why wait so long before writing to him?"

"Most probably because she was too scared, especially when she discovered Dennis Dunscumbe had supposedly committed suicide and, if this Boon woman is all I take her to be," he nodded, "I can't say I blame her. All I can hope for," he sighed, "is that she'll talk to me."

"I sure hope so!" Bill sighed. "Because if she doesn't, then we can't prove any of this, not that I see a jury taking the word of a hooker!" he nodded, "and, don't forget," he pointed his cigar at him, "there's every chance she no longer lives at that address and, even supposing she does or you track her down, what makes you so sure she'll tell you anything?"

"I'm sure of nothing," Tony replied grimly, "but damn it all Bill there are four deaths to be answered for! Not to mention what Lady Collett has endured all this time!"

"You don't think they've done this woman in as well, do you?" Jerry asked thoughtfully. "If she was one of this Eliza Boon's girls," he nodded, "an' she did see or 'ear somethin'…"

"I have to admit," Tony confessed, "that that possibly had not occurred to me, but since you mention it," he shook his head, "I can't see it." Upon seeing the look of doubt descend onto Bill's face, Tony pointed out, "She wrote that letter to Sir Philip sometime after Dennis Dunscumbe's supposed suicide and from this address in Holborn, which means that she was no longer at Periton Place when she wrote to him. I can't say how or when she left there, Bill," he shook his head, "but she must have done. You both know as well as I do that most of these girls have either run away from home or have no one who cares about them, and had she been murdered," he pointed out, glancing from Bill to Jerry, "then surely her unidentified body would be on that list," indicating the piece of paper on Bill's desk with a nod of his head. Then, turning to Jerry, said, "Jerry, I want you to find out who owns this fifty-one Periton Place and who owned it before, in fact I want you to find out everything you can about it."

"Right you are, Guv," he nodded.

"And Bill," Tony smiled, "I know you 'can't pull stiffs out of the air' as you so delicately put it, but keep on digging about Mitchell."

"You got it," he grinned. "Mary Stanley too?"

"Yes," Tony nodded, "keep trying, although it may well be that if you come up with nothing in or around Dagenham I shall have to resort to speaking to Lady Collett about her after all to find an address of some kind, but I would much rather wait until she's recovered a little, besides," he pointed out, "I don't want to upset or worry her over Mary unnecessarily especially as I have every reason to believe that far from being permanently got rid of she is in fact safe and well."

Even though Tony regarded it as a foregone conclusion that Collett would try something in the way of removing Eleanor from the safety of Mount Street, he was quite unable to answer Bill's question as to what moves Collett was likely to make to bring it about, much less when, but that he would not take too long Tony was certain. He was firmly convinced that Eliza Boon's visit to fifty-one Periton Place must mean something and, unless his instincts had grossly misled him when he had told Jerry he felt sure it was connected with the supposed suicide of Dennis Dunscumbe and his brother's brutal murder, he was certain of it. Had Tony the least guess that it was to set plans in motion to lure Eleanor back to Cavendish Square he would have returned to Mount Street straightaway instead of going directly to Holborn.

Having successfully completed her mission, Eliza Boon left Periton Place some two hours later with a reluctant Molly beside her, but for a woman of Eliza's domineering nature and forceful personality, who was not used to being denied, she was very far from happy over the way she virtually had to beg Reggie Wragge for a favour. Were it not for the urgency attached in removing Lady Collett from her sanctuary in Mount Street and without Lady Shipton or her brother suspecting she had a hand in it, Eliza would have known no hesitation in bringing the full force of her bullying disposition to bear on Reggie Wragge. But no matter how desperate she regarded the situation facing her and Sir Braden she had retained enough self-restraint to hold her tongue, besides, she knew that such threatening and bullying tactics would not have served.

It was all very well for Reggie Wragge to calmly assert that he did not trade in human beings, but the fact remained he was making a very tidy living from the men who sought the company of the girls night after night within the confines of fifty-one Periton Place, men who, as Eliza knew only too well, were more than ready to pay through the nose to indulge their unusual proclivities as well as for that all important element of discretion, precisely as she had done. Despite his unruffled claims that he was a businessman and not a pimp or a slave trader, Reggie Wragge had an awful lot to lose should his more illegitimate dealings become known, and had he proved obstinate in rendering himself agreeable to her request, Eliza would have had no compunction in paying him back in a way he would not forget in a hurry; just like *'Mother Discipline's Daughters'*, he would have come to know the meaning of gainsaying her!

Molly Clark, who knew from painful experience precisely what it meant to be one of *'Mother Discipline's Daughters'*, had no doubt at all that Eliza was more than capable of carrying out the threats she had subtly whispered in her ear about the harm she could do Reggie if she failed to help her; Eliza did not make idle threats! Reggie had been good to her, in fact he was good to all the girls who worked in Periton Place, and whilst Molly knew as well as anyone that the authorities would not look upon him as a benevolent employer but as the owner of a house of ill repute, even as a man living off immoral earnings, the fact remained she liked him too much to see him hurt or his reputation ruined and it was because of this that she had agreed to do what Eliza asked.

As Molly had never been forced to ply her trade on the streets to pay her rent or a pimp as well as keeping her in gin or whatever tipple took her fancy but in the protected confines of a most comfortable establishment, her beautiful face had not suffered from the ravages of her livelihood, and no one looking at her as she left the house in company with Eliza would have had the least guess as to what her profession was. Indeed, none of the girls bore any telltale signs as to their occupation, not even when they formed part of *'Mother Discipline's'* elite group. Eliza, for all her faults and the strict discipline she employed as well as the fear she instilled into them, ensured they were well looked after and when Molly arrived in Mount Street half an hour later she no less than Eliza had every confidence in that no member of Lady Shipton's household would have the least suspicion of how she earned her living.

Having been cautioned by Tony before he left the house to be extra vigilant about whom she allowed into the house, Beatrice had listened to Bennett informing her of the arrival of a young woman by the name of Miss Molly Clark with mixed feelings. She knew Tony was going to speak to Jerry about arranging for someone to be close by as it was not possible for either himself or Tom to be always around to offer her and Eleanor protection should Collett decide to show his hand, but in spite of the telephone call from Bill so far Harry had not yet put in an appearance. Beatrice, unable to rid her mind of the sneaking suspicion that this Molly Clark may well not be all she appeared, thought it might be advisable if she instructed Bennett to deny her, but common sense soon asserted itself telling her that she had nothing to fear, especially in broad daylight with a small army of servants for her to call upon should the need arise, and therefore she requested Bennett to inform the young woman that she would be with her directly. After checking on Eleanor, who, Sarah whispered, had been sound asleep for the past hour and more, Beatrice made her way downstairs to meet, for the second time that day, a visitor who was quite unknown to her. Unlike Mrs. Timms, Molly's appearance and demeanour gave no hint as to her true calling and, upon coming face to face with her, Beatrice found herself looking at a young woman of about thirty years of age, a little taller than herself with a good figure, whose rich brown hair was neatly confined beneath a hat unadorned by any decoration, and her clothes, which were serviceable rather than stylish, clearly advertised her domestic service status. It occurred to Beatrice that this remarkably good-looking young woman would not have looked out of place at a society gathering, and those large hazel eyes, which held a hint of humour beneath the openness, could well be the undoing of more than one impressionable young man. Beatrice, having not the slightest inkling that this was precisely what did happen, almost every night, only to men who were very far from being young and susceptible, glided towards Molly where she stood just inside the front door holding her bag in front of her with two small and shapely hands, enquiring politely, "Miss Clark?"

Molly bobbed a curtsy. "Are you Lady Shipton?"

"Yes," Beatrice nodded, "I am Lady Shipton. How may I help you?"

"Beggin' your pardon, m'lady," Molly bobbed another curtsy, Eliza's faith in her talent for acting not misplaced; her articulation precisely what one would expect of an upstairs parlour maid, "but Sir Miles Tatton 'as asked me to come an' see you."

"Sir Miles?" Beatrice repeated, a little bewildered.

"Yes, m'lady." Molly nodded.

"I don't understand." Beatrice shook her head. "Has Sir Miles returned to town?"

"No, m'lady, 'e's still in Suffolk," Molly replied smoothly.

"But I…" Beatrice began.

"I'm sorry, m'lady," she apologised, "I should 'ave said that I work for Sir Miles, a parlour maid, m'lady," she further explained. "Well, it so 'appens that my mother's been taken poorly an' Sir Miles 'as granted me leave to go an' see her. Well, the thing is m'lady," she told her, "Sir Miles asked me if I would stop off an' come an' see you to ask if you would give this letter to 'is daughter, Lady Collett," pulling the oblong envelope out of her bag.

Beatrice, totally confused, shook her head. "For *me* to give to her?"

"Yes, m'lady," Molly confirmed.

"But I don't understand!" Beatrice cried.

"'E'd be ever so grateful, m'lady," Molly smiled.

Beatrice's brain may well be awash with astonishment and misgivings, but she was not so lost to the fact that under no circumstances could she divulge to this young woman that at this very moment Sir Miles Tatton's daughter was enjoying sanctuary under her roof. Even if Tony had not warned her about being prepared for some underhanded tactic on Sir Braden's part, there was no denying that the unexpected arrival of this young woman, supposedly on Sir Miles Tatton's behalf, was extremely suspicious, but mentally pulling herself together Beatrice said, as calmly as she could, "But why should Sir Miles ask me such a thing? Surely, it would be better to take it directly to Lady Collett in Cavendish Square."

"Yes, m'lady," Molly replied without a blink, "but the thing is you see, Sir Miles does not wish Sir Braden to know that 'e 'as written to 'is daughter, which 'e will if I take it there."

"Does not wish…!" Once again Beatrice found it necessary to pull herself together, saying, with as much composure as she could muster, "I should, of course, be delighted to hand the letter to Lady Collett, but," she shook her head, "it is a regrettable circumstance that I do not see as much of her as I was once used to."

"No, m'lady," Molly sadly shook her head, "Sir Miles is aware of that, which is why 'e 'oped you would slip it to 'er, quiet like, when next you *do* see 'er," giving Beatrice no time to refuse by hurriedly depositing the envelope into her suddenly nerveless fingers.

As Beatrice had never seen a sample of Sir Miles Tatton's handwriting, or Sir Braden's for that matter, she could not say with any degree of certainty whether Sir Miles had penned the letter or not, but since her visitor seemed to take it for granted that she would hand over the letter to Lady Collett, Molly bobbed a curtsy and made ready to leave. Beatrice, utterly at a loss, found her voice sufficiently to say, "But Miss Clark, indeed I cannot… I mean, I have not the least idea when I shall run across Lady Collett again!"

"Sir Miles was most insistent, m'lady," Molly told her politely.

Looking uneasily down at the envelope in her hand then back at Molly, Beatrice sighed, "Very well, I shall endeavour to do so, but I cannot say when it is likely to be."

"Thank you, m'lady," Molly bobbed a curtsy, then, turning on her heel, let herself out of the house before Beatrice could say anything further.

As everything about Molly Clark suggested she was precisely what she purported to be, it was not the young woman herself who unsettled Beatrice so much as the unexpectedness of her errand. Since she had no idea who went to make up Sir Miles Tatton's domestic household she could only guess whether this Miss Clark did indeed form part of it or whether she was in fact acting for Sir Braden in his efforts to lure his wife back to Cavendish Square as Tony had every expectation of him doing. She could only speculate how often Eleanor saw her father, but considering the treatment Sir Braden meted out to her Beatrice doubted it would be very often as Sir Miles would surely recognise his daughter's injuries for what they really were, and even though she and Tom were firmly of the belief that he had sold Eleanor into marriage Beatrice did not think that he would sit calmly by and do nothing to stop it. It was common knowledge that Sir Miles did not venture into society much now, in fact he was so seldom to be seen in town that one could almost describe him as a recluse, and therefore Beatrice felt it reasonably safe to assume that the two men did not associate with one another very often. There could, of course, be a more personal motive to account for them keeping their distance and, if her supposition was correct, then it could well be that Sir Miles had, for some reason or other, been forced into sanctioning the marriage against his better judgement, which certainly added a ring of truth to what Miss Clark had told her about him not wishing to let Sir Braden know he had written to his daughter.

It was all so very perplexing and by the time Beatrice made her way upstairs to see if Eleanor was awake, she was not at all sure whether the errand and the reasons behind it were genuine or not. It had crossed her mind to ring Tony and put her concerns to him, but since there was every chance he had left Bill's office by now to visit this address in Holborn, Beatrice was not quite sure whether to hand Eleanor the letter or not. She supposed that from a legal standpoint if nothing else, she had no right whatsoever to withhold correspondence which was expressly addressed to Eleanor and marked 'private' into the bargain, but such was the uncertainty of Beatrice's mind that she wondered whether it was best to wait until Tony returned or Tom arrived home to discuss it with them. As it happened however, the decision was for the moment taken out of her hands as Eleanor was still sound asleep when she quietly entered the guest room, a circumstance Beatrice was not entirely sure whether to be glad about or not.

The arrival of Harry some fifteen minutes later, a tall and muscular young man who bore all the hallmarks of being able to fend off any number of desperate persons, and the reassuring content of Tony's note, went some way to calming Beatrice's nerves, and by the time she had made arrangements to see he was comfortably established, she was feeling a little more like her usual self. Upon hearing of Her Ladyship's unexpected visitor and the questionable letter she had delivered, Harry, who was wise enough to keep his opinion to himself in that it could well be nothing more than a preliminary skirmish to check out the lie of the land, told her that he felt sure it was nothing to alarm her and, after a reconnoitre of the house to check the windows were all secured and any possible means of surreptitious entry, he settled himself down in a comfortable chair in the hall with a bowl of hot soup provided by his hostess.

Unaware of the events taking place all around her, Eleanor opened her tender and sore left eye several hours later to see that Sarah was sitting quietly beside her bed busily engaged with her embroidery, and felt considerably reassured by her comforting presence. Although Eleanor's body still ached it was not so painful to move, and her left eye, escaping most of Braden's brutal attack, was now almost fully open and, for the first time, she was able to gain a clear, though slightly misty, look at Sarah. The sluggish movement of her head on the pillow brought Sarah's head up and her cheerful rosy face broke into a smile, laying aside her embroidery. "How do you feel now, dearie?" she asked in a motherly voice, gently raising Eleanor's head in order for her to have a sip of water.

"Better, thank you," Eleanor managed faintly. "What time is it?"

"Now there's no need for you to be worrying your head over the time," Sarah soothed, gently plumping up the pillows. "'Sides, it doesn't make 'apporth of difference what time it is, you're not going anywhere, nor will for a good while yet!"

Looking up into the warm-hearted face smiling down at her, Eleanor asked, a little shyly, the colour which flooded her cheeks easily discernible beneath the bruises, "Tony?"

"Now," Sarah said briskly, "don't you go worrying over His Lordship," regarding their budding romance indulgently. "He went out this morning not long after seeing you, and," she nodded, forestalling the question she knew was coming, "he won't be back until he's ready." Seeing that Eleanor was about to say something Sarah chided gently, reminding her patient of her old nurse, "Now it's no manner of use asking me where he's gone because I can't tell you. Now you just lie there and do as Sarah tells you," preventing Eleanor from saying anything further as she began to gently apply some of the arnica Doctor Little had left.

Having decided, after much deliberation, to give Eleanor the letter, Beatrice quietly entered the room just as Sarah had finished treating her patient, and Eleanor, who was on the point of asking Sarah if she thought she was looking better, caught sight of the letter in Beatrice's hand and felt a momentary feeling of dread, driving everything else out of her mind. Beatrice, who was still finding it extremely difficult to look upon her dear friend's battered face without wanting to burst into tears at the wickedness of such a vile desecration, managed to clamp down on this overwhelming impulse and, instead, summoned up her lovely smile and asked how she was feeling. Eleanor, telling her that although she still felt as though her body seemed to be made of lead as well as giving her a little discomfort when she moved she was nevertheless feeling much better, but when she quickly followed this up by offering her indebtedness for all the kindness she and Tom were showing her, Beatrice patted the small hand lying on top of the cover, chiding gently, "Such nonsense, my dear! I want to hear no more of it! We are both of us delighted to have you here even though the circumstances are to be deplored, but we are quite decided that you are to remain here, and *nothing*," she stressed, "will prevail upon us to send you back to Cavendish Square!" Upon seeing the tears stream down Eleanor's bruised and swollen face, Beatrice, having to fight the inclination to burst into tears herself, said gently, "You must know, my dear that you are quite safe here. Why, Tony has even arranged for us to have our very own security guard to protect us while he and Tom are out! Yes," she nodded as Eleanor looked an enquiry, "he is at this very moment downstairs so, you see my dear, there is no way Sir Braden or anyone can get into the house to steal you away from us!"

"Tony's done that?" Eleanor cried, choked.

Beatrice nodded. "Yes. I told him there was not the least need as we shall be quite all right with Bennett and everyone else, but he would have it his way, but then," she smiled, "he loves you very much."

Quite overcome, Eleanor said tearfully, "Oh, Beatrice, what can I say?"

"There's nothing *to* say," she assured her. "Now," she said bracingly, more to prevent herself from succumbing to her emotions than anything else, "I have something here for you," indicating the letter she held in her hand. Despite her own misgivings her voice was quite calm, admirably concealing her concerns, "It was delivered by hand a little while ago. It's from your father."

"My father?" Eleanor repeated, her feeling of dread increasing.

"Yes," Beatrice smiled, going on to tell her about Miss Clark.

Unless her father had employed a new member of staff, Eleanor had never before heard of Molly Clark, but since she had not seen him for some little time he could well have done, yet somewhere in the pit of her stomach she had the sickening feeling that he had not and far from having written the letter her father knew nothing about it, and just one look at the writing on the envelope handed to her was enough to confirm this suspicion as well as her worst fears. Not wishing to alarm or distress Beatrice, she took the letter from her and upon being asked if she would be able to read it all right or if she wished her to do so for her, Eleanor smiled and shook her head, assuring Beatrice that she could see sufficiently through her left eye. Waiting only long enough to gently prop Eleanor up against the pillows, Beatrice left her friend to read her correspondence, devoutly trusting that she had done the right thing in handing it to her.

Considering Eleanor had known Tony for such a short time the fact remained she only felt safe when he was near her and although she could not expect him to be within call every minute, she nevertheless missed his comforting presence. He may not have told her in so many words, but she knew he was investigating the death of Sir Philip Dunscumbe and although she had wanted to tell Tony the truth this morning about what she had walked into that night, she instinctively knew that he was already aware that it was her husband who had killed him without the need for her to do so. She suspected that Tony had not told her it was necessary for him to go out so as not to alarm her, but now, in view of Braden's letter, she could only view his absence as providential because if she was right, and she was certain she was, then she had a pretty shrewd idea of the message it contained and, under no circumstances, could she let him or Beatrice read it.

Eleanor's fears were not misplaced. Braden's handwriting, glaring menacingly up at her from the sheets of white vellum, precise and to the point, left her in no doubt of the consequences which would result should she fail to comply with his letter. She supposed she should have known that Braden would realise where she was as well as not letting her escape him for long and the very thought of returning to Cavendish Square and Eliza Boon filled Eleanor with such dread that she shivered, red-hot tears stinging her already sore cheeks. Braden may have promised her that he would not carry out his threat by having her committed if she returned to him of her own free will, but so desperate was he to prevent the truth from leaking out that he would promise anything. Even supposing Braden kept his word, she would be even more confined than she had so far. Her life had already been restricted enough since the horrifying events of that night; her every movement watched as well as never being allowed out alone, but once she returned she could expect even more stringent restrictions being placed upon her, Eliza Boon would see to that! Yet, what choice did she have? If she refused to go back to him her father would suffer for it and she knew Braden well enough to be certain that he would ruin him, not only that, but he could do Tony so much harm, Tom and Beatrice too and, at all costs, she could not allow that to happen. If it were only herself who stood in danger of being harmed or threatened, then she would be quite prepared to take the risk and defy Braden, but as it was he could hurt people she dearly loved, one of whom she knew perfectly well she could not live without. Eleanor could not explain how it was possible to fall in love with someone almost at first sight, but that was precisely what she had done and since Tony had come to mean more to her than anyone else, she resigned herself to the heartbreaking thought that tonight would be the last time she would ever see him. If nothing else, she could count on Braden for that!

If Beatrice noticed any telltale signs that Eleanor had shed more than one tear over the message contained in her letter or that it had distressed her very much, she gave no sign of it when, over an hour later, she put her head round the door. Having put the letter back into its envelope and slid it under the mattress, Eleanor, who knew that Beatrice would not demand to see it, hoped that she sounded as relaxed as she tried to appear when asked how her father was and if he had given any intimation as to when they could expect to see him back in town.

"It seems my father is enjoying the peace and quiet of Suffolk too much to want to return just yet, in fact," she told Beatrice, "he says he wishes I could join him for a week or two as he feels the country air is far more beneficial than that of London."

Under normal circumstances Beatrice would never dream of being impertinent by asking to see someone's private correspondence, but so unsettled was she in her mind over what was happening and the doubts she still harboured about the author of that letter, it was with an effort she reminded herself that good manners demanded she refrain from doing so. She could not prove that Sir Miles had not written that letter or that Collett had, but so concerned was she that she could hardly wait for Tony to return to pour her worries into his ears and, instead, had to content herself with what Eleanor told her with as much calm and composure as she could. "He is quite right, of course, especially when one considers these dreadful fogs we have," Beatrice smiled.

"Yes," Eleanor agreed in a quiet voice, hating the lie she was giving to one whom she had long come to regard as very much her friend.

Realising she would get no more out of Eleanor, Beatrice rose to her feet recommending she rested, adding, with a lightness she was far from feeling, "It will not do for Tony to come home to find you are looking no better than when he left."

Eleanor gave her a perfunctory smile, trying not to think about Tony, but as soon as Beatrice had quietly closed the door behind her, Eleanor buried her face into the pillow and burst into tears. Whether this emotional eruption was because she hated treating Beatrice with a contempt she did not deserve or because Tony was as good as lost to her, she did not know; all she did know was that she had never felt so wretched in her life before.

Chapter Eighteen

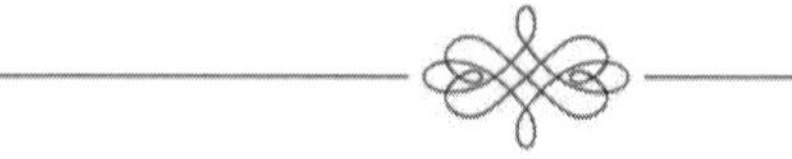

Having walked the relatively short distance from Fleet Street to Holborn, Tony, strolling past such ancient monuments of the legal profession as Lincoln's Inn and Gray's Inn, eventually came upon Fisher Street situated halfway down Gray's Inn Road on the right-hand side. Given the bustling activity of this extremely busy thoroughfare with its shops and commercial premises, where everyone seemed to jostle everyone else as they hurriedly went about their business and the noise from the horsedrawn trams as well as carriage wheels on the cobbles together with shouts from hackney drivers as they yelled abuse at heedless pedestrians trying to dash across the road in front of them, Fisher Street, apart from the odd passer-by, was a surprisingly quiet haven.

Sizeable houses, conventional and respectable, whose well-kept frontages were at the moment liberally covered in soft and glistening white, lined both sides of the tree-lined avenue and, from the handful of wheel grooves in the snow blanketed road, it appeared that Fisher Street had not had a particularly busy morning. Passing number three, Tony crossed over the road and walked down the left-hand side of the street where, over halfway down, he saw number thirty-six. Only one set of footprints, clearly those of a man, were visible on the five stone steps leading from the house to the pavement before turning right heading for Gray's Inn Road and, from the looks of the windows, whose pristine white curtains hung in neat folds to the inner windowsill, it was evidently a clean and eminently respectable dwelling.

After mounting the steps, Tony struck the highly polished brass knocker against the plate and while he waited for a response he took out his card case from his inner pocket and pulled out a card, but no sooner had he returned the case to his pocket than the door was cautiously pulled open just wide enough for a woman to poke her head round it to see who the caller was.

"Yes?" She cocked her head.

"I am sorry to disturb you," Tony apologised, doffing his hat, "but I am trying to trace a woman…"

"Oh, yes!" raising a sceptical eyebrow.

"Yes," Tony smiled. "It is unfortunate that I do not know her name, but…"

"I've 'eard that one before!" she jeered.

"Well," Tony inclined his head, "I wouldn't know about that."

"That's wot they all say," she nodded. She looked him over from head to foot, then, as if deciding he was harmless enough, she opened the door a little wider. "Wot meks yer thinks 'ers 'ere?"

"This is the address I have for her," Tony informed her.

She thought a moment. "Wot der yer wont 'er for?"

"If you are the woman who had occasion to write to Sir Philip Dunscumbe some time ago, I will tell you," Tony smiled, noting the shuttered expression which suddenly descended onto her face, telling him she was most definitely the woman who had written that letter.

"An' 'oo might you be when you're at 'ome?" she asked suspiciously. After reading the card Tony handed her, she looked up sharply, her eyes narrowing. "The newspapers!"

"Well, yes," Tony smiled, "in a manner of speaking."

"Wot d'yer mean?" she asked warily. "I ain't got nuthin' ter say ter no newspapers," she told him without giving him time to answer. "'Sides," she nodded, "wot's a toff like you doin' wi' newspapers?"

"If you are the one who wrote that letter to Sir Philip and," he nodded, "I believe you are, then I will tell you that as well."

"An' if I did," she shot at him, "wot's that ter you? 'E wos an MP was'n 'e?"

"Yes, he was," Tony agreed, "but not for this constituency!"

"Gawd!" she cried. "You're a sharp 'un!"

"Not that sharp I do not need your help," he told her, drawing a bow at a venture.

She eyed him narrowly for a few moments, querying at length, "My 'elp?"

Tony nodded. "Very much so."

She hesitated, then, after deliberating a moment or two, opened the door a little wider, saying, "Well, I dunno."

"I promise you," Tony smiled, "I mean you no harm; I merely want to talk to you about the letter you wrote to Sir Philip."

She had not been one of *'Mother Discipline's Daughters'* for nothing! During her past, if not very virtuous, career, she had quickly learned to sum up her clients with unerring accuracy, knowing precisely what they wanted before they told her and, unless she was very much mistaken, this man was so far removed from the type she had entertained at Periton Place that she knew she had nothing to fear from him but, more importantly, he did not look like a man who would either know Eliza Boon or visit her establishment. "Very well, then," she nodded, stepping aside to allow him to enter.

"Thank you," Tony smiled, removing his hat and gloves as he stepped inside.

She sniffed. "In 'ere," opening the door into the lofty front parlour on the left-hand side of the narrow entrance hall, indicating a wing chair with the nod of her head as she closed the door behind her. Tony thanked her and sat down, whereupon she followed suit in the one opposite and, after making herself comfortable, asked, "Now, abart this letter to Ser Philip; wot's your int'rest in it?"

"May I first of all begin by asking your name?" Tony enquired.

She shrugged. "Joanie, Joanie Simms."

He nodded. "Well, Miss Simms, I…"

"Call me Joanie," she invited, "everybudy does."

"Thank you, Joanie," he smiled, gaining the very strong impression that beneath the red hair, which, from the looks of the roots, she was attempting to grow out, her natural colour being brown, she was younger than she looked. Around the eyes he detected one or two faint scars and, just above her short upper lip, was the silvery outline of a cut about half an inch in length. She was a little taller than Eleanor as well as having a much fuller figure, but her corsets, which not only kept it admirably confined but made it seem as though she had a much narrower waist than she actually did. "I noticed the footprints on the steps," Tony commented. "I take it you do not live here alone."

"I wos right!" she cried, her eyes sparkling. "You *are* a sharp 'un!"

"Too sharp to be taken in," he told her meaningfully, "which is what you have attempted to do." Apart from the fact that Tony had an ear for accents, over the years he had come to understand as well as appreciate the different distinctions and sounds in Cockney speech which were as diverse as those of the various districts of New York and, from the moment she had opened her mouth, he had been unable to pinpoint where in London she was actually from until he came to realise that, for some reason, her accent was being deliberately adopted. He may naturally use words and expressions which were purely American, but there were only faint traces of the accent in his speech, but he had never purposely assumed a manner of speaking to deceive, which he felt sure she was doing now and, for one moment, he was a little at a loss to understand why, but after only a very little thought he shrewdly guessed that she was probably scared which, if she was the one who had written that letter, and he was certain she was, he could not wonder at it.

She eyed him steadily, a slow appreciative smile touching her lips. "Not in the way you mean," she told him, in a totally different voice, "but until I was sure about you I thought it best."

"If what I believe to be true *is* true," Tony nodded, "then I can see why you were cautious, but," he suggested, "what do you say we begin again and, *this* time, a little more openly!"

She nodded. "Yes, of course." She glanced at the card still held between her finger and thumb, saying, "Are you really a newspaperman?" He nodded. "Forgive me," she apologised, "but you do not look like one!"

"And what are newspaper men supposed to look like?" Tony smiled.

She pulled a face. "Untidy and, perhaps, a little down-at-heel, but certainly not dressed like you."

"Well," Tony inclined his head, "I am sorry to disillusion you by not wearing a dishevelled mackintosh or gripping a well-worn notebook!"

"No," she said thoughtfully, "it's more than that." Tony raised an enquiring eyebrow at this. "I beg your pardon, but I know a toff when I see one, and you are *definitely* a toff! Yes," she nodded when he gave her a rueful smile, "I thought so, but what are you doing…?"

"I am not here under false pretences," he assured her, "but merely to discover the truth, although," he confessed, "I admit I am what you might call a toff," going on to give her a brief outline of his antecedents.

"I see," she nodded, "and you say your newspapers are investigating Sir Philip's death?"

"Yes," Tony confirmed, "and the supposed suicide of his brother, Dennis."

"You… you said, I think," she said hesitantly, "that you wanted to know about the letter I wrote to Sir Philip."

"Yes," he nodded, "I do."

"How do you come to know about it?" she asked, curiously. "You see, the police have never questioned me."

"They wouldn't," he told her. "You see, they have no idea you exist much less that you wrote Sir Philip a letter."

"But I don't understand," Joanie Simms shook her head, "if the police don't know anything about it, or of me, how come you do?"

"Before I answer that," he replied, "will *you* tell *me* something?" She nodded. "Am I right in thinking that you know Sir Braden Collett?"

She sighed, putting a hand to her forehead, but at no time did she flinch under Tony's steady gaze. "Yes," she said resignedly, "I know Sir Braden and, before you ask, I know him very well." Tony nodded and she said, quite philosophically, "You are not here by chance; you know, don't you?"

"Apart from one or two gaps which need filling in, pretty much," he inclined his head.

Joanie Simms thought a moment, then, after seeming to debate the issue, said, "Well, I suppose I should have known that sooner or later that letter would come light."

"It didn't," Tony shook his head, going on to briefly explain his visit to Hallerton and the outcome of their meeting, "so, you see," he explained, "having read it Sir Philip burned it, after which he left his rooms at Westminster and was not seen again until his body was found about three days later at Greenwich."

"I wish I had never written it!" she cried fervently. "Had I not have done so, he would still be alive today."

"Well," Tony stated reasonably, "that's as may be, but you clearly had a reason for doing so, and whilst I am pretty sure what that reason was, if Sir Philip's murder is to count for anything, not to mention the death of his brother, I think it's time you told me everything."

"Yes," she agreed, "I think it is." After taking a moment to make herself comfortable, she eyed Tony squarely, saying, though not without some difficulty, "Up until seven or eight months ago, I was... well," she grimaced, "let us just say that my profession was not what you would call respectable, if you know what I mean!"

"Yes," Tony said considerately, "I know what you mean," her admission coming as no surprise to him.

"I was sixteen when I left home," Joanie told him, "no doubt," she grimaced, "I thought the grass was greener on the other side, but I wanted more than I had and, with a schoolteacher for a father whose strict discipline extended beyond the classroom, I longed to break free."

"That accounts for the good speaking voice," Tony smiled.

"Yes," she nodded. "My father made sure that my sister and I did not fall into bad habits with our speech or adopt the local slang and although I fought against it, like I did everything else," she shrugged, "it has nevertheless stood me in good stead. So," she sighed, resuming her story, "there I was, newly arrived in London with nothing in my purse but a couple of shillings which I had managed to save up and no idea how I was going to live or afford lodgings."

Tony, who had a good idea what was coming, the story being all too familiar, asked gently, "And what did the woman who approached you, offer you?"

She smiled gratefully at him. "The usual," she shrugged, "a clean bed and a hot meal until I got myself sorted out." He nodded. "Oh, I'm not excusing myself," she sighed, "but I was young and inexperienced and took her at her word."

"And you remained in this establishment until when?" Tony shrugged an enquiry.

"About eight months ago," she replied. "You see," she explained, "when you become one of *'Mother Discipline's Daughters'*, you remain one."

"*'Mother Discipline's...!*" Tony repeated, a little taken aback.

"I promise you," Joanie assured him, "she did not acquire that title for nothing."

The very name was more than enough to tell him of the kind of activities conducted in her establishment and, instinctively knowing the answer before he asked the question, enquired, "And this *'Mother Discipline'*, would I be right in thinking her real name is Eliza Boon?"

"You know her?" she raised a surprised eyebrow.

"No," Tony shook his head, "but I know of her. She has," he informed her, "figured largely in our investigations."

"I see," Joanie nodded comprehendingly.

"And this establishment," Tony pressed, "would it by any chance be fifty-one Periton Place?"

"Yes," she confirmed, "it would. And Peterson?" she queried. "You know about him?"

"Yes," Tony nodded. "We know too that Sir Braden Collett and Dennis Dunscumbe were regular visitors, but what we *don't* know," he told her, "is what happened to bring about Dennis Dunscumbe's so-called suicide!"

Joanie swallowed. "I… I take it then, that you know of Sir Braden's temper and his… his tendency for…"

"Yes," Tony nodded, "we have good reason to know that," he said firmly, thinking of the brutal treatment he had continually handed out to Eleanor. "And Dennis Dunscumbe?" he raised an eyebrow. "Our information is that he enjoyed slapping women around!"

"Yes," she sighed, "he did, so too did Sir Braden; that's why they came to Eliza's. They knew they could indulge their inclinations in a way they could not elsewhere." Tony nodded and she went on, "Sir Braden had been a regular client of Eliza's well before I went there, but one evening he brought along Dennis Dunscumbe. You see," she explained, "no one went to Eliza's unless they were personally recommended by a client and none of them, not even us girls, were ever allowed to enter or leave through the front door which could give the neighbours cause to suspect just what went on inside." Tony nodded. "Unlike some clients," she told him, "Sir Braden did not have a favourite girl it was simply a case of who took his fancy on the night, but Dennis Dunscumbe *did*, but the thing is," she explained, "when she was not available one of us had to go with him and… well," pausing to collect herself, "we… we didn't like what he asked us to do sometimes, but Eliza had a way of making us," pointing at the scars on her face, "as well as making sure we did whatever the client wanted. I told you," she reminded Tony when she saw the look of horror on his face, "she did not acquire that title for nothing, and not only with the girls. It may seem hard to believe," she told him, "but I understand when she was younger she was most sought after by her clients, which," she added, "is surprising when you consider where her natural leanings lie, if you understand me?"

"I do," Tony replied in a hard voice, having to curb his anger at the thought of Eleanor being held a virtual prisoner by these people as well as the unspeakable brutality they had subjected her to.

'Mother Discipline'," Joanie grimaced, "had a way of bullying whoever had taken her fancy. Oh, no," she shook her head in response to his look, "I never did, I am glad to say, but she did not take no for an answer." She took a moment to calm herself, during the course of which she responded to Tony's solicitous enquiry as to whether she felt up to going on by assuring him she was perfectly all right. "You would not think so to look at her," she nodded, "but due to Eliza providing the kind of entertainment that appeal to men like Sir Braden and Dennis Dunscumbe, she is quite a rich woman, particularly as she made them pay through the nose for it, but they never argued the price."

"Did she pass any of her profits on to you and the other girls?" Tony asked.

"Yes," she nodded, "but not as much as we believed we deserved although," she admitted truthfully, "despite how it may seem had it not have been for Eliza and Periton Place our lives could have been very much worse. You see," she explained, "everything was always provided for us; a bed, food, comfortable, almost luxurious surroundings, so we did not have to walk the streets to try to earn money to pay rent or anything like that."

"Yes, but even so…" Tony began, unable to see it from her point of view.

"I know what you are thinking," Joanie smiled, "and I suppose if I am honest I have to agree with you, but even though Eliza is by nature cruel and domineering and never thinks twice about adopting harsh methods to get her own way," indicating her face with the flick of a finger, "she did look after us."

Tony, who did not call handing out such brutal treatment as looking after someone, kept his views on this to himself and, instead, returned to the matter of Dennis Dunscumbe.

"Eliza always had one evening a week free of clients," Joanie explained, "usually a Thursday, but for some reason that particular Thursday Sir Braden and Dennis Dunscumbe turned up unexpectedly.

Eliza was very strict about this, but she did not turn them away. Sir Braden asked for me and, not surprisingly, Dennis asked for Annie Myers, the girl I said was his favourite," she nodded. "As always Annie asked Eliza to send another girl as she hated going with him, but Eliza forced her, telling her that she was not going to risk losing a valued client because of her and if she knew what was good for her, then she would do as she was told. We were both of us in adjacent rooms on the first floor, the rooms on the top floor being used by us girls when we were not working. When I left Sir Braden sometime after," she further explained, "Annie was still with Dennis Dunscumbe, so I began to make my way upstairs, but just as I put my foot on the first step the other door opened and he came hurrying out, but just the sound of his voice was enough to tell me that something was wrong. Sir Braden immediately went to him, and Eliza, who had just come up the stairs from her room on the ground floor, heard Dennis telling Sir Braden that Annie was dead. I pinned myself against the wall of the stairs so they could not see me and I heard Dennis Dunscumbe telling them that he had accidentally killed Annie; apparently he had asked her to do something which she did not want to do and he lost his temper and hit her and, when she still refused, he hit her again, but somehow she stumbled backwards from the force of it and struck her head on the brass bedstead."

"So, that's how it was!" Tony said slowly.

Joanie nodded. "Yes. Eliza could not afford to have the police involved nor could Sir Braden and Dennis Dunscumbe; their reputations would be ruined and Eliza's place shut down; so Peterson, who is entirely devoted to Eliza, wrapped Annie in a blanket and dumped her body several streets away in some derelict houses."

"I can understand you not reporting it to the police because you were afraid," Tony told her, "but surely the other girls must have suspected something!"

"They did," she nodded, "but Eliza can be very plausible. She told them that following an argument between Annie and Dennis Dunscumbe, who had threatened to boycott the place if Annie remained, she had packed her bags and left."

"And they believed her?" he asked, surprised. "Even though they knew her to be his favourite!"

"Yes, or, at least," she corrected herself, "they pretended they did. Whichever way it was, they never questioned Eliza about it."

"Tell me," he asked steadily, "what did Annie look like?"

Joanie thought a moment. "Well, she wasn't what you would call beautiful," she told him, not unkindly, "but there was something about her which was very attractive; I can't explain it, but everyone liked Annie. In fact," she smiled reminiscently, "she said herself that her only claim to beauty was her thick blonde hair."

"How old was she?" he wanted to know.

"No more than twenty-one or twenty-two," she told him.

"Was she very tall?" Tony enquired.

"No," she shook her head. "Annie was only about five feet four inches or, possibly, five," she told him, "and slim, quite slender in fact."

Tony thought a moment, saying at length, "Were you aware that the body of a young woman fitting that description was found about eight months ago in the cellar of one of those houses?"

She shook her head, pressing a hand to her throat. "No," she said faintly, "I wasn't. Was it Annie?"

"We believe so," Tony told her quietly, "in fact, your description of her corresponds precisely with what our investigations have uncovered, but sadly," he shook his head, "her body was never identified or claimed."

"Poor Annie!" she cried.

"Did she have any family to your knowledge?" he asked.

"No," Joanie shook her head. "I know that because I remember her telling me once that she wished she had a family and that perhaps if she had then her life could well have been very different. You see," she smiled, "despite what you may think, all of us girls were very good friends, in fact we often talked about…"

"What you mean is," Tony smiled, "you compared notes!"

"Yes," she laughed, "if you like."

"Getting back to Dennis Dunscumbe," he cocked his head, "I take it you know something about his supposed suicide or you would not have written to his brother?"

She nodded. "Yes, and I wish I didn't," she confessed. "If Eliza so much as suspected I knew the truth I would… well," she shrugged, "I'm afraid she'll find me; that's why I was cautious at first when you came here."

"You thought she had hired me to find you, is that it?" he smiled.

"Yes, I did think that," she acknowledged. "I can see now I was wrong, but I told you the truth when I said that I'm afraid of Eliza ever finding out that I know what happened or where I live."

"She will never discover either from me," he assured her.

"Thank you," Joanie smiled gratefully. "Well, about Dennis Dunscumbe," she sighed, "I *can* tell you that he was causing Eliza and Sir Braden a few worries. You see," she told him as he raised a questioning eyebrow, "after what happened to Annie he didn't come near the place for almost two weeks then he turned up several times after that for well over a week, but not for one of the girls but to speak privately to Eliza and Sir Braden. I don't know what was actually discussed between them, but I do know that Eliza seemed quite preoccupied, not her usual self at all. Then, one night, I happened to overhear a conversation between Eliza and Sir Braden; it was a Thursday so all the girls were upstairs which is why I think the door to Eliza's room had not been properly closed because they thought we were all upstairs and there was no possibility of being overheard."

"But you weren't upstairs," Tony pointed out, "why was that?"

"Well, one of the girls wasn't feeling too well so I just popped down to ask Eliza if she had something I could give her."

"I see," he nodded, "please, go on."

"It was just as I got to the door that I heard Sir Braden's voice," she explained, "he sounded quite agitated, which is not unusual when he is either worried or anxious. He was asking Eliza what they were going to do about Dennis because nothing he said to him would dissuade him from reporting Annie's death to the authorities. Eliza told Sir Braden that she too had been unable to make him change his mind and since she had no wish to come to the notice of the authorities any more than he did there was really only one way of ensuring Dennis Dunscumbe's silence." She paused and swallowed. "I heard Sir Braden ask her if she was mad to which she replied she was not, but that he must be if he thought for one moment that Dennis was bluffing. It was then I heard Eliza ring her bell for Peterson, so I quickly hid in a little recess, then, as soon as he went in, I went back to the door."

"Are you saying you actually *heard* them planning to murder him?" Tony urged.

"Yes," she confirmed, "I heard them planning Dennis Dunscumbe's murder. I remember Sir Braden arguing against it, but Eliza told him that unless he wanted to face public condemnation with his reputation in shreds and she herself in the dock for keeping a house of ill repute, then they had no choice but to silence him!"

"So you are saying that it was *definitely* Eliza Boon who planned it?" Tony confirmed.

"Yes," she nodded, "it was definitely Eliza. By then it was about eight o'clock and she told Peterson that he was to go to Dennis Dunscumbe's house in Hertford Street because she knew that every Thursday evening his manservant always went out and Dennis Duncumbe usually visited his club. Peterson was to wait for him to return home and tell him he had a message from Eliza; once inside the house he was to shoot him in the temple to make it look as though he had taken his own life. In fact," she surprised Tony by saying, "it was her own gun which she gave Peterson to use."

"Her own gun?" he repeated, taken aback.

"Yes," she nodded, "she always kept it in the drawer of her desk."

"Are you saying that Peterson went along with it without asking any questions?" Tony shook his head in disbelief.

"Oh, yes," she nodded. "Like I told you, for whatever reason he is utterly devoted to Eliza and when she gave him his instructions on what to do when he arrived in Hertford Street he never said a word."

"Miss Simms," Tony urged, leaning forward a little, "can you tell me, and this is *most* important," he stressed, "do you recall Eliza Boon or Sir Braden telling Peterson to bear in mind that Dennis Dunscumbe was left-handed?"

She thought a moment. "No," she shook her head, "I can't remember them mentioning it."

"Did *you* know he was left-handed?" he asked.

"Yes," she nodded, a wry smile twisting her lips, "we all did. There wasn't much we didn't know about our clients."

Tony nodded. "So when you read of his supposed suicide in the newspapers you knew it was no such thing." She nodded. "So, you wrote and told Sir Philip the truth?"

"Yes, but not straightaway," she told him. "The truth is," she grimaced, "I'd had enough of that kind of life and I suppose I wanted to become respectable, but once you became one of *'Mother Discipline's*

Daughters' Eliza made sure you remained one, but after what had happened to Annie, then reading about Dennis Dunscumbe, I was really scared. I knew if Eliza so much as suspected I knew about any of it I should be made to suffer, so," she shrugged, "I decided to leave."

"That was very brave of you," Tony smiled.

"Well," she pulled a face, "I suppose in a way it was, but I knew if I didn't not only would I be there for the rest of my life but go in fear of it."

"So, how did you manage it?" Tony asked.

"I stole out of the back door one night when everyone was asleep," she smiled. "I had to be careful, not only of disturbing the girls but Eliza as well, then there was Peterson. He never seemed to sleep," she explained, "always wandering around the house, but that night he'd had a little too much to drink so I was able to pass his room and into Eliza's and remove the back door key from her desk drawer. I was absolutely terrified someone would hear the sound of the bolts being pulled back, but no one did."

Tony thought of Eleanor's escape and how terrified she must have been in desperately trying to gain her freedom from those who were trying to restrict it. "I take it you didn't come straight here?" he enquired.

"No," Joanie shook her head. "After I left Periton Place, I had no idea where I was going," she explained. "I couldn't go back home to my parents and I had no friends other than the girls so," she shrugged, "I found some cheap lodgings for a few nights. I soon started to look for work, but there wasn't anything, at least," she grimaced, "nothing I was qualified for at all events, but then I was fortunate to see an advertisement for a housekeeper, here," she nodded. "His name is Joe Wilkinson," she told Tony. "He's a manager at a brewery. He's a widower with no children," she explained, "and, for whatever reason," she shrugged, "he likes me and," she smiled, "I like him, in fact, we are to be married soon."

Tony smiled. "Congratulations. I am very happy for you."

"Thank you," she nodded, "but in case you are wondering, yes, he knows about me. He's a good man and an honest one and deserves the truth. Naturally, he was extremely shocked at first, but he neither judged nor condemned me."

"Did you tell him what you had overheard?" Tony asked.

"Yes," she sighed, "I did. You see, I wanted our life together to be free of anything to do with my past; I did not want to be looking over my shoulder or afraid of meeting someone when I was with him who had known me before." Tony nodded. "So, after talking to him about it, I wrote to Sir Philip."

"Why was that?" Tony enquired.

She bit her bottom lip before saying, a little defensively, "Because I thought he should know the truth and, also," she told him, "because Annie was my friend. I didn't like Dennis Dunscumbe and, you are right," she nodded, "he did enjoy slapping women around, quite often he did far worse than that, nevertheless, when it came to it he was decent enough to know that through him a young woman had died and wanted to do something about it."

"And this letter," Tony pressed, "what precisely did you write?"

Joanie sighed. "I told Sir Philip I knew something about his brother's death which I thought he ought to know, and if he would contact me to arrange a meeting I would tell him what I knew."

"And did he contact you?" Tony asked.

Joanie nodded. "Yes, in fact, he came here to see me. He told me he had come in response to my letter he had received only that morning."

"So, he *did* come here?" Tony mused.

"Yes," she inclined her head. "I was rather surprised because I thought he would write to me or something to arrange a meeting, but when I told him what I knew he was understandably very angry. He told me that he knew his brother had for a long time been mixed up with a set of men he was firmly convinced would ruin him, but he had no idea just what he was actually involved in. He said that these types of establishments were a disgrace and he would make it his business to raise questions in the House about them as well as bringing Sir Braden, Eliza and Peterson to account for the murder of his brother."

"He told you that?" Tony questioned, his eyes narrowing slightly.

"Yes. He also told me that when he left here he was going directly to Cavendish Square to see Sir Braden, which he must have done," she said firmly, "because when I read in the newspapers several days later about his body being found, I knew that either Sir Braden or Eliza must have had a hand in it!"

In view of what she had told him, Tony could well understand her fears. Like Eleanor, Joanie Simms held damaging information which could do untold harm to Collett and his cohorts, but in spite of Sir Philip's anger it was clear he had not told Collett from whom he had received his information. Eliza Boon, who had already shown herself to be a woman who did not shrink from perpetrating brutality in order to get her own way, had also proved that she was a woman who was not easily daunted and one, moreover, who had demonstrated just how capable she was of ridding herself of a threat. With calm deliberation she had planned the cold-blooded murder of Dennis Dunscumbe, a man who, despite his temper and aggressive leanings, had clearly experienced some measure of guilt over what had happened to Annie Myers, but had then made the fatal error of informing Collett and Eliza Boon of his intention of going to the police to report her death. Just as he had suspected, it came as no surprise to Tony to learn that Eliza Boon had taken steps to prevent Dennis Dunscumbe from going to the police with such damning information and in a way which would not only ensure his permanent silence, but by means whereby no one would suspect that his death had come about by any other than that of his own hand and, once again, had used a most willing Peterson to further her ends. Sir Braden's participation in helping cover up the unfortunate death of Annie Myers had stemmed from an urgent need to save his own as well as his friend's reputation; under no circumstances could he let it be known that he and Dennis Dunscumbe regularly visited a house of more than ordinary ill repute. Unfortunately, Dennis Dunscumbe's unexpected attack of conscience had threatened to undo all their efforts to avoid an out-and-out scandal, and Sir Braden, whose attempts to dissuade his friend from taking such a reckless step having gone unheeded, had found himself with no choice other than to go along with Eliza's plan of ensuring their protection against public condemnation and the repercussions of the law.

Considering the lengths to which Eliza Boon was apparently prepared to go to achieve her ends it had struck Tony more than once that she had been extremely remiss in not taking into account the vital fact that Dennis Dunscumbe was left-handed which, considering her resource and enterprise, was quite surprising, which is why he had always been convinced that Peterson must have been the one at fault by forgetting his instructions. Tony had always believed that the idea and planning of Dennis Dunscumbe's death had been Eliza Boon's and not Collett's and, according to Joanie Simms, he was right, but in view of what she had told him Tony was now given to wondering whether Eliza Boon had deliberately kept the essential fact that Dennis Dunscumbe was left-handed to herself when imparting her instructions to Peterson in order to provide them with a get-out clause should the truth ever leak out about Annie Myers and her connection with Dennis Dunscumbe, thereby leading the police to look again at his supposed suicide and questions were inevitably asked. Tony had no doubt that her line of defence should she ever be questioned by the police would be why, if she had indeed arranged for Peterson to kill Dennis Dunscumbe by putting a bullet through his temple to make it seem as though he had taken his own life, would she be stupid enough not to tell him to shoot him in the left temple and so open herself up to charges of inciting murder and Sir Braden Collett and Peterson as accomplices? The more Tony thought about it the more plausible it seemed, in fact it was quite a brilliant strategy and, even though it went very much against the grain with to him say it, even inspired, but whilst it roused no admiration in him it certainly went to reinforce his belief that Eliza Boon was a most formidable adversary.

As for Dennis Dunscumbe's manservant not noticing that the bullet had entered the right temple instead of the left when questioned by the police, Tony could not discount the reasonable argument that it was most probably through shock or, failing this, simply because all he had registered was his employer's dead body and nothing else. The same was equally true of Sir Philip who, upon identifying his brother's dead body, had made no mention of it to the police for which Tony could only attribute the reason as being the same as his brother's manservant but, if nothing else, such an oversight on the part of both men had certainly kept the police from Eliza Boon's door as well as presenting themselves in Cavendish Square. Had such vital information been disclosed by either man then the police would automatically have instigated a murder investigation which would have inevitably led to his death being linked to the unfortunate loss of life of Annie Myers and, perhaps, even prevented Sir Philip's own death shortly afterwards. Although Tony still felt confident enough to ascribe such a lack of alertness in failing to spot something which should have been blatantly obvious to two men who knew Dennis Dunscumbe better than most down to shock and not from any ulterior motives, he nevertheless found it a little difficult to understand such an oversight. However, Tony was in no doubt that Sir Philip, who, at best, could be described as being somewhat inattentive when identifying his brother's body, once having learned the truth from Joanie Simms, his confrontation with Sir Braden following his departure from Fisher Street, had most definitely cost him his life.

Bill, having fully expected Tony to find the occupant of thirty-six Fisher Street to be either uncooperative or dead or, even, which was more than likely, not the writer of that letter to Sir Philip or, which would not have surprised him, done a moonlight flit at some point, he was naturally pleased to learn that not only was Joanie Simms very much alive but Tony's visit had not been a wasted journey. Bill was not entirely certain whether to feel shocked or not upon hearing of the callous, almost dispassionate, way in which Sir Braden and Eliza Boon had disposed of obstacles which could have denounced them, but when Tony had finished telling him what had passed between himself and Joanie Simms as well as answering all his questions, he shrewdly suspected from the frown which had descended onto Tony's forehead that in spite of a successful visit to Fisher Street something was troubling him. "Okay, kiddo," he nodded, "let's have it; what's on your mind?" When Tony made no immediate reply to this, he said, "I thought you'd be pleased to have your suspicions confirmed."

"Having my suspicions confirmed is one thing, Bill," Tony sighed, "but proving them is quite another."

"But I thought you said you believed her!" Bill reminded him.

"I do," Tony nodded, "but she is of no more help to us in proving what we know than Lady Collett is," to which Bill cocked an eyebrow. "You know as well as I do that Lady Collett cannot give evidence in court if that evidence is injurious to her husband, which it is," he nodded, "and, Joanie Simms," he pointed out, "because even if the prosecution did put her into the witness-box, which is doubtful, Collett's defence, apart from most probably claiming her evidence as being nothing but hearsay, would soon discredit her as an unreliable witness by tearing her character to shreds! No jury," he shook his head, "would find Collett guilty on the word of a woman whose past profession is utterly condemned. I couldn't put her through her that, Bill," Tony told him firmly.

"So," Bill sighed, as Tony rose to his feet and walked over to the window to stand staring down into the street, "we're back to where we started!"

"Perhaps," Tony said thoughtfully.

Bill saw the frown deepen on Tony's forehead and waited for him to say something, but after several minutes had elapsed without him saying a word, he asked, "What are you thinking?"

"I was thinking of my father," Tony told him reminiscently. Then, turning round to face him, asked quietly, "Do you remember what he used to say, Bill," he raised an eyebrow, "about the rules being there for our guidance and not to hide the truth or to prevent us from seeking it?"

"Sure, I remember," Bill smiled expressively. "So," he nodded, "you're going to break a few rules!"

"No," Tony shook his head, resuming his seat, "just bend them a little," he smiled. Bill raised a questioning eyebrow, to which Tony replied, "Since we cannot prove what we know, then we shall just have to let Collett and the others prove it for us."

Bill's eyes narrowed and, after removing the cigar from his mouth, asked, "When did you come up with this?"

"Just now," Tony told him. "It's not as mad as it sounds, Bill," he smiled ruefully.

"I know I'm going to regret asking this," Bill sighed, "but what *do* you have in mind exactly?"

"We're going to set a trap," Tony told him seriously.

Bill's eyes narrowed even more as he thought it over, finally shaking his head. "Collett'll never fall for it!"

"Yes, he will," Tony told him firmly.

"Huh huh," Bill shook his head again. "He's no fool, you said so yourself!"

"Yes, I did," Tony agreed, "but he's worse than a fool, Bill," he nodded, "he's desperate, and it's this desperation which will ultimately cloud his judgement and lead him into making a mistake." Upon seeing the doubt which still lingered on Bill's face, Tony leaned forward, saying urgently, "Look Bill, since Lady Collett and Joanie Simms can't give evidence because in their own way they are both ineligible, this is the only way we can bring Collett and the others to account for what they have done; it's all we've got."

Bill chewed his cigar for a moment. "Okay," he conceded at length, "suppose we set a trap and he falls into it, what then?" He shrugged. "It doesn't prove a thing; it's just going be our word against his!"

"Not if Dawson at the Yard was in on it?" Tony told him.

A slow appreciative smile spread across Bill's face. "Now *that's* what I call cute!" he grinned. "And they didn't teach you *that* at Cambridge. So," he asked slowly, "have you figured it yet?"

"Not quite," Tony grinned, "but pretty much," going on to tell him what he had in mind.

"I like it," Bill nodded, leaning forward on his elbows, "but what makes you think Dawson'll go for it?"

"He's a cop, Bill!" Tony told him. "And, like cops everywhere, he won't like to think he has a case of murder on his hands that he has not solved, especially when the victim is someone like Sir Philip!"

"Yeah," Bill said thoughtfully, "you're right, but what about this Mrs. Timms? What makes you so sure she'll go along with it?"

"Because she's devoted to Lady Collett," Tony said simply.

"You're going tell her the truth?" Bill enquired, not at all sure this was a good thing, at least, not at this stage.

"I shall have to," Tony nodded, "but I don't think she will be as shocked as you seem to think and, like I said earlier," he reminded him, "she will stand very much our friend." Upon seeing the doubtful look which crossed Bill's face Tony said firmly, "I know you don't like it Bill, but without her help we may as well scrap the idea now because not only do we have no one else on the inside to switch the real newspapers for the phoney ones, but for the life of me," he shook his head, "I can't come up with anything else halfway good enough to fool Collett and the others sufficiently to get them to take the bait and thereby prove their own guilt."

"Okay," Bill shrugged, "I'll go with that, which just leaves Barton at *'The Echo'*, George Buckle at *'The Times'* and Courtney at *'The Telegraph'*. Think they'll go for it?" he raised an eyebrow.

"They're newspaper men, Bill," Tony told him practically.

"Yeah," he agreed, "but you of all people know that it's one a hell of a job we're asking them to do! To insert a piece in only one copy of a run is…"

"I know," Tony nodded, "but if we want Collett to take the bait we have no choice. Mrs. Timms may already take *'The Echo'*, but even if she doesn't, I'm sure she won't mind on this occasion and, as for Collett," he shrugged, "I don't know whether he takes *'The Times'* or *'The Telegraph'*, perhaps both, but whichever one it is," he nodded, "you can bet he will read his copy a soon as Mrs. Timms lets it fall about what she has read in her newspaper and, unless I miss my guess, he will immediately ask to see hers to make sure what he has read in his is true.

We can't risk printing the phoney story to give the copy to Mrs. Timms," he said firmly, "not only because it will make Collett instantly suspicious when he sees it's one our newspapers, but because you can lay your life that he is already wondering about me and what I know or, at least, may have guessed, and since he knows his wife is taking sanctuary in Mount Street his suspicions are going to increase tenfold, which is why if he reads something in one our newspapers it could well have the opposite effect to the one we want." After checking the time and seeing that it was just a few minutes after four o'clock, Tony returned the watch to his pocket and rose to his feet, saying, "I'd better be getting back to Mount Street, but here's what I'd like you to do for me, Bill…"

"Sure! You got it, Tony," Bill nodded when Tony had finished.

"By the way, Bill," Tony raised an eyebrow, "anything on Mary Stanley yet?"

"Not yet," he shook his head.

"Well, see what you can do," shrugging himself into his overcoat, "but I get the feeling it's going to be a case of asking Lady Collett, although I'd rather not bombard her with questions just yet if I can help it."

Lady Collett meanwhile, was herself none too eager to have Tony ask her any questions. Prior to the arrival of that letter from Braden she had been quite ready to tell Tony the truth about the unforgettable events of that night, but now she knew she could not. At all costs she had to protect her father from scandal and public humiliation, even at the cost of her own freedom which, inevitably, would mean never seeing Tony again, the very thought bringing a sob to her throat. It was too cruel of fate to give her a brief moment of happiness only to take it away from her almost before she had come to believe such joy existed, much better to have kept her in complete ignorance of what could be. Once she returned to Cavendish Square, somewhere Eleanor had never thought of as home, Braden would make sure that no further contact was ever again made between herself and the inhabitants of Mount Street, Tony in particular, and even though she could only hazard a guess as to the alternative her husband had in mind to having her put away, she could not delude herself into thinking that her liberty would not be even more curtailed. Her whole body may cry out in outrage, her pain all the more unendurable as she thought of Eliza Boon and Peterson; both of whom would stop at nothing to make sure there was no reprieve from her prison sentence, but if she did not want to see her father ostracised and his name tarnished forever and Tony and Tom with their reputations in shreds, then somehow she had to find the strength to endure what she knew was to come. Her only solace being that whatever Tony may have guessed or worked out, without her corroborative evidence there was nothing he could do to either put his findings to the police or openly charge Braden, thereby ensuring her father's reputation as well as his own and Tom's.

No matter how resigned Eleanor was to the inescapable, albeit reluctantly, she was by no means reconciled, especially when she thought of Beatrice, a woman who had proved to be very much her friend, and the thought of leaving without even so much as a word of thanks made her feel the worst kind of traitress and that what she was about to do was nothing short of betrayal to one who had shown her nothing but kindness and generosity, both of which she could never sufficiently repay. Tom too, who had opened his heart as well as his door to her, offering her sanctuary when she had needed it most! Then, of course, there was Tony! Eleanor closed her eyes on an agonised sigh at the thought of him, a stray tear falling down her cheek, swallowing the lump which formed in her throat. She knew it would be far better for her not to think about Tony because if she did then what little resolution she had would desert her completely, but no matter how painful she could not dismiss him, not only because the thought of never seeing him again was too unbearable to contemplate, but because she knew she would somehow have to find a way of hoodwinking him. Tony was by far too clever and astute to be taken in by a trick, and yet at all costs she somehow had to try to persuade him that she did not need an overseer tonight. Fortunately, that overwhelming nausea and giddiness resulting from the concussion, whilst not having completely deserted her, were far less severe, but she could not pretend feeling strong enough to making it downstairs and then, after struggling with the bolts on the front door, to walking along Mount Street to the corner of Davies Street where Peterson and Eliza Boon would be waiting for her in the carriage. Even so, Eleanor knew she had no choice other than to force her aching body into doing what she had no mind for, but the distressing image of her father, humiliated and publicly disgraced once Braden had denounced him, danced in front of her eyes, relegating her own wretchedness and inclinations to the back of her mind.

But by the time Doctor Little called to see her just after half past three she had somehow managed to school herself into appearing quite calm, and since he was extremely pleased to discover that the effects of the concussion were no longer so acute he pronounced himself quite pleased with her progress. Over her head he told Beatrice and Sarah he was reasonably confident that with continued care and rest her cracked rib would heal within a few weeks, as would the cut to her head and, as for her bruises, he was confident that by regularly applying the arnica he had left in Sarah's charge they too would soon begin to fade. Bearing in mind Tom's brother-in-law's confidences, Doctor Little refrained from plying Eleanor with questions, but as he took one last look down at her swollen and bruised face he devoutly trusted that the perpetrator of such an outrage who, from the wedding ring on his patient's finger, he had no doubt was her husband, would soon be brought to account. Beatrice, after assuring herself that Eleanor did not need her for anything, accompanied Doctor Little down the stairs leaving Sarah to make sure their patient swallowed some of the sustaining broth which she had brought up with her, unaware that beneath Eleanor's calm exterior her heart was crying out against what her mind was unwillingly formulating. Naturally, Beatrice was immensely relieved to know that Doctor Little was very pleased with his patient, indeed, there was no denying that Eleanor was looking very much improved to when Tony had brought her here last night, and whilst Beatrice knew there was some way to go before Eleanor fully recovered, it was nevertheless a tremendous relief to know that no irreparable harm would result due to Collett's brutal assault.

Beatrice may still hold doubts as to the writer of the letter delivered earlier in the day by Miss Clark and the wisdom of handing it to Eleanor, but she would have been deeply distressed had she known that its contents had caused her dear friend such misery and agonising soul-searching. Beatrice felt reasonably certain that Tony would say she ought to have waited for him to return before giving Eleanor that letter, but in her own defence she told herself that there really had been no way she could possibly have withheld it from her because whatever her suspicions it *was* after all addressed to Eleanor.

Arriving back in Mount Street just after half past four, Tony, after a brief discussion with Harry, calmly ushered his anxious sister, who had come into the hall to meet him, into the drawing-room, listening to her pouring the day's events following his departure into his ears almost before he had closed the door behind him. "I know you are most probably going to tell me that I should not have given it to her," Beatrice told him when she came to the end of her recital, "but indeed Tony I could…"

"It's all right, Bea," he smiled, giving her hand a reassuring squeeze, "of course you could not have kept it from her."

"Well," she sighed, "I'm glad you think I did right, but I can't help feeling that it was not from her father at all!"

"Did she show you the letter?" Tony asked.

Beatrice shook her head. "No, and I could not demand she let me read it! Although when I asked her if her father had given any indication as to when he was likely to return to town she said no, only that he wished it were possible for her to join him in Suffolk as he thought the change of air would be good for her!" She saw the frown crease his forehead, asking, worriedly, "What is it, Tony?"

"Tell me Bea," he cocked his head, "have you ever seen this Miss Clark before whenever you have called in Bruton Street?"

"No," Beatrice shook her head, "I have no recollection of having done so and… well, I did not like to question Eleanor about her, but," she shrugged, "even though she looked every inch what she purported to be I cannot help feeling something is not quite right. Oh, Tony!" she cried, agitatedly clasping and unclasping her hands. "You do not think that the letter *was* from Collett, do you?"

"I think it stands a pretty good chance!" he nodded.

"I admit," she said apprehensively, "that I did wonder. But why?" she cried, hunching a helpless shoulder.

"To frighten her," Tony told her grimly.

"To frighten her!" she gasped. "Why?"

"Because she knows too much," Tony said firmly. "Collett knows that once she has recovered sufficiently from her injuries she will tell me everything about what happened that night, which inevitably will direct me to the events leading up to Dennis Dunscumbe's murder as well as that of his brother. Yes, Bea," he nodded, in answer to her wide-eyed enquiry, "my visit to Holborn today was more than worthwhile."

He may have given her a somewhat edited version of what had passed between himself and Joanie Simms, but it was nevertheless enough to hold Beatrice speechless for several minutes, looking at her brother as though she could not take in what he had told her. "B-but that's monstrous!" she cried when she finally managed to find her voice.

"You got that right!" he ground out.

Beatrice thought a moment, "But if this letter *is* from Collett and his intention is to frighten her, what does he hope to gain by it? I mean," she shrugged, "what does he think she will do?"

"Leave here of her own free will!" Tony replied seriously. "Look, Bea," he told her earnestly, "I figured that Collett would find a way of getting Eleanor back to Cavendish Square; he cannot risk leaving her here in case she talks. He knows, as we do, that he cannot come here asking for her, let alone demanding we relinquish her to him, not after that Peterson guy told me she had gone into the country to stay with friends," he shook his head. "I admit," he conceded, "that I had not expected Collett to be so subtle, but little though I like admitting it," he nodded, "I have to acknowledge that he's been very clever."

"*Clever!*" Beatrice echoed in disbelief.

"Sure! If I know our friend Collett," Tony told her, "and I believe I do, it's a pretty safe bet to say that he's threatened her into leaving here and, once she does, he knows there's not a damn thing we can do about it! In fact," he said grimly, "in view of what I have discovered today it would not surprise me to learn that this whole idea is out of Eliza Boon's head rather than Collett's."

"Hateful creature!" she exclaimed.

"And some!" Tony said firmly, "but *this* time," he nodded, "she's got me to deal with! There is no way," he said unequivocally, "that I am going to step aside and allow Eleanor to return to Cavendish Square!"

From the look of grim determination on his face Beatrice did not doubt it, but even though it had disappeared by the time she came to the end of telling him about the outcome of Doctor Little's visit, she knew that nothing would turn her brother from his purpose once he had made up his mind. Upon asking him what he intended to do to counteract this move by Collett, he merely smiled, saying, "I'll know that once I know what's in the letter. Now, I must go up and see Eleanor."

Chapter Nineteen

Eleanor, having come to the painful conclusion that unless she wanted harm to come to those whom she loved, there was really nothing else she could do but follow Braden's instructions, awaited Tony's return with mixed feelings. Part of her tingled with excitement and anticipation at the thought of seeing him walk in through the door, but the knowledge that she was about to deceive him, resulting in her never setting eyes on him again, filled her with despair and heartache.

It seemed she had been right after all in deeming death as being her only release from Braden and the prison-like existence she had endured, and would continue to endure, because she could see no escape from a future which would be nothing short of intolerable. Even supposing Braden kept his word about not having her locked away, Eleanor could not view the rest of her life with anything other than apprehension because with all ties to Mount Street severed, kept away from her friends and only being allowed to see her father in Braden's company, there would be no one to whom she could turn for relief or help, and as Tony's business interests in America would very soon see him return there, she could not even cling to the frail hope that he would be in a position to rescue her. Stifling the sob which rose to her lips, she turned her head on the pillow away from Sarah so she would not see the stray tear which ran down her cheek; the thought of never seeing Tony again and her imminent act of betrayal to those who had shown her so much kindness, causing Eleanor more pain than any one of the injuries Braden had inflicted on her.

But by the time Tony entered her room sometime later she had her emotions sufficiently under control, or so she believed, to avert any suspicion in his mind, her face lighting up at the sight of him, momentarily forgetting everything as she watched him hold the door open for Sarah before walking towards her. "Tony!"

"How's my favourite girl?" he smiled, sitting down on the edge of the bed and taking hold of her hands in his.

"Much better for seeing you," she told him truthfully.

"Now *that's* what I like to hear," he smiled, kissing her fingers. "Missed me?" he asked softly.

"You must know I have," she told him earnestly, deliberately shutting everything out of her mind except the joy of being near him.

"I'm glad," he smiled, his voice a caress, "because I have missed you; terribly."

"Y-you have?" she faltered, her fingers trembling in his.

"You'd better believe it!" he said in a deep voice.

"I like being missed by you," she told him shyly, her body, despite the pain and soreness of her ribs, quivering at the look in his eyes. "Oh, Tony!" she cried, knowing that never again would she have any opportunity of telling him how she felt, "I know we have not long known one another, a bare forty-eight hours and, try as I do," she shook her head, "I can't explain it, but I do love you, so *very* much!"

Unable to resist the temptation, Tony released her hands, then, leaning forward, gently raised her and took her in his arms; holding her close against him. "I know Doctor Little is rather pleased with your progress," he told her a little unsteadily, "but you are still far from well and, certainly, not well enough to enable me to show you how much I love you in the only way which expresses how I feel." He felt her tremble in his arms and held her tighter. "My darling," he told her in a deep voice, "I knew you were the only one for me the moment I saw you through those opera glasses, and that there would never be anyone else."

"Oh, Tony!" she mumbled into his shoulder.

"I love you, Ellie!" he told her wholeheartedly. "Don't ask me to explain it or how it happened because I can't," he admitted, gently easing himself away from her to look down into her upturned face, "all I know," he smiled, "is that I am never going to let you go."

"Never stop loving me, Tony!" she pleaded as he tenderly brushed a strand of her hair from her face. "I couldn't bear it if you did!"

"There's no fear of that," he assured her lovingly. "I shall love you until the day I die and, come what may," he smiled ruefully, laying a gentle hand against her swollen cheek, "I am afraid you are stuck with me!"

Her face might be sore and tender, but the light, almost delicate touch of his hand against her cheek and the warm strength of his body against her own, made her heart cry out for more, but like the man who was looking down at her with so much warmth and love she knew she was in no condition to receive his kisses, kisses she desperately longed for. Instead, she tried to take comfort from treasuring this moment in his arms and hearing those wonderful words 'I love you'; words she knew she would never hear again any more than she would feel his arms around her as he held her close against him. It was a painful thought and one she would much rather not dwell upon, but if nothing else it intensified her ever-growing dread at the daunting prospect of the insupportable and hopeless future which awaited her, but unless she wanted to alert Tony to the truth as well as convincing him that she did not need him or Sarah to keep vigil over her tonight, she managed to stifle the sob which formed in her throat, allowing her to respond to his casual comment about that supposed letter from her father more calmly than she felt.

To her immense relief, like his sister, apart from agreeing that a visit to her father, when she had recovered a little, would do her good, besides which he had fully intended to place her in her father's care, Tony neither doubted that Sir Miles had written the letter or what she told him about its contents, nor did he put forward any nerve-racking questions she could not possibly answer, merely taking her word on trust, a circumstance which only served to make her feel even more wretched. She was not at all certain whether to be glad or not that she had scaled such a delicate hurdle so successfully because she was honest enough to admit that had Tony questioned the letter more closely it would not have been long before she confided its contents to him and, for her father's sake as well as his, not to mention Tom and Beatrice, this was the one thing she could not do. Unfortunately, however, her coaxing but faltering appeal that she be allowed to forgo an overseer was instantly met with a concerned look and a doubtful shake of the head, causing her to feel a moment's alarm, but upon her firmly expressed belief that, as she was feeling much better, she did not expect a disturbed night, on the contrary she was firmly convinced she would have no trouble sleeping, she saw him hesitate. Pressing home her advantage, she said softly, "Indeed, Tony," resting the palm of her hand against his cheek, "I shall be perfectly all right. You said yourself I am quite safe here. Besides," she smiled, trying to ignore the pain around her heart, "I cannot expect Sarah to sit with me during the day as well as all night, any more than I can of you. I know you will not admit it," she said gently, "but you must be tired after sitting up with me last night!"

"Oh," he smiled, kissing the palm of her hand, "I got all the shuteye I needed."

"But it must have been dreadfully uncomfortable for you!" she said steadily, not daring to think what she would do should he decide to stay with her.

"Is this your way of telling me that you have had enough of me already?" he teased, his eyes smiling warmly down at her.

His gentle teasing, instead of making her feel more relaxed, only served to compound her misery, rendering it impossible for her to do more than shake her head, saying fervently, *"Never!"*

He seemed to consider for a moment, before saying, "Very well, if that is what you want."

Having fully expected him, if not to argue the point, then certainly to question it further, so relieved was she that he agreed so readily to her request she could only nod her head, but her pain was so unbearable that the only response she could give to a loving word he whispered in her ear was to bury her head into his shoulder, taking what little comfort she could from feeling his arms hold her even closer to him.

Considering that Tony's opinion corresponded precisely with his sister's regarding that letter in that they both believed it was Collett's way of intimidating Eleanor into either remaining silent or, which seemed most likely, leaving Mount Street of her own free will and not from Sir Miles at all, Beatrice was somewhat puzzled to learn that he had not questioned Eleanor about it, but had accepted what she told him. Beatrice had no regrets whatsoever in offering sanctuary to Eleanor, in fact she had spoken no less than the truth when she had told Tony last night that there was no way she was going to allow Eleanor to return to Cavendish Square and that brute of a husband, but that letter had seriously alarmed her. Beatrice's greatest fear, she told Tony seriously, was that Eleanor, who was far from well enough to think rationally, could quite easily allow that letter, which she had no doubt at all contained all manner of threats, persuade her into leaving their protection, but upon hearing her brother's soothing assurances that Eleanor, apart from being perfectly safe upstairs out of Collett's clutches, was hardly in a physical condition to go anywhere. Having given it a little more thought Beatrice was eventually brought to accept that he was right and that she was allowing her nerves to get the better of her and since Tom, having heard all about the day's events over the dinner table following the discreet exit of Bennett and his attendants, agreed with his brother-in-law, most of her fears had finally been allayed.

However, it was not until Beatrice had retired to bed that Tony, fortified with a glass of whisky in the comfort of Tom's study, told his brother-in-law about the outcome of his visit to Holborn and his informative talk with Joanie Simms. Tom was not at all surprised to learn that Tony had not told Eleanor anything at all about the visit and that what he had told Bea had only been the bare bones of it, but by the time Tony had finished telling him what had actually passed between himself and Joanie Simms and what he thought could well account for Dennis Dunscumbe being shot in the right temple and not the left, all left Tom reeling in shocked disbelief.

"Good God!" he cried, sitting bolt upright. "It's worse than I thought!"

"Well," Tony sighed, inclining his head, "I must admit that I did think it was something along those lines." Upon seeing the look which crossed Tom's face, he explained, "Look Tom," he nodded, "there had to be a reason for Dennis Dunscumbe's death, and having discounted financial difficulties the motive had to lie elsewhere. Once I learned that he had something of a reputation for slapping women around and a buddy of Collett's into the bargain, who we know is pretty fond of beating up defenceless women," he said grimly, "besides his connection with Eliza Boon, whose establishment both men visited regularly, it figured that something must have happened and," he nodded, "when Bill told me that the body of a young woman had been found only a couple of blocks away everything began to make sense. Joanie Simms merely confirmed what I already suspected."

"So," Tom shrugged helplessly, quite impressed how Tony had pieced together a medley of fragmentary information, "Dennis Dunscumbe was murdered to prevent him from telling the police about what had happened to that unfortunate young woman?"

Tony nodded. "Dunscumbe's attack of conscience left them in something of a quandary, and as nothing they could say would dissuade him from going to the police they were left with no option other than to silence him before he could do so, and in a way that would make it appear as though he had committed suicide. Under no circumstances could they let the truth come out. For Collett," he shrugged, "he would probably have found himself answering a charge of failing to report the death of Annie Myers or even helping to illegally dispose of her body, perhaps other charges," he shrugged again, "and once it became known that she worked in a certain kind of establishment which he regularly patronised his reputation would be ruined, as would Dennis Duncumbe's, who, by the way, would also have found himself having to answer similar charges. I have absolutely no doubt," he inclined his head, "that it was not Dunscumbe's intention to kill Annie Myers, but whether he would have been charged with manslaughter I don't know, but I doubt very much that it would have been looked upon as an accidental death, but even if Dunscumbe had not found himself being charged with manslaughter I fail to see how either man would not have faced answering charges of some kind, perhaps even a probable prison sentence. Peterson too most likely! As for this Eliza Boon," he pointed out, "the same goes, to which she would also be charged with keeping a house of ill repute and living off immoral earnings with a prison sentence staring her in the face for that alone!"

"And Collett," Tom summarised, after digesting what Tony had said, "upon finding Sir Philip on his doorstep after learning the truth from Joanie Simms, challenging him about the death of his brother, as well as informing him that he fully intended to raise questions in the House about these kinds of establishments, killed him; and Eleanor, arriving home early from the concert, either walked in on it or stumbled onto something!"

"That's about the size of it, Tom," Tony confirmed grimly. "However," he nodded, "until I have spoken to Eleanor about that night I can only guess which way it was, but the fact remains she knows enough to see Collett hang, which is why she has been kept a virtual prisoner ever since!"

"But, surely," Tom stated incredulously, "they don't seriously think they can keep all of this a secret forever?"

"What's to prevent them?" Tony cocked an eyebrow. "They don't know that Joanie Simms was a witness to any of this or that it was she who alerted Sir Philip to the truth about his brother's death, much less that she has told me. As far as they are concerned the only one they have to worry about is Eleanor. She may not know about Annie Myers or Dennis Dunscumbe, but she knows a hell of a lot about Sir Philip's death, and Collett," he nodded, "knows perfectly well that once she starts talking, whether to me or to the police, it's only a short step to discovering the rest. He may have killed Sir Philip in a moment of panic, but it's still murder, and whilst I am firmly convinced that it was Eliza Boon who incited Peterson to get rid of Mitchell, in the same cold-blooded way she did Dennis Dunscumbe, the fact remains that Collett was a party to both, which is why," tossing off the rest of his whisky, "they have to try to prevent Eleanor from disclosing the truth."

"But why didn't Eleanor tell you the letter was from Collett?" Tom shrugged, puzzled. "Why did she pretend it was from her father?"

"Because she's afraid, Tom," Tony replied grimly, "which is why I did not press her to show me the letter, but accepted what she told me."

"But if she loves you!" Tom shrugged.

"At the moment," Tony told him, "her fear of Collett overrides everything else, even her feelings for me, and had I pressed her to tell me the truth she would not have done so, not because she does not trust me," he shook his head, "but because Collett has instilled so much terror into her that she firmly believes he has the power to harm me or, even," he nodded, "get Peterson and that Eliza Boon woman to try to steal her away from here at dead of night, and so the slightest urging on my part would only have increased her fear. However," he conceded on a sigh, "I must admit that whilst I had a pretty good idea they would try something I could only hazard a guess what it would be, but I had not expected them to be so quick off the mark."

"But Eleanor must surely know she's safe here!" Tom exclaimed.

"She knows," Tony told him, "but she's been frightened, beaten and bullied for so long that she's terrified of Collett, and whatever threats were in that letter you can be damn sure she believes he will carry every one of them out! He knows that he can't come here asking for her any more than he can get Peterson to break in and forcibly remove her at dead of night, but although it gives me no pleasure to say this sending that letter was a pretty shrewd move, clever too!"

"But…!" Tom began.

"Look Tom," Tony broke in, "he knows that Eleanor is afraid of him because she knows what he is capable of, and so he knew he could rely on her fear to corroborate this bogus maid's story as well as being certain that she would not show that letter to either me or to Bea. I'm only guessing here," he shrugged, "but I'd lay you any money that it was Eliza Boon's idea and not Collett's because there's no getting round it she's a pretty cool customer."

"I won't argue with that!" Tom said with feeling. "If you are right about her deliberately not telling Peterson about Dunscumbe being left-handed so he would naturally shoot him in the right temple purely as a line of defence if things went wrong, then I would put nothing beyond her!"

"Neither would I!" Tony agreed. "Especially when you remember that she and Peterson have just as much to lose as Collett! Her treatment of Eleanor alone," he pointed out, a harsh note creeping into his voice, "more than proves how far she is willing to go to make sure the truth never sees the light of day."

"That poor child!" Tom cried. "It doesn't bear thinking of as to what Collett threatened her with, but," he shrugged, "what does he hope to gain from it?"

"Until I've seen that letter I can only guess as to what he threatened her with, but it doesn't take too much figuring out," Tony said grimly. "As to what he hopes to gain from it, well," he shrugged, "ensuring their protection obviously, but whether he means to secure it by intimidating her so she will be too terrified to say anything or whether he is trying to coerce her into leaving here of her own free will, remains to be seen. Whichever way it is he's pretty certain it will work."

Tom eyed Tony thoughtfully, remarking at length, "I get the feeling you already know which aim he has in mind!"

"Pretty much!" Tony nodded.

"But you're not going to tell me, is that it?" Tom nodded.

"Not yet, Tom," Tony smiled, "but I'll know for certain in a little while. Needless to say, though," he assured him, "no harm will come to Eleanor or to Bea."

"You don't have to tell me that," Tom said earnestly, "I know it won't; otherwise you would never have set this Jerry's son on to sit guard during the day. But getting back to the rest," he frowned, "I don't mind saying that it's the most diabolical thing I ever heard!" rising to his feet to take Tony's empty glass. "And the worst of it is," he pointed the whisky decanter at him, "you can't prove any of it! Neither Eleanor nor this Joanie Simms are eligible to give evidence in court!"

"No," Tony sighed, shaking his head. "It's doubtful whether the prosecution would put Eleanor into the witness-box and, as for Joanie Simms," he sighed, "the same goes, but even if they did Collett's defence would make easy work of discrediting her. Her evidence," he told him, "even if she got as far as giving it, would most probably be put down to hearsay."

"So, this plan you're concocting to trap Collett and the others," Tom said thoughtfully, handing Tony his refilled glass, "what makes you think they will fall for it? I mean," he shrugged, resuming his seat, "they're not fools!"

"No," Tony agreed, "far from it, but do not forget," he pointed his glass at him, "at the moment, apart from the risk Eleanor poses, they believe they have eliminated all loose ends, but once they see that the police could possibly have overlooked something which could well incriminate them, they dare not ignore it."

Tom inhaled on his cigar as he considered this. "Yes, I see that, but do you really think you can get this Superintendent Dawson, Mrs. Timms *and* three newspaper editors to go along with it?"

"You're beginning to sound like Bill," Tony laughed, "but yes, I think they'll go for it! And what about you?" He raised an eyebrow.

"Me?" Tom echoed, flicking cigar ash into the fire.

"I take it you still want in?" Tony grinned.

"If that means what I think it means," Tom replied gamely, rising to his feet, "then, as you Americans say, 'I go for it'! Why, I wouldn't miss it for the world!" Then, quite spoiling the effect, said, a little sheepishly, "Only one thing though, Tony," upon seeing his brother-in-law raise an amusing eyebrow, he implored him, "for the Lord's sake, don't tell Bea! She'll only say I'm too old for this sort of caper!"

Tony burst out laughing at this and, rising to his feet, slapped Tom on the shoulder, "And, as you say over here, 'my lips are sealed!'"

Leaving Tony to finish his whisky and to scan the evening edition of the newspaper, Tom wished him goodnight and made his way upstairs to join Beatrice, little realising that within minutes of closing the study door behind him his brother-in-law tossed the newspaper aside, strode into the hall and, after checking that he had disappeared from sight, turned off the light then re-entered the study, leaving the door slightly ajar before casting the room into total darkness, resuming his seat just as the clock struck half past eleven. As he was not of a timid or nervous disposition, Tony sat in complete ease in front of the dying embers of the fire; neither the creaking sounds which were natural to a house settling down for the night or the odd noise which met his ears causing him any concern, but continued to sit calmly back in his chair waiting for what he firmly believed would be the outcome of that letter. His belief was not misplaced, when, just as the clocked chimed the midnight hour, the sound he had waited for met his ears.

As Eleanor expected, Tony took a look in on her just before going downstairs a little before seven o'clock and, as was customary, he was dressed for dinner, but the sight of him in his white tie and impeccably tailored evening clothes, admirably suiting his tall lean figure, brought a lump to her throat. A finely balanced mix of relief and sadness enveloped her when he bent down and gently kissed her forehead, telling her softly that he would not disturb her again tonight and would see her in the morning, but felt certain that Beatrice would come and say goodnight to her before she retired. Through a haze of tears Eleanor watched as he walked over to the door, forcing a smile to her lips when he turned to take one last look at her, but by the time Beatrice floated in to say goodnight to her some hours later in a rustle of pale blue silk she had managed to get her emotions reasonably under control, but upon being asked if she was certain she did not want Sarah to sit with her, Eleanor knew one awful moment of panic. Assuring Beatrice that she was quite certain nothing would disturb her as she was so tired, she received a warm smile and a kiss on the cheek, with the promise that she would not be disturbed, Beatrice having not the least idea of Eleanor's plans or of Tony's suspicions and counterattack. Having learned from Beatrice that Tony and Tom usually sat talking in the study for a time before retiring, Eleanor knew she dared not make any kind of move to leave the house until she heard them come upstairs, particularly as Tony may well decide to take a look in on her before going upstairs to his room after all. As there was nothing she could do for the moment other than wait until she heard the sound of their voices on the landing, she rested her head back against the pillows, trying not to think of what awaited her in Cavendish Square; it was her last conscious thought until over an hour later, opening her eyes to the starling discovery that she had inadvertently fallen asleep.

Although Eleanor hurriedly flung off the bed covers it was somewhat gingerly that she sat up and put her feet to the floor because although the worst of the unpleasant effects of the concussion had left her, she was nevertheless uncomfortably aware of the slight dizzy sensation in her head and that her body, thanks in part to her cracked rib but also because she had been inert for some days, was extremely stiff and sore, but step by gradual step she reached the door and cautiously opened it. No sound met her ears and, managing to cross the landing, rested her hands on the banister to lean rather painfully forward to see if any lights were visible downstairs, but like this landing and the one above, it was in total darkness. Taking this to mean that Tony and Tom had retired she went back to her room and walking over to the far wall where a huge wardrobe stood in which Beatrice kept several items of spare clothing, she quietly turned the catch and pulled the door towards her. Peering inside Eleanor saw several dresses hanging up next to two short capes and one old full-length, fur-lined one and, on the bottom shelf, several pairs of well-worn though perfectly serviceable shoes and slippers. Removing the long fur-lined cape and draping it around her shoulders, she then picked up a pair of leather slippers which, even though they were several sizes too large, would at least protect her feet as she made her away along the frozen pavements to where Braden had said the carriage would be waiting for her. Retrieving his letter from under the mattress and putting it inside the pocket of the cape, Eleanor picked up the slippers, then, after casting a last glance around the room, took a deep and tearful breath and walked out onto the landing towards the stairs, trying not to think of Tom and Beatrice in the room across the way, two people whose kindness she was repaying with such a cruel betrayal. Stifling the sob which rose in her throat Eleanor secured the slippers under her arm with hands that visibly shook, then, gripping the rail, started to make her way sideways down the wide staircase, her legs weak and trembling as she slowly descended one step at a time, desperately trying not to recall her escape from Cavendish Square last night which, in her distressed state of mind, seemed like an ironic jest.

Just the thought of Braden's bullying and Eliza Boon never letting her out of her sight, whose horridly tactile fingers filled her with revulsion, not to mention Peterson constantly standing guard, rendering her life hideous and insupportable, made Eleanor tremble with fear, causing her to pause halfway down the stairs to wipe away the tears as they began to steadily fall down her cheeks. She never wanted to see twenty-nine Cavendish Square again and the mere thought of returning there made her feel sick with apprehension, but Braden had given her no choice and since she could not bear the thought of those she loved suffering because of her refusal to do as he told her, there was nothing she could do other than go back. Having descended the last step she bent down to put on the slippers, a gasp leaving her lips as the movement caused a sharp pain to shoot through her ribs as well as everything to swim nauseatingly around her, making it necessary for her to pause a moment to still the buzzing in her ears, gripping the banister post to steady herself. Slowly the dizziness passed, then, after casting a quick glance all around the darkened hall to make sure she was still alone, she trod carefully over to the front door, but unfortunately her borrowed slippers, several sizes too large, kept slipping off her feet and their leather soles, much to her horror, had a habit of tapping abnormally loud on the highly polished floorboards, but to her relief she eventually reached the door where she stood for a moment to catch her breath. It was just as she was about to reach up to pull back the top bolt when the hall suddenly flooded with light.

"That's not the answer, Ellie," came a deep and familiar voice from behind her.

Spinning round, Eleanor's left eye widening as far as it was able with shock and incredulity, she saw Tony's tall figure slowly approach her. *"Tony!"* she cried in a strangled voice.

"You know as well as I do what will happen to you if you return to Cavendish Square," he said gently, having by now come up to her.

For one awful moment she thought she was going to faint, but managing to remain standing on her own two feet, she looked anxiously up at him, asking faintly, "H-how did you know?"

"Call it a hunch," he shrugged, smiling down at her.

"Oh, Tony!" she cried, laying an urgent hand on his arm, her now almost fully opened left eye reflecting her fear and anxiety. "If… if you love me you will let me go!"

"It's because I love you," he told her softly, covering her cold hand with his warm one, "that I can't. Even if I didn't love you," he told her, "what kind of man would I be to turn a blind eye? Knowing full well that you are going back to a man who has not only treated you shamefully, but who has made no secret of his future intentions. I can't do it, Ellie," he shook his head, "you know I can't."

"Oh, Tony!" she cried fretfully, haunted by visions of Peterson attempting to enter the house to forcibly remove her because she had not gone to them willingly. "You… you *don't* understand!" she cried tearfully.

"Oh, but I do," he assured her gently.

"No," she shook her head, "you don't. *Please*," she begged, "let me go."

"Huh huh," he shook his head, "no can do, Ellie."

"Please, you *must* listen to me!" she urged.

"And so I shall," he smiled, picking her effortlessly up in his arms, "once I have you safely back in bed."

Her feeble attempts to wriggle out of his arms proving quite futile, she burst into distraught tears, but upon feeling his arms tighten around her she instinctively wrapped her own around his neck and, burying her face into his shoulder, gave herself up to the tumult of emotions running riot inside her as he leisurely climbed the stairs. Tony could feel the sobs racking her body as he held her close against him and, not for the first time, he felt such a surge of anger towards those who had, without remorse or pity, systematically perpetrated physical and mental cruelty on a woman who, even when not in their presence, was too terrified to go against them.

Having reached the top step he could see the door to the guest room standing ajar out of which a ray of light filtered onto the landing and, treading softly across the highly polished floorboards, he nudged the door back on its hinges with his shoulder, kicking it shut behind him with a well shod foot and, without a backward glance, carried Eleanor over to the bed. Removing the cloak from around her shoulders and tossing it onto the chair, the slippers having fallen off somewhere between the hall and the landing, he gently eased her down onto the bed, then, sitting down beside her, took her trembling body in his arms, his warm strength going a long way to calming her.

Somewhere in the far recesses of Eleanor's mind a jumbled mass of thoughts tussled one with the other, not the least being Peterson and Eliza Boon's fruitless wait on the corner of Davies Street; what Braden would do once he knew she had failed to do as he had bidden her and, worst of all, the risk to her father, but as she leaned comfortably against Tony's strong hard body, feeling the warm strength of his arms as they cradled her to him, she was far too worn out to give any of it any further thought tonight. Although her sobbing gradually subsided, her emotions, which, during the course of the day, had wavered between fear of not complying with her husband's demands and what awaited her in Cavendish Square if she did as well as the thought of not seeing Tony again, not to mention the heavy burden of knowing she was deliberately deceiving those who had shown her nothing but kindness, culminating in being rescued at the eleventh hour, took their toll, leaving her limp and exhausted in Tony's arms.

Tony, who knew that it would take a long time before Eleanor's fears would disappear completely, had a pretty good idea of what was going through her mind and, after gently kissing the top of her head, asked helpfully, "Would you like to tell me about it?" Although he received a rather unsteady 'yes' she made no attempt to raise her head, seemingly content to remain with her cheek nestling snugly against his white waistcoat, but upon feeling a gentle forefinger under her chin tenderly tilting her head, she raised a tearstained face to his. She saw him smile warmly down at her as he retrieved a handkerchief from his pocket and began to carefully wipe the tears from her eyes and face before smoothly brushing several stray tendrils of damp hair off her forehead. "That's better," he said softly.

"Oh, Tony!" she cried huskily. "What must you think of me!"

"You know what I think of you," he smiled lovingly, kissing the hand he was holding.

"I am so sorry," she told him on a stifled sob. "Can you ever forgive me?"

"Ssh," he soothed, "you have no need to be sorry, and there is certainly nothing to forgive."

"Oh, but there is," she insisted in a choked voice, her fingers clutching his hand. "I lied to you and Beatrice… and… well, oh, Tony, it was because I was so afraid!"

"I know," he said in the same soothing voice, "but there is no need for you to be afraid any more. Don't you know," he asked gently, "that I would never let any harm come to you? I have you quite safe, my darling," delicately stroking her cheek with the back of his forefinger. He felt her tremble in his arms and, holding her tighter, asked, "Did you really think that I would let you to go back to Cavendish Square?"

She shook her head. "No," she replied a little unsteadily. Then, looking up at him, asked, "H-how did you know? You… you said it was a hunch. What is that?" She shook her head.

"Ah!" he smiled. "Well, it's what we mean back in the States as a guess – an educated one, of course!" he pulled a face.

"Oh!" she nodded. "It was that letter, wasn't it?"

"Yes, although," he nodded, "that just went to prove what I already knew. You see," he told her in answer to her look of enquiry, "Collett cannot afford to have you telling me or Bea what you saw or stumbled upon that night." He felt her shudder at the recollection and tightened his hold. "He knows that once your injuries begin to heal it's only a matter of time, perhaps days, before you tell us the truth; he cannot allow that to happen."

"Are you saying that you knew he would write me a letter?" Eleanor asked, surprised.

"No," Tony confessed, "although I did know he would try something; the only thing was I had no idea what it would be, that's why I've arranged for Jerry's son to be here during the day while Tom and I are out, but the moment Bea told me about that supposed maid delivering a letter from your father, I knew straight off who it was from. So," he inclined his head, "the way I figured it, since Collett cannot come here asking for you or remove you by force, he could either threaten you into keeping silent or getting you to leave here of your own free will." Something between a choke and a sob left her lips at this, to which he responded by kissing the top of her head. "You see, my darling," he said softly, "the fact that you did not show me the letter or Bea either, as well as how you tried to persuade me into leaving you alone tonight, I knew beyond doubt it was from Collett and that it was more than likely he was trying to get you to leave here." Wiping away a stray tear, he said gently, "I knew that whatever threats were in that letter you would not tell me because you were too terrified of him carrying them out and so, my darling," he said softly, "I decided to wait upon events." He felt the convulsive movement of her hand in his and, after warmly kissing it, said gently, "My darling, I know you are afraid, but surely you must know that I would never let any harm come to you! Why didn't you tell me? Don't you trust me enough?"

"Oh, Tony!" she cried, raising her eyes to his. "You know I do! It's just that…"

"Just what?" he urged softly. When she made no immediate reply, he asked quietly, "Did he threaten you through me, or Tom, perhaps?"

She nodded. "Both of you, and my father."

"Your father?" he queried, a puzzled frown creasing his forehead.

"Yes, you… you see," she faltered, "Braden knows…" unable to say anything further.

"Ellie," he asked quietly, "do you still have that letter?" She nodded. "May I see it?"

"Yes," she nodded again. "It's in the pocket of that cape."

Gently easing her back against the mound of pillows and pulling the covers over her Tony strode over to the chair and felt inside the pocket of the cape, removing an oblong envelope on which the name 'Eleanor' was written in a bold hand. Coming back to sit beside her on the edge of the bed, he pulled out the three sheets of vellum, his eyes hardening as he read:

Eleanor,

I know you have taken refuge in Mount Street and that Childon, although by what means I know not, conveyed you there, but had you considered a little before embarking upon such a dramatic flight you would have realised the utter futility of such an action. I shall refrain from commenting upon Childon's conduct except to say that it is hardly befitting that of a gentleman, but I would remind you that I am *your husband, which means I do have certain rights.*

I feel sure it is not in the least degree necessary for me to point out how ill-advised it would be were you to impart your knowledge to others any more than I need to expand on what will result should you do so. I flatter myself that I am not without influence in many quarters and should I decide to bring it to bear, suffice it to say, that Sir Thomas Shipton as well as Childon will feel its far-reaching and disastrous effects in a way which would cause you as much distress as it would them ruination. Should this most unwelcome thought not be enough to dissuade you as to the folly of disclosing the most distressing events of that night, then perhaps the thought of your father will. I beg you to consider how humiliating it would be for a man of Sir Miles Tatton's integrity to discover that his name had shamefully been brought into disrepute and for a transgression which contravenes every code of honour by which a gentleman lives, and thus it behoves me, painful though it is, to remind you that it is in your hands to prevent a most distressing occurrence should your father decide not to face society's condemnation.

I feel sure I can rely upon your good sense, my dear Eleanor, to show this letter to no one or reveal its contents and that I shall have the good fortune of welcoming you home this evening. In view of this, Peterson will be waiting with the carriage at midnight at the corner of Davies Street and Mount Street to convey you to Cavendish Square and, in order to relieve my mind of care as to your safety, you may look upon Eliza's escort as you would my own.

In the full expectation of your compliance to my wishes, I offer you, as a token of good faith, my assurance that I shall take no steps, either now or in the future, to approach Sir Wilfred Moore, but should you decide to disregard my guidance as well as deprive me of my earnest wish to have you safely restored to my protection, then I will not hesitate to honour every *promise I have made to you.*

Braden.

Whatever else Tony may accuse Sir Braden Collett of it was certainly not a lack of skill in the epistolary art; this literary example was a masterpiece of coercion, carefully crafted to put fear into the heart of its reader, but as the expression on Tony's face testified it aroused neither admiration nor endorsement in his breast. With every intimidating word Collett had played on Eleanor's fears with such cruel refinement that her response could not have been anything other than what he intended, leaving Tony in no doubt that, despite Collett's assurances about not approaching Sir Wilfred Moore, her future, once back in Cavendish Square, was anything but promising.

"You're very angry, aren't you?" Eleanor broke anxiously into his thoughts, laying a gentle hand on his arm.

"Yes," Tony nodded, the severity leaving his face, "but not with you," he assured her, taking her hand in his and giving it a reassuring squeeze.

Her fingers moved in his. "I have been in an agony of despair ever since I read that letter," she told him huskily, "but I knew if I didn't do as Braden said he would… oh, Tony!" she cried fervently. "If… if anything were to happen to you and Tom or my father because of me I… I couldn't bear it. Y-You do understand that, don't you?" she asked urgently.

"My darling, of course I do," Tony told her earnestly, kissing her hand.

"I… I couldn't tell you," she cried. "I wanted to leave a note, but… I… I… didn't know what to do and, oh Tony," she shook her head helplessly, "I still don't!"

"Don't you?" he asked, his voice a caress. She shook her head. "Then it's a good thing I do, isn't it?" his eyes smiling warmly down at her before taking her in his arms and holding her close.

She nodded and sniffed, but said fearfully, "But what about Eliza and Peterson?"

"I'd say it looks like they're in for a pretty long wait," he told her, not without a touch of satisfaction, kissing the top of her head.

"You don't think they will…?" she asked apprehensively, shuddering at the thought.

"Huh huh," Tony assured her, holding her closer to him, "not a chance!"

"But you don't know them, or Braden, as I do!" Eleanor told him urgently, raising her head to look up at him.

"You are quite wrong, Ellie," Tony shook his head, forestalling her by lightly placing the tip of his finger against her still slightly swollen lips as she opened her mouth to speak. "They might be desperate to get you back into their clutches before you start talking, but they are not so lost to common sense that they don't know the terrible risk they would be running should they make the attempt to break in and remove you," he assured her. "It would be far too dangerous. As for your father," he said gently, "it's clear that Collett has some sort of hold over him, but as you are far too exhausted to tell me about it tonight, it will keep until tomorrow."

"But I am so afraid for him!" she cried fearfully.

"I know," Tony nodded, "but there is not the least need, I promise you. No harm will come to him, or to Tom. Truly," he smiled, "there is no need for you to worry over your father or anything else, and certainly not for me. All you need do," he said warmly, kissing her forehead, "is trust me. You *do* trust me, don't you?"

"You know I do," she said fervently, clutching his hand.

"There is no need for you to be afraid anymore," he said softly.

"I am not afraid when I am with you," she confessed, "it's just that," shaking her head, "I'm still a little…"

"I know," he said soothingly, "which is why I am staying with you tonight." Somehow managing to stem his natural impulses upon feeling the relief run through her, Tony eased her back against the pillows, saying, as he rose to his feet, "First though, I need to get out of this," indicating his dinner suit by tugging the lapel of his jacket with his thumb and forefinger, "so I must leave you for a few minutes." She nodded. "No running away while my back is turned," he teased.

She shook her head. "I won't."

He looked down at her, a look of mock doubt on his face, pointing a warning finger. "Promise."

"I promise," she smiled.

"Good girl," he nodded.

It was just as he reached the door when she said, "You… you always seem to be coming to my rescue."

"Like the proverbial knight-errant?" He pulled an amusing face. She nodded. "I'm hardly that, Ellie," he said genuinely, slowly shaking his head. "I'm just an ordinary guy doing all he can to try to protect the woman he loves."

Her heart gave an ecstatic little jump at this. "I'm glad," she said huskily, "because you see, I… I don't want a knight-errant; I only want you."

When Tony had told her he had fallen in love with her at first sight but that he could neither explain nor understand how it had happened, he had not exaggerated any more than when he had told Beatrice that he would know the only woman for him the moment he laid eyes on her, all he knew was that he had never once doubted or questioned this long-held belief; instinctively knowing it was true. It was also true that he had wanted to kiss Eleanor from the moment he had seen her through those opera glasses, and having held her in his arms and felt her soft pliant body against his own had done nothing to dispel this need. That Eleanor felt the same about him was patent and, as he looked down at her now, he was honest enough to admit that had circumstances been different he would have known no hesitation in kissing her, but to take advantage of her in such a way would not only be unforgivable, but really quite despicable, yet her heartfelt declaration did nothing to help him restrain his natural impulses, but somehow managing to clamp down on them, he pulled a face. "I'm glad to hear you say that because not only am I not knight-errant material, but trying to find a white charger, much less riding around on one, could give people a very odd idea of me!"

Eleanor gave a shaky little laugh as he had intended, but she too was honest to enough to admit that if her nearness put his self-restraint to the test, then so too did his with her own. She could not claim to having any amatory experience, on the contrary before her marriage the young men of her acquaintance, whilst really most agreeable and amusing, had done nothing to make her heart beat any the faster and, as for Braden, far from inspiring love and desire he had merely increased the fear and dread she had always had of him. She did not hate her father for permitting the marriage, after all Braden had caught him at his most vulnerable and taken full advantage of it, knowing no compunction in using it against him by offering him an ultimatum which had left no room for manoeuvre, in fact it had placed him in the intolerable position of either having to sacrifice his daughter to a man she feared or witnessing his own public demise. She had gone on fearing Braden and until Tony had entered her life she had come to believe that love was going to be denied her, and although she had no real idea how she would feel should it ever come her way she instinctively knew she would recognise it instantly, which was precisely what she had done the moment Tony entered their box at Covent Garden, although she was honest enough to admit that she had not been prepared for quite such an emotional upheaval. The swiftness with which it had happened and the intensity of her feelings may surprise her, but she was neither ashamed of them nor disinclined to explore them further. Nevertheless, she knew perfectly well that regardless of her fear of Braden she *was* his wife and therefore not free to love another man or express that love, but she was honest and woman enough to admit that not only did she enjoy being in Tony's arms, but was fully conscious of the fact that she wanted him to kiss her. She may be inexperienced, but she had seen the love and warmth in his eyes whenever he looked at her as well as sensing the urgency which emanated from him every time he held her, and although he may have said he was no knight-errant, his behaviour towards her only went to prove that this was precisely what he was.

Beatrice, suddenly awoken by a noise she was unable to determine, sat bolt upright in bed, assailed by visions of someone trying to gain entry into the house, but just as she was on the point of rousing her husband she wondered if it was nothing more than Tony checking on Eleanor. Slipping out of bed and putting on her dressing gown she tiptoed silently across the room and quietly opened the door, totally unprepared for the blaze of light she could see coming from the hall, her heart beginning to beat uncomfortably fast as the sound of someone moving around downstairs came to her ears. For one awful moment she felt as if she had taken root to the spot, but upon seeing Tony walk from the back of the hall to check the front door wearing his pyjamas and dressing gown a sob of pure relief left her throat causing him to look up, whereupon she ran down the stairs with a multitude of whispered questions tripping off her tongue, almost stumbling into his arms.

"It's all right, Bea," he told her in a hushed voice, giving her a reassuring hug, "there's nothing to worry you."

She caught sight of the slippers on the floor, raising questioning eyes. "But…" she began, shaking her head bewildered. "Tony," she asked urgently, "what's happened? And don't say nothing because I…!"

"No one has tried to get into the house," he told her, "in fact," he smiled, "quite the opposite!"

She looked up at him in bemusement, laying an urgent hand on his arm. "Tony, are you saying that…?"

"Yes," he nodded, "that's precisely what I'm saying."

"So, that letter *was* from Collett after all and not her father!" she exclaimed.

"Yes," he nodded, "and, having read it," he said grimly, "it explains her behaviour today and why she wanted to be left alone tonight. I can well understand why she has been afraid. Not that I needed to see that letter to know just how terrified she has been, and still is."

"Do you mean she has shown it to you?" He nodded. "Oh, that poor child!" she cried, when Tony had come to the end of telling her about Eleanor's attempted escape. "Why could she not have told me?"

"She's afraid, Bea," he nodded, "and with good cause."

"Oh, what I would not like to do to Collett!" she cried from the bottom of her heart. "And that *dreadful* woman!"

"I'm afraid you will have to stand in the queue for that," he smiled.

"But surely they won't still be waiting for her now!" she asked incredulously, casting a glance at the grandfather clock, its fingers showing almost half past one.

"If they are," he nodded, not without satisfaction, "they will be frozen to death."

"Good!" she said firmly. "Although that will be nothing compared to what they have done to Eleanor." She looked worriedly up at him as a thought suddenly occurred to her. "You… you don't think they will try to get into the house, do you?"

Tony shook his head. "No, there's no fear of that," he promised her, picking up the slippers before walking over to the light switch and turning it off. "That's the one thing they dare not do."

"But…" she began.

"Look Bea," he said calmly, pulling her hand through his arm as they mounted the stairs, "they might be desperate to get Eleanor back to Cavendish Square before she starts talking, but they won't do anything which could bring the law down on them, and attempting to enter someone's home by stealth in the dead of night is the one sure way of doing that!"

Tony's calm good sense went a long way to settling her nerves, and by the time they reached the first landing she was a little more inclined to relax. She was not in the least surprised to learn that he was fully intending to sit up with Eleanor again, but upon offering to be her overseer in his place, stating that he would be fagged to death by losing another night's sleep, he shook his head.

"It will take more than the loss of two nights' sleep to do that," he grinned. "Don't worry," he assured her, kissing her cheek, "I manage to get enough shuteye." She was about to say something but he forestalled her, saying seriously, "I cannot leave her, Bea. You must not ask it of me." She nodded, then, after taking the slippers from him, gave him a quick hug and wished him goodnight.

By the time he returned to the guest bedroom Eleanor was sound asleep, which was not at all surprising considering the emotional turmoil she had experienced. With her left cheek resting on the palm of her hand and her dark blonde hair spread invitingly on the pillow, she presented an irresistible picture to the man looking down at her with his hands dug deep into the pockets of his dark blue brocade dressing gown and a deep frown creasing his forehead. He knew perfectly well that Eleanor's stay under his brother-in-law's roof rendered his own position extremely awkward, but he would have been more than human not to be affected by seeing her like this and less than honest not to admit that when he held her close against him to offer her much-needed comfort and reassurance, her very nearness tested his resolve. He had not expected a harmless evening at the opera to bring him face to face with the woman he had instinctively known was the only one for him any more than he could have foreseen the events which had followed hard upon its heels, but he could no more have left Eleanor to her fate than he could stop loving her. That he and Jerry had been in Cavendish Square at the precise moment she was attempting to make her escape had been purely coincidental, not to say providential, but had he turned his back and left her to either freeze to death or fall into the hands of those who had ruthlessly mistreated her would have made him no better than them. Tom had told him that this was his home too and that he would have been extremely hurt had he taken Eleanor to her father in Bruton Street had he been in town, and whilst Tony had no need to hear his brother-in-law say any of this, knowing it to be true, the fact remained that Eleanor's presence in Mount Street would test his self-restraint to the utmost. He had at one point toyed with the idea of putting up at a hotel in order to protect Eleanor from malicious gossip should it ever become known that they had resided under his sister's roof at the same time, but only a moment's thought had been enough to tell him that this would not answer, not only because it would inevitably lead to questions being asked as to why he had suddenly moved out of his brother-in-law's home, but also because it could well reach Collett's ears and the chances were that he could well take advantage of his absence by trying to remove Eleanor from Mount Street. Tony had no regrets about the part he was playing in trying to bring cold-blooded murderers to justice any more than he had about any of his actions so far, and certainly not in taking the decision to bring Eleanor here to his sister, but as he prepared to watch over Eleanor's sleep he could not fool himself into thinking that Collett would not try again to get her back to Cavendish Square any more than he could fool himself into thinking that he could remain immune to her.

Chapter Twenty

At no time did it even occur to Eliza Boon that Molly would fail in her mission, in fact so convinced was she that Lady Shipton would be completely taken in that Eliza never even contemplated failure, in truth there was no reason why she should; Molly was an extremely good actress and passing herself off as an upstairs parlour maid would pose no difficulty for her whatsoever. It came as no surprise when Eliza learned from Molly that Lady Shipton had accepted her tale and, apart from enquiring if Sir Miles had returned to town, she made no comment as to the letter's authenticity, but promised to give it to Lady Collett when next she saw her. Of course, it had to be acknowledged that Molly had been greatly assisted by the fact that Lady Shipton had no idea who made up Sir Miles Tatton's domestic household, for which keeping Eleanor as far away from her as possible was responsible unless, of course, she was accompanied by either herself or Sir Braden and, from this standpoint alone, Eliza had considered it to be a pretty foregone conclusion to say that Lady Shipton would neither question nor doubt Molly.

As far as Eleanor was concerned, it could not be argued that her escape from Cavendish Square was most unfortunate as well as being quite unforeseen, but it certainly proved what Eliza had suspected for some little time in that her prisoner had not been totally cowed into submission and, in view of this, the sooner they removed her from Mount Street the better. For the moment at least there was no immediate danger of Eleanor succumbing to Lady Shipton's persuasions or those of her brother, but once she began to recover the danger they posed could not be underestimated particularly as it was patently clear that Childon and Eleanor had taken a liking to one another, but whilst this was a possibility which could not be overlooked, unless Eliza had grossly erred she could not see Eleanor putting a man she had not long met before her own father. It was therefore without any misgivings that Eliza knew Eleanor would not show the letter to either Lady Shipton or her brother as well as being relied upon not to contradict Molly's story when it was later related to her by Lady Shipton. As for Eleanor doing precisely what Sir Braden had instructed her to do, despite the flickering embers of independence which continued to linger and could so easily be fanned into a flame of total defiance by Lady Shipton or her brother, Eliza believed they had instilled enough fear into her over the preceding months to make her submission a foregone conclusion.

Unfortunately, however, Sir Braden did not share Eliza's optimism. She had not needed to hear him voice his doubts and uncertainties about the success of the scheme they were hatching to get Eleanor back home before she could start talking, they were clearly etched into every inch of his face. He had great faith in Eliza, in fact he placed a considerable amount of trust in her, but although he admitted that he had never known her make an error of judgement or wrong decision, despite her confidence in Molly Clark, he nevertheless envisioned all manner of things going wrong. He could not find fault with Eliza's reasoning in that since they could not go to Mount Street either enquiring after Eleanor or demanding they give her up, let alone trying to force an entry to remove her, there were no options open to them other than coercing her into leaving Lady Shipton's protection of her own accord, but it was not Lady Shipton who worried him so much as her brother.

Admittedly their paths had crossed only once at the Kirkmichaels', and then briefly, but however much he had taken Childon in instant dislike, a feeling he instinctively knew as being entirely mutual, there had been no disguising the fact that Childon had taken a real liking to Eleanor, and he knew his wife well enough to say that she had taken a liking to him too. Sir Braden Collett may find Beatrice Shipton's brother objectionable for any number of reasons, not the least of these being he did not hold with Colonials taking up hereditary titles and then commencing their aristocratic careers by aping their betters, but the truth was Sir Braden's dislike stemmed not from Childon's nationality so much as intuitively knowing that he was very far removed from this firmly entrenched belief as well as being a man with an inflexible determination. But more than this, he had read the silent condemnation behind the politeness confirming that Childon must have witnessed his treatment of Eleanor the previous evening, and whilst he still had not been able to work out just where this man fitted into his wife's escape, that he had assisted her he was in no doubt. One look at Eleanor would more than suffice to tell Childon how she had come by her injuries, and if he was the type of man Sir Braden took him to be, and he was certain he was, then as soon as Eleanor was well enough to talk to him he would not sit back and ignore it. Left unchecked Childon could do untold damage and, from what Collett had seen of him, he was determined and intelligent enough to arrive at the truth, and with his newspapers behind him it would not be long before his crimes were made public and he was being charged with murder; the very thought making him recoil.

Eliza may have every confidence in Eleanor complying with that letter, but as the minutes ticked by while Sir Braden waited for Eliza to return to Cavendish Square, his mood hovered dangerously between seething anger at his wife placing him in this invidious position and anxiety should she fail to do as he instructed or, which was infinitely worse, fear that Molly Clark may not have convinced Lady Shipton and she could well have opened the letter herself and even shown it to her brother. Had he the least suspicion that Childon did not need to see the letter to know who it was from and that he and his accomplices were being closely watched and followed twenty-four hours a day as well as Childon having discovered his involvement in recent events, Sir Braden's anxiety would have increased tenfold.

Like Sir Braden, Eliza could think of nothing more unfortunate than knowing that the man who had clearly taken a fancy to Eleanor and was evidently determined to come to her aid, was none other than the brother of a woman both she and Sir Braden had taken care to keep at a distance. It was also most unfortunate that Childon just happened to be the owner of certain newspapers whose pages, like those of other publications, even now, were reporting on the unexplained death of Sir Philip Dunscumbe, a story he would be very familiar with.

Tony may have entered into Eliza Boon's calculations only as far as he concerned Eleanor, but certainly not to the extent that he was investigating what she firmly believed he could possibly have no knowledge of without Eleanor's testimony of what occurred that night in Cavendish Square. As it was, Eliza had no idea that he had ascertained the reason to account for those times when Eleanor had found it necessary to withdraw herself from society over recent months and then, when she did appear, never being allowed out alone as well as accurately interpreting her response to a newspaper article about Sir Philip and that, from these three seemingly unimportant circumstances, he had pieced together the facts surrounding his death. Unlike Sir Braden, Eliza had not laid eyes on Lady Shipton's brother, but that did not prevent her from recognising the danger he posed, and the longer Eleanor was in his company the greater that danger would become and it was for this reason Eliza had acted swiftly and decisively, giving Eleanor no time to feel at ease in his company and thus encouraged to open her mind to him.

It was therefore in an optimistic frame mind that Eliza made her way back to Cavendish Square; totally confident that her plan could not fail and utterly oblivious to the fact that she and her accomplices were being kept under close observation. It was perhaps as well for her continued peace of mind that she had no idea fifty-one Periton Place had come to the notice of the man she had no hesitation in deeming their biggest threat and that he had, with a determination which matched her own, found out about Joanie Simms by way of a letter she had no idea even existed and was, at this very moment, on the point of interviewing her.

Had anyone asked Eliza if she remembered Joanie Simms she would have said yes, in fact she remembered her very well, though not with kindness, especially considering how she had taken her in and given her a roof over her head, only to be repaid with her leaving without a word or explanation. Eliza had liked Joanie, in fact she would have been hard put to bring to mind one person who did not, particularly certain clients, but upon reflection she would have said that Joanie had never really been committed to her work and had, for some little time prior to her sudden departure, expressed a desire of wanting to leave. Had she pressed the point Eliza would have done everything possible to prevent it, but the stealthy way in which she had left her establishment had by no means pleased her, but since she had never even so much as suspected that Joanie had left armed with such damaging information which could see her and her collaborators facing the Queen's Bench, Eliza had soon dismissed her from her mind.

A rapid review of the situation facing them having brought to light no other loopholes which could possibly denounce them, Eliza entered the impressive portals of twenty-nine Cavendish Square supremely confident that they had frightened Eleanor enough to get her to do precisely what they wanted. Totally unaware of the part Joanie Simms was about to play in turning their schemes to ashes and Tony's resolve to bring them to account for their actions, Eliza was able to give Sir Braden a most favourable report of the morning's events, blissfully ignorant of the storm clouds gathering overhead.

Just one glance at Sir Braden was enough to tell Eliza exactly how he had spent his time during her absence and, from the looks of the decanter on his desk, she would say that he had been drowning his sorrows for some considerable time rather than setting his mind to the problem facing them. She fully appreciated his anger over the awkward position Eleanor had placed them in by escaping, in fact she was herself furiously angry over such an unfortunate occurrence, but taking solace from the brandy decanter would not solve their difficulties. Sir Braden, as Eliza knew very well, did not perform well under anxiety and it seemed that now was no exception, but if she thought her assurances that Lady Shipton had accepted Molly's story without question, promising to hand the letter to Eleanor when next she saw her, just as she had predicted, would assuage his doubts, Eliza was quite wrong; not even her guarantee that she would have his errant wife back in Cavendish Square this evening allaying his fears.

"But what if you don't?" he demanded, his blue eyes staring fixedly at her. "What if she has shown that letter to Beatrice Shipton or that brother of hers?"

It came as no surprise to Eliza to discover that during her absence this morning he had worked himself up into a state of considerable agitation, exacerbated by what she guessed as being the consumption of several glasses of brandy, but since letting one's imagination run riot or seeking comfort from the contents of the decanter would not serve the purpose, she told him firmly, "She won't, not if she wants to protect her father. She loves him too much to run the risk of him being disgraced."

Sir Braden rose a little unsteadily to his feet, the legs of the chair scraping on the polished floorboards, tossing off the remainder of the amber liquid in his glass before saying reprovingly, his voice just a little slurred, "This is *your* doing!" pointing a thick accusing finger. "You should have kept a closer eye on her!"

Eliza's eyes narrowed at this and, taking a step nearer to him, said severely, "It's no use laying this in my lap! You told me there was no need to stay with her! I was simply following your orders. Besides," she nodded, "how was I to know what was in her mind?"

"Damn it, Eliza!" he exclaimed, taking several unsteady steps away from his desk. "You're the one who has been looking after her!"

"Yes," she bit out, her eyes flashing, "and a pretty piece of work I've had of it! You should have had her put away where she could do no harm well before now, like I suggested; instead of which you decided to keep her here, and now see what's come of it!"

"So," he nodded, his colour rather high, "it's my fault, is it?"

"Yes," she shot at him. "By not approaching Sir Wilfred Moore about having her committed you've put all three of us at risk! Don't forget," she reminded him, "I have as much to lose as you; so does Peterson!"

"So, what are you saying," he said a little peevishly, hating the thought that he could ever be in the wrong, "that once I have her back here I go back on my promise?"

"There's nothing else you *can* do, Sir Braden," she said realistically, "she knows too much. If she escaped once she can do it again."

He thought a moment, his colour darkening. "And what of this Childon tyke?" he demanded.

"He need not concern us for the present," Eliza told him practically. "The first thing we have to do is to get Lady Collett back here; once we have her safe, then we can deal with her, after that," she shrugged, "if this Childon begins to make a nuisance of himself or starts asking questions, then we shall deal with him too!"

The idea was not without its merits, in fact it was the only sensible thing they could do to protect themselves because it was no use pretending that Childon would calmly sit back and do nothing especially having involved himself already by coming to Eleanor's assistance and offering her his protection. It was logical to assume that at some point his business affairs in America would see him return there, but as it was most unlikely that he would notify him of when he meant to depart these shores, Sir Braden could only hazard a guess as to how much longer he would be in England, but the longer he remained here the greater the risk of denunciation would become. It seemed to Sir Braden that this nightmare they had stepped into would never end, but as he looked at Eliza Boon's thin and determined face he knew no other course was open to them but the one she had intimated.

From the beginning, they had found themselves forced into covering up one crisis after another following the unfortunate death of Annie Myers, culminating in the deaths of three more people, one of whom was a prominent Member of Parliament and close friend of Lord Salisbury and now, if Eliza had her way, it would mean that a peer of the realm would be included in that number. Of course, Sir Braden knew very well that bemoaning the difficulties which beset them would not make them go away, but he could not help thinking that if only Dennis had not been so violent; if only he had not decided to report the accident to the police; if only Sir Philip had not called on him charging him as being responsible for his brother's death and warning him that he was going to raise questions in the House about the type of establishment he and his brother frequented and worse, if only Eleanor had not returned home earlier than expected, then none of this would be happening. Of course, it was much too late now for regrets, they were in too deep to call a halt and, as far as Sir Braden could see, all they could do was to see the matter through to the bitter end until all possible sources which could denounce them were finally dealt with. As Sir Philip had not told him from whom he had learned the truth about his brother's death being cold-blooded murder and not suicide, then, like Eliza, Sir Braden was of the belief that Dennis must have confided in him and, after mulling things over, Sir Philip had eventually drawn his own conclusions, and so all they need concern themselves with was Eleanor because even in Sir Braden's anxious state of mind it seemed unlikely that she had, within so short a time, said anything to Beatrice Shipton or her brother. He had no wish to climb the scaffold for his part in recent events any more than he had to see his name brought into disrepute and, from what he could see of it, only his wife could put his life and good name at risk, but once she was back in his safe custody with no possibility of her being in a position to relate what she knew, then both dangers would be permanently eliminated. As far as Childon was concerned, Sir Braden would be a fool to either dismiss him or believe he would leave well alone until he returned to America, but however much he may dislike another death on their hands the fact remained that he could neither minimise the risk Childon posed nor ignore it, but – well, that was for the future – for now, all that mattered was getting Eleanor safely back here. Had Sir Braden the least idea that one of Eliza's girls held such damaging information and was on the point of confiding it all to Childon, as well as the trap he was in the process of laying which would see them proving their own guilt in the deaths of four people, then Sir Braden would not have looked upon getting rid of him, even with Peterson's help, as being the relatively easy matter he envisaged but, more than this, what little fortitude he had would have completely deserted him.

He may have discarded the brandy decanter, but as the day wore on Sir Braden's nerve as well as his optimism fluctuated alarmingly, and Eliza, not at all certain whether to be glad or not he made no effort to venture out of the house, informed Peterson that if they were not careful he would bring all to ruin. Peterson, whose suspect career had been closely aligned to Eliza's for a long time, was prepared to take on all-comers in her cause and if this included Sir Braden, then so be it. He may not possess the sharpest intelligence but he knew danger when he smelled it and, like the woman to whom he was extremely partisan, he sensed that Sir Braden, should Lady Collett fail to respond to his letter and not show herself tonight, then his nerves could well collapse altogether, leading him into saying or doing something which could bring the law down on them. As for this lord or whoever he was who came knocking on the door enquiring after Lady Collett and who had apparently unsettled Sir Braden, he may look like a man who knew how to take care of himself but Peterson had no doubt that he would be able to deal with him adequately enough, in fact he was rather hoping he would show himself tonight. But whatever hopes or expectations the inhabitants of twenty-nine Cavendish Square had of Lady Collett doing what they wanted, it was not long before it became obvious that they were clearly doomed to disappointment.

Arthur, having handed his morning's vigil over to his brother, had gone home to catch up on his sleep before resuming his watch later that evening in company with his father and eldest brother Samuel, both of whom were already waiting for him when he arrived just after half past nine. Armed with freshly baked pasties, thoughtfully provided by Mrs. Kent, a kind-hearted woman who came in to cook and clean for them since Mrs. Taylor's death three years before, to sustain them through the nighttime hours and a small bottle of whisky, just to keep the cold out, they positioned themselves in the gardens of Cavendish Square to wait upon events. Jerry fully agreed with Tony that they would try something to get Lady Collett away from Mount Street, but considering the importance they obviously attached to getting her safely back to Cavendish Square Jerry had been rather surprised to hear that, apart from Eliza Boon's trip to Bloomsbury, no one else had left the house. He doubted very much that it was the weather which was keeping them indoors, but no sooner had Harry told him about that letter which had been delivered by a supposed maid in Sir Miles Tatton's household and the suspicions it had aroused, Jerry was left in no doubt that they were up to something and whatever it was that letter formed a major part of it.

After warning his sons to keep their eyes peeled, he set off to patrol the Square's garden and the immediate vicinity, returning an hour later to be told that Peterson had left the house to go to the stables round the corner that served the local residents, but was only gone for about twenty minutes. "They're up to somethin'," Jerry told his sons. "Mark my words, one or the other of 'em must be goin' somew'ere an' I'll lay my life it's Mount Street," he told them. "Somethin' to do with that letter 'Arry said 'ad been delivered." Since they were all agreed that the only reason Peterson could have had for visiting the stables was for the sole purpose of ordering Sir Braden's carriage, they waited expectantly for something to happen, but it was not until half an hour later that they finally saw Sir Braden's smart town carriage leave the stables to make its careful way towards number twenty-nine before slowly pulling up in front of the house. As the carriage blocked his view of the front door, Jerry crept cautiously towards the snow-covered bushes just across the path in time to see Peterson step out of the house and speak to the driver on the box who immediately jumped down and walked back to the stables. Within seconds Eliza Boon stepped out of the house and, following a nod of her head at Peterson, climbed up into the carriage before the equipage moved steadily over the frozen cobbles towards Oxford Street. Unless Jerry's instincts were grossly at fault, he intuitively knew they were making for Mount Street, and it was therefore without any loss of time that he and Samuel followed in the carriage's wake.

By half past eleven the streets were almost deserted, only the most hardened or foolhardy venturing out on such a raw cold night, the pavements as treacherous as the roads, but the man sitting huddled over the reins on the box and the solitary occupant of the carriage parked on the corner of Davies Street and Mount Street seemed impervious to the weather as they waited expectantly for Eleanor. As no vehicle could be seen either arriving or leaving this select thoroughfare, signifying that none of the inhabitants was leaving their homes to keep an engagement or receiving guests, the lights in the houses went off one by one, only the street lamps illuminating the stark white scene. The temperature, which had dropped steadily over the last few hours, rendered Eliza's wait inside the carriage rather cold and uncomfortable, but since she did not expect Eleanor to fail she was easily able to put her discomfort to one side. Every few minutes Eliza found it necessary to wipe the continual build-up of ice and condensation off the glass with her gloved hand to peer through the windows and when, for the third time of looking, she caught sight of a hurrying figure coming towards her she was just about to open the door when she realised that Eleanor's condition would automatically prevent her from hurrying, Eliza's lips pursing upon seeing the huddled form disappear down the basement steps of one of the houses; no doubt a maid who had been out to meet her young man. Slowly the minutes ticked by until a little over two hours had elapsed and, by quarter past one, with no sign of Eleanor, Eliza's mood of optimism began to turn into despair as she considered the consequences resulting from Eleanor's failure to show herself, but her temper, exacerbated by growing uneasiness, prevented her from abandoning the wait. Just as Beatrice had hoped Eliza grew steadily colder, but after two and a half long hours of waiting and hoping that Eleanor would, even now, come to them, she reluctantly accepted that she was not going to, and so it was in a voice she knew must be her own that she instructed Peterson to return to Cavendish Square, totally oblivious to the two pairs of watchful eyes from their vantage point down the basement steps of a neighbouring house.

Apart from a harrowing dream in which Eliza Boon and Peterson were attempting to break into the house and take her away, Eleanor's sleep was mostly undisturbed, but so real were the visions which danced in front of her eyes that her fretful cries soon brought Tony to her side. Sitting on the edge of the bed and taking her two small agitated hands in his warm ones, his deep voice breaking through the layers of her nightmare into her consciousness assuring her she was quite safe, had the immediate effect of making her sleepily open her partially functioning left eye to look up at him before drifting contentedly back into a dreamless sleep for what remained of the night.

Sarah, who, despite her misfortunes in love, was an incurable romantic at heart, and liked nothing better than to know a budding romance was blossoming just as it should, but if the star-crossed lovers needed a little push to bring this about, then she was only too happy to oblige. In her opinion, nothing could be better than His Lordship, a man it was impossible not to like, and his sister's young friend falling in love, and when, around five o'clock, she softly opened the door to Eleanor's room to assure herself she was in fact all right, being of the belief that she had spent the night alone, Sarah was not altogether surprised to see Tony, with his head resting against the back of the chair he had drawn up beside the bed and his long legs stretched out in front of him, holding Eleanor's right hand as it lay on top of the coverlet with his left one. To one of Sarah's romantic disposition they presented a moving picture, but deciding to leave them undisturbed she quietly left the room and went back to bed with a clear conscience, not only because she knew His Lordship was not one to overstep the line but also because if his presence meant that Eleanor slept in peace, a remedy Sarah firmly believed in, apart from which Eleanor badly needed it after the treatment she had received from that brute of a husband, then that was all that mattered. Had Sarah seen the smile which touched Tony's lips the minute she closed the door behind her, she would have felt fully justified in boxing his ears.

If Tony saw a gleam of indulgence in her eyes when he entered Eleanor's room several hours later, bathed, shaved and fully dressed following a substantial breakfast, he gave no sign of it, but Sarah, having known him for many years as well as treating him like a favourite nephew, was by no means fooled. As he held the door open for her to take away the remains of Eleanor's breakfast tray she could not resist casting a mischievous glance up at him, commenting favourably as she did so upon their patient being the better for a good night's sleep.

"Much better," Tony agreed, not quite able to suppress the twitch at the corner of his mouth, but when she followed this up with the solicitous enquiry as to whether he too had managed to get some sleep, he smiled disarmingly down at her, to which she was by no means impervious, saying, without the least sign of embarrassment, "You must know I did." She eyed him knowingly. "You were up and about remarkably early this morning, Sarah!" he told her conversationally.

"So," she nodded, the primness of her lips belied by the twinkle in her eyes, "you were *not* asleep."

Tony shook his head, his eyes alight with amusement. "'Fraid not."

"*Well!*" Sarah exclaimed, her cry of shock falling very short of the mark. "*Mr. Tony!*"

"Ah," he smiled, "we're back at 'Mr. Tony' are we? I wondered when you were going to stop calling me 'my lord'."

"*Mr. Ton... my lord!*" she hastily corrected herself. "Let me tell you that you are not too big nor too old for me to box your ears!"

Tony grinned. "I've heard you say that before."

"Well," she nodded, trying very hard not to laugh, "perhaps if you behaved yourself I wouldn't have to!"

"I might just do that, Sarah," he laughed, kissing her cheek before she left the room with an unconvincing sniff of disapproval.

Eleanor's dreams had certainly been harrowing, in fact so lifelike were they that for one awful moment she actually believed that Peterson and Eliza Boon were in her room, and when she felt a pair of hands take hold of her own for one horrifying moment she thought they were pulling her out of bed to take her back to Cavendish Square. Eleanor's frantic efforts to free her hands seemed as ineffectual as her desperate cries for help, but little by little the sound of a deep and familiar voice telling her she was quite safe penetrated the layers of sleep, and upon briefly opening her almost fully functioning left eye to find Tony sitting on the edge of the bed warmly clasping her agitated hands, she gradually grew more calm until falling back into a deep and dreamless sleep. When she drowsily opened her left eye again sometime later it was to find Tony stretched out in the chair beside the bed with her hand comfortingly held in his warm one as it rested on top of the coverlet, but far from being shocked she experienced such a feeling of wellbeing that she wanted it to go on forever, but even before she could take time to savour the most wonderful moment of her life she fell into a deep and happy sleep.

As Tony turned towards her after closing the door behind Sarah, the laughter in his eyes combined with a look Eleanor had no difficulty in defining, brought the colour flooding to her cheeks. She may not have set out to fall in love with Tony, but since she had done she did not regret it, and she was honest enough to admit that if the opportunity arose whereby she could stop loving him at a stroke she would not take it. She knew perfectly well that irrespective of her feelings for Braden and the fear he had instilled in her she *was* his wife and therefore neither free to love another man nor at liberty to express it, in fact it would be quite wrong of her to do so, but even though there might be some who would say he had done nothing to deserve her fidelity, she could not easily set aside her own standards of behaviour. Unfortunately, though, the promptings of her heart, which were not only in perfect tune with Tony's but apparently impervious to common sense, besides continually arguing against doing what she knew to be right, rendered this extremely difficult. Braden's demands, which were at no time welcome to her, could not be termed either gentle or considerate let alone loving, never encompassed tenderness or affection, on the contrary they were brutal and abhorrent, calculated only to please and gratify himself, so very different to the man who could, without any effort whatsoever, demolish her defences. Even before taking refuge in Mount Street, she had been conscious of Tony's consideration towards her and since two nights ago even more so, but whilst his nearness gave her the comfort and security she desperately needed, she was honest enough to admit that she loved him too much to derive no small amount of pleasure from feeling his arms around her. As Braden had never exercised either restraint or thoughtfulness in his dealings with her, such consideration as Tony exhibited was a totally new experience and, as for her feelings, although they may still make her catch her breath in surprise, never having believed herself capable of such intense emotion, she was not ashamed of them.

Before her marriage, apart from a fond embrace from her father and a fraternal, if somewhat casual, salute on her cheek from her brother, the young men to whom she had regularly been introduced had done nothing more daring than raise her hand to their lips. As for Braden, his brutal and vicious usage had, apart from inflicting acute pain, proved his contempt as well as his disregard for her, and therefore it was not until the advent of Tony in her life that she had been made to feel as though she was the most precious thing in the world. If nothing in her well-ordered life had prepared her for what she could expect with Braden, then neither had it prepared her for the way Tony would make her feel just by looking at her, and if he could make her heart pound in her breast and her senses reel just by holding her in his arms, she trembled to think what his kisses would evoke.

She would never be able to repay the kindness and unstinting care bestowed on her by Beatrice and Sarah even though she instinctively knew they neither wanted nor expected any reward, but the tender and demonstrative attention she had received from Tony during the short time she had been here was something she had never known before. Tony's presence went a long way to calming her nerves, particularly now when she needed it most, especially as she could not rid her mind of the fear that Eliza Boon or Peterson may attempt to remove her. Just knowing Tony was here, watching over her while she slept and keeping her safe, was very reassuring, but to awaken at some point to see him stretched out in the chair beside the bed comfortingly holding her hand, far from producing shock and dismay, it had been the most intimate and intensely stirring moment of her life.

"Sarah's right," Tony said softly, breaking into her thoughts as he sat gently down on the edge of the bed, correctly interpreting her awkwardness, "you *do* look better for a good night's sleep," taking hold of her hands in a firm warm clasp, "and Sarah," he smiled, "*always* knows best!"

"Yes," she managed huskily, "she… she does." Even though her feelings were still so very new to her it was not this that brought about her momentary loss of composure, but her acute awareness of just how susceptible she was to him. Then, swallowing uncomfortably, her fingers trembling nervously in his, said, "And she… she is *so* kind."

"Mm," Tony nodded his agreement, his eyes revealing all he felt as he looked down at her bent head, her attention fixed on the pin in his pale grey cravat, "she is, *very* kind."

"Yes," she said again. She paused a moment, then, raising her eyes to his, her colour still a little high, faltered unsteadily, "Y-you told S-Sarah you were n-not asleep. I'm s-sorry if you were uncomfortable?"

"No," Tony said tenderly, "I was not uncomfortable, far from it, in fact I got all the shuteye I needed." He may well have done, but being in such close proximity to her throughout the night had nevertheless tested his self-possession, even so he could no more leave her alone at night with her fears than he could stop loving her. But however insecure his defences he was far too attentive to her feelings as well as her agitation to do anything which could add to her obvious awkwardness on finding herself spending part of the night in such immediacy to him because although she was by no means unaffected by it he needed no telling that she was quite unused to sharing such an intimacy. Despite being married for just over twelve months he accurately deduced that Collett, who had proved how violent he was in his dealings with her, far from showing her consideration, much less love and affection, was not only ruthless in his personal attentions to her, but totally indifferent to her feelings.

Tony knew as well as Eleanor that under normal circumstances he would not have spent two whole nights in her bedroom and certainly not while she was lying in bed, but these were not normal circumstances. She had received a most vicious and brutal beating which would not only take time to get over but had rendered her extremely fearful, but as his presence not only had a calming effect on her but made her feel safe and secure, encouraging her to fall into untroubled sleep, then he for one was quite prepared to disregard convention in order to ensure it. Nevertheless, when he had told her last night that he was just an ordinary guy this was no less than the truth, but being an ordinary guy he needed no reason or excuse to show her how much he loved her and had refrained from kissing her simply because she was in no condition for him to do so. As for making love to her, it would be quite wrong of him, indeed it would be unforgivable, but this was not out of consideration for Collett, but simply because she was enjoying his sister's and Tom's protection and, also, when he did make love to her he wanted it to be under his own roof; when *his* ring was on her finger and not Collett's. Tony knew beyond doubt that Eleanor loved him and that in time her shyness over any intimacies between them would naturally leave her, but since he had no wish to intensify her discomfiture or make her feel ill at ease over something which was an intrinsic, and really quite irresistible, part of her nature, he merely squeezed her hand and commented favourably on the pale blue bed jacket she was wearing, to which she told him that Beatrice had kindly lent it to her until other arrangements could be made.

If Eleanor could have read Tony's thoughts she would have agreed that her memories of Braden as well as her experiences with him were painful and not pleasurable, a man whose natural tendency towards aggression only served to increase the fear she had always had of him, so very different to Tony's warm and tender demonstrations of love. She might be unused to having such consideration shown to her welfare as well as attentiveness to her feelings, but she had to admit that his affectionate expressions of love, which she knew did not even scrape the surface, were more than enough to weaken the defences she was trying to erect to withstand the promptings of her heart, an organ which seemed to have suddenly taken on a life and mind of its own. Had anyone ever asked Eleanor if she thought she was capable of feeling this way she would have replied with a categorical no, but since Tony had entered her life she had been forced to admit to herself that she was most certainly capable of it and, more than this, she longed for the day when her own needs and desires could be fulfilled with the same eagerness as the man who had brought the love she never thought she would have into her life.

By the time Tony had gently teased her about her borrowed wardrobe, sadly shook his head and sighed, "Poor Bea will have nothing left at this rate!" although Eleanor's colour was still a little high, she was far more calm and therefore able to respond to his solicitous enquiry as to whether she was feeling strong enough to tell him about last night and, after assuring him that she was, he smiled, then, kissing the hand he was still holding said softly, "Ellie, tell me, what hold does Collett have over your father?"

She lowered her eyes and bit down lightly on her bottom lip, the swelling having gone down during the night and the cut at the corner healing nicely, but it was not until Tony gave her hand a reassuring squeeze did she raise her eyes to his, faltering, "I… I take it Beatrice has told you about… my brother."

"Reginald?" He nodded. "Yes," he said gently, "she told me how your father settled his gambling debts before sending him to your uncle's in Ceylon."

She nodded, then, after lowering her eyes again to study the pattern on the quilt, as if by doing so it would help her find the right words, she slowly raised them to his, saying, not a little awkwardly, "Yes, but the thing is you see, they… they totalled far more than Reginald had led him to believe."

Tony was not at all surprised by this. It seemed that no hardened gamester had the least awareness as to how much money they put down or the number of *IOUs* they handed over, seemingly blind to everything except the run of the cards, and if Reginald Tatton formed one of this group, and from what Bea had told him he did, then he could well understand such a discrepancy. As it was obvious Eleanor was having difficulty in finding the right words to tell him something which she clearly found extremely painful, he gave her hand another encouraging squeeze, saying gently, "It's all right, Ellie; take your time." After several attempts to try to explain something which really was quite inexcusable, especially about her own father, Tony smiled, saying considerately, "Is it so bad that you cannot tell me?" She compressed her lips and nodded. "Is it something your brother did other than accumulate gambling debts?" Tony prompted gently.

"No," she managed at length, shaking her head, "n-not Reginald; my father."

"Your father?" he repeated, his eyes narrowing a little.

"Yes," she sniffed, turning her head away.

Aside from a palpable disregard for his daughter's happiness and wellbeing by sanctioning her marriage to a man he must have known she hated and feared, Tony knew nothing of Sir Miles Tatton other than what Tom and Bea had told him, but from the look on Eleanor's face whatever it was that Sir Miles Tatton had done that no one else other than Collett knew about it was clearly something which could do his reputation irreparable harm should it ever become known, were it otherwise Eleanor would never have attempted to return to Cavendish Square last night as Collett had coerced her into doing in his letter. "Ellie," Tony said quietly, gently turning her head round to face him, "if I am going to help your father, no matter what it is he has done, you *must* tell me." He felt her fingers tremble in his. "Is it because you think when I know the truth it will alter my feelings for you?" he smiled. She nodded. "It won't," he assured her in a deep voice, "nothing could."

"Y-you mean that?" she sniffed.

"Cross my heart," he smiled, suiting the action to the words.

She threw him a watery little smile before crying, "Oh, Tony, it has all been so horrible! My father would n-never have done such a d-dreadful thing had he n-not have been so distraught over my b-brother's debts!"

"And what was this dreadful thing?" he asked gently.

She took a moment to answer, taking comfort from the warm strength of his fingers firmly clasping her own, then, taking a deep breath, said unhappily, "B-Braden caught m-my father ch-cheating at cards." If Tony was a little taken aback at this he did not show it, but whatever he had expected Eleanor to confide it was certainly not this. "I know w-what you must be th-thinking," she cried, distressed, breaking into his thoughts. "It was very w-wrong of him; but my father is not a card cheat, truly he is not!" she shook her head. "He w-would never have d-done such a dreadful thing were it not for the shock of d-discovering the exact amount of Reginald's debts."

Tony found his anger equally divided between her husband and his cohorts and Sir Miles Tatton, all of whom it seemed had used Eleanor to suit their own ends. It came as no surprise to Tony that she was beside herself with fear and anxiety; not only because she had to make such a damaging confession about her own father, but also because of all the emotional and physical traumas she had experienced over the last twelve months or more, but upon seeing her turn her head away from him as though she was too ashamed to face him and feeling her fingers convulse in his was more than he could bear, and instantly gathered the distraught and trembling bundle of the woman he loved in his arms.

From the disjointed and muffled account poured tearfully into his shoulder, Tony gleaned that her father, upon discovering the exact sum owed by his son to those members of his clubs to whom he had carelessly handed over numerous *IOUs*, had reeled in shock at the staggering total. Unlike Sir Braden Collett, Sir Miles Tatton, thanks to wise investments and being a man with no extravagant pastimes to indulge, was financially secure rather than wealthy, imposing no hardships on his family or domestic staff, enabling him to maintain a comfortable household without the need for exercising caution in expenditure, but the heavy burden of his son's gambling debts had seriously put this at risk. It seemed that Sir Miles Tatton, having had to assemble the financial wreckage brought about by his own father's addiction to gambling, when faced with the startling reality that his son's predilection for the cards was equally ruinous as his grandfather's, together with the horrendous prospect of finding himself yet again facing grave financial difficulties, had suffered a brief emotional collapse. Sir Miles may have inherited a natural aptitude for cards, but he lacked that burning passion for them which saw men like his father and son regularly taking their places at the gaming tables, and since he did not have that obsessive need to repeatedly pit his skill he was an infrequent player and seldom to be seen in the card room at his club.

From Eleanor's halting account of that fatal night, Tony understood that Sir Miles, having laboured under severe shock for some weeks as well as being in the throes of temporary depression and despair had decided, after some deliberation, to accept an old friend's invitation to join him for dinner at his club in the hope that it would help divert his mind, temporarily at least, from the misfortune which had befallen him. Norton Gwyn, unaware of his friend's inner turmoil, whose own love of the cards was as well-known as Sir Miles Tatton's infrequent participation, despite his skill, somehow managed to persuade him to join him in the card room at the poker table, if not to play then merely to keep him company. Sir Miles, regardless of the fact that his son's staggering gambling debts were constantly at the forefront of his mind, allowed himself to be persuaded, surprised to find that while his attention had momentarily been taken up with something Norton had said to him and not on the dealer, he had automatically been dealt a hand.

Eleanor, burying her face into Tony's shoulder at the painful recollection of her father's transgression, falteringly explained that due to a club steward entering the card room and whispering something into Norton Gwyn's ear, resulting in him excusing himself for a few moments without even looking at his hand, the players, apart from turning over their cards to look at the hand dealt them, deferred starting the game until his return. Her father, having taken a cursory look at his cards to find it was not the best hand he had ever been dealt, in fact it was not even good enough to enable him to gain the lowest hand of a high card let alone a one or two pair hand, laid them back face down onto the table, conscious of thinking that Reginald's bad luck had attached itself to him. As not even Sir Miles could explain what happened next much less the sudden and unaccountable urge which came over him, it seemed that due to a momentary diversion at the other end of the card room which saw his fellow players turn their heads to see what the commotion was about, he surreptitiously slid his hand to where Norton Gwyn's cards lay face down in readiness at his place on the table, his deft fingers lifting the corners of his friend's cards to enable him to see that the hand held no less than three aces and a king.

At this Tony let out a long low whistle. "One ace short of four of a kind! The third highest hand a man could have!"

"Is… is that good?" Eleanor managed on a hiccup.

"Good!" Tony shook his head. "My darling, the odds of a man winning with a third highest hand is several thousand to one, but to be dealt those cards straight from a shuffled deck is quite incredible! He sure was a lucky guy!" Then, feeling her body convulse in his arms and hearing the choked sob which ripped from her throat, he looked down into her flushed and tearstained face, asking gently, "Ellie, are you saying that your father switched cards?"

She nodded, confirming, hardly above a whisper, "Yes."

Sir Miles, who knew as well as any man that being dealt such a fortunate hand was somewhat remote to say the least, had, in an unguarded moment of acute vulnerability and at his most weakest, taken advantage of the disorder at the far end of the room and the brief absence of his friend to exchange three of his low numbered cards for Norton's three aces. Momentarily losing sight of the gross betrayal of trust between friends and the codes governing gentlemanly behaviour, especially in all matters of play, by which Sir Miles had always lived, no one sitting at the table in the card room of *'The Stephenson Club'*, least of all his old friend Norton Gwyn, had the least idea that he had acquired an unjustifiable advantage as he played his way to a four card hand win, rising from the table several thousand guineas to the good.

He may seldom display his skill at cards but everyone knew of it, even those members of *'The Stephenson Club'* of which Sir Miles was not a member but an honoured guest of one and, when he left the card room sometime later, it therefore entered no one's mind to question the legitimacy of his win; all but one man it seemed had seen that fleeting exchange of cards. But for a man like Sir Miles, whose very life was firmly grounded in honour and integrity, he could no more explain such an uncharacteristic and ungentlemanly act to himself any more than he could to Sir Braden Collett when he called upon him in Bruton Street the following morning to once more request his permission to marry his daughter; a request he knew would not be denied again.

"So," Tony mused, when Eleanor had come to the end of her heartrending confession, "that is how Collett coerced your father into agreeing to the marriage."

"Oh, Tony!" she cried, lifting her head from his shoulder. "I… I know it was very wrong of my father, but I love him; that is why I married Braden. I could not see his name tarnished. I can't condone what my father did," she sniffed, "but neither can I bear to think that you hate him for it!"

Tony had no doubt that under normal circumstances Sir Miles Tatton would not have resorted to such a deception and that only his disturbed state of mind could explain it, but Tony could not see his fellow players viewing his sleight of hand in quite the same light should they ever discover it. For himself, it was a despicable act of deceit which was really quite unforgivable, but as Tony felt reasonably sure that Sir Miles knew this as well as anyone he could not find it in him to hate him. Nevertheless, it could not be argued that Eleanor had paid an extremely high price for his momentary lapse to make sure his reputation remained unsullied and, for this reason alone, Tony could neither condone nor defend it. "Ellie," he sighed, laying the palm of his hand against her cheek, "even though I believe your father acted out of character due to the immense strain he was under and not from a deliberate intention to deceive, I can't condone it any more than you can," he said calmly, "but no," he shook his head, "I don't hate him, all the same," he told her truthfully, "the fact remains that his actions not only forced you into a most intolerable marriage, but was also the reason Collett used to try to coerce you into going back to him last night."

"Yes, I know," she nodded, "but I can't let Braden hurt my father. Y-you do understand that, don't you?" she pleaded, gripping his hand.

"Of course I do," he soothed, kissing her forehead, "but he won't; I promise."

"But Tony," she urged, "I know Braden and what he is capable of."

"I thought you trusted me," Tony said softly.

"You know I do," Eleanor said fervently, easing herself out of his arms in order for her to sit up facing him, resting the palms of her hands against his chest, "but Braden is…"

"Braden," Tony interrupted firmly, "is going to have far more important things on his mind to worry about than your father, and sooner than he thinks," he assured her.

"You… you mean Sir Philip's death?" she said hesitantly.

"Yes," he nodded, "I mean Sir Philip's death."

Eleanor bit lightly down on her bottom lip, asking at length, "Tony, do… do you know why Braden killed him?"

"Yes," he confirmed quietly, "I know. I know too how you returned home earlier than expected and either walked in on it or stumbled upon something to alert you to the truth," he said gently, "and although I do need you tell me about what actually happened that evening, it will keep for now. *Now,"* he smiled, easing her back against the pillows, "I want you to rest, *or*," he shuddered, "I shall have Sarah on my tail!"

The memory of that night was all too vivid in Eleanor's mind, so much so that she knew she would never forget it, but upon seeing the look of mock horror on Tony's face and the exaggerated shuddering of his shoulders at the thought of Sarah taking him to task had the effect of momentarily driving all thoughts of Braden from her mind and prompting a barely stifled choke of laughter out of her, which is what he had intended; having a pretty shrewd idea of the images which had crept into her mind about the events of that night.

"You're not afraid of her, are you!" she managed a little unsteadily, responding easily if a little shyly, to his drollery.

"Oh, terrified!" he shuddered again, his eyes laughing down into hers.

"But what has poor Sarah ever done to make you so afraid of her?" She shook her head, a little bewildered.

"What *hasn't* she done you mean!" He pulled a face. Upon hearing another barely stifled choke of laughter he looked down at her saying, with all the air of one who could tell many a tale, "It's all very well for you to laugh," he nodded, "but you would be surprised at the number of scolds she's given me!"

"Yes, I would," she managed, biting down on her bottom lip.

"You don't believe me?" He raised a questioning eyebrow, to which she shook her head. "Well," he shrugged helplessly, as though he could not believe his ears, "and here I was thinking you would!"

"Oh Tony," she laughed, no longer able to resist the bubble of laughter inside her, "you *are* funny!"

"No, am I?" He raised an eyebrow, his voice deepening.

"Yes," she nodded, "you know you are."

"And *you*, my darling," he told her, his voice a caress, "are utterly adorable! So adorable in fact, that I could very easily forget everything and kiss you," then, tracing her lips with a gentle thumb, confirmed softly, "so *very* easily."

If she was honest she wanted him to forget everything and kiss her, but although her colour deepened she did not avert her eyes from his, but when she felt his thumb brush gently over her lips it was almost as though he had kissed her, her heart suddenly taking flight and her breath stilling in her lungs, in fact when he left her moments later she felt quite bereft. Even if Braden did manage to steal her away from Mount Street as well as ensuring she never laid eyes on Tony again, nothing could take away the joy and pleasure she felt at being with him, and certainly not his parting words.

Sarah, entering the room only minutes after Tony had left, could not fail to notice the glow on Eleanor's face as she rested contentedly back against the pillows, and as Sarah glanced sideways at her she had no difficulty in understanding why Mr. Tony had fallen in love with her. Eleanor had taken quite a beating from her husband, but the fact remained she was an extremely beautiful and desirable invalid and one, moreover, who clearly returned the feelings of the man who unquestionably adored her.

Chapter Twenty-One

Sir Braden Collett, walking into the hall as soon as he heard Eliza enter the house following her long and fruitless wait for Eleanor, did not need her to tell him that his wife had failed to show herself, just one look at Eliza's face and the very fact that she was alone were more than enough. Her plan to bring Eleanor home had clearly miscarried just as he knew it would, but finding himself proved right in no way eased his temper or allayed the fear escalating inside him, on the contrary the horrendous prospect of denunciation and a walk to the gallows, which had assailed him ever since she escaped, suddenly took a giant leap closer.

He did not have far to look for the reason to account for his wife's failure to comply with his bidding; this brother of Beatrice Shipton's was proving rather a nuisance, and unless his persistent interference in his affairs was speedily brought to an end, then he could look forward to a most unpromising future. Of course, he had not one shred of evidence to prove Childon's involvement in Eleanor's escape or in preventing her from leaving Mount Street, but no matter how he tried he could not acquit him of having no hand in either; Childon had been quite cunning there! As things stood at the moment, Collett had no idea just how much Beatrice Shipton's brother knew about recent events and his involvement in four deaths and until he did he dare not approach him, but of one thing he was absolutely certain and that was until this meddlesome Colonial was either safely back in America where he could do no harm or permanently dealt with, then he could neither ignore the danger Childon posed nor dismiss his participation as merely the actions of a man coming to the aid of a woman for whom he had taken quite a liking.

Sir Braden could not fool himself into believing that Childon was in any way ignorant of Sir Philip Dunscumbe's death any more than he was to that of his brother, after all his newspapers had covered both stories the same as every other, even so he failed to see how Childon could possibly know the reason for either much less question Dennis Dunscumbe's suicide, any more than he could know of Annie Myers and the terrible tragedy which had occurred, setting in motion a string of events which seemed to be fast catching up with him. Until his wife had effected such a dramatic escape he had been reasonably safe; with Eliza and Peterson to constantly keep watch over her there had been no real cause for alarm, but now, with her safely housed in Mount Street and Childon just waiting for her to recover from her injuries, it was only a matter of time before this prying American arrived at the truth.

Sir Braden had gone along with Eliza's plan simply because no other viable alternative presented itself, but now this had failed other strategies would have to be thought of. Since gaining admittance to Mount Street either openly or surreptitiously was out of the question for very practical reasons and coercing Eleanor back to Cavendish Square of her own volition had failed, then other lines of attack would have to be considered. So far, both he and Eliza had concentrated solely on his wife and the danger she posed once she recovered sufficiently from her injuries to impart what she knew to Beatrice Shipton or, which was more than likely, to her brother, but what if, instead of stemming such damning information at source, they silenced the man who would use it against them?

Eliza Boon may have no qualms about doing whatever she considered necessary to protect her own interests, but upon learning what Sir Braden had in mind she vigorously argued against it on several grounds, earnestly suggesting they try one more time to manipulate Lady Collett into returning home of her own accord. Sir Braden, shaking his head, vehemently pointed out that if the thought of her father's public demise had not moved her into leaving Mount Street, then he failed to see what other inducement could be offered her to make her change her mind besides which, for all he knew she could already have told Childon everything. Eliza, her face screwed up in thought, vetoed this idea on the grounds that unless Eleanor had made a miraculous recovery over the last thirty-six hours it was most unlikely that she had said anything to either Lady Shipton or her brother, an observation which Sir Braden was soon brought to see was most probably right; neither of them giving a moment's thought to the healing effects Tony's love would have on Eleanor. Eliza, still pondering Sir Braden's suggestion that it was perhaps better to deal with Childon rather than concentrate on Eleanor, was still far from convinced that this was the answer and felt it behoved her to draw his attention to the fact that Childon's sister and her husband would not be fooled into thinking that his death was anything other than deliberately contrived and would know immediately at whose door to lay the blame. Collett may have no liking for another death on their hands, in fact all Eliza said was true, but the fact remained that whether they liked it or not Childon would have to be got rid of, and even supposing Sir Thomas and Lady Shipton did suspect them they would not be able to prove it especially once the police had ascertained that the cause of Childon's death had been the result of a brutal assault committed by person or persons unknown. As for Eleanor, she may know precisely where to look for the culprits, but knowing the awful truth would frighten her more than any threats made against her father, apart from which, Collett could not see the Shiptons sanctioning her continued stay with them once Childon was out of the way. His sudden and tragic end therefore, would not only effectively deal with his meddlesome interference and the damage he could do to them, but would also see Eleanor returned to Cavendish Square with the prospect of being locked away unless she kept the secret of that night firmly to herself. Sir Braden had no doubts whatsoever that Childon could more than adequately take care of himself in a fair fight, but if that fight was cunningly contrived at some out-of-the-way venue involving more than one assailant, confident that Peterson knew any number of suspect individuals who would be willing to undertake such a job for monetary reward, then Childon would stand no more chance of defending himself than a babe unborn.

Considering Sir Braden did not perform well under duress or anxiety, Eliza Boon was somewhat surprised to discover that, despite its flaws, he had nevertheless come up with the only practical solution to their difficulties, but not quite in the way he had it worked out. As far as she could see Sir Braden's idea of luring Childon to some secluded destination was doomed to failure at the outset because even though she had never laid eyes on him, she doubted very much whether he would be fool enough to fall for something which he would know instantly was a blatant trap. As far as she could see taking him completely unawares was going to be the only way which would guarantee success which necessarily meant waylaying him, a circumstance which made Collett purse his lips and shake his head. Upon pointing out to him that should it turn out that Lady Collett had already told Childon the truth after all, then she could not see him hanging back with such damaging evidence and so it was logical to assume he would report it to Bow Street or

Scotland Yard at the earliest opportunity, which left them with very little time, a few more hours, if that. From the look on Collett's face Eliza could see he was coming round to her way of thinking, and as she knew he had no wish to go to the gallows any more than she wished to spend several years in prison for conspiring to commit murder and goodness only knew what else besides, she persuasively enlarged on her theme by mellifluously outlining the best way of tackling this man without any fingers being pointed in their direction, ending by saying that Peterson, a man in whom she had always had great faith, would make sure Childon told no one anything!

Sir Braden, having consumed almost half a decanter of brandy during the last two or three hours while he had anxiously awaited the return to Cavendish Square of his errant wife in Eliza's safe custody, listened to her revised version of how Childon's demise would actually be brought about in a most receptive frame of mind and, having given it as much thought as he could in his somewhat inebriated condition, finally gave it his full approval. Eliza, immediately going in search of Peterson and finding him stretched out on top of the bed in the small attic room with a couple of empty bottles of brown ale on the table beside him, impatiently shook him awake. Not unexpectedly it was several minutes before he eventually opened his bleary eyes in response to her urgent tugging to see her sharp features looking down at him, but after heaving himself up into a sitting position and knuckling his eyes, he listened to her brisk but detailed instructions about dealing with one more obstacle without a blink or qualm of conscience. Satisfied that he had taken in all she had told him, Eliza made her way to her own room just as the clock in the hall struck half past four, sliding into bed with the same unconcern as the man who slavishly followed her every order.

After leaving Eleanor, Tony leisurely made his way downstairs reaching the hall just as Harry arrived and, following a brief discussion with him, read the note he handed to him before going in search of Beatrice, tracking her down in the small sitting room sorting through a basket of silks. "You will be pleased to hear, Bea," Tony smiled, waving the note in the air, "that according to Jerry our friends waited until half past two this morning before deciding that Eleanor was not going to show herself."

"Good!" Beatrice declared roundly. "And were it not for the poor horses being out in such dreadful weather, I hope they were frozen to death!"

"I'd say it stands a pretty good chance," he smiled.

"Well," she nodded, a martial light in her eye, "it serves them right for treating Eleanor so despicably!"

"That's for sure!" Tony agreed, pocketing the note.

"I just hope this does not mean they will attempt something else," she said thoughtfully, casting the basket aside and rising to her feet. "Do you think they will?" she asked, walking towards him.

Taking hold of her hands he smiled reassuringly down at her, "I don't think you need worry over that." She looked an enquiry. "You see, Bea," he told her, refraining from telling her of Sir Miles Tatton's faux pas, "very soon now, our friend Collett and his cohorts are going to have something other than Eleanor to think about."

Beatrice looked closely up at him, her pretty lips compressing, asking a little cautiously, "Are you planning something, Tony?"

"Too right I am!" he said firmly. "And by the time I have finished with them whatever Eleanor may or may not have said to me will be totally irrelevant." Upon seeing her raised eyebrow he smiled, "I can't tell you too much at the moment Bea except that since we can't prove their guilt, then we are just going to have to let them prove it for us."

She considered a moment, saying at length, "Well, I shan't tease you to tell me what it is you are planning, but you will be careful won't you, Tony?"

"Sure I will," he promised, kissing her forehead.

"And you will tell me all about it," she said hopefully, "when it is all over?"

"I'll give you a blow-by-blow account," Tony smiled. "By the way," he raised an eyebrow, "I take it Tom has left?"

"Yes," she told him, "while you were upstairs with Eleanor." He nodded. "Speaking of Eleanor," she enquired, "I know you told me over breakfast that apart from a nightmare she spent a reasonably comfortable night, but tell me, how did you leave her a moment ago?"

"*Very* reluctantly," he inclined his head.

"Yes, of course," she nodded, "the poor child must still be dreadfully upset over… oh!" She nodded, catching the laughter in his eyes. "That's not what…"

"No, Bea," Tony smiled ruefully, giving her hand a playful little shake, "that's *not* what I meant."

"No, of course not," she smiled. "How stupid of me!"

"Are you thinking that…?"

"No, I'm not," Beatrice broke in firmly, "I know you too well for that, but Tony," she shook her head, a little perplexed, "if you are hoping to marry Eleanor…"

"Not hoping, Bea," he told her purposefully, "determined."

She knew from experience that it was useless trying to change her brother's mind once it was firmly made up to something, and although she could think of no two people better suited for one another, she felt it incumbent upon her to remind him of something which he had appeared to have lost sight of. "Tony, you don't need me to tell you what I think of Eleanor, or of you," she smiled, squeezing his hand, "but aren't you overlooking Collett? What I mean is," she faltered, "once his dealings are eventually made known it is bound to come out that you and your newspapers had a hand in bringing him to justice and… well," she said hesitantly, "it could be that some people, when they know you have married his widow, which she will be," she nodded, "because it is useless to suppose he will not hang for his crimes, not that he does not deserve it or those other two either, well…" she faltered again, "it could be that they may think you deliberately engineered his downfall just so you could marry her."

"I'm a newspaperman, Bea," Tony reminded her, "and even if I weren't, I couldn't turn a blind eye knowing that someone had committed cold-blooded murder."

"Yes, I know," she agreed, "but you know how people talk."

"Worried about my reputation, Bea?" he smiled. "Because if you are, there's no need; I can stand a lick or two and, as for Eleanor, she's done nothing she has to either apologise or answer for."

"I know," Beatrice agreed, "neither of you have, but Tony," she shook her head, "you know as well as I do how spiteful some people are."

Tony nodded. "Yes, I know, but I have no intention of allowing them to weigh with me either now or in the future." He saw she was going to say something, but forestalled her, "Listen Bea," he soothed, warmly clasping her hands, "up until a few short days ago I never knew Eleanor existed, but now that I do," he told her, "*I* couldn't exist without *her*. If it is my position as Viscount Childon you are thinking of," he smiled, "then I wish you wouldn't. I may not have come into my grandfather's title for much over a few months, but I take the responsibilities which come with it very seriously, but without Eleanor everything I have means nothing at all; including my title."

"Yes," she nodded, "I know, but…"

"Look Bea," he said earnestly, "people can speculate and gossip all they like, but regardless of my feelings for Eleanor we must not forget what Collett and his clique have done to her or that they are responsible for no less than three deaths, four if you take what happened to Annie Myers into account, and," he nodded meaningfully, "if my participation can help in bringing them to account for such vicious crimes as well as releasing Eleanor from a most brutal marriage, then I shall not sleep any the less soundly for that!"

"Oh, Tony," she cried, "you are absolutely right!" Then, standing on tiptoe to kiss his cheek, smiled, "As well as being really quite wonderful!"

"Yeah, sure I am!" he grinned, giving her a hug. "Just make sure you tell Bill that next time you see him!"

She laughed, but when, five minutes later, he left the house and she made her way upstairs to see Eleanor, it was more than obvious that she thought Tony was quite wonderful too. Like Sarah, just one look at Eleanor's face was more than enough to tell Beatrice just how she and Tony had parted earlier because despite her injuries nothing could hide the glow on her face or the sparkle which was clearly visible in her partially opened left eye, and had she been asked if she had ever seen Eleanor look more beautiful, irrespective of the bruises, than she did at this moment, she would have to say most definitely not. Beatrice did not need it spelling out that her friend was as much in love with Tony as he was with her and his confession that he could not exist without Eleanor was, without any doubt, entirely reciprocated.

If it had been at all possible for Eleanor to read Beatrice's mind, she would have totally agreed with her, even though she could not explain any of it. For some inexplicable reason Eleanor felt she had known Tony all her life instead of just a few short days but, more importantly, how empty her life would be without him. Even now she could still feel the touch of his thumb on her lips, soft and warm and gently coaxing, evoking sensations which she never knew existed, but although Tony had by no means given rein to his feelings, the woman inside her instinctively knew he was a very passionate man. All the same, his somewhat restrained and extremely tender caress against her lips had nevertheless given her an exciting, if all too brief a glimpse, of not only what she could expect to feel when he did kiss her but how much he loved her.

Apart from happily informing Eleanor how pleased she was to learn from Tony that she had spent a fairly restful night and how extremely relieved she was to see her looking so much better, Beatrice tactfully refrained from mentioning that she knew precisely where to look to account for her surprisingly swift recovery. Eleanor, upon having her confession and sincerely voiced contrition about last night gently waved aside by Beatrice as being perfectly understandable given the circumstances and she was not to give it a moment's thought, Eleanor shook her head, saying, rather ashamed, "It was a dreadful thing to do, especially after all the kindness you and Tom have shown me."

"Now, that's enough of *that*!" Beatrice smiled, taking hold of Eleanor's hand as it rested on top of the coverlet. "You were sadly placed in a most awkward position, my dear."

"Yes, but…" Eleanor sniffed.

"No 'buts'," Beatrice shook her head, "and no more talk of our kindness, in fact," she smiled, "except to say that I am very glad Tony was around to prevent you from leaving here, which," she nodded, "I am extremely relieved he was because I don't want you to return to Collett or Cavendish Square any more than he does, or Tom either, I want to hear no more about it," she smiled.

"But it was such a gross act of betrayal and…!" Eleanor exclaimed.

"My dear," Beatrice soothingly cut in, laying the palm of her hand against Eleanor's flushed cheek, "this is merely irritation of the nerves, and no wonder after all you have undergone! You have betrayed no one, my dear," she assured her, taking hold of her agitated hand, "and if Tom were here now he would tell you the same and, as for Tony," she smiled, "well…" she nodded meaningfully, "you don't need me to tell you that he would move heaven and earth to protect you."

No, she did not, and the thought made Eleanor tremble, and Beatrice, reading the quivering movement of her fingers in her own with unerring accuracy, only wished that she could answer her enquiry about what Tony had planned for today, but when she finally left her to rest, her mind, like Eleanor's, was almost wholly taken up in what he was going to do. Beatrice may have told him that she would not tease him about his plans, but even so she could not help worrying over him, especially when she considered the type of people they were dealing with. If Sir Braden Collett could cold-bloodedly bludgeon a man to death as well as treating his wife in a manner which could only be described as iniquitous, then he would not think twice about doing harm to a man who stood on the brink of calling him to account for his actions.

Lingering only long enough to have a brief word with Harry, whose cushy duties had been the subject of some lively sibling leg pulling, Tony left the house. Having descended the steps, he made his way along Mount Street towards Davies Street, but even before he came within a few yards of the junction he spotted Arthur slouching towards him with his hands dug deep into his pockets and his head bent down, but just as they came up with one another Arthur deliberately bumped into him and, with a dexterous movement of his head, let his cap fall onto the wet pavement, to which he said belligerently, "'Ere! Watch where you're goin', Guv!"

"I beg your pardon," Tony apologised, making a show of bending down.

"Well, watch it next time," Arthur warned, also bending down to pick up his cap, saying in a lowered voice as they stood up, "Davies Street, alleyway, first on the right – Peterson."

Tony nodded, whispering, "Thanks, I owe you one." Then, in his usual voice, said, "I am so sorry."

"That's all very well," Arthur called after him as Tony began to walk away, "but you don't own the street y'know!"

Even before Arthur had deliberately bumped into him Tony knew that his being here could only mean that he had found himself obliged to follow one of their suspects, most probably Peterson, whose intention was either to keep an eye on himself or the comings and goings of the inhabitants of Mount Street with a probable view to spotting his chance of removing Eleanor, but now there could only be one reason for Peterson concealing himself in the alleyway. Tony knew that Collett and the others would stop at nothing to keep their dirty secrets, but this latest tactic of attempting to waylay him in broad daylight when, despite the dreadful weather conditions, any number of people could so easily be abroad, was more than enough to tell him just how desperate they considered their situation. Collett, who knew perfectly well that his wife was safely in Mount Street and would, once having recovered sufficiently from her injuries most probably divulge all she knew, was in the unfortunate position of having no precise idea of the full extent of his own involvement or just how much he knew, but clearly Collett regarded him as a threat and, once again, had called upon

Peterson to deal with it, a man who had already proved not only what he was capable of but also that he was not prone to attacks of conscience in doing whatever might be asked of him. Tony may not immediately see the reasoning behind this new strategy to try to get rid of him as it made no sense, unless, of course, it was merely a warning for him to lay off!

No one who happened to pass Tony as he continued on his way along Mount Street would have had the least guess from his totally unconcerned demeanour that he was mentally preparing himself for the forthcoming encounter with Peterson and, as he turned left into Davies Street where, just a short distance down on the right-hand side was the narrow thoroughfare which led on to New Bond Street, his every instinct was on the alert. By now it was almost fifteen minutes past ten o'clock, but although any number of hardy wayfarers and a few hackney carriages were abroad in Mount Street and Davies Street, due to the treacherous weather conditions this narrow cobbled roadway was quite deserted, and no sign of life could be evinced in any one of the buildings on either side. Due to a severe frost overnight the sound of Tony's well shod feet on the roads and pavements seemed to crunch abnormally loud in the stillness, and the leaden sky, which not only promised more snow before the day was out, cast a dull grey light over the scene all around him. Tightening his hold on the walking cane in his right hand he strolled into this side street with a leisureliness which totally belied his alertness, and whilst he still believed that to ambush someone in broad daylight was taking a huge risk, the fact remained that this was not a bad spot for someone to lie in wait for their hapless victim, but as he was far from being a hapless victim he continued to walk calmly on waiting for his assailant to come upon him.

Tony did not have to wait too long. Almost before he had walked past the first two houses on the right-hand side, he heard the sound of crunching footsteps on the icy cobbles coming up behind him, slowly and somewhat cautiously at first then at a rushing speed, but even before his attacker had time to reach out and grab hold of him, Tony dropped his cane and swung round and landed him a flush hit to the face with his right fist which had the effect of sending Peterson sprawling to the ground. It was not only adequate testimony to his resilience due to his long experience in the ring but also evidence of a life steeped in considerable violence that Tony saw him get to his feet almost straight away to come rushing towards him, but although the swinging right Peterson threw at him went glaringly abroad he quickly followed this up with a straight left to the head which Tony skilfully ducked before landing Peterson a punishing right to the stomach. Momentarily winded, Peterson shook his head before coming on once more, but Tony, more than ready for him, gave him another flush hit to the jaw which saw him reeling backwards against the wall, but hardened and resilient, Peterson immediately dug a hand into his coat pocket to pull out a cudgel about seven inches long to finish off the job, an ugly look descending onto his battered face. Holding out his right arm with the cudgel firmly clasped in his hand he moved away from the wall, holding out his left one as he did so and beckoning Tony to come on as he took several steps towards him, but with a swiftness which took Peterson completely by surprise Tony reached out and gripped his right wrist, hitting it several times against his raised left knee until the cudgel finally fell from Peterson's fingers. A string of expletives left his fast swelling lips at this, but Tony, giving him no time to finish his verbal assault, grabbed hold of his left shoulder and gave him a powerful right to his already painful jaw, instantly sinking him to his knees.

Having waited until he saw Tony disappear into Davies Street Arthur quickly followed him, entering the narrow side street leading off it in time to see Tony more than adequately defend himself. Running up to him he stood looking up in admiration at his father's client before staring down at Peterson temporarily winded on his knees in front of him, saying, somewhat disappointed, "I see you've not croaked 'im!"

"Not quite," Tony grinned, then, after taking a moment to recover his breath, he bent down and pulled Peterson up to his feet by the lapels of his jacket before pushing him up against the wall. "Go back to Cavendish Square," he told him ominously, "and tell Collett I'm coming after him; not only for the brutish treatment of his wife, but for the four violent deaths he has on his hands. Tell him too," he said grimly, "that he will have to do better than this if he wants to rid himself of me!" whereupon he unceremoniously released Peterson, watching unmoved as he slumped half dazed to the ground, believing it to be no more than he deserved for treating Eleanor so appallingly as well as his utter lack of conscience and remorse over his dispassionate conduct towards those whose lives he had helped bring to an end and disposed of so callously. Removing his gloves in order to rub his knuckles, Tony smiled down at Arthur, confessing, "I enjoyed that," to which Arthur grinned. "Now," Tony nodded, pulling on his gloves, "I want you to go to Mount Street and tell your brother what has happened, *but*," he stressed, gripping his shoulder, "neither of you are to let Lady Shipton or Lady Collett know anything about this." Arthur nodded. "Just tell Harry to be extra vigilant, not that I expect them to try anything else today," Tony inclined his head. "I would like you then to return to Cavendish Square."

"Righto, Guv," Arthur nodded. "You're not goin' back there yourself?" he asked, indicating Mount Street with a nod of his head.

"No," Tony shook his head, "I must see Bill, and there are things I have to do. I doubt very much whether I shall be back before this evening."

Arthur nodded, but found himself unable to refrain from commenting favourably upon Tony's pugilistic skills.

Tony laughed. "It's been quite a while since I needed them," picking up his hat and cane from the pavement, "but I had an extremely good teacher in my father." Peterson, having by now opened his eyes to stare dazedly all around him, caused Arthur to ask Tony what they were going to do with him because left to himself he would rather hand him over to a constable. Tony, who fully agreed with this, said reluctantly, "He certainly deserves it, but he's no good to us either dead or being held in a police cell following his arrest for brawling in the street. I think we can let him make his own way back to Cavendish Square. By the way," Tony smiled, "thanks Arthur. That was neatly done."

Arthur, clasping Tony's outstretched hand, grinned, "Jus' wait until I tell me dad about that punishin' right of yours!"

Tony laughed, then, following a few final words of caution to Arthur to be careful, he waited only until he had seen him turn the corner on his way back to Mount Street before casting a cursory glance down at Peterson, still winded and on his knees with his arms wrapped around his stomach. After assuring himself that he would be up on his legs pretty soon, Tony continued on towards Bond Street to pick up a hackney to take him to Fleet Street where he hoped to see Mrs. Timms as well as to hear favourable news from Bill in that he had managed to get not only his competitor newspaper editors to agree to his scheme but also that he had been able to persuade Superintendent Dawson of Scotland Yard to see him.

Mrs. Timms, taking no small amount of comfort from Lord Childon's assurances that no harm would come to Lady Collett, returned to Cavendish Square in a more calm, even hopeful, frame of mind. She could not deny that she had taken quite a liking to Lady Shipton and her brother, whose relaxed manner and earnest assertions that she was not to worry herself over her mistress had gone a long way to easing her concerns, nevertheless, she gained the impression that Lord Childon knew more than he had let on, although what this could be she had no idea. She may not have had a fine education but she was a no-nonsense woman who knew more than seven as the saying went, and nothing would rid her mind of the feeling that something pretty irregular was going on and that this Eliza Boon woman and that thatch gallows Peterson who acted as butler, was heavily involved in it and that Sir Braden knew a great deal about it.

Mrs. Timms knew nothing to Sir Braden's detriment, except of course his aggressive manner and violent temper, which, she would take her dying oath, he had more than once subjected her mistress to, and that far from suffering from an intermittent nervous disorder, it was more than likely a case of too much maltreatment by Sir Braden! As for that squinty eyed woman who called herself Eliza Boon, nothing would please Mrs. Timms more than to give her a piece of her mind and the only thing which prevented her from doing so was because she clearly had Sir Braden's support as well as his trust. Not only that, but it could have unpleasant consequences for Lady Collett and since the dear sweet creature already seemed to be enduring more than enough one way and another, Mrs. Timms had no wish to make her situation worse than it was, even so, despite Lord Childon's assurances it would greatly relieve her mind if she could see her mistress just once to assure herself she was in fact all right.

The opportunity came sooner than she expected, in fact almost immediately upon her return from seeing Lady Shipton and her brother. Having removed her hat and coat, admonished Pearl for not doing her work thoroughly enough during her absence quickly followed by briskly instructing her to put the kettle on, Ellen came in carrying a tray with the information that Sir Braden had shut himself up in his study with orders that he did not want to be disturbed and Eliza Boon had gone out. "Not more than an 'our ago!" Ellen nodded to Mrs. Timms, putting the tray down on the table. "You should 'ave seen 'er!" Ellen said, impressed. "Dressed up as fine as fivepence she was!"

As this dispensed with Eliza Boon, Ellen, leaving Pearl to clear the tray, left the kitchen to resume her duties upstairs, little realising that Mrs. Timms, despite her apparent unconcern, was very interested in the activities of her employer and Eliza Boon. No sooner had Ellen left the kitchen than Mrs. Timms went to her own room and, after taking off her coat and putting her bag away, she removed a key from the ring of keys Lady Collett had very early on given her in case of emergencies and which she kept hidden in one of her drawers. Slipping the key into her pocket she returned to the kitchen to find that Pearl, having put the kettle on to boil with the teapot ready to warm, was finishing off cleaning the silver, but not wishing to fill her ears Mrs. Timms told her to carry on with her work while she went to the huge pantry to check if they needed anything. As it was not possible for Mrs. Timms to show herself in the main body of the house in case anyone saw her, which would be bound to raise questions, once having closed the kitchen door behind her she made her way up the same back stairs Eleanor had used to make her escape, pausing to catch her breath before silently opening the door which would lead her onto the first-floor landing where Sir Braden and Lady Collett's rooms were situated. Having assured herself that no one was hovering about in the hall by peering cautiously over the balustrade, Mrs. Timms quietly walked past Sir Braden's room until she came to Lady Collett's, where, after putting her ear to the door and hearing neither voices nor movement, she hurriedly retrieved the key from her pocket and inserted it into the lock, carefully turning it before silently opening the door, removing the key before entering the room and closing and locking it behind her.

Although the heavy brocade curtains were drawn back the blind was pulled down, but there was more than enough light for her to see. Nothing to suggest that an act of brutality had taken place here the other night was visible, Eliza Boon having removed every shred of evidence, the room as neat and tidy as it always was with not a thing out of place, but of Lady Collett there was no sign. The big four-poster was unoccupied and the covers and pillows undisturbed, clearly indicating that it had not been slept in, and all Her Ladyship's brushes and combs together with her favourite perfume and those little personal items she treasured, were carefully arranged on the dressing table as usual. Looking about her in dismay, Mrs. Timms called out in a hushed voice several times in case her mistress was in Sir Braden's dressing room, but upon receiving no response she poked her head round the door to see that she was not there nor was she in his bedroom. Hurrying back into Her Ladyship's room Mrs. Timms promptly opened the double doors of the two huge wardrobes set against the far wall only to discover, much her to disquiet, that not one item of clothing had gone and, anxiously pulling open the drawers to the cabinets, she saw that every glove, scarf, stocking, in fact every item of underwear and accessory, were still there, neatly laid out the same as always. Managing to stifle the sob of dread which formed in her throat, she closed the drawers and, after taking one last look around the room, left as quietly as she had entered it, her fears for the safety and welfare of her young mistress growing, not daring to think what they had done to her, wishing she had discovered her absence earlier this morning before she visited Lady Shipton. So concerned was she over Lady Collett and what could have happened to her that for the rest of the day Mrs. Timms was unable to think of anything else, but since she could not approach either Sir Braden or Eliza Boon her mind was awash with conjecture, and it was therefore not surprising that her sleep that night was rendered hideous by the visions which danced in front of her eyes.

The following morning, Jerry, carrying out Tony's instructions passed on to him by Bill, descended the basement steps of twenty-nine Cavendish Square just as his client was busily tackling Peterson in that narrow side street. Having been told by Edward that his brother Arthur had left his vantage point an hour or so earlier to follow Peterson, Jerry nodded, but although he was a little bewildered as to where Peterson could be going so early, he was nevertheless somewhat relieved. He had no doubt that he could more than adequately deal with Peterson, but his absence meant that there was no likelihood of him coming down to the kitchen while he was there talking to Mrs. Timms, the last thing any of them wanted was their investigations being discovered at this stage!

Pearl, being briskly told by Mrs. Timms, who had hardly closed her eyes all night in worrying over Lady Collett, to see who was at the basement door, returned to the kitchen a minute or so later to disinterestedly tell her there was a man wanting to see her, shrugging her shoulders as she told her she thought he was trying to sell her something. Bustling out of the kitchen to make her way along the narrow passageway to the basement door, Mrs. Timms, forestalling any opening sales pitch, roundly informed Jerry that she did not deal with door-to-door salesmen. Upon being told that he was not a member of this fraternity, Mrs. Timms looked warily at him before asking what he was doing here if he was not trying to sell her something.

From Harry and Tony's description Jerry had no difficulty in recognising Mrs. Timms, Sir Braden Collett's cook, but when he asked her to confirm if she was in fact Mrs. Timms she told him somewhat sharply, "Yes, I'm Mrs. Timms," adding, "an' 'ave been for more years than I care to remember, although what it 'as to do with you I *don't* know! An' there's somethin' else I don't know," she nodded, "an' that is who might you be an' what you're wantin' with me since you say you're not tryin' to sell me somethin'!"

Jerry, after casting a glance up at the top of the basement stairs, told her in a conspiratorial voice, "The name's Jerry Taylor," he doffed his hat, "private investigator," pulling out a rather dog-eared looking licence from his inside pocket.

Mrs. Timms, looking as bemused as she felt, mechanically took the licence he was holding out to her with rather unsteady fingers, but not until she had read with her own eyes that *'Mr. Jeremiah Elisha Taylor of 312, Wellington Road, Marylebone in the County of London was duly authorised to ply his trade as private investigator…'*, did she unbend towards him and, after handing him back his licence, asked, in a far more friendly tone, "An' what would a private investigator be wantin' with me?"

Following another quick glance at the top of the basement steps, he whispered, "'Is Lordship, Lord Childon that is," he nodded, "asked me to come an' see you."

As soon as he mentioned Lord Childon's name she instinctively knew it had something to do with Lady Collett, and upon having this confirmed by the man who was all the time keeping one eye fixed on the basement steps, all her fears resurfaced, and it was with barely concealed dread that she asked him if something had happened to Her Ladyship.

After quickly assuring her that nothing had happened to Lady Collett, Jerry pulled out the card Bill had given him on which Tony had written a couple of lines as added proof that Jerry's visit to Cavendish Square was legitimate and, after briefly scanning it, Mrs. Timms nodded, telling him they could not talk in the doorway and stepped aside for him to enter. Removing his bowler he stepped into the passageway and followed Mrs. Timms towards the warm kitchen where a tantalising aroma of recently cooked bacon met his nostrils, and Pearl, looking from one to the other quite agog, almost dropped the plate in her hand. Mrs. Timms, having no wish to talk in front of Pearl, a good girl but one who could not keep her tongue between her teeth, quickly told her to leave the washing up and make herself useful by tidying up the store cupboard, a job she felt sure she had told her to do yesterday. Pearl, who longed for something exciting to happen, had the nerve to tell Mrs. Timms that she had told her no such thing, but upon being admonished to watch her manners it was with something of a lagging step Pearl left the kitchen, but hopeful of gleaning something of their conversation from the store room just the other side of the kitchen, deliberately left the door slightly ajar only to find, much to her disappointment, that Mrs. Timms firmly shut it for her.

Needing no persuading to take a seat at the huge scrubbed topped table, especially in such raw cold weather as this, Jerry, who had taken an instant liking to Mrs. Timms, gratefully accepted the hot mug of tea she put in front of him, commenting favourably as he helped himself to several spoonfuls of sugar that there was nothing like the smell of freshly cooked bacon. Mrs. Timms, whose shrewd judgement had never yet failed her, had taken one look at Jerry and liked what she saw, by no means disapproving of his scarcely veiled inference, and as she knew from her own experience when Mr. Timms was alive that men, no matter how much you fed them, always seemed to have room for more, she was not at all surprised when he accepted her offer of a bacon sandwich. Taking it upon himself to cut two thick slices off the loaf of bread she placed on the table in front of him Mrs. Timms, having put several rashers of bacon in the pan, joined him at the table and asked him what it was His Lordship wanted.

Having taken an instant liking to Tony, especially as it seemed he had her mistress's interests at heart, Mrs. Timms was by no means averse to helping him, but upon asking Jerry what it was he wanted her to do precisely, he took a quick glance around the kitchen before leaning forward on his elbows, saying quietly, "I think it best if 'Is Lordship tells you. 'Owever," he nodded, "I can tell you that it will 'elp 'Er Ladyship."

Mrs. Timms, needing to know nothing more than this, nodded her head and, after voicing her concerns to him about Lady Collett, promised to meet Tony at Bill's office in Fleet Street just as soon as she had finished here, strenuously refusing the fare Jerry handed her, but upon finding it thrust into her hand and being told that His Lordship was most insistent she was not to be out-of-pocket by his request, she was eventually persuaded to accept it. Unfortunately however, it was not until well over an hour after Jerry had left that Mrs. Timms was able to leave Cavendish Square, but it was not until she was actually seated in the hackney on the way to Fleet Street that she wondered why His Lordship had arranged to meet her in a newspaper office, but since she had no doubt everything would be explained to her, she sat back against the squabs in quiet contemplation until her destination was eventually reached.

As Jerry had no idea what could have taken Peterson out so early or how long it would be before he returned to Cavendish Square so he could get a report off Arthur, he only had time to warn Edward, huddled behind the bushes in the Square's garden, to keep his eyes peeled, before he made his way to Fleet Street. Like Bill, Jerry was in complete ignorance of Tony's brush with Peterson earlier that morning, but as he sat and listened to Tony's account of what had happened, despite his relief in learning that Arthur was unhurt, so surprised was he that he let out an expletive which, had Mrs. Timms been privileged to have overheard, she would have severely taken him to task for using such language, but since neither Tony nor Bill was either offended or shocked by it, it was not commented upon.

"I'd say Collett's getting jumpy!" Bill pointed out, sitting back in his chair.

"He's more than jumpy, Bill," Tony said firmly, "he's desperate, were it otherwise he would never have arranged for this little shindig this morning."

"But why come after *you*?" Jerry asked. "Surely it's Lady Collett who's the danger!"

"Yes, I know," Tony nodded, "and whilst I admit that it had me licked for a while, I think I now know why." In response to a raised eyebrow from Bill, Tony explained, "Thanks to Jerry here, I now know that Eliza Boon and Peterson waited until half past two before they gave up waiting for Lady Collett to show herself. Neither Collett nor Eliza Boon expected Lady Collett to fail to comply with that letter, I don't include Peterson," he nodded, "because he's nothing more than a 'yes man' who carries out their dirty work, but the fact that she *did* fail to comply could only lead them to suppose that she had nothing to fear because she had already confided to me about what happened that night. Up until I arrived on the scene they really had only Lady Collett to worry about, and although she was kept a virtual prisoner to keep her away from all her friends and acquaintances, they knew that if she somehow managed to be alone with any one of them, Bea especially, and confided the truth and they took it to the police, even though they would be obliged to question Collett, the chances were it would not be taken to the point where he would be arrested and, don't forget," he reminded them, "once the police interviewed Collett's household staff and they learned from them about Lady Collett's so-called mental disorder and how she regularly hurt herself during a supposed hallucination, any claims put forward by Bea or anyone would be dropped and," he nodded, "even if they did arrest him and it went to Court, Lady Collett could not stand up in the witness-box and give evidence which would be damaging to her husband, besides which, her supposed nervous condition would immediately render her an unreliable witness. Whichever way it went Collett would still have got away with cold-blooded murder and being a party to three more, the only damage would have been to his reputation, and it's *this*," he pointed out, "which has rendered Lady a Collett a threat. He might not be the most popular man you will ever meet," Tony remarked, "but his name is so far unsullied, and he will do anything to ensure it remains so!"

"Then you came along," Bill supplied, fishing out a cigar.

"Precisely!" Tony inclined his head. "As things stand now, should I take what Lady Collett knows to the police without hard evidence to back it up, the chances are that the outcome will be the same, but," he pointed his cigarette at Bill, "it's not that which worries him so much as the fact that I am in a prime position to investigate what the police can't, based solely on what they would believe to be the detrimental, even mentally unstable, evidence of Collett's wife, and also that it would not be long before I discovered the truth about Annie Myers and the others. This morning's exercise," he nodded, "was a desperate attempt to silence his wife's messenger before I could set in motion the very thing he has dreaded."

"So," Bill nodded, "by silencing you before you can do anything to damage them they saw it as the next best thing to getting Lady Collett back to Cavendish Square?"

"That's about the size of it! Very neat," Tony conceded reluctantly.

"*Neat*!" Bill and Jerry exclaimed in unison.

"Sure," Tony shrugged, unable to resist a smile as he saw the look of horror on their faces. "By getting me permanently out of the way," he told them, "I am firmly convinced he is relying heavily on Bea blaming Lady Collett for my death and therefore no longer prepared to offer her sanctuary or, if she doesn't blame Lady Collett, then, at the very least, the chances are that she would probably think it rather inappropriate to continue offering her shelter. Collett knows that whichever way it went his wife would have no choice other than to return to Cavendish Square or, failing this, then to her father. Should she decide to return to Collett then her life would simply revert back to how it was before or, even," he inclined his head, "Collett could well carry out his threats by having her put away. If, on the other hand, Lady Collett felt she could not return to her husband and would much prefer to live with her father, then Collett is still a winner because even though my death would be reported as the direct result of a brutal assault by person or persons unknown, Lady Collett would not be taken in. She would know that he was the one responsible for getting rid of me and *this*," he pointed out, "would frighten her more than any one of the threats in that letter because Collett knows she would be too terrified to say anything, even to her father, thereby running the risk of being disposed of as well."

"And Sir Philip's death would remain on police files as unsolved and Dennis Dunscumbe's death still recorded as a suicide," Bill supplied disgustedly.

"Like I said," Tony nodded, "very neat."

Bill thought for a moment, his eyes narrowing slightly as he looked at Tony through a cloud of cigar smoke, conceding at length, "Sure it's neat, but," he nodded, feeling compelled to point out one important factor which Tony appeared to have overlooked, "you may have handled yourself well this morning, but damn it Tony…!"

"Save it, Bill," Tony broke in, "I know what you're about to say but there's no need." Bill, casting an exasperated look from Tony to Jerry then back at Tony was just on the point of opening his mouth to say something when Tony forestalled him. "Look Bill, up until now Collett has been only able to hazard a guess as to what, if anything, I know which, for a man in his position, is unnerving to say the least, but now," he nodded, "I've told him precisely what he needs to know and…"

"You got that right!" Bill cut in, frustrated. "And in doing so you've also given him a reason to come after you again!"

"Finished, Bill?" Tony smiled.

"Argh!" Bill cried frustrated, waving an exasperated hand.

"By telling him what I know," Tony explained amiably, fully conscious of Bill's concern for his safety, "I have merely made it impossible for him to do anything other than what we want him to do when he reads the piece we are going to have inserted in the newspapers. He's going to be far too worried about any possible evidence in Hertford Street to spare a thought for getting rid of me."

"You have it all off pat, don't you?" Bill said goaded, to which Tony grinned. "Yeah," he nodded, relighting his cigar before pointing it at him, "sure you do! Wise guy!" not without a touch of pride.

"Never mind that!" Tony dismissed, a laugh in his eyes. "Tell me how you got on with Courtney at *'The Telegraph'* and the others and this Superintendent Dawson."

"Oh, Courtney and the rest will go for it!" Bill assured him. "Just let them know which run you want it included in, but," he nodded, a gleam in his eye, "they told me to tell you that it'll cost you – big time!"

Tony laughed. "Sure, they got it!"

"They also think you're crazy!" Bill added, unable to resist Tony's smile.

"Crazy or not," Tony said determinedly, "I want that piece inserted as soon as Dawson agrees to our plan. Now," Tony urged, "about Dawson?"

Bill sighed and leaned back in his chair. "I'm afraid he was not so easy to win over, Tony, however," he nodded, in answer to the frown which had suddenly descended onto Tony's forehead, deciding not to tell him that Dawson had needed some convincing that he was serious and not wasting his time, "I did manage to persuade him to at least talk to you about it; he'll meet you here at two this afternoon." Bill pursed his lips, asking, "What if he doesn't agree to it?"

Tony thought a moment, the frown on his forehead deepening. The instant Eleanor had escaped from Cavendish Square, he had known that it was only a matter of time before Collett would try something to get her back; under no circumstances could he allow her to disclose what she knew, and certainly not to one such as himself. However reluctant Tony was to give Collett and his accomplices credit, he had to admit that even though he knew how urgent it was for them to get Eleanor back into their custody, they had nevertheless taken him by surprise by the swiftness with which they had moved. They knew as well as he did that they could not openly approach Beatrice about Eleanor any more than they could attempt to break into the house and forcibly remove her so, instead, they had come up with a cunningly daring plan which had not only been quite cleverly executed, but should have worked. But however much their promptness to deal with a difficult situation may have surprised him, they had misguidedly failed to take in to account that he had fully expected them to try to remove Eleanor from the safety of Mount Street one way or the other. Tony was totally convinced that the planning and execution of such a brilliant strategy had come out of Eliza Boon's mind and not Collett's, but just because last night's scheme had failed Tony knew perfectly well that it did not mean they would not try again; that was, until this morning.

Their sudden change of tack in deciding that it would be far more sensible to permanently silence him, a far better option from their point of view he would have thought than just warning him off, certainly relieved his mind where Eleanor's immediate safety was concerned, but it also meant that his strategy for tricking them into proving their own guilt had unfortunately made it necessary for him to bring his timetable forward. Had it not have been for this morning's attempt to try to rid themselves of him, proving beyond doubt the risk he posed, Tony had calculated he had several more days in which to arrange for his plans to be put into effect, but in view of this new and desperate line of attack, it meant that he could not afford to delay matters any longer than was necessary. He knew his parting words to Peterson had not only confirmed that he knew the truth about their crimes but that he had opened himself up to further attempts on his life but, more importantly, they gave vital credence to the articles Collett would read in his newspapers, convincing him that it was imperative he visit Dennis Dunscumbe's house in Hertford Street before the police arrived to carry out further investigations.

Tony knew just as well as Bill that it was not a small matter to add an article in just one copy of a run, but he had never doubted for one moment that Courtney of *'The Times'* nor Buckle and Barton of *'The Telegraph'* and *'The Echo'* would refuse, not only because they were newspaper men but also because they had no stomach for seeing cold-blooded murder going unanswered any more than he did. As for Mrs. Timms, apart from having taken a liking to this no-nonsense woman who clearly had Eleanor's interests at heart, Tony had seen enough of her to know that she was honest and law-abiding and would not hesitate to help them waylay Collett and his cohorts by the heels. As for Superintendent Dawson, Tony still believed that in spite of his obvious reluctance he was enough of a policeman to want to apprehend individuals who had broken the law, especially those who had committed such a vicious and brutal murder as that perpetrated against Sir Philip Dunscumbe. Tony did not need Bill to tell him that without Dawson's help then they may as well give up the idea now because should Dawson refuse and he and Tom together with Jerry and one or other of his sons go ahead regardless, then it would simply be a case of their word against Collett's, in which case the chances were very good that no charges would be brought against him; as for themselves, then the chances were equally good that they could well be charged with all manner of things.

Until Collett had forced the issue by sending Peterson to deal with him permanently, Tony's plans had been carefully calculated so that the relevant parties concerned would have time to get things moving their end, but now he was unfortunately faced with a period of time which left very little room for manoeuvre. He knew Bill would feel far more comfortable knowing he had Dawson's support and, to be honest, so would he, but he realised that if he delayed the opportunity may not present itself again for some time, besides which, it would give Collett and the others an undeserved reprieve as well as ensuring that he would be constantly looking over his shoulder, but worse than this was knowing that Eleanor would never know a moment's peace of mind. Even so, somewhere at the back of Tony's mind he felt sure that Dawson would agree to his scheme to lay Collett and the others by the heels if for no other reason than his own sense of right and wrong, but also because like cops everywhere he had his pride and would not like to think that a case he was in charge of, particularly one as serious as murder on such a prominent figure as Sir Philip Dunscumbe, remained unsolved. Be that as it may, should Dawson agree to the plan they were hatching there would be no way he could go ahead with it without it being approved by the Commissioner of Police if for no other reason than the man they were trying to trick into admitting his own guilt was none other than Sir Braden Collett. Then, of course, there was every possibility that Dawson would want to speak to Eleanor before he approached the Commissioner to get her side of the story from her own lips, perfectly understandable of course, but apart from this very necessary procedure delaying the winding up of this matter Tony wanted to talk to Eleanor himself first about what had actually happened that night as well as preparing her for a visit from a police officer.

"Tell me, Jerry," Tony asked almost absently, "have you ever had occasion to work with this Superintendent Dawson?"

"Yes," he confirmed, "I 'ave."

"And?" Tony urged.

"'E's a good man who knows what 'e's doin'," he told him, "but 'e does things 'is own way, if you know what I mean."

"Yes," Tony said thoughtfully, "I know what you mean."

"'E gets results," Jerry told him, "and I ain't never known 'im turn 'is back on information, nor," he added, "is 'e too proud to listen to another side o' things."

"Let us hope that this is not one occasion when he does turn his back," Tony sighed hopefully. Then, turning to Bill, cocked his head. "He will be here at two, you say?" Bill nodded. Pulling out his watch, Tony pursed his lips, saying, "It's almost twelve now; let's say it takes us about an hour and a half to speak to Mrs. Timms and for Dawson," he shrugged, "more or less the same." He paused and thought a moment, then, returning his watch to his pocket, said slowly, "It's no good Bill; I think it looks very much as though we shall have to sit on that story for a day or two," briefly explaining what he believed would happen should Dawson agree.

Bill knew from long experience that Tony was a man who acted decisively and one who certainly got things moving, but since there was nothing any one of them could do for the present to hasten matters, Bill was at least able to give him some good news about Mary Stanley. It seemed that when she was discharged from Sir Braden's employ she had returned to Dagenham to live with her mother and, according to Bill's contact on a local paper, she was now working in a draper's shop, but since she could not tell the local reporter anything more than they already knew, he failed to see the need to question her further. Tony was certainly relieved to hear that she was safe and unharmed as well as not having to question Eleanor about her, which would naturally plant a seed of doubt and fear in her mind about the welfare of one she was very much attached to. As for Mitchell, Bill still could not tell Tony anything as to his whereabouts, assuming he was alive, or, if he was in fact dead, which looked more than likely, then it seemed the exact location of his body would only come to light once Collett and his confederates had finally been arrested.

Upon being asked how his enquiries were going regarding Periton Place, Jerry told Tony that as far as his friends in the Metropolitan Police were concerned they knew nothing against the address as nothing had come to their notice about anything illegal taking place, with regards to his other enquiries he had discovered that the current owner of number fifty-one was a Mr. Reggie Wragge who had purchased the house about ten months or so ago from a woman fitting Eliza Boon's description. Bill, eyeing Jerry with widened eyes, almost dropped his cigar, telling Tony in answer to his raised eyebrow that unless there were two Reggie Wragges then this guy was a wealthy businessman who was well-known and respected in the City and whose reputation was beyond dispute and, more than this, was known to entertain those in high places at his home in Belgravia. Jerry, upon seeing the crease which had descended onto Tony's forehead informed him that according to his discreet enquiries in and around Periton Place, it seemed that some of the residents did occasionally see a most respectable looking gentleman enter and leave the house, usually in the mornings, but apart from nodding his head in acknowledgement to one or the other, he seemed to keep himself very much to himself. "If 'e is usin' the premises for the same line o' business as Eliza Boon," Jerry concluded, "then it's all pretty 'ush 'ush because from what I can discover number fifty-one is as respectable as all the other 'ouses in the neighbour'ood, an' always 'as been."

Bill, who knew perfectly well what was going through Tony's mind, knew too that he may as well save his breath as remonstrate with him when he had decided on something, which, unless he had grossly misread that look on his face, he most certainly had, so leaving him to clear up one or two points with Jerry, Bill went into his secretary's office to return minutes later with a piece of paper which he handed to Tony.

Glancing from the paper in his hand on which Bill had written down two addresses to his resigned face, Tony smiled, "Thanks, Bill. You've read my mind."

"Don't thank me," Bill shook his head, "because I get the feeling I'm doing you no favours!" Then, pointing his cigar at him, warned, "You just be careful."

"You know me, Bill," Tony smiled, pocketing the piece of paper.

"Too right I know you!" he shot at him. "That's why I'm telling you to be careful."

Tony was just on the point of saying something in response to this when Bill's secretary walked in following a brief tap on the door to announce that Mrs. Timms was here.

Chapter Twenty-Two

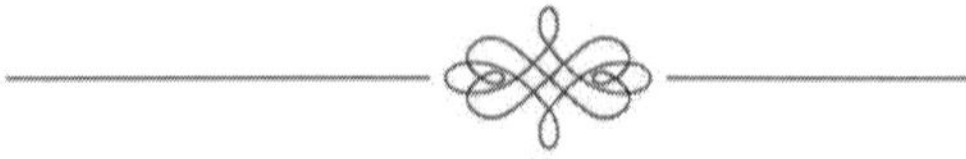

When Eliza Boon had agreed to sell her profitable little business and move into Cavendish Square it had been on the understanding that it was to guard Lady Collett and not to keep coming up with contingency plans to extricate them from one crisis after another. For a woman of Eliza's deviousness and ingenuity as well as a natural inclination for self-preservation, coming up with strategies to fend off disasters which could denounce them posed no great difficulty for one of her mental agility, but the truth was she had not bargained for this and were it not for protecting herself and Peterson she would willingly let Sir Braden sink or swim on his own. The fact that she could not do so, simply because he could not be trusted to keep his mouth shut, especially when under duress or panic set in, she had no choice but to see matters through to the bitter end, and if this meant doing away with a peer of the realm, then so be it!

Sir Braden's tendency to lose his head in moments of anxiety had more than once required her stepping into the breach by coming to his relief in drawing up plans to ensure his protection, in fact had she not have done so then all three of them would have undoubtedly been arrested and sentenced long since. In view of this then, she had been somewhat surprised at the plan he had devised to deal with Lord Childon and the threat he clearly posed because it was useless to suppose that he could be persuaded into leaving well alone.

Lady Collett's failure to show herself last night may or may not have been due to Childon's intervention, but the fact remained that without his interference she would never have escaped in the first place. It seemed to Eliza that Childon had somehow or other imbued Lady Collett with a resurgence of self-worth but, more importantly, the courage to think and act on her own initiative because there was no denying that before he entered her life, even though there were definite signs pointing to the fact that she had not been totally cowed into submission, she had nevertheless been reasonably compliant and manageable. Now though, it was becoming increasingly clear that no further reliance could be placed upon her doing what they wanted and therefore Sir Braden's idea of dealing with Childon first then Lady Collett after the dust had died down, made perfect sense.

Eliza knew just as well as Sir Braden and Childon that Lady Collett's eyewitness account of what happened that night could not be given in evidence as no wife could testify against her husband if that testimony was in any way harmful to him, even so, Eliza could only be thankful that Lady Collett's accidental stumbling into Sir Philip Dunscumbe's brutal murder had not put her in the way of what had brought it about. Even if the police gave credence to Lady Collett's claims prompting them to question Sir Braden, it was extremely doubtful it would get to court and, supposing it did and, supposing again Lady Collett was actually allowed to give evidence, once the jury heard of her mental disorder and frequent hallucinations, especially once the servants had verified it, and with no other witness, the case would be thrown out of court, but the damage it would do to Sir Braden's reputation would be incalculable. It was an unfortunate circumstance, but regrettably mud did have a habit of sticking and although Sir Braden would survive the police enquiry as well as a court case, if it ever got that far, there would be no way his name would survive the scandal. Now though, with this Childon tyke interesting himself in Lady Collett as well as involving himself in their affairs, they were facing an entirely different situation because he and his newspapers, more so than the police, were in a prime position to investigate matters in more depth, especially as Childon knew perfectly well that Lady Collett was as sane as anyone and what she saw that night, far from being a hallucination, was in fact the cold hard truth.

But it was not only Sir Braden Eliza was thinking of but herself and Peterson, whose positions were far more precarious than Sir Braden's and certainly less secure. Sir Braden may have killed Sir Philip in a moment of panic as well as covering up the death of Annie Myers besides being a party to all that followed but she, with calculated deliberation, had incited Peterson into murdering Dennis Dunscumbe as well as Mitchell. Eliza was conversant enough with the law to know that once Childon concluded of all this, even without Lady Collett's testimony, there would be no way Sir Braden and Peterson would escape the gallows whilst she would certainly find herself facing a lengthy prison sentence which, depending on how magnanimous the judge was, could be with or without hard labour, but she no more than Peterson could claim momentary loss of rationality to help her case nor rely upon a long-established title to protect her.

Sir Braden's idea, surprising for one in his escalating nervous condition, was not without its merits, in fact it was nothing short of inspired, but however imperative it was to dispose of Childon, and as soon as possible, it had to be done in such a way that no finger of blame could be pointed in their direction. Eliza's faith in Peterson, which had never once been misplaced, was more than enough to convince her that he would have no difficulty in making Childon's death appear anything other than precisely what would be construed from it, the result of a vicious attack, and when it became known that his clothes had rigorously been searched and the pockets emptied of their contents, no one would ever doubt it. Once this meddlesome Colonial was permanently out of the way, then they could deal with Lady Collett who, without Childon's support and Lady Shipton's protection, because it was not to be supposed that she would continue to look upon her protégée in quite the same way, Lady Collett would not be so disobedient or inclined to rebel, and certainly not disposed to imparting her knowledge.

Sir Braden's nerves, as Eliza Boon had rightly assessed, were beginning to overtake him, so much so that should anything else arise which needed to be dealt with to ensure their protection, then he doubted very much whether he would be able to face it. As he shut himself away in his study awaiting Peterson's return he considered, and not for the first time, that too many things were going wrong, it seemed that no sooner had they averted one crisis than they were confronted by another, each one more threatening than the one before. He may have met Lord Childon only once and then briefly, but there was something about this man which told him that he was by far the biggest threat they had yet encountered and, with the power and influence of his newspapers behind him, doubly so. Sir Braden had no liking for another death on their hands, but in this instance he could see no other way of dealing with a man he instinctively knew would not give up any more than he could be bought and, like Eliza, his faith in Peterson was such that the thought of him failing in his task to rid themselves of this menace never so much as entered his head. It may not have entered his head but it did not prevent him from pouring himself a generous glass of brandy just to steady his nerves because even with Childon out of the way, giving them much-needed time as well as room to manoeuvre, Sir Braden knew it did not mean they were out of the wood.

Had Dennis not lost his temper that night, then none of this would be happening and, upon reflection, Sir Braden supposed that it would have been far better to have reported the girl's death and faced the consequences, at least by doing so they would not have found themselves saddled with three more deaths on their hands, but the consequences had been far too horrendous to contemplate. The very thought of him regularly visiting a house of ill repute, particularly one that catered for those such as himself and Dennis Dunscumbe, being spread all over the newspapers and discussed by all and sundry, was something he could not even bring himself to think about. As Sir Braden had not the least idea that Joanie Simms had left Periton Place armed with such damaging information, and Sir Philip had not disclosed his informant, he still believed that the only way he could have discovered the truth was from his brother Dennis, and therefore at no point during the last eleven months or so had Sir Braden even taken this woman into consideration and the very real danger she presented. For one in his highly nervous state it was perhaps as well that he remained in total ignorance of the damage she could do much less that she had imparted knowledge none of them knew she possessed to the very man who could bring them to ruin.

So lost in unpleasant thought was he that he entirely failed to hear Eliza's tap on the study door or her silent entrance, and it was not until he heard her say, "Sir Braden," did he realise that he was no longer alone.

"Oh, it's you," he sighed, raising his head to see who it was. "Has Peterson returned yet?" he asked, looking at the clock on the mantelpiece.

"No, Sir Braden," she shook her head, "not yet. That's what I came to tell you."

He let out an anxious sigh, then, after swallowing a mouthful of brandy, said, a little tetchily, "Where the devil is he? He should have been back by now!"

"I know," Eliza nodded, having looked to see him before now, "but I expect he has had to wait for Childon to show himself."

Sir Braden, finishing off his drink, rose to his feet, a deep frown creasing his forehead. "Childon!" he scorned. Then, pulling himself together, he nodded meaningfully, "You know what will happen if this fails?" striding over to the fireplace.

"It won't fail," she said firmly.

"That's what you said about my wife returning home last night," he sharply reminded her, "and yet," he pointed out, "she is still in Mount Street."

Not liking the way he was again trying to lay the blame at her door for their plans going awry, she reminded him that Lady Collett's failure to show herself last night had not been because her scheme for getting her back to Cavendish Square had been faulty but, on the contrary, undeniable proof that she was on far more comfortable terms with Childon than they had originally supposed. "Either she or Lady Shipton must have shown him that letter or told him about it or," Eliza nodded, her eyes narrowing, "he guessed who it was from and put two and two together."

"Which is why it is imperative we rid ourselves of this man!" Collett said sharply. "Even now," he said irritably, "we can't say for certain whether Eleanor has told him anything or not."

"It makes no difference whether she has or not," she shook her head, "because when Peterson has finished with him he will be in no position to do anything about it."

"Assuming Peterson *does* finish him!" he bit out, his colour deepening.

In view of his growing agitation, and not wishing to exacerbate it which could well lead him into losing his head altogether, Eliza bit down on her temper in favour of adopting a more conciliatory attitude, saying practically, "If it turns out that Childon did not show himself or things did not go to plan, then," she nodded, "we'll try again tomorrow, and the day after if we have to."

"And the day after and the day after until there are no 'days after' left!" he cried impatiently, his eyes protruding alarmingly and his hands clenching and unclenching at his sides, signs Eliza knew well. "Damn it, Eliza!" he exclaimed. "He could bring all to ruin!"

"I know that!" she snapped. "But Peterson won't give him the chance to. Trust me, Sir Braden," she urged, "Peterson won't fail."

Sir Braden had certainly never known him to, but considering the way things seemed to be going of late he could not prevent the horrendous thought from entering his head that this could well be one time when he would. An encroaching Colonial upstart Childon may be, but he nevertheless bore all the hallmarks of being a man who could more than adequately take care of himself, a circumstance which by no means helped to curb the growing unease inside him. Sir Braden compressed his lips as he considered the possibility that Peterson, no stranger to this kind of work, may find it a little more difficult to overpower Childon, but before he could go any further with this idea a thought, equally worrying, suddenly occurred to him and, after deliberating a moment, asked abruptly, "Have the servants said anything about Lady Collett?"

"No, Sir Braden," Eliza shook her head, "not a thing, although," she added truthfully, "I can't deny they're curious. Ellen asked me again this morning if she was to take Lady Collett some breakfast."

"And what did you say?" he asked curtly.

"That Her Ladyship was still asleep," she informed him, knowing as well as Sir Braden that this pretence could not be maintained indefinitely.

"And she believed you?" He raised an eyebrow.

"Why shouldn't she?" Eliza wanted to know.

"Has any one of them asked to see Her Ladyship?" he queried, inwardly shying away from the thought.

"No," she shook her head, "there's no reason why they should," she shrugged, "they are far too used to her nervous disorders and the need to keep her quiet."

"What are they saying downstairs?" he demanded sharply. "Do you know?"

She shrugged. "No, how should I? You must know that I am no favourite with them, although" she offered slyly, "I would not put it beyond Mrs. Timms to make it her business to find out what's going on."

"Mrs. Timms?" He raised a surprised eyebrow. "What's she been saying?"

"It's not what she's been saying so much as her attitude," she told him firmly.

"Her attitude?" Sir Braden repeated, looking a little blank. "What do you mean?"

"Well," Eliza shrugged, "I can't help thinking that she does not believe Lady Collett is ill at all, in fact," she pursed her lips, "I think she could cause a bit of a problem by insisting on seeing her."

"Then you must make sure she does not," Sir Braden bit out.

"That's all very well," Eliza told him sharply, "but for one thing she's no fool and for another," she nodded, "she's always enjoyed a good understanding with Lady Collett."

"So, what are you suggesting?" he demanded. "That we get rid of her too!"

"No," Eliza shook her head, "at least, not yet."

"Not yet!" Sir Braden echoed. "For God's sake, Eliza!" he exclaimed. "We can't afford another death on our hands!"

"Nor can we afford to allow Mrs. Timms to know the truth!" she threw at him. "Her position in the household and the length of time she has been with you and your family renders her dangerous because there's no getting away from it that the younger members of staff look up to her, and only one word from her would be enough to set them thinking."

Just the thought of having to overcome yet another obstacle was too horrendous to contemplate, but as Sir Braden stared with horrified eyes at Eliza he knew that if Mrs. Timms ever did take it into her head to insist on seeing Eleanor or somehow managed to secretly enter her room, little realising that this was precisely what she had done, then she could do as much damage as Childon. Of course, there was every chance that Eliza had read far more into Mrs. Timms's natural concerns than was actually the case, even so, it would not hurt to keep an eye on her because the last thing he wanted was to have to either dismiss her, which would by no means solve the problem as she was bound to talk, or adopt far more unpalatable methods of keeping her from knowing the truth which, with Childon just hovering in the background, would be suicidal. Unable to bring himself to agree with what Eliza was blatantly suggesting Sir Braden shook his head, saying firmly, "No, Mrs. Timms must not be laid a hand on. Just keep an eye on her for the time being."

Eliza, by no means convinced that this was the right decision, argued strenuously against the sound wisdom of not dealing with her before she could do any harm, but Sir Braden, whose nerves would not tolerate much more, began to realise that Eliza was in fact far more ruthless than he had ever suspected. He admitted that without her help matters would have reached crisis point well before now, in fact he would go so far as to say that were it not for her clear thinking and decisive actions all three of them would doubtless have faced the Queen's Bench long since, but whether from a belated attack of remorse or merely because he was looking to his own self-protection, he remained adamant that unless it was absolutely essential Mrs. Timms was to remain unmolested.

Eliza, seeing he could not be persuaded into her line of thinking, at least for now, was firmly of the belief that once he had given it more thought he would eventually come to see that the threat this woman posed could seriously jeopardise their position and in so doing accept that no option was open to them other than to ensure her silence once and for all. Believing she had done all she could for the time being to impress upon him the urgency of dealing with Mrs. Timms before it was too late Eliza left him to mull things over, confident that he would soon come to see that her solution for dealing with this fresh difficulty was not only sensible but the only one in the circumstances, little realising that her stalwart had failed in his mission and Mrs. Timms was on the point of helping to seal their fate once and for all.

Mrs. Timms knew perfectly well that her mistrust and dislike of Eliza Boon was entirely mutual, but she would have been extremely disturbed to learn that this hard-nosed woman was actually contemplating disposing of her to obviate the potential risk she posed. Nevertheless, Eliza Boon was right in thinking that Mrs. Timms, irrespective of the possible dangers to herself, would put a spoke in their wheel if she could because Eliza intuitively knew that this rather forthright woman had at no time believed what she had told her about Lady Collett's mental disorder resulting in frequent hallucination attacks.

Mrs. Timms had known for some time that something was dreadfully wrong, but try as she did she could not put her finger on what it could possibly be. As she was neither fanciful nor over imaginative, she had ruled out the possibility that Sir Braden was trying to place his hands on his wife's assets by pretending she was mentally unbalanced. Sir Braden was a wealthy man who had no need to marry for money, and as his wife before her marriage had been almost a pauper in comparison Mrs. Timms had never really taken this theory seriously, nevertheless, nothing would rid her mind that Lady Collett stood in danger, and upon discovering no sign of her in her room and none of her belongings had either been removed or disturbed, her fears increased alarmingly. Despite Jerry's encouraging assurances earlier that she was not to worry her head over Lady Collett, Mrs. Timms remained extremely fearful for the safety and welfare of her young mistress, so much so that she was barely able to wait for Tony to thank her for coming following a few short words of introduction to Bill to pour forth her concerns over what she had discovered yesterday morning upon her return to Cavendish Square. "What could 'ave 'appened to 'Er Ladyship, m'lord?" She sniffed into her handkerchief. "Not a sign of 'er could I see, an' not one of 'er things gone!"

"I am afraid I owe you an apology, Mrs. Timms," Tony said remorsefully. "You see," he explained, "when you called to see my sister yesterday and I told you there was no need for you to worry yourself over Lady Collett, I should also have told you that she was, even then, safely installed in Mount Street."

She eyed him dumbfounded. "Mount Street!" she cried, looking up at him bewildered.

"Yes," he nodded.

"But… I… I don't understand, m'lord!" She shook her head. "What's 'Er Ladyship doin' in Mount Street? Not that it's not a relief, I can tell you!" she nodded.

"Well," Tony sighed, inclining his head, "I am afraid that is rather a long story, but believe me when I say I had not meant to cause you any distress by not telling you Lady Collett was safe," he told her sincerely.

Mrs. Timms eyed him thoughtfully for a moment, her eyes narrowing before asking shrewdly, "Is it your doin' she's there, m'lord?"

"Yes," he smiled, not a little ruefully, "I am afraid it is."

No, she decided, Lord Childon was not what you could call a handsome man, not with that nose you couldn't and that deep cleft in his square chin, and yet there was something about him which was very attractive and, like Sarah, Mrs. Timms was by no means impervious to that smile. She pursed her lips a little, then, after some thought, asked, "Is that why you asked me to come 'ere', m'lord, to tell me about 'Er Ladyship?"

"Partly," Tony nodded, "but also because we need your help."

She saw the look Bill cast up at Tony and wondered, not for the first time since leaving Cavendish Square, just what he was doing in a newspaper office in Fleet Street, and felt impelled to ask before she said or did anything which could harm her young mistress, not that she really believed any harm would come to her through this man. "Beggin' your pardon m'lord an' meanin' no offence I'm sure, but just what 'ave you got to do with this 'ere newspaper office?" catching the smile in his eyes as he glanced from her to Bill and back again.

"Well, you see Mrs. Timms," Tony admitted, almost apologetically, "I own the newspapers." Upon seeing her eyes open to their fullest extent, he smiled and nodded confirmation before going on to give her a brief explanation of his antecedents.

"Well!" she gasped, dropping her plump hands onto her lap, the discovery that he was in fact half-American coming as more of a surprise than learning he owned the newspapers. "I would never 'ave thought it because no one would think it to 'ear you talk."

"Thank you," Tony said meekly, inclining his head, the laughter in his eyes confirming what she had thought yesterday when she had met him in company with his sister.

A lord he may be as well as a press whatever they called it, not that it mattered because she had seen at a glance he was a real gentleman who by no means stood on his dignity any more than he was one to puff off his own consequence, unlike Sir Braden, but Mrs. Timms was astute enough to recognise that beneath his easy-going and relaxed manner there lay hidden a strength of purpose and a determination that she shrewdly guessed were quite inflexible, as Bill could have told her, and instinctively knew that if anyone could help her mistress, then it was this man so, nodding her head, said, "Just what is it you want me to do, m'lord?"

Drawing up his chair nearer to hers, Tony leaned forward, saying quietly, "Before I tell you that, Mrs. Timms, you need to know *why* we are seeking your help, but I am afraid," he shook his head, "it will come as something of a shock."

To say the story which unfolded came as a reeling blow was a gross understatement, so horrified and appalled was she that it was several minutes after Tony had finished telling her all that happened before she could find her voice to speak. Forthright and plain speaking she may be, but she was no prude, accepting that everyone had their little quirks, even so, she had her standards which most certainly did not include approving the type of establishment it seemed Sir Braden had frequented, and definitely not murder. She knew Sir Braden had a most unpredictable temper as well as being naturally aggressive, and despite her long-held conviction that he quite often subjected his poor wife to rather harsh treatment, it had never so much as crossed her mind just how harsh that treatment actually was or that he had patronised a certain establishment to gratify his more brutal tendencies. She knew of course that some men did lean towards this rather unfortunate inclination and that there were houses where they could go to indulge it, but at no time had she ever suspected that Sir Braden formed one of this group, but what shocked her as much as all the rest was that it was Eliza Boon who had presided over the very establishment he had patronised and that Peterson had been a part of it. That these visits of Sir Braden's to her premises had eventually resulted in covering up such a violent death which had set in motion a string of others that had been deliberately calculated, culminating in Lady Collett either witnessing such a horrifying spectacle in her own home or stumbling upon something to alert her to it then, on top of this, being kept a virtual prisoner, left Mrs. Timms so appalled that she could only gasp her shocked disbelief.

Tony had thought long and hard about how much to tell Mrs. Timms, after all it was far from suitable for a woman's ears, nevertheless, two things had swayed him to tell her the truth; the first was that she was far too astute to be taken in by only half a tale, and second, that there was no other way of explaining recent events without telling her all the facts. "I am sorry to have to be the one to break such dreadful news to you," Tony sighed apologetically.

"No," she shook her head, "I'm glad you 'ave." She took a moment to blow her nose and swallow a much-needed drink of tea before saying, "I knew somethin' wasn't right, but I never suspicioned nothin' like this, no," blowing her nose again, "not for a minute I didn't! Sir Braden too!" She shook her head, bemused. "I'd never 'ave thought it! 'E 'as a temper I know, in fact," she nodded, "'e can be downright nasty when 'e's a mind, but I never thought 'im capable of murder! An' 'Er Ladyship," she wanted to know, "are you sayin' that it was because of what she'd seen or stumbled on that they kept 'er a prisoner an' made on she 'ad nervous disorders?"

"Yes," Tony confirmed gently, perfectly aware of what a shock it had all been for her. "Sir Braden had not expected to find Sir Philip Dunscumbe on his doorstep that night, in fact," he told her, "I would say he never expected him at all and, as for Lady Collett, he had not looked to see her return home early from the concert, but having done so and accidentally walked in on such a brutal act, because I am absolutely convinced that is precisely what she did do," Tony nodded, "even though Lady Collett is not yet well enough to confirm it, he could not allow her to tell anyone, in fact," he sighed, "it was far too dangerous to let her go out alone, which is why Eliza Boon was brought in to keep constant guard over her and to look after her in place of Mary as well as threaten her into doing what they wanted."

The very mention of Eliza Boon brought a martial light to her eyes. "If I thought for one minute that that woman 'ad ever laid an 'and on 'er," she said firmly, "I'd…"

Tony may only have caught a brief glimpse of Eliza Boon when she accompanied Eleanor to Mount Street, but the impression he had of her more than confirmed what Joanie Simms had told him about her treatment of the girls. Tony doubted very much that Collett, despite his own brutal treatment of Eleanor, would allow someone else to physically harm her, and even though she had not said anything to him about Eliza Boon hitting her at any time, Tony was more inclined to believe that, apart from her menacing presence, which in itself was bad enough, her brutality had been more in the way of threats than actually laying a hand on Eleanor, and so he felt able to confidently assure Mrs. Timms, "No," he shook his head, "she did not."

Mrs. Timms sniffed. "Well, that's small comfort, m'lord, I don't mind sayin', but as for Sir Braden," she blew her nose, "I often thought 'e 'andled 'Er Ladyship 'arshly even before all this. More than once he called me up to 'is study to tell me that 'Er Ladyship was unable to see me as she always did every mornin' because she was feelin' unwell or 'ad a migraine and was lyin' down quiet in 'er room, and often and often I saw bruises on her wrists that she tried to 'ide, but that 'e should beat 'er like 'e did is downright wicked. If only she'd come to me, m'lord," she blew her nose again, "I'd 'ave 'elped 'er."

"I know," Tony said gently, "but she was too afraid."

Mrs. Timms, quite overcome by it all, took a moment to compose herself. "Thank goodness you were both there, m'lord, when 'Er Ladyship escaped!" looking from Jerry then back at Tony, dreading to think what would have happened otherwise.

"Our presence was certainly timely," Tony nodded, "because she would not have survived long in such freezing temperatures."

She nodded, then asked, "About Mary, m'lord, she's not…?"

"No," Tony shook his head, "Mary is quite safe I promise you and is, as we speak, living with her mother."

"Thank God!" Mrs. Timms cried.

"Sir Braden dismissed her merely to get her out of the way," Tony assured her.

Mrs. Timms nodded. "But what about Mitchell, m'lord?" she asked, her face suddenly puckered in thought. "Are you sayin' that 'e wasn't dismissed after all?"

"We're not sure," Tony told her truthfully. "The thing is, Mrs. Timms," he said gently, "we have found no trace of him, and had he been dismissed and simply moved away he would doubtless have contacted the police after learning of Sir Philip's death because he would naturally have let him into the house that night. The fact he has not done so can only lead us to believe that he was…"

"Murdered!" she said with a resigned acceptance.

"I am afraid it looks very much as though that is the case," Tony confirmed quietly, "even though our investigations reveal that no unidentified body fitting his description has been found."

Taking a moment to dab at her eyes and vigorously blow her nose, Mrs. Timms looked from Bill to Jerry then back at Tony, saying firmly, "Well, if anyone's done away with Mitchell, I'd lay my life it's that Peterson!"

"Yes," Tony agreed, "we think so too."

"They'd no call to do that to 'im," she sniffed. "'Onest as the day's long 'e was and been with the family since I don't know when." She finished her tea, then, looking straight at Tony said, "And that poor girl! 'Er death may 'ave been an accident, but they'd no right to throw 'er body in an empty 'ouse like an old carpet, no matter 'ow 'er earned 'er livin'. Poor little mite," she shook her head, "they'd no right to do anythin' so wicked; they shouldn't ought to 'ave done it, m'lord!"

"No," Tony agreed wholeheartedly, "they should not."

"An' 'Er Ladyship," Mrs. Timms said unsteadily, wiping her nose, "when I think of what they did to 'er an' then threatenin' to 'ave 'er put away!"

"They have a lot to answer for," Tony told her, "and, with your help, we are going to make sure they *do* answer for their crimes." She raised tear-filled eyes to his warm and reassuring ones and felt greatly comforted. "So," he pressed gently, laying a hand on hers, "will you help us bring them to justice, Mrs. Timms?"

She nodded. "You may be sure of it, m'lord," she said firmly, "because no matter 'ow you look at it, what they've done is wrong! You just tell me what it is you want me to do, an' I will do it!"

"Four down, one to go!" Bill commented when Tony returned from seeing Mrs. Timms safely into a hackney. "Let's hope that Dawson is as easy to convince!"

Tony hoped so too, but when, twenty minutes later, Superintendent Dawson was shown in, it was not certain from his expression as he looked from one to the other what he was thinking much less whether he would be prepared to go along with them once he discovered the truth. Jerry may have no qualms about meeting Superintendent Dawson, in fact he was one of the very few senior officers who, apart from knowing what he was doing, had never had a run in with him, nevertheless he felt it prudent to suggest to Tony that he would probably find it easier to convince him if he made himself scarce. Tony cocked a laughing eye at Jerry who, totally unabashed, grinned, "Best be on the safe side, Guv!" whereupon he donned his hat and coat and made his way back to Cavendish Square.

Superintendent Dawson had been a police officer for a good many years, in fact if he was honest he would have to say for far more years than he cared to remember, even so, he was highly respected by those with whom he worked and, as Jerry had rightly pointed out, one of the few who knew precisely what he was doing. He was known for being thorough and tenacious, but he was also known, as often as not, to go with his instincts which, however much it irritated certain members of the police hierarchy, had nonetheless seen him solve the vast majority of the cases which had crossed his desk as well as a richly deserved promotion to superintendent and being awarded The Albert Medal. Over his long career he had naturally been in charge of any number of murder investigations and suspicious death enquiries, most of which had come under the full glare of the press and, whilst he was not claiming to have solved them all, he could say, and with justifiable pride, that he had apprehended the perpetrators in most cases.

With only two years left to his retirement it had tentatively been suggested by one or two in the corridors of power at Scotland Yard that he might like to consider sitting out the rest of his time at a desk in order to make room for a number of up and coming young men whose ideas were somewhat more forward thinking than his own, but which he knew to mean not so insubordinate and prepared to go their own way. Times and methods may have changed considerably since he was a young constable on the beat as well as during his time in the Criminal Investigation Department, but it was not new procedures or techniques you needed for apprehending criminals but a nose, a view which only exacerbated the frustration of those eager to be rid of him. It was this flagrant disregarding of the rules and shunning progressive innovations as well as his persistence in continuing to carry out his investigations in the same old way which, some said, only went to prove how important it was for him to step aside for far more open and pioneering minds. As he had no more liking for having his hand forced any more than he did for those who were trying to force it he had adamantly refused, a rejection which would have seen storm clouds gathering over his head had not the Commissioner of Police, Sir Edward Bradford, requested him, on the personal recommendation of the Prime Minister, Lord Salisbury, to conduct the investigation into the murder of Sir Philip Dunscumbe MP.

No one could say of Superintendent Dawson that he was either egotistical or prone to boasting of his achievements, on the contrary he was a man who expected neither praise nor reward for his work, but he would have been more than human had he not admitted to feeling that such an application, and from the Prime Minister himself, had certainly justified his methods in carrying out his duty. It certainly silenced those who were eager for him to step aside, but as time passed with him no nearer finding the perpetrator of such a vicious crime, much less a reason for it, their doubts as to his methods as well as his so-called instincts resurfaced with a vengeance proving once and for all that a man of his archaic techniques should hand the case over to a younger and far more energetic man. Sir Edward Bradford, a fairly easy-going man with a military background and a mind for administration, upon being earnestly requested to remove Dawson from the case on the grounds that Scotland Yard would be made a laughing stock over its failure to apprehend the murderer of so prominent a figure as Sir Philip Dunscumbe, MP, had maintained his faith in Superintendent Dawson as well as keeping his word to Lord Salisbury by firmly overruling their request.

Superintendent Dawson had applied the same diligence and commitment to the murder of Sir Philip Dunscumbe as he did to every case he handled, but in spite of his painstaking efforts and the vigorous investigation he had set in motion, he had been at a loss to find a reason for such a brutal crime, much less the perpetrator. It seemed that Sir Philip Dunscumbe, having left his rooms at Westminster, had simply disappeared off the face of the earth until his body had washed up at Greenwich three days later, with not even one eyewitness who saw or heard anything unusual. Everyone he had interviewed connected with Sir Philip, from his domestic staff and political colleagues as well as members of his club, including his personal and private secretary, could offer no indication as to his probable destination or the reason for his sudden departure from his rooms, which would help in his investigation. From what Superintendent Dawson had been able to discover, Sir Philip was meticulous in his political dealings with not even a hint of corruption attached to his name which could possibly give rise to a line of enquiry and, as far as his private life was concerned, apart from his natural shock and grief over his brother's suicide, there had been nothing in his behaviour prior to his death to suggest something was causing him concern. Superintendent Dawson could not even open a line of enquiry into any amorous affairs either past or present indicating a possible scandal was brewing as it seemed Sir Philip, unlike his brother, other than visiting his club, had led a very abstemious and quiet life in Curzon Street.

And so, after months of intense effort followed by a scrupulous re-examination of the facts and going over statements to try to piece them together into a clear picture, Superintendent Dawson was no nearer solving the murder of Sir Philip Dunscumbe than he ever was. He knew that certain individuals at Scotland Yard were only waiting for him to fail to prove their point, but it was not their personal expectations which concerned him so much as the fact that he had no liking for a case to remain unsolved, especially one as serious as murder. He may not be an arrogant or conceited man, but he would at least like to solve what bore all the hallmarks of being his last case, but although Jerry was right in that he had never known him turn a blind eye to new evidence or information, Superintendent Dawson had nevertheless been somewhat reluctant to agree to a meeting in Fleet Street to discuss the Dunscumbe case.

Superintendent Dawson had nothing against newspapers, in fact he could bring to mind a number of occasions when their coverage of a case had greatly assisted police investigations, but at the same time he could not deny that some of the less scrupulous reporters for those newspapers who were more concerned in selling copies than the truth, had only succeeded in impeding their lines of enquiry. However, this could not be said of *'The Daily Bulletin'* or *'The London Chronicler'*, their reputations, like *'The Times'* and *'The Daily Telegraph'* along with others, were above reproach and, after giving it a little further thought, he decided that he had nothing to lose by at least talking with this Lord Childon and if he had discovered something which would help him solve the case as Bill Pitman had indicated, then all well and good.

As only to be expected over the course of his long career,

Superintendent Dawson had either parried or answered questions put to him by reporters and even met several of the editors in Fleet Street on occasion, and he was certainly no stranger to Bill, but when he had told him that it was the owner of *'The Daily Bulletin'* and *'The London Chronicler'* who wanted to discuss the case with him, he had been a little surprised. It was seldom, if ever, the owner of a newspaper involved himself so particularly in a case, even one of such headline news as Sir Philip Dunscumbe's murder, and Superintendent Dawson could not help wondering if this half-English half-American lord was serious or just idling away the time until he returned to America when he could boast of being involved in a prominent murder case! However, it took no more than a matter of moments for him to sum Tony up and, deciding he liked what he saw and that he was very far from being the happy-go-lucky young aristocrat he had envisioned him to be playing at being a newspaperman or the amateur detective, Superintendent Dawson began to see that there was far more to this tall loose-limbed American than he had thought.

But Tony could not say the same of Superintendent Dawson, a tall and somewhat angular man he saw at a glance as being precisely what he was; a no-nonsense plain speaking guy who was not afraid to use the common sense he clearly possessed. There may well be those at Scotland Yard who regarded him as being what Tony would call a maverick cop who preferred to go his own way rather than follow a rule book, but there was no hiding the shrewdness in those deep-set dark grey eyes as they expertly weighed him up, during the course of which Tony neither flinched nor averted his eyes. As it seemed that each man approved of the other Tony was given some hope in that Superintendent Dawson may just be persuaded into going along with his plans after all, he hoped so because if he did not, then the chances of Collett and his associates getting away with murder seemed likely or, at least, for the time being.

As Bill had only said enough to arouse his curiosity sufficiently to persuade him into coming here this afternoon, Superintendent Dawson had only been able to surmise what Tony wanted to talk to him about regarding the Dunscumbe case, but to tell the truth he thought that at best it could only be to inform him that he had come across some evidence which had either been overlooked or just come to light, but at no time had he suspected the precise nature of what it was Tony wanted to discuss. Superintendent Dawson, being a man who firmly believed that members of the upper classes were just as capable of committing crimes the same as everyone else, the discovery that a man of Sir Braden Collett's reputation and standing in society had not only murdered Sir Philip Dunscumbe but was heavily involved in the supposed suicide of his brother as well as the death of one other victim, all of which had resulted from an accidental death which he had assisted in covering up, was by no means the shock as it had been for Mrs. Timms. Superintendent Dawson could not fault Tony's investigations any more than he could his explanation about recent events, which was concise and to the point, nevertheless, he could not help interrupting at certain points in Tony's narrative to clarify one or two details. He could not deny that Tony had presented a well compiled case, logically and meticulously put together and delivered in a way which left no doubt as to its veracity, but even though the disclosure may not have been what he had expected he knew it could neither be ignored nor dismissed, nonetheless, he felt it incumbent on him to point out one or two pertinent facts.

"I am sure you do not need me to tell you that Sir Braden Collett is a man of impeccable credentials and one, moreover," Dawson nodded significantly, "who has very influential friends; not to mention his association with the Prince of Wales?"

"I am well aware of his standing in society as well as his connections," Tony acknowledged, "but that does not alter the fact that he helped cover up the accidental death of Annie Myers to save both his and Dennis Dunscumbe's reputations as well as committing cold-blooded murder and being a party to two more and, let us not forget," he pointed out grimly, "the brutal treatment he regularly meted out to his wife!"

Superintendent Dawson could not argue against this, in fact the evidence Childon had uncovered about Sir Braden Collett's complicity was too strong for doubt, nevertheless, there was one aspect which he could not disregard if, for no other reason, than Collett's defence most certainly would not. In their efforts to defend their client they would stop at nothing to discredit Lord Childon by any means available thereby casting serious doubts on the claims he had put forward, and even though Dawson suspected that Childon was as aware of this as anyone, he nevertheless felt it incumbent upon him to raise it with him no matter how delicate. Slowly pulling out a box of matches from his pocket, he took a moment to light his pipe and only when he seemed satisfied that it was burning properly did he look up at Tony, eyeing him closely for a moment or two before enquiring, "Tell me, Lord Childon, just what is the precise nature of the relationship between you and Lady Collett?"

Tony, who had fully expected to be asked this question at some point as well as knowing the connotations which could be drawn from it and that Collett's defence would have no compunction in using it against him, replied unambiguously, "My relationship with Lady Collett has neither compromised her reputation nor undermined her as a witness."

"But you do have feelings for her," Dawson observed perceptively.

"Yes, I do," Tony nodded, "very much so."

"Would I be right in thinking then," Superintendent Dawson raised a bushy grey eyebrow, "that you have aspirations in that direction?"

"If by that you mean is it my intention to marry Lady Collett at some point in the future?" Tony replied evenly. "Then the answer is yes."

"So it could be construed," Dawson commented reasonably, fanning his pipe with his match box, "that your feelings for Lady Collett have somewhat clouded your judgement where Sir Braden is concerned, and that your accusations against him are nothing more than an attempt to discredit him in order to further your own ends regarding his wife."

"I have no doubt there are some who will construe that, yes," Tony replied composedly.

"Sir Braden's defence most certainly will," Dawson nodded, "as I am sure you are aware."

"Of course," Tony agreed, "that goes without saying, but if you are wondering whether the prospect of being harangued in the witness-box makes me want to retract everything I have said, it doesn't."

"I didn't suppose it," Superintendent Dawson assured him.

"But you do believe what I have told you?" Tony urged.

Taking a moment to relight his pipe, Dawson eyed Tony steadily before saying, "Since you do not strike me as being a man either prone to exaggeration or fabricating evidence to either suit your own ends or sell newspapers and I am not one who believes that a title precludes a man from breaking the law, you may take it that I do."

"Thank you, Superintendent," Tony nodded, relieved.

"However," Dawson inclined his head, "I feel it only fair to tell you that even if I had been a little reluctant to believe you, the attack on you this morning would have been enough to convince me as to the truth of it and that it proves how dangerous you have become to Sir Braden and his accomplices. You do realise, of course," he offered, giving Tony no time to respond, "that they could well try again."

"Yes, I realise that," Tony nodded.

"In that case, do you not think," Dawson suggested, "that it may perhaps be advisable to keep your head down for a while?"

Tony, unable to resist glancing across at Bill, whose expression was more than enough to not only bring a smile to his lips but to tell Dawson that trying to get Tony to do something was only guaranteed to make him do the complete opposite, looked back at Dawson, smiling, "Advisable, yes," he nodded, "but not at all convenient, Superintendent."

Superintendent Dawson had seen enough of Tony to know that he was not the type of man to hide himself away until the danger had passed and had therefore not needed to see the look on Bill's face to confirm his own opinion of the man who was looking a little amusingly at him, nevertheless, he felt it necessary to point out, "Convenient or not, next time you may not be put on your guard as you were this morning by Jerry Taylor's son."

"I have a lot to thank him for," Tony acknowledged, "but should the day ever dawn when I am caught napping by Peterson and his ilk, then I shall certainly deserve all they mete out."

Like Bill, Superintendent Dawson was coming to accept the inevitable in that trying to get Lord Childon to do something he was in no mind for was equivalent to leading a horse to water without making him drink so, instead, acknowledged, "You have put together a well compiled case, my lord, and in a remarkably short space of time."

"Only because over the last few days I have been put in the way of certain things which you have not," Tony assured him.

"All the same," Dawson added significantly, "you must know, as I do, that not only has it rendered you something of a threat to Sir Braden's peace of mind but also that his defence will do everything possible to discredit it by making great play of your feelings for Lady Collett and," he nodded, "my experience of defence barristers tells me that your relationship with Lady Collett will be the least of their allegations to try to besmirch you should this case ever get to court, which," he nodded, "is doubtful considering the ineligibility of your two witnesses, which," he sighed, "leaves us having to rely solely on Sir Braden and his associates stepping into the trap you want to bait them with in order for them to admit their own guilt, but you clearly know all this otherwise you would not have put such a proposal to me."

"And do you agree to my proposal?" Tony cocked an eyebrow.

Dawson thought a moment, saying at length, "Since there appears to be no other witnesses, and I am as loath as you to see cold-blooded murder go unanswered, yes."

Tony heaved a sigh of relief. "Thank you, Superintendent."

"Well," Dawson warned, "do not thank me yet because however much I believe it is the only way we shall bring Sir Braden Collett and his associates to account, laying a trap to ensnare a man of his reputation will require the approval of the Commissioner of Police."

"I realise that, but surely," Tony shook his head, "when he knows the circumstances he won't withhold it!"

"Sir Edward Bradford's a good man," Dawson told him, "but he will need convincing."

"Then convince him!" Bill shrugged.

"You may believe me when I tell you that I shall certainly try to do so," Dawson replied. He thought a moment. "Tell me," he raised an enquiring eyebrow at Tony, "did you believe Hallerton when he told you why he had not mentioned that letter to me?"

"Yes," Tony nodded, crossing one leg over the other, "I did. I also believe he was telling the truth when he said that the reason he did not tell you about it once the shock of Sir Philip's death had worn off a little was because he thought the letter may contain something harmful to either Sir Philip or his brother and therefore did not want to risk damaging Sir Philip's reputation."

"Nevertheless," Dawson sighed, inspecting his pipe, "it's a pity that he withheld such vital information in a murder investigation, had he not have done so then, as you rightly said," he acknowledged, "it is more than likely this matter would have been concluded by now."

Tony could not deny that when he spoke to Hallerton he was himself rather vexed to think that through his failure to tell the police about that letter he had not only withheld vital information from them which could have closed this matter long since, but had also ensured that Eleanor's unbearable existence had unnecessarily been prolonged. Now though, having given it more thought, Tony could see very little to be gained by charging Hallerton with something which had stemmed from the best of motives and not deliberately intended to impede the police with their enquiries, but when he pointed this fact out to Superintendent Dawson he replied noncommittally, "I shall of course decide what action, if any, to take against him once I have interviewed him again. So that letter," he said thoughtfully, as though there had been no digression, "is what took Sir Philip out of his rooms that day?"

"Yes," Tony replied. "However," he admitted, "it was not until I spoke to Miss Simms that I learned he went straight to see her in response to that letter rather than arrange a time and date as she had suggested. As we now know," he nodded, "it was due to what she told him that Sir Philip called on Sir Braden in Cavendish Square accusing him of being in some way responsible for his brother's death as well as how he fully intended to raise questions in the House about the kind of establishments he and his brother frequented. I can only assume," Tony shrugged, "that Sir Philip did not tell Collett from whom he received his information about his brother's death, had he have done so," he sighed, "then Miss Simms would have most probably been dealt with in the same way as the others!"

Superintendent Dawson nodded his head, then, after pursing his lips in thought, asked, "What makes you so sure this Miss Simms told you the truth?"

"Because Superintendent," Tony told him frankly, "apart from the fact that I trust my own judgement, I have been in the newspaper business long enough to know when someone is lying. Not only that," he nodded, "but her fear of Eliza Boon was not feigned but very real, and until she is finally arrested and no longer around to pose a threat, Miss Simms remains in fear of her; the same goes for Sir Braden and Peterson. All three of them," he pointed out, "have too much lose to ignore the danger Miss Simms poses should they ever discover what she knows."

"So," Dawson said thoughtfully, "they silenced Dennis Dunscumbe because he threatened to report what had happened to Annie Myers."

"Yes," Tony nodded. "It seems that his attack of conscience was something they had not bargained for."

"Nor apparently was your intervention," Dawson nodded significantly, "and," he pointed out, "neither was Miss Simms!" He considered a moment. "About Mitchell, I shall of course make some enquiries, but it is doubtful if they will establish anything more than your own. I would say," he nodded, "that we shall only discover Mitchell's whereabouts or that of his body when we interview Peterson, but what I don't quite understand," he frowned, "is why kill him in the first place, assuming they did?"

"I think we can safely take it that they did," Tony said firmly, "as for why," he shrugged, "it can only be because he let Sir Philip into the house that night and once he learned of his brutal death he would have been bound to know that Sir Braden was most probably the last man to see him alive especially as he did not show him out. He may not have been able to give the police chapter and verse, but he certainly knew enough, or so Collett and the others believed, to do them tremendous damage."

"And you say Lady Collett has no idea why her husband murdered Sir Philip?" Dawson questioned.

"No, none," Tony shook his head. "She knows nothing about Annie Myers and the others and, I am pretty sure," he added firmly, "that she has no idea her husband frequented such an establishment."

"Well," Dawson sighed, putting another light to his pipe, "there's no denying it's going to come as a shock to her when…"

"Superintendent," Tony interrupted, "I know you will have to speak to her at some point, but if you have no objection I would much rather tell Lady Collett the truth myself first."

Dawson considered this a moment as he pulled on his pipe. "Very well," he agreed, then, nodding his head, pointed out, "but even though her evidence will count for nothing in court I shall, as you rightly say, need to speak to her myself, in fact," he told him, "I shall need to speak to Lady Collett before I approach Bradford to approve this plan of yours, and indeed," he nodded, "to this Miss Simms," an announcement which came as no surprise to Tony.

Tony had every intention of telling Eleanor the truth as well as hearing her account of what actually happened that night, but he had so far refrained from doing so because he much preferred to wait until she was feeling a little stronger. Now though, there was no time for that as Sir Edward Bradford would need all the corroborative evidence he could get his hands on before sanctioning their scheme, and since time was of the essence Tony knew there was nothing he could do but agree to Superintendent Dawson visiting in Mount Street tomorrow morning to officially interview her following his visit to Holborn to interview Miss Simms.

Having given Tony his assurance that he need have no concerns about him compromising Miss Simms given she was at risk and also that due to Lady Collett's present condition and the circumstances surrounding her stay in Mount Street he need have no fears about his discreet handling of the interview, he immediately followed this up with the heartfelt utterance that in view of what Tony had told him about her maid being found alive, he would not have to relate any further bad news to her than was necessary. It was just as he was about to take his leave that he looked at Tony, asking curiously, "Just one thing, my lord," to which Tony raised an enquiring eyebrow, "are you seriously telling me that you have actually managed to persuade three newspaper editors," waving a copy of the notice Tony had handed him to show the Commissioner, "as well as a member of Sir Braden's domestic staff to go along with this scheme of yours?"

Tony smiled. "'Fraid so, Superintendent."

Dawson sighed. "I don't suppose it's any use asking you to tell me how you managed it?"

"Huh huh," Tony grinned, "no can do, Superintendent."

"No," Dawson sighed again, "I thought not," whereupon he shook hands and left.

Chapter Twenty-Three

Doctor Little may well be pleased with Eleanor's progress, in fact the speed with which her injuries were healing far exceeded his expectations, especially when he recalled the serious condition she had been in when he first attended on her, even so, he was most reluctant to accede to her request that she be allowed to get out of bed in favour of resting on the day bed, particularly when his examination established that she was still experiencing pain from her cracked rib. Left to Beatrice and Sarah she would most definitely have remained where she was for a little longer, but Eleanor, earnestly stressing that she was not an invalid and felt certain she would recover more quickly if allowed to leave her bed, eventually managed to persuade that diligent professional to allow it.

Sarah, who really had taken to her patient for her own sake and not simply because of Mr. Tony, clucked and tutted and prophesied disaster in leaving her bed too soon, but Beatrice, having given it a little more thought, decided that it may not be such a bad thing after all and, following a quick inspection of her own wardrobe, pulled out a rose pink dressing gown she no longer wore for her friend's use. Pursing her lips in disapproval, Sarah reluctantly helped her patient out of bed and into the bath which had not long before been brought up and placed in front of the fire, muttering and scolding as she gently sponged Eleanor's bruised and aching body, rounding off her catalogue of protests as she wrapped a huge towel around her by stating that it was no use coming crying to her if she suffered a relapse which, Sarah nodded vigorously, would not surprise her in the least. "Yes," she said briskly as Eleanor gave a little laugh, "you can't fool me into thinking that it's not for Mr. Ton… I mean His Lordship," she amended hastily, "that you're in a hurry to leave your bed." Eleanor coloured slightly, but Sarah, an incurable romantic at heart, softened her scolding by saying indulgently,

"Not that it matters to him one bit because he's quite betwattled about you as it is!" Had she have seen Tony when he entered Eleanor's room upon his return to Mount Street several hours later she would have seen with her own eyes just how right she was.

Tony, lingering only long enough to ascertain from Harry that nothing untoward had occurred as a result of his encounter with Peterson, then asked him to wait a few minutes while he wrote a note that he wanted him to hand deliver tonight to which Harry, who, like his father and brothers, had taken a real liking to Tony, nodded his head. Taking only moments to scribble a few lines in Tom's study, Tony returned to the hall just as Harry was shrugging himself into his overcoat who, after safely depositing the envelope into his inside pocket and promising to deliver it, grinned, "Fancy me goin' to an 'ouse in Belgravia! Who'd 'ave thought it?" Tony laughed, then, following some words of caution for him to be careful, closed the front door behind him and went in search of his sister to give her a brief account of the day's events and to allay any remaining fears she may have, carefully omitting telling her about his run-in that morning. Beatrice had suspected that the police would at some stage have to speak to Eleanor, but she had not thought it would be so soon, and could not help saying a little worriedly, "Yes of course I realise it is very necessary, but I do hope he will be patient with her. She is still far from well."

"I know," Tony nodded, "and I would do anything to spare her such an ordeal, but apart from the fact that she is a vital witness to a murder, in fact the *only* witness to Sir Philip's murder, Dawson's an okay guy."

As Beatrice trusted Tony implicitly she did not question it further, but could not help reiterating her fears for his safety, particularly as matters seemed to be coming to a head, a circumstance he seemed totally unperturbed about. She knew perfectly well that Tony was more than capable of taking care of himself, but had she known that he had been attacked it would have upset her very much, but her brother, affectionately casting aside her entreaties to him to be careful, kissed her forehead, saying, "Never mind about me, what did Doctor Little have to say about Eleanor?"

Beatrice was naturally pleased to be able to tell him that Doctor Little had found his patient recovering quite nicely, however, upon hearing her expressed wish to be allowed to leave her bed he had been extremely reluctant to allow it, but after cautiously conveying his doubts he had finally allowed Eleanor to persuade him into permitting it. Tony was naturally relieved to learn that Doctor Little was very pleased with her progress, but upon learning that she had cajoled him into allowing her to rest on the day bed instead of remaining in bed a little longer a worried frown creased Tony's forehead, to which Beatrice sighed, "I am afraid she was most insistent, and whilst at first I was doubtful as to the wisdom of it, I do feel that she may indeed recover more speedily by not feeling quite such an invalid."

Ascending the stairs a few minutes later with a leisureliness which completely belied his eagerness to see Eleanor, Tony opened the door to her room following his brief tap, whereupon the worried crease on his forehead instantly lifted.

The swelling to Eleanor's lips, which had receded over the last twenty-four hours together with her fully opened left eye, had certainly gone a long way to restoring the symmetry of her face, but as Tony looked at her now he could see that during the day her right eye had partially opened while the bruises, thanks to the arnica regularly applied by Sarah, had faded to the point where only a blue-yellowish tinge was visible and would, over the next few days, disappear completely. Even though her cheeks were still rather puffy and the cut not quite healed, it was certainly a heavy weight off his mind to know that she was recovering from Collett's brutal beating, but the sight of her resting on the day bed wearing a soft cashmere dressing gown in a deep rose pink with her head eagerly turned in his direction and her hair dressed and carefully arranged by Sarah's clever and deft fingers to hide the gash on her head, made Tony catch his breath. "So," he mused, closing the door behind him, "I've got mutiny on my hands, have I?" walking over to the day bed.

"Well, not mutiny precisely." Eleanor smiled, blushing a little at the look in his eyes as he sat down beside her, taking hold of her left hand in his. "You see," she explained in response to his raised eyebrow, "Doctor Little was very pleased with my progress and therefore felt persuaded into allowing me out of bed."

"Oh, I see," Tony teased affectionately, his eyes laughing down into hers, "is that how it was?" She nodded. "It couldn't be," he shook his head doubtfully, "that it was *you* who convinced *him?*"

She looked contrite and bit her bottom lip. "Oh, Beatrice told you?"

"Mm," he nodded, "Bea told me."

She stole a glance up at him from under her lashes asking, not a little shyly, "Aren't you pleased to see me out of bed?"

"You must know I am," he told her warmly, kissing the hand he was holding, "it's just that I don't want you doing too much too soon; it's still very early days."

"Yes, I know," she nodded, "but I promise not to do anything I should not." She felt the pressure of his fingers on her hand and, giving him a shy little smile, confessed, "I… I looked at myself in the mirror today."

"Did you?" he asked softly. "And what did you see?"

"Well," she said a little thoughtfully, "I don't think I look quite such a fright as I must have when you first brought me here."

"No," Tony said lovingly, "not *quite* such a fright."

"No," she agreed a little unsteadily. "Do you think I look better?"

"I think you look adorable," he told her in a deep voice.

"Y-you do?" she managed, thrilling at these words, her trembling fingers in his telling him precisely what she was feeling.

"Mm," he nodded, "although," he mused, screwing up his face as if in an effort of memory, "I thought I told you so this morning, in fact," he told her, giving her hand an affectionate little shake, "I'm sure of it." He hesitated for a moment as if deliberating something, but upon seeing the colour deepen in her cheeks as she nodded her head in confirmation of this it was as if the decision whether or not to kiss her was no longer his to make, being taken out of his hands by a force stronger than himself and, slowly lowering his head, he gently brushed her lips with his own.

If Eleanor thought that the feather-like stroke of his thumb against her lips before he had said goodbye this morning was stirring, then the delicate, almost elusive touch of Tony's lips against her own, so very different to Braden's ruthless and brutal demands, proved how wrong she was; the fluttering of excitement coursing through her, the like of which she had never experienced, causing something between a cry and sob to leave her lips, feeling just a little bereft when Tony eased himself away from her.

"What is it?" he asked softly. "Didn't you want me to kiss you?" When she did not answer straightaway he said quietly, "I'm sorry, perhaps it *was* a little too soon."

"No," she managed somewhat huskily, her fingers gripping his, "oh, no!"

"Then what is it?" he asked gently. "Didn't you like it?"

"Yes," she assured him a little breathlessly, "oh, yes I… I liked it very much; it… it's just that…"

"Just what?" he urged softly, his eyes warm and dark and telling her the most marvellous things.

"It's just… well, I… I never knew a kiss could be like that," she told him breathlessly.

"Like what?" he pressed.

"So… so beautiful and… and exciting!" she told him unsteadily.

"Well, it can, and just to prove it's no fluke," he smiled, lowering his head, "I am going to do it again."

It may not have been a passionate kiss, on the contrary it was extremely light and gentle, but those delicate caresses against her receptive lips were electrifying enough to set her whole body tingling in excitement, filling her with the need to be closer to him, and instinctively brought her free hand up to rest flat against his chest.

"You see," he said gently, when his lips released hers, "it was no fluke."

"No," she huskily confirmed at length, "it… it was no fluke."

Tony looked thoughtfully down at her for a moment before saying a little doubtfully, "Mm, I don't know though," shaking his head, the look in his eyes as they searched her flushed face thrillingly contradicting his pensive expression, sending a quiver of awareness running through her, "I could be wrong," he said on a deep sigh, covering the trembling hand resting against his chest with his left one, "but although you say it was no fluke I somehow get the feeling you are not quite sure."

"Do you?" she asked, raising a surprised eyebrow, realising that this affectionate teasing, which had up until now not only been absent in her life but which she had unconsciously longed for, was very stimulating.

"Mm," he nodded. "Of course," he sighed again, "if you don't like my kisses then there is nothing more to be said; a great blow to my vanity, that's all," he shrugged, his eyes laughing down into hers, "but if it is simply a case of you needing more convincing then…" Upon feeling her fingers move in his and hearing the little choked laugh which left her lips, he said in the voice of one forced into doing something which he knew to be completely pointless, "Very well," he conceded, "I shall try once more to convince you, but, quite frankly," he told her, his voice deepening as he lowered his head, "I think I am wasting my time," giving her no opportunity to respond by gently kissing her. "Do you still doubt it or that I love you?" he asked lovingly when he released her lips.

"No," she breathed huskily, making no effort to stop him when he released her hands for him to gather her in his arms and kiss her again.

Had Doctor Little witnessed this scene he would have known no hesitation in reminding his patient that being held in a passionate embrace was hardly conducive to repairing a cracked rib, and when he had reluctantly acceded to her request to leave her bed so she could rest on the day bed this was not what he had in mind. His erring patient, however, was not only perfectly happy to overlook any discomfort in the arms of the man she loved as she welcomed his kisses, but gave not a moment's thought to that diligent professional's advice about resting being the best remedy to aiding her recovery and nor, from the looks of it, did the man holding her close against him and agreeably kissing her.

Tony's assertion to Superintendent Dawson that his relationship with Lady Collett had not compromised her reputation was true in that he had not singled her out in public giving anyone the least cause to suspect that an affair had begun between them or, if not that, then imminent. He may want to make love to her with every fibre of his being, but the truth was he did not want an affair with Eleanor; he loved her and wanted to make her his wife, and since no one beyond the confines of thirty-six Mount Street knew anything about their feelings for one another, much less that she was taking sanctuary under his sister's roof, her reputation would remain intact and he for one was fully determined it stayed that way. Loving Eleanor as much as he did, Tony knew that such a resolve would put a great strain on his self-control, but he knew too that should he not do so then he would be totally unworthy of the woman without whom he could not imagine the rest of his life.

Eleanor, resting her head comfortably against Tony's shoulder with his arms still wrapped around her several minutes later, did not need reminding that she was a married woman and therefore not free to love another man, but the truth was she was conscious of only one thing and that was she was where she wanted to be, now and always. Unfortunately, as matters stood at this moment she realised all too painfully that it was as impractical to look forward to a life with Tony as it was impossible to predict what was going to happen in the immediate future with regards to Braden and the brutal killing of Sir Philip Dunscumbe, but one thing she did know and that was no matter what the outcome of this, she could not return to Cavendish Square.

She shrewdly suspected that Tony knew far more than he had told her, nor was she blinded to the fact that any future they had together could only be realised once Braden had been found guilty and punished for the brutal murder of Sir Philip Dunscumbe because if he were not, there was no possibility of him ever agreeing to a divorce. Even though she was very far from conversant with the requisites of the law she knew enough to be certain that as Braden's wife her evidence would go for nothing, and so she had no idea how Tony and the police would begin to prove Braden guilty of such a vicious crime. Her feelings for Braden might be very far removed from love or even liking, but whilst it was horrifying enough to know that even a man of his aggressive and bullying nature had murdered someone for no reason she could see, to know that he had been a party to three more deaths would have profoundly shocked her. Eleanor was not at all sure whether to feel relief or not that her evidence would carry little or no weight in a court of law even though she had the sneaking suspicion she would be interviewed by the police because although she knew that such a serious matter as murder could not go unanswered, to find herself being required to stand up in the witness-box and give evidence which would see her husband hang, albeit a man who had bullied and beaten her consistently, was something one of her gentle nature could not contemplate without a shudder. Not only that, but her fear of Braden was very real and somewhere at the back of her mind was the disturbing thought that should she be required to give evidence after all and Braden was ultimately discharged of murder in spite of it, then she could not see him letting such a humiliation pass.

Tony had a very good idea of what was going through her mind and although he did his best to dispel her fears he knew as well as she did that the memory of that night would stay with her for a long time, not only that, but any future they had together was totally dependent upon factors which were, for the most part at least, outside their control. He was confident that Sir Edward Bradford would see that the plan outlined by Superintendent Dawson was really the only chance they had of bringing Sir Braden Collett and the others to justice for such brutal crimes, and would give it his approval. Tony was equally confident in that Sir Braden, once having read the article in his newspapers announcing that due to new evidence having come to light the police were reopening the case of Dennis Dunscumbe's suicide which meant they would be revisiting his home in Hertford Street where he had allegedly taken his own life, he dared not ignore it and would try to gain admittance to the house before the police arrived to assure himself that

Peterson had left nothing incriminating which the police could use against them. Tony had not needed Superintendent Dawson, or Bea for that matter, to tell him what conclusions society would draw when it became known that he and his newspapers had been responsible in the downfall of a man whose wife he fully intended to marry, and although Tony cared nothing for the gossip which would follow, whether ill-informed or not, he wanted to shield Eleanor from it as much as he could. Of course, if their plans failed, then not only would three felons escape the law, but it would mean his chances of marrying Eleanor were going to be anything other than straightforward as Sir Braden Collett could most certainly be relied upon to not only refuse to sanction a divorce but make things extremely difficult for her, and should Eleanor file for one, on no matter what grounds, even supposing it was in fact granted, it would open her up to vicious criticism.

But all this was for the future; right now the important thing was to acquaint Eleanor with the truth and to tell her about Superintendent Dawson's visit tomorrow morning, but first Tony needed to hear from her own lips what had actually happened that night, and when he gently asked her if she was feeling up to confirming what he knew as being pretty much the truth, she nodded and haltingly began telling him what she had witnessed upon her return home from the concert earlier than expected.

"So, I was right; you *did* walk in on it," Tony said gently, holding her as tightly as he dared.

"Yes," she nodded. Then, taking several moments to compose herself, told him falteringly, "There was b-blood on Sir Philip's head and on the c-carpet, and Braden," she managed faintly, "was still holding the poker, and there was blood on his hands and his shirt and w-waistcoat. Oh, Tony," she cried, "it was horrible!" burying her face into his chest, her body shivering at the recollection, taking comfort from his strong arms as they held her closer to him. "I remember screaming and r-running t-towards the door to g-get help, but B-Braden stopped me and c-clamped his hand over my mouth before hitting me. I… I don't remember anything else," she mumbled into his chest, "until I opened my eyes the next m-morning to find Braden and that w-woman in my room."

The disjointed account of what followed came as no surprise to Tony. It seemed that right from the very beginning Collett and Eliza Boon had threatened her into silence by telling her they would have her put away as well as exposing her father and, not content with this, they had cold-bloodedly kept her a virtual prisoner. He could well imagine what life must have been like for her these past months, made even more intolerable by Collett's regular cruelty, but he had told Beatrice no less than the truth the other night when he said that nothing or no one was going to hurt Eleanor ever again, and he for one was going to make sure of it. The last thing Tony wanted was to add to her distress by telling her about the sequence of events which had led to Collett murdering Sir Philip, but just as he was striving to find the right words he felt Eleanor move in his arms and raise her head to look up at him, her face a little flushed and her eyes sparkling with tears. "Tony, can I ask you something?"

"Sure you can," he smiled, "anything," gently removing a strand of hair off her face before tenderly kissing her forehead.

"You said you knew why Braden had murdered Sir Philip." Her left hand clasped the lapel of his coat. "Is… is that true?"

"Yes," he nodded, "it's true," his right hand covering the agitated fingers gripping his lapel.

Taking comfort from his warm strength, she swallowed, faltering. "It's just that… well… I… I need to know and…"

"It's all right," he soothed, "I realise you need to know the truth to help you understand why they have treated you in the way they have." She nodded, giving a little sniff. "I had every intention of telling you," he said considerately, "but I wanted to wait until you were feeling strong enough." After assuring him she quite understood this, she falteringly told him that she would much rather hear what she suspected was going to be bad news now than later, Tony told her as gently as he could the awful truth surrounding Sir Philip's death.

But the shuddering sobs which racked her body as she clung to Tony bore adequate testimony to the fact that the awful truth was so very far removed from what she had expected that she could barely take it in. Tony knew that she was no coward, but if there had been any way he could have spared her this he would, but as she was bound to discover the truth at some point he would far rather Eleanor hear it from him than in a court of law, forcefully presented by the prosecution and heatedly disputed by the defence or reading it in the newspapers.

Shocked and dazed by all she had heard, Eleanor, taking solace from Tony's comforting arms as they held her close to him, cried uncontrollably into his shoulder, her mind too numb to take it all in, not at all certain which aspect of it appalled her the most. It had been bad enough witnessing her husband committing a most brutal act of violence, but that he had been party to other vicious crimes was too base even to contemplate. His regular visits to an establishment, presided over by the very woman who had been nothing short of her gaoler all these months, almost took her breath away, but although it came as a terrible shock it seemed as nothing in comparison to the callous treatment they had meted out to Annie Myers or the coldly calculated death of Dennis Dunscumbe. It was of course a tremendous relief to know that her dear Mary, as much a friend as an attendant, was safe and well, but the thought of Mitchell, who had never done anyone any harm and who had proved himself a very good friend to her, had been pitilessly and viciously done away with for no other reason than he had let Sir Philip into the house, shocked her to the core. "I can't believe it!" she cried into Tony's shoulder, when she had recovered a little from the shock. "It's worse than I thought!"

"I wish I could have spared you this," Tony pressed against her hair, "but…"

"No," she sniffed, easing herself a little away from him, "I… I had to know. I needed to make some sense of it all. It… it's just such a shock," her eyes reflecting the horror she felt. "I… I never suspected anything like this!" she cried. "Eliza Boon too!" She shook her head, bewildered. "When I think… oh, Tony, it has all been so horrible!" she sobbed. "The look in her eyes whenever she… oh, I couldn't bear her to come anywhere near me!" She shuddered at the recollection.

"I know," Tony said soothingly, gently lifting her chin with his forefinger to allow him to tenderly wipe away her tears, "but there is no further need for you to fear Eliza Boon."

Despite her valiant attempt to calm herself, Eleanor was palpably distressed, as Tony had known she would be and, as he held her securely against him, his nearness giving her the comfort and solace which no words possibly could, he was content to just hold her as she gave in to the natural repercussions such a shock had brought about. It was clear from her distraught outpourings that she had been afraid of Eliza Boon from the moment she had opened her eyes the morning following Sir Philip's murder to find her standing beside Braden in her room, and had continued to be afraid of her. It was not only because she never allowed Eleanor out of her sight as well as threatening her with all manner of dire consequences if she did not do as she was told, but because she had seen from the outset that Eliza Boon had taken a more than ordinary liking to her, but apart from assisting Eleanor with her dress, something she would have dispensed with had it been at all possible, Eliza Boon had at no point raised a hand against her or attempted to further her partiality. Just as Tony had rightly supposed, at no time had Eleanor entertained the idea that her husband had sought extramarital amusement, and certainly not the kind presided over by Eliza Boon at her establishment in Periton Place, a woman who had not only generated so much fear in her, but had proved more than once just how ruthless she was. But no matter how difficult Eleanor found it to understand Braden's preference for such aggressive amusement, it certainly explained his rough treatment of her in and out of the bedroom, experiences she was in no hurry to repeat, the very thought of which made her recoil. Even now, folded safely in Tony's arms, she shrank from the look she had seen in Eliza Boon's eyes whenever Braden had beaten her in her presence and, for the first time, Eleanor was now able to fully comprehend the meaning of that glint which had lurked in those cold sharp eyes. She could well imagine Eliza Boon's detached indifference upon discovering the death of that poor young woman and her equally callous unconcern in instructing Peterson to dispose of her body, and because of her own experiences at Eliza Boon's hands Eleanor knew she must have displayed the same lack of sympathy in dealing with Sir Philip Dunscumbe's body and his brother's death and, regrettably, Mitchell's.

It was all too horrendous to contemplate, but gradually Eleanor became less agitated and after blowing her nose in Tony's already mangled handkerchief, managed unsteadily to ask him several questions, which he did his best to answer without distressing her further. No one knew Braden's temper better than she did and how he frequently failed to keep it under control, and that his customary method of venting his anger was in adopting brutal tactics which had more than once required her to keep to her room, but until that never to be forgotten evening she had never believed him capable of murder. To witness such a cold-blooded act had been a horrifying experience, but to discover that her husband had been a party to two more brutal deaths resulting from his collusion in assisting to cover up the accidental death of a young woman was devastating, but no matter how carefully Tony expressed his answers to her questions nothing could disguise the awful truth of Braden's actions.

Tony had tried his best to break such dreadful news as gently as possible, but he knew no words of his could really minimise either the seriousness or the magnitude of what Collett and the others had done or the shock it had engendered in the woman he would give his life to protect. Tony understood Eleanor's need to know why she had been kept a virtual prisoner only too well, but whilst it would be some time before she would be able to put such an appalling episode behind her, he had every hope that in time it would become nothing but a memory, if not entirely forgotten, then at least far distant enough to no longer hurt her. But although she now knew the truth about her husband's crimes there remained the task of proving him and his accomplices guilty, and whilst Tony had no intention at this stage of telling her any more than he had told Beatrice, it was essential for Eleanor to know the difficulties they faced in trying to bring them to justice and why it was so important that Superintendent Dawson had to speak to her. Knowing she was safe in Mount Street as well as being acquainted with the truth may be the beginning of Eleanor's emotional recuperation, but considering her distress Tony could only hope that being questioned by a police officer about her husband's crimes would not impede that recovery, but upon informing her of the Superintendent's intended visit tomorrow morning, it was clear that she had expected it.

"I thought perhaps I would be," she managed unsteadily, "but Tony," she urged, laying a hand on his arm, her eyes a little fearful as they looked up at him, "about going to court; I… I know you said that Miss Simms's evidence could easily be discounted and that my evidence w-would not be admissible b-because it… it is damaging to Braden, but…"

"Ssh," Tony soothed, covering her hand with his warm one, "you must not worry over that."

"It's just… well," she faltered, "I know what Braden and the others have done is not only unpardonable but very wicked and that they have to answer for their crimes, but I could not b-bear to think that I sent them to the g-gallows!"

"My darling," Tony said softly, "they did that themselves the moment they murdered Dennis Dunscumbe. You have nothing to blame or reproach yourself for. Do not forget," he reminded her, "you too are a victim of their scheming."

Eleanor shuddered at the recollection, trying not to think what would have happened to her had Tony not come along when he did because honesty compelled her to admit that she had long past the point where anything was preferable to such an existence. Between them, Braden and Eliza Boon together with Peterson, had rendered her life intolerable; the beatings which had kept her to the house, being frequently locked into her room, never being allowed out alone even to go shopping and, worse, the fear they had instilled into her heart by threatening her with being committed as well as warning her as to what her father could expect if she failed to do as she was told, all of which haunted her dreams. Even now, safely installed in Mount Street, her fear of them was such that she could not entirely rid herself of the thought that they would not make another attempt to remove her, but not only this, she failed to see how such cold and ruthless people could be brought to step calmly into whatever trap Tony was planning to set for them, providing of course it was approved. However, Tony's calm assurances that he had no doubt it would be, particularly when Sir Edward realised it was the only way of proving Collett and the others guilty, then it was a foregone conclusion they would fall into it, if for no other reason than they could not afford to ignore anything which could possibly incriminate them, reassured her.

"I… I thought I knew w-what Braden was c-capable of," she faltered, "but never anything like this!"

"A man who can beat his wife without the least compunction," Tony said reasonably, "is capable of anything, which is why, my darling," he smiled fondly, "even if he had not committed murder, there is no way I can let you return to a brute of a man who deserves to be horsewhipped for what he has done to you."

"I couldn't bear it!" she cried fervently, shivering at the thought.

"Neither could I," Tony told her with feeling, laying the palm of his hand against her cheek, his eyes warm as they looked down at her. "When I told you that you are stuck with me, I meant it; and that, my darling," he nodded, "means permanently!"

She covered his hand with her own, saying lovingly, "I like the idea of being stuck with you permanently."

"So do I," he concurred in a deep voice, taking her back in his arms and tenderly kissing her.

"You will be with me tomorrow when this Superintendent calls, won't you?" she asked huskily when he finally released her.

"You know I will," Tony assured her, not very hopeful of this considering the relationship between them, but deeming it wiser to keep this to himself said, "but there's nothing to worry you I promise; he's an okay guy."

She did not doubt it, but no sooner had Tony left her some minutes later than all her uncertainties and fears returned. Her knowledge as well as her experience of Braden were such that she only felt safe when Tony was with her and whilst she knew he could not remain by her side all the time, it was nevertheless true to say that when she was alone she could not entirely banish her fears from her mind. Like Beatrice, Eleanor had not the least idea that Braden and Eliza Boon had set Peterson on to attack Tony with a view to putting him out of the way, had she done she would not have relaxed at all, but if nothing else it would certainly have reinforced her conviction that, despite Tony's assurances that Braden was in no position to either ignore or discount whatever plan he was setting in motion, he was not so reckless as to calmly step into it. She had every faith in Tony, but no one knew Braden better than she did, a man who had so far proved himself to be one of infinite resource, were it otherwise he would surely have answered for his crimes long since!

Beatrice, who knew no more than Eleanor as to what Tony had in mind for Collett and the others, kept her word by not teasing him into telling her, but had she the slightest idea that her husband, whose innocent demeanour over dinner gave her no cause for suspicion, had freely offered his services to her brother, she would not have been so complacent. Tom, shrewdly suspecting that his brother-in-law had not told Beatrice and Eleanor the full sum of the day's events, refrained from questioning him until they were alone after dinner, but upon learning that Peterson had lain in wait for him, although it had not prompted Tom into withdrawing his services, on the contrary he was as determined as he ever was, it nevertheless seriously alarmed him. Knowing Tony as well as he did, Tom was not at all surprised to find his warnings about another such attack being attempted cast aside as most unlikely. Whilst he could not argue that Collett would very soon have more to worry about than silencing his brother-in-law, assuming of course Tony's plan was given the thumbs up, Tom nevertheless felt it necessary to point out that although Collett had no idea that a trap was being set for him, there was still enough time between now and when it was actually put into operation for him to try again, adding, somewhat forcefully, "For God's sake Tony! The very fact that he sent Peterson after you surely goes to prove he suspected you of knowing the truth before you told Peterson you were coming after them and the danger you pose!"

"I don't know so much," Tony said thoughtfully, inclining his head, a smile entering his eyes as he watched Tom struggle for words, but giving him no time to find any told him what he had told Bill and Jerry in that

Collett, who was by no means stupid, would know that there had been no time for Eleanor to tell him what she had seen that night and therefore there was no way he could have found out about Annie Myers and the others, and so sending Peterson to waylay him had been more in the way of silencing the messenger.

"Even more so now that she has!" Tom said candidly. "And, stupid or not," he reminded him, "Collett knows that it's only a matter of time before she does, but Bill's right," he nodded, "Collett may not know how much, if anything, you have deduced much less knowing about this scheme of yours, but just because their attempt to rid themselves of you this morning failed doesn't mean they won't try again; and next time," Tom warned, "you may not be so lucky in having Jerry's son close at hand!"

"So, what are you saying, Tom?" Tony raised an eyebrow. "That I hide myself away until it's all over? Huh huh," he shook his head, "nothing doing! Between them, they have frightened Eleanor to death until she's too terrified to fight back, well," he nodded, "they don't frighten me and I *can* fight back and," he said firmly, "that's precisely what I'm going to do!"

"Even if the police don't approve of your plan?" Tom enquired.

"Even if they don't approve of my plan," Tony confirmed unequivocally.

Tom knew that Tony was neither stupid nor lacking in intelligence and that he was perfectly aware of the risks he was running, but Tom knew Tony too well to try to change his mind about keeping his head down, but if he was honest he could not blame Tony for taking such a rigid stance, in fact, had he been in his shoes he would do precisely the same thing. It came as no surprise to Tom to learn that Tony had not told his sister or Eleanor about his run in this morning with Peterson, not only because he did not want to worry them but also because he was not the type of man to boast about such an encounter. What did surprise Tom however, was Sir Miles Tatton's conduct which, no matter how one looked at it, went far beyond an indiscretion, in fact it contravened every code by which a gentleman lived, so much so that not even his temporary loss of rationality could possibly excuse or condone what was nothing short of a contemptible transgression, but if nothing else it at least explained why he had sanctioned Eleanor's marriage to Sir Braden Collett. Even though their paths had crossed many times, Tom could not claim to be on anything like intimate terms with Sir Miles

Tatton, even so, it seemed to him a pretty rum do when a father was willing to sacrifice his daughter to a man like Collett merely to save his reputation. In fact, so disgusted was Tom that he knew no hesitation in telling Tony that Sir Miles had, however unintentionally, more than adequately played his part in contributing to the unbearable life Eleanor had endured; a sentiment to which Tony wholeheartedly agreed. "I'm not questioning his love for his daughter," Tom nodded, "but he must have known she was afraid of Collett, why," he pointed out, "Tatton himself barely accorded him a bow in passing even before he agreed to the marriage!" Without giving Tony time to respond he went on, with more vehemence than Tony had ever yet heard from him, "I don't pretend to understand Tatton's reasons for doing what he did; perhaps he was suffering a reaction of some kind resulting from the shock of knowing the full sum of Reginald's gambling losses, but nothing can excuse his conduct where Eleanor is concerned."

"I agree that Sir Miles certainly has a lot to answer for regarding his daughter," Tony nodded, "but as to whether he knew of the treatment Collett handed out to her is another matter. He may have sold Eleanor into marriage to save his reputation as well as recouping his losses by whatever settlement he and Collett agreed upon, but considering that Collett only let her visit her father in his company, giving Eleanor no opportunity to tell him the truth, I feel we must exonerate Sir Miles of condoning Collett's treatment of her because no matter how callously he disregarded her feelings to protect himself, I can't see him calmly ignoring her suffering without trying to put a stop to it."

"Well," Tom sighed thoughtfully, conceding the point, "I have to say I think you're right, but it does not make it any the more acceptable to me."

"Do you think it does to me?" Tony raised a questioning eyebrow. "I assure you it doesn't. Like you," he nodded, taking his refilled glass from Tom, "I can only speculate on the reason behind Tatton's deceit; perhaps it was a reaction resulting from the shock of discovering the full extent of his son's gambling debts as Eleanor thinks, but whatever it was," he shook his head, "I can't condone it any more than you, even though I can, at a push, understand it, but condemning Tatton won't help Eleanor and certainly not divulging it. As for Bea," he inclined his head, "I've not mentioned it to her, I think you will agree that must be for Eleanor to do should she feel so inclined."

Tom nodded. "Yes, I agree, after all," he sighed, "it's not something one wants to become known about one's father."

"No, it's not, and yet," Tony nodded, "it seems Eleanor does not hate him for it."

"Well," Tom acknowledged, "that doesn't surprise me, although," he admitted, "after all she has been through I wouldn't blame her if she did. Last night for instance," he nodded, "had it not have been for you deducing Collett's intention from that letter she would now be back in Cavendish Square subjected to all manner of abuse."

"Yes, she would," Tony agreed at length, a frown appearing on his forehead, knowing only too well what would have been in store for her had he not prevented her from leaving the house.

"Well, all I can say," Tom said firmly, "is that by the time they realised Eleanor was not going to show herself I hope they were frozen to death!"

"I think it stands a pretty good chance that they were, but if nothing else," Tony smiled, "it's no more than they deserve."

"I'll drink to that!" Tom grinned, taking a generous mouthful of whisky, to which Tony raised his glass. "So, this Superintendent Dawson," Tom enquired, "do you think he will be able to persuade Sir Edward Bradford to your scheme?"

"I think so," Tony replied thoughtfully. "Dawson's a down-to-earth guy who knows there is no other way we can apprehend Collett and the others since the two witnesses we have are practically disqualified from one cause or another. Of course," he sighed, "even though Eleanor realises Dawson must speak to her, I wish I could spare her such an ordeal until she is fully recovered, but unfortunately he must do so as well as to Miss Simms before he approaches Bradford." Pausing only long enough to swallow some of his whisky, he asked, "Tell me Tom, have you ever met Bradford?"

"Yes, I have," Tom nodded, "but only once mind you; at a dinner in the City. I *can* tell you though," he told him, "that he is very highly thought of and has done wonders with the Metropolitan Police since he became Commissioner nine years ago. He was an officer in the Indian Army so he's used to command and he does have an air of authority about him, but he is generally considered rather easy-going for all that. I can also tell you that he is a Knight Commander of the Bath and was made a Knight Grand Cross of the Bath only two years back," to which Tony raised a praising eyebrow, "but if you are going to ask me if I think he will agree to your plan, then yes," he nodded, "I do, if for no other reason than he has shown himself determined to reduce crime on

London's streets, which," he pointed his glass at Tony, "has been more than adequately demonstrated."

"Some guy!" Tony said impressed.

"Well," Tom smiled, "as you say in America, 'you'd better believe it!'"

Tony laughed and, after lighting a cigarette, said, "Just one more thing Tom, have you ever come across a guy by the name of Reggie Wragge?"

"Don't tell me he's involved in this!" Tom said, a little startled.

"I don't know what he's involved in, yet," Tony shrugged, "but I take it from your surprised expression that you do know him."

"Not personally I don't," Tom shook his head, "and I've never done business with him, but he's well-known in the City. A respectable businessman who has his finger in any number of pies." His eyes narrowed slightly. "Why are you asking about him?"

"Oh," Tony shrugged, "it's just that his name came up today."

"Well, if his name came up," Tom pointed out reasonably, "it could only be because he is in some way connected with what's going on with Collett! I can see no other reason to account for it."

"It was," Tony said simply, going on to explain how Harry had followed Eliza Boon to fifty-one Periton Place and the results of Jerry's enquiries.

"Good God!" Tom exclaimed, some of his cigar ash falling onto his jacket in his surprise. "You don't mean…?"

"I'm not sure what I mean, Tom," Tony told him truthfully, "but one thing is clear, and that is he must know Eliza Boon, a woman who visited there yesterday morning don't forget, the very day that young woman came here carrying that supposed letter from Sir Miles. I can't say for certain that he *is* conducting illicit business from the premises, but considering he has a house in Belgravia then I doubt he is using it as his place of abode, so," he shrugged, "he must have bought the place for a reason and, if I am right, he bought it from Eliza Boon, which suggests the chances are he *is* carrying on where she left off," he nodded significantly, "and that this Molly Clark works for him."

"You mean she's a…?"

"I'd say it stands a pretty good chance," Tony broke in. "I'm only guessing here, I know," he admitted, "but I think this Reggie Wragge bought Eliza Boon's business and is now running it himself, and this Molly Clark used to be one of her girls, which would account for her visiting the premises yesterday to enlist her help in delivering that letter." After swallowing some of his whisky he said, "I may be wrong, but I get the feeling that this Reggie Wragge runs more than one illegitimate business, were it otherwise," he nodded meaningfully, "how would he and Eliza Boon have known one another, much less sell her business to him?"

Tom stared aghast at Tony. "Good God!"

"Why not?" Tony wanted to know. "You said yourself he has a finger in any number of pies; why not illicit ones as well as legitimate? After all," he shrugged, "a man who has made a name as well as a reputation for himself in the City has to be a hard-headed businessman who knows his way around, and therefore," he nodded, "I doubt he would have any difficulty in keeping his more seamy enterprises well hidden from prying eyes."

"But how would that be possible?" Tom demanded, leaning forward in his seat. "I mean, surely to God something would have leaked out before now if that was the case!"

"Well," Tony grimaced, "the way I figure it, if you've got something you don't want anyone to know about you will find a way of hiding it."

"Yes," Tom nodded, "that's true enough," several prominent businessmen who had at one time or another found themselves caught out in their illegal dealings involuntarily coming to mind.

"Of course," Tony conceded, "I may well be wrong, but if he was totally legitimate," he shrugged, "I fail to see why his name should have come up much less why Eliza Boon paid him a visit."

Tom thought a moment, saying at length, "You know something, Tony, it seems the more you dig the worse it gets!"

"You got that right!" Tony nodded.

"Yes but," Tom shook his head, "even supposing Wragge is carrying on where this Eliza Boon woman left off, it doesn't mean he knows anything about that poor girl or Sir Philip and his brother, or Mitchell if it comes to that!"

"No, it doesn't," Tony conceded, throwing the end of his cigarette onto the fire, "and if he wants to run a certain type of establishment, then that's his affair not mine," he told him truthfully. "All I'm interested in is whether he knows anything about what happened to them or not because if he does," he nodded, "then he could have something to answer for. If he's not involved," he shrugged, "and merely bought Eliza Boon's business in good faith, then as far as I am concerned that's it." Upon seeing the look which crossed Tom's face, he smiled, "Look Tom, I don't understand men who visit these establishments that cater for the Colletts of this world any more than you, but if this Reggie Wragge guy has nothing whatever to do with those four deaths, then I am not going to waste my time by hauling him up in front of the authorities for keeping a bawdyhouse; *that,*" he stressed, "will come to him sooner or later without any help from me."

"So," Tom cocked an eyebrow, taking Tony's empty glass, "you're going to see him, are you?"

"You bet!" Tony said firmly, telling him about the letter Harry had delivered for him to Reggie Wragge's home arranging a meeting. "But *not* at fifty-one Periton Place," he grinned in response to his brother-in-law's amused expression. "I thought a more neutral venue would be better."

"I agree." Tom nodded. "So, where *have* you arranged to meet him?"

"At my club." Tom raised a questioning eyebrow at this, to which Tony smiled. "*'The Palatine Club'*, remember? My grandfather made me a member while I was up at Cambridge."

"Yes, of course," Tom nodded, "I was forgetting, but," he asked a little worriedly, "do you think it will answer?"

"Well," Tony sighed, "he's more likely to open up to me in such relaxed surroundings than he is anywhere else."

"But what makes you think he will talk to you?" Tom asked reasonably.

"If you were in his shoes, Tom," Tony asked, taking his refilled glass, "who would you rather talk to, me or the police?"

Tom smiled and resumed his seat. "I take your point."

"And so will he," Tony said firmly.

Tom thought a moment as he looked meditatively at the rich amber liquid in his glass before raising his eyes to look at Tony, saying, "Tony, you don't need me to tell you what I think of you or how much I admire the way you've gone to work with this case, you already know, but if Reggie Wragge is in some way involved what's to stop him from telling Collett?"

"Nothing at all," Tony shrugged, touched by his brother-in-law's concern.

"Damn it, Tony!" Tom exclaimed, frustrated. "There's already been one attempt made on your life! Why not let the police deal with it?"

"I can't, Tom," Tony shook his head, "you must not ask it of me."

"I know you're doing this for Eleanor," Tom told him earnestly, "and I commend you for it, but…"

"Yes," Tony nodded, "I'm doing it for Eleanor, but also," he said purposefully, "there are four people whose deaths have to be accounted for. If I were I turn my back on them I should not only be condoning cold-blooded murder, which would make me no better than Collett and the others, but I would be going against everything I believe in and all my father stood for! I can't do it, Tom," he told him resolutely, "even though it means I'm putting myself at risk."

Tom, who had expected no less from a man of Tony's integrity, knew it was useless to continue trying to dissuade him from taking any further part in this matter himself, merely nodded, even so, he could not help reiterating the need for caution, ending by reminding him that his offer of help still held. Tony, who fully reciprocated Tom's feelings, indeed, he knew of no finer man than his brother-in-law, was not unmoved by his concern, but having no wish to worry Beatrice by the look of anxiety on her husband's face, told Tom that he could more than adequately take care of himself, concluding by laughingly telling him he was fully counting on his help, but that he need not worry because his lips were firmly sealed where Bea was concerned.

Tom knew perfectly well that Tony could take care of himself, but when he thought of the people they were dealing with, who had already demonstrated how far they were prepared to go to protect themselves, he could not totally abandon his fears. Reggie Wragge may well be involved in underhand dealings, he certainly would not be the first businessman to do so, but that did not make him either a murderer or a party to murder as Tony himself admitted. Tom knew Tony was shrewd enough to see through evasion and lies, however convincing, but as he had pointed out to him, even if it turned out that Reggie Wragge was totally innocent of any participation in wrongdoing Tony could well be opening himself up to goodness only knew what as Reggie Wragge, for reasons best known to himself, may feel it incumbent upon him to alert Eliza Boon that Tony was making enquiries. Should this be the way of it, then considering the attempt on his life this morning, it could well turn out to be open season on Tony, and next time, bearing in mind Peterson's failed efforts today, goodness only knew who they would hire to make an end of him. Tom devoutly trusted that his prediction would be realised in that Sir Edward Bradford would sanction the plan Tony had put forward to force Collett into proving his own guilt, because only when he and his accomplices were safely in a police cell would Tony be safe.

Beatrice, detecting nothing in her husband's demeanour when he eventually joined her upstairs to alert her to his concerns, had not the least idea of his anxiety about her brother's safety or his worries over what Collett and his associates would do next in their efforts to thwart Tony from exposing their crimes. In complete ignorance of the attack on her brother this morning she had no idea that at the back of her husband's mind was the dreadful thought that Peterson, either single-handedly or with others, may make another such attempt tomorrow and, despite the fact one of Jerry's sons would most probably be on hand, Tony might not be so lucky.

Tony was neither unmindful of nor unmoved by Tom's warnings and concerns, in fact he had merely echoed what Bill had said earlier in that just because their attempt this morning had failed it did not mean they had given up on the idea of disposing of him, he knew it perfectly well. Collett and his associates, who, up until his arrival on the scene, had been pretty secure in the knowledge that no one knew of their recent activities and with Eleanor well and truly watched and guarded with the threat of being institutionalised should she make any kind of move to say anything, there had been no real cause for concern, now though, they were facing a very different future indeed. Such uncertainty had not only rendered them reckless in their attempts to salvage the situation but would, the longer Tony continued to pose a threat, make them exceedingly dangerous, and even though they were walking a very fine line with none of them feeling very secure their position was such that they could not afford to either ignore or disregard him.

Tony did not need it reinforcing that his involvement had exposed him to whatever stratagems they may employ to rid themselves of him, particularly so since he had Eleanor safe, but he had spoken no less than the truth when he told Tom that irrespective of the dangers he was totally committed to the story he was investigating. As he leisurely climbed the stairs some minutes later in Tom's wake, he was conscious of no regrets in uncovering the truth and, even supposing Reggie Wragge did inform against him to Eliza Boon thereby intensifying the risk to himself, it in no way deterred him in his determination to bring to justice those who had callously and cold-bloodedly taken the lives of three people as well as being heavily involved in the unfortunate death of Annie Myers. Then there was Eleanor; a woman who had come to mean more to Tony than life itself, sold into marriage to a man she hated and feared purely to protect her father's reputation, then systematically and heartlessly subjected to the most diabolical treatment to which had cruelly been added the most inhuman of threats. For Eleanor's sake as much as those other victims whose lives had been unceremoniously cut short Tony could not, in all conscience, shelve his responsibilities by walking away just because things were becoming a little too hot; not only because it was not in his nature to give up on something, especially when it was something he knew to be right, but to do so would be unforgivable.

By the time he left his room some twenty minutes later to go downstairs to Eleanor's room, so lost in thought was he that the look on his face was quite daunting, but the unexpected sight of his five-year-old niece had the immediate effect of softening his features. Just one look at the miniature replica of his sister sitting on the bottom step of the stairs which led up to the nursery, clutching her rather tattered bear with a strip of plaster stuck over its right eye in her right arm and knuckling her eyes with her left hand, was enough to tell him the reason for her being out of bed at this time of night. Crossing the short distance from his room to the foot of the stairs, his slippers making no sound on the highly polished floorboards, Tony squat down in front of her and, raising her down bent head by gently tilting her chin with his forefinger, he smiled tenderly, his voice calm and comforting. "Has my special girl had a bad dream?"

Alice shook her head, her little face puckering. "Bertie has," she sniffed.

"Bertie?" he repeated surprised, sternly suppressing the twitch at the corner of his mouth as he wiped away her tears with a gentle finger. She nodded. "It's not like Bertie to have a bad dream, is it?" he said softly. She shook her head. "Can't he go back to sleep?" he asked. Again, she shook her head. "Well, we can't have that, can we?"

A little sob left her lips, telling him huskily, "He's frightened."

"Well," Tony soothed, picking her effortlessly up in his arms, "he needn't be frightened any more; Uncle Tony's here."

Wrapping her arms around his neck she snuggled against him as he carried her up the stairs to the nursery, her description of Bertie's dream tearfully relayed into his shoulder, to which he responded by kissing the top of her blonde head and soothingly allaying her fears. His comforting voice soon had its effect and by the time he tucked her up in bed she was more calm, so much so that she told him Bertie loved him almost as much as she did, to which he smiled and said he was glad because he loved them very much too, bending down to kiss her goodnight.

"Uncle Tony, will you stay until Bertie's gone to sleep?" she asked in a drowsy voice.

"Yes," he smiled, "I will stay with you until Bertie's gone to sleep, although," he nodded, indicating the somewhat threadbare bundle of golden fur she cradled to her, "I think he very soon will be."

She nodded and yawned, saying, "He's been poorly; look," removing her hand from under the blankets to point out the plaster.

"What has he been doing?" Tony asked, concerned.

"He fell off the chair," she told him, pointing towards the one beside the bed.

"Well," he sighed, his eyes alight with amusement, "he *has* been in the wars, hasn't he?"

"Yes," Alice stifled a yawn, "but he's getting better now. Mummy's friend is poorly too, isn't she?"

"Mummy's friend?" Tony repeated softly.

She nodded and yawned. "Mummy said she's been poorly and staying here."

"Yes," he said quietly, "Mummy's friend has been poorly too, but she's getting better now."

"Has she had a bad dream like Bertie?" Alice asked drowsily.

"Yes," Tony said quietly, "she's had a bad dream just like Bertie."

"Did you have to carry her up to bed too?" she yawned sleepily.

"Yes," Tony said in a hushed voice, sternly suppressing the smile which hovered on his lips at this innocent question, "I had to carry her up to bed too," rising to his feet and pulling up the covers a little as she fell asleep on a contented sigh, her blonde head snuggled comfortably against her favourite cuddly toy.

Tony stood looking down at her for a moment, his hands thrust deep into the pockets of his dressing gown, wondering, and not for the first time, how any father could sell his daughter into marriage with a man she not only hated but feared as well. He fully endorsed Tom's sentiments in that no matter how straitened his circumstances nothing would induce him to hand his daughter over to a man who neither loved nor deserved her and when, several minutes later, Tony stood beside Eleanor's bed as she lay asleep against the pillows, he vowed that no matter what happened there was no way he was letting her go.

Chapter Twenty-Four

Had anyone ever told Peterson that he would be worsted in a fight he would never have believed them, but as he watched Tony disappear from sight through a blurry mist he knew that this was precisely what he had been. It was a completely new experience for him and one he had no taste for and swore he would get his own back, but for now it was all he could do to recover his wind, managing, after several futile attempts, to rise unsteadily to his feet. The tentative touch of his calloused fingers against his jaw was enough to tell him that although it was steadily swelling and already extremely tender, it was not broken, but he knew it would take several days to heal, but as he picked up his cap and the cudgel from the gutter where Tony had kicked it he realised that his aching face was a small matter compared to his victim walking away unharmed. To be honest, he had not expected Tony to be so handy with his fists, but within the space of a few nicely timed hits he had demonstrated that getting rid of him was not going to be the easy matter he had thought. As Peterson eventually made his slow and ponderous way back to Cavendish Square, oblivious to the weather as well as to the stares of those whom he passed as he entered more frequented thoroughfares, he set his mind, as far as he was able, to formulating a fitting revenge on the man who, by his own parting words, knew what they had been trying to hide all this time.

It was perhaps a most unfortunate circumstance, but Peterson, whilst perfectly capable of carrying out plans, was very far from capable of devising them, something Eliza Boon and Sir Braden knew very well, but in fairness to him however, he did, with all the mental agility at his command, attempt to work something out as he plodded along the frozen streets. Regrettably though, the escalating pain of his fast stiffening jaw was progressively taking his mind, not very agile at the best of times, off the matter in hand, so much so that by the time he arrived back in Cavendish Square, nothing remotely resembling a scheme had sprung to mind.

Having left Sir Braden in his study to contemplate the ever-growing difficulties facing them in a dangerously balanced mood, Eliza Boon anxiously awaited the return of Peterson in an equally apprehensive frame of mind, not quite able to blot out the unwelcome thought that he had failed in his mission. Somehow she had managed to hide her disquiet from Sir Braden, but as she apprehensively watched the minutes tick relentlessly by as she sat in her sitting room with no sign of Peterson, she was reluctantly forced to face up to the fact that their plans had gone dreadfully wrong. Unable to be still, she walked into the hall to begin pacing restlessly up and down, nervously kneading her hands in between periodically peering through the side windows of the front door in the hope of catching sight of him, oblivious to the fact that Jerry's eldest son, Samuel, was keenly watching her from his vantage point in the Square's garden.

As his dad and Arthur had not yet joined him Samuel had no way of knowing about the stirring events which had taken place earlier, but from what he could see of it he was quite convinced that something mighty peculiar was going forward and when, ten minutes later, he caught sight of Peterson approaching holding his swollen face, he was sure of it. Stepping a little further back behind the snow-laden bushes, Samuel watched Eliza Boon fling open the front door, her eyes wide in shock as she stood staring at Peterson open-mouthed before grabbing his arm and hurriedly pulling him inside. Samuel knew that Arthur had followed Peterson when he left the house earlier and for one awful moment he wondered if he had spotted his brother and decided to tackle him, which seemed quite likely in view of Peterson's condition. Samuel knew that under normal circumstances Arthur could more than adequately take care of himself, but when he considered the disparity between Peterson's hefty build and Arthur's slighter one he could not prevent the sickening feeling which invaded the pit of his stomach when he thought that his youngest brother could be lying hurt somewhere, and for one indecisive moment Samuel was anxiously torn between standing his post or going in search of him. However, he was happily spared having to make such a decision as Arthur, thankfully without a mark on him, suddenly came up to him, whereupon the brothers immediately imparted to one another what had taken place, ending with Samuel heartily wishing he had seen Tony tackling Peterson. After describing the encounter in exhaustive detail, Arthur then nodded towards twenty-nine Cavendish Square, telling his brother that he would give anything to be a fly on the wall when they learned that their attempt to rid themselves of Tony had failed. He would not have been at all disappointed.

Just one look at Peterson's face was enough to tell Eliza Boon that the morning had gone badly and any faint hope she may have had that Childon had finally been dealt with in spite of Peterson's injuries, were immediately dashed when he told her that Childon had walked away without even taking a punch. It was bad enough knowing that yet another plan to rid themselves of the risk this man posed had gone horrendously awry, but upon being further told of Tony's parting words of warning that he was coming after them, her anger, which had been steadily mounting, became tinged with a panic she had never experienced before. It was clear from Peterson's description of the morning's events that Childon had not only been aware of his approach but also knew how to take care of himself, were it otherwise he would by now be lying on a mortuary slab identified by the police as an unfortunate victim of a street robbery, instead of which he was very much alive and armed with damaging information; information which would see her serving a prison sentence and Sir Braden and Peterson hanging from the end of a rope.

Even supposing Eleanor had told him what she had seen that night, Eliza failed to see how Childon could possibly know about Annie Myers and the others because neither she nor Sir Braden had told Eleanor, in fact, they had strictly forbidden her to mention that night let alone question it. Where then, had Childon got his information from? Considering the police had still not come up with a motive for Sir Philip's murder and his brother's death was still officially a suicide and no one knew about Annie Myers or Mitchell, Eliza was momentarily at a loss to even begin to think how Childon could know they had four deaths on their hands. That he was astute went without saying, even so, there was still no way as far as she could see that he could possibly have deduced the truth from the confession Eleanor must have made, and since Eliza remained in total ignorance of the fact that Joanie Simms had overheard everything between herself and Sir Braden and had in fact imparted what she knew to Childon, her mind was awash with speculation.

Eliza's anger may be aimed at Tony and not Peterson, but she needed to vent her spleen on someone for the difficult position this morning's fiasco had placed them in and from which she could momentarily see no way out, and turned it on the man who had never once failed her. When Joanie Simms had told Tony that Peterson had an unaccountable attachment to Eliza Boon she had spoken no less than truth; from the very beginning he had slavishly followed her every instruction and, in spite of this verbal annihilation, not the first by a good way, it looked as though he would continue to do so. Experience had taught him that to argue the toss with Eliza would serve no purpose and he therefore listened in unaffected silence as she tore his character as well as his intellect to shreds, but eventually her temper wore itself out as he knew it would, and merely nodded when she ended by recommending that he put something on his jaw.

With so much on his mind Sir Braden had neither the wish nor the inclination to keep any of the engagements that filled his diary, a circumstance which caused Eliza a little concern stating that his continued absence from society and his non-appearance at his club, could only raise questions. It may well, but until this business of Childon had been satisfactorily dealt with Collett was in no frame of mind to enjoy the company of his friends, pointing out that his lack of enjoyment, which would certainly not go unnoticed, could equally give rise to questions.

Like Eliza, he fully blamed Childon for their present difficulties and, for this reason, he experienced no qualms or twinges of conscience at the prospect of putting a permanent end to his existence. Once this had finally been achieved then not only could he relax a little, but eventually bend his mind to the vexed question of getting his erring wife safely back to Cavendish Square, something he owned would be a relief off his mind. Being a man who refused to acknowledge that he had any shortcomings, Sir Braden would have been rather indignant had he known that Eliza had been somewhat surprised at his idea of taking Childon by surprise by setting a trap for him, particularly when she considered the increasing agitation of his nerves, but even though the plan had undergone some modification the idea still had a lot to recommend it, in fact Sir Braden himself was fully convinced of its infallibility. This conviction, which had its roots firmly planted in his personal knowledge of Peterson, a man who had never yet failed to fulfil every task asked of him, gave Sir Braden no reason to doubt that this would be another occasion which would meet with success. For a man like Peterson, whose past was steeped in violence in and out of the ring and more than adequate testimony to his capabilities, he would surely have no difficulty in ensuring that this meddlesome American was no longer in a position to say or do anything to their detriment. Sir Braden felt sure that Peterson, having taken Childon totally unaware, would have no trouble in overpowering him before doing whatever was necessary without any finger of suspicion falling onto them, leading the police to believe that he had, sadly, been the hapless victim of a brutal street robbery.

It was all very reassuring, not to say comforting, especially when Sir Braden thought of all he had to lose once Childon reported his findings to the police, unhappily though, the longer it took Peterson to return from his mission the more his conviction diminished. Eliza's assurances that nothing could possibly go wrong had not entirely assuaged his fears, and as the minutes ticked relentlessly by without any sign of Peterson the more fearful he became, but when, just over half an hour later, he was informed by Eliza that their efforts to deal with Childon had regrettably failed, Collett looked for all the world as though he had been poleaxed.

Eliza's fierce defence of Peterson in that Childon had put up an unexpectedly good fight of it, in fact it was almost as though he had expected it, made no difference; Collett's anger, exacerbated by fear and panic at the thought that this man had somehow discovered what they were striving to hide, and the question as to where they went from here, exploded over her head. She by no means liked the idea of Sir Braden venting his spleen on her, but she knew from experience that whilst he was in this highly emotional state no sense would be got out of him, and therefore listened with as much endurance as she could until his temper burned itself out. Not for the first time she was conscious of wishing she could leave him to sort out his own problems, but the unpalatable truth was, whether she liked it or not, they were her problems too, and Peterson's. If Sir Braden went down so too would they, and it was for this reason only that she withstood his spluttering accusations and vituperative allegations as to her and Peterson's incompetence and inability to sort this damned mess out before they all took a walk to the scaffold!

For the moment at least Eliza had no more idea than Sir Braden about what to do next especially as Childon seemed to thwart them at every turn, but one thing she did know, and that was this interfering Colonial had to be dealt with and as soon as possible. She knew as well as Sir Braden the risk Childon posed, even more so now he knew the full extent of their crimes, and that the longer he remained alive the less chance they would have of extricating themselves from the dire situation facing them, and since she had no more wish to face the Queen's Bench than Sir Braden it was imperative that between them they come up with a foolproof plan of dealing with him. But until Sir Braden's anger had abated sufficiently for him to even begin to listen to reason, no semblance of a plan could be put together which, had she but known it, considering the ploy the man she had no hesitation in deeming their archenemy was devising, would be to no avail in any case.

Their archenemy, having consumed a hearty breakfast, wholly unperturbed by the disagreements he knew must now be raging in the enemy camp following their failure yesterday to put a period to his existence, strolled leisurely into the hall just as Harry arrived, whereupon he was immediately handed an envelope of the finest quality from which he retrieved a gilt-edged sheet of notepaper and, after reading the few lines, Tony nodded his head, saying, "Thanks, Harry."

Harry, who envied his brother Arthur witnessing Peterson receiving his comeuppance yesterday and had in fact told Tony so last night, could not help reiterating that he would have given anything to have been there. "Arthur 'as all the luck!" he told him disgustedly.

"Next time," Tony smiled, "I'll make sure you're on hand instead of your brother."

"Real chuffed me dad was," Harry grinned, "said 'e knew from the off that you'd strip to advantage!"

Tony laughed. "Sure I do!" clapping him on the shoulder, contentedly exchanging boxing reminiscences with him before mounting the stairs.

Sarah, who had prevented Tony from seeing Eleanor before he went downstairs to breakfast, telling him as indignantly as she could that just because he sat with her during the nighttime hours this did not automatically mean he could walk in and out of her room as and when he pleased. Trying not to catch Tony's eye which Sarah knew was brimful with laughter, she told him tartly, the slight quiver in her voice quite spoiling the effect of her scolding, "A nice thing I *must* say! Entering a lady's room even before she is fit to be seen or had her breakfast either!" She sniffed. "'Sides, she is still in bed, *where,"* she nodded, "she'd stay left to me, not trying to make it over to the day bed."

"Now *that's* where I can help," Tony told her solicitously.

"Hm!" Sarah sniffed again, not quite managing to stifle the choke which rose in her throat.

"It will only take a moment to carry her from one side of the room to the other," he assured her, reaching out a hand for the handle.

"Mr. Ton… my lord!" Sarah hastily amended, barring his entrance to Eleanor's room by standing with her back to it as though prepared to take on all-comers. "*Will* you behave yourself!"

"I always do," he defended himself.

"So you say," she nodded, having no difficulty in understanding why Eleanor had fallen in love with him.

"I *do* say," Tony confirmed, sternly suppressing the twitch at the corner of his mouth.

"Hm!" Sarah nodded, twinkling up at him.

Tony laughed, then, bending down to kiss her cheek, said, "I love you too, Sarah," before making his leisurely way down the stairs.

By the time he had given his final instructions to Harry then spent a little time with his sister, who had by now learned from her daughter about her adventures the night before as well as being told by Patrick as he and his brother were sitting down to breakfast in the nursery day room that Toby had shown Uncle Tony his newt. "Such a horrid thing!" she shuddered. "I can't understand why he wants it!" It was over an hour later before Tony warily put his head round the door of Eleanor's room following his brief tap, asking in the manner of one who was extremely apprehensive at being caught, "Is it safe to come in?"

Eleanor, who had by now breakfasted and had her hair arranged, was resting comfortably on the day bed, dressed in the same pink dressing gown which had been generously loaned to her by Beatrice, had heard the bantering exchange between Tony and Sarah earlier, and turning a smiling face towards him nodded her head.

As if unsure, Tony stood holding the edge of the door while he scanned the room, asking in a hushed voice, "No Sarah?"

Eleanor shook her head, confirming, "No Sarah," her eyes laughing up into his as he cautiously crossed the room towards her. "Are you *that* afraid of her?" she teased shyly.

"Oh, terrified!" Tony shuddered as he sat down beside her, taking her hands in his and warmly kissing them. "I told you so yesterday, but you didn't believe me!"

"I still don't!" she laughed.

"I can't imagine why not!" he said with wide-eyed innocence.

"Nor can anyone else," Eleanor smiled, "when it is obvious she likes you very much."

"I will let you in on a secret," Tony told her in a conspiratorial whisper, "I think Sarah's pretty wonderful too."

"I think she probably knows," Eleanor smiled, returning the gentle pressure of his fingers.

"You know," Tony nodded, as if making a sudden discovery, "I think she probably does."

Eleanor laughed. "You know she does."

"And do *you* know," Tony said softly, his eyes reflecting all he felt as they looked deeply into hers, "how much I love you?" holding her hands a little tighter.

"Yes," Eleanor breathed huskily, her fingers moving in his, "I know, and I can't tell you how happy it makes me."

"You don't have to, I know," he told her lovingly, "as I hope I don't have to tell you that knowing you love me makes me happy too."

She lowered her eyes at this, then, after a moment, raised them to his, asking a little shyly, "Can I tell you something?"

"Sure you can," Tony said softly, "anything."

"I… I missed you last night," she confessed unsteadily.

"Did you?" he asked tenderly. She nodded. "Well, I was here," he told her, "sitting in that chair," nodding his head towards the wing chair, "but you were asleep, in fact you slept undisturbed throughout the night, for which I am not at all sure whether to be glad or sorry."

"Y-you're not?" she managed faintly.

"No," he said slowly, shaking his head.

"Why?" she asked a little breathlessly.

"Because my darling," he told her, quite unashamedly, "it meant I had no reason to hold you."

Considering Doctor Little had cautioned against too much excitement, advising rest and quiet, this admission, deliciously exciting, was definitely guaranteed to do the complete opposite, but as far as his patient was concerned it was precisely what she wanted to hear. "Do you need one?" she asked huskily, putting up no resistance as he released her hands and gently gathered her in his arms.

"No," he said lovingly, drawing her closer to him, "none at all."

"Y-you don't?" she managed, her arms seeming to fold themselves around his neck of their own volition.

"Too right I don't!" he told her, his voice a caress, proving his point by proceeding to gently, but agreeably, kiss her; her response ensuring that close on a full minute elapsed before he released her.

Eleanor had no need to be told that not everyone was like Sarah or Tom and Beatrice, who knew that nothing improper was going on between her and Tony, but unfortunately there were some who would look upon them being together like this as quite wrong, especially as she had a husband. Useless to tell them that her husband had committed cold-blooded murder and had brutally treated her as well as threatening to have her put into an asylum, and that for the past twelve months she had found herself forced into keeping up the unbearable pretence of an agreeable marriage for appearance's sake; hiding the truth and living a lie to protect Braden as well as her father and that it had all made her very fearful and unhappy. Somewhere in the far recesses of her mind hovered the thought that no matter what Braden had done two wrongs did not make a right, but as Tony held her against his strong hard body, his tender kisses evoking the most wonderful sensations, all she knew was that she loved him and because she loved him she could not believe that what they shared was wrong.

Tony was very sure that what they shared was not wrong. From the moment he had seen Eleanor across the space which had separated them at Covent Garden he knew that at long last he had found the woman for whom he had unconsciously searched his whole life, but although he may find it impossible to resist kissing Eleanor at no time had he ever had the smallest intention of taking advantage of her by attempting to make love to her. For himself, he cared nothing for society's narrow-minded criticism, but for Eleanor's sake he could not dismiss the chorus of disapproval from the censorious which he knew would be directed at them should they ever be privileged to witness scenes such as this. It seemed ironic to him that society much preferred to accept the superficial pretence of a marriage rather than exposing the truth hiding behind it, and whilst he would not go so far as to say people would condone or overlook cold-blooded murder, they certainly adopted these conveniences when it came to a husband's vicious treatment of his wife.

Since it appeared that Sir Miles Tatton had no immediate intention of returning to town, Tony knew that until Eleanor was well enough to go to him her continued refuge under his sister's roof must not become known beyond the walls of Mount Street, should it ever do so then society could certainly be relied upon to judge and condemn her and, at all costs, Tony had to protect her from the malicious and painful gossip which would result. In the eyes of society as well as the law Collett was still Eleanor's husband which not only gave him rights that he himself did not hold, but automatically rendered Collett the aggrieved husband, and even though he may not be the darling of society his wife's apparent disloyalty to her husband would nevertheless ensure him their sympathies. Until the truth about Collett emerged Eleanor did not deserve the unjust condemnation of her world, and having already suffered at the hands of others for merely doing as she was told, it would be cruel in the extreme to subject her to any more misery. It was therefore imperative that Superintendent Dawson did everything possible to persuade Sir Edward Bradford into agreeing to the scheme to lay Collett and his associates by the heels. Should he not do so, then not only would they escape answering for their crimes, at least for the foreseeable future, but any hope Tony had of marrying Eleanor would be anything but a foregone conclusion because it was not to be supposed that Collett would agree to a divorce, especially when he knew the so-called co-respondent was the very man who had caused him so much aggravation.

Tony was as reluctant to leave Eleanor to go downstairs to await the arrival of Superintendent Dawson as she was, but by the time he entered her room with Tony some fifteen minutes later she had managed to calm herself sufficiently to give the Superintendent no cause to think that her rather heightened colour was anything other than a natural nervousness at being interviewed by a police officer.

Tony, after listening to Superintendent Dawson recount his interview earlier that morning with Miss Simms, who had confirmed everything she had told him, was not all surprised when Superintendent Dawson expressed his regret in that it was out of the question for him to sit in on the interview as it was essential he speak to Lady Collett alone, but when it came to offering a reason for Tony's prohibition, he suddenly knew a moment of embarrassment.

"It's okay, Superintendent," Tony smiled, "I rather expected you to say no."

"You did?" Dawson asked, raising an eyebrow.

"Sure I did," Tony nodded, not in the least embarrassed. "Your refusal is quite understandable in view of my relationship with Lady Collett."

Relieved to have this very delicate hurdle scaled for him, Superintendent Dawson hastened to assure Tony that no offence was intended.

"None taken," Tony told him affably, accepting Dawson's assurance that he was not accusing them of any collusion to try to discredit Sir Braden Collett to get him permanently out of the way. "I never supposed it, Superintendent," Tony told him calmly, "it is simply that Lady Collett has not yet fully recovered from her injuries as well as being extremely fearful, in fact," he informed him, "she is still under the doctor's care," to which Superintendent Dawson nodded.

"Just go easy with her, Superintendent," Tony advised, opening the door to Eleanor's room and following him inside.

Superintendent Dawson's well-trained eye told him that the couple exchanging a few quiet words together some little distance away from him were very much in love and also that, although Lady Collett accepted Childon's explanation for his absence during their interview, she was nevertheless quite upset by it. Dawson's detractors at Scotland Yard might be eager to be rid of him and what they termed his old-school approach to policing, but one thing they could not lay at his door was his lack of tact and diplomacy when dealing with ladies in a delicate condition or fragile state of health and, from what he could see, Lady Collett was certainly fragile.

Eleanor, looking anxiously at the door Tony had quietly closed behind him on his way out then back at Superintendent Dawson, a man who suddenly seemed to take on a menacing aura, it was noticeable to his experienced eye that without Childon's reassuring presence and support she became just a little fretful. Considering her facial injuries, the results of the brutal beating inflicted upon her by her husband, and not the first by all accounts, added to which was the horrifying spectacle of what she had seen that night, it was hardly surprising, but it spoke volumes for Superintendent Dawson's sensitivity and consideration in dealing with a woman who was clearly still very much afraid that Eleanor soon found herself relaxing.

It could not be said that her account of what she had seen that night was smoothly delivered, in fact it was rather faltering and disjointed with several pauses in between, but it was nevertheless made with more ease than she would have thought possible.

But however skilful Superintendent Dawson was in drawing Eleanor out as well as making her feel at ease, the fact remained that certain points needed clarification and, however regrettable, he knew that most of them would clearly upset her. "You say your husband used the brass poker?" he queried gently when she had thankfully come to the end of her description of events.

"Yes," she nodded, blowing her nose on the handkerchief she had pulled out of her dressing gown pocket, "he was still holding it in his hand when I entered the study."

"And you say Sir Philip was already dead when you entered?" Dawson pressed gently.

"Yes," she nodded again, shivering at the recollection. "H-his face was all covered in blood and…" she shuddered, "it was rather distorted, and there was blood on the carpet."

"You said, I think," Dawson raised an eyebrow, "that you were not acquainted with Sir Philip, but you recognised him from photographs you had seen of him?"

"Yes," Eleanor sniffed into her handkerchief.

"You said also," Dawson reminded her, "that upon asking your husband why he had attacked Sir Philip, a man with whom he was unacquainted, he refused to tell you?"

She nodded. "He never spoke of it, in fact he forbid me to question him."

"Forgive me, Lady Collett," Dawson said considerately, "but you did not actually see your husband strike Sir Philip, did you?"

"No," Eleanor shook her head, blowing her nose, "b-but he was leaning over him with the poker in his hand, I told you that."

"Yes," Dawson agreed, "you did, but you see, Lady Collett," he pointed out carefully, "your husband's…"

"But there was b-blood all over Braden's clothes," she broke in agitatedly, "and the poker too, besides the pool of b-blood on the carpet! Why would he have blood over his c-clothes if he had not killed him?"

"Do you know what happened to your husband's clothes?" he asked calmly.

"No," Eleanor shook her head, "I… I assume he must have burned them or something!"

"And the poker?"

"The… the poker?" she repeated, a little bewildered.

"Yes," Dawson smiled encouragingly.

"It… it's still in the study," she managed.

"And what about the carpet?" he further encouraged.

"The… the carpet?" Eleanor repeated, raising a distracted hand to her forehead.

"Yes," Dawson pressed gently. "I understand it was taken up."

She thought a moment. "Yes," she confirmed hastily, "it was, but I can't tell you when precisely."

Dawson nodded. "Now, going back a moment to when you arrived home; you told me you let yourself into the house that night." Eleanor nodded. "Was that usual?"

"No," she shook her head. "You see, it was seldom I went out without my husband."

"But you did that night," Dawson remarked.

"Yes," she confirmed faintly.

"Why was that?" Dawson asked calmly.

"Well, you see," Eleanor explained, "I particularly wanted to see the performance at The Royal Albert Hall, and as a friend of mine wanted to see it too we went together."

"Your husband did not mind?" he queried. "Or raise objections?"

"H-he would have much preferred to have accompanied me," Eleanor explained, "but in view my friend…"

"He gave his consent," Dawson supplied, to which she nodded. "Did you let yourself in with a key or did Mitchell open the door for you?" he invited quietly.

"I didn't have a key," Eleanor explained unsteadily, "you see, not being used to going out without my husband I had forgotten to take it with me, but I knew the door would be unlocked."

"Is the front door usually kept unlocked?" he wanted to know.

"Yes… no… that is… I mean," she faltered, "Mitchell always locked the doors before he retired."

"But you didn't see Mitchell at all when you returned home?" Dawson raised an enquiring eyebrow.

"No, there was no sign of him," Eleanor said agitatedly.

"When was the last time you saw Mitchell?" Dawson asked.

Eleanor thought a moment, a trembling forefinger rubbing her temple. "It… it was just before I left home to attend the concert."

"And what time was that?"

"It was about half past four," she told him.

Dawson nodded. "Tell me, Lady Collett," he asked calmly, "why did you go to your husband's study that night? You told me yourself that you seldom entered it."

"Why?" she repeated.

"Yes." He inclined his head.

"I just wanted to let my husband know that I had returned home," she explained.

"So he didn't see or hear you arrive?" Dawson queried.

"No," Eleanor told him, twisting the handkerchief in her fingers.

"How did you know he was in the study?"

"B-because there was no s-sign of him in the d-drawing-room," she faltered, "b-but I saw the light shining from under the d-door of his study."

"Did you knock on the door or just walk in?" he smiled.

"I… I just walked in," she told him helplessly.

"So he wasn't expecting you to arrive home early," he cocked his head.

"No," she shook her head. "As I told you, Superintendent, the concert finished earlier than scheduled."

"Tell me, Lady Collett," he said gently, "what do you remember after your husband hit you to keep you silent?"

"Nothing," she said faintly. "I… I remember nothing more until I opened my eyes the next morning. I was still lying on top of the bed where my husband had left me."

"And from that moment on Eliza Boon and Peterson have been constantly in attendance?" he stated, to which she gave an inaudible 'yes'. "Did you ask your husband who they were or question him about Mitchell and your maid, Mary?"

Eleanor nodded. "Yes, but as I told you he forbid me to mention anything about what had happened the night before or question it or enquire about Mary and Mitchell," wiping away a tear with nervous fingers.

"In what way did he forbid you, Lady Collett?" Dawson pressed gently.

"He…" Eleanor drew in her breath on a choke, "he threatened to have me committed to an asylum if I said anything and… well he…"

"Hit you on more than one occasion," to which she gave a barely audible 'yes'. "And so to account for your injuries which kept you to your room he informed his household that it was because you suffered from mental disorders which brought on delusional attacks when you hurt yourself, which is why he brought in Eliza Boon to take care of you, but whose real role was to guard you and make sure you told no one what you saw?" A choked sob and a nod of the head was the only answer he received to this. "And you had no idea that your husband's acquaintanceship with Eliza Boon and Peterson was due to his regular visits to her premises?"

It was several painful moments before she could manage in a barely audible voice, "No. I… I had no idea he visited such a place."

"And you had no idea that Sir Philip's unfortunate death at your husband's hands was in any way connected with this establishment and what had happened to Annie Myers or Dennis Dunscumbe?" he pressed gently.

She shook her head. "No," she replied faintly.

"And when you heard of Dennis Dunscumbe's suicide you had no reason to doubt what you read in the newspapers?"

"No," she managed in a stifled voice, "no reason at all."

"Thank you, Lady Collett," he smiled, "you have been most helpful," returning his notebook to the inner pocket of his overcoat. "I realise it has all been quite distressing for you," he told her sympathetically, "and I am sorry I have had to ask you some rather pressing questions, but your husband's defence will…"

"Y-you mean I shall have to go to Court and give evidence?" she asked, horrified, her wide blue eyes staring at him.

"Given that your evidence is incriminating to your husband, I think that is a most unlikely contingency, Lady Collett," Dawson assured her. "I was simply making you aware of what questions could be asked you by your husband's defence should that eventuality arise."

"Do you think it will?" Eleanor asked faintly, as he rose to his feet to take his leave of her.

"Frankly, no," Dawson smiled down at her, "in fact," he nodded, "I shouldn't let it worry me if I were you," briefly taking her hand in his.

"Thank you," Eleanor smiled unsteadily, watching him stride towards the door. "Superintendent," she called, just as he put a hand on the handle, "I… I know I did not actually see my husband murder Sir Philip, but if he did not, then why was he holding the poker? And why should he have blood all over his clothes as well as keeping me…? I mean you… you *do* believe me, don't you?" she urged.

"Believe you!" Dawson raised an eyebrow. "Why yes, Lady Collett," he smiled, "I believe you; implicitly!"

As soon as Tony heard Superintendent Dawson come down the stairs he strode into the hall from the drawing-room where he had anxiously been waiting with Beatrice, relieved to learn that Eleanor's ordeal was over. "However," Superintendent Dawson told him, after relating the interview to him, "I did have to ask some very necessary questions which naturally upset her a little, but I think I can safely say that from what you have told me as well as what I have discovered from Lady Collett and Miss Simms I should be able to persuade the Commissioner into going along with your plan." After putting on his hat and gloves, he paused a moment to eye the weather through the side windows of the front door, then, turning back to Tony said, quite conversationally, "I have arranged to see him at one o'clock, and needless to say as soon as I have his decision I will let you know."

"Thank you, Superintendent." Tony shook his hand. "However, I do have to go out quite shortly, so if you could let Bill know."

"Of course," Dawson nodded, opening the door, "and please, offer my apologies to Lady Collett."

After saying goodbye to Superintendent Dawson, Tony waited only long enough to have a quick word with Beatrice who had entered the hall, before mounting the stairs two at a time. He had not needed Superintendent Dawson to tell him that Eleanor had found the interview quite distressing, he had known she would, but upon opening the door to her room without even knocking just one look at her tear-stained face as she turned it towards him was more than enough to tell him that it was not answering the Superintendent's questions which had distressed her so much as re-living the events of that night. Within a few strides Tony was at her side, sitting down beside her and taking her in his arms. "It's all right my darling," he soothed, "I'm here. It's all over."

"Oh, Tony!" she cried into his shoulder. "I…"

"I know," he said gently, "it was pretty tough and I wish I could have been with you, but there's nothing more for you to worry about except getting well," holding her securely against him as she gave vent to her feelings.

With so much emotion pent up inside her she had a lot of feelings to vent, but the more she tried to pull herself together the more tears she seemed to shed, but thanks to Tony's soothing assurances in response to her disjointed and tearful account of the interview, she eventually managed to stem the flow and, raising a tear-stained face, sniffed, "I'm sorry! I… I seem to do nothing but cry and… oh," she dropped her head, "you must be wishing you had never met me!"

"Sure I do," he told her, his voice a caress, gently lifting her chin with his forefinger, "just about every minute of every day!" his smile as well as his words not only banishing the remainder of her fears, but causing a deliciously warm quiver to unfurl somewhere inside her, her skin tingling as he tenderly wiped away her tears.

As her father had only uttered the occasional witticism and she had hardly laid eyes on her brother, while Braden's idea of humour was passing caustic comments which only he seemed to appreciate, before Tony had entered her life she had never come across anyone with such a droll sense of the ridiculous. Her own mischievous sense of humour, although not instantly discernible beneath her natural shyness, had never really been allowed to materialise and certainly not during her marriage to Braden, but the man who was at this moment looking down at her with so much warmth and love in his eyes had not only untapped this vital part of her personality, but had triggered a responsive chord inside her to his own sense of humour. She had been very conscious of it at the Kirkmichaels' party as well as how much she enjoyed his teasing, but having spent time with him over the last few days she had to acknowledge it gave her as much pleasure as did his kisses.

"As often as that?" she smiled on a sniff, all her fears forgotten as he drew her closer to him. "I didn't know."

"Mm," Tony mused, the puzzled expression which descended onto his face at variance with the look in his eyes, "I could have sworn I had made my feelings quite clear, in fact," he inclined his head, "I'm sure of it."

"Do you think it would help if you made them clear again?" she suggested huskily, her eyes smiling shyly up into his.

"Yes," he said slowly as if giving it serious thought, "I think it just might, at least," he caressed against her lips, "I'm prepared to have a shot at it!" which he did, to their mutual satisfaction.

Right from the beginning Tony had seen the real Eleanor Collett hiding beneath the surface of her fear and shyness and knew that although it was very early days, given time, the vibrant woman he loved and could not live without, would gradually emerge from the chrysalis which concealed so much. Had matters not progressed so far he would not have left her, not only because he could not bear being parted from her or because he was enjoying kissing her, but she was still far too vulnerable. He knew she felt herself to be in no better hands than Beatrice and Sarah, both of whom adored and petted her, but it was clear Eleanor only felt truly safe when he was with her, but whilst she had made no demur when he left her, he had seen the fear she could not quite hide, a resurgence of anger sweeping through him towards those who had so callously used her. He was still thinking of Eleanor when he arrived at his destination three-quarters of an hour later fully aware that until Collett and his associates had been arrested for their crimes she would never feel entirely safe, and hoped that Superintendent Dawson would be able to persuade Sir Edward Bradford into going along with laying the trap Tony was totally convinced Collett and the others would have no choice but to step into.

'The Palatine Club', established in 1689 by a privileged few who had either known or served with Prince Rupert of the Rhine, had relocated from its original site near St. James's Palace in the late eighteenth century to an angled Georgian end terraced building in St. Anne's Gate, a quite imposing edifice and one Tony had only seldom visited. It had a well-deserved reputation for serving the best luncheons and dinners in London, and where its members could be assured of quiet and solitude within its impressive walls and elegant apartments. A copy of a portrait of Prince Rupert as a young man painted by Van Dyck and another when he was older painted around 1669 by Sir Peter Lely hung on opposite walls of the entrance hall, a lofty and imposing vestibule which Tony wished he had time to appreciate in more detail. Having signed the register and handed his overcoat, hat, cane and gloves to the hall porter he enquired after his guest whereupon he was unassumingly informed that Mr. Wragge was awaiting him in the upstairs green anteroom, to which Tony thanked him. Taking only a moment to check his card case

he climbed the elegant staircase to the upper floor, its pale blue walls exhibiting paintings of Prince Rupert's campaigns from Edgehill to when he later commanded *'The Constant Reformation'* on his voyage to the West Indies and his time as General-at-Sea after the Restoration.

Apart from the reading room, *'The Palatine Club'*, unlike some, did not have rules on maintaining a permanent silence within its precincts, and so by the time Tony reached the first floor a steady flow of voices wafted through to him from the dining room and other apartments which led off the wide and lofty corridor. The green anteroom, a small apartment overlooking the street, had only one occupant enjoying its quiet opulence, a rather tall and distinguished looking man in his mid to late fifties with silver-grey hair sitting at his ease in a wing chair by the fire glancing through a periodical, who, upon seeing Tony enter, instantly dropped it onto a nearby table and rose to his feet.

Regardless of whatever secondary or illicit business enterprises Reggie Wragge may be involved in, Tony was not at all surprised to find himself looking at an eminently respectable and impeccably dressed man, but it was otherwise with Reggie Wragge who was not quite able to disguise the questioning look which entered his intense blue eyes at the sight of Tony, a man who was as immaculately dressed as himself. "Mawdsley?" He raised an enquiring eyebrow.

"Yes," Tony smiled, extending his hand, "how do you do? You must be Mr. Wragge."

"Yes," he nodded, shaking Tony's hand.

"It is good of you to see me at such short notice," Tony acknowledged.

"Your note," Wragge told him, "*was* rather intriguing."

"I'm sorry," Tony smiled, "I did not mean it to be obscure."

"Didn't you?" Wragge raised a sceptical eyebrow, to which Tony neither disclaimed nor averted his eye. "You know," he told him composedly, "it's not often I am invited to luncheon by a newspaper reporter, since that is what I inferred you were from your note, and certainly not one who could afford to dine in such an exclusive club," indicating his surroundings with a wave of his hand, "or dressed such as yourself, but even though my curiosity eventually overrode my caution and persuaded me to accept, I cannot help wondering," he suggested, eyeing Tony knowingly, "if you are here under false pretences?"

Totally unperturbed by this, Tony smiled, "Yes, I suppose I am, but not in the way you mean," pulling out a card and handing it to him.

"Perhaps this will help."

Looking at the card Tony handed him for a moment then back again, Reggie Wragge nodded his comprehension. "Of course, Mawdsley-Dart, I remember now; Viscount Childon. You came into your grandfather's title some months ago." Tony nodded. "If I remember correctly," he mused, "your father was an American." Again Tony nodded. Reggie Wragge thought a moment, then, as enlightenment entered those piercing blue eyes, he nodded. "Of course, now I begin to understand your note; *you* own *'The Daily Bulletin'* and *'The London Chronicler'*!"

"Yes," Tony confirmed, "as well as newspapers back in the States."

"So," Wragge pondered, handing Tony his card back, "to what do I owe the purpose of this meeting? A meeting," he inclined his head, "which you requested in a most – how shall I say? – interesting manner!"

"I was rather hoping we could discuss that over luncheon," Tony replied affably.

Reggie Wragge thought a moment. "Why do I get the feeling you want me to sing for it? Very well," he shrugged, "after all, what do I have to lose?"

"That, Mr. Wragge," Tony smiled, "wholly depends upon what you tell me over luncheon."

The dining room, dominated by a white marble Robert Adam fireplace over which hung a Louis XIV mirror, was a spacious and elegant apartment which had changed very little since it was built well over a century ago for its then present owner. Set at discreet angles to afford the utmost privacy were tables sheathed in pristine white covers and laden with silver cutlery which glinted in the glow from the roaring fire and the chandeliers which hung from either end of the beautiful Adam ceiling, while lambrequins of rich red silk and taffeta covered the windows, harmonising perfectly with the rich colours of the Aubusson carpet.

Being a man of impeccable taste and a fondness for the finer things in life, all of which were well within his financial sphere, Reggie Wragge fully appreciated the luxury of his surroundings as well as the many dishes which were on offer and certainly took his time over the menu, discussing in detail various dishes with the waiter. Having finally come to a decision he elected to begin his meal with a warm salad of scallop and prawns with ginger confit and pear purée, followed by steamed fillet of sea bass with oyster veloute and caviar, then, after toying with the main course decided on cutlet of venison forestiere, not only instructing the waiter on how he liked it cooked but discussing at length the merits of several complementing wines before making his selection. Tony had seen from the outset that his guest was not only a well-educated and cultured man, but one who certainly had a taste for rich living and, judging from his choice of dishes, a discerning palate, but as his own taste favoured more simple cuisine he ordered nothing more exciting than warm smoked chicken with wild mushroom salad, followed by braised halibut and ending his meal with fillet of beef.

"I see you do not have an adventurous palate, Childon, but are in fact a man of simple tastes," Reggie Wragge commented as soon as the waiter had departed with their order.

"Do you disapprove of that?" Tony raised an enquiring eyebrow.

"Not at all," Wragge assured him, "each man to his own as they say, but I can't help wondering how you reconcile your simple tastes with being a member of a most exclusive club!"

"Exclusivity does not preclude personal preference, Mr. Wragge," Tony told him amicably.

"Very true, even so," Wragge commented, "something tells me that you do not partake of its exclusiveness every day," indicating their surroundings with a wave of his hand. "Am I right?"

After taking a quick glance around him, Tony brought his gaze back to rest on Reggie Wragge's rather gaunt yet striking face, inclining his head. "Yes, but that is because the opportunity to do so does not often come in my way. Travelling regularly back and forth from New York to London on business," he explained in answer to his guest's raised eyebrow, "means I seldom find myself with enough time to take advantage of my membership."

"A pity," Reggie Wragge remarked, "but I do understand the demands of business," he acknowledged, "and yet you have found the time to invite me here today. How is that?" He raised a questioning eyebrow.

"Because Mr. Wragge," Tony told him, "I thought both our interests could best be served if this conversation was perhaps conducted in less formal surroundings."

Reggie Wragge's intense blue eyes narrowed slightly, but his voice was perfectly controlled. "Are you by any chance considering putting a business proposition to me, Childon?"

Waiting only until the waiter, whose approach had been remarkably unobtrusive, had departed, having filled the two glasses he had placed carefully in front of them with the rich amber liquid from a crystal decanter, did Tony shake his head, saying, "Not quite."

Taking a moment to savour his sherry, Reggie Wragge looked over the rim of his glass, his eyes contemplative. "So," he said slowly, "I was right; you *do* want me to sing for my luncheon." Putting his glass down with slow deliberation, he raised an enquiring eyebrow. "And what is it you want me to sing, precisely?"

Tony eyed him squarely, saying calmly, "The truth, Mr. Wragge."

"The truth?" Wragge repeated, a little bewildered, his eyes narrowing. "The truth about what?"

"Periton Place," Tony replied evenly.

Reggie Wragge's hand stilled in the act of raising his glass to his lips and a slightly wary expression had entered his eyes, repeating in an odd voice, "Periton Place?"

"Number fifty-one," Tony supplied helpfully. When his guest made no attempt to answer he asked, "Are you going to tell me you have never heard of it?"

Eyeing Tony thoughtfully for a moment, Reggie Wragge slowly put his glass down onto the table, his eyes meditative as they pondered the rich amber liquid as it danced in the light from the chandelier, then, raising his eyes back to Tony, whose expression told him more than any words could, sighed resignedly, "I think that would be quite pointless, don't you agree?"

"Yes," Tony nodded, "quite pointless." As the waiter had by now arrived with their first course, the discussion naturally had to be held in abeyance, but no sooner had this discreet individual placed their dishes in front of them followed by a polite enquiry if there was anything else, to which both men shook their heads, he made his unassuming exit, whereupon Tony raised an eyebrow, saying, "Well, Mr. Wragge?"

Before his guest could respond to this prompt, a second waiter arrived with a bottle of wine which he held up for Reggie Wragge's inspection and, after receiving a confirming nod of the head, set about uncorking it before pouring a small amount into his wine glass, waiting patiently while he expertly tasted it, eventually nodding his head in approval. Waiting only until this impassive individual had filled both glasses followed by carefully wrapping a pristine white napkin round the bottom and placing it in the cooler on the stand beside the table before bowing himself away, Reggie

Wragge shrugged, "As you have already clearly deduced, Childon, you must know that I own fifty-one Periton Place."

"Yes," Tony nodded, "I had already deduced that, and since you have a most eminent address in Belgravia we both know you are not using it as a residence!"

"So," Wragge enquired, sampling a prawn, "since you are not here to put a business proposition to me by making me an offer, what is your interest in it?" His eyes narrowed suddenly, then, raising a surprised eyebrow, said doubtfully, "Do not tell me you are seeking membership?"

"Huh huh," Tony shook his head, "not in my line, Mr. Wragge."

"I didn't think so," Reggie Wragge replied calmly, "which is why," he nodded, "I don't understand what Periton Place is to you?"

After taking a moment to savour a forkful of smoked chicken, Tony said affably, "Well, I'll tell you, Mr. Wragge; the woman from whom you purchased it, Eliza Boon, or *'Mother Discipline'* as she was once known," he cocked a knowing eyebrow, "is presently under investigation for conspiring to commit murder," grimacing, "not to mention a small matter of terrorising a young woman."

If Tony thought that this disclosure would impair his guest's appetite he was mistaken, but it did make him pause in the process of putting a forkful of scallop into his mouth. "Murder!" he repeated, a little shaken.

"Two counts to be precise," Tony supplied, cutting himself another small segment of chicken, "all of which," he explained, "came about as the direct result of an accidental death which took place at fifty-one Periton Place."

An arrested expression entered Reggie Wragge's intense blue eyes as he realised the damning significance of Eliza Boon's sudden desire to sell her business and the awkward position it had placed him in, and so angry was he that it took him several moments to regain control over himself. "These are serious charges; I hope you can explain them, Childon," he said as calmly as he could.

"We shouldn't be here now if I couldn't, Mr. Wragge," Tony assured him and, over the next three courses, gave him a faithful account of the series of events which had led to this luncheon today, ending by saying, "*That*, Mr. Wragge, is what Periton Place is to me."

Reggie Wragge, an educated and cultured man as well as hard-headed and successful in business, had long since come to believe that nothing could possibly surprise him. Over his long career he had seen and heard it all, but Tony's unexpected disclosure immediately gave the lie to this long-held belief, so much so that had any of his acquaintances seen the shock and incredulity on his face as he stared at Tony, they could well have been forgiven for thinking that they were not looking upon Reggie Wragge at all. Not until Tony had signed his bill and handed it back to the waiter inside its discreet leather folder with a request to bring their brandy and sodas to them in the smoking room, did the full significance of all Reggie Wragge had heard hit him and, as he accompanied Tony into this comfortable apartment, his brain reeled at the revelation.

Reggie Wragge had always known that Eliza Boon, despite her shrewdness in business, was really quite ruthless, but setting this aside as well as her natural proclivities and the strict way she had dealt with the girls, particularly those who had taken her fancy, he had never once considered her capable of such infamy. Now though, to learn the desperate lengths to which she had gone to protect her interests and Sir Braden Collett's reputation, including arranging the supposed suicide of Dennis Dunscumbe due to his sudden attack of remorse and all that had followed, shocked Reggie Wragge out of his calm assurance, but however genuinely appalled he was he was also very conscious of a far more urgent and personal concern.

For a long time now he had managed his licit as well as illicit affairs with dexterity and discretion, so much so that no one who knew this refined and successful man and one, moreover, who could proudly claim to be on friendly terms with any number of people in high places, had the least cause to question either his integrity or respectability. His impeccable reputation as a businessman had seen him dining at the Mansion House in the company of no less a dignitary than the Lord Mayor as well as eminent City bankers and, as a private individual, he was known to regularly entertain distinguished politicians and people of note at his luxurious home in Belgravia. But now, thanks to Eliza Boon, he stood on the brink of public disgrace and humiliation, even ostracism, because although society may look a little indulgently at certain foibles and frailties of personality, it would not look upon running several certain establishments in quite the same way and, at all costs, he had to prevent this from happening.

Tony, who shrewdly suspected what was going through his mind, was not at all sure whether to feel sorry for him or not because although Reggie Wragge's abhorrence was patently clear, he was, just like Sir Braden Collett, equally desirous of protecting his name and reputation.

When Tony had told Superintendent Dawson that he not only trusted his own judgement but he had been in the newspaper business long enough to recognise the truth when he saw and heard it he had not exaggerated, but even though Reggie Wragge had not spoken one word, much less in his own defence, his reception of the disclosure was so far removed from guilt that Tony was easily able to exonerate him of complicity or knowledge.

It was seldom, if ever, Reggie Wragge lost his composure or succumbed to his emotions, but not until he had fortified himself with a generous and much-needed mouthful of brandy and soda was he able to regain the one and control the other, at least sufficiently enough for him to express his profound shock. "I had, of course," he sighed in conclusion, "heard of Dennis Dunscumbe's suicide and the tragic death of his brother, but I had never suspected the truth." Tony waited patiently while he lit a cigar. "I knew Dennis of course," Reggie Wragge nodded, "but I was not so well acquainted with his brother. Sir Philip," he sighed, "was, as you know, a quiet and reserved man who, I am reasonably sure, had no idea of his brother's activities or, I should say," he corrected himself, "his more cloaked ones. As for Sir Braden," he shrugged, "well, we are not friends you understand, but our paths have crossed socially many times and, of course, I have seen him at Periton Place. Both he and Dennis were regular visitors to Eliza's," he nodded, "but at no time have I ever been given cause to believe that Sir Braden, despite his aggressive sexual tendencies, is a man capable of inflicting such harm on his wife or committing such a vicious act as murder, even though I know he has a most uncertain temper and can, when he's a mind, make himself quite disagreeable." He paused a moment to swallow some of his brandy and soda. "You must forgive me, Childon," he apologised, "but I am finding it extremely difficult to come to terms with everything you have told me." He inhaled heavily on his cigar, then, looking directly at Tony said, "I am not going to ask if there is any possibility you could be wrong, you would not be here now if you were not certain of your facts, but it is a dreadful business."

"Yes," Tony agreed, "very."

"I hope I have no need to tell you, Childon," Wragge nodded, "that I do not condone murder or that I knew nothing of any of this."

"No need at all, Mr. Wragge," Tony assured him, lighting a cigarette, "but tell me, how did you come to acquire Periton Place?"

Reggie Wragge thought a moment, then, heaving a sigh, said

resignedly, "Well, I suppose you may as well know, if you don't already, I do have other business interests like Periton Place."

"I figured you did," Tony inclined his head.

"Yes, well," Wragge sighed, "despite that, I know a good business when I see one. I had had my eyes on Eliza's place for some time," he explained, in response to Tony's raised eyebrow, "in fact, I had made her several offers, all of which she had turned down. Then, about ten or eleven months ago, she approached me and asked if I was still interested in buying her place. She even named her own price!" he grimaced.

"And?" Tony prompted.

"It was somewhat extortionate," Wragge inclined his head, "but even without looking at Eliza's books I knew it was a profitable business. I may not be overly fond of her," he admitted, "but I'll say one thing for Eliza, she has a shrewd business head on her shoulders."

"What reason did she give for selling up?" Tony enquired.

"Only that she was retiring from business," Wragge shrugged. "I saw no reason to disbelieve her."

"You say you had had your eye on her business for some time," Tony queried, leaning forward to pick up his glass, "I take it then that you must have visited the premises at some time to spy out the land as well as meet the girls?"

"Yes," he admitted, "I did, including Annie Myers."

"So what did Eliza Boon tell you about her disappearance once you took possession?" Tony pressed.

"Only that she had left Periton Place for pastures new a few weeks before," Wragge replied, finishing off his drink. "I was though," he confessed, "quite surprised because Eliza looked upon the girls as her own personal property, apart from which, Annie was very popular, but I had no reason to question it," he shrugged, "particularly as the girls corroborated it." Taking a moment to ask a passing waiter to bring two more brandy and sodas, to which Tony declined another one, Reggie Wragge eyed him thoughtfully for a moment, saying at length, "You know, Childon, even though I can't pretend to being anything other than shocked over what you have told me; indeed," he nodded, "it was the last thing I had expected, what you said about what happened to Annie Myers did not really surprise me. I can only hazard a guess who told you, but it must have been one of Eliza's girls. Oh, don't worry," he shook his head when he saw the look which descended onto Tony's face, "I don't expect you to betray your sources; not that I have any wish to know who it was, but I can tell you that it sounds about right. Knowing Dennis Dunscumbe as well as I did he would not have taken her refusal kindly, especially as Annie Myers was a particular favourite of his."

"Some favourite!" Tony derided, sitting comfortably back in the leather wing chair.

"Yes, well," Reggie Wragge sighed, "her death is to be regretted, of course, but although Periton Place caters for those with unusual tastes Dunscumbe's were a little more extreme."

"Yes," Tony agreed in a hard voice, "I understand he had a habit of slapping women around, only that night he went further and, accident or not," he bit out, "he hit her hard enough for her to stumble backwards and strike her head against the bedstead which killed her instantly. Dunscumbe and Collett, fearful of the harm it could do their reputations and Eliza Boon equally fearful of the harm it could do her business if it became known that a death had occurred on her premises, instructed Peterson to dump her body in a derelict house not two blocks away from Periton Place like a piece of garbage!"

"And then Dennis is unexpectedly attacked by a fit of remorse," Reggie Wragge sighed, "which resulted in his supposed suicide and all that followed, including Lady Collett being kept a virtual prisoner to prevent her from talking. I'm sorry," he apologised, "I…" breaking off as the waiter brought his brandy and soda, then, after making sure he was out of earshot, resumed, "I should have known Eliza was up to something when she came to see me the other day. So," he mused, "that's what she wanted Molly Clark for! But…"

"The young woman who passed herself off as one of Sir Miles Tatton's housemaids, yes," Tony broke in. "Eliza Boon may well be a hard-headed businesswoman, Mr. Wragge, but she is without doubt extremely ruthless and," he nodded, "considering her past profession, I should say a very good actress." Finishing off his drink, he said firmly, "She not only engineered two murders, but callously ordered the disposal of a young woman's body, not to mention Sir Philip's, without a moment's thought. Between them Mr. Wragge, they are responsible for three deaths, four if you count Annie Myers, and irrespective of whether it was an accident or not, just because she adopted a certain profession which society frowns upon does not mean she is not entitled to justice like the other three, she is," adding determinedly, "and I for one aim to make sure she gets it!"

"I hope you do," Wragge told him.

"You may be sure of it, Mr. Wragge," Tony said firmly.

"And *you* may be sure that I shall never repeat what we have discussed today," he assured him. Tony did not doubt it. "I realise of course," Wragge acknowledged, "that you had to determine what part, if any, I had played in this tragedy if, for no other reason," he grimaced, "than to bring me to account, for which I hold no resentment towards you. You could," he nodded, "had you been so minded, interviewed me at your offices in Fleet Street or at one of my places of business, perhaps even at Scotland Yard, but your discretion and courtesy in discussing such a delicate matter with me in private not only does you credit, but earns my gratitude."

"My sole aim throughout this case, Mr. Wragge," Tony assured him, rising to his feet, "has been to bring the culprits to justice and not to accuse or embarrass the innocent which," he nodded, "unless I've figured you all wrong over the past couple of hours, I'm pretty sure you are."

"Does that mean I can rely upon your discretion?" he asked hopefully, looking up into Tony's resolute face as he too rose to his feet.

"If by that you mean am I going to print your name on the front pages of my newspapers or approach Scotland Yard," he told him, "then the answer is no. Your secondary business affairs are no concern of mine, Mr. Wragge; helping bring murderers to justice is!"

"And if I *had* been a party to it or, even," he enquired curiously, eyeing Tony thoughtfully, "known about it but kept silent to save my reputation?"

"Had either been the case, Mr. Wragge," Tony told him evenly, "then I am very much afraid that you could neither have looked for nor relied upon my discretion."

"No, that's what I thought," Wragge smiled, shaking Tony's outstretched hand.

Chapter Twenty-Five

When Tom had told Tony that Sir Braden Collett had powerful friends to whom he could apply should he become something of a nuisance, he had not exaggerated. These friends, influential in the City as well as the world of commerce, were certainly ideally placed to damage Tony's personal reputation or that of his newspapers, either of which would ruin him; his name would not be worth the paper it was written on. No one, least of all Scotland Yard, would take the word of a man whose integrity had not only been called into question, but found to be sadly wanting especially when they knew that his motives for making allegations against a man of Sir Braden's impeccable credentials stemmed from his illicit relationship with his wife. Of course, it was only to be expected that Childon's title and rank would assure him a certain amount of deference, but society, although as fickle as the weather, would never be brought to accept a man into its ranks once it became known that he had lured Lady Collett out of her home and away from her husband's love and protection, then maliciously fabricated a tale to denounce him. Childon would be ostracised completely!

But however pleasing a picture this presented to Sir Braden Collett, who seemed permanently thwarted by a man of inflexible determination, it was very soon rudely brought home to him that his own somewhat delicate position rendered achieving this most gratifying accomplishment as quite out of the question. It was not because his friends would refuse to come to his aid, after all it was not as though they had not pulled beneficial strings in the past, but he could not afford to have them enquiring into the reason he was seeking their help. They may be prepared, for certain inducements, to influence a decision in turning the tide in favour of one company rather than another or something equally beneficial to themselves or a friendly party by putting the word about of scurrilous dealings by an individual or corporation, but they would not be so happy or eager to help a man in furthering his aims to cover up cold-blooded murder.

As it was impossible for Sir Braden to call upon those he had long since called friends to rid him of this meddlesome American, whose persistent thwarting of his plans was beginning to become a fixed obsession with him, he had to look elsewhere for the answer. As Peterson's bundled attempts yesterday morning to lay Childon by the heels once and for all had gone drastically wrong and Eliza seemed to be at a loss to know what they should do next, besides their failed attempt to get Eleanor back into their safe custody, all served to exacerbate Sir Braden's temper and increase his fear. As he sat in brooding silence in his study contemplating the dilemma facing them, he came to the horrifying conclusion that unless a miracle occurred or Childon was suddenly struck down by lightning or some other means of divine intervention, then nothing could possibly save them from the full penalty of the law. Unfortunately however, miracles were proving to be somewhat elusive and divine intervention remarkably unwilling to come to his rescue whilst time was ticking remorselessly by with a swiftness which did nothing to assuage his alarms. Sir Braden had not needed to hear of Childon's parting words to Peterson in that he was coming after them, he had known this all along, what did shock him however, was knowing that Childon knew about Annie Myers and the others. Sir Braden had no idea how he could possibly have deduced all of this, but one thing he did know and that was, for now at least, he was utterly at a loss to see what could feasibly be done to frustrate Childon's schemes, and unless Eliza put something together and soon, then one thing was certain, and that was they could expect a visit from Scotland Yard before many days were out.

Since Eleanor had clearly shown which side of the fence she was on and any pressure he may bring to bear on her to persuade Childon to call a halt to his investigations would not yield the response he wanted, and Childon himself had proved just how well he could defend himself, it seemed the only bargaining power Sir Braden had which would bring forth dividends was Sir Miles Tatton. He had already seen to what good effect his father-in-law's transgression could be put over recent months and he saw no reason why it could not be used in the same way again, only this time his threats would not be directed at his wife.

Sir Braden had no notion where the idea had come from but it was both brilliant and risky, but for a man of his pride and arrogance it was also quite offensive. It went very much against the grain with him to have to go cap in hand to the very man he loathed above all others, but when faced with the unpalatable alternative he was reluctantly forced to admit that presenting a bargaining plea was far better than having his neck stretched. Of course, he fully expected Childon to discount it out of hand, in fact the chances were very good that he would throw it back in his face, but Sir Braden had seen enough of this tenacious young man to know that he was realistic enough to face the facts for what they really were. He may find the very concept of approaching Childon as being quite repugnant, but the one thing which would help ease his humiliation and make it all worthwhile was that should this objectionable Colonial refuse to submit to his terms, then Eleanor, upon discovering her husband had denounced her father and that Childon could have prevented it, she would never forgive him. He may not get Eleanor back, but then neither would Childon; what more fitting revenge then for his effrontery in daring to compromise him? As far as Sir Braden could see there was not the slightest chink in this plan's armour and, if he was honest, he could not imagine why he had not thought of it before now, but having done so he felt sure that Eliza would fully approve.

She did, but to say she was taken aback was a gross understatement, quite frankly, considering Sir Braden's state of mind she was utterly astonished at the way he had put together such a clever plan, but managing to hide her amazement she eagerly threw herself into implementing it. Like Sir Braden, she saw no chink in its armour, in fact she failed to see how it could fail, especially when she knew that Childon and Lady Collett had taken more than a liking to one another; the glow on her prisoner's face and in her eyes the evening she returned from the Kirkmichaels' had been more than adequate testimony to this fact, so too was the way Childon had taken her under his protection in Mount Street. Admittedly, Eliza had never laid eyes on him, but if he was the type of man she took him to be, then she could not see him refusing Sir Braden's proposition which, no matter how one looked at it, would leave this meddlesome American very little room for manoeuvre. This did not mean to say he would like it, far from it, but experience had taught her that it was surprising what a man in love, or in the throes of intense and aroused excitement, would agree to and, unless she was grossly mistaken, Childon would be no different. She could not see him refusing to agree to Sir Braden's proposal, not when he knew that Eleanor, whose love for her father had already been more than adequately demonstrated, would never forgive him when she learned that he had put his personal desire for a story before helping protect her father from disgrace and scandal. It was therefore in complete confidence that Eliza summoned Ellen to arrange for Albert the boot boy to deliver Sir Braden's letter to Mount Street.

Although no more than a light flurry of snow had come down during the past thirty-six hours it was still bitingly cold, but Tony, too used to the winters in New York and Montana, was totally impervious to it, and therefore upon leaving *'The Palatine Club'* just a little before half past three, he walked to Fleet Street instead of hailing a hackney. He knew Superintendent Dawson had arranged to see Sir Edward Bradford at one o'clock, but even though that was two and a half hours ago it did not mean that he would have arrived at a decision in so short a time. From what Tom had told him it seemed to Tony that Sir Edward Bradford was a man determined to reduce crime in the Metropolitan area, and whilst it was inconceivable that he would condone murder or even allow it to go unanswered, he could well feel somewhat hesitant in sanctioning a plan deliberately calculated to ensnare a man of Sir Braden Collett's reputation and standing in society. Sir Edward may also feel that although the evidence strongly pointed to Collett's guilt, considering the only two witnesses were disqualified for different reasons, it might be better to wait until more substantial proof came to hand. Should this in fact be his decision, then Tony failed to see where more proof would come from, particularly when he considered how Collett and his associates had so far effectively covered their tracks.

The same thought had also crossed Superintendent Dawson's mind, but although this could not be discounted he knew enough of Sir Edward Bradford to feel fairly confident that he would ultimately agree, but to say that Sir Edward, having listened to the story which unfolded in disbelief, was profoundly shocked, was a gross understatement. To learn that a man of Sir Braden Collett's reputation and standing in society had not only visited a certain type of establishment but had been present when Dennis Dunscumbe had accidentally killed Annie Myers and colluded in disposing of her body was bad enough, but to learn that he had cold-bloodedly murdered Sir Philip Dunscumbe and colluded in the death of his brother Dennis and, from the looks of it, a member of his own household as well, came as a reeling blow.

But no matter how surprised Sir Edward was to discover that the owner of several newspapers, and a lord at that, had actually carried out reporting investigations instead of leaving it to his reporters, he could not find fault with the case he had put together. Even so he could not help thinking it was a great pity that the witnesses, if not unreliable, were certainly not qualified to stand up in the witness-box to give their evidence, but even though this plan of Lord Childon's had a lot to recommend it, there were no guarantees that Sir Braden or one of his accomplices would fall into it. All the same, Sir Edward had no liking for murderers going free of the law no matter who they were, besides which, there were four deaths to be accounted for, and in view of there being no other witnesses and the chances of any further evidence coming to light seemed remote, he decided that the scheme proposed by Lord Childon appeared to be the only way forward. He still found it hard to believe that Childon, despite his title, had managed to persuade three respectable newspaper editors to insert the typewritten piece he presently held in his hand, providing of course he agreed to it, but since Childon *had* persuaded them, and no other options presented themselves to waylay the culprits by the heels, he gave the plan his approval. Nevertheless, he could not help expressing his sincere regret that uncovering the truth had been down to a newspaperman and not the police, but as far as the surveillance operation in Hertford Street was concerned Sir Edward would have Superintendent Dawson know that although he could not really forbid Lord Childon to take part in it, particularly as it was his idea as well as all the work he had put into the case, it was to be a police undertaking and not in any way attributable to any newspaper. Considering the criticism which had unfortunately been directed at them over the delay in discovering the truth surrounding Sir Philip Dunscumbe's murder, Sir Edward went on to suggest that Superintendent Dawson meet with this Childon as soon as possible to discuss the details of the surveillance in Hertford Street, in the meantime he would acquaint The Prime Minister of this new and startling development. Although Sir Edward had no doubt that it would be just as much a shock for him as it was for himself he could not see Lord Salisbury putting forward any objections, particularly given his friendship with Sir Philip.

Since Sir Edward did not approve of telephones or typewriters and would not have either in any police station under his jurisdiction, he had nevertheless ensured that they were all installed with a telegraph machine and therefore Superintendent Dawson, immediately upon leaving the Commissioner's office, was able to send a message to Bill in Fleet Street.

By the time Tony strolled into Bill's office half an hour after leaving *'The Palatine Club'* wheels had already been set in motion; an office boy had promptly been sent hurrying to Cavendish Square to tell Jerry he was needed here straightaway and Courtney, Buckle and Barton of *'The Telegraph', 'The Times'* and *'The Echo'* respectively, had all been given the nod to run the article for tomorrow's editions.

"With luck," Bill nodded, "Collett will read it in his copies tomorrow morning."

"What would I do without you, Bill?" Tony smiled, removing his hat and coat, relieved that Sir Edward Bradford had agreed to the plan. "Okay," he grinned, in answer to Bill's raised eyebrow, "I'll skip that one."

"They told me to tell you," Bill pointed his cigar at him, his eyes smiling up at Tony, "that they still think you're crazy as well as owing them one – like big time!"

"Sure," Tony laughed, pouring himself a cup of coffee, "they got it!"

"So," Bill sighed, "you still think Collett will go for it?"

"He'll be a fool if he doesn't!" Tony inclined his head, easing himself into the chair on the opposite side of Bill's desk.

"Which we know he's not," Bill nodded.

"Huh huh," Tony shook his head, "but he sure is desperate!"

"Desperate enough to visit Hertford Street before the police?" Bill raised an eyebrow, eyeing Tony through a cloud of cigar smoke.

"He can't take the risk of not going, Bill," Tony said firmly. "If there's the slightest chance of him finding any incriminating evidence which Peterson could possibly have left after he shot Dennis Dunscumbe which got overlooked by the police when they first checked the house, then he can't afford to leave it there!"

"And if he does take the risk and not show," Bill wanted to know, "what happens then?"

"Do you mean to me or to Collett?" Tony grinned.

"Both," Bill shrugged.

"As far as Collett is concerned," Tony told him, "we shall just have to keep digging, as for me," he shrugged, "well," a smile playing at the corner of his mouth, "I shall most probably find myself answering charges of wasting police time or bringing false allegations against one who is allegedly beyond suspicion!"

"Sure he is!" Bill scorned. "A real nice guy is Collett!"

"You said it!" Tony derided.

"So," Bill cocked his head, "did you see this Wragge guy?" Tony nodded as he swallowed some coffee. "And?"

"No go, Bill," Tony shook his head, going on to tell him what had passed between them.

"So then—?" Bill shrugged a question.

"Huh huh," Tony shook his head, correctly interpreting this. "Like I told Tom last night, I may not approve of Wragge's illegal business enterprises, but they're no concern of mine."

"Okay," Bill pulled a face, "it's your ball game. By the way, how is Tom?" relighting his cigar.

"You know Tom," Tony smiled.

"Sure! A great guy!" Bill grinned.

"He sure is!" Tony agreed. "Thing is though," he smiled, not a little ruefully, "he's determined to be in on this at Hertford Street."

Bill almost dropped his cigar. "You're kiddin' me!"

"Straight up," Tony laughed.

"Well I'll be…!" Bill cried.

"You said it!" Tony grinned, finishing off his coffee.

Bill eyed him narrowly. "You agreed to it, didn't you?"

"Mm," Tony nodded, his eyes alight with laughter.

Bill thought a moment. "I hope you know what you're doin'!"

"I do," Tony assured him, "'sides, Tom's a useful guy with his fives, apart from which," he pointed out, "he doesn't approve of murder or beating up women any more than we do." Suddenly his shoulders shook as Tom's rueful expression and urgent plea danced in front of his eyes. "Thing is, I'm sworn to secrecy."

"Beatrice?" Bill raised a knowing eyebrow.

"Beatrice," Tony confirmed.

"For the love of Mike!" Bill cried between amusement and exasperation. "What a way to run a newspaper!"

Jerry, arriving a few minutes later, not only expressed his satisfaction to know that Tony had given Peterson what for, but also that things were beginning to move, quickly following this up by voicing his surprise over the way Collett had not left the house since the evening they rescued Eleanor. "Ain't stepped a foot outside the 'ouse!" He scratched his head.

"I think you will find, Jerry," Tony nodded, "that our friend Collett has other things on his mind at the moment than keeping his engagements."

It was just as Jerry was snorting his disgust of Collett's engagements that the door opened and Bill's secretary announced Superintendent Dawson. Jerry may have no qualms about coming face to face with him, after all he had been one of the few senior officers he had not come into conflict with, but Dawson could not fail to be aware of the frustration felt by his colleagues over his frequent questioning of orders. Tony, watching their affable reunion with an amused eye, could not resist casting a sidelong glance of pure enjoyment at Bill as Jerry, totally unabashed, answered Dawson's enquiry about how his private detective business was faring followed by several minutes of exchanging reminiscences. Superintendent Dawson knew perfectly well that Jerry Taylor had been far from popular with the hierarchy at Bow Street, but he knew too that he was a man who knew what he was doing and could be relied upon totally, and had not been at all surprised when Tony had told him yesterday that he had recruited him on Bill's recommendation. Recommendation or not, Superintendent Dawson had nevertheless considered it prudent to keep Sir Edward in the dark about Jerry's participation in this case as he felt reasonably certain that it would have done very little if anything to advance his application for approving Tony's scheme.

Considering it was Tony who had pieced the case together as well as coming up with a way of apprehending the perpetrators of such vicious crimes, Superintendent Dawson felt just a little awkward upon informing him that Sir Edward, whilst perfectly happy for his officers to comply with whatever details Tony worked out with regards to the surveillance in Hertford Street, nevertheless deemed it only right that it should be regarded as a police operation.

"I quite understand, Superintendent," Tony nodded, quite unperturbed by this.

"Thank you, my lord," Superintendent Dawson nodded, "but I did think that you could well take…"

"Offence?" Tony broke in. "Huh huh," he shook his head, "all that matters is that Collett and the others are finally brought to account for what they have done."

"That's true enough, my lord," Superintendent Dawson acknowledged.

"You know, Superintendent," Tony smiled, unable to resist casting a glance at Bill, "if you have no objection, I would prefer it if you called me Tony or," he suggested, "if you feel you can't, then Childon or Mawdsley will do just fine!"

"That's very good of you my l…Childon," he nodded.

"Not at all, Superintendent," Tony smiled. "Now," he nodded, "I'll put you in the picture as to where we are so far."

However surprised Superintendent Dawson was to learn that the notice they wanted Collett to read in the newspapers would be included in tonight's run for the first edition tomorrow, being of the belief that such a project would take several days at least, he could not help being impressed with the swiftness Tony and Bill Pitman had gone to work on this. "That quickly?" he raised a surprised eyebrow.

"That quickly, Superintendent." Tony smiled, opening out the street plan Bill handed him and stretching it out on the desk as he did so.

"So, what have you in mind?" Superintendent Dawson cocked his head, retrieving his pipe from his pocket.

"Here is Dennis Dunscumbe's house," Tony told him, pointing out the house number on the plan, "and, as you can see," he nodded to Dawson, "it's just three doors along from the corner of Stanhope Row, which helps us a great deal."

"Yes," Dawson agreed, resting his hands on the desk to look down at where Tony was pointing. "I'll put some men on duty there in case they try to make a run for it. I can't see them legging it all the way to Old Park Lane," he admitted, "but just to be on the safe side I'll have that covered as well."

"Assuming it's Collett who turns up," Tony inclined his head, "and I am certain he will, Peterson too, if for no other reason than to effect an entry, I can't see either of them making it that far should they try to escape, but it certainly won't hurt to have that end of Hertford Street covered. I think it will also be as well, Superintendent," Tony smiled, "if you tell your men that two of Jerry's sons will also be on the watch outside."

Dawson nodded, then, having made sure his pipe was lit, he leaned over the map and, after pinpointing other possible routes of escape, told Tony that he would make certain they too were sufficiently manned. "Now, about inside?" he queried.

"You and I and Jerry will be inside," Tony told him, "so too will my brother-in-law. I'll explain about Tom tomorrow." He grinned in answer to the surprised look on the Superintendent's face. "I promise you he's a useful guy."

Accepting this, Dawson suggested, "We had better have two uniformed men inside."

"I agree," Tony nodded.

Dawson thought a moment, saying at length, "I'd say the basement door is their most likely means of entry. No one is going to see them force a door down the basement steps."

"That's my guess, which is why," Tony pointed out, "I am firmly convinced Collett will take Peterson with him, not only that, but Collett may need him to run through precisely what he did that night."

"And Eliza Boon?" Dawson queried, puffing on his pipe.

"She could well," Tony conceded, "but quite honestly I fail to see the need for the three of them to go."

Dawson nodded, then, after going over various other aspects of the plan for tomorrow with Tony and Jerry, a crease descended onto his forehead as he turned something over in his mind. "There's just a couple of things, Childon," to which Tony raised an eyebrow. "Bearing in mind we don't want Collett becoming suspicious, I take it that the article you have arranged to be inserted in three different newspapers will actually be worded differently."

"Yes," Tony assured him, "even though the message will mean the same thing. The last thing we want is to raise doubt in Collett's mind."

Dawson nodded. "And how are you going to make sure that he reads the newspapers we want him to?"

"According to Mrs. Timms," Tony told him, "every morning the boot boy goes and purchases *'The Times'* and *'The Telegraph'* for Collett. Having done so he takes them straight to the kitchen where she puts them ready for Ellen, the upstairs parlour maid, to take upstairs to leave on the table in the hall. Tomorrow," he nodded, "when the boot boy returns with the newspapers, Mrs. Timms will exchange them for the ones we want Collett to read only *this* time," he smiled, "she will take them upstairs herself with the excuse that, due to Lady Collett being unwell, she needs to speak to Collett about some domestic matter which won't keep, during the course of which she will slip into the conversation about the dreadful piece she has read in her newspaper about 'poor Mr. Dunscumbe'!"

"Alerting Collett to the urgency of picking up his copies," Dawson supplied. Tony nodded. "I see, but how do we know that Eliza Boon does not take a newspaper?"

"She doesn't," Tony shook his head. "According to Mrs. Timms she always reads Collett's when he has finished with them."

Dawson nodded, then, after checking his pipe, asked, "But how do we get our copies to Mrs. Timms?"

"As soon as *'The Telegraph'* and the others have printed our copies they will then be brought straight here tonight to Bill where Jerry will be waiting for them. He will then make his way to Cavendish Square where he will hand them over to Mrs. Timms via the basement door for her to keep safely hidden until tomorrow morning ready for when the boot boy Albert returns with the copies he has just bought. We can't risk handing them over to Mrs. Timms in the morning because it will be cutting it pretty fine. Jerry will also hand her a copy of *'The Echo'* for herself."

"So that's why you had it inserted in her copy too in case Collett demands to see it," Dawson said, impressed.

"You'd better believe he will!" Tony said firmly. "Having read the story in three different newspapers Collett will be in no doubt that Scotland Yard, on information received, are looking again at Dunscumbe's supposed suicide and that his death could well be tied in with that of his brother Sir Philip. To assist the police in their investigations it will be necessary for them to conduct another search of Dennis Dunscumbe's home in Hertford Street to make sure no vital evidence was overlooked first time round, which is due to take place the day after tomorrow."

"The information received," Dawson nodded, "supposedly coming from yourself."

"That's about the size of it, Superintendent," Tony nodded. "Collett may not be entirely certain what I have discovered, but he knows enough to believe I pose a threat to him and the others, and bearing in mind my parting words to Peterson as well as Lady Collett taking refuge in my sister's home, there is no way he can take the risk and not visit

Hertford Street. Of course," he sighed, "I have to admit we've been lucky in that the house has not been sold or let since Dunscumbe's death, had it have been," he shrugged, "we would have had to come up with another idea."

Dawson nodded. "Yes, we've been lucky there."

"That's for sure!" Tony agreed. "However, having taken the bait Collett will know he can't afford to waste any time and that he must get there before the police, which means he will have to go to Hertford Street tomorrow," he nodded, "but he can't effect an entry in broad daylight so he will have to wait until it starts to get dark before he can make a move, and when he does," he smiled, "we'll be waiting for him."

"Yes," Dawson said thoughtfully, fanning his pipe with a match box, "but considering the position he's in he might take a chance before it gets dark; in which case," he raised his eyes to Tony, "we have to make sure we get there well ahead of him."

"Yes," Tony agreed, "we can't risk leaving it too late."

Superintendent Dawson, staying only long enough for certain final arrangements to be agreed for their meeting up in Hertford Street the following morning, took his leave.

"Jerry," Tony cocked his head, when Dawson had left, "when you get back to Cavendish Square you will have to spot your chance to speak to Mrs. Timms to let her know that it's on for tomorrow and that you will be delivering the phoney newspapers later," to which Jerry nodded, by no means averse to seeing Mrs. Timms again.

Upon seeing the gleam which had entered Jerry's eyes when he mentioned Mrs. Timms, Tony sternly suppressed the twitch at the corner of his mouth, telling him, "Tomorrow, I want Harry to stay where he is in Mount Street. Samuel and Edward will be on the watch outside in Hertford Street from certain strategic points, but Arthur is to remain in Cavendish Square." Jerry cocked an eyebrow. "I can't see the three of them descending on Dunscumbe's house," Tony shook his head, "and I'd stake my life Eliza Boon will stay behind, but just in case they've concocted something and she leaves the house, then I want Arthur to follow her," to which Jerry agreed, then, after a brief discussion, took his leave. "Well, Bill," Tony sighed, "I think that's everything covered. All that's needed now is for you to wish us luck!"

"You got it!" Bill said firmly, rising to his feet.

"Depending on how things go," Tony told him, shrugging himself into his overcoat, "I may or may not see you tomorrow, but I'll try to keep you posted."

Bill nodded. "Hey, Tony," he warned, gripping his hand, "you take care, you hear?"

Tony grinned, "Sure I will. So long Bill, and thanks," closing the door quietly behind him.

Beatrice, being assured by Tony before he left for *'The Palatine Club'* that although Eleanor had been rather upset by the interview with Superintendent Dawson, he had nevertheless left her feeling more calm, told him that she would go up to her because the poor child, apart from just having undergone a most dreadful ordeal, would welcome some company. Fully expecting to find Eleanor just a little pulled after her ordeal, it was something of a surprise to Beatrice to see that, despite the fading blue and yellow of her bruises and the residual swelling to her cheeks, although by no means as distended as they had been, far from being any such thing, Eleanor looked positively radiant and knew instantly how Tony had taken her mind off the interview, but not for the world would Beatrice embarrass her by mentioning it. Eleanor, who had no idea her face glowed or that her fully opened left eye and partially opened right one sparkled from Tony's kisses, happily made room for Beatrice to sit beside her on the day bed, and as neither of them had any idea of what Tony was planning with regards to Sir Braden Collett or that Tom had wholeheartedly pledged himself to it, they were both able to relax and enjoy a good gossip in blissful ignorance.

Sarah, who had by now learned the truth about Sir Braden's iniquities, had always been fully committed to her mistress and nothing or no one would ever change that, much less prise her away from her, but it could not be denied that she had taken to Lady Collett the moment Mr. Tony had carried her lifeless body into the house. Upon setting eyes on the full extent of her injuries, Sarah had vowed there and then that no matter what she was determined to do everything in her power to prevent Eleanor from returning to a man who neither loved nor deserved her, but it had not taken many minutes for her to see that there was no need for her to worry as Mr. Tony would make sure she did not. Sarah could think of no two people more suited to one another, but upon taking a look in on Eleanor only minutes before Beatrice tapped on her door one look at that glowing face was enough to tell her just how suited they really were, and should anything happen to prevent them from spending the rest of their lives together then all she had to say was that there was no justice in the world!

Doctor Little, extremely pleased with Eleanor's progress, saw no reason why his patient should not be allowed to venture downstairs, providing of course she did not do anything too strenuous, advising that although her bruises were healing nicely her cracked rib still required her to rest. Receiving this news with relief, Eleanor, on legs which still felt a little unsteady and Sarah's supporting arm around her waist, while Beatrice plumped up cushions in the rear sitting room in readiness, Eleanor slowly descended the stairs, entering this cosy domain just as the clock struck four o'clock.

Harry may not have recognised the handwriting on the envelope when it was hurriedly pushed through the letterbox a few minutes before Beatrice came down the stairs followed by Eleanor and Sarah, but thanks to his surveillance duties outside twenty-nine Cavendish Square he had certainly been able to recognise the boot boy Albert descending the steps as he caught sight of him through the side windows of the front door. It did not take much ingenuity to know that the letter was from Sir Braden Collett, but bearing in mind Tony's instructions that his turn up with Peterson was not to come to the ears of Lady Shipton or Lady Collett Harry felt sure he would not want them to know about this letter either and so slid it into his pocket until Tony returned a few minutes after half past five. Recognising the handwriting immediately, Tony tore open the envelope and read the single sheet with its half dozen or so lines with a deep frown creasing his forehead, then, after checking with Harry that nothing untoward had occurred followed by informing him of tomorrow's events and thanking him for not showing the letter to his sister he wished him goodnight, whereupon Tony perused the letter's content again. It was certainly unlooked-for but clearly Collett had a reason for requesting his attendance this evening in Cavendish Square, but before Tony could go any further as to Collett's motive the door to the rear sitting room opened and Beatrice walked towards him, his frown lifting instantly.

If she wondered about the letter she saw her brother slide into the inner pocket of his coat it was only briefly, smiling, "Tony, I am so glad you're here at last!"

Hanging his hat and overcoat on the stand he bent down and kissed her cheek, taking her hand in his and giving it an affectionate little shake. "Are you," he smiled. "Why?"

"I have a surprise for you; in the sitting room," she told him. "You go on through and I'll join you in a little while."

"You're looking very conspiratorial. Just what have you been up to, Bea?" He cocked his head.

"Why, nothing at all!" she said innocently over her shoulder as she began to climb the stairs.

Striding leisurely down the hall to the rear sitting room Tony pushed open the door to the surprising, but not unwelcome, sight of Eleanor resting back against a mound of cushions on a sofa wearing a dressing gown of pale blue which Beatrice had assured her would become her far better than it did herself, besides which she had not worn it this age. "So," he mused, his dark grey eyes laughing down into Eleanor's, "I see you are still determined on mutiny!"

She laughed. "You must blame Doctor Little. He said I may come downstairs."

"Did he?" Tony raised an enquiring eyebrow, coming to sit down beside her. "You know," he said thoughtfully, "it seems to me you can twist him round your little finger."

"Well, perhaps just a little," Eleanor smiled, laying a hand on his arm. "Aren't you pleased?"

"You must know I am," he told earnestly, covering her hand with his, "but as I told you last night, I don't want you doing too much too soon."

"I shan't," she promised him, "but I shall be glad to be up and about again instead of reclining on a day bed or a sofa."

"I'll second that," he assured her softly. It was just as he was about to kiss her when he heard Beatrice making play with the handle of the door and, smiling down at Eleanor, whispered amusingly, "You can't deny she plays fair!"

Almost immediately Beatrice floated into the sitting room looking innocently from one to the other, not finding it in the least degree shocking that her brother was sitting beside Eleanor with her hand tucked into his, saying with great aplomb, "I really must ask Bennett to take a look at that handle! I can't imagine why it has suddenly started to jam!" Without waiting for a response Beatrice smiled at Tony, her colour just a little high as she caught the laughter in his eyes, asking, "Well, and how did you like your surprise?"

"As much as you knew I would," he grinned, rising to his feet. "I suspect that's why the door suddenly jammed!"

She laughed and placed her hands in his as he bent down to kiss her cheek, saying impishly, "It *was* rather clever of me, wasn't it?"

"Oh, *very*," he agreed readily, squeezing her fingers affectionately. "Tactful too."

"Yes," she smiled, "*I* thought so."

"So," he teased, "having played Cupid you're not going to play gooseberry!"

"Certainly not!" she cried, her indignation belied by the laughter in her eyes, "the very idea, although," she admitted, "I must own I am looking forward to the four of us sitting down to dinner."

He sighed, saying ruefully, "Sorry Bea, but I am afraid you will have to hold me excused."

She eyed him a little disappointed. "Oh, Tony, no!" she cried, gripping his fingers. "Do not say you have to go out!"

"I'm sorry, Bea," Tony shook his head, "but I must; it's important."

"But you can't," she protested, "not on Eleanor's first evening downstairs! Surely it can wait until tomorrow!"

"I'm afraid not," he said meaningfully.

"But…" She was just about to entreat Eleanor to persuade him into remaining at home when she caught a warning look in his eyes and instinctively knew it had something to do with Sir Braden which he did not want Eleanor to know about, so quickly changed what she was about to say. "Very well, if you must you must, but I don't know what you deserve for this!"

He laughed and kissed her cheek. "I have no doubt you will think up a fitting punishment while I am gone."

"You may be sure of it!" Beatrice nodded, but unable to resist his smile added that she promised it would not be too dire, whereupon she kissed his cheek and left the sitting room.

"Phew! I'd say I've just managed to avoid the doghouse! Although," Tony sighed, inclining his head, "it was a pretty close run thing!"

"Yes," Eleanor smiled, holding out her hand to him, "I think it was."

"Are you cross with me too?" he asked contritely, taking her hand in his and resuming his seat beside her.

"No," she shook her head, "but I must own to being disappointed."

Tony nodded. "I know, and I'm sorry," he sighed, "but you must know that if it were not so important I would not go."

She bit down on her bottom lip, her eyes looking a little mischievously up at him. "I thought for a moment," she teased shyly, her fingers moving in his, "it was your way of telling me that you do not wish for my company?"

"Mm," he mused, looking lovingly down at her, "and here I was thinking I had carried it off with such flair!" gathering her in his arms and kissing her. "*That,*" he told her in a deep voice when he eventually released her, "is how much I don't wish for your company."

Easing herself a little away from him in order for her to look up into his face, she said a little huskily, "I… I don't mean to tease you, but is the reason you are going out tonight something to do with Braden? Yes," she sighed, interpreting the look in his eyes, "I thought so."

"It's nothing for you to worry about," he assured her, not wishing to alarm her by telling her he was going to see her husband. "I do not expect being gone long," he told her gently. "I promise I'll be back before you know it."

"It's not that," Eleanor shook her head, "but you will be careful, won't you?"

"Cross my heart," he promised, suiting the action to the words.

"It's just… well," she faltered, her colour a little high, "it's because I love you that I couldn't bear anything to happen to you!"

"Nothing's going to happen to me," Tony assured her softly, taking her back into his arms, "and as for loving me," he smiled, "you'd better because I sure love you!" silencing any further concerns she had by agreeably kissing her.

Half an hour later, Beatrice, relinquishing Tom to her brother with the dire warning what she would like to do to him if only she were a few inches taller, left them alone together in the study, telling them as sternly as she could that she was going up to the nursery. Had Beatrice the least idea that while she was reading stories to their children, her husband, having listened to his brother-in-law tell him about his luncheon with Reggie Wragge as well as about the arrangements which had been set in motion for tomorrow eagerly followed up with his own readiness to take part, she would not have been so contented. But although Tom was by no means unwilling to lend a hand in bringing cold-blooded murderers to justice, on the contrary he was looking forward to it, especially when he considered the treatment which had ruthlessly been handed out to Eleanor all this time, he was by no means easy about Collett's letter, and not even a second reading of it would convince him that it was not a trap.

Childon,

In view of recent events, I feel sure there is no need for me to explain the reason for this letter or to warn you of the consequences which will result should you persist on your present course. I am confident that, after due consideration, you will see the wisdom of attending in Cavendish Square this evening at seven-thirty in order for us to discuss the matter.

Collett

"You're surely not going!" Tom exclaimed, handing the letter back.

"Too right I'm going," Tony replied firmly, returning the letter to his inside pocket.

"But how do you know it's not a trap!" Tom cried.

"I don't," Tony shook his head, "but I doubt it."

"You doubt it!" Tom echoed, aghast. "After what happened to Sir Philip in that very house," he pointed out, "not to mention the attack on you yesterday, how can you possibly discount it?"

"I don't like Collett and the others any more than you do," Tony inclined his head, "and come what may I aim to see them answer to the law for what they have done, but what happened to Sir Philip was not premeditated but a spur-of-the-moment thing. No," he shook his head, "I'd stake my life that Collett did not want a death in his own home, but when faced with Sir Philip's unexpected visit and his accusations about him being responsible for his brother's death as well as informing him of his intention of raising questions in the House about such establishments as Periton Place, Collett lost his head and struck him with the poker in the throes of an uncontrollable rage brought on by sheer panic."

"Yes," Tom nodded, "that's all very well, but what happened to you yesterday…"

"Was an act of sheer desperation," Tony told him, "resulting from their failure to remove Eleanor from under this roof before she could tell me anything about what happened that night."

"Yes but…"

"The way I figure it, Tom," Tony smiled in response to his brother-in-law's doubtful expression, "is that they've had a change of heart, which is why Collett wants me to go and see him. It's my guess," he nodded, "that Collett is going to try to coerce me into dropping my investigations."

"You mean by threatening you with Eleanor?" Tom supplied worriedly.

"Either Eleanor or her father." Tony inclined his head.

"Yes," Tom said thoughtfully, "I think you're right, but I don't like it, Tony!"

"Well," Tony sighed, "like it or not, I have to go."

"But what about tomorrow?" Tom wanted to know.

"As there is no inducement Collett could possibly put forward to make me drop this case," Tony told him firmly, "that's still on!"

Since nothing Tom could say would dissuade Tony from going to see Collett and he laughingly turned down his offer of accompanying him on the grounds that Bea would not speak to either of them for a month if they both left the house, Tom was left to take what comfort he could from knowing that Jerry would be outside within call should his brother-in-law find himself in need of assistance.

Jerry may have been of the same mind as Tom, but he was even more forthright in his opinions about Collett's motive as well as what they had planned for him, but although Tony expressed his thanks for his concerns it was clear he was taking no more heed of his warnings than he had to those of his brother-in-law. It was in a mood of considerable disquiet therefore that Jerry watched Tony unobtrusively leave the Square's gardens to stride over the road towards Collett's house, casually mounting the steps for all the world as though he was attending a soiree, saying darkly to Samuel and Edward that he hoped this would not be the last time they would ever set eyes on him.

In view of recent events, Tony could not blame Tom or Jerry for thinking that Collett was setting a trap for him so they could do away with him, but although he had considered this possibility himself it had been no more than a fleeting thought. Collett may lose his head when faced with an unexpected crisis or in the throes of an ungovernable rage, but Tony could not see him taking such a monumental risk as Collett would know that he would not be fool enough to visit in Cavendish Square without telling people he was doing so. Of course, considering the desperate straits in which Collett and his accomplices found themselves one more murder more or less was not going to make much difference, but as Tony waited for Peterson to open the door in response to his tug on the bell, now, no more than upon first reading Collett's letter, did he believe that they would be reckless enough to put an end to his life. The expression on Peterson's swollen face, however, told Tony that this was precisely what he would like to do, but since neither man had the least desire to converse with the other Tony merely followed him down the hall to Collett's study, stopping for a moment to look up as he caught sight of Eliza Boon standing on the first landing looking down at him. For the first time Tony was able to take a good look at the woman who had helped to terrorise Eleanor, recognising the cruelty on her thin and unsympathetic face as well as that ruthless determination which had not only seen her and her confederates avert one crisis after another, but kept them from the gallows, leaving him in no doubt that left to her he would not leave twenty-nine Cavendish Square alive.

At no time could it be said that Sir Braden Collett was a man who took very kindly to his behaviour or actions being questioned, much less having to justify them, and certainly not to a man he had taken in violent dislike. It went very much against the grain with him to have to placate anyone, deeming himself far above such a need, but that he must do so now and to Childon of all people was insufferable, but as this man was not going to go away of his own accord he somehow had to swallow his pride sufficiently to persuade him into doing precisely that. As it was not in Collett's nature to conciliate or compromise, considering both as being far beneath his dignity, the thought of having to do so now made him furiously angry, and were it not for Eleanor's dramatic escape there would not be the least need for him to do so. He may bitterly regret the urgent necessity of having to demean himself, especially to the man who was adamantly bent on his downfall, but since he had he was firmly determined to conduct the interview on his own terms and not Childon's. Unfortunately, however, when he had decided upon this last-ditch attempt to solve the problem regarding the danger Tony posed, Collett had entirely failed to take one important point into consideration and that was just the mere sight of Tony would be more than enough to not only test his self-control but demolish it altogether, rendering his plan null and void before it even got off the ground. From the moment Collett had sent that letter he had painstakingly rehearsed what he would say to this man, in fact so calm and persuasive was he that he eventually won Childon over to his way of thinking, delicately pressing the point that he would become estranged from Eleanor if he did not do so, and as Collett waited for this thorn in his flesh to arrive he was supremely confident that the outcome of this meeting would be precisely as he had imagined it. Unhappily though, the sight of Tony's tall lean figure strolling quite unperturbed into his study had the immediate effect of arousing the very worst in Collett, bringing all his grievances against this man bubbling to the surface, and Tony's apparent unconcern, in total contrast to his own feelings of desperation, was all that was needed for him to relinquish the frail hold on his self-control. The very idea of having to go cap in hand to this meddlesome American, a bitter pill to swallow at the best of times, to barter for his silence as well as his own liberty was more than Collett could stomach, and so consuming was his resentment and rage that he not only felt deprived of speech but completely lost sight of this evening's intention.

Tony, having a pretty shrewd idea of what was going through Collett's mind, eyed his efforts to bring his temper under control dispassionately, saying tersely, "I don't intend making a long stay, Collett; so, let's have it! What is it you want?"

Quite unused to such dismissive treatment as this, not to mention the undignified position he was in as well as the humiliating recollection of being sent on a fool's errand by this man at Covent Garden, Collett, with his temples pulsating and his eyes protruding alarmingly in his reddening face, looked for all the world as if he was about to burst a blood vessel. He may have lost sight of the reason for Tony's visit but he had certainly not lost sight of his dignity or what he believed was due to his name, and so affronted was he at this man's brusque dismissal of both that in his overwhelming need to let Tony know that he was not dealing with someone of no importance, every other consideration was forgotten. "Tell me," he asked pompously, determined to let this insufferable upstart know he was not a man to be trifled with, "are all you Colonials so ill-mannered?"

"We just believe in telling it like it is!" Tony told him bluntly. "You should try it sometime, Collett!" he suggested provocatively.

"You want conduct, Childon," Collett reproved, heatedly.

"If by that you mean I don't have your taste for dissimulation," Tony told him candidly, his eyes hard and uncompromising, "you're right!"

"You will find, Childon," Collett told him with barely suppressed anger, his chest heaving and his colour darkening, "that over here good manners and codes of behaviour are not taken lightly."

"Coming from a man who is treading on rather thin ice when it comes to good manners and codes of behaviour," Tony told him bluntly, "I think it best if we skip that one!"

As Collett had by this time lost all sight of the real purpose of this meeting, his only desire now was to get the better of this man in any way he could, but for one who did not perform well under duress and prone to losing his head when faced with a crisis or unlooked-for eventuality, Tony's scarcely veiled reference to his own conduct did nothing to either calm him or assuage his ever-growing discomfort. The one thing Collett must avoid at all costs was to let this man standing totally unperturbed in front of him gain the upper hand, and so in a determined effort to not only assert himself but to let Tony know that his blasé attitude would not be tolerated, he said with credible hauteur, "I have no doubt there are those who find your brash American humour quite entertaining; I do not. These crude, gung-ho cowboy tactics you Colonials are fond of adopting rouse no admiration in me, indeed," he sneered, "they are very far removed from conduct befitting gentlemen!"

Tony raised a sardonic eyebrow at this, saying coldly, "So is cold-blooded murder and the vicious bullying of your wife! Or don't they count?" Without giving Collett time to respond Tony told him uncompromisingly, "Before very long I am going to enjoy giving you a lesson in conduct befitting gentlemen! You're very fond of beating up defenceless women, Collett," he told him harshly, "but you are going to find out what it's like to tackle someone your own size before I'm through with you!"

"Why you insufferable upstart!" Collett fumed, his eyes bulging. "Think to teach me manners, do you? Why, I'll break you with my bare hands!" he raged, holding them out in front of him as he stepped out from behind his desk. "I'll tear you limb from limb like the mongrel cur you are! I'll make you wish you had never meddled in my affairs or taken it upon yourself to remove my wife from the safety and protection of her home and husband. I'll teach you to mind your betters and know your place!"

It had not taken this uncontrollable outburst to tell Tony that Collett was not only on the defensive but also quite incapable of controlling his temper; his ever-darkening colour, the rapid throbbing of the pulse at his temples and the constant opening and closing of his hands as well as the over bright glint in those protruding blue eyes, did so equally as well. Tony had never for one moment underestimated Eleanor's fear, on the contrary he had seen it on her face and in her eyes, felt it permeate her beaten and battered body every time he held her, but now, as he stood face to face with Sir Braden Collett in the confines of his study, with Peterson and Eliza Boon hovering within calling distance, he could easily imagine the terror twenty-nine Cavendish Square and its inhabitants had instilled in her. Sir Braden Collett may come from a long and distinguished line as well as being an educated and cultured man, but Tony saw him for what he actually was; a sadistic bully who took pleasure in inflicting pain and torment on those who were too frightened and overawed and in no position to fight back. Well, he was neither frightened nor overawed of this man who had, without compunction or remorse, not only been involved in three deaths and covering up another, but had beaten and terrorised his wife to the point where she had considered anything was preferable to the unbearable life she was living, even death itself, rather than endure it any longer.

"That's some temper you have there, Collett," Tony remarked composedly, quite undaunted by the bulging eyes spitting hatred and the fleshy cheeks suffused with colour. "Did you lose it on the night Sir Philip called to see you about his brother?" He cocked his head inviting an answer. "You certainly didn't need to lose it for terrorising and beating your wife then leaving her for dead, did you? Nor for threatening her with an asylum to terrify her into keeping silent about what she saw that night!"

"Why you…!" Collett thundered, taking a step nearer to Tony.

"You're a sadistic bully, Collett," Tony told him contemptuously, "and if I had my way I'd horsewhip you for what you have done to your wife!"

"Why you miserable…!" Collett barred his teeth, clenching his fists suggestively as he took a step towards him.

"Don't push it, Collett," Tony warned uncompromisingly, "I'm already fighting a powerful urge to beat the hell out of you!" his eyes cold and hard as they looked purposefully at the flushed and excited face only a couple of feet away from him. "Understand me," Tony told him unequivocally, "I'm no more intimidated by you than I am of that henchman you sent after me yesterday. I know what happened to Annie Myers and Dennis Dunscumbe as well as what occurred that night when Sir Philip came here to charge you with his brother's death. I know too that you got rid of Mitchell in case he put two and two together and told the police as well as dismissing Mary Stanley so that you could bring in Eliza Boon and Peterson to keep your wife from talking about witnessing such a violent act by keeping her a virtual prisoner."

"Damn you, Childon!" Collett thundered, shocked at just how much this man actually knew. "It's a pity Peterson did not make an end of you yesterday!"

"You'd better believe it!" Tony said firmly. "I'm not so easily got rid of, Collett," he told him sternly, "any more than I can be bought or coerced into calling a halt to my investigations," he nodded in response to Collett's surprised stare. "I figured that was the reason you asked me to come here tonight in some misguided attempt to try to threaten me into doing precisely that. How did you intend doing it, Collett?" he demanded. "Did you think to force my hand through Eleanor or her father? Huh huh," he shook his head, "your thinking is way off line, Collett! Besides," he nodded, "I think you've overdone that one!"

Anger, disbelief and sheer panic engulfed Collett like a tidal wave and, as Eliza Boon knew only too well, nothing else was needed for him to lose what reasoning he had. For a man of his rather corpulent proportions he nevertheless moved with surprising agility, lunging at Tony with his hands outstretched and had it not have been for the swiftness with which Tony sidestepped him, those huge paws would have been around his throat. With nothing to break the propelling of Collett's body as it hurtled forward he careered headlong into a wing chair just to the side of the fireplace, crashing forcefully into it before sinking to his knees, but it only took a moment for him to gain his breath as well as his legs, having more than enough strength left to throw a forceful if wild right at Tony who easily stepped back out of range. Collett, fuming with rage, followed this up with an efficient left to the right side of Tony's head which missed its mark by the quickness Tony ducked, but Collett, not through yet, attempted a lunging head butt to Tony's stomach, but before contact was even made Tony delivered a right to his jaw quickly followed by a punishing left to his stomach which saw Collett double over before crumpling to the floor.

Without waiting for him to recover his breath Tony bent down and, with no effort whatsoever, pulled Collett to his feet by the lapels of his coat with one hand, thrusting him unceremoniously onto the chair. "Get up, Collett; you're not dead yet!" he told him, ignoring Collett's spluttering oaths as he straightened up.

From the moment Tony had read Collett's letter asking him to come here tonight he had shrewdly guessed that his intention was to try to coerce him into dropping his investigations, but Tony had not expected such a proposal to follow hard upon the heels of yesterday's failed attempt to put an end to his life. For a man of Collett's temperament and self-importance, Tony would have thought that such a manoeuvre would have only been attempted as a last resort when other and more devious methods of putting a period to his existence had failed. That Collett was adopting such a tactic now could only mean that he was reluctant to find himself with another body on his hands, but whether this strategy had Eliza Boon's approval remained to be seen, although from the look on her face as she had peered down the well of the stairs at him Tony gained the very strong impression that left to her he would not leave here alive. Even so, he was honest enough to admit that he had no regrets about coming here if, for no other reason, than he had, in some small measure, paid Collett back for the brutal treatment he had meted out to Eleanor, but it did mean a little sidestepping was now required if he wanted Collett to walk into the trap set for tomorrow. Had he not requested this meeting Tony knew that Collett would, upon reading those bogus articles in tomorrow's editions, know, or at least strongly suspect, that the information received by Scotland Yard had come from him, but irrespective of the source of information Collett would have no choice but to visit Hertford Street. Now though, if Tony wanted this man to do precisely that as well as not alerting him to the fact that his investigations had progressed to the point where he had called in Superintendent Dawson, he had no choice but to make Collett believe that he had no hard evidence to prove his crimes but, more than this, Tony must not give Collett the slightest cause to suspect that those articles were false and merely the mechanism which would see him fall into the trap which had deliberately been laid for him. At all costs Tony must not give Collett any reason to doubt what he would read in his newspapers tomorrow, besides which, he did not want to put Joanie Simms or Mrs. Timms at risk and therefore he knew no hesitation in deliberately misleading Collett by making him believe that he was still missing certain pieces to the jigsaw puzzle.

Looking dispassionately down at Collett, Tony said coldly, "That was no more than you deserved, Collett, but you can count yourself extremely fortunate that unlike you I can control my temper. Now," he said firmly, "I think it's time we got one or two things straight."

"Damn you!" Collett bit out.

"About Mitchell," Tony said forbiddingly, ignoring this outburst, "I'm guessing it was Peterson who did your dirty work for you, am I right? No," he shrugged when Collett made no answer, "you don't like that one!" He raised an eyebrow. "Then how about this? Where did Peterson leave his body?" The only answer he received to this was a ferocious glare. "Mm," Tony mused, "not very talkative all of a sudden, are we? Then try this one on for size, Collett; whose idea was it to murder Dennis Dunscumbe and make it look like suicide? No," he shook his head, "you don't like that one either; or is it because you can't begin to think how I know all this?" He raised a questioning eyebrow. "It wasn't really that difficult. Once Lady Collett told me about what she walked into that night everything else just fell into place. Do not tell me you have forgotten I'm a newspaperman?" he asked in mock surprise when he saw the questioning look which crossed Collett's face.

"I'll ruin you for this, Childon!" Collett fumed when he eventually found his voice, his eyes bulging.

"I'm all for optimism, Collett," Tony told him with maddening calm, "but you really are stretching it. You see," he nodded, "I may be missing one or two pieces of the jigsaw puzzle before I can put this whole thing together and take to Scotland Yard, but I *will* find them, you can bet on it! I'm coming after you, all of you," he told him firmly. "Do not think for one moment that just because the only witness I have is your wife who cannot give evidence against you in court because it would be damaging to you as her husband, I've given up on you; I've not. I'm going to keep digging until I get the evidence which will see the three of you receive the justice you deserve. Sooner or later," Tony told him unequivocally, his eyes cold and hard as they looked down at him, "you're going to pay for your crimes! As for Lady Collett," he said determinedly, "she remains under my sister's protection, and should you dare pull another stunt like the other night to try to remove her I promise you it will be the last thing you ever do!"

"Damn you! You think you have me beat!" Collett fumed, breathing hard. "Well, let me tell you that I am not without influential friends. I'll ruin you, Childon! I'll break you and your newspapers! You will regret the day you ever interfered in my affairs!"

"Save it, Collett!" Tony dismissed, picking up his hat from off the floor.

"I'm not done with you, Childon," Collett spluttered, breathing hard, his face unhealthily flushed, "don't think it. I'll… I'll…"

"You'll do squat!" Tony broke in tersely, dusting his hat with a flick of his hand. As this expression had not yet come in Collett's way he understandably looked a little confused to which Tony smiled, infuriating the man who, despite his threats, knew he was beaten. "You're done for Collett and you know it. By all means call on these influential friends of yours if you dare, but you won't; to do so would mean you'd have a hell lot of explaining to do and that, as we both know," Tony nodded, "would finish you."

"Don't be too sure, Childon," Collett warned, rising to his feet, "I may just finish you first."

"Like I said," Tony nodded, putting on his hat, "you're stretching optimism too far." It was just as he was about to leave when the door to the study suddenly burst open and Peterson strode purposefully in with his fists suggestively clenched and an ugly look on his pitted face and in his scarred eyes as he stared across at Tony.

Having spent the last ten minutes hovering outside the study with his ear to the door Peterson could not fail to hear the commotion coming from the other side and Eliza, who had joined him some minutes before, needed no telling that Sir Braden, yet again, had allowed his temper to override his judgement. The plan he had outlined to silence Childon once and for all had been well-nigh perfect, but regardless of her surprise at the way he had managed to formulate such a scheme in his agitated state of mind she had failed to see how it could possibly fail, unless of course Sir Braden lost his temper, which, from the sound of it, was precisely what he had done. She had no intention of spending time in a prison cell merely because Sir Braden could not control his temper and therefore deemed the only way of ensuring this was to get Peterson to finish Childon now. He could not be allowed to leave the house alive!

Upon seeing who had entered, Tony prepared himself for Peterson's rushing dive by nimbly stepping out of the way, but no sooner had Peterson come to a halt than Tony grabbed him by the right shoulder with his left hand and, turning him round to face him, let him have a flush right hit to his already swollen jaw. Peterson staggered back from the force of Tony's fist, almost stumbling into Collett who was not quite quick enough to get out of his way, but Peterson soon regained his balance and came in again with a wide right swing to Tony's head which he swiftly ducked, hitting Peterson in the stomach with a nicely timed right before he well knew what had happened. Winded and stunned, Peterson lay gasping for breath on the floor at Collett's feet, quite unable to make another attack, but Eliza Boon, having watched with startled eyes the neat way Tony had dealt with her stalwart, decided it was time to make an end of this meddlesome American in the only way which would guarantee his silence. Digging her hand into the pocket of her skirt to pull out the pistol Joanie Simms had told Tony she always carried on her, looked horror-struck down at her empty hand, remembering too late that she had left it in the drawer of her dressing table.

Eliza may deprecate the way Sir Braden Collett lost his temper at the slightest provocation, but as she stared aghast at Tony she found herself filled with the same hatred and rage which had almost consumed him, and for the first time in her life lost that control and clear-sightedness which had enabled her to deal with more than one crisis. She snarled and barred her teeth and her eyes narrowed into cruel slits as she suddenly flew across the room at Tony with her hands stretched out like the claws of a cat, but to her frustration she found her wrists being caught and held in an iron grip before being flung into Collett's vacated chair. Something resembling a hissing sound left her misshapen lips as she glared with venomous dislike at Tony and had it not have been for Peterson, who had by now slowly managed to get to his knees, placing a restraining hand on her arm preventing her from getting to her feet to make another attack, she would certainly have done so.

Tony's hard grey eyes skimmed dismissively from one to the other as he flexed his fingers and stretched his leather gloves over his hands, saying inexorably, "Like I said, Collett; I'm not so easily got rid of, and if you're looking to those two to do it," nodding his head towards Peterson and Eliza Boon, "forget it; they're just not makin' it!" whereupon he picked up his cane and strolled out of the study and into the hall, opening the front door and descending the steps.

Jerry, relieved to see Tony leave the house in one piece, left Samuel and Edward to watch the house while he surreptitiously made his way down the Square's gardens, eventually meeting up with Tony who was waiting for him at the corner of Hollis Street. His account of the evening's events came as no real surprise to Jerry, but although fending off Collett and Peterson in tonight's set-to had posed no real problem for Tony, a man Jerry knew as being handy with his fives, he knew that he could have done nothing about a loaded pistol aimed at him from such a close range. Trying to buy Tony off was one thing, even going so far as to waylay him, but attempting to permanently silence him by putting a bullet through him was quite another, proving beyond any doubt just how dangerous they regarded him. Upon Tony pointing out that making an end of him had not been premeditated but a reckless reaction resulting from panic, Jerry, removing his hat and slapping it against his thigh, exclaimed, "Dang me! It makes not an 'apporth o' difference whether it was or it wasn't! You could be cockin' up your toes now!"

"I could," Tony smiled a little ruefully, only too aware of his narrow escape, "but I'm not."

"No," Jerry said forcefully, "you ain't, and thank God for it! But I tell you to your face," he nodded, "that you should 'ave let me go in with you like I wanted!"

"Believe me, Jerry," Tony told him, "that would have served no purpose."

It was clear from the look on Jerry's face that he would have liked to take issue with him on this point, but instead gave vent to his feelings by offering his disparaging and graphic opinion of the inhabitants of twenty-nine Cavendish Square and of Eliza Boon in particular, to which Tony wholeheartedly agreed. *"But,"* Jerry ended on a warning, "I ain't lettin' you out of my sight tomorrow, so don't you think it! I know you're stubborn," he nodded, forestalling Tony as he opened his mouth to speak, "but so am I."

"On the contrary, Jerry," Tony smiled, touched by this, "I am wholly relying on you."

Not the first to succumb to Tony's smile, Jerry nodded, somewhat mollified, but said firmly, "Well, just as long as you know."

They parted on the best of terms a few minutes later, but as Tony made his way back to Mount Street, a deep frown creasing his forehead, he could not deny that Jerry had spoken no less than the truth in that a bullet fired at such close range would surely have been fatal. Dealing with Collett and Peterson had been easy enough, but Tony knew perfectly well that he had been very lucky tonight because had that pistol been in Eliza Boon's pocket as she thought, he would, in Jerry's own words, most definitely have been cocking up his toes!

Chapter Twenty-Six

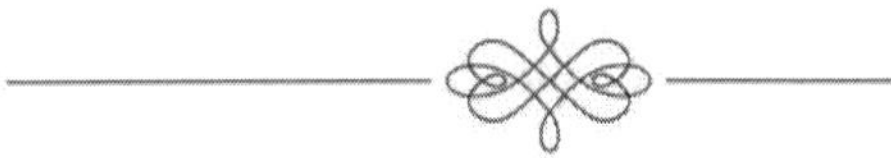

Apart from those intimate moments he shared with Beatrice, Tom had never sat down in company with a woman wearing nothing but a nightdress and dressing gown and certainly not at the dinner table, but since he was truly delighted to see that Eleanor's injuries had healed sufficiently enough to persuade Doctor Little into permitting her to leave her room, he accepted her attire without a blink. Even though Tony's departure from the house was certainly regrettable, dinner was nevertheless the same as it always was, an enjoyable and relaxed affair which placed no demands on anyone. Nevertheless, it was noticeable to Tom and Beatrice that Eleanor, in spite of her contribution to the conversation, appeared a little preoccupied which seemed to them to go deeper than just missing Tony or recovering from her injuries, or even to her natural shyness.

Beatrice, having watched Eleanor grow up, knew that from childhood she had always been a little shy, yet at no time could it ever be said that she was either aloof or standoffish, on the contrary in her quiet and gentle way she was delightful to be with. But it was not until Tony entered her life that the vital woman behind the reserve began to emerge; a young woman whose innate sense of humour and mischievous hint of fun matched his own and which he found totally irresistible. Over the past few days Beatrice had noticed the subtle change in Eleanor and had no difficulty in attributing this to not only knowing she was safe here in Mount Street, but also that Tony loved her. In her unobtrusive way Beatrice had seen how her brother's natural easy manner and gentle teasing had begun to strip away the layers which hid so much of the real Eleanor, gradually revealing the woman Beatrice knew he could not live without.

This was no less than truth. As far as Braden was concerned, even when his mood had been fairly tranquil, dinner in Cavendish Square could at no time be described as anything other than strained, Eleanor having vivid and horrendous recollections of sitting on the very edge of her chair just waiting for something to ignite his temper as well as being very conscious of Eliza Boon and Peterson hovering in the background. The only time Braden had ever spoken to her over dinner was to either deliver a sharply worded rebuke or offer a sarcastic observation, but at no time had he ever made the least effort to make conversation. Eleanor's own attempts to introduce one, at least at the beginning of their marriage, more to lighten the oppressive atmosphere than wanting to be on companionable terms with him, had been indifferently received at best or, more often than not, unattended to. But now, to find herself seated at the dinner table with a flow of light-hearted and amusing conversation taking place and in such a happy and relaxed atmosphere with those whom she loved, took her a little time to adjust to.

As for Tony, she had no need to read Beatrice's mind to know that it was all too true. Loving Tony was the most natural thing in the world, as was missing him, as well as responding to his kisses and those demonstrative expressions of love which, inexperienced though she was, knew only scraped the surface of his feelings. Eleanor longed to see his tall figure walk in through the door and could not resist glancing hopefully at it every time it opened, disappointed to see that it was only Bennett or one of the maids who had entered and not Tony. Beatrice understood Eleanor's disappointment only too well and wished she could have produced Tony for her, but had she known that at this very moment her brother was doing verbal as well as physical battle with Sir Braden and Peterson or of his narrow escape at the hands of Eliza Boon and that tomorrow would see him joining Superintendent Dawson in a surveillance in Hertford Street, to which Tom had eagerly pledged himself, she, no more than Eleanor, would have eaten a morsel let alone closed her eyes all night.

No one looking at Tom as he laughed and talked with Beatrice and Eleanor in the drawing-room where he sat with them for half an hour after dinner before he retreated to his study to go through some papers, would have had the least guess that his mind was wholly taken up with what was happening in Cavendish Square. He knew Tony was more than capable of taking care of himself should Collett actually have laid a trap for him as he was more than inclined to think, but since Tony had dismissed this as unlikely and insisted on going alone Tom could only hope that his brother-in-law, for once in his life, had not miscalculated. It may ease his mind to know that Jerry and one at least of his sons would be on the watch in the Square's garden should Tony need help, but it could well be that should anything happen he may well be unable to get word to them, and were it not for the fact that Tom did not want to leave Beatrice and Eleanor alone he would have taken a walk to Cavendish Square himself to find out what was happening.

As Beatrice and Eleanor were unaware of Tom's concerns for Tony, they settled cosily down in front of the sitting room fire to spend a pleasurable hour looking through any number of fashion journals, and as they both had an eye for colour and style they freely expressed their flattering endorsement or strong disapproval on the various ensembles. But Eleanor's excursion downstairs had taken rather a lot out of her, and Beatrice, upon turning a smiling face towards her to make a none too favourable comment about a black velvet evening dress with swags of black net decorated with a myriad of diamanté, saw that she had fallen asleep. Collecting the journals and putting them onto the table Beatrice rose to her feet just as the clock struck half past nine followed within seconds by the sound of the front door opening and closing. Quietly leaving the sitting room she saw Tony removing his hat and coat and exchanging a quiet word with Tom who had emerged from his study some minutes before to peer anxiously through the side windows of the front door to look for him, but upon setting eyes on her brother she hurried forward and laid a hand on his arm, saying relieved, "Oh, Tony! Thank goodness you are back safe!"

"I've not taken part in the gunfight at the OK Corral, Bea!" Tony laughed, bending down to kiss her cheek, deliberately avoiding his brother-in-law's eye.

"At the O…?" she asked, bewildered. "Oh… well, never mind!" she smiled up at him. "Not that I know what that is anyway, but it doesn't signify even if I did!" she shrugged, as he burst out laughing. Then, almost without pause, told him that he must be ravenous and she would send a message to the kitchen to have something brought up to the study for him because she had no doubt, looking mischievously from one to the other, he wanted to talk to Tom. "Because I can see you are not going to tell me where you have been! Yes, I know," she reminded him, "I told you I wouldn't tease you and I don't mean to, but considering the warning look you threw at me earlier I did think that perhaps…! Oh, very well, then," she conceded in response to the rueful smile which touched his lips, "I'll not press you, but," she laughed, standing on tiptoe to kiss his cheek, "I think it's most unfair!"

"I couldn't agree more!" Tony smiled.

"You couldn't…!" Beatrice gasped. "Well, let me tell you that you have an awful lot of explaining to do at some point, and not just to me!" she warned him, quite unable to resist his smile. "Poor Eleanor couldn't stay awake any longer!" telling him that she was at this moment still in the sitting room, having fallen asleep on the sofa.

"Thanks, Bea," Tony nodded. "I'll go to her," then, turning to Tom, told him that he would join him in the study in a few minutes.

Tom, waiting only until Tony disappeared into the sitting room, drew his wife into the study where, following a quiet word with her, he wished her a long and affectionate goodnight, her colour just a little high as she went away some minutes later to arrange for some supper to be taken into the study.

Even though Tony had promised himself to even the score with Collett and his accomplices for their treatment of Eleanor, he had not intended this evening to turn into a bout of fisticuffs, but since it had unexpectedly been forced upon him he was honest enough to admit that he did not regret it. Tony had no doubt that Eliza Boon would have shot him if the pistol had been in her pocket as she thought, but her ferocious attempt to attack him instead merely proved how brutal and vicious she actually was. As he stood looking down at Eleanor curled up asleep on the sofa, her long blonde hair having partially escaped from the confining clips so carefully inserted by Sarah, with her left cheek cradled in her hand as it rested against the cushion, his eyes softened perceptibly, experiencing no qualms in offering her either his protection or the sanctuary of Mount Street. He had no difficulty in imagining her terror; alone and vulnerable in a house whose ruthless occupants were firmly bent on keeping her silent by all manner of threats, doing everything possible to make sure she told no one about her husband's cold-blooded actions.

Eleanor did not stir when he bent down to lightly kiss her forehead, but upon feeling his arms slide around her as he gently picked her up in his arms to carry her upstairs she opened her eyes for a moment and smiled sleepily up at him, his name a barely audible hush on her lips, contentedly resting her head against his shoulder and folding her arms around his neck just seconds before sleep reclaimed her. As he carried her effortlessly up the stairs he was conscious of no remorse in his dealings with Collett and his attempts to bring him and the others to justice for their crimes and certainly not for sending them sprawling, which was nothing compared to what they had meted out to Eleanor, and when Tony had told Collett that it was no more than he deserved, he had meant it. It was just as he laid his precious burden down onto the bed, carefully removing her arms from around his neck and kissing the top of her head that Beatrice came in, telling him in a hushed voice that she would take care of her. Tony nodded, but even though he was reluctant to leave Eleanor he knew must, and following a few words with his sister made his way downstairs to join Tom.

As soon as Tom saw his brother-in-law enter the house just one look had been enough to tell him that something quite unexpected had happened at twenty-nine Cavendish Square, but as there had not been much time to go into any detail due to Beatrice coming out of the sitting room, he had waited with what patience he could until Tony joined him in his study some minutes later. Not surprisingly, Tom was just as horrified as Jerry upon hearing what had taken place and his reaction, though not so colourfully phrased, was nonetheless just as vehement. "Good God!" he cried, almost choking on his whisky. "Jerry was right," he said firmly, "you should not have gone there alone. I should have insisted you let me go with you instead of allowing you to persuade me not to; either that," he nodded, "or you should have taken Jerry in with you. Why," he shuddered, appalled, "anything could have happened, which," he pointed his glass at him, "very nearly did."

"Well," Tony inclined his head, fully appreciative of his brother-in-law's concerns, "it didn't."

"But it could have done!" Tom told him firmly. "Tackling Collett and Peterson was one thing, but…!" he exclaimed, almost lost for words. "A gun!"

"You know, Tom," Tony smiled, "I *can* take care of myself."

"Yes," he shot at him, "in a fair fight, but, I mean to say," horror-struck at the thought, "a gun!"

"Not quite what I expected, I admit," Tony grimaced, setting aside his supper tray, "although," he sighed, "bearing in mind what Joanie Simms told me about Eliza Boon possessing a gun, I should have."

Tom, understandably exasperated, said, goaded, "This is not a matter to be taken lightly, Tony!"

"Do not think for one moment that I do," Tony assured him. "I don't."

"Well," Tom conceded, "that's something at least, although," he added seriously, "you could have fooled me. The fact that this Eliza Boon woman did not have the gun in her pocket as she thought is quite beside the point." Without giving Tony time to respond to this, he went on, "You could have been killed! You *do* realise that?"

"Yes, but I wasn't," Tony smiled.

"No," Tom returned abruptly, "but it was certainly not for the want of them trying! Don't misunderstand me, Tony," he shook his head, "I realise why you took this job on and I admire you for it, but for the life of me I can't understand why you didn't let Bill put someone on to this?" he demanded. An infuriating grin was the only response to this and Tom, sighing his frustration, told him as sternly as he could, "You know what your trouble is, Tony?" he pointed his glass at him, to which Tony smiled and raised a questioning eyebrow. "You're never happier than when you're knee-deep in trouble or finding yourself in a tight corner. Well," he nodded, "I can't imagine any more of a tight corner than this one tonight. Why you insist on carrying out investigations yourself when God knows you've a small army of reporters to do it for you, I can't think!"

"Has it ever occurred to you, Tom," Tony asked good humouredly, "that I might enjoy it?" The only answer he received to this was an exasperated frown, to which Tony laughed, "You know, Tom, you're getting to sound like Bill; *he* worries too much."

This was too much for Tom, exclaiming, "It seems to me that someone has to worry over you since you don't worry over yourself! Yes, and I'll tell you something else," pointing his cigar at him, "as I've no wish to be the one to relate bad news to Bea or Eleanor any more than I want to see you being carried back here on a stretcher, I'm not letting you out of my sight tomorrow, so don't think it!"

"Well," Tony pulled a comical face, a smile lighting his eyes, "with you on one side and Jerry on the other, not to mention Superintendent Dawson hovering somewhere in between, I've got nothing to worry about!"

"I'm serious, Tony," Tom said firmly, eyeing his brother-in-law steadily. "I like you too much to see anything happen to you."

"Do you think I don't know that, Tom?" Tony said earnestly. "Well, I do. Do not think for one moment," he shook his head, "that I don't appreciate your concerns, or Jerry's either because I do. I realise perfectly well that I was damned lucky tonight, and it was sheer good fortune that the gun was not in her pocket because had it have been she could not have missed at that range. Believe me, Tom," he said with feeling, "I do not take what happened tonight any more lightly than you or Jerry, nor do I need to have it spelled out that, like Sir Philip and most probably Mitchell, by now my body could well be floating in the Thames to come ashore in a few days' time!" Rising to his feet and taking Tom's empty glass, he shook his head. "Huh huh, I'm not so flippant that I take my life so casually, nor so conceited that I don't know full well that I was damned lucky to walk out of there!"

"I'm sorry, Tony," Tom apologised, "I never meant to give you a lecture. I only meant…"

"You didn't," Tony threw over his shoulder, "and I know what you meant," replacing the stopper on the decanter. "As my sister's husband you are naturally concerned for my safety and, as for our personal friendship," he smiled, handing him his refilled the glass, "the same goes."

"It does," Tom said emphatically. "I'm glad I've no need to tell you that."

"You don't," Tony smiled, resuming his seat, "any more than I need to tell you it is entirely reciprocated."

"Well," Tom inclined his head, a smile touching his lips, "I know the banking business can be pretty hairy at times, but it's hardly in the same league as tracking down cold-blooded murderers!"

Tony laughed. "Perhaps not, but confess, Tom," he nodded, "if you knew someone was milking the cream off you'd not stand by and let it happen."

"No," Tom conceded, "I wouldn't, but it's not quite the same thing or," he amended, "I should say, not so dangerous."

"Maybe not," Tony agreed, "but it still comes down to right and wrong, Tom."

Tom nodded, then, as if a thought had suddenly occurred to him, said a little pensively, "You know Tony, I've just thought of something. In view of tonight's fracas as well as you leading Collett to believe you have insufficient evidence to take to the police, because don't forget," he reminded him, "the idea was that Collett would think the information came from you, are you sure that he and the others will still step into this trap tomorrow?"

"You'd better believe it, Tom!" Tony said firmly. "Their situation is such that they dare not ignore it. As for the information coming from me," he shrugged, "I didn't expect that letter from Collett, so I couldn't risk telling him too much in case it made him put two and two together when he reads his newspapers in the morning. No," he shook his head, "they'll turn up in Hertford Street tomorrow and, when they do," he nodded, "we'll be waiting for them!"

Tom nodded, but it was obvious to Tony that something was on his mind and, in response to his enquiry, was pensively told, "I've just thought of something else. If the gun which was found beside Dennis Dunscumbe's body was Eliza Boon's own, then what made her think to put her hand in her pocket to get hold of it to try to shoot you?"

"You know, Tom," Tony confessed a little ruefully, "I never thought of that, but since you mention it, either she had forgotten that she had instructed Peterson to leave it or," he nodded, "she has more than one!"

"Good God!" Tom cried, not daring to think what else she may have in her armoury.

"I know," Tony replied meaningfully, finishing off his drink.

"Tell you what though, Tony," Tom smiled, "I'd give anything to be a fly on the wall in Cavendish Square right now!"

"You know something, Tom," Tony grinned, "so would I!"

Had this been at all possible they would not have been disappointed. From the accusations which hurled back and forth between Eliza Boon and Sir Braden Collett, realising too late that he had allowed his temper to get the better of him resulting in him losing sight of his purpose and ending in his humiliating encounter with Tony, it was clear that both blamed the other for this evening's shambles. Sir Braden, telling Eliza Boon in no uncertain terms that before Peterson's unlooked-for pugilistic demonstration which, he accused fiercely, had fared no better than the previous one, he had had the matter well in hand, but what he most certainly did not want was another body in the house. Eliza Boon, well past the point of showing him any courtesy or respect, said viciously that had he not lost his temper in the first place then none of this would have happened, and if he thought that by letting Childon walk out of here in one piece he had heard the last of him, then he was a bigger fool than she thought. Not surprisingly, this indictment merely served to fuel the flames of Sir Braden's temper reminding her angrily that she would do well to consider to whom she spoke, going on to ferociously point out that if they were talking of fools, then she most certainly could count herself one as anybody with only half a mind would have more sense than to attempt to pull a gun on a man who was not stupid enough to come here without telling someone he was intending to do so. Both combatants, incandescent with rage and refusing to take the blame, firmly believing the other was solely responsible for the way things had turned out, eventually parted company on very bad terms, the one convinced that they would receive a visit from the police first thing in the morning and the other trying to think of something to avert another crisis; a crisis which was to come sooner than expected.

Although Mrs. Timms had known for some time that something was very wrong at no point had she suspected the truth, but Tony's disclosure had come as a tremendous shock, in fact it would be a while before she recovered from it. As far as Sir Braden's regular visits to a certain type of establishment was concerned, despite his aggressive temperament, she would not have thought it of him, and whilst it was not for her to sit in judgement on his personal activities she did not hold with cold-blooded murder, any more than she did with the way he had beaten and bullied her young mistress. It had been downright cruel the way he and that squinty-eyed woman between them had treated Her Ladyship, not to mention Peterson and, seemingly not content with harrying and beating her, they had threatened her with all manner of things so she would not divulge their secret. She could only imagine the shock and horror Lady Collett must have felt upon witnessing her husband committing such a gruesome and ghastly act and then, if this was not bad enough, to suddenly find herself deprived of two people, one of whom she had a great fondness for, as well as her liberty.

Mrs. Timms was neither a vengeful nor a vindictive woman, indeed she considered herself to be as liberal minded as the next person, but surely it could not be right when cold-blooded murder went unanswered. What they had done was beyond pardon and fully deserving of the full penalty of the law and, left to her, so would their hounding and bullying of Lady Collett, and therefore it was without any qualms or twinges of conscience that she knocked on Sir Braden's study door the following morning to carry out Tony's instructions.

Armed with Sir Braden's supposed copies of *'The Daily Telegraph'* and *'The Times'*, brought round by Jerry last night, a man Mrs. Timms was far from averse to sharing a cup of tea with, surreptitiously replacing the newspapers Albert had gone out to buy only an hour before, she entered Sir Braden's study in answer to his curt, "Come in," with such a look of innocence on her face that no one could possibly have accused her of being part of a deception.

Sir Braden, whose temper had not improved overnight, for which the horrendous images which had haunted his dreams were largely responsible, stared at Mrs. Timms as though in a daze, fully expecting it to be Eliza offering an apology or, failing this, a solution to their difficulties. As Mrs. Timms seldom, if ever, found it necessary to speak personally to him, her presence now made him start in alarm fearing that she wanted to talk to him about Eleanor, Eliza's suspicions about this woman suddenly springing to mind, but upon hearing her tell him that due to Lady Collett being indisposed she needed to speak to him upon a rather urgent domestic matter, he waved it irritably aside saying that it would have to keep as he had far more important things to think about at the moment.

"Very well, Sir Braden," Mrs. Timms nodded, knowing perfectly well what these other matters were as well as how he had acquired the slight bruising to his jaw, thanks to Jerry's gleeful account of last night's events. "May I ask, Sir Braden," she ventured, "as to when *will* be convenient for you?"

Apart from the fact that he had far more urgent concerns on his mind than domestic issues, his protruding blue eyes had by now caught sight of the newspapers she held in her hand and, totally ignoring this question, he nodded, "I take it those are mine?"

"Yes, Sir Braden," she replied calmly, looking from his darkening face to the copies in her hand. "I thought as I was comin' upstairs to see you I might as well bring them with me." Walking over to his desk she deliberately unfolded the newspapers to show the front page, laying them carefully down well within his reach, those damning headlines jumping mercilessly up at him, obviating the need for her to point out what she had read in her own newspaper, his protruding eyes staring down in horror as if he could not believe what he was looking at.

Had anyone asked Mrs. Timms for her opinion, she would have had no hesitation in saying that it looked for all the world as if Sir Braden had suddenly been struck with a paralysis as for almost a full minute he neither moved nor spoke, and it was not until she said, "Will there be anythin' else, Sir Braden?" did he raise his head, completely forgetting she was still here.

Gradually his bulging eyes brought her into focus, and after what seemed like an eternity he found his voice sufficiently to say, somewhat strained, "No, nothing," he shook his head. It was just as she was about to reach for the door handle and let herself out of the study when he forestalled her, asking, "Mrs. Timms, do you take a daily newspaper?"

"Why yes, Sir Braden," Mrs. Timms nodded, looking innocently at him.

"Would you," he managed, feeling as though the ground had unexpectedly been kicked from under him, all the colour leaving his face, "allow me to see it?"

"Yes, of course, Sir Braden," she smiled. "Now, Sir Braden?"

"Yes, now," he said absently, sitting heavily forward in his chair and reaching for the newspapers on his desk with fingers that no longer seemed to belong to him.

"Very good, Sir Braden," she nodded, leaving him to read Tony's bogus articles.

They did not make inviting reading, on the contrary they acted on Collett like a body blow, and while he waited for Mrs. Timms to return with her newspaper, he read with a sickening feeling in the pit of his stomach:

POLICE TO RE-OPEN DENNIS DUNSCUMBE'S DEATH - NEW EVIDENCE CASTS DOUBT ON SUICIDE

Dennis Dunscumbe, whose body was found in his Hertford Street home almost a year ago, following what was apparently a case of suicide, is to be re-investigated by police. According to Scotland Yard, this new investigation is due to information being received which would seem to indicate that his death was the result of foul play and not suicide.

Superintendent Dawson of Scotland Yard who has been conducting the investigation into the vicious murder of the Right Honourable Sir Philip Dunscumbe MP, older brother of Dennis, believes that the two deaths could be connected. Although the police are not saying what this new information is, they confirm that it will be necessary to revisit Dennis Dunscumbe's home in Hertford Street, which has remained empty since his death, as a vital first step in their new enquiries. Although Superintendent Dawson has confirmed that the search of Dennis Dunscumbe's Hertford Street home is due to be carried out tomorrow, he has kept a discreet silence as to what he hopes the search will reveal as well as if this new evidence that has come to light will lead to an arrest.

Dropping the newspaper onto the desk as though it were a live coal, Sir Braden picked up the other with fingers that shook uncontrollably.

THE TRAGEDY OF THE DUNSCUMBE BROTHERS

What has become known as the tragedy of the Dunscumbe brothers, whose deaths occurred within a short space of time of one another, appears to have taken a quite unexpected turn. Superintendent Dawson of Scotland Yard who has been in charge of the investigation into the brutal murder of the Right Honourable Sir Philip Dunscumbe MP is to re-open the case on what has always been believed to be the suicide of his younger brother Dennis.

It has been confirmed by Scotland Yard that new evidence has come to hand which suggests that the death of Dennis Dunscumbe may not have been suicide and that the brothers' deaths could well be linked. Dennis Dunscumbe's home in Hertford Street where his body was found almost twelve months ago will, as from tomorrow, once again be the focus of police attention as they search for vital evidence which will assist in their enquiries. Superintendent Dawson, who will lead the search at Dennis Dunscumbe's home in Hertford Street, declined from commenting whether this new line of enquiry will lead to an imminent arrest.

Shock, incredulity and an overwhelming sense of panic engulfed Collett all at once, and when, ten minutes later, he read the report in Mrs. Timms's copy of '*The Echo*', they increased a hundred-fold; his hands shaking so much that he could hardly retrieve his handkerchief from his pocket to mop his perspiring brow:

SCOTLAND YARD OPTIMISTIC - NEW EVIDENCE IN THE DENNIS DUNSCUMBE SUICIDE CASE

New evidence suggests that Dennis Dunscumbe's death may have been murder and not suicide....Superintendent Dawson at Scotland Yard.....now looks like brothers' deaths could be connected......reopening investigations......Police to visit Dennis Dunscumbe's house in Hertford Street tomorrow......No confirmation yet as to whether the police are looking to make an arrest in the immediate future.

Staring as one in a daze down at the newspapers in front of him, the bold black print seeming to jump mockingly up at him, Sir Braden's only conscious awareness was of a pounding in his temples and an overwhelming sense of nausea, his mouth so dry that for several stunned moments he was quite incapable of calling for Eliza.

Up until the arrival of Childon in his life and the precipitate flight of his wife, no one had been able to point the finger of suspicion at him, much less of accusation, but from the moment Eleanor had escaped and this meddlesome busybody had offered her sanctuary in Mount Street, all that had changed. Since then, Sir Braden had lived on a knife-edge, never quite knowing from one minute to the next what was going to happen, attempting to ward off one crisis after another to protect himself, and all to no purpose which, for a man whose tendency it was to fall into panic at the least provocation, merely served to increase his fear. He had tried to remove Eleanor from Mount Street and failed; he had sent Peterson to make an end of Childon and failed and, last night, he had attempted to coerce him into leaving well alone which, again, had also failed and, on top of this, he was trying to keep up the illusion that his wife was indisposed in her room. And now, if all this was not bad enough, the police were looking again into Dennis's death and, by all accounts, Sir Philip's too!

Since Childon had told him only last night, and in this very room, that he had no proof of their complicity in murder to take to Scotland Yard, Sir Braden never even associated those write-ups in the newspapers with him and that they formed the basis of a trap which would see him and his co-conspirators incriminate themselves. For a man in his overcharged state of nerves it never so much as crossed his mind that Childon had engineered the whole thing, little realising that his name and reputation in Fleet Street were such that he was able to persuade three newspaper editors, and with the backing of the Commissioner of Police to boot, to insert a false article. In view of this then, Sir Braden could only guess where this new evidence had come from let alone what it could possibly be that Scotland Yard considered important enough to not only connect the brothers' deaths but call for a new investigation into Dennis's supposed suicide, but worse than this was their proposed visit to Hertford Street tomorrow, a circumstance which seriously alarmed him and, for the life of him, he could not even begin to imagine what they hoped to find. Not unexpectedly, this new initiative by the police only served to intensify Collett's panic, made infinitely worse by uncertainty and fear, and by the time Eliza Boon entered his study some minutes later to discuss the situation facing them, one look at his protruding and staring eyes and the darkening of his fleshy cheeks, told her instantly that something untoward must have occurred. But nothing quite prepared her for the garbled and excited explanation which left his lips and, upon having the newspapers thrust nervously at her, read for herself the damning significance of what he had disjointedly told her; her cold hard eyes narrowing into slits and her lips compressing into a thin ugly line.

With the single exception of yesterday evening, unlike Sir Braden, Eliza had never been known to lose her head in a crisis, but this, as she knew very well, was more than a crisis; it was a catastrophe of mammoth proportions and, for several horrifying minutes, felt just as inadequate to combat this latest setback as he did. A multitude of thoughts and ideas chased one another in her chaotic brain, but even though she was momentarily incapable of sorting out the jumbled mass into anything remotely resembling order, of one thing at least she was certain and that was, having come this far, she was not now going to be detained at Her Majesty's pleasure!

Like the man sitting uneasily in front of her mopping his perspiring forehead, it never so much as crossed her mind that it was part of a cleverly contrived scheme by Tony to lure them into proving their own guilt, but she did share Sir Braden's concerns over this new evidence which had come into Scotland Yard's possession and why they needed to visit Hertford Street again. She found it inconceivable that Peterson had left something incriminating as Sir Braden had feverishly suggested a moment or two ago because whilst her stalwart may not possess the sharpest of minds he was not so stupid that he would leave the house without first checking he had left nothing behind or some telltale sign that Dennis Dunscumbe's death had not been suicide, even so, it would be foolish to take it for granted that he had not done so.

For a man who was by now in a highly developed stage of panic and fast losing what little reasoning he had left which, considering all he had been through over the last few days as well as everything he and Eliza had so far attempted in the way of averting a disaster having fallen by the wayside, it seemed to Sir Braden that there was nothing else they could do to stave off the inevitable. He failed to see how even this unpleasant but resourceful woman could find a solution to this new and unexpected development, but after what seemed an inordinately long time before she said anything in response to this fresh setback she eyed him narrowly, putting forward a counter-plan which not only took him completely by surprise but one he immediately vetoed.

Eliza, knowing from experience that when Sir Braden was in this mental state not only was he unable to focus his attention on the matter in hand with even a modicum of calm but that his temper became even more volatile, but in view of what was at stake she bit down her impatience and persevered in outlining the advantages of her scheme. He was by no means convinced and his astonished cry of, "Go to Hertford Street! Why, it's insane!" considerably annoyed her, and not all her painstaking efforts to convince him that it was the only thing they could do would change his mind. He continued to argue against it on several grounds, not the least being it was taking a terrible risk especially as they had no idea when the police would take it into their heads to descend upon Hertford Street tomorrow, if they had not done so already, despite what this Superintendent had told the newspapers. Without giving her time to question this, Collett further argued that the way their luck was running it would not surprise him in the least to see the police turn up at the house while they were inside searching for something they had no idea what they were supposed to be searching for in the first place.

For a man in his delicately balanced state of nerves this was a very sensible point of view, but it found no favour with Eliza, stating sharply that given the circumstances she failed to see an alternative, unless of course, she added with awful irony, he had something better in mind because if he had, then she would be extremely pleased to hear it.

He may be in the throes of panic and alarm, but he had not missed that touch of derision in her voice, and he by no means liked it, telling her sharply, "As it happens, I *do* have an alternative. In fact," he added belligerently, "there is nothing else we *can* do."

Unfortunately, his alternative was received with even more anger than his refusal to accept her suggestion of going to Hertford Street, in fact so shocked was she that it took her a few moments to digest it. "Go to the police!" Eliza cried at length, her eyes widening to their fullest extent. "Are you mad?"

"You must see that it's all we can do now," Sir Braden told her, his voice a nice mix of belligerence and hopelessness, spreading his hands helplessly over the newspapers on his desk. "There's nothing left. The police know too much already otherwise why would they be reopening Dennis's death?"

"Nothing left!" she almost spat at him, her face contorted with rage. "Well, let me tell *you* something, Sir Braden," she bit out, "if you want to dangle at the end of a rope then go ahead, but you're not taking me and Peterson with you!"

"It's no use, Eliza!" he urged fearfully. "You must see it's hopeless.

It's only a matter of time before the police come knocking on the door. Then there's Childon! He knows too much!" Collett mopped his forehead. "I really can't take any more of this cat and mouse game. It's hopeless!" he cried again. "Everything has gone wrong and nothing we try can prevent us from…"

"Why you lily-livered coward!" she flung at him, rage consuming her, any pretence at respect disappearing. "A few setbacks and you're crying like a baby! Well, you sit here and whine and feel sorry for yourself if you want, but I'm not. I'm not giving up now having come this far."

"What are you going to do?" Collett asked anxiously, rising unsteadily to his feet.

"What *you* should be doing!" Eliza snapped. "Seeing about going to Hertford Street with Peterson to see what can be done to salvage things! In the meantime," she suggested sarcastically, "see what you can do to control yourself!"

"Damn you, Eliza!" Sir Braden said angrily, by no means liking her dismissive treatment. "You dare to speak to me like that?"

"Dare!" she disparaged, her lips curling as she looked him over disdainfully. *"You* can ask *me* that?" she scorned. "*You*, who can't even keep your wife in check let alone anything else! The blame is yours," she threw at him. "Had you not allowed your temper to get the better of you by murdering Sir Philip we should not now be in this mess!"

Anger, frustration and an overwhelming fear had Sir Braden Collett in their grip and before Eliza even knew what was happening he took several steps towards her and struck her a tremendous backhanded blow across the face sending her reeling to the floor, colliding with two chairs as she did so.

When Joanie Simms had told Tony that for some unaccountable reason Peterson had a profound attachment to Eliza which went beyond all understanding, she had not exaggerated and therefore upon hearing the crashing of furniture coming from the other side of the study door, having spent the last few minutes hovering outside, he burst into the room to offer Eliza support. Upon seeing her dazedly trying to get to her feet he turned to Sir Braden, his eyes narrowing and his lips drawing angrily back, snarling, "Yoo 'ad no right to tuch Eliza!"

Sir Braden, considerably startled at his unexpected entrance, stared furiously at him, but even before he could order Peterson out of his study he rushed towards him with such an ugly look on his face that Sir

Braden instinctively took a step backwards.

"You shudn't awt to 'ave dun that!" Peterson growled between gritted teeth. "Nobudy tuches Eliza, see!"

"Why you insolent wretch!" Sir Braden managed, having recovered a little. "I'll teach…!"

Whatever it was he was going to teach him, no one got to find out, the words dying on his lips as Peterson, surprising not only Sir Braden but Eliza as well, suddenly lunged forward and gripped him around the throat, the force of Peterson's unexpected attack pushing Sir Braden back against the desk.

Sir Braden, by no means a slightly built man, clawed ineffectually at those strong and calloused hands as he tried to remove them from around his neck as they slowly squeezed tighter and tighter, but to no avail, Peterson's thumbs pressing relentlessly into his throat. Sir Braden's chest heaved as he gasped for much-needed air, feeling his heart was going to burst, Peterson's snarling face, only inches from his own, so close in fact that Sir Braden could smell the faint tinge of stale drink on his breath, rapidly becoming enmeshed in a mist in front of his bulging and glassy eyes. Sir Braden's frantic efforts to force Peterson off him or to at least push him to one side proved quite useless as with every second the strength drained from his body, his desperate fight for life growing weaker, the buzzing in his ears and the gushing noise in his head so loud that he failed to hear Eliza order Peterson to let him go. Eliza, looking at the spectacle in front of her in utter disbelief, hurried unsteadily over to the desk still clasping her hand to her right eye, but even before she reached Peterson to try to pull him away she heard the ghastly choking rattle which left Sir Braden's throat. It was then, to her horror, that she saw the uncontrollable jerking of his legs and body followed seconds later by his arms slumping heavily to his sides, his body thudding unceremoniously to the floor as soon as Peterson removed his hands from around his throat. Peterson, breathing hard, stepped back to look totally unmoved down at the man whose pale blue eyes stared hideously up at the ceiling while his mouth gaped wide open, revealing the lodging of his tongue in the back of his throat, adequate testimony to how he had desperately fought for air. Eliza, looking horror-struck at the gruesome sight on the study floor in front of her was left in no doubt: Sir Braden Collett was quite dead!

Being a woman who always kept a clear head as well as one who thought and acted decisively, Sir Braden's tendency to fall into a state of panic at the least provocation was something she had never understood, much less had any time for, even so, she had always managed to talk him round to her way of thinking. Nevertheless, ever since that fatal night when he had lost his temper and bludgeoned Sir Philip to death the hold on his nerve, which had been fragile at best, could not be said to inspire confidence, but from the moment this Childon tyke had taken a hand in their affairs she had seen just how unsound Sir Braden's grip on his mental state actually was. She had always known that should the finger of suspicion ever be pointed in his direction then no reliance could be placed upon him keeping his mouth shut, indeed when faced with a barrage of questions by the police he could be depended upon to lose what little reasoning he had and blurt out the truth. In view of this then, she had recognised early on that the time would come when Sir Braden would have to be dealt with especially if she was to avoid serving a prison sentence and Peterson the gallows, even more so since Childon had completely unnerved him, but the last thing she had wanted was this hasty and unplanned death, and certainly not in his own study.

For a woman who was by nature self-serving and insensitive to the feelings of others, except when it came to pandering to their needs for monetary reward, she nevertheless had a genuine fondness for Peterson which she knew perfectly well was fully reciprocated. Although their association was of long duration its origins had long since been buried in the mists of time, neither party able or willing to recall their first encounter, but it could not be denied that a very comfortable relationship existed between them. Over time Eliza had come to rely heavily on this man who was never very far from her side and knew that he would do anything for her, but this fatal attack on Sir Braden was the last thing she had expected, much less wanted. This latest example of Peterson's continued protection, particularly coming at a moment when matters were so precariously balanced, especially with Childon asking questions and the police looking again into Dennis Dunscumbe's death, may prove his attachment to her, but he had, however unintentionally, taken them one step nearer to their inevitable reckoning.

She could not deny that those damning articles in the newspapers had come as something of a shock to her, but for Sir Braden they had been all that was needed to not only set the seal on his mental fragility, but also to convince him that nothing was left to them other than to surrender a position she by no means regarded as hopeless. He had been quick to condemn the idea of going to Hertford Street and, if she was honest, she had to admit that he had made a valid point when he said that they had no idea when the police would take it into their heads to visit Dennis's house irrespective of what this Superintendent Dawson said, but to her way of thinking it was imperative. If Peterson had accidentally left some clue behind, then they had to find it before the police did because if they did not, then everything they had worked for all this time would go for nothing. Over the last ten months or so she had more than once been obliged to keep a tight rein on her temper in her dealings with Sir Braden, but since Lady Collett's unexpected escape and all that had followed, this resolve had proved too much for her self-control, and whilst Eliza had not meant to lose her temper with him this morning the provocation had been too much to ignore. Had Peterson not decided to take a hand in the affair she had been quite willing to overlook that blow Sir Braden had dealt her, at least until they had cleared this latest hurdle, but since her devotee had elected to take matters into his own hands he had, however unintentionally, turned a looming catastrophe into an unmitigated disaster by the added burden of not only having to rid themselves of Sir Braden's dead body but to try to explain away his sudden disappearance.

Her familiarity with Peterson was such that she knew it was useless to expect him to formulate a strategy which would extricate them from the difficulties surrounding them and also that, yet again, it was going to be left to her to try to assemble the wreckage. To a lesser mind assembling the wreckage would have been daunting to say the least, but Eliza Boon, whose resourcefulness seemed to know no bounds when faced with a crisis, rapidly considered the options available to them and decided that their main priority, however risky, was to try to gain access to Dennis's house Hertford Street. At no time did it even occur to her that they would be better off by confessing the truth to the police as Sir Braden had suggested and, as for attempting to make a run for it, she never gave it more than a moment's thought. For one thing, she knew the police would be bound to catch up with them sooner or later once they had enough evidence against them, evidence which she shrewdly suspected would be gained in Hertford Street and, for another, spending the rest of her life on the run with the prospect of what awaited her and Peterson if they were caught, held no appeal for her whatsoever.

As raking Peterson down would serve no real purpose, not only because his mental agility was such that nothing she could say or do would help him to grasp the seriousness of his actions but also because the damage had already been done, she nevertheless felt unable to refrain from saying sharply, "You bloody fool! Now see what you've done!" Pushing him unceremoniously aside, she knelt down beside Sir Braden's dead body to hurriedly rifle through his pockets, her thin fingers finally finding what she was looking for. Clutching the key to the study door she rose to her feet and, without wasting any time now on recrimination, it was in a mood of grim determination that she quickly locked the door before sharply ordering Peterson to help her hide Sir Braden's body.

Unaware of the stirring events about to be played out in Cavendish Square Tony left his room to saunter leisurely down to the next landing to take a look in on Eleanor, having spent the night in his own room. Apart from that brief moment when she had opened her eyes to find herself in his arms, snuggling comfortably against him, she had not opened her eyes again and Tony, having carefully laid her down on her bed, deemed it quite safe to leave her. Sarah, knowing he would come to see Eleanor before going down to breakfast, had tried her best to keep an eye open for him, but as it happened missed him, his light tap on the door some minutes later taking her unawares. Stepping outside and pulling the door to behind her, she told him in a hushed voice and a finger over her lips that Lady Collett, having spent an undisturbed night, was still asleep, to which he nodded, saying that he would come up and see her after breakfast.

Having accepted her husband's announcement that he might be a little late arriving home tonight with a smile and a nod, Beatrice had kissed him goodbye without the least suspicion that he was on the point of participating in her brother's well-thought-out trap to ensnare Sir Braden in company with Superintendent Dawson and half of Scotland Yard. As the brothers-in-law had already decided that their actions this morning were to be no different to that of any other to prevent alarm bells ringing in Beatrice's head, Tony's casual, "Has Tom gone?" occasioned no comment from his sister other than, "Yes, although he did say he might be a little late back tonight."

"Oh!" Tony raised a credibly surprised eyebrow.

"Yes," she smiled, "a late meeting with a client."

"Oh, I see," Tony nodded, helping himself from the serving dishes on the sideboard. Like Tom, he hated not telling either Beatrice or Eleanor about what was going forward today until it was all over, especially as they already knew about recent events, but as both men felt it more than likely that should either of them ever get wind of it the chances were they would only worry themselves into a state, fully expecting one or the other of them to be brought home on a stretcher any minute.

"You know, Tony," Beatrice broke musingly into his thoughts, "I have been thinking. I know you are intending to place Eleanor in her father's care just as soon as you can, but when all this is over I thought perhaps it would be nice if I took Eleanor down to Childon for a while. I am sure a spell in the country would do her good. That is," she coaxed, "if you do not mind?"

"And why should I mind?" he smiled, returning to the table with a healthy plateful. "It's your home too, don't forget."

"Yes, I know," she nodded, putting down her empty tea cup, "but I thought you might…"

"Might what?" he laughed. "Get upset if you did not ask my permission?"

"No," she shook her head, "not that, but I did wonder whether you would much prefer to be the one to take Eleanor to Childon first… I mean as your…"

He looked up from his plate, a smile lurking at the back of his eyes. "As my bride?" She nodded and smiled. "I have every intention of doing so," he told her, "but I am not so blind that I cannot see the merit of your suggestion, especially as I may not be able to get down there for some considerable time, but neither am I so insecure that I feel you are trying to deprive me of what you may consider to be a husband's right!"

"*Never that!*" she assured him fervently.

Putting down his knife and fork he took hold of her hand which was resting on the table saying softly, "No, never that. You're a real treasure, Bea, and I love you very much. If Tom can spare you to go with Eleanor to Childon Manor then I have no objection, and I am sure Sir Miles will not either. In fact," he smiled, giving her hand an affectionate little shake, "it will do you both good."

"Only if you are sure!" she stressed.

"Sure I'm sure, besides," he grinned, "just because she has been there before in your company it will not alter the fact that when I take Eleanor to Childon she will be there with me as my bride!"

The thought brought a tear to Beatrice's eye, but firmly blinking it away asked, "Do you plan on being out most of the day?"

"'Fraid so, Bea," Tony nodded, inserting his fork into a crisply grilled slice of bacon, "there are a number of things I have to do."

"I see," she nodded. Then, pursing her lips, asked thoughtfully, "Tony, is this business with Sir Braden and the others nearly over?"

"Pretty much!" he inclined his head.

"Is… is that why we shan't see much of you today?" she asked quietly.

"Yes," he sighed, "I'm afraid it is. Worried about me, Bea?" he smiled, refilling his coffee cup.

"Yes," she nodded, "you know I am."

"Don't be," he shook his head. "I can take care of myself, I promise you."

"Yes, I know," Beatrice agreed, "but you are the only brother I have and I couldn't bear anything to happen you."

"Nothing's going to happen to me," he assured her, rising to his feet as she walked around the table to stand beside him, giving her a reassuring hug.

"That's all very well," she sighed into his shoulder, "but Sir Braden could do you a lot of harm."

"Huh huh," he grinned, easing himself a little away from her and smiling down into her worried face, "it'll take more than Collett to do that."

She hoped he was right, but leaving him to finish his breakfast she went upstairs to the nursery in complete and blissful ignorance of what he and Tom were intending to do to bring this matter of Sir Braden to a conclusion.

Eleanor had certainly missed Tony's company at dinner last night, even so, she had enjoyed her foray downstairs, but she too had wondered how he was progressing in his investigations regarding Braden. She knew Tony was careful in what he told her to prevent her from worrying too much, but like Beatrice she could not help being concerned about him especially as she knew only too well what Braden and the others were capable of, so much so that had she the least idea why Tony had found it necessary to leave the house last night or what had so nearly resulted from his visit to Cavendish Square, she, no more than Beatrice, would have closed her eyes all night. But when, half an hour after waking from a deep and undisturbed sleep, Eleanor, having by now been gently eased into her borrowed bed jacket and her hair carefully brushed by Sarah, who had periodically taken a look in on her during the night, she heard Tony's tap on the door, no thoughts of her husband intruded in Eleanor's mind as she saw him enter her room.

"Good morning," Tony smiled, sitting gently down on the edge of the bed as she made herself comfortable against the pillows, "and how's my favourite girl?" taking hold of her one small hand.

"Much better," she smiled, her fingers returning his grip.

"Mm," he mused, pulling a face as he looked thoughtfully down at her, "now," he teased, giving her hand a playful little shake, "is that because of the undisturbed night Sarah told me earlier you had or for seeing me?"

"For an undisturbed night, of course!" Eleanor told him mischievously, her colour deepening.

"Ah!" he exclaimed painfully, clasping a theatrical hand to his heart and agonisingly closing his eyes. "You have wounded me to the heart!" he cried dramatically.

"H-have I?" she managed unsteadily.

"Yes," Tony shook his head sadly, his eyes laughing down into hers, "I shall *never* recover from your cruel rejection!" he told her soulfully.

"Never!" she repeated faintly.

"*Never!*" he sighed, shaking his head. "In fact," he told her mournfully, "it would not surprise me if I went into a decline!"

"Oh, Tony!" Eleanor laughed. "You *are* funny."

"And *you*, my darling," Tony told her in a deep voice, gathering her in his arms, "as I have already told you, are utterly adorable."

Tony may have somehow or other managed to curb his very natural impulses but his kiss was nevertheless moving enough to bring a little satisfied cry from deep within her throat, a low provocative sound which rendered it even more difficult for him to keep a hold on his self-control. Tony, no more than Eleanor, wanted the kiss to end, and it was with great reluctance that he slowly eased himself away from her, but even though he was honest enough to admit that he could have cast everything aside and remained with her locked in his arms all day, he knew he could not. As Eleanor felt the same there was no need for him to tell her this, but as she knew he had things to do apart from extracting his promise that whatever it was he had planned for today he would be careful, she posed no questions which he was presently in no position to answer. Laying a gentle hand against her cheek he affectionately warned her not to run off while his back was turned, then, after tenderly brushing her lips with his he was gone, leaving her to lie comfortably back against the pillows with her arms behind her head, a soft contented sigh leaving her lips, reliving again those moments in his arms until Sarah came in.

Chapter Twenty-Seven

At fifteen minutes to eleven o'clock, following Tony's carefully thought out timetable to make sure they were duly installed in Hertford Street well ahead of Collett gaining entry, Tom left his place of business in that prestigious square mile known as the City, to hail a hackney to convey him to Hertford Street. Due to the continued freezing temperatures over the past week the roads and pavements had been extremely treacherous, but although the unexpected thaw which had begun some twenty-four hours previously had come as a welcome relief to everyone it had by no means lessened the hazards for travellers whether on foot or horsedrawn transport, as the melting ice and snow, turning into a slippery slush, had rendered them equally risky. Tom's progress along Cheapside and Newgate Street was therefore slower than usual, but by the time Old Bailey was eventually reached the driver had managed to pick up enough speed to give Tom every reason to hope that he would be in Hertford Street on time after all, but just as he was on the point of consulting his watch to confirm this he was unexpectedly jolted forward in his seat, the driver having suddenly brought the vehicle to a juddering standstill only yards from Holborn Viaduct. Upon asking the driver what had happened, he was frustratingly told that a private vehicle almost immediately in front of them had overturned and not only had the horse taken fright and broken loose from its harness but its two occupants had unfortunately been pitched into the middle of the road, ending by saying somewhat tetchily over his shoulder, "'Opes yer ain't in any 'urry Guvna! Luks like we'll be 'ere a spell!"

Pulling out his watch to see that it wanted only three minutes to quarter past eleven and Tom had arranged to meet up with Tony and Superintendent Dawson at half past, he jumped out of the vehicle, informing the driver that he would be quicker walking past the obstruction and picking up another hackney on the other side, tossing him a coin before setting off in that direction. The driver, pocketing the coin, shook his head over the vagaries of toffs, huddling further into his coat and muffler as he continued to sit with what patience he could muster until the overturned vehicle had eventually been cleared away and the horse brought under control, spotting his recently departed fare flagging down a hackney some little way ahead.

Leaving Mount Street a few minutes after eleven, Tony walked leisurely along South Audley Street to Hertford Street where, on the corner of the Old Park Lane end of this quiet and exclusive thoroughfare, he saw Superintendent Dawson talking to Jerry and his sons, Samuel and Edward. Superintendent Dawson, informing Tony when he came up to them that the three police constables he had waiting in readiness in case Collett or Peterson decided to make a run for it were already in place, nodded his head in their way. After casting a brief glance in their direction, Tony was then told that police officers had also been positioned at various concealed points along Hertford Street with two more standing by in Stanhope Row and also that a police vehicle was unobtrusively parked near Shepherd Street.

"Seems as though we've got all the relevant points covered," Tony nodded, looking up and down the street.

"Yes," Superintendent Dawson corroborated, raising his eyes from his pipe to look up at Tony, "that is," he pointed out, "apart from the mews which runs parallel to Shepherd Street and Curzon Street, but as they can't escape that way without being seen, assuming they do try to make a run for it that way, they won't get far."

Tony nodded and, looking at his watch, said, "Now all we need is Tom."

"I… er… I take it," Superintendent Dawson said tentatively, casting another glance up at Tony, "that your brother-in-law will…!"

"Don't worry, Superintendent, Tom wouldn't miss this show for anything." Receiving a doubtful look in reply to this, Tony smiled, saying amusingly, "And I suppose *I* can take it that you have collected the keys from the agent!"

"You *can*," Dawson assured him, rattling his pockets. "Can't have Scotland Yard forcing an entry into private premises!"

"No," Tony shook his head, his eyes alight with amusement, "that would never do!"

"No," Dawson concurred on a cough, avoiding Tony's laughing eye by focusing his attention on his pipe until suddenly recalling something to mind. "Oh, by the way, I saw Hallerton first thing."

"You *have* had a busy morning, Superintendent," Tony told him with perfect gravity, sternly suppressing the twitch at the corner of his mouth.

Superintendent Dawson, eyeing him very much as he would a mischievous child, sighed resignedly, realising he was not impervious to Tony's sense of humour. "Yes, well," he sighed, "it seems you were right."

"Are you going to charge him with him anything?" Tony asked.

Dawson shook his head. "Well," he sighed again, "I suppose I should for withholding vital evidence if nothing else but, quite frankly," he admitted, "I see little point in that. His reasons were not criminal after all said."

Tony considered a moment. "No, they weren't. His main concern was for Sir Philip's reputation."

Superintendent Dawson agreed to this, then, tapping his pipe on the heel of his boot to empty the bowl, sighed, "I get the feeling it's going to be a while before my next pipe, assuming that is," he said meaningfully, casting a glance up at Tony, "this plan of yours works."

"It will," Tony said firmly.

"Well, if it doesn't," Dawson told him with resignation, "we're both for the high jump!"

Tony was just about to respond to this when Jerry cocked his head, asking, "Is this 'im Guv?"

Looking in the direction Jerry had indicated Tony saw Tom hurrying along Hertford Street towards them, approaching the group a little out of breath, his hackney having unfortunately dropped him the opposite end of the street. Tony, slapping him on the shoulder, laughed away his apologies, then, having made him known to his co-collaborators, decided it was time they were making a move, whereupon they walked along the pavement until they came to Dennis Dunscumbe's house.

The five-storey double-fronted house of white Portland stone was every bit as respectable as all the other houses which lined both sides of this fashionable thoroughfare, leaving Tony to wonder how Dennis Dunscumbe had managed to maintain a most impressive house in such an exclusive location on his limited financial resources. Unlike most of its neighbours the path, although only a shallow step up from the pavement, extended for several feet leading to the front door, the black painted railings on either side at right angles with those running along the pavement, concealing the double fronted basement steps. Surprisingly, it had not suffered any external deterioration during its vacancy nor, for that matter, had the interior, but even though the rooms still housed the late owner's furniture and the curtains still hung at the windows, the atmosphere was ice-cold rendered infinitely worse by that distinctive smell of emptiness nothing could quite disguise.

It was not a death on the premises which had deterred potential buyers or tenants, after all it was only to be expected that people died in their own home more often than not, it was the knowledge that the death had supposedly been brought about by Dennis Dunscumbe's own hand which had resulted in a lack of enthusiasm even to make enquiries. Consequently, apart from the occasional visit by the agent to check the premises, it was obvious no one had been inside the house for some appreciable time, and as Collett would not yet have had time to recruit his forces, it was therefore deemed safe to make a brief reconnoitre. As Dennis Dunscumbe had not got round to having electricity installed the lights were then tested to see if there was still a gas supply connected and, upon seeing there was, Superintendent Dawson then sent two uniformed police constables to check the upper floors while he went to look over the basement and kitchen area with Jerry and Tony and Tom surveyed the ground floor.

The door giving access to the room to the right of the main front door, when compared with viewing it from the street, although lofty, was deceptively small, and in view of the floor to ceiling bookshelves either side of the black granite fireplace and the covered leather chair and desk, there could be little doubt that it had clearly been used as a study by its late occupant. Having cast an eye all around what was evidently the room in which Dennis Dunscumbe had spent most of his time when he was at home, Tony, upon seeing nothing to suggest anything untoward had taken place, decided that nothing could be gleaned from it, walked across the black and white tiled hall floor to the room immediately opposite with Tom following closely behind. Like all the front facing rooms in the house, this lofty and spacious apartment had its cream blinds pulled down, concealing the interior from the curious stares of passers-by, but as with the study there was more than enough light for the two men to see clearly. The only item of furniture which had not been wrapped in a protective cover was a half-moon spindle-legged table standing against the wall between the two sash windows, elegantly festooned with pale blue and gold brocade curtains, acting as perfect foils for the carpet of the same hue and the tinted walls in warm yellow. Above the white marble fireplace hung an oval shaped mirror in the style of the second French Empire, an attractive piece which Tony suspected had cost a considerable sum, but whose glass, clearly visible where its protective cover had begun to fall away, was sadly beginning to blacken at the edges. Except for an intricately carved centre piece, from which hung an ornate chandelier protected in swathes of calico, the ceiling was surprisingly plain, but regardless of this and the fact that everything was well covered it could be easily seen that the room was elegantly and tastefully furnished.

"Dennis Dunscumbe certainly had taste," Tom remarked, eyeing the room. "Pity about that though, don't you think?" nodding to where an old rug had haphazardly been placed just to the left of a wing chair. "Not my cup of tea decor," he admitted, "leave all that to Bea, but I'd say it looks rather out of place."

"Yes, it does," Tony said slowly, following his glance. "You know, Tom," he mused, "I'd say that rug was never intended for this room at all but just put there and," crossing over to the chair, "unless I miss my guess, I think I know why." Bending down Tony lifted one end of the rug with his gloved fingers, then, looking up at Tom, said, "As I thought."

Tom stared at the faded reddish brown tinge with horrified eyes. "Good God! Do you mean…?"

"This is where Peterson shot Dunscumbe," Tony nodded, "and the room where they will head for!" replacing the rug and rising to his feet.

"But I thought it happened in his room!" Tom jerked a thumb upward.

"Yes," Tony admitted, "so did I. A pretty natural assumption to arrive at given that it was his man who found him." His eyes narrowed in thought, saying at length, "According to Bill, the only information the police released about Dunscumbe's suicide was that his body was found in his own home, they did not specify which room; so when the story went to press there was nothing reported about it actually taking place in here."

"But Superintendent Dawson…!" Tom began.

"He was never in on this case," Tony shook his head. "It was apparently handled by the local police at Vine Street, and since they had no reason to doubt his death as being anything other than suicide, Scotland Yard was not brought in. In fact," he nodded, "I'd say they still have it marked down as such."

"Looks like they're in for a bit of a shock then!" Tom remarked, casting an eloquent glance at his brother-in-law.

"Too right they are!" Tony agreed. "Now though," patting Tom on the shoulder, "I think it's time we took a quick look over the other rooms."

Had anyone asked the two police constables assigned to this duty for their opinion, they would have had no hesitation in saying that whoever had dreamed up this little caper needed his head examining because as far as they could see no one in their right mind was going to return to the scene of the crime after all this long time. Since they were both of the same mind they whiled away the time in the hall as they waited to report to Superintendent Dawson that the upstairs was clear by bitterly complaining about such a pointless duty. "'Ow many of us roped in on this?" Constable Short demanded scornfully. "Those poor buggers outside an' us in 'ere. A bloomin' waste o' time! 'Oos idea wos it?" he asked his colleague in a belligerent under voice, indicating the drawing-room from where movement could clearly be heard through the partly open door. "That's wot I wont to know!"

"Serposed ter be teckin' the missis out tonight," Constable Moore told him cantankerously, rubbing his hands together behind his back.

"Ha! Yer've got no chance, mate!" Constable Short told him irritably. "We'll be 'ere till bloomin' midnight at this rate, you wotch! An' for wot?" he demanded of his colleague in a fierce whisper, keeping an eye on the drawing-room door. "A wild goose chase, that's wot! Brass monkeys out there," nodding towards the street, "an' brass monkeys in 'ere!" going on to colourfully describe the various methods by which he would like to deal with the man responsible, sentiments his colleague fully shared.

"'Ere, Ed," Constable Moore wanted to know, darting a wary glance around the hall, "'oo's this geezer wi' the Boss, anyway?"

Constable Short shrugged his broad shoulders, saying out the corner of his mouth, keeping one eye cocked for the Superintendent and one on that partly open drawing-room door, "Newspaperman I 'eard."

"Get away!" Constable More exclaimed. "'E ain't no newspaperman, not in them togs! 'Ere," he cocked his head, a thought just occurring to him, "yer don't think 'e's the one…"

"Wotch it," Constable Short warned as the drawing-room door opened and Tony and Tom emerged into the hall, "sumone's cumin'."

Tony, who had caught the last few vehemently expressed comments through the partly open door, had no need to hear the tail end of this exchange to know precisely how they were feeling or what they would like to do to him, but by the time he drew abreast with them nothing could be detected in their demeanour or from the respectful touch of their helmets to suggest this. Unlike these two men Tony knew how important this surveillance was, even so, he fully sympathised with every one of their embittered opinions, and the temptation to say, "Quite so, Constable!" as he walked past them, albeit a little ruefully, was irresistible.

Tom, casting a brief look over his shoulder, was just in time to see the looks exchanged between the two constables, but catching the laughter in Tony's eyes, raised a questioning eyebrow, only to be told, "I'm the guy they'd like to string up by the thumbs! Be honest Tom," Tony smiled in answer to Tom's bewildered look, "where would you rather be," opening a door at the rear of the hall, "at home with Bea or hanging around here in the freezing cold for goodness only knows how long?"

Not surprisingly the other ground floor rooms, comprising a dining room, a small sitting room and what appeared to be a billiards room, were also shrouded in protective covers, but if the reams of calico could not quite hide their taste and elegance, they certainly did little to dispel the eerie emptiness which pervaded them, but since they did not form part of the matter in hand, both men returned to the front drawing-room with no sign of Constable Short and his colleague in the hall.

Superintendent Dawson, having conducted his search of the basement quarters, was looking pensively down at the stain on the carpet, looking meaningfully up at Tony as he walked into the room. He fully agreed that this was where Dunscumbe had met his end as well as being the room Collett would make for while Jerry, quite at a loss for words, merely pulled off his hat and scratched his head.

As it was generally agreed that Collett and Peterson would not try to gain entry by way of the front door simply because it was running too much of a risk in drawing attention to themselves but through the basement door, it was therefore considered essential that the bolts be left securely fastened so as not to make them suspect a trap.

"I agree the basement is favourite," Superintendent Dawson said thoughtfully, looking from one to the other, "in fact," he nodded, "they'd be foolish to try to force an entry by way of the front door, but that one downstairs is heavy, at least two inches thick," he pointed out. "This Peterson is going to have to be pretty strong to shoulder it open."

"'E's that all right!" Jerry confirmed. "Used to be a bruiser."

"Jerry's right," Tony nodded, "but if this Peterson guy is all I take him to be he won't come unprepared. What is it you call a jimmy over here, Jerry?" he smiled, cocking a humorous eyebrow. "A jemmy?"

"That's it!" he grinned.

"Well," Tony inclined his head, "you can bet he'll bring one with him."

Accepting this as more than likely, Superintendent Dawson briefly glanced at his watch, sighing, "Well, gentlemen, since there's nothing more we can do now but wait, I'd say it's time we took up our positions. It's quarter to one now," he nodded, "and although I can't see them making an attempt until it gets dark, we can't take that for granted."

Upon learning that the two police constables had already been posted to a vantage point just on the bend in the stairs, Tony could not help wondering what was going through their minds, particularly as there was nothing they could do to while away the time, but if nothing else stringing him up by the thumbs would be the most minor punishment they would come up with.

Superintendent Dawson may be no stranger to lying in wait in some dingy alley or side street for something to happen, but on those occasions he had at least been able to smoke his pipe whereas now to do so in a house which had been empty all these months would only serve to make their presence known. Jerry, never being tempted into using tobacco, going without a smoke for what could be several hours was not something that troubled him. As he was himself no stranger to these kinds of jobs he knew that not only could they be in for a very long wait but also being in such close proximity to a man who regularly indulged his habit could end up being somewhat fraught and, in view this, had had the forethought to bring a pack of cards with him. He was not saying it was a substitute for tobacco, but if nothing else it would go a long way to taking Superintendent Dawson's mind off it and, as the hours dragged endlessly by, this smart move, together with recalling past cases and colleagues, their wait was thankfully rendered less frustrating than it would otherwise have been.

Having decided to take up their positions in the small sitting room at the rear of the hall within feet of the camouflaged door entrance to the stairs which led to the basement and kitchen just to their left, Tony and Tom made themselves as comfortable as possible. Pulling up an upright chair and placing it a slight angle to the door which he left slightly ajar, giving him an unrestricted view of the hall, Tony sat down and, crossing one long leg over the other, prepared himself for a long wait. His brother-in-law, having finally settled himself in a wing chair which looked far more comfortable than it actually was, made worse by the protective cover riding up every time he moved, propped his chin in his hand and regarded Tony with a thoughtful eye.

"Okay Tom," Tony smiled, "let's have it! What's on your mind? You think I've got this all wrong, is that it? Or are you thinking that Collett won't rise to the bait?"

"What!" Tom cried, sitting bolt upright, dropping his hand onto the arm of the chair. "Lord no!" he assured him. "You haven't got it wrong it at all! Collett'll rise to the bait because he can't afford not to. No," he shook his head, "someone will come, no question, it's just that I can't help feeling we're in for the devil of a long wait!"

"Well," Tony sighed, "I can't argue with that, but no matter how desperate Collett is he can't risk showing himself in broad daylight any more than we could have left arriving here any later!"

"Do you really think Collett *will* show himself," Tom raised a questioning eyebrow, "or do you think he will leave it to Peterson and this Eliza Boon woman?"

"I'm convinced of it," Tony nodded. "Peterson's okay for the strong-arm work, which will certainly be needed to prise open that basement door, and naturally Collett will need him to go through precisely what he did that night, but he's nothing but a yes-man when all is said and done and Collett dare not leave something of such importance as identifying incriminating evidence to him. As for Eliza Boon," he shrugged, "who knows? Although I must admit that at first why she should come at all escaped me, but now," he nodded, "having given it some thought, she may decide to if for no other reason than to prevent Collett from losing his head and 'blowing the gaff' as Jerry would say, but that she will come in place of Collett, huh huh." He shook his head. "There is no way Collett will remain behind in Cavendish Square; he's far too nervous for that!"

A deep frown creased Tom's forehead as he considered something before saying thoughtfully, "Supposing she *does* come," eyeing his brother-in-law meaningfully, "in view of last night," he nodded, "I'd say we had better be on our guard!"

"Too right!" Tony agreed firmly. "That woman is one tough cookie!"

Sir Braden's death, resulting from Peterson's momentary loss of rationality, could not have come at a worse time for Eliza Boon, but even though it had undoubtedly shocked her, her well-thought-out actions following this unfortunate occurrence certainly proved just how tough a cookie she actually was. Being faced with the task of keeping a lid on what had happened so as not to alert the servants until they could get rid of Sir Braden's dead body without anyone being the wiser, not to mention the urgency attached in keeping up the illusion that Lady Collett was still indisposed in her room as well as visiting Dennis Dunscumbe's house before the police descended on the premises tomorrow, may be considered by some as being rather daunting to say the least, but Eliza Boon was not of their number. She may not have expected things to turn out in this way, but since they had she saw no use in repining or wasting time by wishing things were different, and it was with a determination bordering on callousness that she set about salvaging what she could from this debacle. With Peterson's help, within the space of thirty minutes there was no evidence to suggest that a violent death had taken place; the room being fully restored to order, so much so that had anyone managed to find a spare key to the study and later chanced to put their head round the door, there was not the slightest sign to suggest that Sir Braden's gruesome corpse was actually bent into a foetal position behind a leather club chair in the far corner out of view.

Since visiting Dennis Dunscumbe's house could not even be considered until it started to get dark and it was impossible to dispose of Sir Braden's body in broad daylight, Eliza Boon took advantage of the lull in proceedings to carry out a task that she dared not leave undone. Sir Braden may not have inspired loyalty in the hearts of his domestic staff, but they were not so unconcerned that they would not notice his continued absence from home and the last thing she wanted right now was to start them thinking, particularly Mrs. Timms. Should this rather forthright woman take it into her head to come upstairs to retrieve her newspaper only to find the study door locked, Eliza would not put it past her to question Sir Braden's whereabouts, and therefore decided it prudent to nip any flights of fancy in the bud straightaway. Once she had done this as well as recovering what, if any, incriminating evidence Peterson may have left in Hertford Street followed by disposing of Sir Braden's body once the staff had retired for the night, what happened after that she would deal with it as and when it came along, now though, her chief aim was to grant herself and Peterson enough time to act.

Mrs. Timms, always suspicious of Eliza Boon, received her copy of *'The Echo'* together with the news that Sir Braden had found it necessary to go out and did not know when he would be back without a blink, believing he was merely doing what His Lordship wanted him to do in response to the article he had caused to be inserted in the newspapers. Mrs. Timms may consider Sir Braden's attempt at gaining entry into Dennis Dunscumbe's house in broad daylight as being somewhat risky, but not wishing to alert this woman to the fact that she not only knew the truth but was a party to the trap which had been laid, she merely took her newspaper before asking about luncheon and whether Lady Collett, who, over the past few days, had hardly touched a morsel of the food Eliza had taken in to her, would be requiring anything, some sustaining broth perhaps? Had Eliza the least inkling that Mrs. Timms knew that Lady Collett, far from being indisposed in her room, was safely installed in Mount Street following her escape and that she herself had cunningly disposed of some of the food she had supposedly taken in to her to allay suspicion, she would not have been quite so optimistic about her plans. As it was, the last thing Eliza wanted was to alert Mrs. Timms to the fact that Lady Collett had escaped as well as making sure that no one tried to enter her room while she and Peterson were in Hertford Street this afternoon, let alone the drastic incident in the study and how, as a result, the very thought of food at such a moment was quite nauseating. However, Eliza responded quite calmly to this perfectly natural enquiry by saying that she had given Lady Collett a sedative and she was now asleep and would remain so for several hours, but the sustaining broth would be most welcome when she eventually awoke and, as for herself, she would take her luncheon in her sitting room and Peterson, as was proper, would take his down here as usual. As Mrs. Timms had no more liking for Peterson than she had for this woman who had rendered her young mistress's life such a terrible ordeal, she simply nodded and acquainted her with the menu, to which Eliza's thin lips parted into the merest semblance of a smile, saying she was quite sure it would taste as delicious as ever.

But when Ellen later carried her luncheon upstairs, Eliza Boon, unlike Peterson sitting totally unconcerned at the scrubbed topped table in the kitchen eating his meal with the same sullen enjoyment as he always did, she could do no more than push the food around on her plate as she sat in her sitting room pondering the dilemma facing them.

It was not that she was overly squeamish, far from it, but this morning's fiasco had completely taken away her appetite. It had been bad enough reading those articles in the newspapers about a new police investigation necessitating a visit to Hertford Street, a circumstance which could, if she was not careful, see her and her confederate facing the Queen's Bench, and it was therefore in an agony of suspense that she waited with what patience she could for dusk to fall. As it was Sir Braden's custom to lock his study door whenever he went out, Eliza Boon, with the key safely in her pocket, knew that there was no fear of his dead body being found by one of the maids and, just as the clock in the hall struck half past four with the daylight fading fast, she felt it safe for her and Peterson to leave the house and make their way to Hertford Street. Somewhere at the back of her mind Eliza could not rid herself of the nagging thought that Sir Braden could well have been right when he said that the police may have already visited Dennis Dunscumbe's house irrespective of what it said in the newspapers or, which she fervently hoped would not be the case, unexpectedly turn up while they were there. But although she told herself that there had really been no time for the police to organise a search of the house given that their intention had only been made known in the newspapers this morning, besides which it was most unlikely they would conduct a search at this late hour of the day, it did not quite set her mind at rest. Nevertheless, by the time she and Peterson arrived at their destination with neither sight nor sound of any police activity within the vicinity she was able to breathe more easily before bending her mind to the task ahead of them, confident that she would be back in Cavendish Square in time to prevent either Ellen or Mrs. Timms attempting to enter Eleanor's room.

From his vantage point in the Square's garden, Arthur saw them leave the house and descend the steps, pausing only long enough to look all around them before making their way towards Oxford Street, knowing precisely where they were heading, but of Sir Braden there was no sign. As Arthur was well acquainted with the plan of action he could not quite understand why Sir Braden was not with them and since no one had left the house prior to Eliza Boon's and Peterson's departure a few minutes ago, it could only mean that Sir Braden had decided to remain behind. Considering the seriousness of his position, Sir Braden, who had no way of knowing that this was merely a well-thought-out scheme to entrap him, was certainly behaving blasé to say the least about something as important as this. Had the police really intended visiting Hertford Street and during the course of their search they actually found something which could tie him in with Dennis Dunscumbe's death and all that had followed, Arthur was a little at a loss to understand why Sir Braden had elected to stay at home instead of doing everything possible to obviate this risk. To Arthur's way of thinking what made Sir Braden's failure to show himself even more inexplicable was that so far Tony's reckoning had been spot on, and unless Arthur was very much mistaken he did not see him being wrong now in that Sir Braden would be forced into visiting Hertford Street to assure himself that there was nothing there which could incriminate him. It could be of course that he intended to follow on in a little while, but as the minutes ticked by with no sign of him Arthur began to suspect that something did not ring true, and the longer he waited behind the frozen bushes rubbing his gloved hands together for Sir Braden to leave the house, this suspicion eventually turned into utter conviction.

Firmly convinced that something was dreadfully wrong inside twenty-nine Cavendish Square, Arthur took the decision to investigate. Keeping a wary eye cocked all around, he cautiously emerged from his hiding place and hurried over the road which separated the gardens from the houses, quietly opening the basement gate before carefully descending the steps which, although the slush had all been cleared away by the ever-complaining boot boy, Albert, they were still rather treacherous, but eventually he reached the bottom and knocked on the door. In view of the part Mrs. Timms had played in their plans, at no time did it cross Arthur's mind that she would either shut the door in his face or refuse to help him; and nor did she.

Pearl may have set her heart on Albert, a young man who, though not averse to passing a few illicit moments in pleasurable dalliance with her when Cook's back was turned, was remarkably slow to come up to scratch and so in her efforts to force his hand she ogled every young man who came within her orbit hoping that it would make him jealous enough to pop the question. So far this strategy, which she implemented with enthusiasm, had failed in its object, but upon opening the door to find herself looking at a young man who was by far the most good-looking yet to come in her way, she was given every reason to believe that at long last she had found the very person who could not fail to make Albert jealous. Arthur, who could not see Albert standing watching Pearl from down the passage, was instantly thrown into a little confusion when she unexpectedly grabbed the sides of her skirt and swished it from side to side, but it was the provocative look she cast up at him from under her lashes which positively alarmed him and when she asked, in a voice she mistakenly believed was laden with feminine seduction, what she could do for him, it took all his resolve to stand his ground.

Fortunately for Arthur, the sound of Mrs. Timms's voice calling to Pearl from the kitchen doorway asking if she was going to keep the basement door open all night and let the cold air in, brought her down to earth with a shattering thud. With the colour flooding her cheeks, Pearl lowered her eyes and invited Arthur to step inside and, after asking what he wanted, she hurried down the corridor to tell Mrs. Timms that a young man wanted to see her. It was not to be expected that Albert had missed Pearl's attempt to make him jealous, in fact he had known all along what game she was playing and was extremely flattered by it, but upon setting eyes on Arthur, far better looking than the others Pearl had flashed her eyes at, gave him pause for thought. This pause for thought quite naturally found its outlet in tackling Pearl the instant she came up to him, but Mrs. Timms, looking at Arthur over their heads with his cap in his hands, soon bustled the arguing couple about their business, telling them that if they had nothing to do then she could easily find them something.

Mrs. Timms may not have set eyes on Arthur before in her life, but the likeness between father and son was quite pronounced, and therefore recognised him instantly as Jerry's son and that together with his father and brothers he was taking it in turns to watch the house. She did not pretend to understand the intricacies of keeping up a surveillance, but she did know that something untoward must have occurred to cause him to leave his post and come to the house, and could not help wondering if the plan His Lordship had set in motion had failed. Arthur was just about to tell her the reason for him being here when she forestalled him, saying in her motherly way that they would be far more comfortable in the kitchen where it was a great deal warmer than standing in a cold and draughty passageway, allaying his concerns by adding that since Ellen and Susan were out running errands and not expected back for half an hour or more and the warring love birds were in the rear pantry, there was no fear of them being disturbed or overheard. "Now dearie," she smiled, "I take it your dad 'as sent you!"

"Well, no," Arthur confessed, gratefully accepting the mug of scalding hot tea she handed him, going on to tell her what had made him decide to leave his post and come and speak to her.

"Sir Braden!" Mrs. Timms echoed. "You must be mistaken, dearie. Accordin' to Eliza Boon 'e went out early this mornin' an' so far 'e's not come back yet," handing him a thick slice of fruit cake. "I must say though," she confessed, putting the lid back on the tin, a slight frown creasing her forehead, "it did cross my mind that 'e might go straight to 'Ertford Street…"

"But 'e can't 'ave gone out, Mrs. Timms," Arthur told her earnestly, "I've been on watch all day an' I've seen no one leave the 'ouse except Eliza Boon an' Peterson not fifteen minutes back. They must be goin' to 'Ertford Street. I thought Sir Braden would be goin' with Peterson an' that Eliza Boon would stay 'ere, same as the Guvna did," he nodded, "that's why 'e wanted me to stay on watch 'ere in case she went somew'ere so I could follow 'er, but I've not seen Sir Braden leave the 'ouse. She must be goin' instead of 'im!"

Mrs. Timms knew precisely who he meant when he referred to the 'Guvna' and since she had as much faith in Tony as Jerry and his sons clearly did, she could not see him being wrong about Sir Braden. "Well!" she cried, shrugging helplessly, not at all sure what to make of it all, "if Sir Braden 'asn't gone out, what's 'appened to 'im? 'E 'asn't been in 'is study because Susan went up earlier to dust an' do, forgettin' 'e'd gone out," she nodded, "an' the door was locked, just as it always is when 'e steps out," she told him, "an' 'e always keeps the key on 'im."

Arthur, chewing a generous mouthful of cake, thought a moment, then, putting his plate and mug down onto the table said, "I don't suppose there's a spare key is there, Mrs. Timms?"

"Spare key!" she repeated. "No, lovey," she shook her head. "'Er Ladyship did give me a spare set of keys, but not for the study. Sir Braden's the only one who 'as a key to it." She looked closely at him for a second, a horrid suspicion entering her mind. "Never tell me you think somethin's 'appened to 'im!"

"Somethin' must 'ave 'appened to 'im, Mrs. Timms," Arthur nodded, "otherwise 'e would 'ave shown 'imself. I've got to get into that study," he said firmly. "If somethin' 'as 'appened, I've got to let the Guvna an' the police know."

Mrs. Timms needed no more persuading and, determinedly nodding her head, told him she would take him upstairs to Sir Braden's study and, after making sure that Pearl and Albert were still in the rear pantry, led Arthur up the back stairs and through the door which gave access to the rear of the hall. As Eliza Boon and Peterson had left the house Mrs. Timms knew there was no fear of being disturbed by either one of them and, as Arthur reminded her, there was no fear of them returning to Cavendish Square because once they stepped foot inside Dennis

Dunscumbe's house they would be arrested. Treading softly across the black and white tiled floor to the door which Mrs. Timms had indicated with a nod of her head as being Sir Braden's study, Arthur put his ear against it and, when no sound could be heard from the other side, slowly turned the handle and gently pushed the door which remained firmly shut against him. Deciding that he had no choice but to pick the lock he dug a hand into his inside coat pocket and pulled out what Mrs. Timms thought was a leather wallet, but upon seeing him open it to display a row of instruments carefully secured by small tabs she put a hand to her throat, watching almost mesmerised as she saw Arthur kneel down and put his eye to the keyhole to see which hook would be most suitable, then, removing a long thin piece of metal with hooks at both ends, he inserted it into the lock.

"Never tell me your dad taught you to do that!" Mrs. Timms gasped.

Smiling mischievously up at her, Arthur nodded. "Knows a thing or two, does me dad!" he said proudly. "'Sides," he added, "it's better than breakin' the door down."

Upon reflection she had to agree and waited with bated breath as she watched him carefully turn the pick inside the lock, her eyes round with wonder when she finally heard it click. Removing the lock pick from the keyhole, Arthur rose to his feet and returned it to the wallet which he put back into his pocket, telling Mrs. Timms to stay where she was while he went inside, the door opening easily in response to the turn of the handle. Sir Braden may not as yet have got round to having a telephone connected but, like so many others who could afford it, he had certainly had electricity installed, this modern technology enabling Arthur to illuminate the room by merely flicking the switch on the wall just to his right. Although the fire had long since died the room was still fairly warm and at first glance everything appeared perfectly normal with nothing out of place; even the newspapers Sir Braden had read earlier that morning were neatly folded on his desk next to his correspondence which, surprisingly, had not been opened, but reading nothing untoward in this Arthur crossed over to the window and closed the curtains. Certainly the orderliness all around him gave the lie to his feelings that something was wrong, but for some unaccountable reason his instinct was telling him that something was in fact very wrong, and were it not for the fact that he had been in a perfect position to see all the comings and goings he could so easily have believed that Sir Braden had indeed left the house without him noticing. According to Mrs. Timms Sir Braden always locked the study door when he left the house, but Arthur would stake his life he had never set foot outside the front door but also, from what she had told him, when the maids had gone about their duties they had never once clapped eyes on him. It was doubtful that Sir Braden would have locked the door to his study had he merely been in another part of the house, but surely he could not be in another room all this time and no one see him! The more Arthur thought about it the more convinced he became that something was not right, and it was just as he was about to leave the study to conduct a search of the house when he caught sight of the leather club chair in the far corner jutting out at a slightly awkward angle. It was of course perfectly possible that being as there was no carpet covering the highly polished floorboards the chair had naturally moved a little out of position when being used, but Arthur, not at all convinced of this, stepped over to the chair and pulled it out. Whatever he had expected it was certainly not the sight of Sir Braden's dead body, suddenly released from the confines of the back of the chair and the wall, to roll over onto its back and lie staring up at him out of those bulging blue eyes with the mouth almost frozen open revealing a purple tongue lodged at the back of the throat, causing Arthur to jump involuntarily back a step or two gasping in shock.

It was several moments before he could gather himself together, but after taking several deep breaths he knelt down to have a closer look at Sir Braden's body, his rather unsteady fingers carefully moving his head from side to side, exposing the severe bruising around his neck and throat. Arthur could only guess as to what had brought this about, but he did know that it was not Eliza Boon who had put an end to Sir Braden's life. She may be mentally strong, possessing a determination to overcome all obstacles at no matter what cost, but she was certainly not physically strong enough to strangle Sir Braden, which meant it had to be Peterson.

Mrs. Timms, watching anxiously from the doorway, no sooner saw Arthur's startled reaction followed by him bending down behind the chair, and she knew instinctively what he had discovered. Clapping her hands to her cheeks, she watched Arthur rise to his feet and walk towards her, his face as pale as her own, and upon him confirming that Sir Braden was dead, she exclaimed, "Lord ha' mercy! You can't mean it!"

Although neither of them were in any doubt that Sir Braden's death must have had something to do with the articles in the newspapers this morning and that it was Peterson who had killed him, they were utterly at a loss to understand what could possibly have happened to cause him to do such a thing. However, the more Arthur thought about it the more likely it seemed that it was a case of thieves falling out, but as it was imperative he set off for Hertford Street as soon as possible to tell Tony and the Superintendent what had happened, there was no time now to consider it any further.

Mrs. Timms may not hold with what Sir Braden and the others had done, but neither did she hold with such goings-on as this, and it was several minutes before she could pull herself together. If it was a case of thieves falling out after all as Arthur seemed to think, then considering the full extent of their crimes as well as the anxiety they must have felt knowing that sooner or later the law would catch up with them, exacerbated all the more by reading the article in the newspapers, it was perhaps not surprising that Sir Braden had met his end by the hand of one with whom he had collaborated. From the moment Tony had asked her to help him and the police bring Sir Braden and the others to account for their transgressions, she had experienced no twinges of conscience especially when she considered all her young mistress had endured, but whilst she admitted that she would have much preferred Sir Braden to have received his just deserts through the due processes of the law, his death at the hands of Peterson could be said as being nothing short of poetic justice. Be that as it may, however, she could not pretend to being anything other than profoundly shocked, and as Arthur made sure she did not see the body, not that she had any wish to, the very thought making her shudder, she easily allowed him to shepherd her away from where she was standing by the open doorway into the hall, nodding her head in full agreement as he impressed upon her how important it was that none of the servants knew what had happened.

After switching off the light and closing the door, Arthur once again inserted the lock pick into the keyhole to lock it, after which he told Mrs. Timms he would return as soon as he could with Tony and the police, smiling reassuringly down at her and telling her not to worry as she let him out of the house by the front door, turning up his coat collar before running as fast as he could in the slushy conditions to Hertford Street.

Chapter Twenty-Eight

By half past four, Constable Short and his equally long-suffering colleague, sitting uncomfortably on the bend in the stairs in fast-growing darkness, were still bitterly bemoaning the fact that they were on a wild goose chase, and if the boss and that other geezer had nothing else better to do, then they did. The other geezer, who, at no time, had even so much as considered this surveillance as being a wild goose chase, had sat comfortably back in his seat throughout the long wait contentedly exchanging low voiced observations with Tom, wholeheartedly agreeing with him when he said with feeling, "If only we could smoke!" It was perhaps as well for Tom that he happened to catch sight of an old newspaper, taking his mind off the cigars in his inside pocket as he glanced through it until half an hour ago when the last remnant of daylight coming in through the window had gone. As there were no chimes from any of the clocks to indicate what time it was as they had all long since wound down, Tony, rising to his feet and striding over to the window, pulled out his watch and held it up to the pane just managing to see that it wanted only two minutes to quarter to five and, after returning it to his pocket, walked back to his chair and returned it to its original position. "Shouldn't be too long now, Tom," he said in a hushed voice in response to his brother-in-law's cocked eyebrow, putting his head round the door which still stood ajar to look into the hall.

Tom, feeling a little stiff, rose to his feet and strode over to where Tony was standing, but because he was by no means as tall as his brother-in-law he had to stand on tiptoe to peer over his shoulder into the dark empty hall just in time to see Jerry step out of the study and tread softly over to them. Standing aside to allow him to come into the small sitting room, Tony whispered, "Everything okay with you, Jerry?"

"Apart from Dawson dyin' for a pipe," he grinned, "everythin's fine, Guv."

"He's not on his own in that!" Tom whispered with feeling.

"Well, we shouldn't have too long to wait now," Tony said quietly. "Are you and the Superintendent ready, Jerry?"

"Just about we are." Jerry nodded, rubbing his hands together, then, looking back over his shoulder into hall, said, "I'd best be gettin' back, Guv."

Tony nodded and, after watching him disappear into the study, turned to Tom, smiling. "Still glad you came, Tom?"

A sheepish grin crossed Tom's lips at this, whispering back, "Do I need to answer that?"

"No," Tony shook his head, "I knew I could count on you," he whispered, peering once more into the hall. "You're a Trojan, Tom," he smiled, looking round at him.

"Well," Tom sighed on a grin, "I hope Bea thinks the same when I tell her what I've been up to!"

"She will, you'll…" Tony broke off as the faint sound of splintering wood from the basement came to his ears and, after standing perfectly still for a moment or two listening intently, turned to Tom and gripped his shoulder.

"What is it?" Tom asked in a hushed voice. "Have you heard something?"

Tony nodded and, pointing a gloved finger towards the basement door just across the way, whispered, "This is it, Tom!" Peering round the door he saw Superintendent Dawson, who, like himself, had heard the faint sound, looking in their direction and, upon receiving a thumbs up from Tony, slipped back into the study to wait.

"Now we're on!" Tom said fervently.

"You *bet* we are!" Tony grinned before swiftly stepping out of the room to the bottom of the stairs to give the signal to the two men sitting in abject boredom just on the bend.

"Blimey!" Constable Short exclaimed, when Tony had disappeared back into the sitting room. "'Oo'd 'a thawt it!"

Constable Moore shrugged. "Betta late than neva I serpose!" to which his colleague fully agreed.

By the time Eliza Boon and Peterson arrived in Hertford Street, totally unaware of the numerous pairs of eyes closely watching them from various vantage points, it was almost quarter to five and the light gone, but there was enough illumination from the street lamps to show them the way to Dennis Dunscumbe's house. Although there were any number of passers-by, the weather was such that in their eagerness to get home out of the cold none of them took the slightest notice of the couple making a discreet but hurried descent down the basement steps of an empty house carrying an old hessian bag. Digging a hand into the cavernous interior Peterson pulled out a crowbar and handed the bag to Eliza who, after a quick look all around her, gave him the nod that all was clear, whereupon he began to ply this effective tool. Although it took several attempts before he was finally able to force the door around the lock, the sound of splintering wood reverberating abnormally loud in the cold stillness, the bottom bolt having given way under the force, the top one held fast. Pausing only long enough for Eliza to give him the nod to carry on after making sure his attempts at illegal entry had not attracted attention, Peterson repeatedly put his muscular shoulder to the door, but although the top bolt stubbornly resisted his powerful persistence for several minutes, eventually it was heard rupturing from its mounting, the force of it propelling him irresistibly into the basement corridor.

Without giving him time to recover his balance Eliza stepped inside and quickly looked around for something to put against the door to keep it shut, her eye alighting on an iron door stopper which she soon had in place. Although there were two windows on the rear wall they were situated too high up for the light to be of any benefit, and therefore the only light to illuminate the huge kitchen was the partial one coming in from the street lamps through the small front window protruding a couple of feet above the basement area, rendering her search for an oil lamp slow and frustrating. Eventually though she found what she was looking for in the far recesses of a large cupboard, but in her eagerness to reach for it she unfortunately knocked over a miscellany of objects which had haphazardly been placed in front of it. Cursing under her breath, she put the lamp down onto the scrubbed topped table and, after checking there was enough lamp oil in the base, grabbed the matches off Peterson and removed the glass top to light the wick while at the same time sharply asking him if he remembered which room it was.

Peterson, who knew precisely what she was referring to, took instant exception to this blatant questioning of his intellect, saying grumpily,

"O'cus I rememba. Wot der yer think I am?"

She threw him a speaking look, saying, "I hope so," thrusting the lamp into his hand, "because I don't want us to be here any longer than we have to," then, pushing him in front of her, they left the kitchen and made their way across the stone flagged corridor to the stairs which led to the hall.

Tony, standing just behind the half open door of the sitting room, had heard the commotion in the kitchen when Eliza had searched for the lamp, but upon hearing the creaking of the back stairs as she and Peterson slowly trod up them one by one, Tony moved closer to the opening, turning to Tom and putting a gloved finger to his lips. "They're here," he whispered.

From his vantage point Tony saw the back stairs door slowly open and the shaft of light from the oil lamp held aloft, keeping perfectly still as he watched them emerge into the hall, somewhat taken aback when he saw that it was Eliza Boon who had accompanied Peterson and not Sir Braden Collett. As it was impossible for Tony to alert Tom to this fact without drawing attention to their presence, he watched Eliza Boon following closely behind Peterson as they crept stealthily along the hall towards the front drawing-room, pausing only for a brief word one with the other before they disappeared into this spacious apartment. Slowly pulling open the sitting room door Tony stepped quietly into the hall with Tom immediately behind him, the light from the lamp being moved about in the front drawing-room clearly visible through the partly open door; the hushed sound of furniture being moved wafting through to them in the stillness as they moved silently forward. As they reached the drawing-room Jerry and Superintendent Dawson were just leaving the confines of the study and Police Constables Short and Moore, glad to stretch their legs at last, had descended the stairs to come up behind them.

During Eliza Boon's heated discussion with Sir Braden following Tony's departure from Cavendish Square last night, it appeared that although he had somehow or other managed to put his hands on the truth he had no proof to substantiate his investigations, therefore rendering it impossible for him to take his findings to the police. She could only guess what this new information was that Scotland Yard now had in their possession or from whom they had received it, but in view of what Sir Braden had told her she was given no cause to suspect that the man she had come to look upon as their most dangerous enemy had merely put out a smoke screen to hide his carefully laid trap. Should their search come up with nothing after all, then all well and good, but under no circumstances could she take it for granted that Peterson had left no incriminating evidence behind him when he had shot Dennis Dunscumbe regardless of his assurances at the time that he had left everything as he had found it, and which had, somehow or other, been overlooked by the police first time round. Whilst Peterson could be depended upon to carry out whatever she asked him to do without the need for explanations or arguments she could not pretend that he had the sharpest of minds, and therefore it could well have escaped him to make sure that he had left nothing, no matter how insignificant, which could point the finger in their direction. Although Sir Braden had adamantly argued against a surreptitious visit to Hertford Street, Eliza had never for one moment disregarded how important it was, in fact she looked upon it as imperative and therefore saw their covert entry as essential. Unless Peterson had got it wrong when he assured her that he knew exactly which room to head for, she knew there should really be no need to search the rest of the house and, wholly oblivious to the forces gathering on the other side of the door in readiness to descend on them, they began their industrious search for any evidence which could see them facing the Queen's Bench.

Being totally absorbed in their task the sound of the door cautiously opening went unheard, and it was not until Tom turned up the gas on the wall sconce just to his right and flooded the room with light did the intruders realise they were not alone, turning horrified eyes in their direction and gasping their shock, but it was Eliza who pulled herself together first. She had no need to see the two uniformed police constables standing at the back of the group or be formally introduced to Superintendent Dawson to recognise him for precisely what he was; she could smell a police officer a mile off, but it was Tony who made her face contort with rage and hatred, realising this was nothing but a trap. *"You!"* she hissed, her hands clenching. "I should have known this was nothing but a trap!"

"Yes, you should," Tony said coolly. Her eyes spat venom at him. "The fact that you did not recognise it as such merely goes to prove how little faith you have in your accomplice," nodding in Peterson's direction. "Had you have done then you would never have taken the bait, but since you have I feel sure you do not need me to tell you that you have not only proved your complicity in Dennis Dunscumbe's murder and that of his brother Sir Philip but also Mitchell and the events surrounding it. I also feel sure that you have no need for me to tell you what we are doing here and that Superintendent Dawson from Scotland Yard," indicating the man standing next to him, "will shortly be asking you some questions before placing you both under arrest for your various crimes, but before he does so, in view of your attempt to put a bullet through me last night, I would like you to empty your pockets and put the contents on that table," nodding his head towards a little occasional table just to her left. Apart from throwing him a look of pure venom, Eliza Boon made no attempt to either answer him or do as he requested.

"If you refuse," Superintendent Dawson told her steadily, "then I shall have no choice but to get one of my officers to do it for you."

Eliza Boon, who was by no means stupid or lacking in intelligence, did not need to see the hard, implacable look in Tony's dark grey eyes to know precisely what he would like to do to her for her treatment of Eleanor alone, she already knew, the same as she knew that Superintendent Dawson would have no hesitation in ordering his officers to search her. It would give her tremendous satisfaction to refuse but as this would do her no favours she told Peterson to empty his pockets, but apart from a penknife, a ball of string, a box of matches and a screwed-up handkerchief, no weapon was found inside any of his pockets, then, after casting another look of loathing at Tony, emptied her own pockets which, to everyone's relief, contained nothing more dangerous than a handkerchief and a set of keys.

"Now turn out the linings," Tony said firmly, impervious to the look of hatred she threw at him as she did so. "Now unfasten your coat and empty the pockets of your skirt."

The only thing that made Tony's requests bearable was knowing that he had no idea of the secret pouch she had stitched into the lining of her left coat sleeve which cunningly held the little pistol she had taken the precaution to bring with her and, as she resentfully did as he asked, she could not help regretting her failure to make an end of him last night. "Satisfied?" she snarled.

Ignoring this, Tony asked curtly, "Where is Sir Braden?"

When she made no effort to reply to this, Superintendent Dawson, mindful of Tony's warning, was extremely relieved her pockets had contained nothing in the way of a weapon, took a step further into the room, saying severely, "I would strongly recommend you tell us where Sir Braden is."

Peterson, who was by now just a little confused over this unprecedented turn of events, especially as Eliza had assured him that nothing could go wrong, he stared somewhat bemused at the Superintendent for a moment or two before growling out, "'E cudn't cum!"

"Be quiet you fool!" Eliza shot at him. "Can't you see this is nothing but a trap?" mentally berating herself for being stupid enough not to have seen the truth before now in that those articles had been nothing but a fabrication by the man she hated above all others to lure them here.

"What do you mean, he couldn't come?" Superintendent Dawson pressed.

"Say nothing!" Eliza warned Peterson, taking a step nearer to him. "Can't you see what they're trying to do?" throwing a look of pure malice at Tony.

"Don't make things any worse for yourselves than they already are," Superintendent Dawson advised them.

"They don't know anything," Eliza Boon told her stalwart, laying a reassuring hand on his arm. "They're just putting the frighteners on."

"Where is Sir Braden?" Superintendent Dawson urged. "Is he at home?"

Upon finding himself being verbally assailed from both sides Peterson looked as bewildered as he felt, glancing from Eliza to the Superintendent as though one in a daze, but one thing he did know and that was this unexpected state of affairs boded no good for him. "I told yer," he ground out, "'e cudn't cum," shaking off Eliza's hand.

Tony saw the veiled look which suddenly entered Eliza Boon's eyes at this and the darting glance she cast at Peterson, but no matter how incredible the thought which came into his mind, he could not dismiss it. He was still pondering this when the sound of someone entering the house by way of the front door caught his attention and, upon turning his head to see Arthur whispering in Constable Short's ear, one look at his face was enough to tell Tony that his instincts had not erred.

By the time Arthur reached Hertford Street, having run all the way from Cavendish Square, he was considerably out of breath, but from the looks of the lights shining out from the hall and the front drawing-room window as well as the uniformed officers who had converged outside the house and the police vehicle that was just pulling up, the culprits had obviously been apprehended. At first it seemed he was going to be denied entry into the house, but thanks to his two brothers catching sight of him, both of whom vehemently confirmed his identity to the constables on the door, he was eventually allowed inside.

It was just as Constable Short was about to attract Tony's attention when he saw him step into the hall, and Arthur, seeing Tony cock his head, hurried over to his side where he breathlessly poured his findings into his ear. "Thanks, Arthur," Tony sighed, gripping his shoulder. "That must have been no pleasant sight! Are you okay?"

"Yes, Guv," he nodded, removing his cap and wiping his brow with the back of his hand.

"And Mrs. Timms?" Tony enquired.

"It's okay, Guv," Arthur assured him, "I didn't let 'er see anythin'."

Returning to the drawing-room in time to hear Superintendent Dawson demanding an answer to his question about whether Sir Braden was at home, Tony touched him on the shoulder and, after he had turned his head to look up at him, whispered the startling truth into his ear. Jerry, looking back into the hall to see what had attracted Tony's attention, was somewhat surprised to see his son standing in the hall and Tom, after following his glance, cast an enquiring look up at his brother-in-law, but before Tony had time to say anything, Superintendent Dawson, having recovered from the shock, turned to Eliza Boon, his lips compressed into a forbidding line.

From where she was standing Eliza Boon could not see who had entered the house, but that uncanny intuition which had never failed her was once again at work telling her that they had found Sir Braden's body, and when Tony re-entered the drawing-room a few minutes later the look on his face was more than enough to confirm this. She may not be a woman given over to self-recrimination and now, no more than at any time during the last twelve months, did she feel remorse over her actions, on the contrary she looked upon them as merely protecting her interests, but she could not pretend to looking upon Sir Braden's death in quite the same light. Even supposing they believed her if she told them that his death had not been at her instigation, the fact remained that it had come about as a direct result of their collusive scheming which had its origins in the unfortunate death of Annie Myers, but devious and conniving though Eliza was, she was no self-deceiver. However much it went against the grain with her to admit it, there was no denying that Childon was right when he said that had they had no hand in Dennis Dunscumbe's death they would never have found it necessary to come here and search for any possible any evidence which could denounce them. Their presence in Hertford Street was a damning self-indictment to their involvement in four brutal deaths and more than enough to send Peterson to the gallows whilst she could expect to find herself enjoying sparse comforts in a prison cell! It was an inescapable fact which to a lesser mortal would certainly have been more than enough for them to throw in the towel and accept defeat, but not Eliza Boon; she had not come this far to be beaten now even though the odds were overwhelmingly stacked against her! No matter how dire the situation facing them, unlike Sir Braden, she had never really lost sight of common sense and this was now telling her that trying to escape her accusers, all of whom were congregating by the door to prevent any move she made to make a run for it, would not only be madness but virtually an admission of guilt. Her agile brain, seemingly never at a loss, quickly sought a way out of this dilemma by coming up with a last-ditch attempt to save herself from losing her freedom for a rather lengthy spell, and it was as she listened with only half an ear to Superintendent Dawson as he informed them of their findings in Cavendish Square, that she realised deliverance was at hand, in fact had been all along!

Had Childon and the police any evidence against them, then this charade would not have been necessary, proving beyond doubt that, apart from Lady Collett, whose testimony would go for nothing, they had no witnesses to prove their complicity, meaning there was really no case to answer. No jury could find one guilty on supposition alone, if that were so, then they would never have found themselves forced into engineering this well laid trap in the first place. Even had Eliza known that Joanie Simms held such damning information and had told Childon what she had overheard, although Eliza would have been furiously angry at such a betrayal, she would not be alarmed because in her own way Joanie Simms was just as ineligible to give evidence as Lady Collett. As far as Eliza could see the only charge to answer was being found red-handed in Dennis Dunscumbe's house which, she felt sure, could be easily explained away in a court of law and, as for Sir Braden's unfortunate death, she had had no hand in that whatsoever, in fact she had tried to persuade Peterson into releasing him besides, what did she possibly have to gain from his death? Sir Braden's untimely demise, tragic though it was, did not suit her at all and, furthermore, she felt sure that once this was eventually explained the police would have no choice but to withdraw the charge against her and place the blame where it rightly belonged.

The unfortunate death of Annie Myers was to be regretted of course, but at no time was it Eliza's intention to do a stretch at Her Majesty's pleasure and now was no different. The truth was she would much rather save her own skin than anyone else's and if this meant throwing Peterson to the wolves, a man who, for whatever reason, had stood loyally by her and done her every bidding, then she was quite prepared to do it. As a great believer in self-preservation she looked upon using him as a scapegoat in the same clinically detached way she had everything else she had put her hand to since this whole thing began and, if she played her cards right, then she had every expectation of walking away from this completely unscathed.

Unfortunately, Peterson was not so adept as Eliza in thinking on his feet nor, to do him justice, so disloyal as to abandon her in the face of Superintendent Dawson's allegations of her inciting the murder of Sir Braden Collett. Yet again, Peterson was more than ready to defend the woman who was, even now, considering how best to serve him up as a sacrificial lamb on the altar of her own self-interests and, in complete ignorance of this pending treachery, growled, "It wasn't Eliza!" little realising he was playing into her hands.

"Are you saying *you* killed him?" Superintendent Dawson asked.

"'E shudn't 'ave 'it Eliza!" Peterson said adamantly. "Nobudy don't tuch Eliza!"

"Is that why you strangled him," Superintendent Dawson pressed quietly, "because he hit her?" stepping further into the room and seeing for the first time in the full glare of the light the faint bruising on the side of her face. "Was there a disagreement?" he encouraged.

"Sed 'e wos goin' ter the puleece," Peterson said gruffly. "Sed 'e cudn't tek eny more."

"Take any more what?" Superintendent Dawson asked.

"Dunno," Peterson shrugged. "Summut in the papa," he said vaguely. "Summut ter do wiv cumin' 'ere."

"What about coming here?" Superintendent Dawson urged.

"Dunno," Peterson shrugged again. "Sed there wos nuthin' else ter do but go ter the puleece!"

"Is that why you killed Sir Braden, because he and Eliza Boon had an argument about what they read in the newspapers this morning?" Superintendent Dawson urged.

Peterson nodded, saying gruffly, "Ee shudn't awt ter 'ave 'it Eliza.

Nobudy don't tuch Eliza, see!"

It came as no surprise to Tony that Collett's murder had come about due to an argument between himself and Eliza Boon after reading the article in the newspapers, what did surprise him, however, was hearing Peterson say that Collett had talked of going to the police. Such an intention had been the furthest thing from his mind last night, in fact he had made it clear to Tony that his visit to Cavendish Square had been for the sole purpose of trying to silence him by threatening him with Eleanor and her father and not to discuss terms of surrender; this change of tack therefore was clearly the direct result of what Collett had read in the newspapers. For a man in Collett's position Tony could well understand his reaction to the news that the police were reopening the case of Dennis Dunscumbe and that the death of his brother could well be linked to his supposed suicide. Such an announcement would, if nothing else, have brought about a state of unbridled panic, and whilst Tony very much doubted Collett's suggestion of going to the police had its roots in remorse, it certainly proved that he knew it was only a matter of time before the truth came out. Apparently though, this idea had not found favour with Eliza Boon who, according to Peterson, had argued heatedly with Collett on this very point, an argument which had not only resulted in him striking her, but which had brought about his death by the hand of the very man who had carried out his dirty work.

Peterson's strenuous defence of Eliza Boon neither filled her with shame nor brought about a change of heart in setting him up as a scapegoat, in fact she could not have been more pleased with his answers any more than if she had primed him beforehand. Every word he had uttered all went to exonerate her of any blame in Sir Braden's death, but unfortunately her delight as well as her confidence were short-lived when Superintendent Dawson demanded to know who had killed Dennis Dunscumbe. Superintendent Dawson did not need his years of experience in dealing with the criminal fraternity to tell him that Eliza Boon was as tough as they come because like Tony he had seen her for what she was immediately he laid eyes on her, and therefore knew that no questions of his would elicit a response, and decided instead to aim them at Peterson.

Peterson may not have the sharpest of minds, in fact he was precisely how Tony had described him as being nothing but a yes-man who carried out Eliza Boon's dirty work, but in fairness to Peterson his faith in Eliza had never once wavered. Now though, thanks to her constant interruptions expressing her innocence and her urgent pleadings insisting he tell them the truth in that she had had no involvement whatsoever in any of it except being asked to look after Lady Collett, and that by trickery and deceit, although going unheeded by Superintendent Dawson, from the look on Peterson's face it was clear he was having some difficulty in understanding Eliza's forceful denials. Her repudiation of any wrongdoing as well as her insistence that it was him and Sir Braden between them who were solely responsible for what had happened as well as manipulating her into the unfortunate position in which she now found herself, took Peterson's confused brain by surprise, giving him a little pause for as much thought as it was possible for him to muster. As he was by nature a follower and not a leader as well as being used to merely doing as he was told as opposed to thinking for himself, it therefore took him a little time to assimilate the meaning of her vigorous protestations that she was entirely blameless. Tony, who knew instantly what Eliza Boon was trying to do, saw the look of doubt and confusion on Peterson's face as he stared at her somewhat bemused, but before long Tony saw that her attempt to absolve herself of all culpability was beginning to slowly permeate the dense layers of Peterson's not very agile brain, gradually coming to realise that she was trying to shift the blame.

Peterson's rendering of this morning's events could not have suited Eliza Boon better, but like Tony she recognised the effect her vigorous disclaimers of being a party to, or having knowledge of, any criminal act had upon her stalwart. To her horror, under Superintendent Dawson's skilful handling, Peterson's sudden loquacity, as surprising as it was totally unexpected from a man of few words and no thoughts of his own, Eliza was soon brought to see that far from exonerating her his exposé, including what had happened to Mitchell, could only serve to incriminate her. Her determined efforts to stem this voluble transformation, a nice mix of threats and cajolery with the added attempt at appeasement by petitioning him to trust her, not only because she knew precisely what she was doing but also because he must know she would never fail him, unexpectedly fell on deaf ears. She had always known that Peterson could, on occasion, prove a little awkward, even wilful, but where, before today, she had never once doubted she could handle him, she saw now that she had grossly underestimated her influence and, from the look in his eyes, very much that of a hurt and bewildered kitten, her treachery and abandonment had inflicted a grievously deep and painful wound. In his shoes, she was honest enough to admit that she would feel exactly the same, particularly when she considered his unwavering loyalty, but right now the only important thing was saving herself from the consequences of her actions. As she looked at Peterson through narrowed eyes, totally unmoved by his shock at her betrayal, the only thing on her mind was the unpalatable thought that due to his thoughtless and unexpected volubility, deeming it as quite irrelevant that it was her disloyalty that had prompted it, the confines of a prison cell were getting ever nearer and any hope she may have had of buying an acquittal fast receded. "You bloody fool!" she cried, incensed, fear welling up inside her, taking a step nearer to Peterson and punching his shoulder. "Can't you see what you've done?"

"That's enough of that!" Superintendent Dawson ordered, signalling to Constable Short and his colleague. "Eliza Boon and James Peterson," he said firmly, "I am arresting you both for the…"

Considering the lengths to which Eliza Boon had gone to make sure she would never arrive at the point where she would be arrested, upon seeing the two police constables enter the room pulling out their handcuffs from their pockets and hearing Superintendent Dawson resolutely utter those fatal words, she experienced such an overwhelming sense of panic that, for the first time in her life, she completely lost sight of rationality. Tony, watching Eliza Boon closely, saw her step back several paces as Constable Moore approached her, her eyes looking wildly around her before coming to rest on himself, her lips curling back in a snarl of pure loathing as the sight of him rekindled her antipathy towards him. "I should have made an end of you last night!"

"Don't make things any worse for yourself," Superintendent Dawson warned.

"Don't just stand there!" she cried at Peterson, ignoring this warning. "*Do something!*"

Peterson, who had by now been handcuffed by Constable Short and was in the process of being escorted from the room, was in no position to do anything, a circumstance which did nothing to assuage Eliza Boon's panic, but even though a prison sentence may be beckoning before they shut the door on her and threw away the key for several years she was absolutely determined to have her revenge on the man she held totally responsible for their downfall. To this end she did her best to obstruct Constable Moore's passage towards her by kicking out a small foot stool to impede his progress, but although he maintained his balance he was not quick enough to prevent her from evading his apprehending hand. Eliza Boon, having by now lost sight of everything except having her revenge, managed to position herself behind a wing chair and, sliding her right hand up the left sleeve of her coat, pulled out the serviceable little pistol from its hiding place and, keeping it well out of view by holding it against her right side, aimed it at Tony. The movement, so swift and proficient, would have gone completely unnoticed had it not have been for Constable Moore just catching sight of the light momentarily glinting on the short barrel, but even though he shouted a warning and managed to grab hold of her left arm which jerked her off balance she still managed to pull on the trigger.

Jerry and Tom, having stepped back into the hall to make room for Constable Short to escort Peterson off the premises, heard rather than saw Eliza Boon's desperate attempts to evade arrest, and it was not until they heard Superintendent Dawson warning her to come quietly that they realised she was putting up no small resistance. Tony, not altogether surprised at this, was just turning his attention away from Peterson being safely conducted off the premises by Constable Short into the waiting police vehicle when he heard Constable Moore's shouted warning followed by a loud report which, thanks to that alert young man causing Eliza Boon to lose her balance, the bullet, missing Tony by a fraction, lodged itself in the frame of the door.

Discovering that Eliza Boon had actually secreted a weapon on her person in as cunning a hiding place as one would find after ascertaining there was nothing in her pockets, was just as big a shock to her intended victim as her last-ditch attempt to have her revenge by trying to shoot him. Tony had no need to look at the bullet embedded in the door frame no more than two inches from where he had just been standing to realise that he had had a very lucky escape because even though it was only a small calibre pistol she had used, firing at such a close range the wound would have been extremely serious, if not fatal. Eliza Boon's attempts to escape did not cease when Constable Moore and Superintendent Dawson between them eventually managed to handcuff her and, as they half dragged and half carried her out of the drawing-room as she kicked and struggled to break free, the look of pure hatred she threw at Tony as she stumbled past him left him in no doubt just how vicious she really was.

Tom may have no regrets about taking part in today's events, in fact he would not have missed it for anything, even so, he was visibly shaken by Eliza Boon's cold-blooded attempt to put a bullet through his brother-in-law, a man who had thwarted her and her accomplices at every turn. It had been horrifying enough to learn of Tony's narrow escape last night, but to actually witness an attempt on his life first-hand was really quite harrowing and something Tom would not forget in a hurry, but even though he managed to pull himself together it was nevertheless with a rather ashen face that he stared across at his brother-in-law.

Jerry, whose own face had paled, stared aghast at Tony as though he could not believe he was still alive following such a pretty close shave. Like Tom, he mentally berated himself for not keeping a closer eye on him as he had promised, but Tony, blaming no one but himself for failing to realise Eliza Boon might well adopt such deceitful and ruthless measures, silenced their concerns as well as dispelling the conscious stricken look on their faces for not trying to prevent it by smiling considerately down at them. "I wish you two would stop blaming yourselves for what happened. If anyone is to blame, it's me. I should have foreseen something like this."

"Yes, but…" Tom began, taking a step nearer to him, "you could have been…"

"Well, I wasn't," Tony smiled. "As you can see, I am quite unhurt," reassuringly gripping Tom's shoulder. "Tell you what though, Tom," he grinned, forestalling the words he knew was on the tip of his tongue, "if you have that hip flask of yours with you," he nodded, "I sure could use it!"

Tom, handing the flask he pulled out of his overcoat pocket to his brother-in-law, did not fail to notice that despite Tony's outward show of calm over what had just happened, his hand was nevertheless far from steady as he put the flask to his lips to swallow a generous mouthful of brandy. This reaction did not escape Jerry's notice either, exchanging significant glances with Tom, but by the time Tony handed the flask back to Tom, as much in need of a stimulant as his brother-in-law, the fiery liquid had already had its beneficial effect before Jerry even had time to take a most welcome drink of the restorative contents of Tom's flask. While waiting for Superintendent Dawson to return from overseeing the transport of the prisoners, Tony took a moment to gently prise the damaged projectile out of the door frame with his penknife before picking up the pistol which Eliza Boon had dropped on the floor and removing the second bullet, looking inscrutably down at them in the palm of his gloved hand for a moment before thrusting them into his pocket.

Had Superintendent Dawson the least idea of what was going to happen he would have happily vetoed today's surveillance or, failing this, strictly forbidden Tony to come anywhere near Hertford Street. He could not deny that it was a tremendous relief to finally solve the case of Sir Philip Dunscumbe's murder and that of his brother's supposed suicide, not to mention Mitchell and what had happened to Annie Myers, but the truth was the cost of apprehending the perpetrators could have well ended up being far too high a price to pay. But upon voicing these thoughts and concerns to Tony he received the same calm response of dismissal as Tom and Jerry, even so, Superintendent Dawson could not refrain from saying that at least Tony must allow him to offer his thanks because he knew it was due to his industrious investigations that he could now close what had been a rather baffling case.

"Don't mention it, Superintendent," Tony smiled. Then, digging a hand into his pocket, said, "By the way, I think you had better take these," handing him the pistol and one remaining bullet together with the one he had prised out of the woodwork.

Having put them into his pocket Superintendent Dawson looked up at Tony, but just as he was on the point of reiterating what a lucky escape he had had, he saw the look in those dark grey eyes and thought better of it, not at all sure whether to be glad or not when Tony forestalled him by asking about the prisoners. "They're on the way to Vine Street where they will spend the night in the cells. I doubt very much if anything will be got out of them tonight, but I'll be interviewing them in the morning. Well," he sighed, pulling out his watch, "I suppose it's time I was making my way to Cavendish Square." He paused a moment, saying at length, "I er… I don't suppose that…?" casting a hopeful glance up at Tony. "It's just that… well," he cleared his throat, "I thought as you knew Mrs. Timms…"

"You know something, Superintendent," Tony smiled, "I was rather hoping you would ask me that," then, turning to Tom and cocking his head, was at once assured by his brother-in-law that he would gladly keep him company. "Jerry?" Tony raised an eyebrow, not at all surprised to receive a categorical 'yes'.

By the time the two horsedrawn police vehicles pulled up outside twenty-nine Cavendish Square it was almost half past seven, and Mrs. Timms, who had been on the watch for them in between trying to keep Sir Braden's death a secret from the servants, was heartily pleased to see them. She was not at all sure whether to feel relief or not when she saw two police constables alighting from the second vehicle, but the reassuring sight of His Lordship certainly made her feel more comfortable and no sooner had he stepped inside the house and firmly took hold of her agitated hands and solicitously enquired after her than she burst into tears. "Oh, m'lord!" she cried. "Am I glad to see *you*! I don't know whether I'm on my 'ead or my 'eels, an' that's the truth. To think that in that very room…" indicating the study with a nod of her head, "Sir Braden…" she dabbed at her eyes. "I've not breathed a word of this to anyone," she told him, "but I've been awful worried. What's the world a-comin' to m'lord?" She shook her head. "I never liked Sir Braden I know, but never in all my days did I suspicion anythin' like this!" blowing her nose vigorously into her handkerchief.

Before Tony could respond to this Superintendent Dawson strode into the house and, after briefly introducing him to Mrs. Timms, Tony watched him approach the study where he pulled out the set of keys which had been in Eliza Boon's pockets. Upon seeing him unlock the door, Mrs. Timms broke into fresh tears, but when Tony said soothingly, "Mrs. Timms, I know this has all been a terrible shock for you, but would you do something for me?"

"Anythin' m'lord," she assured him, pulling herself together.

"What do you say to making us all a cup of tea?" he smiled, laying a comforting hand on her arm.

This perfectly mundane request acted on her like a tonic and after opening the basement stairs door for her to pass through, Tony joined Superintendent Dawson in the study where he was already kneeling down beside Sir Braden Collett's dead body.

"He's dead all right!" he sighed, looking up at Tony after examining the body, rising slowly to his feet just as Tom and Jerry walked in. "Strangled; just like Peterson said," he confirmed. "His fingers are just beginning to stiffen," he nodded as Tony stood looking down at the body, the bruises around the neck clearly indicating the cause of death, "which, considering the room is still rather warm," Dawson remarked, "is not surprising. Peterson clearly used some force," he pointed out. "Those bruises to his neck and throat are severe."

"He's one strong guy, Superintendent." Tony nodded. "Collett would not have stood much of a chance!"

"Yes," Dawson sighed, "and you would know," he said significantly.

"That's for sure!" Tony agreed.

Jerry, looking from the ghastly face of Sir Braden Collett to Tony's grave one, exclaimed, "Gawd love us! Peterson's seen to 'im right enough!"

"You got that right, Jerry," Tony replied grimly.

"It's hard to believe he's dead!" Tom shook his head, staring a little bemused at the lifeless form of Sir Braden Collett. "What's even more hard to believe," he exclaimed, "is that he met his end by the very man he had come to rely upon!"

"Thieves falling out," Superintendent Dawson supplied. "Not the first time either. Well," he sighed, having taken a quick look around the room, "it seems there's nothing more we can do now but wait for the doctor followed by the removal of the body."

By the time they had all been fortified with the strong tea provided by Mrs. Timms, the staff, agog with curiosity at the unexpected official invasion, being called together in the kitchen, were naturally shocked at the news imparted by Superintendent Dawson. Ellen and Pearl burst into tears and Susan dabbed at her eyes with the corner of her apron while Albert, staring open-mouthed at the group who had descended on Cavendish Square, was not entirely sure what to feel about the unexpected goings on upstairs. After answering Superintendent Dawson's questions, Susan and Ellen, being assured by Mrs. Timms that there was no need to worry about Lady Collett as she would make sure she was all right, declared in unison that nothing would induce them to sleep in the house tonight, despite Superintendent Dawson's assurances that it was most unlikely anything further would happen. Not even when he told them that a police constable would be standing outside all night had the power to make them change their minds, adamantly refusing to stay, and since he could hardly force them he finally relented on condition they let him know where they could be contacted. Pearl, from the moment she had learned the truth, had no wish to remain one more night under the same roof where the master had been brutally murdered and lying dead nearly all day and would rather go home, but the minute she knew a police constable would stand his post throughout the night, she immediately underwent a change of heart and eagerly announced her intention of staying.

"And what about you?" Superintendent Dawson demanded of Albert.

Albert had seen how Pearl's eyes had lit up upon learning that a police constable would be on duty outside all night and was not at all surprised to learn of her change of mind, knowing perfectly well that she would try again to make him jealous enough to pop the question. He had every intention of doing so, in his own good time that was, but as he would not put it past Pearl to make any excuse to draw the police constable's attention, nodded his head and said he would stay. Superintendent Dawson then turned his attention back to Mrs. Timms, enquiring about Sir Braden's family or nearest relative, to which she unsteadily informed him that his only living relative was a cousin, Hubert Collett, who lived Wimbledon way and, after furnishing him with his address, vigorously blew her nose.

Upon being informed that the doctor had arrived as well as the mortuary vehicle, Superintendent Dawson left the kitchen and made his way upstairs, but Tony, remaining where he was a moment, tried to persuade Mrs. Timms into removing herself from the house until matters were a little more settled, a suggestion she firmly vetoed. "That's most considerate of you, m'lord, I'm sure," she told him, touched by his concern, "but I'll be just fine 'ere. Thankin' you kindly, m'lord."

He was just about to press the point when Jerry intervened, saying that there was no need to worry because he would be popping in regularly to make sure things were all right and, from the tinge of colour which stole into Mrs. Timms's ample cheeks, it seemed she had no fault to find with this suggestion, pouring him another cup of tea laced with something from a bottle she retrieved from a cupboard. Casting a surprised glance at Tony, whose eyes were brimful with laughter, Tom decided against saying anything until they were out of earshot, but the moment they mounted the basement stairs to the hall, whispered, "You don't think…?"

"I'd say it's a pretty safe bet, Tom," Tony smiled over his shoulder. "Quite smitten with Mrs. Timms is Jerry!"

By the time the doctor had carried out his preliminary examination and pronounced life extinct followed almost at once by Sir Braden's body being carried out of the house, it was almost quarter to nine and Superintendent Dawson, after arranging for a couple of police constables to be placed on duty over night outside the derelict house in Sunshine Terrace where Peterson had confessed to leaving Mitchell's body, stated there was nothing else they could do tonight, decided it was time to call it a day. Tony, staying only long enough to have a final word with Superintendent Dawson, declining his offer of taking them up as far as Mount Street, much preferring to walk the short distance, followed by a quick word with Jerry who, not surprisingly, announced his intention of remaining in Cavendish Square a bit longer, the brothers-in-law finally made their way home.

Chapter Twenty-Nine

As Beatrice had never been given any cause to either question or doubt what her husband told her, she had accepted his reason for being late home this evening without the slightest suspicion that he was being deliberately secretive, but as the afternoon gave way to evening with no sign of him she began to grow rather uneasy. She had no idea who Tom's late client was, but she found it difficult to believe it would take all this time to transact his affairs, and as the thought of a clandestine assignation never so much as entered her head, she was left with no other explanation to account for Tom's continued absence except that it must have something to do with her brother. She knew Tony had told her over breakfast that he was looking to be out most of the day, particularly as this affair with Collett was almost at an end, and even though she could not begin to imagine what it was he had planned, she had certainly expected him home before now and could not understand why he had so far put in no appearance since he left here just after eleven o'clock this morning. As her discreet enquiries with Harry, remaining steadfastly at his post until relieved by Tony no matter what time he returned, had elicited no favourable response, she grew more and more convinced that her husband was with Tony, especially when she considered how deeply he had confided in Tom.

In view of what she had learned about Sir Braden Collett and the lengths he and the others had gone to keep their crimes a secret, by the time the clock on the mantelshelf in the drawing-room showed eight minutes to nine o'clock with no sign of her brother or her husband, Beatrice became seriously alarmed. She tried her best not to let her mind dwell on what could possibly have happened to either of them because nothing would convince her that they were not together, but as she was only too mindful that Eleanor was still far from recovered as well as being plagued with the same concerns as herself, Beatrice made a quite valiant effort to play down her own fears by comfortingly telling her young friend that they were most probably worrying over nothing. Eleanor knew no more than Beatrice as to what Tony had planned for today, but she had certainly not expected him to be out for this long and, like Beatrice, was growing more convinced that Tom was with him, and could only hope that whatever it was they were doing they would return home safely, and soon.

Ignoring Eleanor's claims that she could not eat a thing, Beatrice, perfectly aware that she needed something considering she was still far from well, persuaded her into taking a little soup if nothing else, but even though Eleanor managed to swallow every mouthful, the thought of dinner was something she could not face. As Beatrice felt exactly the same she sent word to the kitchen to delay dinner until Tom and Tony arrived home, but as the minutes ticked remorselessly by she was beginning to think that dinner would end up being a very late supper. But in spite of her growing unease over Tom and her brother, Beatrice was not so insensitive nor so blind that she could not see how Eleanor, over the last half hour or so, was finding it more and more difficult to stay awake, and upon gently pointing out that whilst she appreciated her anxiety she had been out of bed for far longer than she should have which surely could only impede her recovery, Beatrice eventually managed to persuade Eleanor into allowing her to help her upstairs to bed.

"Oh, my dear," Beatrice cried, patting her cold hand as she eased her back against the pillows, "you must not think that I do not understand your very natural concerns, I do, but I am sure Tony would not wish you to make yourself ill by worrying over him."

"I know," Eleanor acknowledged in a choked voice, "it's just that I couldn't bear anything to happen to him!"

"Nothing is going to happen to him," Beatrice told her with more confidence than she felt. "In fact," she smiled, "I expect them both to walk in any moment."

Had they have done so she would have felt perfectly justified in boxing their ears, but within fifteen minutes of returning to the drawing-room after helping Eleanor upstairs the sound of the front door opening and closing followed by two familiar voices wafting through to her, this very natural inclination died a death. Heaving a heartfelt sigh, Beatrice rose hastily to her feet, firmly clamping down on the urge to run into the hall to meet them, but after several minutes of standing nervously in front of the fireplace the door to the drawing-room opened and Tom walked in, her brother taking a moment to have a word with Harry. Upon setting eyes on her husband, apparently none the worse for wear after what must have been an extremely eventful day, not surprisingly her pent-up emotions found their natural release and the tears which filled her eyes began to fall freely down her cheeks, casting herself into his arms and enjoying a good cry. Hearing her brother enter the drawing-room several minutes later, Beatrice raised her head from her husband's shoulder and, looking somewhat tearfully up at Tony, gave him a rather wan little smile.

"I'm sorry, Bea," Tony said contritely. "Don't blame Tom, it's all my fault."

"I-I'm sorry I…" she began, easing herself out of Tom's arms. "It's just that we have been so worried," stretching out a hand to him. "We wondered what had happened to you."

"I know," Tony sighed, comfortingly squeezing her hand and giving it a little shake. "The last thing either of us wanted was to worry you, but I am afraid I shall have to leave Tom to explain things to you for now. I take it Eleanor is upstairs?"

"Yes," she nodded, "not twenty minutes ago. In fact," she told him on a sniff, "she was falling asleep on the sofa, but she would not go to bed because she was so worried about you, but eventually I managed to persuade her," wiping her nose on the handkerchief Tom handed her. "I would not be at all surprised to find that she is fast asleep." She saw the frown crease his forehead, asking, "Won't it keep until tomorrow?"

"Don't worry," Tony assured her, the frown lifting, "if she's asleep I shan't disturb her."

She did not need to see the glance which passed between the two men to know that all was not well, but apart from giving her brother a hug and a tearful scold followed by promising she would have some food sent into them, she forbore to tease him and, after kissing her cheek, Tony left her alone with Tom.

Having fought off sleep for as long as she could, determined to stay downstairs until she knew Tony was safe, Eleanor finally gave in to Beatrice's persuasions about going to bed, but so fearful was she that even after Beatrice had left her she could not be easy in her mind. In view of the lengths which Braden and the others had gone to prevent their crimes from ever seeing the light of day, Eleanor knew they would not hesitate to do everything they could to prevent Tony from either investigating further or putting his findings to the police. She may not know about his visit to Cavendish Square last night and his narrow escape, but no one knew better than she did what Braden was capable of and the harm he could do to Tony, and Tom too for that matter, and the longer it took them to return home the more she feared for their safety. The very thought of something happening to Tony was more than she could bear, so too was never seeing him again, in fact both were too horrendous to contemplate, and as she lay back against the pillows watching the minutes tick steadily by with no sign of him, the more harrowing her fears became. But no matter how hard Eleanor tried to stay awake until he returned her eyelids gradually closed of their own volition and even though she fell into a deep sleep, thanks to the hideous images which haunted her dreams, it was far from undisturbed.

Tony may be able to exonerate Eliza Boon and Peterson of physically harming Eleanor, but their ominous presence alone would have been enough to make her extremely fearful, putting her under an intolerable emotional strain and, left to Tony, they would not only be charged for their other crimes but also for perpetrating such contemptible cruelty which was as despicable as it was deliberately calculated. As far as Sir Braden Collett was concerned, he may have received nothing short of poetic justice by the hand of his accomplice, but Tony could not help thinking that he had got off extremely lightly for his crimes. What he had done to Eleanor alone was fully deserving of the due processes of the law because no matter which way Tony looked at it Collett's treatment of her, both mental and physical, had been nothing short of criminal, but his own feelings aside, Tony knew that even though Eleanor had never loved Collett, in fact she had stood in fear of him, she would not be unaffected by his death.

Tony knew that it was his responsibility to break the news to Eleanor before she read about it in the newspapers, but having already been called upon to try to take in the full sum of her husband's activities as well as all she had endured at his hands and her ongoing recovery both physically and emotionally because of it, Tony was only too aware of how very vulnerable she was right now. He was no coward, on the contrary he had never once been known to shelve his responsibilities, but as he stood looking down at Eleanor he was not at all sure whether to be glad or not that she was fast asleep. He was honest enough to admit that his narrow escape this evening, more so than last night, had shaken him and the need to hold Eleanor close against him to reassure himself he was still alive was so strong that he toyed with the idea of waking her, but as he was neither a selfish nor an uncaring man he decided to let her sleep. It would do no harm to leave off telling her about Collett until the morning and, after bending down to kiss her forehead, quietly left the room.

Beatrice, torn between admiration at her brother's ingenuity in putting together such a clever plan and her concerns for the safety of the two men she loved most in the world, listened to Tom's edited version of the day's events in shocked disbelief as she sat beside him with her hand comfortingly held in his warm one. She was naturally pleased to learn that Eliza Boon and Peterson had finally been arrested which, she told him firmly, was no more than they deserved, but she could not hide her surprise upon hearing that the woman who had tormented Eleanor's every waking moment had ruthlessly done her utmost to put all the blame onto her confederate. As for Sir Braden Collett's brutal end she was palpably shocked and could do nothing more than stare aghast at her husband for several stunned moments before she could find her voice sufficiently to put one or two questions to him, all of which he did his best to answer as diplomatically as he could without going into gruesome detail or alerting her to Tony's near miss.

Tom may have no secrets from Beatrice, but on this occasion he fully agreed with Tony in not telling her, or Eleanor either, about his lucky escape last night as well as earlier this evening nor, for that matter, his run-ins with Peterson. Tom knew his wife well enough to say that even though her brother had miraculously walked away unscathed from Eliza Boon's two attempts on his life, it would cause her great distress, in fact he would go so far as to say that she would never again know a moment's peace of mind where Tony was concerned. As it was her only worry, apart from knowing they must have spent a most uncomfortable day in Hertford Street, was the effect the day's events would have on Eleanor, but when, not long afterwards, Tony returned to the drawing-room, it was clear from the short time he had been upstairs that Eleanor was asleep and so there had been no opportunity for him to break the news to her.

"Oh, Tony!" Beatrice cried on a sniff, jumping up off the sofa and eagerly holding out her hands to him. "Thank goodness you and Tom are safe! Tom's been telling me all about it. What a day you have had!"

"That's for sure!" Tony said with feeling, taking her hands in his and giving them a warm squeeze, looking a little contritely down at her. "Does this mean I am forgiven?" he asked ruefully.

She paused a moment as if considering, then, smiling irrepressibly up at him, teased, "I will tell you tomorrow."

"No," Tony urged persuasively, giving her hands a playful little shake, "tell me now – *please.*"

"You know you are," she smiled, kissing his cheek, "both of you. Besides, there is nothing to forgive."

"Indeed there is," Tony nodded. "The last thing I wanted was to worry either you or Eleanor, which is why I did not tell you what we were meaning to do," he told her, "but I see now," he sighed, "that by not telling you I did precisely that."

"Well," she smiled, "I suppose that knowing you as well as I do I should have known better than to worry," missing the significant glance which passed between the two men over her head, "but I can't help it," she shrugged helplessly, "Eleanor too! In fact," she told him, "in the end I had to insist she go to bed; she could barely keep awake. I take it she is asleep."

"Yes," Tony nodded. "I thought it best not to disturb her."

"That poor child!" Beatrice shook her head. "I know she had no love for Collett, but it's still going to come as a dreadful shock to her. Just how much more does she have to endure? Collett dead!" She shook her head, bewildered. "I simply can't believe it! Peterson of all people too!"

"I know," Tony sighed, "and the thing is," he confessed, "I never saw it coming."

"How could you?" Beatrice asked reasonably. "Oh Tony," gripping his hands, "you must not blame yourself!"

"It's not that," he shook his head, a frown creasing his forehead, "it's just…"

"You think Collett has got off extremely lightly, is that it?" She raised an enquiring eyebrow.

"Well yes, there is that," Tony conceded, "but I was thinking of Eleanor. Collett's death or, I should say," he corrected himself, "his murder, is just going to spin things out for her. She's been through enough as it is without this."

"Yes," Beatrice sighed, "she has." A slight frown creased her forehead and, casting a look up at Tony, said thoughtfully, "Mitchell too! His death will hit her very hard because from what she has told me he had always stood very much her friend. It's as well you didn't disturb her, I mean," she explained, "it's one thing to know that your husband will sooner or later be tried and sentenced by a court of law for what he has done, but quite another to be faced with something like this."

"Exactly," Tony replied with feeling, "which is why I decided not to disturb her. I'm not saying the news will be any less of a shock for her tomorrow than it will tonight," he nodded, "but I think a good night's sleep will do her far more good than lying awake worrying over something that can't be mended."

She wholeheartedly agreed to this, then, after reiterating her concerns to which her brother assured her there was not the slightest need to worry over him, she said, "Yes, I know, you have told me often that you are quite capable of taking care of yourself, but I do worry over you, Tom too." As the only response to this was a rueful grin, she quickly followed it up by telling him as sternly as she could that it would serve them both right if she washed her hands of them. "And I suppose," she nodded, the smile in her eyes in complete contrast to the tartness of her voice, "that you are waiting to be rid of me so you can talk privately with Tom!"

"And here was I thinking you'd never get the message," Tony teased, his eyes laughing down into hers, giving her hands a final squeeze.

"It would serve you both right if I let you starve!" Beatrice smiled before affectionately kissing both of them goodnight with the promise that she would have some supper sent into the study for them, a cosy room into which the two men immediately repaired and made themselves comfortable.

As Tony was as much in need of a stimulant as his brother-in-law, he thankfully took the glass of whisky Tom handed him and tossed it back in one go. "You know, Tom," he said with feeling, "I needed that!"

Having witnessed his reaction following that horrifying incident in Hertford Street Tom could well believe it and, after making short work of his own drink, nodded, "And no wonder!" refilling their glasses.

"I think we both did," Tony smiled, taking out his cigarette case.

"Tony," Tom said steadily, raising his eyes from the decanter to his brother-in-law's face, a slight frown suddenly descending onto his forehead, "I know you don't want to talk about what happened earlier, but I'm afraid I must." Apart from a raised eyebrow Tony made no reply to this and waiting only until he had handed him his refilled glass did Tom say, concerned, "I don't mind saying that for a minute there I thought you were…"

"A goner?" Tony supplied.

"Frankly, yes," Tom told him truthfully, not fooled by his unruffled response, "I did. So too did Jerry."

"You know something, Tom," Tony admitted, "for a minute there, so did I! A fraction more to the left and I would have been." Upon seeing the look which crossed his brother-in-law's face, Tony forestalled the words on his lips by saying earnestly, "There's no need to say it, Tom," inclining his head, "I know damn well it was a pretty close shave!"

"Close!" Tom echoed, almost choking on his cigar. "I should rather think it was! And not for the first time!" he pointed out meaningfully, easing himself into the comfortable club chair beside the fire.

Taking a moment to light his cigarette, Tony eyed his brother-in-law thoughtfully, saying at length, "You know Tom, not every story I cover ends up with someone taking a potshot at me."

"A good thing too," Tom said firmly, "because as I told you last night," he nodded, "I have no wish to be the one to carry bad news to Bea and Eleanor."

"Do you think that's what I want?" Tony asked, resting his arm along the mantelshelf.

"No," Tom shook his head, "I don't, but you seem to forget," he reminded him, "you don't have nine lives."

"Which is why I'll take precious good care of the one I *do* have," Tony nodded. Upon seeing the look which descended onto Tom's face, he smiled. "Don't look so worried, Tom; as I told you last night, I'm not so casual with my life."

"I know," Tom nodded, "but you certainly seem to possess the knack of putting yourself at risk."

"Not my intention, Tom, I promise you," he told him, raising his glass to his lips.

"That's as may be," Tom conceded, "but the fact remains that in less than twenty-four hours you have had two miraculous escapes!" After taking a much-needed drink he pointed out, "Just because Eliza Boon did not have the gun in her pocket last night as she thought does not alter the fact that your life was in danger; had she have been able to put her hands on it you would not be standing here now. As you said yourself," he reminded him, "she could not have missed at that range, and as for this evening," he nodded, "you came as close to death as any man could and I came as close as I hope I ever shall again to witnessing it! That gun going off was no accident, Tony; it was a deliberate attempt to kill you! An act of pure revenge."

"Damn right it was!" Tony said with feeling, sitting down in the wing chair opposite his brother-in-law. "She sure is one tough cookie, Tom!" He inclined his head.

"You can say that again!" Tom said wholeheartedly. "And not one to be crossed!"

"You'd better believe it!" Tony nodded. "But I'm sorry, Tom," he apologised, "I never meant to put you and Jerry through that."

"Or yourself if it comes to that, but it's not me I'm thinking of," Tom told him, genuinely concerned, "or Jerry, it's you. And before you say anything," he forestalled him, pointing his glass at him, "I know you said that there's no need to worry over you, but if anything were to happen to you not only would I lose a brother-in-law but a man who I am proud and honoured to call friend! As for Bea," he inclined his head, "well," he shrugged eloquently, "it doesn't bear thinking of; she would lose a brother whom she loves and adores whilst Eleanor…"

"Do you think I don't know all this, Tom?" Tony cut in steadily. "Well," he nodded, "I do, but even though it was just as much of a shock to me as it was to you to find myself in the firing line," he admitted, "I don't regret one of my actions in trying to bring them to justice. Nevertheless," he smiled, "I'm damn glad you were there!"

"If it comes to that," Tom grinned, "so am I; your run-in apart."

"You know, Tom," Tony smiled ruefully, crossing one leg over the other, "I must be slipping because I never saw that coming any more than I did Collett's death."

"Well," Tom said practically, "there was no reason why you should have anticipated Collett's death, or anyone else if it comes to that! As for Eliza Boon," he pointed out, "there was no way any one of us could have known she had that pistol hidden up her sleeve."

"I know," Tony conceded, "but considering her track record I should have guessed she'd try something."

"Well," Tom sighed, "at least she is where she can no longer do anyone any harm."

"I'll drink to that!" Tony said with feeling, swallowing the rest of his whisky.

"Speaking of Eliza Boon," Tom raised a questioning eyebrow, "do you think Dawson will get much out of her?"

"If you mean a confession," Tony shook his head, "I doubt it. In fact," he sighed, "I'd say the chances are she will do all she can to exonerate herself of any wrongdoing; precisely what she tried to do earlier by laying the blame equally between Collett and Peterson!"

Tom nodded, then, after considering the contents in his glass for a moment, raised his eyes, saying thoughtfully, "You know Tony, I never thought I should ever feel sorry for anyone like Peterson, but I don't think I shall ever forget the look on his face when it dawned on him what she was trying to do."

"I know," Tony sighed. "Some kick in the teeth, huh! Talk about hard-boiled!"

A crease suddenly appeared on Tom's forehead and, after finishing off his whisky, said slowly, "You know, a thought has just occurred to me," to which Tony raised an eyebrow. "Well, I know it may sound stupid, but you don't think Peterson is in love with Eliza Boon, do you?"

"Well," Tony sighed, throwing the end of his cigarette onto the fire, "that would certainly explain his almost slavish devotion to her as well as the reason he came to her defence and ended up murdering Collett, but if he is it cannot be said he's gained much by it! In fact, I'd say her attempt to drop him in it this evening was the reason he opened up the way he did, and," he nodded, "unless I miss my guess, I'd say she killed any feelings he had for her at a stroke, even though her personal preferences naturally rendered him out of the running!"

"Assuming he *had* feelings for her, but whatever the truth of it," Tom shrugged, "at least we now know what happened to Mitchell," a reminder which had the immediate effect of bringing a deep frown down onto Tony's forehead.

He would have liked nothing more than to be proved wrong about Mitchell, but from the very beginning Tony had found it difficult to believe that Collett had paid him to disappear and keep silent about Sir Philip's visit that night simply because Collett could not afford to take such a risk. He would know that there was no way Mitchell could have accused him of Sir Philip's murder, but Collett would know that Mitchell knew he was most probably the last man to see him alive and whilst this would not have been enough for the police to charge Collett, it would have done tremendous damage to his reputation. Then, of course, there was always the possibility that Mitchell, having put two and two together, could attempt extortion and Eliza Boon, no more than Collett, could have allowed such an eventuality to arise and run the risk of being bled dry; therefore to let him walk away unmolested would have been an act of gross stupidity. From all Eleanor had told him about Mitchell and his many kindnesses towards her during her unhappy time in Cavendish Square and how he had proved himself a good friend, Tony doubted very much that such a thought would have entered his head, but it was a risk that neither Collett nor Eliza Boon could afford to take.

Tony had suspected all along that it was Eliza Boon who called the shots because it had been clear from the outset that Collett, despite his aggressive manner and violent temper, could not be relied upon to keep a clear head in a crisis whereas she, no matter what dire exigency befell them, never seemed to be at a loss to extricate them from the difficulties which beset them. Time and again she had rescued them from a situation which could so easily have denounced them, but due to her devious scheming and Machiavellian thinking she had managed to fend off the inevitable, and whilst Tony doubted Peterson would have had the least idea whose concept it was he would say that it was she who had persuaded Collett into getting rid of Mitchell. Tony could only hazard a guess as to whether Tom was right about Peterson's feelings for Eliza Boon, but the fact remained that he had dispassionately carried out whatever she had asked of him without question or conscience and Mitchell's brutal death, executed with cold and calculating precision, had been no different. Peterson's account of how he had dealt with Mitchell may have been somewhat inarticulate, but it had nevertheless been delivered without any emotion or pretence of remorse and no matter how welcomed the confession, its chilling effect could, even now, send a shiver down Tony's spine.

Peterson's days in the ring may have been over long since, but Tony's two recent encounters with him were more than ample proof that although he had lost some of his timing when throwing punches and his ungainly proportions were not so agile, he still retained enough of the skills which had kept him in the ring for so long; skills which had been more than adequate to put an end to an unsuspecting Mitchell!

Mitchell, whose only concern about Sir Philip Dunscumbe's visit was that he had not been on call to see him out of the house when his interview with Collett ended as he had inadvertently fallen asleep in his pantry, harboured no suspicions about his employer. Mitchell had certainly felt the lash of Collett's tongue the following morning, but far from being dismissed for stealing he had merely been sent out on an errand, and however much Mitchell may have resented being treated no better than the boot boy Albert he had been far too relieved to escape so lightly for his dereliction of duty the night before to argue the point. Not that it would have mattered if he had because Collett, who brooked no argument or insubordination from his staff, was more than capable of dismissing him there and then irrespective of his long service to the family, nevertheless, the insult, for Mitchell regarded it as nothing less, continued to eat away at him as he left the house to carry out his orders. Turning the interview over in his mind as he made his way towards Oxford Street as well as taking pleasure from imagining what he would say to Sir Braden Collett if it were at all possible, a man who was as different to his father as any man could be, meant that he was totally oblivious to Peterson leaving the house from the basement steps in full accordance with his instructions and stealthily following him at a discreet distance. If Mitchell wondered what Sir Braden Collett's business was with this Mr. Parker in Acton, and at such an early hour, it was only briefly, his grievances taking up his entire thinking, but as he hailed a hackney halfway down Oxford Street, he was honest enough to admit that he would dearly love to know what was in the sealed note Sir Braden had handed him to give to this Mr. Parker.

As Sir Braden had given no inkling where Lion Street was actually situated and Mitchell had never before set foot in Acton, he decided that if anyone should know then it would be the hackney driver, but upon making enquiries of this surly-faced individual he was sullenly told that it was no manner of use asking him because he did not know either, besides, he pointed out sulkily, he was no travel guide. However, he did relent sufficiently to tell Mitchell that he would drop him off at the next corner where, hopefully, he could stop and ask a passer-by or a shopkeeper, but as there were not many people about this early in the morning and most of the premises had not yet opened their doors for trade, Mitchell held out very little hope of this. Alighting somewhat despondently from the hackney, watching uncertainly as the driver whipped up his horse and drove unconcernedly away without a backward glance, Mitchell began to walk along the almost deserted High Street when, almost at once, a second hackney pulled up almost immediately alongside him. Taking no notice of the passenger who had jumped down onto the pavement, he was just about to stop and ask directions of a man walking towards him when, suddenly, he found himself cheerfully buttonholed by the man who had alighted from the second carriage, having come up to him within a few strides. As Mitchell had no idea that he had followed him all the way from Cavendish Square he looked up at the man who had suddenly fallen in to step beside him, turning up his coat collar against the wind and rain and grumbling about the weather, without the slightest suspicion that it was all part of a devious scheme to make an end of him, and as his companion seemed harmless enough Mitchell politely agreed that it was terrible weather. As the oncoming pedestrian from whom he had intended to seek directions had now walked past them, he decided to ask his unknown companion if he knew where he could find Lion Street, not at all surprised when Peterson, who Mitchell took to be local to the area, exclaimed, suitably surprised, "Well! That's an 'appenstance an' no mistake!"

"Do you know where I can find it?" Mitchell asked hopefully.

"Lor' luv yer, Guvna!" he grinned. "I'm goin' to the very place meself!" Upon Mitchell raising an eyebrow, he explained, "Lives there yer see; me, the missus and five yung 'uns, wi' anotha on the way. Gawd 'elp us!"

As there was nothing in Peterson's demeanour to suggest he was anything other than what he purported to be, a night watchman at a warehouse, Mitchell accompanied his newly found acquaintance along the High Street in blissful ignorance that he was being cleverly lured to a secluded destination. So loquacious was Mitchell's companion, giving him no opportunity to reply to his jovial conversation, that it never once occurred to him to question how a man with a wife and five children with another one on the way could possibly afford to spare the money for hackney fares, but more than this close on ten minutes had gone by before he realised they had turned off the main street and were walking down a dingy cobbled alleyway. Mitchell had no recollection of being steered away from the main street, but just when he enquired how much farther it was to Lion Street, unable to think who Sir Braden could possibly know who lived in such a run-down area, Peterson nodded, "Jus' down 'ere on the left it is, Guvna," at the same time surreptitiously sliding his hand into the right pocket of his coat and pulling out a small heavy cosh. "See them 'ouses there," he pointed with his left hand, "that's Lion Street."

"But surely no one lives there!" Mitchell exclaimed. "They're derelict!" staring round at his companion just in time to see the ugly look which crossed his face and the cosh raised in his right hand, knowing no more as a black chasm opened up before him.

Following a quick look up and down the alleyway to make sure no one had entered from either end, Peterson rained down blows onto the already bleeding and battered head of Mitchell and, when satisfied that his quarry was dead, he returned the cosh to his pocket. Considerably out of breath from his exertions, Peterson took a moment to steady himself before picking up Mitchell's damp and crumpled bowler from where it had toppled to the wet ground before roughly pulling his lifeless body to its feet and setting his hat onto his bloodstained head. Bearing in mind Eliza Boon's instructions, which had been repeatedly drummed into his head that he was to dump the body where there was no chance of it being found for some appreciable time, Peterson staggered as though drunk with his arm around his dead companion towards the empty houses he had pointed out a few minutes ago to his hapless victim.

Although Acton was a middle-class district with some very desirable houses there were unfortunately still peripheral areas such as this neglected and run-down quarter, which were little more than slums. Peterson, who knew this locality well, knew too that the residents of this poor and dilapidated neighbourhood would not find anything unusual in seeing two men, even this early in the morning, staggering home drunk. For a man of Peterson's muscular physique dragging Mitchell's thin and lifeless body the short distance to the row of back-to-back derelict houses posed no difficulty whatsoever and, as he rightly predicted, their seemingly inebriated condition brought forth neither stares nor comment from passers-by on their way to work.

The nearer Peterson got to Sunshine Terrace the more gloomy his surroundings became, but for a man who had grown up in a similar locale the dark and filth ridden narrow alleys and the searing cries of fractious children and the strident voices of arguing adults which emanated from the run-down houses as well as emaciated dogs foraging in the gutter, left him totally unmoved. Looking to neither right nor left he continued on his indifferent way until he finally arrived at what could only be described as the most inaptly named street imaginable, but since this was something he did not bother his head about Peterson merely took a quick look all around him before shouldering open the wood blistered front door of the third house in the front row. Stepping hurriedly inside and kicking the door shut without a backward glance he dispassionately shrugged off Mitchell's body, slumping heavily onto the cracked tiled floor, and began to look around him for a suitable hiding place, his eyes eventually alighting on the space beneath the fractured enamelled sink in the corner hidden by a torn and dirty curtain.

Impervious to the rain which was blowing in through the small and broken window which overlooked a tiny backyard, as grimy as it was gloomy, and the small pools of rainwater which had gathered on the narrow window sill, he dragged Mitchell's body across the floor with no effort whatsoever and, after kneeling down, he bent his victim into a foetal position and unceremoniously bundled the body under the sink. Getting to his feet he then placed the sole of his boot against Mitchell's back in order to push him further into the recess, finally pulling the curtains together across the slackened length of string without a qualm of conscience, whereupon Peterson left number five Sunshine Terrace as unmoved as he had entered it.

"God damn, Tom!" Tony ground out, the cold and callous images Peterson's confession had conjured up flashing in his mind's eye. "The guy never stood a…!" breaking off as Bennett, following a light tap on the study door, wheeled in a trolley laden with food, the sight of which was more than welcome to two men who had not eaten since breakfast.

"What was it you were going to say about Mitchell before Bennett came in," Tom cocked an eyebrow when they were alone, "about how he never stood a chance?" lifting the lids from the serving dishes. "Well, I quite agree."

"Too right he didn't!" Tony said grimly, coming to stand beside Tom. "No wonder his body has never been found!"

"Well," Tom sighed, helping himself to several slices of roast beef, "if Superintendent Dawson is right, and I've no reason to doubt he is, then this Sunshine Terrace has not been demolished yet, which means," he looked meaningfully up at Tony, "that Mitchell's body will be no pretty sight after all this time!"

"That's for sure!" Tony agreed wholeheartedly, cutting himself several generous slices of beef.

"What I don't understand though," Tom mused, pausing in the act of cutting a slice of ham, "if these houses have not yet been demolished, why has the body never been found? I mean," he shrugged, "one would have thought that somebody would have stumbled upon it; a tramp looking for shelter for the night perhaps or possibly children playing or, even," he suggested, "a Council official inspecting the buildings ready for demolition!"

"I can't answer that, Tom," Tony sighed, "but Collett and his crew were certainly lucky in that no one did enter the house and discover it!"

"Are you planning on being there tomorrow with Superintendent Dawson?" Tom asked, inwardly shuddering at the thought of what would meet their eyes.

"Huh huh," Tony shook his head.

"Well," Tom sighed, "I can't say I blame you. I'm not tickled stomached you understand," he nodded, "well…" he corrected himself, "for most things I mean, but not for something like this!"

"It's not that," Tony shook his head, "although," he confessed, "I must admit I don't envy Dawson that task, but apart from the fact that I have never laid eyes on Mitchell and so there is no way I can identify him, not that there will be much to identify," he said meaningfully, "except perhaps his clothes or possibly a ring or, even," he shrugged, "some distinctive scar or something that is still visible after nearly twelve months of decomposition, I shall be of very little use to him, I have to see Bill as well as breaking the news to Eleanor about Collett."

"Yes," Tom agreed slowly, a frown descending onto his forehead as he helped himself from the array of serving dishes, saying thoughtfully, "I've been thinking about that. I know she has to be told about Collett, after all," he pointed out, "it's not something that can possibly be kept from her, but no matter what her feelings for him it's going to come as rather a shock to her."

"Yes it is," Tony sighed. "It's one thing to know that your husband will sooner or later be convicted and hanged for murder, but quite another to know that he was actually murdered by one of his accomplices!"

"Yes," Tom agreed, "which is why," he told him, "I feel you were right when you told Bea that Eleanor will be all the better for a good night's sleep before she's faced with something like this. But about Mitchell," he queried, "surely you're not going to tell her how Peterson bludgeoned him to death!"

"Believe me, Tom," Tony said wholeheartedly, "if there was any way I could avoid it I would, but sooner or later she will learn the truth, if not from the newspapers then at the inquests for Collett and Mitchell because it's useless to suppose she won't have to attend Mitchell's as well; she will, simply because both deaths are inextricably linked to the same thing. Then, don't forget," he nodded, "there will be the court hearing. As far as giving evidence against Peterson and Eliza Boon goes, particularly now Collett is dead, Eleanor may or may not have to give evidence, but I fail to see how she can avoid attending. Believe me,

Tom," he said firmly, "if I could spare her any more pain and distress I would, but I would far rather Eleanor hear the truth from me than anyone else!"

Tom, who had suddenly been struck by a horrendous thought, nodded a little absently to this before saying meditatively, "You don't suppose that Dawson will ask Eleanor to identify Mitchell's body, do you?"

"I think that most unlikely," Tony shook his head, "in fact," he admitted, "I'd be astonished if he did. My guess is," he nodded, "that Dawson will accept the body as being that of Mitchell in view of Peterson's confession."

"Yes," Tom conceded after giving it a little thought, "I think you're probably right. Speaking of the inquests though," he commented, sitting down in his favourite chair and balancing his tray on his lap, "they're going to be pretty grim!"

"Too right they are," Tony acknowledged, picking up his tray and taking his seat opposite Tom, "and the Coroner will have no choice but to call Eleanor."

"Yes," Tom nodded, "but you too will be called, don't forget."

"That goes without saying." Tony pulled a face.

Tom looked pensively across at Tony, knowing that what he had to say was far from pleasant, but after chewing thoughtfully on a forkful of food, sighed, "Tony, I've no wish to sound like Job's comforter, but…"

"There's no need to say it, Tom," Tony broke in, a rueful smile touching his lips, "I know as well as you do that Collett's inquest will naturally be more of an ordeal for Eleanor than Mitchell's because the Coroner will ask some pretty pertinent questions; questions which will certainly demand answers about Sir Philip's death and why she did not come forward as well as why she was not at home when Peterson murdered her husband, all of which," he inclined his head, "will inevitably lead to Collett's treatment of her and, unless I miss my guess, it won't take them long to figure out the part I played in bringing her here. Like you and Dawson," he nodded meaningfully, "I know how people talk, and they *will*," he stressed, "particularly when it becomes known that my newspapers played a major part in discovering the truth about Collett's activities!"

Tom could not argue with this, knowing it was only too true. Society, with its narrow-minded prejudices, would be only too ready to believe there had been impropriety between them during Eleanor's stay in Mount Street, but worse than this they would need little or no persuading into believing that Tony had exposed Collett, not in the interests of justice, but merely as a means to coveting his wife. "Yes," Tom scorned, "they'll put two and two together and come up with five!"

"Too right they will!" Tony grimaced. "What they don't know they will assume and what they *do* know will naturally be added to in the telling which will end up bearing no resemblance to the truth, but what's worse," he said disgustedly, "they will enjoy doing it! I don't want Eleanor exposed to that!"

"Well," Tom said sympathetically, "I can understand your wanting to protect her from malicious tongues, but I hope you know without me saying it that I know nothing improper has taken place between you and Eleanor, and also," he nodded, "that she is more than welcome to stay here for as long as is necessary."

"You don't have to tell me any of this, Tom," Tony broke in, "I know," smiling a little ruefully as he admitted, "nevertheless, I can't deny to having…"

"Kissed her?" Tom raised an eyebrow.

Tony grinned. "'Fraid so!"

"Do you think I didn't kiss Bea before we got married?" Tom cocked his head.

"I'm sure you did," Tony smiled, "but the cases *are* a little different."

"Do you think so?" Tom raised an eyebrow. "Well," he conceded, "maybe they are, but you know, Tony," he told him, "there's a vast difference between kissing the woman you love and taking advantage of her, and that is something I know you would never do."

"No," Tony shook his head, "I wouldn't, but I could no more stop loving Eleanor than you could Bea, and I am certainly not going to apologise for the way I feel about her just to suit society's over-inflated sense of morality, all the same," he nodded, "you must admit that the longer Eleanor remains here the more she runs the risk of being talked about, particularly as it is known that I am staying here at the moment, *which*," he stressed, a frown descending onto his forehead, "will be all the censorious will need to feed their suspicions that something went on between the two of us even before Collett died, and that is something I am fully determined to shield her from."

"I can understand that," Tom said sympathetically, "but even though I know it has been your intention from the beginning to take Eleanor to her father in Suffolk as soon as she is well enough to leave here, in view of what's happened today, particularly the longer Sir Miles remains there, that might not be possible for several days, perhaps even longer, and so I can't see how that will help."

Ordinarily Sir Miles Tatton's protracted stay in Suffolk would not have posed a problem, but given the unprecedented set of circumstances in which they found themselves his obvious wish to enjoy the peaceful seclusion of his country retreat for as long as possible instead of returning to town had certainly created an extra difficulty, but Tony, after eyeing his brother-in-law meditatively for several moments as he turned over an idea in his mind, said at length, "You know Tom, I think there may be a way of protecting Eleanor from gossip after all."

Raising a surprised eyebrow at this, Tom said truthfully, "Well I hope so because for the life of me *I* can't see how it can possibly be done!"

"Neither did I until a moment ago," Tony admitted. "Look Tom," he explained, "I never expected Collett's death, let alone anticipated it, but you're right, it *has* changed things, certainly as far as Eleanor is concerned as well as putting a completely different complexion on the matter altogether because once it becomes public knowledge, which by this time tomorrow it most certainly will," he nodded, "as well as the circumstances which brought it about, you can lay your life that people will be wondering about his widow. Eleanor may be recovering more quickly than we could ever have hoped for, but she is still far from well enough to undertake a journey into Suffolk and, under no circumstances," he said firmly, "can Eleanor's stay under this roof be made known. As for her remaining here," he shook his head, "like you I can't see how that will stop the gossip."

Tom, who was looking just a little mystified, shrugged helplessly, "Yes, but…"

"Where else would a daughter go but to her father to escape her bullying husband?" Tony stated calmly.

"To escape her…!" Tom repeated faintly.

"It's perfect, Tom," Tony smiled. "Not only will it safeguard Eleanor from vicious gossip, but it's precisely what people would expect her to do under the circumstances, particularly when you remember how they raised their eyebrows in surprise when they learned of the marriage."

Tom pursed his lips in thought as he considered this, then, looking up at Tony, nodded. "Yes," he said slowly, "I see what you mean, at least," he confessed, "I think I do, but will it answer?"

"I see no reason why it shouldn't particularly when you bear in mind that no one other than ourselves and Mrs. Timms knows that Eleanor's been staying here, in fact," Tony nodded, "as far as Collett's household is concerned she has been secluded in her room for several days apparently recovering from another nervous relapse."

"So?" Tom shrugged, not at all sure what his brother-in-law was driving at.

"*That,*" Tony smiled, "was just a story Collett put out to save his face."

"A story!" Tom repeated faintly. "*Collett?*"

"Sure!" Tony smiled in response to the look of bewilderment on Tom's face. "Look Tom," he explained, "having arrived home from the Kirkmichaels' party Collett lost his temper with Eleanor, the reason is immaterial," he shrugged, "but it resulted in one brutal attack too many on Eleanor and because Collett had no wish for his staff to know that his wife had left him that morning and gone to stay with her father in Suffolk, where, incidentally," he nodded meaningfully, "she has been all this time, he used the same old excuse about her succumbing to this so-called nervous disorder."

Almost dropping his knife and fork Tom looked every inch his disbelief, so much so that it took him a moment to find his voice sufficiently to say, "It will never work!"

"Yes it will," Tony said firmly.

"But how?" Tom demanded, rising to his feet. "Don't forget," he reminded him, setting his tray somewhat ungainly down onto the trolley, "apart from Mrs. Timms, every one of Collett's staff is under the impression that she *has* been prone to these nervous disorders; you said so yourself."

"Yes I did," Tony acknowledged, getting to his feet and putting his tray down beside Tom's on the trolley, "but that's only because Collett has continually led them to believe that," he pointed out. Seeing that Tom was not quite convinced, he explained, "Look Tom, when it becomes known that Collett had a habit of beating his wife not one of them will be in any doubt that it was these regular beatings which made it necessary for her to keep to her room now and then, and that far from suffering from nervous or mental disorders it was simply an excuse because Collett did not want them to see her bruises, therefore putting two and two together about how she acquired them."

Although it made perfect sense Tom, foreseeing one major pitfall at least, shook his head. "Yes, but aren't you forgetting Eliza Boon and Peterson? What I mean is," he pointed out, pouring out two glasses of whisky, "when it becomes known that Collett murdered Sir Philip and Eleanor accidentally stumbled in on it, forcing him to bring in those two to keep a constant guard over her, as well preventing her from leaving the house without one or the other of them accompanying her, not to mention how they kept her locked in her room, how could she possibly leave the house without them knowing?"

"You're forgetting two things, Tom," Tony smiled as he took his glass. "First, it's not likely that anyone will get to know that her bedroom door was always kept locked when she was in her room, and even if they do it will soon be lost sight of in view of everything else and, two," he nodded, "Mrs. Timms."

"Mrs. Timms?" Tom raised a questioning eyebrow.

"A woman who, you will agree," Tony smiled, "is by no means half asleep and one, moreover, who never believed the tales that Collett and Eliza Boon put out about Eleanor suffering from mental disorders, in addition to her sincere attachment to Eleanor which," he nodded meaningfully, "has already been more than adequately demonstrated."

"Tell me," Tom smiled, raising his glass, "how many of these have I had because I'm not sure I follow you?"

"Don't you see, Tom?" Tony raised an eyebrow. "Having heard Collett raking Eleanor down on their return home from the Kirkmichaels' party, not the first by a good way, Mrs. Timms knew from experience that it would end in only one way, and in her genuine concern for her mistress helped her leave the house the following morning without anyone being the wiser."

"She did, did she?" Tom asked sceptically, casting another suspicious glance at his glass.

"Yes," Tony smiled, "she did. Okay, Tom," he grinned, "I know it's full of holes at the moment and the details of it will have to be worked out, but if you can come up with anything better to protect Eleanor from gossip, then I'd sure be glad to hear it!"

"Well," Tom said firmly, "I can't, so it seems we're stuck with your idea." He thought a moment. "What of Sir Miles?"

Tony sighed and shook his head. "He may have sold his daughter into marriage to save his name and reputation, but I doubt he's so far lost to all fatherly feeling that he'd give the lie to his daughter's word!"

"Yes," Tom said slowly, looking pensively at the end of his cigar, "I think you're right. By the way," he nodded, eyeing his brother-in-law, "just to set your mind at rest, I don't blame you for trying to protect Eleanor, after all I would do exactly the same thing for Bea."

"You don't have to tell me, Tom," Tony smiled, "I'd already figured that!" he assured him, finishing off his drink. "I don't like deceit or dissimulation any more than you do," he told him, "but in this instance I believe the end justifies the means. For myself," he nodded, "I don't give a damn what people say or think about me, but it's Eleanor that concerns me now; she has suffered enough at the hands of Collett and the others without having the added burden of putting up with the unspoken censure, even downright shunning, of her acquaintance. Eleanor has done nothing she need lie about or apologise for at any time," he said firmly, "and certainly not while she has been under this roof, but you know how people talk as well as I do, and I for one fully intend to protect her from that in any way I can!"

"And so will her father, I'm sure," Tom nodded, taking Tony's empty glass and refilling it.

"Tell me," Tony cocked an eyebrow, "do you know if Sir Miles has had the telephone installed at his place in Suffolk?"

Tom pulled a doubtful face as he refilled his own glass, "I shouldn't have thought so," he shook his head. "I am not that well acquainted with Sir Miles," he sighed, handing Tony his glass before resuming his seat by the fire, "but from what Bea has told me I gain the impression that he is a man who is not overly fond of anything modern and it would not surprise me to learn that he has not had a telephone installed in Bruton Street either."

"Well," Tony sighed, taking his seat opposite Tom, "I figured as much, but it does mean he will read about what's happened in the newspapers before I can put the facts to him."

"That's going to come as rather a shock," Tom acknowledged.

"Too right it is!" Tony agreed. "Which is why I was hoping to speak to him before that happens. Now though," he sighed, "it looks as if I shall have to explain everything in a letter, as far as I am able that is," he inclined his head, "about everything that has happened."

Tom, who had been savouring his whisky, looked across at Tony with a slightly puzzled expression on his face and, in response to a raised eyebrow, said, "I can understand why you need to speak to him, and given that he most probably is not connected up to the telephone a letter will have to suffice for now, but do you think it worthwhile Eleanor travelling into Suffolk only to return within what?" He shrugged. "Twenty-four hours!"

"Eleanor's not going into Suffolk, Tom," Tony smiled.

"Not going… but I thought you said…!" sitting bolt upright.

"We're just giving the illusion that that is where she has been for the past few days," Tony said calmly.

"But…!"

"Eleanor will remain here until her father returns to Bruton Street," Tony explained. "Once he does," he smiled as he saw the look on his brother-in-law's face, "she will join him there, but more to the point," he pointed his glass at him, "she will have been with her father all this time."

"You know, Tony," Tom sighed, looking helplessly from his brother-in-law to the glass in his hand, "I'm not at all sure whether I've had one whisky too many after all or somehow or other stepped into a Jacobean drama!"

"Neither," Tony laughed, "and, before you start wondering, no," he shook his head, "I'm not crazy!"

"Not crazy, no," Tom grinned, "just a little touched in the upper storey that's all, in fact," he pointed out, finding it difficult to keep a straight face, "I can't understand why it has not occurred to me before now!"

"No," Tony laughed, "neither can I!"

At this his brother-in-law proceeded to recount several instances which more than adequately bore out his theory, but just as he was about to bid him goodnight almost half an hour later he suddenly bethought himself of something, saying thoughtfully, "Just one thing, Tony; about Reggie Wragge?" to which Tony raised an enquiring eyebrow. "Well," Tom mused, "I know you told him you were not going to print his name in your newspapers or approach Scotland Yard with what you know about his illicit enterprises, but in view of the way things have turned out this evening I fail to see how his name won't come up."

"Well," Tony sighed, "I can't pretend that hasn't crossed my mind this last few hours because it has, particularly when I think how ready Eliza Boon was to drop Peterson in it! If she can do that to a man who, no matter how reprehensible his crimes, certainly deserved better from her, then she would not think twice about doing the same to Reggie Wragge if she thought for one moment that it would serve her ends. Of course," he shrugged, "what motive she could have for doing so I don't know, especially as he knew absolutely nothing about what had happened to Annie Myers and all that followed and merely bought her business in good faith, believing her tale about retiring. To be sure," he nodded, "he was genuinely shocked, but I fail to see what threat he poses to Eliza Boon other than knowing about her past profession, which," he pointed out, "will come out in court anyway. As for Superintendent Dawson," he shrugged again, "he may or may not investigate the questionable activities which took place at Periton Place during her tenancy which will inevitably lead to him discovering that Reggie Wragge bought her business but," he nodded, "unless I've figured Reggie Wragge all wrong I'd say he has already set plans in motion to not only disassociate himself with Periton Place and Eliza Boon but to get shot of anything which could possibly link him to either!"

Knowing something of Reggie Wragge's reputation as an astute businessman and one who knew his way around, Tom had no difficulty in believing this and, after agreeing with Tony's very logical observation, suggested that as it was getting rather late he postponed writing his letter to Sir Miles until tomorrow.

"Huh huh," Tony shook his head, having walked across to the desk and sat down, pulling out several sheets of paper, "no can do, Tom. I know I can't explain all that has happened in a letter, but I'll not have enough time to write everything I feel Sir Miles should know tomorrow." Tom nodded, but just as he was about to pull open the door Tony forestalled him, looking up at him with a rather rueful expression in his eyes, smiling. "Tom, thanks."

"For what?" Tom cocked his head.

"Oh," Tony shrugged, "just thanks."

"Goodnight, Tony," Tom nodded, waving away his thanks as totally unnecessary before closing the door quietly behind him.

By the time Tony had finished his letter it was well after half past twelve, but despite Tom's firmly held belief that he must be feeling quite worn out after such an eventful day the truth was that sleep had never been further away than it was at this moment. It was not just Collett's violent death by the hand of his accomplice which was responsible for Tony's present insomnia nor the events in Hertford Street, but what he knew was to come as a result of his investigations.

In spite of having witnessed Collett's brutal treatment of Eleanor at Covent Garden, when Tony had set out to discover the truth behind her fears he had not the least idea what his enquiries would unearth, but he had certainly not expected to find that her husband kept her a virtual prisoner in his attempts to cover up multiple murder. Regardless of the three attempts on his life, Tony had told Tom the truth when he said that he had no regrets about any of his actions in attempting to bring the culprits of such vicious crimes to justice, not only because of his own sense of right and wrong but also because four deaths needed to be accounted for!

Despite Sir Braden Collett's generous donations to various charities and his continued support of the arts as well as his association with the Prince of Wales, with whom he had often been seen at race meetings, apart from a few like-minded cronies he had not been the most popular member of society, for which his volatile temperament and aggressive manner were responsible. But regardless of his shortcomings his impeccable credentials had ensured that every door was always open to him, and since no breath of scandal had ever been attached to his name it was unlikely that any hostess would have failed to send him a card of invitation.

Tony knew that Collett's violent death, which had stemmed directly from his involvement in four others, one being the brutal killing of Sir Philip Dunscumbe MP and executed by his own hand, all having come about due to his regular visits to a certain establishment, would not only send shockwaves through society but kill at a stroke any respect it may have had for him. Patronising a house of ill repute was one thing but to frequent an address which catered for those with out of the ordinary tastes was quite another, so too was being a party to or actually committing murder. It was only to be expected that Collett's death and the events leading up to it would outrage society because whilst he had not been overly liked by many, indeed there were those to whom he had given grievous offence, he had, in the main, been accepted, but even though society may have a dread of personal scandal beneath that surface layer of morality it seemed to delight in those of others, which was why Tony's main concern was for Eleanor and not for what people would say of her husband. He knew perfectly well that once the story broke there would be little if any escape for her from the gossip and rumours, all of which she would find extremely distressing, but although he was absolutely determined to do all he could to shield her from the worst of it, he realised only too well that this aim was largely dependent upon her father.

He knew there was every possibility that Sir Miles Tatton would read the stark truth in the newspapers before he received Eleanor's letter and his own accompanying one, and Tony could only hope that, having explained the pertinent points as far as he was able, they would suffice to allay any fears Sir Miles may have about his daughter. Tony also hoped that such tragic news together with Sir Miles Tatton's concern for Eleanor would see his immediate return to Bruton Street because the longer he lingered in Suffolk the greater the risk would become of people knowing about her stay in Mount Street, especially as it could not be taken for granted that no visitor would call in Cavendish Square either from a genuine wish to offer their condolences or merely to satisfy their curiosity.

Tony knew that Eleanor's reputation needed no defending, indeed it was above reproach, but should it ever become known that she had stayed in Mount Street at the same time as himself it would be seen to be compromised by association. The tale would lose nothing in the telling; the malicious tongues of the narrow-minded would see to that! Far from seeking sanctuary with her mother's dearest friend to flee the brutal treatment of her husband, nothing short of conducting a torrid liaison with Lady Shipton's brother would suffice to feed the outraged sense of morality of the self-righteous.

Tony may have no liking for dissimulation, indeed it was anathema to him, but he was fully determined to protect the woman he loved from censure and criticism by every means at his disposal, but even before he had reached the first landing he realised it was imperative he discuss matters with Mrs. Timms without any loss of time to plug one of those holes in his theory he had mentioned to Tom.

Chapter Thirty

Opening her eyes just as the clock struck eight o'clock, Eleanor could not honestly say that she felt very much refreshed following her night of uninterrupted sleep, for which her chaotic dreams were responsible. But in spite of the lethargy which seemed to have her in its grip as she rested back against the pillows, her first waking thoughts were of Tony, her eyes instinctively glancing towards the door in hopeful expectation of seeing him walk in. There may not have been anything she could have realistically done to hasten his return last night, but just being downstairs had rendered waiting for him to come home not quite so unbearable, but it had been from sheer exhaustion that she had eventually allowed Beatrice to persuade her into going to bed. Eleanor had tried her best to stay awake until she knew Tony had returned home, but without her being aware of it her eyelids had begun to close of their own volition until she knew no more until a few minutes ago. But her fears for Tony's safety had not disappeared overnight, on the contrary she was still extremely worried, but although common sense told her that if anything had happened to him she would certainly have been told of it by now, she could not be easy in her mind and so eager was she to know he was safe that anything was preferable to lying here worrying.

Thanks to the arnica which Doctor Little had left with Sarah and who was applying it daily to her patient, Eleanor's bruises were fading far more quickly than they otherwise would have, but her ribs were still rather tender, while her legs, unused to too much exercise over the last few days, proved just a little unsteady, but totally disregarding any discomfort as inconsequential compared to Tony's safety, she pushed back the covers and put her feet to the floor, taking a moment to steady herself before reaching out for her dressing gown draped across the foot of the bed. Having got a little shakily to her feet she slid her arms into the sleeves of this borrowed garment, but no sooner had she fastened the buttons than the door silently opened and Tony walked in and, thinking it was Sarah, Eleanor could do no more than stare at him in unutterable relief.

Having taken a look in on her before he went to bed Tony had not been at all certain whether to be glad or not to find that she was still asleep. It was not because he wanted to tell her about Collett, but simply because he was both human and honest enough to admit that after what had happened earlier in Hertford Street the need to hold her close was so strong that it had taken all his resolution to return to his own room without waking her. His narrow escape at the hands of Eliza Boon, more so than the previous evening's attempt to make an end of him in Cavendish Square, had certainly shaken him, but it had also served to intensify his love and need for the woman without whom his life would be completely meaningless, a woman who, despite only having entered his life a few short days ago, felt like the other half of himself. But seeing her now, her face flushed and her hair tousled as it fell halfway down her back and her eyes revealing all the love she had for him, made him catch his breath, and not surprisingly it was several moments before he was able to ask, an odd inflection underlying the amusement in his voice, "And just where do you think you're going?" coming to stand in front of her within a couple of strides.

Eleanor felt the colour deepen in her cheeks and faltered, "I… I was going downstairs."

"Downstairs!" he repeated in mock surprise, raising an eyebrow, clamping down on his natural impulses.

"Yes," she nodded.

"I see," Tony mused, his eyes smiling down at her. "Why?" he asked gently, already knowing the answer.

"W-why?" Eleanor managed.

"Mm," he nodded, taking hold of one of her agitated hands.

"Well I… well… because…" she shrugged helplessly, "I…" then, her relief at seeing him alive and safe overcoming her, cried, "Oh, Tony!" unable to prevent the catch in her voice. "I…" covering her face with her free hand while the fingers of her other gripped his, "I have been so worried about you." Then, raising her eyes to his, said unsteadily, "I couldn't stay in bed another instant until I knew you were safe!"

As words seemed totally inadequate to express how he felt, Tony took her in his arms and held her, closing his eyes on a heartfelt sigh as he recalled with vivid clarity just how close he had come to never seeing her again, but other than brushing his lips against her hair he made no attempt to kiss her, content for the moment to just hold her tight against him, but Eleanor sensed the urgency and the need he had for her leave his body with every breath he drew. Up to now when Tony had held her in his arms it had always been when she was either sitting up in bed or on the day bed, but to find herself standing full against him, crushed against the strong hard length of his body wearing nothing but her nightdress and dressing gown, was as exhilarating as it was arousing. But even though it was a completely new experience, all Eleanor knew was that being locked in his arms felt like the most natural thing in the world and that in some inexplicable way she had come home and, as she melted into him, she knew beyond any doubt that it was where she wanted to be.

Tony also knew beyond any doubt that holding Eleanor in his arms was the most natural thing in the world as well as where he wanted her to be, but he knew too that his love for her rendered him acutely susceptible to her, and just to feel her soft and pliant body against his own tested his defences to the uttermost. It was only after a hard-fought inner struggle therefore that he managed to stop himself from throwing caution to the wind and unreservedly kissing her, but even though he somehow or other managed to keep his emotions on a fairly tight leash his kisses were by no means as restrained as they had been so far.

From the moment Eleanor first met Tony she had instantly recognised him as being a most caring man, but in spite of her inexperience she had intuitively known that he was also a deeply passionate one, and whilst this neither frightened nor shocked her she could not say the same about herself. She had never believed it possible that she could be equally as passionate or love a man so intensely, and it was something of a revelation to discover that she could, particularly when she considered her past experiences.

Hovering somewhere at the back of her mind was the painful recollection of Braden's repellent and inconsiderate demands which, at no point, had either been acceptable to her or filled her with the desire to respond, on the contrary they had left her feeling ashamed and tarnished and certainly in no hurry to repeat the experience. But Tony's tender and considerate expressions of love, the very opposite to what her husband had subjected her to, had not only shown her just how very pleasurable it was to exchange intimate caresses, but elicited a response for which she was by no means embarrassed or ashamed, and certainly not now when his kisses were far more demonstrative than ever before, in fact when Tony eventually released her lips she felt quite deprived.

So too did Tony, but although he wanted nothing more than to hold her in his arms all day he knew he could not, not only because her very nearness put a severe strain on his self-control but there were matters he must discuss with her, even so, it was several moments before he could finally bring himself to release her.

"Oh Tony!" she cried when he eventually eased himself a little away from her. "I have been so worried! I thought something had happened to you!"

"Nothing has happened to me," he assured her, cupping her face in his none too steady hands. "As you can see," he smiled, "I am quite safe," taking her back in his arms.

"And Tom?" she asked unsteadily.

"And Tom," he confirmed, feeling the relief run through her. "I'm sorry my darling," he pressed against her hair, "I never meant to worry you. Forgive me."

"My darling," she cried huskily, "there is nothing to forgive."

"Indeed there is," he told her on a deep sigh, holding her tighter still, "I never meant you and Bea to be anxious."

Easing herself out of his arms she laid the palms of her hands against his chest, looking lovingly up at him, saying softly, "If I didn't love you so much I wouldn't be, but it's because I do love you," she confessed huskily, bringing the palm of one hand to rest against his cheek, "that I *do* worry; so very much, and the reason I was going downstairs. I couldn't lie in bed another instant until I knew you were safe."

"My poor darling," he soothed, kissing the palm of her hand, "I have used you abominably!"

"No," Eleanor assured him earnestly, shaking her head, "you haven't, you must not think that. You did whatever it was you had to do, but it's because I love you so very much that I sense something has happened."

Tony could claim no more of a liking for Sir Braden Collett now that he was dead any more than when he was alive, but the fact remained that through his devious scheming he had met his brutal end by the hand of the very man who had more than once carried out his dirty work; a clear case of thieves falling out, just as Superintendent Dawson had rightly claimed! Eleanor may not have loved Sir Braden Collett, in fact she had lived in fear of him, nevertheless, Tony knew that the news of his death would be a terrible shock to her and, after planting another kiss into her soft palm, he nodded, saying quietly, "Yes, I am afraid something *has* happened."

She looked fearfully up at him, but not until he had gently sat her down on the day bed and wrapped his arms around her did she say, "Tony, is what happened something to do with Braden and Sir Philip?"

"Yes," he sighed, holding her close against him, "I'm afraid it is."

Tony knew perfectly well that the truth could not be withheld from her, but as he had fully expected by the time he had come to the end of recounting yesterday's events, purposely omitting telling her of his narrow escape, Eleanor was profoundly shocked and distressed, so much so that she buried her face into his shoulder.

Having suffered the unbearable bullying and vicious treatment which her husband had meted out to her as well as living in constant fear of being locked away, Tony would not have blamed Eleanor had she expressed relief or pleasure of some kind upon discovering that Collett had been viciously strangled by one of his accomplices. That she did neither came as no surprise to him, on the contrary her reception to such distressing news was precisely how he knew it would be for one of her kind and gentle nature and for whom such brutality was beyond her comprehension.

Having come to believe that no one knew the truth about what had happened, Eleanor could well imagine her husband's anger and incredulity upon reading the article Tony had arranged to be inserted in the newspapers, even so, Braden's suggestion they go to the police and tell them the truth considerably surprised her. Like Tony, she doubted very much that such a proposal stemmed from a sense of remorse for what he had done, but whatever the reason it had certainly not met with Eliza Boon's approval. Ever since this woman had become a permanent resident of twenty-nine Cavendish Square Eleanor had never once known the two of them argue or disagree or, if they had, she had no knowledge of it, but clearly Eliza had been against going to the authorities to make a full confession. Her refusal to agree to Braden's astonishing suggestion had inevitably resulted in an argument between them which ended with him striking her, culminating in Peterson coming violently to her defence in a way that was as brutal as it was certainly unexpected and, apparently, with no more thought than when he had so callously disposed of Mitchell. Despite Eleanor's fear and hatred of Braden as well as knowing that it was only right he answered for his crimes, his death had not been the just punishment decreed by a court of law duly carried out following his trial, but cold-blooded murder committed by one of the two people he had come to rely heavily on. The mental picture of her husband's body lying dead on the study floor suddenly danced in front of her mind's eye causing her to shudder in Tony's arms and a choked sob to leave her lips, but even though she took much-needed comfort from his reassuring presence and the soothing words he whispered in her ear, Eleanor could not totally banish the horrendous images which only went to increase her horror.

As Tony held her safely in his arms he wished, and not for the first time, that he could have spared her the brutal truth, not only about Collett but also about what had happened to Mitchell, a man for whom she had no little affection. Eventually though, Tony managed to calm the shivering bundle of disbelief in his arms and, after vigorously blowing her nose on the handkerchief he pulled out of his pocket, sniffed, "I'm sorry. I…"

"There's no need to be sorry," Tony said gently, "it's a lot to take in. I only wish I could have spared you."

"No," she shook her head, wiping her nose, "I had to know, no matter how dreadful; it's just that… well, I… I can't believe it!"

"I know," he soothed, removing a stray tendril of hair off her face.

"Oh, Tony," she cried on a shudder, "it's all so horrible!"

The only response he made to this was to tighten his hold, knowing that only time would erase the images in her mind as well as the memory of what she had suffered.

But no matter how shocked and distressed Eleanor was at the dramatic turn of events she was perfectly well aware of the harsh and inescapable realities which lay ahead, and even though the very thought of all the official formalities was extremely painful she knew they were unavoidable. From the moment she had found herself safely installed in Mount Street her profound hope was that never again would she have to set foot inside twenty-nine Cavendish Square, and therefore upon learning of Tony's intention to take her to her father as soon as she was well enough to travel and with whom she would live until matters were eventually settled, had relieved her mind of this overwhelming dread. Now though, Braden's unforeseen and brutal death had changed things resulting in Tony having to hastily adjust his well-ordered plans for her protection, but she was not fooled by his tactful explanation to save her any embarrassment. She was not so naïve that she did not know as well as he did the gossip which would follow should it ever become known that she had lived in the same house with him all this time irrespective of the continued presence of Tom and Beatrice, and whilst Eleanor had come to expect no less from a man of Tony's integrity she was deeply touched by his consideration for her feelings. Having promised to write to her father today in order for both their letters to catch the evening collection, she gently eased herself out of his arms and, laying the palms of her hands against his chest, smiled up at him, saying, "I can't see my father delaying his return to town once he knows what has happened," adding a little awkwardly, "any more than he will deny me his protection against any gossip."

A deep sigh racked Tony's body at this. "Ellie, I…"

"No," she said soothingly, laying her hand against his cheek, "it's all right, I *do* understand."

"I know," Tony sighed, covering the hand resting lightly against his cheek with his own, "it's just that I want to…"

"Shield me?" She smiled. "Yes I know, and such concern for my feelings only makes me love you more, but whilst I know nothing improper has taken place between us," she shook her head, "I *do* know that just being together in the same house will inevitably be seen as having compromised my reputation."

"Damn the gossips!" he bit out.

"Yes," Eleanor conceded sadly, "they can be very cruel; really quite vicious, but my father is just as aware of this as we are; which is why," she assured him, "he will not delay his return to Bruton Street so I can go to him. Indeed, Tony, it is for the best," she urged upon seeing the frown crease his forehead.

"I know," Tony heaved a deep sigh, kissing the palm of her hand, "but I can't bear being parted from you, and certainly not for such a reason as pandering to the narrow-minded!"

"I feel the same," Eleanor told him earnestly, "but even though it is all so very cruel, I cannot see my father refusing permission for you to visit me in Bruton Street."

"Just let him try!" Tony said resolutely, taking her back in his arms.

"Are you saying you would disregard him?" she asked, breathless at the thought.

"You'd better believe it!" Tony told her in a deep voice, feeling the shudder of excitement course through her. "I'd disregard anyone who tried to keep me away from you!"

"Y-you would?" she asked huskily.

"Too right I would! Meanwhile though," he told her between amusement and need, lowering his head, "what the gossipmongers don't see won't hurt them!" proceeding to agreeably kiss her.

Beatrice, who was as kind as she was generous, would like nothing better than to have Eleanor remain in Mount Street until such time that she and Tony could be married, but like her husband and brother Beatrice knew that it would not do. She had not exaggerated when she had told Tony the other morning of how cruel and malicious people could be because whilst no one enjoyed going more into society than she did, she hated the gossip and tale-bearing which formed part of the world she adorned, and did not need it reinforcing about the connotations which would be drawn from Eleanor's stay in Mount Street at the same time as her brother. Had Tony been a married man or even a widower, his presence under her roof at the same time as Eleanor's own would be perfectly acceptable, but unfortunately he was neither; on the contrary he was a most eligible bachelor and one, moreover, who had exposed the truth about Eleanor's husband! Maybe Tony could stand a lick or two as he had told her the other day, but the truth was Beatrice could not bear to think of him being maligned and certainly not by those who would not only make it their business to spread malicious rumours, but who would never even consider taking the trouble to discover the truth. The same went for Eleanor. She did not deserve the harsh condemnation of her world which, unless Beatrice had totally miscalculated, could well lead to her young friend being wholly ostracised from society; a society which, however fickle, could do Eleanor's reputation far more harm than Tony ever could.

Even if Tony had not told her about his feelings for Eleanor, Beatrice would have to be blind not to recognise the love which existed between the two of them and that, at long last, her brother had finally found the woman with whom he wanted to spend the rest of his life. She could think of no two people more suited, indeed they were made for one another, but although she knew beyond question that at no time had Tony either compromised Eleanor or behaved improperly towards her, it was nevertheless imperative that no one knew of her stay in Mount Street. Tony's suggestion that Eleanor live with her father was, as far as Beatrice could see, the only solution to the problem; whether society would believe that Eleanor had been with Sir Miles for the better part of a week however, remained to be seen! That she would miss Eleanor went without saying, even so, Beatrice was quite ready to do everything possible to protect her young friend from spiteful tongues, telling Tony as he tucked into a substantial breakfast following his visit to Eleanor that she would be happy to go with Sarah to Cavendish Square later that morning to help Mrs. Timms pack her belongings.

It would be an exaggeration to say that Beatrice did not know Sir Miles, she did, but the truth was she had never been on such close terms with him as she had been with his wife and could not say with any degree of certainty how he would react to Tony's letter or the one from Eleanor. Even if she had known that Eleanor's marriage to Sir Braden Collett had its roots in her father's faux pas, Beatrice did not think he would fail to come to his daughter's aid in such an extremity as this, particularly when he learned of everything she had endured at her husband's hands and would own herself astonished if he did not respond to Eleanor's plea.

Beatrice fully shared Tony's concerns for the future, particularly with regard to the inquests and the court hearing, all of which Eleanor would find extremely distressing, but since there was no way the official procedures attached to these matters could be avoided, all Beatrice could hope for was that they would not drag on too long. As for her brother's marriage to Eleanor, nothing could be done until her period of mourning was over because even though she had not a thought in common with Collett, in fact she had hated and feared him, it would create a very odd appearance if his widow flouted convention by disregarding what was due to her husband's memory by immediately marrying the very man who had exposed him. Then, of course, there was Sir Miles to consider. Amelia Tatton had told Beatrice herself that Eleanor would not reach her majority until she was twenty-five which meant that, widow or not, she would still need her father's permission to re-marry, a circumstance which, when Beatrice pointed this out to Tony, seemed not to bother him at all. In fact, his only reply to this most important point was an acknowledging nod of the head followed by an unperturbed, "I can't see him withholding it."

She had no idea what made him think so, but of one thing she was certain and that was her brother, once he had made up his mind to something, did not give up on it and, as far as marrying the woman he had set his heart on was concerned, he most definitely would not. But this was for the future, for now, there were more practical matters for her to set her mind to and no sooner had she said goodbye to Tony, whose first port of call in what was going to prove a rather full day was Cavendish Square, she made her way to the nursery to spend a little time with Alice before seeing Eleanor to discuss collecting her belongings and to recruit Sarah's capable help.

Mrs. Timms may have accorded Sir Braden Collett all the respect which was due to him, not only as a knight of the realm but also as her employer, but at no time could it be said that she had a liking for him. His volatile temper and aggressive manner were not conducive to creating a happy household, but providing his staff carried out their duties without question or argument the daily running of the house had been relatively smooth that was until he had brought in Peterson and Eliza Boon. Never having believed the tales about Her Ladyship's mental disorder, Mrs. Timms had regarded both of these individuals with suspicion from the moment they had stepped foot across the threshold, but since it was not her place to question Sir Braden's decisions she had, like the rest of the domestic staff, to make the best of things. Nevertheless, unlike Ellen and Susan, she had held serious doubts about Lady Collett's delicate state of health and had more than once been forced to bite her tongue, particularly as Eliza Boon looked to be very far removed from the nurse Sir Braden had said she was. But whatever Mrs. Timms may think as well as what she personally believed as being the real cause of Lady Collett regularly withdrawing to her room for days on end, nothing had quite prepared her for what Tony had disclosed and so shocked and appalled was she that had Eliza Boon suddenly appeared before her she would not have been answerable for her actions.

As for Sir Braden Collett, despite his faults, Mrs. Timms had never thought him capable of murder, and as far as visiting a certain kind of establishment was concerned – well, the least said about that the better! But that he had met his end by a man who clearly had no qualms about committing the most vicious of crimes, was no more than poetic justice! She hoped she was not a vindictive woman, but when she thought of what he had done to her young mistress, the kindest and gentlest of souls who had never done a mite of harm to anyone, it was no more than he deserved and therefore she had known no hesitation in doing all she could to help bring him and those other two to account. Even so, to think that Sir Braden had lain dead nearly all day in his study without anyone being the wiser made her shiver, and she was honest enough to admit that it would not have taken much for her to pack her bags and leave, just like Ellen and Susan. Had it not have been for her concerns about Lady Collett and how important it was to keep the truth from the rest of the staff, at least for the time being, Mrs. Timms would most certainly have done so because although Superintendent Dawson had done his best to set her mind at rest that nothing else was likely to happen, it had been Tony's reassurances she had taken comfort from. It had, of course, afforded her some peace of mind to know that the Superintendent had posted a police constable outside all night, but she could not deny that Jerry's presence long after the others had left had gone a long way to allaying the worst of her fears, a man for whom she admitted to having taken rather a liking and, as Tony had rightly told Tom, it was fully reciprocated.

She was at once pleased and relieved to receive a visit from Tony, and after responding to his concerns about her wellbeing told him that she would be only too pleased to help Lady Shipton and her maid sort out Lady Collett's belongings and to make sure they were safely delivered to Mount Street. Having listened to him outline his idea for Lady Collett and the best way of shielding her from gossip, Mrs. Timms, who had no qualms whatsoever in letting it be known that she had helped her young mistress leave Cavendish Square following another brutal attack by her husband, fully agreed that nothing could be better than putting it about that Lady Collett was with her father in Suffolk, and had been for the better part of a week because, she told Tony forthrightly, nothing did more damage than the tongues of tittle-tattling busybodies. As for the staff here in Cavendish Square, Mrs. Timms told him not to give it another thought as she would make sure they were left in no doubt as to the truth of things and that, having arrived home from the anniversary party given by the Kirkmichaels at The Park Grove Hotel, Her Ladyship, following yet another brutal assault, had found herself unable to cope with such vicious treatment any longer and that she had personally assisted her in leaving the house. "There is just one thing, m'lord," she nodded, having turned something over in her mind, "this Eliza Boon woman, do you think she will say anything, if only out of spite?"

"We can't discount that possibility, of course," Tony shook his head, "but quite frankly, Mrs. Timms," he said truthfully, "I doubt it, in fact," he shrugged, "I fail to see how it would serve her purpose," to which she nodded in agreement.

It seemed her only other concern was informing Sir Braden's cousin as to the tragedy, "Because," Mrs. Timms told Tony justly, "it wouldn't be right for 'im to read it in the newspapers."

"There is no need to worry yourself over that, Mrs. Timms." Tony smiled encouragingly. "Even though the story will be in this evening's editions of *'The Chronicler'* and *'The Bugle'* Superintendent Dawson will have already advised him of Sir Braden's death as well as his involvement in all that has happened when he visits him today."

She nodded, then, looking slightly troubled, sighed, "About Mitchell, m'lord; 'e will be given a proper burial, won't 'e?" still shocked at what Tony had told her.

"Yes," Tony confirmed quietly, "I promise you that, Mrs. Timms."

"Downright wicked it was what they did to 'im!" she cried, wiping her nose. "They'd no right to do that to 'im, m'lord."

"No," Tony confirmed gravely, "no right at all."

"What 'e must 'ave suffered!" Mrs. Timms sniffed into her handkerchief. "It doesn't bear thinkin' on."

"If it helps at all, Mrs. Timms," Tony told her quietly, "I doubt very much whether he felt anything. That first blow would have been more than enough to render him unconscious."

"That's little comfort, m'lord," she told him truthfully, "but it's good to know that 'e wouldn't 'ave felt anythin'." Giving her nose one final and forceful blow she returned the handkerchief to her apron pocket, then, looking straight at Tony said cautiously, "There is one thing I'd like to ask, m'lord."

"Anything at all, Mrs. Timms," Tony smiled.

"Well," she nodded, "the thing is, I've been right worried over 'Er Ladyship, an' that's the truth, an' I wondered if I could per'aps go an' see 'er."

"Of course," Tony smiled. "I know I can speak for my sister as well as myself when I say that you will be most welcome in Mount Street at any time."

"Well," she nodded, her bosom swelling, "that's most kind of you, m'lord, I'm sure."

"Not at all," Tony shook his head. "As for Ellie – Lady Collett," he hastily corrected himself, "she would very much like to receive a visit from you as soon as may be convenient."

"So," Mrs. Timms mused, the shrewdness in her eyes tinged with indulgence, "*that's* the way the wind's blowin', is it?"

Having taken a real liking to this no-nonsense and plain-speaking woman, Tony looked straight at her, an irrepressible smile dancing in his eyes, but said, somewhat ruefully, "Yes," by no means surprised that she had picked upon on his slip of the tongue, "*that's* the way the wind is blowing."

Mrs. Timms pursed her lips, "Well," she nodded, "I must say I did suspicion it. Not that I'm not glad, mind you!" She nodded again. "It's about time that dear sweet mite 'ad a bit of 'appiness in 'er life!"

Tony fully agreed with this sentiment and, after shaking her hand and pulling on his gloves, he looked down at her, smiling, "You know, Mrs. Timms, Jerry sure is one lucky guy!"

She did not pretend to misunderstand him. "Give over m'lord, do!" she chided as though she had known him all her life. "At my time o' life! Such nonsense!" to which Tony laughed. He saw the colour deepen a little in her cheeks as she seemed to consider something before saying a little hesitantly, "I take it, m'lord, you will be seeing Jerry today?"

"Yes," Tony smiled, "very soon in fact. Is there something you would like me to tell him?" he asked, already knowing the answer.

"Nothin' important, I'm sure," Mrs. Timms shrugged, not very convincingly, trying not to catch the twinkle in Tony's eyes, "it's just that 'e did say somthin' about poppin' in and… well," she shrugged again, "I'm not goin' anywhere if 'e'd like to come round."

"I shall be pleased to convey your message to him, Mrs. Timms," Tony assured her, suppressing the twitch at the corner of his mouth.

"I take that very kindly in you, m'lord," she told him.

"Not at all," Tony smiled and, after reiterating his thanks and promising to convey her message to Jerry, left her to her own thoughts, which had undergone no change.

Yes, she had been right about His Lordship. He was not handsome, no, but there was something mighty attractive about him all the same! Of course, there was no mistaking that air of calm authority which hung about him, but there was no starch to him; not like Sir Braden! As for Lady Collett, well, all she could say was that a better man than His

Lordship she would never find, not if she looked ever! Without a doubt, she will receive no harsh treatment at his hands.

It had been obvious to Tony from the beginning that Jerry had taken a liking to Mrs. Timms and, from what he could see of it, it was entirely reciprocated. As a result of this mutual partiality Tony had not been in the least surprised when Jerry had elected to stay behind in Cavendish Square last night long after the rest of them had left to allay any fears she may have had. Tony felt it pretty safe to assume that Jerry would have been in no hurry to leave the warmth and comfort of Mrs. Timms's kitchen, not only to help him thaw out following what had been a long cold wait in Hertford Street but also to further his acquaintance with her, and Tony, upon strolling into Bill's office after leaving Cavendish Square, could see Jerry had the same gleam in his eyes as Mrs. Timms.

But there was no gleam in Bill's eyes. Having learned from Jerry precisely what had happened when Tony had visited in Cavendish Square the night before last and all that had happened yesterday in Hertford Street, the news that Eliza Boon had yet again attempted to take Tony's life outweighed any satisfaction he had about her arrest and that of Peterson following his confession. The quick actions of Constable Moore had certainly averted a tragedy by fractionally diverting her aim, but Bill could not pretend to being anything other than shocked and appalled to discover that this ruthless and determined woman had tried one final time to take Tony's life. Over the years Bill had told himself he really should know better than to worry over Tony who had more than once found himself in a tight corner as a result of covering a story, but somehow or other he had always managed to come out of it in one piece, but this latest attempt to kill him had been the closest call yet. To Bill's way of thinking it was far too serious to be taken lightly much less ignored, but although there was a rueful smile in Tony's eyes as he looked at him, he made no mention of it. A look of sheer exasperation descended onto Bill's face as he watched Tony casually remove his hat and gloves followed by his overcoat before unconcernedly pouring himself a cup of coffee as though nothing had happened and, goaded beyond endurance, Bill threw him a fulminating glance, Tony's second near miss being of far more importance than the arrest of Eliza Boon and Peterson or, even, the death of Collett by the hand of his accomplice.

"You don't have to say it, Bill," Tony sighed inclining his head, not needing to have his expression interpreted.

Opening his eyes to their fullest extent, Bill asked with awful irony,

"Say what? Why should I say anything?" Upon encountering an eloquent look, he shrugged innocently, "Did something serious happen yesterday?"

"Okay, Bill," Tony sighed again, "I know damn well it was a close call," sitting down on the chair he had just pulled out and crossing one long leg over the other, "too damn close for my liking if you must know!"

"*Never* learn, do you!" Bill shot at him between impatience and frustration, a tone he always adopted to hide his anxiety. "How many times have I told you that you never…?" breaking off to pat his waistcoat pockets in search of a cigar.

"Some!" Tony nodded good humouredly, knowing it was pointless telling Bill he could take care of himself.

"Too right I have!" Bill nodded. "And what notice have you ever taken?" lighting the cigar he finally pulled out of his pocket.

"Look Bill…"

"None!" Bill cut him short. "I've never known anyone like you for attracting trouble. How come it doesn't happen to the others?" he demanded, cocking his head. "How come they cover a story without someone taking a potshot at them or putting them in hospital with a broken leg or ending up concussed for days on end! Tell me that?" He nodded.

"I don't go looking for it, Bill," Tony pointed out.

"You don't have to," Bill shot at him, "it just comes right round the corner at you!" going on to remind him of just a few instances which fully proved his point, concluding by pointing out firmly. "And I daresay if it had not been for Jerry telling me about either of your near misses you'd have said squat!"

"Won't let me get a word in, will you?" Tony said affably, taking out his cigarette case.

"*And*," Bill finished firmly, ignoring this, "if yesterday's little clambake was not enough to make you realise that you're pushing your luck, nothing will. Yes," he nodded, as a thought occurred to him, "and that's another thing; what about Beatrice and Lady Collett? Have you stopped and thought how they'd feel if…?"

"They don't know, Bill," Tony broke in steadily, "and, what's more," he said meaningfully, "they aren't going to."

"God damn!" Bill cried. "Are you…?"

"Skip it, Bill," Tony said firmly. "I have no intention of telling them about yesterday or the other night nor, if it comes to that," he stressed, "about that set to with Peterson because all it would do is worry them unnecessarily. As for the rest," he nodded, "it made me realise a lot of things; not the least of which is that I am in no hurry to have a repeat performance; but since none of us could possibly have foreseen that Eliza Boon would have a pistol hidden up her sleeve and I'm still here in one piece…"

Like his father, it was impossible not to like Tony, a man who went about his work in a quiet and methodical way and one, moreover, who neither boasted about his achievements nor drew attention to his confrontations. Bill knew perfectly well that in a fair fight, like his run-ins with Peterson and Collett, Tony could more than adequately take care of himself, but the calm way he shrugged off two of the most closest calls of his life merely highlighted Bill's concerns for the man he freely admitted to having a deep and genuine fondness for, but his untroubled acceptance of what happened in Cavendish Square and again in Hertford Street made Bill angrily demand of Jerry, "Can you *beat* this guy?" waving a hand in Tony's direction.

Jerry's acquaintanceship with Tony may be of short duration, but he had seen enough of him to know that he was a man with a mind of his own and one who could not be pushed and, like Bill and his sister, knew that once he had made up his mind to something it would take an awful lot to change it. Jerry had taken a real liking to Tony, a man after his own heart, but he had been genuinely shocked at the vengeful actions of Eliza Boon and, even now, he could hardly believe that Tony had twice miraculously escaped being killed. It was not often Jerry was caught napping, but no more than Tony or the rest of them had he been prepared for that pistol cunningly hidden up her sleeve yesterday much less it being aimed at him, but apart from expressing his relief and ascertaining Tony was all right before they left Hertford Street, Jerry had refrained from making any further comment about it. Like Bill, he had come to know Tony as being a man who disliked puffing off his successes or drawing attention to something as serious as an attempt on his life and was not at all surprised to learn that he had not told his sister or Lady Collett about what had happened, even so, he could quite well understand Bill's concern.

"Forget it, Bill," Tony nodded, by no means unappreciative of his freely expressed frustration; knowing from experience that this was Bill's way of hiding his feelings.

"God damn, Tony!" Bill cried. "She could have killed you!"

"Do you think I don't know that?" Tony raised an eyebrow. "Well," he nodded, "I do, but it's yesterday's news."

"Yesterday's news…!" Bill echoed when he finally found his voice, dropping his hands onto the arms of his chair. "You've gotta be kiddin' me!"

"Huh huh," Tony shook his head. "It's over! Besides, there's other and more important things to think about."

Biting down the blistering words which rose to his tongue, knowing perfectly well that Tony would just shrug them off, Bill demanded instead, "What's more important than your life?"

"Lady Collett's reputation," Tony told him firmly, giving him a brief outline of what he intended to avert any malicious gossip, "which was the reason for my visit to Cavendish Square this morning," catching the glance Jerry cast at him from out the corner of his eye, suppressing the twitch at the corner of his mouth, "as well as Superintendent Dawson's visit to Sunshine Terrace to retrieve Mitchell's body and to visit Collett's cousin in Wimbledon; not to mention getting the front page ready," he nodded.

Leaning forward in his seat with his cigar held between his fingers, Bill eyed Tony closely, pursing his lips as he nodded his head, saying slowly, "The front page!"

"The front page," Tony repeated. "You know what the front page is, Bill?" He raised an eyebrow.

"Wise guy!" Bill said at length, unable to resist the laughter in Tony's eyes. "You cover a number of stories and think you know it all, huh! Well," he nodded, straightening up, "let me tell you that I knew what a front page was before your old man ever let you loose in the newsroom!" to which Tony burst out laughing. "But hey!" Bill shrugged, opening the drawer of his desk and pulling out a sheet that he tossed onto his desk. "What do *I* know about getting a front page ready? I'm only an editor!"

"I figured we'd get round to that!" Tony grinned, leaning forward to pick up the sheet.

"Damn right!" Bill nodded drawing hard on his cigar as he sat back in his chair while Tony read the sheet in front of him. "It would serve you right if I washed my hands of the whole thing!"

"You won't," Tony smiled.

"Pretty cock sure, aren't you?" Bill nodded.

"You forget," Tony reminded him, "I know you, Bill; there's no way you'd turn your back on a story."

"There's a first time for everything!" He pointed his cigar at him.

"Sure there is," Tony grinned, "but you're too much of a newspaperman for that!"

"Got it all off pat, haven't you?" Bill cocked his head. "Yeah, sure you have!" he nodded when he saw the smile on Tony's lips as he pulled out a pen from his inside pocket. Realising it was pointless to say anything more, Bill sighed his resignation and, turning his attention to the sheet Tony was reading, pointed out, "There are gaps as you can see which need filling in, but once Dawson's removed Mitchell's body it's ready to roll! The print room's on standby ready, but it'll be out for this evening's edition."

"It'll be on standby for a while yet, Bill," Tony told him, crossing out and amending various bits.

"God damn, Tony!" Bill exclaimed, leaning forward. "It's the story of the decade!"

"Sure it is," Tony confirmed, "but until Dawson has informed Collett's next of kin of the tragedy and the circumstances which brought it about, it goes nowhere. I'm expecting to see him here later."

"Son of a…!"

"Sorry, Bill," Tony shook his head, looking briefly up from the sheet to Bill's face, "but for Collett's cousin to learn about it from a newspaper article would be one hell of a shock." Bill was just about to say something when Tony said firmly, "I run a newspaper, Bill; I am not in the business of selling sensationalism or giving people heart attacks because I want us to be first with the news!"

Such consideration came as no surprise to Bill, but after all the work Tony had put into this, not to mention putting his life at risk, he would hate one of the other dailies to beat them to it, but upon pointing this out Tony shrugged, "I'm not responsible for what other editors do, Bill. Don't worry," he smiled, in answer to Bill's scornful expression, "they won't beat us to it."

"You hope!" Bill scoffed.

"Trust me, Bill," Tony smiled.

With this Bill had to be satisfied, but from out the corner of his eye Tony saw the frustrated looks Bill regularly cast at him, but although Tony fully appreciated the thinking behind his old friend's wish to get the story out, he was adamant they were going to sit on it for now. Being first with the news was one thing but to deliberately cause someone untold pain and distress in order to do it was quite another, and therefore Tony sat calmly back in his seat as he leisurely altered the sheet Bill had handed him, totally unperturbed as the minutes ticked by while they waited for Superintendent Dawson.

Resigning himself to the fact that Tony did not want to talk about his near miss yesterday and he would not budge about running the evening's edition until Superintendent Dawson arrived, Bill commented instead on their wait in Hertford Street and Peterson's unlooked-for confession, agreeing with Jerry that it must have had its roots in Eliza Boon's betrayal. "Too right it did!" Tony said firmly, raising his eyes from the sheet he was amending. "Had you seen the look of sheer bewilderment and shock on Peterson's face as he heard Eliza Boon denying any knowledge of wrongdoing and trying to shift the blame onto him and Collett like we did, you'd be left in no doubt."

"Talk about bein' pole-axed!" Jerry exclaimed. "Weren't nothin' to the look on 'is face."

"Too right!" Tony nodded, going on to tell Bill about Tom's theory.

"In love with Eliza Boon!" Bill cried shocked. "God damn! I'd say a more hard-boiled dame you'll never find!"

"Well," Tony sighed, "whatever the reason for Peterson's loyalty to her it sure took a nose-dive yesterday!"

"Big time by the sound of it!" Bill nodded. "Talk about a kick in the teeth!"

"It was that right enough!" Jerry confirmed. "Regular baffled 'e was!"

"That's for sure," Tony agreed, "and were it anyone other than Peterson I'd have some sympathy for him," looking from one to the other, "but as it is I only have to think of Annie Myers and Mitchell to kill it at a stroke."

"About Mitchell," Bill cocked his head, "that sure was one way hell of a way to deal with the guy!"

"You can say that again!" Tony said firmly. "The only consolation, if one can call it that, is that he would not have felt a thing. That first blow would have been more than enough to render him senseless."

"You got that right," Bill nodded, "but I sure wouldn't like to be one of the guys who removes his body! It'll be no pleasant sight after all this time!"

"No," Tony sighed, "I don't envy them that."

Bill agreed, then, after a moment's thought he eyed Tony, saying, "This idea of yours about Lady Collett having sought sanctuary in Suffolk with her father and not stepping foot anywhere near Mount Street; do you think it will fool the gossips?"

"I see no reason why it shouldn't," Tony shrugged, casting a brief glance up at Bill. "Unless I miss my guess," he pointed out, "they're going to have enough to wonder and marvel at as it is without wondering whether Lady Collett was in Suffolk with her father or not."

Much struck by this, Bill nodded. "You got that right!" Then, as if a thought had just occurred to him, he cocked his head. "What about this Eliza Boon dame?" unconsciously echoing Mrs. Timms. "What I mean is," he nodded, "you're not exactly top guy with her! What's to stop her from getting her own back by trying to drop you in it?"

"Nothing at all," Tony shrugged, "but I fail to see what good it would do her," to which Bill raised an eyebrow. "Unless I've figured that woman all wrong, Bill," Tony told him, "her sole aim right now is to get off with as light a sentence as possible which means not only trying to shift the blame onto Collett and Peterson for all that has happened but also to acquit herself of any wrongdoing where Lady Collett is concerned, which is what she claimed yesterday in Hertford Street. She knows as well as we do that by trying to drop me in it will not serve her purpose. Eliza Boon may be one tough cookie," he nodded in response to Bill's eloquent expression, "but she's no fool, in fact," he pointed out, "it would not surprise me in the least to discover that she would rather be accused of keeping a house of ill repute and living off immoral earnings than being charged and sentenced for conspiracy to commit murder or being partly responsible for keeping Lady Collett a virtual prisoner!"

"Why," Bill cried, "the dame's as guilty as hell!"

"She sure is," Tony agreed, "but like I say," he nodded, "she's no fool!"

As Bill seemed at a loss for words to express how he felt about Eliza Boon, he turned instead to an equally pressing question, asking, "Do you think Collett's staff will buy the story Mrs. Timms is going to sell 'em?"

"They'll buy it, Bill," Tony nodded, "not only because they look up to Mrs. Timms but also because they've seen enough over the past few months to make them question things. As for Bea and Sarah calling in Cavendish Square at some point today to see about Lady Collett's belongings being packed and delivered to Mount Street in readiness for her supposed return from Suffolk, bearing in my mind my sister's friendship with Lady Tatton, I can't see them reading anything into that," to which Bill nodded. "By the way, Jerry," Tony smiled across at him, "Mrs. Timms asked me to thank you again for last night."

Jerry looked a little sheepish at this, but not quite able to keep the hopeful note out of his voice, asked, "Did she say anythin' else, Guv?"

"Well," Tony screwed up his face as if in an effort of memory, "it seems you said something about popping in to see her again."

Shifting a little uncomfortably in his chair, Jerry shrugged and pulled a nonchalant face, which did not fool Tony in the least, explaining, "Well I did just 'appen to mention that while things were a bit unsettled 'er might like a bit o' company; you know, Guv," he nodded, "to make 'er feel a bit more comfortable like."

"That's very thoughtful of you Jerry!" Tony commended with exaggerated approval. Then, leaning across to where Jerry was sitting next to him slapped him cheerfully on the arm, grinning, "It's okay, Jerry, she said she's not going anywhere and so she'd be happy for you to pop round whenever you were passing."

A tinge of colour crept into Jerry's cheeks at this and his eyes lit up, asking eagerly, "Straight up, Guv?"

"Straight up, Jerry," Tony smiled.

Bill was just about to pull Jerry's leg about his blossoming friendship with Mrs. Timms when the door opened and Superintendent Dawson walked in. It was clear from the look on his face that he had had a fairly harrowing morning, but upon setting eyes on Tony, who appeared none the worse for his near miss yesterday, he could not help asking if he was all right. Having his enquiry kindly yet firmly dismissed Superintendent Dawson went on to tell them with a barely suppressed shudder that Mitchell's body was in fact where Peterson said he had left it. "It made no pretty viewing after all this time as you can imagine," he nodded, accepting the coffee Tony handed him, going on to tell them that the body had now been taken to the mortuary at the Central Middlesex Hospital before being transported to St. Pancras where a post-mortem would take place. "As you would expect," Superintendent Dawson sighed, "the body was badly decomposed, but it was perfectly clear that he had been viciously struck across the head several times." He took a generous mouthful of coffee. "The worst of it was," he managed, "we had to break his legs to straighten his body before we could lay it on the stretcher, which was not very pleasant as you can imagine."

"Gawd love us!" Jerry exclaimed, leaning forward in his seat.

"That's pretty tough," Tony said quietly.

"Yes," Dawson sighed again, "in fact," he told him, "one young bobby had to rush outside because he couldn't stomach it."

"Well," Tony nodded, "I don't hold that against him!"

"No," Dawson shook his head, "neither do I," going on to unconsciously echo Tom's observations in that it was a miracle the body had never been found.

"Have you informed Collett's next of kin yet?" Tony enquired, helping himself to some more coffee.

"Yes," Superintendent Dawson nodded, fishing out his pipe, "in fact, I've not long left him."

"No need to ask how he took it," Tony grimaced.

"Well," Dawson sighed, looking down at the unlit pipe in his hand, "he didn't take it as badly as I thought. From what Hubert Collett told me," he shrugged in response to Tony's raised eyebrow, "he and his cousin Sir Braden were not close, in fact they seldom laid eyes on one another, so it was not the devastating news I thought it would be, nevertheless he was very much shocked, although," he admitted truthfully, "I think it was the manner of his death and the events leading up to it which took him aback rather than the actual loss of his cousin."

"Well, that's not surprising," Tony sighed, "but it sure will take some living down!"

"Yes," Dawson agreed, pulling out a box of matches, "I am afraid you're right!"

"Tell me, Superintendent," Tony cocked an eyebrow, "have you managed to interview Peterson and Eliza Boon yet?"

"Yes," Dawson nodded, "I have." Taking a moment or two to light his pipe he went on to explain that as far as Peterson was concerned, who, whether from bemusement or resignation, appeared reconciled to his lot, made no attempt to retract any of what he had confessed to in Hertford Street but, on the contrary, told the same story. "As for Eliza Boon," Superintendent Dawson told them, "she is still vehemently denying any participation in murder, and that she had known nothing of what was going on, indeed she had been shocked to learn that Sir Braden Collett, having duped her regarding Lady Collett's mental disorder by leading her to believe she had inflicted the injuries on herself due to her condition, had involved himself in something as serious as murder," to which Tony and Bill exchanged significant glances. "As for Sir Braden's death," Dawson informed them, "she says that they did argue the morning Peterson attacked and killed him because he resented her telling him that a physician should really be called in to see Lady Collett, which he ought to have done long since, and upon asking him why he had not done so he told her it was not her business to question him, but upon her pressing the point it seems he told her that it had something to do with Dennis Dunscumbe's death. Her story is that, after demanding Collett tell her the truth, he told her that he and Dennis Dunscumbe had been involved in something that had gone wrong, but he had become something of a threat and therefore Collett told Peterson to do away with Dennis Dunscumbe, but his brother, Sir Philip, had somehow or other learned the truth and visited Cavendish Square where he openly charged Collett with his brother's death, resulting in Collett losing his temper and killing Sir Philip, but although Collett didn't tell her what it was he and Dennis Dunscumbe were actually involved in, she then accused Collett of asking for her help in looking after Lady Collett by trickery and deceit, whereupon he lost his temper and struck her across the face. If we are to believe her," he sighed, fanning his pipe with his match box, "Collett read the newspaper articles before she spoke to him and had already rung for Peterson to go to his study only she got there first, but it seems that just as she was leaving Peterson entered the study, but so annoyed was she in discovering Collett had used her she listened to their conversation through the gap in the door as apparently Peterson had failed to close it behind him. She said she heard Sir Braden telling Peterson about what he had read in the newspapers and he wanted Peterson to go to Hertford Street to see if he had accidentally left anything incriminating behind him when he had shot Dennis Dunscumbe, but it seems that Peterson resented Collett's manner and they had a bit of an argument and before she could even think what was happening she heard a scuffle, and upon her entering the room she saw Peterson with his hands around Collett's throat, but although she tried her best to stop him she couldn't."

"God damn!" Bill cried, looking from one to the other in disbelief.

"When I asked her why," Dawson told them, "if all she had told me was the truth, then what was she doing in Hertford Street, to which she said that Peterson threatened to expose her past profession as well as implicate her in Dennis Dunscumbe's death and that of his brother if she didn't help him. As for attempting to shoot *you*," he nodded to Tony, "she claims that the gun went off by accident as she was about to hand it over," to which Jerry let out an angry expletive. "She claims that if Constable Moore had not caught her arm, taking her by surprise and causing her to lose her balance, the gun would not have gone off. When I asked her why she didn't hand it over when she emptied her pockets," Dawson told them, "she said she had forgotten all about it and upon being asked why she carried the gun in the first place, she said it was for her own protection. However," he sighed, "she *does* admit to keeping a certain kind of establishment as well as confirming that Annie Myers *was* one of her girls, but although she admits to there being an accident one night when Annie Myers had had too much to drink and somehow or other fallen over and struck her head on the bedstead which unfortunately killed her, she adamantly denies that Dennis Dunscumbe had anything to do with it and, as for Sir Braden, although she says he was a regular visitor to her place, neither man was there that night. She says that she and Peterson disposed of Annie Myers's body between them and told the girls that she had done a moonlight flit."

"So," Bill scorned, rising to his feet, "that's how she's gonna try to beat the rap, is it!"

"If you mean is this is her line of defence," Dawson nodded, "then yes, it is." Then, turning to Tony, who, though frustrated, appeared to be in no way surprised, shrugged and sighed, "I'm sorry, Childon."

Tony, after glancing from Jerry to Bill, whose expressions were eloquent testimony to their feelings, sighed, "I figured she'd come up with something like this, especially after her denials yesterday and her attempts to drop Peterson in it! She sure is one cool customer!" He nodded.

"To be honest," Dawson shook his head, "I can't see her changing her story, which means that," he said a little uncomfortably, glancing down at the pipe held between his fingers, "even though Peterson's evidence should really be enough to find her guilty, it may be that Lady Collett will after all be required to give evidence in court, especially now that her husband is dead and her evidence can't actually incriminate him." He saw the frown descend onto Tony's forehead and his lips compress, but without waiting for him to say anything, Dawson sighed, "I know you don't like it and neither do I if it comes to that, particularly as it will prove most distressing for Lady Collett, but I am sure you will agree that should Peterson's evidence not be enough to convict Eliza Boon then we shall be left with very little choice but to put Lady Collett in the witness-box to substantiate his testimony."

Tony did agree, but he had no liking for it. There may be no way Eleanor could avoid attending the court hearing, but having told her that due to her evidence being harmful to her husband it was most unlikely that she would have to give evidence, only to tell her now that this was a very real possibility because of Eliza Boon's refusal to admit knowledge or guilt, made him feel as though he had betrayed her. It was not something he felt particularly good about especially as it was going to be distressing enough for her to attend the inquests as well as answer questions which the Coroner was bound to put to her, but to stand in the witness-box to have her answers distorted by the defence to exonerate the woman who had really been nothing short of a gaoler, was too cruel. He had seen enough of Eliza Boon to know that she would lie through her teeth in order get a not guilty verdict for her crimes, and since the services of a top barrister were clearly not be beyond her means, who would no doubt do his best to tear Peterson's evidence to shreds, the best Tony could hope for was that Eleanor, bearing in mind her recent bereavement, would be spared too much harsh treatment at the hands of Eliza Boon's defence counsel.

Superintendent Dawson hoped so too because although Peterson was singing like a bird it could not be said that he possessed the sharpest intelligence and a halfway decent barrister would have no difficulty in confusing him and twisting his testimony to Eliza Boon's advantage a woman who, as Joanie Simms had rightly told Tony, was extremely plausible. Eliza Boon may not have committed cold-blooded murder herself, but she had certainly incited it, which would bring a heavy prison sentence, but Superintendent Dawson had seen enough of her to know that she would do everything possible to avoid this eventuality, even at the risk of receiving a lighter prison sentence for keeping a house of ill repute and living off immoral earnings. He felt sure she would not mind this, but for himself he had no liking for felons escaping the full penalty of the law, and certainly not those like Eliza Boon who had caused so much havoc in furthering her ends.

As for Joanie Simms, no prosecuting counsel would even so much as consider for a moment calling her to give evidence as any defence barrister worth his salt would have no trouble in discrediting her. Her past profession meant she was an unfit, even an immoral, witness in a court of a law and her evidence, significant though it was, would be deemed as nothing more than hearsay and therefore not admissible.

"God damn! This Boon dame's as guilty as hell!" Bill cried, not for the first time over the last half hour or so.

"That's as may be," Dawson acknowledged, "but one never can tell what a jury will believe." It was an unsatisfactory state of affairs and one he was by no means pleased about nor, from the looks of it, was Tony, but deciding the least said about it for now the better, asked if he could have a look at the front page which he had caught sight of.

"Sure," Tony said absently, somewhat preoccupied with all that loomed ahead for Eleanor.

"I take it," Superintendent Dawson raised an enquiring eyebrow, "that you are going to run this for this evening's edition?"

"Yes," Tony nodded, his attention now back on the matter in hand, "I was only waiting until you had informed Collett's relative."

Picking up the proof sheet, Superintendent Dawson read the article which covered all the front page with interest, nodding his head now and then, but after reading the last paragraph he looked briefly up at Tony then back at the sheet in his hand, reading it again, but out loud this time, *"Lady Collett, who has today been informed of the death of her husband, commented only that she will be instantly returning to town in company with her father Sir Miles Tatton, with whom she has been staying in Suffolk for the past week, and will, due to the tragic circumstances, be residing in Bruton Street for the foreseeable future…!"* Tapping the stem of his pipe against his bottom lip, Superintendent Dawson eyed Tony thoughtfully for a moment or two, musing at length, "I thought something like this was in your mind."

Tony smiled and, raising an eyebrow, asked, "And will it answer, do you think?"

After taking a moment to check his pipe, Superintendent Dawson looked up at Tony, sighing, "You know, Childon, it is a sad fact but I have all too often seen the irreparable harm and damage gossip can do, so I do not blame you for doing all you can to protect Lady Collett from the tittle-tattle which will follow should it ever become known that, far from being in Suffolk with her father, she was in fact staying in Mount Street during your own stay there, so I do not need to have this pretence explained," pointing the stem of his pipe at the sheet he held in his hand. "As for it answering," he shrugged, "then I have to say yes, I think it will. Unless I am very much mistaken," he nodded, dropping the sheet onto the desk before searching in his pockets for his matches, "I would say that no matter how disagreeable we think it, people are going to be far more interested in the gory details of what has happened than in Lady Collett's domicile over the past few days."

"I am glad you agree, Superintendent," Tony nodded, "because *that* is what I am counting on."

Superintendent Dawson thought a moment as he lit his pipe, then, after making sure it was burning to his satisfaction, he looked up at Tony, saying, "I suppose it *has* occurred to you, Childon, that should it turn out Lady Collett's stay in Mount Street becomes known in spite of your efforts, you too will come under censure?"

"That goes without saying," Tony told him, "however, it's not *my* reputation that concerns me, but Lady Collett's. When I told you that my feelings for her had neither compromised her reputation nor undermined her as a witness I meant it; it was true," then, looking straight at Superintendent Dawson, said unequivocally, "it still is."

"I never supposed otherwise," Superintendent Dawson told him, "but you must admit that it could do you and your newspapers a lot of harm."

"My newspapers need no defending, Superintendent," Tony told him firmly, "as for me," he smiled, "I can stand a lick or two!"

"That's as may be, but you don't need me to tell you…"

"No," Tony shook his head, "I don't." Upon seeing the slight crease which had descended onto Superintendent Dawson's forehead, Tony, although touched by his concern, could not resist saying, a look of pure amusement in his eyes, "Don't worry, Superintendent, if the worst comes to the worst I can always hightail it out of here and board the first available ship back to the States!"

Superintendent Dawson was not the first to succumb to Tony's easy manner and sense of humour, all the same he deemed it prudent not to respond as he had the very strong feeling that this extremely likeable young man could well undo his resolve and said, as matter-of-factly as he could, "I take it for granted Lady Collett's father will not say anything to the contrary?"

"Most unlikely, Superintendent," Tony shook his head. "I can't see Sir Miles saying or doing anything which could possibly expose his daughter to malicious gossip," going on to briefly explain what he was arranging with him.

Superintendent Dawson nodded, then, after pulling out his watch and seeing it wanted only fifteen minutes to two o'clock said that it was time he was taking his leave as not only had he things to attend to, but felt sure they did too to get the newspaper out for this evening's edition. Remaining only long enough to exchange a brief word with Bill and Jerry he wished them good afternoon, adding as he opened the door that he had no doubt he would be seeing them again before too long. Jerry, who also had things to do, not the least being paying a call on Mrs. Timms, stayed for just long enough to exchange far from polite opinions with Tony and Bill about Eliza Boon's attempts to save herself, before saying it was time he too was making tracks, whereupon he donned his hat and overcoat and left.

"So," Bill mused when they were alone, scanning the proof sheet he had picked up, "this is what you were scribbling away at, is it?"

"'Fraid so," Tony grinned.

Bill thought a moment. "You really think it will fool 'em?" He cocked his head.

"I sure hope so!" Tony said with feeling.

"And if it doesn't?" Bill wanted to know.

"Like I said," Tony smiled, "I can always…"

"Yeah, I know," Bill scorned, "you can always hightail it out of here and board the first available ship back to the States! Like hell you would!" he shot at him. "You're too much your old man's son to do something like that! But Dawson's right," he pointed out, "if this turns round and kicks you in the teeth…!"

"If it does," Tony told him calmly, "then so be it. Look Bill," he told him in response to the frustrated sigh which left his lips, "I know damn well Dawson's right about the harm malicious tongues can do, but my father did not raise me to believe that it was okay for me to throw someone to the wolves in order to save myself just because things get a little too hot. You were right, Bill," he nodded, "I *am* too much my father's son to hightail it out of here. Being a human being as well as a newspaperman carries responsibilities, that was one of the first things my father taught me, *you* know that."

"Sure," Bill sighed, "I know. He was a great guy; the best, and you're exactly like him, which is why I can see it's pointless saying anything more."

"Quite pointless, Bill," Tony smiled.

Bill thought a moment, asking at length, "You love her that much?"

"Yes," Tony nodded, "I love her that much."

"So," Bill pondered, "you really think this will work?" pulling the front page towards him and pointing at Tony's handwritten note about Eleanor being in Suffolk with her father.

"Well," Tony shrugged, walking round the desk to stand beside him, "we shall soon find out."

"We sure will!" Bill exclaimed, looking sceptically up at Tony.

"Well, if you can think of anything better," Tony nodded, "I'd sure like to hear it!"

"I can't," Bill told him firmly, "so we'll just have to trust to luck. Now though," he said meaningfully, "we've got a newspaper to get out; *two,* in case you'd forgotten! Unless, of course," he nodded, "you want the others to beat us to it!"

"You know, Bill," Tony said conversationally, "you really must do something about those ulcers of yours!"

"Perhaps if I didn't have you to worry about I wouldn't *have* ulcers!" to which Tony merely laughed as he settled himself beside Bill to begin the final preparations ready for the evening's run, all thoughts of banter forgotten as they worked uninterrupted together against the clock.

However, by the time Tony made ready to leave with a copy of *'The Daily Bulletin'* and *'The London Chronicler'* tucked under his arm it was almost half past four and Bill, after pointing out to him that he had been right when he said it would set Fleet Street alight, leaned back in his seat with a fresh cigar stuck between his teeth, looked up at Tony, saying seriously, "Hey, kiddo, you sure you're okay?"

The casualness of this enquiry did not fool Tony in the least. "Sure I'm sure," he smiled.

Bill sighed. "You wouldn't tell me if you weren't, would you?"

"So long, Bill," Tony grinned, closing the door quietly behind him.

Chapter Thirty-One

Mrs. Timms, having already decided she liked Lady Shipton, and her quick and shrewd appraisal of Sarah was favourable, their visit, within an hour of Tony's departure, was very much welcomed, and it was not long before the three women were enjoying a good gossip as well as a free exchange of views over a cup of tea in the privacy of Mrs. Timms's room. Pearl, having tried in vain to prise information out of Mrs. Timms about the goings-on, was agog with curiosity at such a distinguished visitor arriving on the doorstep so soon after the swell gent earlier, but the only response she received to her enquiry was a sharp reminder to get on with her work. Albert, although still somewhat surprised at the unexpected turn of events which had occurred and the unlawful activities of his late employer, nevertheless was only too happy to take the opportunity offered by Mrs. Timms's brief absence from the kitchen to flirt outrageously with Pearl, whose pouting disappointment at being kept in the dark was soon forgotten. The return of Ellen and Susan first thing this morning certainly gave an air of normality to twenty-nine Cavendish Square, but even though they were willing to continue carrying out their duties until Sir Braden's cousin took up residence or, at least, arrived at a decision about the domestic arrangements, nothing would induce them to set foot inside the study, much less stay in the house overnight. Their reluctance to so much as run a duster over the room was felt to be more than justified, even more so when they learned the truth from Mrs. Timms about Lady Collett and that far from suffering from a so-called nervous disorder as Sir Braden had continually led them to believe she had, over a period of many months, been subjected to the most appalling treatment from him. In view of this, they could quite well understand why Her Ladyship had left her husband to seek her father's protection in Suffolk, and therefore needed no persuading to unearth the trunks from the attics so that Mrs. Timms and Lady Shipton could pack away the rest of Lady Collett's clothing and belongings in readiness for her return to Bruton Street.

Everything in Eleanor's room was just as she had left it, and Beatrice, after exchanging significant glances with Sarah and Mrs. Timms, soon set to work to gather Eleanor's belongings, including the little French enamel clock and all her combs and brushes and other precious possessions which meant so much to her. Between the three of them they soon filled up the two huge trunks which would eventually be conveyed to Mount Street, but Beatrice, recognising Eleanor's urgent need to wear something other than her borrowed nightclothes in the meantime, set aside two dresses and other essential items of clothing and underwear which Sarah neatly packed into a large portmanteau to take back to Mount Street with them. Beatrice knew too that although Eleanor's feelings for Sir Braden were very far removed from love, at some point she was going to have to put herself into mourning, but for now the dark blue dress and the pale grey one which had been carefully folded and placed in the portmanteau would have to suffice. Mrs. Timms, in response to Beatrice's warm thanks as well as her reiterated assurance that she looked forward to welcoming her in Mount Street, dabbed her eye with the corner of her handkerchief, saying that she would be pleased to. "I know 'Is Lordship said you would not mind, m'lady, when 'e came 'ere earlier today," she told her.

"And he was quite right," Beatrice smiled. "You must know, Mrs. Timms, that you are more than welcome to visit in Mount Street whenever you wish."

"Thankin' you kindly, m'lady. Providin' of course," she nodded, "you're sure, m'lady."

"Quite sure," Beatrice smiled, laying a hand on her arm. "Lady Collett I know, is most eager to see you."

Eleanor was certainly eager to see Mrs. Timms as well as being most grateful to Beatrice for her kindness and generosity, not only for giving her sanctuary but also for providing her with every stitch of clothing she stood up in. When Eleanor had told Tony that she hoped she would never again have to set foot inside Cavendish Square she had meant it and although she knew she would have to cross the threshold at some point, the very thought of doing so made her shiver. When Beatrice had told her earlier this morning what she and Sarah intended, she had swallowed her fear and offered to go with them, but this Beatrice would not hear of, stating that apart from the fact that not one of her dresses would fit her and Eleanor could not leave the house in her nightclothes, she was still not fully recovered and certainly not to the point where she could walk abroad in this dreadfully cold weather, not only that, Beatrice had laughed, "but you are now supposedly in Suffolk with your father!" As Eleanor had momentarily forgotten this was how Tony planned to account for her absence from Cavendish Square as well as giving the lie to the fact that she had taken refuge in Mount Street she looked contrite, apologising for being so stupid as to forget, to which Beatrice hugged her, telling her that it was not surprising she had forgotten given everything that was happening. Perhaps not, but Eleanor could not help feeling a little guilty, nevertheless, several hours later the sight of Sarah opening the bulging portmanteau in front of her drove everything from her mind except being able to go downstairs and meet Tony fully dressed.

Sarah, who knew precisely what Eleanor was thinking, refrained from commenting that Mr. Tony, having seen her in her nightclothes and even spent more than one night in her room, seeing her fully dressed was really by the by, merely smiled indulgently as she gently brushed and pinned the thick blonde hair of the young woman who had captured his heart, telling her that she would be dressed all the sooner if she kept still instead of continually looking round at the clock. "Mr. Tony won't return home any the quicker!"

Eleanor knew it was true, but as the afternoon wore on the fluttering of excitement which had invaded the pit of her stomach earlier, resulting in her having to begin the letter to her father a second time due to her mind continually wandering and her slightly trembling fingers on the pen causing the ink to blot, gradually increased until unfurling into a breathless crescendo when, a few minutes after five o'clock, she heard Tony arrive. Beatrice, who had joined her in the drawing-room to spend a little time with her and to tell her that she had arranged for Bennett to have the envelope containing the two letters sent to the posting office, no sooner heard Tony arrive than she excused herself on some pretext, leaving Eleanor to wait excitedly for Tony to enter the drawing-room. She had the sneaking suspicion that Beatrice had deliberately engineered her brief departure to give her a moment or two alone with Tony by laughingly saying that she had just remembered what it was she had meant to speak to Nanny Susan about. "I knew it would come to me when I least expected it!" Beatrice cried, then, after affectionately bestowing a kiss upon her cheek, floated happily away. Through the half-opened door, Eleanor could hear brother and sister exchanging a few quiet words before Beatrice left him to hurriedly climb the stairs, then, waiting only long enough to discard his outdoor clothes, Tony was at the drawing-room door within a couple of strides, which he pushed unceremoniously open just as Eleanor rose to her feet.

For several moments neither of them moved nor spoke, but although Eleanor held Tony's look without any embarrassment the colour which flooded her cheeks at what she saw in his eyes merely confirmed what the man standing watching her already knew. Eleanor supposed that, especially now in view of her recent bereavement, she should really not be feeling like this, but the truth was even if she and Tony had met under different circumstances and her husband had not made her afraid of him or committed cold-blooded murder, she could not have stopped herself from falling in love with Tony. She had never felt this way before and instinctively knew she never would again, but as she watched him shut the door without a backward glance and walk towards her without taking his eyes off her, so overwhelming were her feelings that her legs, which were only now beginning to get their strength back, felt in imminent danger of collapsing under her.

Eleanor knew perfectly well that she was going to have to put herself into mourning, and whilst she would not even have considered for so much as a second flouting convention by not doing so, the very thought of wearing black to mourn a man she had hated and feared made her feel quite hypocritical. She fully intended to rectify her wardrobe as soon as her father returned to town and she placed herself once more under his protection in Bruton Street, but for now all that mattered was that she was with the man she loved, a man who had entered her life when she had least expected it and changed it forever.

"Bea told me I should find you in here," Tony smiled, an odd inflection in his voice, "but she didn't tell me just how beautiful you look," taking her hands in his and holding her at arm's-length.

"I was rather hoping you would think so," Eleanor managed unsteadily, not shrinking from the warmth in his eyes, her fingers moving in his, "particularly after all the trouble Sarah has taken to make me presentable. She and Beatrice have been so kind," she said earnestly. "I don't know what I should do without them."

"And *I,"* Tony told her in a deep voice, releasing her hands and drawing her gently into his arms, "don't know what I should do without you."

Although the colour deepened in her cheeks her heart soared at these words. "You don't?" she managed huskily.

"Too right I don't," he told her, his voice a caress. "You know something?" he smiled, to which she smiled and shook her head. "I have always known that I would know the only woman for me the moment I saw her, which is precisely what happened the instant I saw you through those opera glasses, but what I *didn't* know," he told her, his voice deepening, "was just how you would make me feel."

Removing her hands from his chest and bringing them to rest on his shoulders, she looked up at him, asking a little breathlessly, "How do you feel?"

Lowering his head and drawing her closer to him, he smiled, "Like the happiest and luckiest guy in the world!"

"Oh, Tony!" she cried fervently, folding her arms around his neck. "I do love you, so very much!"

"Like I said," he reminded her against her lips, "I sure am a lucky guy!" quite prepared to set aside the harsh realities which faced them for now as he proceeded to agreeably kiss her.

Like Tony, Eleanor knew there were practicalities which had to be dealt with that could not be shelved or set aside, but for now she was more than happy to relegate them to the back of her mind as she melted into him. Beatrice, whose cautious opening of the drawing-room door some minutes later not surprisingly went unnoticed, decided to leave the couple alone for a while longer making a discreet and silent exit wishing, and not for the first time, that Eleanor had met her brother before Sir Miles had tied her to Sir Braden Collett.

Dinner may have been a relaxed and happy affair but Tony was very conscious of how those newspaper articles which Eleanor had caught sight of and which he had tried to keep from her, at least for the time being, despite her valiant efforts to the contrary, had upset her. Tom and Beatrice, having scanned the front-pages, fully agreed with Tony that it would be better for him to discuss things with Eleanor alone rather than over the dinner table, played their part admirably by commenting on how pleased they were to see her looking more like her usual self, chatting about anything and everything except recent events or the official procedures which faced them. Eleanor was certainly grateful to them, but she knew she could neither delay facing the inevitable nor hide from the harsh realities, and no sooner was she alone with Tony in the rear sitting room than she laid a hand on his arm, saying with quiet resignation, "Tony, about those newspaper articles; people are going to say the most dreadful things, aren't they?"

Removing her hand from his arm and holding it in a firm warm clasp, he looked down at her, sighing, "Yes, I'm afraid they are."

She nodded. "I suspect it has already started."

"Yes," he sighed again, giving her hand a comforting squeeze, "I'd say it stands a pretty good chance. I'm sorry, Ellie," he shook his head, "I should have made sure I put those newspapers somewhere where you would not catch sight of them."

"No," she shook her head, "you must not be sorry; you have merely reported on what has happened and," she smiled bravely, "I was bound to read the newspapers at some point. I can't hide myself away from them indefinitely. It's just that... well," she faltered, "it's one thing knowing it will be in the newspapers, but quite another to actually see it." She paused, faltering a little, "I... I daresay that by tomorrow every newspaper will carry the story." He could not deny it. "Yes, of course," she nodded, "how stupid of me to think otherwise!"

"Ellie, my darling," Tony urged, "you must not think anyone will blame you; you are totally innocent and just as much a victim as Annie Myers and the others."

"It... it's not that," she shook her head, her fingers in trembling his, "it's just that... well, whatever my feelings for Braden it... it's all so horrible! Then, too," she told him fairly, "his cousin is going to find it very difficult to establish himself in the wake of what has happened!"

"Well, I can't deny that," Tony acknowledged on a sigh. "Unfortunately though, things like this always creates innocent casualties, but my main concern," he told her, "is for you."

She looked up at him, her eyes troubled. "Y-you mean the inquests and Braden's funeral arrangements?"

"Yes," he nodded, taking hold of her other hand in a comforting clasp as he told her as gently as he could about the very real possibility of her having to give evidence at the trial of Peterson and Eliza Boon as she was categorically denying everything.

Before Braden's brutal death at the hands of Peterson Eleanor's attendance at court to give evidence had been extremely unlikely due to her testimony being detrimental to him as her husband, but knowing that she may after all find herself standing in the witness-box with Eliza Boon sitting in the dock looking at her, filled her with dread, the thought making her shudder. "Oh, Tony!" she cried, burying her face into his shoulder, taking comfort from his arms as he wrapped them around her. "I can't bear the thought of it!"

"I'm sorry, my darling," Tony soothed. "I know it has come as a shock, but I had to tell you. I wish I could say the next few months are going to be easy, but I can't; they're going to be pretty rough." He felt another shudder run through her and, tightening his hold, asked softly, "You don't honestly think I would leave you to face it all alone, do you? You won't have to, I promise," he assured her. "My darling," he said earnestly, gently tilting her face in order for her to look up at him, "there may be nothing I can do to prevent the inevitable formalities from taking place or about arranging Collett's funeral, much less attending it, but even though I know your father will be with you I am going to be right there beside you come what may."

"I couldn't bear it if you weren't!" she cried. "Truly I could not!"

He smiled lovingly down at her. "Like I said," he told her, his voice a caress, "you're stuck with me – permanently." Without giving her time to respond to this, he spent the next few minutes agreeably proving his point, telling her a little unsteadily when his lips reluctantly released hers that although he knew it was for the best she resided with her father for the foreseeable future, he could not bear the thought of being parted from her. "I love you, Ellie!" he pressed urgently into her hair. "And if I could take you away from all of this I would, but although I cannot see your father failing to give you his support over the next few months," he told her, "I shall be right there at your side."

"Never leave it!" she begged huskily.

"There's no chance of that," Tony assured her. "From here on in I'm a permanent fixture in your life, so much so," he told her warmly, "that there will be no escape from me; not now, not ever; not even when you are in Bruton Street. In fact," he told her, kissing the top of her head, "your father could well be forgiven for thinking I had taken up residence."

"If only you could," she said wistfully, leaning her head comfortably against his chest.

"When all of this is out of the way," he told her in a deep voice, holding her tightly against him, "and your period of mourning is over, I fully intend to marry you, and you and I will never be parted again." He felt the tremor which ran through her at this, but giving her no time to utter the words forming on her lips he proceeded to kiss her to their mutual satisfaction.

"When do you think my father will return to town?" she managed when she finally recovered her breath.

"Well," Tony sighed, "since I understand from Tom that your father most probably does not have a telephone," to which she shook her head in confirmation, "I cannot see him receiving our letters until the day after tomorrow at the earliest, therefore I don't expect to see him back in town before the end of the week. Regrettably though," he sighed again, "it means the chances are very good that he will read the story in the newspapers before he receives them."

"Yes," she said sadly, "I have thought of that too and what a terrible shock it will be for him."

Tony agreed to it, but he doubted very much that Sir Miles Tatton, who he felt sure needed no reminding as to the kind of man Sir Braden Collett was, would be as shocked as Eleanor believed, but keeping this to himself Tony looked down at her, asking gently, "Ellie, will you do something for me?"

She nodded. "You know I will, anything."

"I know it's difficult," he said softly, "but promise me you won't worry too much over all of this."

"I promise," she nodded.

He smiled and, stroking her soft cheek with the back of his forefinger, said considerately, "My darling, I know it's not much comfort at the moment, but even if I had not come along when I did, the truth would have come out sooner or later."

"Yes, I know, but my darling," she said tenderly, looking lovingly up at him, "I can't tell you how glad I am that you did come along when you did, not only because you relieved me of an intolerable burden but also because you brought love into my life; a love you must know," she told him huskily, "I cannot possibly live without!"

As there were no words adequate to describe how he felt upon hearing this, Tony simply gathered her in his arms to spend the next few minutes letting his kisses do it for him.

As Tony had rightly surmised Sir Miles Tatton needed no reminding as to the kind of man Sir Braden Collett was, but his volatile temperament and aggressive manner notwithstanding Sir Miles had, at no time, believed him capable of committing cold-blooded murder.

Collett's brutal death at the hands of his accomplice, ensuing as a direct result of their actions, whilst tragic, had, at least in Sir Miles's view, been nothing short of poetic justice and, try as he did, he could rouse neither sympathy nor regret. When it came to Collett's treatment of Eleanor Sir Miles was profoundly shocked because although he had never suspected Collett of ill-treating her he had nevertheless believed that his behaviour towards his daughter was, for the most part, rather harsh and, on the occasions she had visited him in Bruton Street, he had detected from her pale face and lacklustre eyes that she was very far from happy. Sir Miles had naturally put this down to the fact that through his own reckless actions he had forced her into a marriage he himself had no mind for and she had never wanted, but whilst she had never once so much as intimated that Collett regularly mistreated her his own fatherly instincts should have told him that more than being married to a man she did not love was the cause of her lassitude. Considering that her visits to him had always been in her husband's company it was hardly surprising they were unable to converse privately, much less Eleanor telling him the truth about her marriage, but as he brooded over the contents of those letters and the stark facts staring ruthlessly up at him from the newspapers lying on his desk, he berated himself for the momentary madness which had brought his daughter so much suffering as well as being blinded to the truth which had been right under his nose.

Of course, this had not been printed in the newspapers, for which he knew this Lord Childon was responsible, but having read his letter which had explained the circumstances in far more detail than Eleanor's as well as his feelings for her, Sir Miles had immediately understood the significance about her being in Suffolk and that she would be returning to town with him. He knew he was most fortunate in his household staff, all of whom had been with him for many years, and knew there was no risk of any one of them revealing the fact that Eleanor, far from having joined him in Suffolk, had taken refuge in Mount Street. There had, of course, been an exchange of letters between himself and his daughter during the time he had been out of town, and whilst Eleanor's had been somewhat guarded, relating only to mundane items of news to which not even Sir Braden Collett could take an exception, although Sir Miles had no doubt that he had skimmed his eyes over them before they were posted, he had been a little surprised at how she had only lightly touched upon what had happened in this latest letter. But one thing if nothing else he had gleaned from it and that was she was by no means indifferent to this Childon, but whilst Sir Miles could claim acquaintanceship with his grandfather this young man, quite naturally considering he had been born on the other side of the Atlantic, was quite unknown to him, he was nevertheless very conscious of the debt he owed him, as well as to the Shiptons. He knew Beatrice Shipton far better than her husband, perfectly understandable given that she had been a close friend of his late wife, but the fact remained that if it had not been for them heaven alone knew what would have become of his daughter.

It may not be within his power to undo either his uncharacteristic actions of that night or the terrible consequences they had for Eleanor, but Sir Miles was nevertheless determined to do all he could to make up for it. Despite what people may say should they ever discover his misdemeanour he dearly loved his daughter, indeed such was the remorse he felt upon learning the true extent of her unhappiness and fear he was instantly filled with shame and self-disgust, and because he could not bear the thought of Eleanor being hurt any more, and certainly not from malicious gossip, he therefore issued instructions to prepare for an immediate return to town.

If it were at all possible for Eleanor to remain in Mount Street until such time that she and Tony could be married she was honest enough to admit that she would certainly do so, but unfortunately such an option was out of the question; so too was resuming residence in Cavendish Square, the very thought of which was too horrendous to contemplate. To live in a house where her husband had brutally murdered Sir Philip Dunscumbe, and in his own study, the very room in which he had himself been brutally murdered by his accomplice, was really quite repugnant to her, added to which were her own painful memories of being kept a virtual prisoner within its walls and, for these reasons, she was by no means averse to returning to Bruton Street. She knew that as Braden's widow Cavendish Square was her home or at least until such time that his cousin came to certain decisions which, considering his large family, she felt sure would not include her continued residence, in which case he may feel himself duty bound to provide for her, a circumstance that she found insupportable, particularly as any provision he made her would naturally come out of his inheritance from Braden. That Braden had made provision for her himself in his will, which would not only include her financial security but her domicile as well, was really a foregone conclusion, even though he had never discussed his will with her, but the truth was Eleanor wanted nothing from Braden – nothing at all! She supposed that as a last resort she could set up her own establishment until her period of mourning was over and she and

Tony could be married, but whilst this was a far better prospect than having to live on what Braden had bequeathed her, not only would it give rise to gossip and speculation, but something she was really rather disinclined to do. The allowance from her father had naturally ceased upon her marriage and although she had not touched the money her mother had left her it fell far short of what she would need to maintain herself over an indefinite period, and knew that the only option available to her was removing to Bruton Street. But as she neither hated nor blamed her father for that momentary lapse of judgement which had brought about her marriage to Braden, on the contrary she loved him very much, she knew no qualms about returning to live under his protection for the foreseeable future.

Eleanor knew Tony was aware of her concerns even though she had not voiced them, but when she raised the matter with him the following morning after breakfast in the sitting room, he easily put into perspective her immediate domestic uncertainties in that relaxed yet assured way which never failed to set her mind at rest. "My darling," he told her simply, taking her in his arms, "you will live happily and contentedly with your father in Bruton Street until your period of mourning is over," he smiled, tilting her chin up a little, "and when it is I shall formally ask his permission to marry you, then, having given it, we shall be married just as soon as it is humanly possible to arrange it," stemming the words forming on her lips by contentedly kissing her. "All I want you to think about from now on," he told her in a deep voice when he reluctantly released her, "is our future together."

"That is such a very easy thing for me to do," she smiled, "in fact," she confessed a little shyly, "I think about it all the time."

"So do I," he said lovingly as he lowered his head, "but agreeable though these thoughts are they do absolutely nothing to make the waiting any easier!"

"They don't?" she managed huskily.

"Huh, huh!" his kisses not only silencing any response but more than adequately proving his point, so much so that she felt quite bereft when he left the house some minutes later.

Within less than hour of Tony leaving the house to see Bill Beatrice announced that she too had found it necessary to go out, but fingers crossed she should not be gone too long. "I would not leave you alone," she assured Eleanor, folding her in a scented embrace and fondly kissing her cheek, "if I was not convinced that you are quite safe here."

Eleanor knew this was true, but having lived in fear for so long she could not help feeling a little nervous as she heard the front door close behind Beatrice, but thanks to Alice, who, despite Nanny Susan's strictures, had wandered downstairs to the rear sitting room as soon as she had turned her back dragging her battered bear behind her, whatever apprehension Eleanor felt soon left her.

"Are you Mummy's friend?" Alice asked, her wide blue eyes looking questioningly up at Eleanor.

"Yes, I'm Mummy's friend, Eleanor; and you," she smiled, looking down at a miniature replica of her mother, "must be Alice." Upon receiving a confirming nod to this, Alice then introduced her to her friend, whereupon Eleanor enquired as to the reason for Bertie's plaster, sadly curling up at the edges, and was confidingly told all about his accident. Having condoled sympathetically, taken her upstairs to apply a new plaster to Bertie's forehead followed by being irresistibly pulled into Toby and Patrick's room in order for Alice to show her Toby's newt, a most pleasurable hour had elapsed. "I think it's beastly," Alice shuddered, "but Uncle Tony thinks it's super!" she told Eleanor as she shut the drawer of the dresser. "I like Uncle Tony, don't you?"

"Yes," Eleanor managed, feeling the colour creep into her cheeks.

"Next to Mummy and Daddy," Alice confided, tucking her hand into Eleanor's and looking innocently up at her, "I love Uncle Tony the most in the world. Don't you?"

Thankfully for Eleanor, who really had no idea how to respond to this, Nanny Susan entered the room, gently scolding her charge for leaving the nursery while at the same time hoping that she had not been a nuisance to Her Ladyship's guest. Eleanor, assuring her that Alice had been no such thing, on the contrary they had spent a very happy hour together, Alice then wished her a reluctant but affectionate farewell before following Nanny Susan out of her brothers' room.

A visit from Mrs. Timms shortly afterwards came as a most welcome and delightful surprise for Eleanor, who thoroughly enjoyed the agreeable hour or so they spent together. Apart from lightly touching upon recent events, waving aside Eleanor's gratitude for everything she had done, Mrs. Timms made no further mention of them, but if this rather shrewd woman noticed the difference in Eleanor since she had been in Mount Street she had not far to look for the reason. Without doubt, Mrs. Timms could not bring to mind one occasion during the time Eleanor had resided in Cavendish Square when she had seen her looking so happy and contented, but even though she kept this reflection to herself she was honest enough to admit that if anyone were to ask her she would have to say that her young mistress, despite the fading bruises, was positively glowing. So too did Sir Miles when setting eyes on his daughter two days later.

Despite his failure to curb his son's reckless gambling and his own frustration in continually being obliged to settle the debts which had accrued because of it, resulting in Reginald's eventual deportation to Ceylon as well as his own unwitting contribution in bringing about Eleanor's distasteful marriage, Sir Miles was a loving and devoted father. Although Eleanor had never been given cause to either doubt or question her father's affection, she knew he was not a man to readily demonstrate it, and was a little surprised, upon his arrival in Mount Street, to find herself being warmly embraced, but so happy was she to see him that she eagerly returned it. Like Mrs. Timms, Sir Miles saw beneath his daughter's fading bruises as well as the looks exchanged between her and Lord Childon and knew that neither had exaggerated their feelings for one another in their letters to him, but in spite of this Sir Miles inwardly winced at the diminishing discolouration and, as he gently traced her face with his forefinger, mentally berated himself for being the one responsible for all that had befallen her. "Forgive me, my dear," he said earnestly.

"There is nothing to forgive," Eleanor smiled.

"Indeed there is," he sighed. "If I had not…"

"Ssh," she soothed, taking hold of his hand, "that is over and done," she assured him softly.

"Had I known!" he pressed against her fingers as he held them tightly in his gloved hands.

"But you didn't," she assured him softly.

"Had I have had the least ounce of courage…!" Then, as if recollecting they were not alone, he pulled himself together and somewhat uncomfortably reiterated his apologies to Tom and Beatrice for calling upon them unannounced as well as his gratitude for all their kindness to his daughter.

Beatrice smiled and disclaimed, stating that no thanks were in the least necessary, and Tom, assuring Sir Miles that although the circumstances surrounding Eleanor's stay were to be regretted, it had nevertheless been a pleasure to have her in Mount Street. Sir Miles nodded, but it was Tony to whom he owed his thanks for learning the full sum of events and to whom he opened his mind a few minutes later in the privacy of Tom's study.

For a modest and rather private man like Sir Miles Tatton, who not only had an intrinsic dislike of scandal and gossip but one whose whole life had always been conducted in a manner which was unimpeachable, his uncharacteristic actions of that never to be forgotten evening, resulting in his daughter's marriage to Sir Braden Collett, went against all his principles. That his reprehensible conduct had never seen the light of day made no difference; he knew he would never be able to reconcile it with his conscience, but this business of his late son-in-law's illegal activities, guaranteed to catapult them into the public eye, shocked and appalled him. "This is a bad business, Childon!" he said gravely, when Tony had come to the end of his account of Collett's dealings.

"Yes, a very bad business," Tony confirmed quietly, walking over to where a table stood against the far wall on which stood several glasses and decanters.

"I don't know when I have been more shocked!" Sir Miles exclaimed, taking the whisky and soda Tony handed him.

"Not very edifying!" Tony nodded, resuming his seat.

Sir Miles stared broodingly down into the fire for a moment, then, raising his eyes to Tony, said, "And you say Eleanor walked into this brutal act which Collett perpetrated against Sir Philip?"

"Unfortunately, yes," Tony sighed. "Collett had no way of knowing that he would receive a visit from Sir Philip charging him with being responsible for his brother's death or that the concert would end ahead of time bringing Eleanor home sooner than he thought. I suspect the last thing Collett expected," he inclined his head, "was to see his wife enter the study at the precise moment he was committing cold-blooded murder."

"That she should have witnessed such cruel villainy!" Sir Miles exclaimed, shaking his head, looking suddenly so much older, his thin face pale and drawn. "It's iniquitous! When I think of what they did to her!" he groaned, covering his eyes with his hand as if to shut out the horrendous images which flashed into his mind. "If only she had confided in me."

"Well," Tony told him grimly, "I'm afraid she was given no opportunity to confide in anyone. As I understand it even Eleanor's visits to you were under supervision."

"Yes," Sir Miles acknowledged on a sigh, "they were. Collett was always with her. More than once I…" he broke off. "To think that I…!" he cried, his voice somewhat ragged. Then, pulling himself together, said, "It appears, Childon, that your newspapers have shown far more circumspection than the others I have been privileged to see over the last couple of days," adding, not without a touch of bitterness as he waved one of the offending newspapers he had fished out of his pocket at Tony, "I see they have wasted no time in delving into my daughter's reasons for supposedly joining me in Suffolk."

"It is unfortunate, of course," Tony agreed, "but however much we may dislike it," he said realistically, "there is nothing I or Superintendent Dawson can do to prevent it."

"Are you saying that members of Collett's staff have spoken to reporters!" Sir Miles cried, aghast.

"Not to mine," Tony said firmly, "but I can't deny that half of Fleet Street has virtually laid siege to twenty-nine Cavendish Square since my newspapers ran this story, and whilst I can vouch for the continued discretion of Mrs. Timms, who has proved herself very much our friend," he nodded, "I think you can take it as a pretty safe bet that one or the other of Collett's staff has said something. As for the rest of Fleet Street, it seems to be split between Collett's cousin, who, I understand, has a horde of reporters camped on his doorstep, while the remainder," he informed him, "are either buzzing around Scotland Yard like a swarm of bees or hovering expectantly in Bruton Street awaiting your return in company with Eleanor."

Sir Miles looked horror-struck. "Are you saying," he managed, "that they expect us to talk to them?"

"I am very much afraid that they do," Tony confirmed quietly.

Sir Miles thought a moment. "These newspaper reporters, are you saying they're paying Collett's staff for information?" he asked, appalled.

"I can't say for certain, but that cannot be discounted." Tony shook his head.

"But can't you stop them?" Sir Miles wanted to know.

"They're not my reporters, Sir Miles. Besides," Tony reminded him, "it *is* a free press."

"But this is monstrous!" Sir Miles cried, his brow creasing.

"I can see why you think so," Tony acknowledged, "but now the cat's out of the bag so to speak it's pretty much fair game and," he admitted truthfully, "speaking as a newspaperman I can well understand that."

"And speaking as the man who loves my daughter," Sir Miles demanded, "do you condone such methods?"

"I should have thought that the methods I have employed to try to protect Eleanor from scandal and gossip would more than adequately have answered that, Sir Miles," Tony remarked coolly.

A tinge of colour crept into those thin cheeks at this. "Yes, of course, forgive me," Sir Miles conceded. "I am well rebuked!"

"No rebuke was intended, Sir Miles," Tony assured him, "but however much you may deplore what you deem a gross intrusion by the press, the fact remains that the truth will come out at the inquests about Collett's treatment of her, in fact," he nodded, "I fail to see how it can possibly be avoided." When Sir Miles made no reply to this, Tony pointed out, "The Coroner will undoubtedly ask some very pertinent questions, none of which Eleanor can refuse to answer, however," he sighed, "the one saving grace to come out of all this is that her reputation remains untarnished. No one outside ourselves knows that I came upon her trying to escape and brought her here, where she has been ever since. All that will most likely be revealed is that Eleanor, being subjected to yet another brutal assault by her husband following their return home from the Kirkmichaels' party, took refuge with you in Suffolk. Even supposing some of Collett's staff have been financially induced to talk to reporters," he pointed out, "thanks to Mrs. Timms, who is most sincerely attached to Eleanor, they can't tell them anything more damaging than that Collett had been brutally mistreating her from the beginning and put her frequent absences down to nervous disorders instead of recovering from a vicious beating to prevent them from knowing how he treated her."

A multitude of thoughts chased one another in Sir Miles's brain, but after several moments of what seemed to be deep mental absorption he looked up from the contents in his glass, saying, "I had hoped to return to Bruton Street with Eleanor, that was the main reason I came directly here after leaving the railway station, but if the house is presently surrounded by reporters as you say," he sighed, "I don't want to subject her to their intrusive questions."

"I can understand that," Tony acknowledged, "but you must agree that nothing will more surely give the lie to what we are trying to do than arriving on your own doorstep without your daughter, especially as we have made it known that she has been with you in Suffolk for the past week."

"Yes," Sir Miles sighed at length, having given it some thought, "you are quite right, of course, but I would give anything to spare her any more distress. You must know without me saying it," he shrugged helplessly, "that I stand very much in your sister's debt; her care of Eleanor has been such that I can never discharge the obligation I am under, but I realise the sooner Eleanor is safely back in Bruton Street the better," finishing off his whisky and soda. "You know, Childon," he heaved a sigh, "this business is worse than I thought! Collett, of all people!" he exclaimed, aghast. "It is beyond everything!" he cried. "To think that he involved himself in murder and what else besides, not to mention regularly visiting a certain type of establishment and then ending up being killed himself by the hand of an accomplice! And as for that woman he replaced Mary with, Eliza Boon, well," he shrugged, "I never liked her, but I never suspected the truth of it for one moment, and Mitchell," he shook his head, "it was such a wicked thing to do to him! Then, of course," he nodded, "there were her attempts on your life…" He shook his head, bewildered. "It goes beyond all bounds!"

"I'm afraid risks come with the territory!" Tony shrugged. "Although," he admitted, pulling a face, Bill's frustration coming forcibly to mind, "I don't mind saying they *were* a little too close to home for comfort."

"I will not disagree with that," Sir Miles nodded.

"Neither did my editor," Tony pointed out ruefully.

Sir Miles thought a moment, his brow creased. "About Eleanor; I realise of course that there is no way she can avoid attending the inquests, but will she have to give evidence in court, do you think?"

"I can't tell yet." Tony shook his head. "I hope not, but when I spoke to Superintendent Dawson this morning he told me that Peterson is still singing the same song as he did in Hertford Street. As for Eliza Boon," he sighed, "she is still denying any knowledge of or participation in what happened."

"So then…" Sir Miles began.

"I'm afraid it depends on how good Eliza Boon's defence counsel is and whether or not the jury can be persuaded into believing her guilt,"

Tony told him. "If they believe Peterson, and we must hope they do," he nodded, "then not only will he convict himself out of his own mouth, but Eliza Boon too will be found guilty."

"But if they don't," Sir Miles said hopefully, "then surely this Simms woman…?"

Tony shook his head. "'Fraid not! There is no way the prosecution would even consider calling her as a witness as the defence would tear her character to shreds, and should she even get to the point of telling the court what she overheard, the chances are very good that it would be discredited on the grounds of hearsay. Not only that," he told him, "but no one other than myself, Superintendent Dawson and my editor knows she exists, which is why there has been no mention made of her in any of the newspapers."

Having considered this, Sir Miles nodded, sighing, "Well, I hope I am not an unfeeling man, but it is to be hoped that Eliza Boon and Peterson get what they deserve, preferably without Eleanor having to give evidence. As for Collett," he said firmly, "I cannot help thinking he came by his just desserts; for his brutal treatment of Eleanor if nothing else!"

"I doubt very much whether you are alone in thinking that," Tony inclined his head, "but you will certainly get no argument from me on that score!"

"I never liked Collett, I know," Sir Miles admitted, "a most disagreeable and argumentative man, but I never thought him capable of such infamy as this!"

"And yet," Tony reminded him civilly, "you permitted him to marry your daughter."

Sir Miles, not shrinking from the accusation in those dark grey eyes, admitted on a sigh, "I served my daughter a very bad turn, Childon, for which I shall never forgive myself. I assure you," he nodded, "I am most conscious of it."

"If it is of any consolation at all," Tony told him, "Eleanor does not blame you."

"No, I know," Sir Miles acknowledged. Then, looking straight at Tony, asked, "And you?"

"I think you know the answer to that," Tony told him candidly, returning his look unflinchingly. "Whilst I easily acquit you of being a practiced card cheat, because of your actions that night," he nodded, "committed with whatever reason or motive in mind, between you, you and Collett must certainly be held responsible for all she has endured."

"Good God!" Sir Miles cried, leaning forward in his seat. "Do you *really* believe that I would have sat back and allowed his treatment of her to continue had I known?" he demanded.

"No," Tony shook his head, "in fact, I feel quite sure that you would have done everything possible to put a stop to it even at the risk of your reputation, but the fact remains that however out of character it was for you to execute a sleight of hand," he acknowledged, throwing the end of his cigarette onto the fire, "in doing so you not only gave Collett a reason for forcing your hand into agreeing to his marrying Eleanor, a man whom you knew full well she hated and feared as well as being an aggressive bully, but effectively gave him licence to treat her in any way he chose, and *that*, Sir Miles," he told him unequivocally, "is something I find hard to forgive."

"I see you are a man who believes in plain speaking, Childon," Sir Miles commented without rancour.

"I'm sorry if that offends you but…"

"It doesn't," Sir Miles shook his head, "on the contrary I much prefer to deal with a man who is not afraid to speak his mind, but you must now allow me to speak mine," he nodded. "I may have had no hand in Collett's crimes, but I need no reminding of the part I played in all Eleanor has suffered, believe me," he assured him, "I am aware that the blame lies with me. I knew perfectly well the kind of man Collett was and how Eleanor felt about him, which is why I refused his requests to pay his addresses to her, and," he sighed, "in the normal course of events nothing would have induced me to change my mind, but as you know," he shrugged, "circumstances intervened which rendered it necessary for me to renege on my refusal. Very well," he conceded upon seeing the look which crossed Tony's face at this, "I was more concerned with protecting my reputation than ensuring my daughter's happiness, but whatever you may think, Childon," he said firmly, "I am sincerely attached to my daughter and no one regrets my decision more than I do indeed," he admitted, "it makes me quite ashamed and," he inclined his head, "if it were at all possible for me to turn the clock back and undo my indiscretion as well as what resulted from it I would gladly do so, but I cannot. *However*," he stressed, "it is my intention to try to make her future as happy as I possibly can."

"*That*, Sir Miles," Tony told him categorically, "is my intention as well."

"You may be thinking it a little late in the day for me to be expressing fatherly concern," Sir Miles said a little wryly, "but I am glad we agree on that, Childon."

"I do not doubt your fatherly concern," Tony assured him, "or your affection for Eleanor, but *you* Sir Miles," he nodded, "must not doubt *me* when I tell you that I love your daughter and fully intend to marry her just as soon as her period of mourning is over."

Sir Miles eyed him thoughtfully for a moment before saying, "Eleanor's letter to me, though not as detailed as your own, nevertheless left me in no doubt as to her feelings for you, and whilst I have not yet spoken to her about it, not that I need to," he shrugged, "because I only have to look at her to know that she loves you very much and is happier than I have seen her in a long time, but in view of what you have told me about wishing to marry her just as soon as her period of mourning is over, I feel it only fair to point out to you that she only turned twenty little more than five months ago and will not reach her majority until she is twenty-five, which means that even though she is now a widow," he informed him, "should it happen that she wishes to marry again before then, she will need my permission to do so."

"So I understand," Tony replied calmly.

"In which case…"

"Are you telling me that you would withhold your permission?" Tony broke in steadily, looking directly at him.

"And if I did withhold my permission?" Sir Miles raised an eyebrow. "You would disregard it; is that what you are you saying?"

"*That*, Sir Miles," Tony confirmed evenly, "is precisely what I am saying."

"Yes," Sir Miles mused, looking thoughtfully across at Tony sitting quite unperturbed opposite him, "that is what I thought you would say; so," he smiled, a gleam of approval in his pale blue eyes, "it is perhaps as well that I shan't withhold my consent. Do not get to thinking," Sir Miles explained, "that it is because you are a very different kettle of fish to Collett, any fool can see that you are by far a better man than he ever was, nor is it because of your title or money or that I feel a reward is due to you for everything you have done for my daughter, but because any man who is not afraid to speak up for the woman he loves as you have just done," Sir Miles told him, "even to her father, has more than adequately proved not only how much she means to him, but that he is more than worthy to marry her. There is no need to say anything." Sir Miles raised a stalling hand as Tony opened his mouth to speak. "For me to deprive my daughter of the happiness she deserves with the man she clearly loves," he explained, "as well as forbidding you to visit in Bruton Street, would not only be unforgivable of me," he nodded, "but infinitely worse than anything I have so far inflicted on her," rising to his feet. "You have spoken your mind very plainly, Childon," he smiled, "and I think none the less of you for it," holding out his hand. "I think we can say," he nodded, "that we understand one another."

"I think so," Tony smiled, rising to his feet and gripping the hand held out to him, "and thank…"

"There is no need to thank me," Sir Miles broke in, shaking his head.

"Nevertheless," Tony smiled, "I do so all the same."

"I stand very much in your debt, Childon," Sir Miles told him sincerely.

"Not at all, Sir Miles," Tony disclaimed.

"You say that," Sir Miles nodded, "but you and I know the truth of it! You have behaved precisely how I would expect a man of your…"

Tony, looking down into the upturned face of his future father-in-law, smiled, saying, not a little ruefully, "I'm no paragon or knight in shining armour, Sir Miles; I assure you I am neither. Despite my money and title I'm just an ordinary guy who loves your daughter and who has done everything possible to protect her and can't wait to make her his own."

Sir Miles, who did not need to have this explained indeed its meaning was plain enough, merely nodded his head before allowing Tony to escort him out of the study.

As returning to Cavendish Square was something Eleanor could not bring herself even to consider and remaining in Mount Street was out of the question, she knew perfectly well that returning to Bruton Street was the only practical course open to her, besides which, she loved her father very much. Even so, somewhere deep inside her she had rather hoped her departure from Mount Street would not be quite yet, but although she was naturally pleased to see her father his arrival had killed this at a stroke, and it was with a tear in her eye that she said goodbye to Beatrice and Tom, and Sarah, having brought her portmanteau downstairs with the promise that she would make sure the rest of her belongings would be safely delivered to Bruton Street tomorrow, sniffed into her handkerchief. Only the knowledge, imparted to her by Tony in a private moment in the small sitting room before Eleanor left, that her father had not forbidden him to visit her, rendered her parting from him more bearable, taking solace as he held her in his arms, telling her in a voice as ragged as her own that when this was all over they would never be parted again before his lips eventually claimed hers.

Chapter Thirty-Two

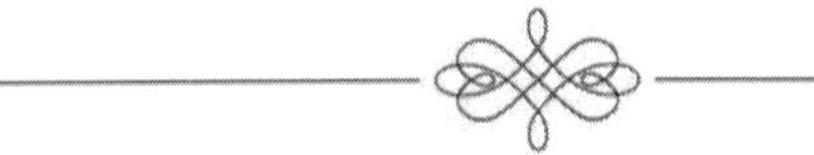

As Tony was not only known to every editor in Fleet Street and to most of the reporters congregating expectantly outside Sir Miles Tatton's house in Bruton Street but also as being the one who had uncovered the story and whose newspapers were the first to run with it which, as he had rightly predicted to Bill, set Fleet Street alight, his visits were clearly deemed to signify that Lady Collett had granted him an exclusive interview. As Tony said nothing to disabuse them of this, some of them, deciding it was pointless hanging around any longer, began to disperse, but the remainder, hopeful of gleaning something, resolutely stood their ground, but when, several days later, Eleanor, in company with her father, attended the inquests, not only were the press benches inside the Coroner's Court packed to capacity but also a horde of expectant reporters eagerly assembled outside.

As Sir Braden Collett's death was inextricably linked with that of Mitchell, the Coroner had taken the decision to conduct the two inquests in one session, a circumstance which Eleanor regarded as a relief, especially when she alighted from the carriage to find a multitude of reporters suddenly converge upon her. Beneath her black veil her face was alarmingly pale and as she clung to her father's arm as they tried to forge a path to the steps leading into the building, not only were they under siege by the incessant clicking of cameras as reporters tried to capture them arriving at court on film, but jostled and shoved and subjected to a barrage of questions, all of which her father refused to answer and Eleanor because she was in no emotional state to do so.

As it was impossible for Tony to arrive at the Coroner's Court in company with Eleanor and her father as it could well lead to tongues wagging, the very thing he was striving to avoid, he had instead made his way there from Mount Street with Tom and Beatrice. Leaving them to find a seat Tony stood just inside the vestibule waiting for Eleanor and her father to arrive, not at all surprised to find half of Fleet Street waiting for them, but the sight of her being besieged by its rowdy representatives proved too much for him to bear, and it was with a total disregard as to how his actions could be construed that he ran down the steps and, without any apparent effort whatsoever, made his way to her side. His reassuring hand beneath her elbow considerably calmed her, filling her with the strength she badly needed, but although she dared not look up at him for fear of betraying herself, the relief she felt at his presence easily conveyed itself to the man who wished he could have spared her this.

The Coroner's Court, filled to the rafters with interested onlookers, all of whom were giving their own opinions to their neighbour, fell silent the moment Eleanor walked in with her father and, for one awful moment, she thought she was going to faint. She did not, but it was only by a superhuman effort that she somehow managed to overcome it sufficiently to allow her father to lead her to a seat at the front while Tony took his own beside Tom and Beatrice in the second row.

Had the inquest related to someone other than Sir Braden Collett, a prominent and respected member of society, the Coroner, an experienced man in his late fifties, knew perfectly well that the courtroom would probably only be half full. As it was every seat and standing space was taken with not another fraction of an inch to be found, necessitating the police constables on duty to bar entrance to those who had arrived late but still hopeful of being able to gain admittance. Not surprisingly, being denied entry did not mean they were going away, and since it was clear they all preferred to congregate outside in the foyer for fear of missing something, one of the police constables was instantly sent out to stay with them and keep order. The Coroner, having warned the assembled company that he would not tolerate any cries or other such protestations or outbursts and that should such interruptions occur he would have no hesitation in clearing the room and conducting the hearing in camera, then placed his spectacles on his nose and, after reading the findings of the autopsy reports for Sir Braden Collett and George Edward Mitchell, began recounting the series of events which had brought them here today.

But the series of events, although calmly and impartially described by that diligent professional, nevertheless produced precisely the kind of response that Eleanor had feared; the shocked gasps, scandalised shakes of the head and even barely stifled sniggers, leaving her sickened and filled with the overwhelming need to run away and hide. A comforting word in her ear by her father went a long way to steadying her nerves, but it was knowing that Tony was sitting right behind her that gave her the strength to see these most painful proceedings through to the bitter end. But the bitter end seemed a long time in coming as Superintendent Dawson and Tony were the first two to be called, both of whom answered the Coroner's questions directly and to the point, then, after what seemed to Eleanor like a never-ending list of witnesses, the moment she had dreaded arrived when the Coroner's voice, authoritative but by no means unsympathetic, called, "Lady Collett."

An expectant buzz went around the courtroom and every eye turned upon the young woman whose legs felt in imminent danger of collapsing under her with every step she took to the witness stand. The spectators, eager to see the face which had been kept veiled throughout the proceedings, looked with keen interest as Eleanor's gloved fingers slowly raised the length of sheer black tulle over her head to reveal a face which, despite the pallor and haunted expression, looked absurdly youthful.

Whenever Eleanor looked back on this most harrowing and traumatic morning she would never be able to say with any degree of certainty how she had managed to answer the questions put to her following the Coroner's reminder, "Lady Collett, I would remind you that this is not a court of law but a Coroner's Court convened to ascertain the circumstances surrounding the death of your husband Sir Braden Collett and not to determine his guilt or innocence, but merely to ascertain the circumstances leading up to his death and that of George Edward Mitchell, butler, and so it will be necessary for me, however distressing," he nodded, "to establish certain facts," to which Eleanor could do no more than nod. After answering question and after question about Mitchell; the last time she had seen him alive; the length of time Mitchell had been in service to the Collett family; what her husband had told her about his dismissal; what explanation he had offered for bringing Peterson into the household and many more, it was therefore with relief that Eleanor heard the Coroner say to the police constable, "A chair for Lady Collett." Waiting until she had sat down and determining she felt able to continue, the Coroner resumed his questioning, but very soon found it necessary to point out, after receiving a nod of her head in response to a question, "I realise this is most distressing for you, Lady Collett," he acknowledged considerately, "but I must ask you to tender verbal replies to my questions."

"Yes," she managed, "I-I'm sorry."

Mrs. Timms, sitting behind Beatrice, had recourse to her handkerchief as she heard her young mistress falteringly answer the questions put to her, whilst Pearl, regardless of the fact that her mistress had been beaten, bullied and kept a virtual prisoner, sat forward in her seat with her chin propped in her hands next to Mrs. Timms as she eagerly drank in every word and gory detail, never having experienced anything as remotely exciting as this in her life before.

Eleanor, upon being asked if, before the distressing events which had brought them here today, she had any knowledge of her husband's regular visits to a certain type of establishment she choked a barely audible 'no'.

"So when you first encountered Eliza Boon you had no idea that she had presided over the establishment your husband had frequented?"

"No," Eleanor replied huskily.

"And James Peterson," the Coroner raised an enquiring eyebrow, "you had never met him before either?"

"No," Eleanor shook her head, "never."

"Had you ever met, or had previous acquaintanceship with, Dennis Dunscumbe?"

"No," she shook her head.

"So when you learned of his death in the newspapers you naturally believed he had committed suicide?"

"Yes," she confirmed faintly.

"And you had no knowledge of Annie Myers?" he pressed.

"No," Eleanor managed, looking down at her hands lying on her lap.

"So it is true to say, Lady Collett," the Coroner pressed gently, "that upon discovering your husband had been brutally killed by the man Peterson as a result of a disagreement over what had gone before, you were profoundly shocked?"

"Yes," she nodded, pressing her handkerchief to her lips.

Beatrice, looking from Eleanor's pale face to her brother's unusually stern one, was in no doubt that left to him he would put a stop to the proceedings as Eleanor was far too distressed to continue, laid a trembling hand on her husband's arm. But Tom, who had kept an eye on his brother-in-law, knowing precisely what was going through his mind, was just about to say something to Tony when he saw him leave his seat and occupy the one next to Eleanor's vacated chair in the front row.

In her distressed state of mind Eleanor was quite unable to bring herself to even glance at the men who made up the jury or look at the sea of faces all around her, all of whom were not only looking expectantly at her but eager to hear every word and sordid description which left her lips. When she was not looking at the Coroner she kept her eyes fixed on an invisible point somewhere in front of her, not daring to look in Tony's direction until, out the corner of her eye, she caught sight of him changing his seat. Taking the opportunity offered when the Coroner directed a reproving look in Tony's direction as well as deeming it opportune to call once more for order, she glanced at Tony as he turned his head as Tom leaned forward to whisper something in his ear and his answering nod before turning back to face her. Across the space which separated them their eyes met and held for just long enough for her to see that beneath Tony's concern was all the love he had for her and, were it at all possible, she would have left the witness stand and flung herself into his arms.

"Now, Lady Collett," the Coroner broke into her thoughts.

What seemed a relentless flow of questions followed, which Eleanor did her best to answer, but her faltering account of the brutal treatment her husband had meted out made it necessary for her to pause and compose herself more than once, relieved that the Coroner had accepted the reason given for her supposed stay in Suffolk with her father for precisely what Tony had intended: to escape from Braden's violent behaviour.

Tom, leaning forward in his seat, laid a stilling hand on Tony's shoulder preventing him from bringing to an end the persistent interrogation of a woman who was not only entirely blameless of any wrongdoing but also in palpable distress. But just when Eleanor had come to believe she could endure no more, it was with the utmost relief that she heard the Coroner tell her that was all and she could resume her seat, whereupon Tom looked knowingly at his wife who, more than once during the proceedings, had fully expected her brother to intervene.

Following Eleanor's release from the witness stand the Coroner, calling no more witnesses, conferred with the jury under the cover of the low-voiced hum which went around the room. Tony, taking the opportunity offered by the lull in proceedings, quietly consulted with Sir Miles who, after nodding his head in agreement, saw his future son-in-law turn round and whisper to Tom who, not at all surprised at what Tony had decided, discreetly turned in his seat to pass on his instructions to Jerry sitting next to Mrs. Timms.

As it was perfectly obvious to the interested assembly that the proceedings they had sat and listened to so enthusiastically for the last two hours and more was an open and shut case, they were not in the least surprised to discover that the Coroner's deliberation with his jury took only a matter of a little over five minutes. That worthy official, after calling for order, eventually gave his summing up, concluding by pronouncing that Sir Braden Collett's death was a clear case of strangulation, committed by one James Peterson, an accomplice of the deceased directly resulting from the aforementioned crimes. Regarding the death of George Edward Mitchell, employee of the late Sir Braden Collett, the evidence clearly showed that as a result of receiving several severe blows to the head he had finally succumbed to the vicious assault perpetrated by the same James Peterson who was being held in police custody by reason of his admission of guilt in both murders and whose case would be scheduled for trial in due course. "With regards to Eliza Boon," the Coroner concluded, "it is not for this Coroner's court to discuss or either prove or disprove her complicity in the crimes mentioned; *that,"* he stressed, "is for a court of law which will convene at a later date to determine guilt or innocence. And *that*," he announced with finality, "concludes these proceedings."

Those members of the press who had managed to get a seat and had spent the last two hours feverishly recording all the relevant points which they considered noteworthy or rather sensational enough to guarantee extra sales, no sooner heard the Coroner bring the proceedings to a close than they made a sudden dash to the door before the rest of the spectators had even made a move to leave their seats. The respect in which Tony was held in Fleet Street may have persuaded three newspaper editors to insert a bogus article on their front pages, but when it came to what they printed with regards to the inquest or the case in general he had neither the right nor the desire to influence their decisions. However, as far as his own reporters were concerned his instructions had been explicit about what he expected of them, and as he could rely on Bill totally Tony knew that only the bare facts would be printed in *'The Bulletin'* and *'The Chronicler'* in order to save Eleanor and her father any further pain or embarrassment.

Since Eleanor had taken up residence in Bruton Street Tony knew that she had not once set foot beyond the front door for fear that the handful of persistent reporters still congregating outside would bombard her with questions she was in no fit condition to answer. He knew too of her strenuous efforts to hide her fears at the thought of what awaited her this morning and, in view of her reception earlier upon her arrival at the Coroner's Court, he could well understand her dread at the prospect of having to face those same reporters on her way out. Tony had no doubt that the welcoming committee would still be there in Bruton Street waiting to waylay her upon her return home in the hope of gleaning something, but as he had no wish to remind her of this and add to her anxiety, he told her that they would stay behind until everyone had left the courtroom and that he had arranged for their carriage to be brought round to the rear of the building to avoid the reporters waiting outside. Not daring to look up at him for all the prying eyes continually glancing in her direction from those who were still slowly making their way out of the courtroom, Eleanor was able to do nothing more than nod her head, but when, some minutes later, he placed a hand under her elbow to help her out of her seat, she was conscious of an overwhelming desire to throw caution to the wind and cast herself into his arms. Left to Tony he would have taken her in his arms there and then and to hell with the consequences, but considering the lengths to which he had gone to avoid the finger of gossip being pointed at Eleanor, setting light to rumours of an illicit affair between them long before Sir Braden's death, this very natural urge had to be strenuously curbed.

As Tony had rightly predicted more reporters had congregated in Bruton Street awaiting their return, swelling the group who had doggedly been hovering outside for days, but as Sir Miles and Eleanor gave not the slightest sign that they were open to answering their barrage of questions, they were thankfully allowed unrestricted passage into the house. If Tony's tall and rather imposing figure alighting from a hackney which had drawn up in the wake of Sir Miles's carriage about ten minutes later occasioned any comment it was merely that he had once again stolen a march on them by being granted another interview with Lady Collett, and as Tony made no effort to contradict this belief he was able to leisurely enter the house without any awkward questions being asked.

Sir Miles, apart from reassuringly patting Eleanor's hand and the occasional quiet word of comfort in her ear, he had maintained a dignified silence throughout the inquest, but no less than Tony had he been extremely concerned over his daughter's palpable distress during the time she had been on the witness stand. Like Tom, he had sensed Tony's frustration over the relentless questioning of Eleanor, for which he did not blame him, in fact he too wanted nothing more than to put an end to her torment, but since an adjournment or even a short break would only prolong the agony for her, it was not entirely without relief that he welcomed Tom's intervention.

In spite of the unwitting part Sir Miles had played in bringing Eleanor to this point, Tony had never doubted his love for her and upon seeing him embrace his daughter and hearing his emotional tribute to her courage before he left her to have a private word with him in his study, clearly proved the depth of his fatherly concern. After discussing the effect the morning's proceedings had had on Eleanor and the pending trial of Peterson and Eliza Boon, Tony, declining Sir Miles's invitation to stay to luncheon due to work he had to go through with Bill that would not keep, Tony shook the hand Sir Miles held out to him, then, leaving him to his own reflections, joined Eleanor in the drawing-room.

Eleanor, shivering with mingled cold and reaction, was standing in front of the fire with her back to the room and her face buried in her hands when she heard Tony close the door quietly behind him. She had of course taken much-needed comfort from her father's support as well as his soothing words of encouragement, indeed she could not have borne it without him, but it was Tony's reassuring presence that had sustained her throughout what had been a most distressing couple of hours. Despite the Coroner's consideration towards her, his questions had nevertheless been intrusive and to the point, rendered all the more difficult to answer sitting as she was in front of those who were morbidly eager to hear every sordid detail of Braden's death and the circumstances leading up to it. She was not entirely sure whether to feel relieved or not in that Tom had prevented Tony from following his inclinations and requesting the Coroner to either adjourn the inquest or grant a short recess in order for her to compose herself because whilst she was glad it was over she was honest enough to admit that she would not have raised any objections to such a request. Tony's consideration for her feelings and welfare only made her love him all the more and when she felt his hands come to rest on her shoulders so he could turn her round to face him, it was the most natural thing in the world for her to melt into him, the emotions which had built up inside her finding their natural release as he folded her comfortingly in his arms.

Not unexpectedly, it was some little time before her tears subsided, and Tony, holding her tightly against him, knew perfectly well that months of living in fear as well as being subjected to brutal treatment by a husband whose death, far from ending her anxieties was only protracting them, would not leave her overnight. If it had not been for Tom pointing out that trying to intervene in the morning's proceedings by requesting the Coroner to either desist in a line of questioning Eleanor clearly found distressing or urging a brief recess in order for her to compose herself, he would only be giving the interested onlookers food for thought about the true nature of their relationship, Tony would certainly have done so. Nevertheless, having to sit there and watch the woman he loved in palpable affliction knowing there was nothing he could do about it unless he wanted to alert the world to the truth thus exposing Eleanor to gossip had been more than he could bear, but now the only thing that mattered was offering Eleanor all the comfort he could. Understandably, it was several minutes before her sobbing subsided and the distraught and muffled words poured into his shoulder gradually died away, leaving her limp and exhausted and grateful for the support of his arms as he held her trembling body close against him. "It's all right, my darling," he soothed, "I have you quite safe."

"Oh Tony!" she cried, resting her head against his chest, "it was all so horrible! All those questions and everybody looking and waiting for me to say something scandalous about Braden!" shuddering at the recollection. "And those reporters!"

"I know," Tony sighed, "it was pretty rough. I only wish I could have spared you," he pressed against her hair.

"I know, but I am so glad you were there!" she told him fervently.

"God knows I did little enough!" he sighed frustrated.

"Oh, but you did!" Eleanor assured him sincerely. "Just knowing you were there was enough. I could not have borne it without you!"

Tony wished he could tell her that from now on she would not have to bear anything alone ever again, but the truth was there was the very real possibility of her having to give evidence in court at the trial of Peterson and Eliza Boon when, probably, he would himself be called to give evidence, which meant he would not be allowed inside the courtroom as she stood in the witness-box to give her even moral support. Then, of course, there was Collett's funeral which, despite Eleanor's feelings towards her late husband, would inevitably be an ordeal for her, so too would the reading of his will, neither of which she could fail to attend and, again, Tony could not be with her for either. He had told her only the other evening that he would be right there at her side even though he had known it would not always be possible, particularly at the trial, but she had been far too anxious for him to even mention the cold hard facts and legal requirements of court procedure. Now though, he deliberately refrained from mentioning these impending and painful proceedings as she had been through more than enough this morning, but upon feeling Eleanor move in his arms he looked down into her upturned face and, after wiping away her tears with a gentle forefinger and telling her how much he loved her, tenderly kissed her.

Whatever disappointment Eleanor may have felt in knowing Tony could not stay for luncheon his warm and tender kisses and the heartfelt words of love he pressed against her lips certainly went a long way to making up for it, but when she walked with him into the hall several minutes later she consoled herself with the thought that there would be many more luncheons for them to share, but more importantly that he loved her. Tony, looking lovingly down into the face smiling a little shyly up at him, could not resist leaving her with a lingering reminder to this very pertinent fact, totally oblivious to Sir Miles's butler. This diligent individual, whose service in the Tatton household was of long duration, having come into the hall in readiness to show Sir Miles's visitor out, found himself torn between his duty and saving Miss Eleanor any embarrassment by advertising his presence at a moment when a third party would most certainly have been *de trop*. He had, of course, been taken fully into Sir Miles's confidence as regards the true state of affairs between his daughter and the man who was presently holding her in a suffocating embrace, but deciding that discretion was, at least at this precise moment, the better part of valour, he tactfully withdrew to his own quarters as silently as he had appeared.

As Sir Miles took no pleasure from adorning society by participating in the numerous functions his peers seemed to delight in and Eleanor had no wish to leave the house quite yet, the group of expectant reporters hovering outside, coming to the conclusion that they were not going to be given a statement by either Sir Miles Tatton or his daughter Lady Collett, soon left their post. In Eleanor's present emotional state it was perhaps fortunate that her dressmaker, a shrewd businesswoman who was quite prepared to do anything rather than lose a client, had no qualms about visiting in Bruton Street to array one whose patronage she would be loath to lose in clothing suitable to her most sorrowful circumstances, even going so far as to take with her a rapidly created black ensemble for her to wear at her attendance at the inquest. At no time could it ever be said that Eleanor lacked sensitivity by failing to show proper respect, but the mere thought of wearing black to mourn a man for whom she had felt not the smallest speck of love and one who had given her feelings not one iota of thought and instilled so much fear into her, made her feel nothing short of a hypocrite. Left to Tony and her father, both of whom felt that Collett's memory deserved neither respect nor consideration in view of the brutal treatment he had meted out to her, Eleanor would not have put herself into mourning, but it certainly did her no disservice in the eyes of Hubert Collett, who, despite the lack of regular contact between himself and his cousin, would have been outraged at such a flagrant show of disrespect by Braden's widow.

No one looking at Hubert Collett would have had the least guess that he was in any way related to Sir Braden; so different were they in appearance as well as manner that the onlooker could be forgiven for thinking that there was no family connection between them. Having already sent Eleanor a polite letter of condolence in which he expressed his regret over her sad loss and in circumstances which he felt sure were as distressing and unexpected for her as they had been for him, he had refrained from commenting further on such a painful subject when he managed to speak briefly to her before her departure from the Coroner's Court. Eleanor knew that Braden's death would have rather a significant impact upon his cousin. Apart from taking on the hereditary title whose origins went back centuries, he would not only find himself living in a most desirable residence in one of the most fashionable parts of town, but would inherit the sizeable fortune which would have been passed on to Braden's son had circumstances been different. Eleanor could not claim a liking for Hubert Collett, whose moderation in all things and the penny-pinching way he ran his neat and orderly household had so exasperated Braden, even so, she was not so unfeeling that she had no sympathy for a man whose cousin had rendered it extremely difficult for him to be accepted into the society he had adorned. It was going to prove no easy matter for Hubert, not to mention his wife and four children, to overcome the prejudice and condemnation of the world they were about to enter, but since he appeared to have more faith in society than Sir Miles did about not being tainted by association, Eleanor decided the less said about it the better.

Having mentally prepared herself for the visit Hubert Collett had told her he proposed making on her when he had briefly gained a few words with her before she had left the Coroner's Court to discuss Braden's funeral, Eleanor, still feeling the effects of her husband's treatment as well as trying to come to terms with his crimes, was only too glad to relinquish the task of overseeing the arrangements into Hubert Collett's hands. She realised of course that as Braden's widow his obsequies were just as much her concern as Hubert's, in fact more so, but the truth was she found herself totally at a loss to know how to begin orchestrating a sanctified service to honour the memory of a man whose life, as a direct result of his machinations, had ended so violently. This, Hubert Collett assured her, leaning forward in his seat to rest a hand on her arm, need not trouble her. He was, he said, more than happy to relieve her of such a burden once Braden's body was eventually released for burial and, smiling encouragingly at her, assured her that all he required from her, if she felt up to it of course, was for her to tell him if there was anything particular she wished him to attend to or any personal detail which she considered proper as the deceased's widow. Upon being sincerely thanked for his kindness and generosity Hubert Collett immediately disclaimed any such thing, but could not help puffing out his thin chest a little at the magnanimity he was showing towards a woman he had only met three times and to a man, who, despite their kinship, hardly met, much less had a thought in common with.

Eleanor, having assured him that she felt sure she could rely on him to do everything that was proper as well as ensuring the funeral would be carried out with dignity, Hubert Collett unhesitatingly promised her it would be, going on to inform her that he had already taken the liberty of speaking to Reverend Goddard at the church he and his family regularly attended in Wimbledon to discover if he would be willing to oversee the burial service of his cousin, to which that diligent ecclesiastic had agreed, providing she approved of course. Considering the hue and cry that still abounded about Braden, rendering a service at St. George's Hanover Square or any other church for that matter within the vicinity as not only inappropriate but guaranteed to be the focal point for every reporter and gossipmonger who had nothing better to do, Eleanor was finally brought to accept that this alternative venue to conducting her husband's obsequies seemed to be the only practical option, and therefore agreed to Hubert Collett's proposal.

And so, a week later, Eleanor, accompanied by her father, paid her last respects to a man whose tyranny could, even now, make her tremble in fear, but not by a word or gesture did she let anyone of Braden's friends or the curious and uninvited observers who, for whatever reason, had flocked to the church, so much as suspect the tumult of emotions running riot inside her. Braden's relations, all of whom came from the highest echelons of society, may have flocked to St. George's Hanover Square upon the unfortunate occasion of their marriage, but Eleanor was by no means surprised to find that not one of them had honoured his funeral service with their presence; clearly, they were extremely eager to disassociate themselves with a man who had not only committed cold-blooded murder but patronised a certain type of establishment. Reverend Goddard's devotion to his calling may far exceed his shock and disgust at the transgressions of the deceased, rendering it impossible for him to expound at length, if at all, on the qualities of the man whose service he was presiding over, but when he quoted *Psalm XXXVIII* from his pulpit, *'O Lord, rebuke me not in thy wrath; neither chasten me in thy hot displeasure. For thine arrows stick fast in me, and thy hand presseth me sore. There is no soundness in my flesh because of thine anger; neither is there any rest in my bones because of my sin…*" no one could possibly deny the earnest cleric's choice was certainly apposite. Eleanor, sitting white-faced and ramrod straight beside her father in the front pew, felt the comforting touch of his hand on her arm, as aware as she was that Reverend Goddard, despite his belief in that every man, irrespective of his sins, had a right to stand before his Maker, clearly believed that he should nevertheless be brought to account in his house before he set out on his final journey.

Hubert, who had generously permitted the doors of his Wimbledon home to be opened to the mourners for refreshment, especially now the reporters had left and would not be around to harass or upset any one of them, had his own reasons for such a magnanimous gesture. He knew as well as anyone that stepping into the shoes of a man who had committed cold-blooded murder as well as a party to others and goodness only knew what else, was going to be no easy thing and that society, who needed very little reason to shun a newcomer to its ranks, wanted to give none of its members the least opportunity to either compare him to Braden or transfer their condemnation onto him and his family. In letting it be seen that he and his wife were on the friendliest of terms with his cousin's young widow and their sole aim was to relieve her of a burden after all she had been through and that she accepted him as her cousin-in-law without regret or misgiving, was an extremely wise move. He also considered it an extremely wise move to maintain a discreet silence should he be asked about Braden or to give his opinion as to the revelations which had emerged over the last couple of weeks, convinced that his good judgement would do him no disservice in the eyes of society proving that he was more than adequately suited to his new role as Sir Hubert Collett; a title and position he had never in his wildest dreams thought would be his.

His wife, who had assumed the role of Lady Collett with no difficulty whatsoever, and certainly with a swiftness that, had Eleanor thought about it at all, betokened a lack of delicacy which was hardly likely to endear her to those with whom she was looking forward to rubbing shoulders, was eagerly anticipating being the new mistress of twenty-nine Cavendish Square before many days were out. She may have happily been formulating plans for their imminent occupation of what could only be described as a most desirable town mansion almost from the moment she had learned of her husband's sudden and unexpected rise up the social ladder, but she retained just enough common sense and discretion to know that Hubert was quite right when he said that no good would result by giving the impression that they were eager to see their young and distraught cousin-in-law permanently evicted from this very eminent address until she was ready. Eleanor had not confided in her, which was hardly surprising considering they barely knew one another, but in view of what had taken place over the last twelve months or so it stood to reason that Eleanor's feelings for twenty-nine Cavendish Square could be nothing other than utter aversion and that it was most unlikely she would leave Bruton Street to return there. Nevertheless, Elvira Collett felt it behoved her and Hubert to assure Eleanor that she was more than welcome to return to Cavendish Square should she so wish until she had arrived at certain decisions regarding her future; not that Elvira really expected her to leave her father's home to go back to a place which could only hold the most distressing memories for her. But the gesture, if nothing else, would go a long way to proving that they were by no means eager to oust Eleanor from the house she had shared with her husband as well as being willing to conciliate on all matters pertinent to her welfare, thereby proving to society that not only were they eminently suited to their new positions but did not deserve to be held responsible for anything Braden may have done. Hubert may hold the purse strings but it was his wife who called the tune, and she knew no hesitation in disregarding his opinion that a funeral gathering was hardly the place to approach Eleanor on such a delicate matter as her occupancy of Cavendish Square. As Elvira was a firm believer in that striking while the iron was hot was always the best policy, she went in search of her cousin-in-law.

Eleanor may have met Elvira Collett only twice, the first occasion being when she had attended her wedding to Braden in company with her husband and the second when she and Hubert had called in Cavendish Square, much to Braden's annoyance, on the flimsiest of reasons which Eleanor could no longer bring to mind, but she had been quick to recognise the longing Elvira Collett had always had to adorn a world which had so far been denied her due to Hubert being the youngest son of a youngest son. His allowance was respectable only, but being a man who counted every penny it had been more than enough to enable him to maintain his family and household without incurring any financial embarrassments, and whilst he was able to ensure his wife was more than adequately turned out it was clear that Elvira Collett looked forward to the day when she could patronise the most stylish of dressmakers.

As it was now common knowledge that Eleanor had sought refuge with her father in Suffolk and was now residing with him for the foreseeable future in Bruton Street, she was rather surprised to find herself being taken a little to one side by her rather forthright cousin-in-law to enquire of her plans about Cavendish Square. Since Elvira's interpretation of tact was more compatible with sledgehammer tactics than discretion and diplomacy, her direct question as to her plans about her domicile took Eleanor a little aback. The mere thought of returning to a house where she had suffered all manner of abuse, leaving her with memories she was striving to forget, was really quite repugnant to her, as was Elvira's insensitivity in putting such an enquiry to her, especially now when she was far too vulnerable. Eleanor's barely audible assurance that she had no intention of resuming residence in Cavendish Square, on the contrary she was quite happy to continue residing in Bruton Street with her father, came as no surprise to Elvira who, despite her assertions that neither she nor Hubert had the least wish to oust her from her home, was secretly delighted with this confirmation. Not only had they shown great magnanimity towards Eleanor, which could only be to their advantage, but Elvira, more so than her husband, was rather eager to take up residence in a house that had a most eminent address; the distasteful thought that her husband's cousin had not only kept his wife a virtual prisoner as well as physically abusing her in addition to committing murder, culminating in his own violent death, within its walls, not troubling her in the least. Then there was Braden's will! Neither Elvira nor her husband could possibly put a figure on what he was worth, but that his fortune was immense they were in no doubt. Although his death had come as complete surprise and the manner of it even more so, it nevertheless meant that she could now adorn the world she had hankered after all her life and, as for Braden's money, it would certainly enable her to afford a lifestyle she would have no difficulty in accustoming herself to, and she was barely able to contain her impatience until tomorrow when they congregated in Cavendish Square in order for Braden's solicitor to read the contents of that all-important document.

It was otherwise with Braden's widow. The mere thought of having to visit twenty-nine Cavendish Square, even for only an hour or so, made Eleanor feel quite sick, but more than this she wanted nothing from Braden. She knew that the bulk of his estate would go to Hubert as his heir and, apart from perhaps certain smaller bequests, the remainder would go to herself, possibly by way of an allowance, but due to Braden's treatment of her and the fear he had instilled in her, the very thought of touching a penny of any money he left her was really quite repugnant to her.

Although Sir Miles fully shared this opinion as well as his daughter's feelings upon the subject, he nevertheless firmly believed that she had more than earned anything Braden had bequeathed to her, but considering her distressed state of mind and her dread of visiting in Cavendish Square tomorrow he refrained from remarking on it. Compared to Sir Braden, Sir Miles's finances could not be regarded as a fortune, but they were more than healthy enough for him to support his daughter irrespective of whether she touched a penny of whatever her husband left her or not, and certainly until such time as he saw her safely handed into the care of a man he had no hesitation in deeming as being totally worthy of her. He had spoken no word of a lie when he had told Tony that he had seen from the outset he was a very different man altogether to Sir Braden Collett and that he had no doubts as to just how important his daughter was to him. Just one glance at Eleanor when he had seen her in Mount Street had been enough to tell Sir Miles that she was very much in love with Tony and, as for her prospective bridegroom, even if he had not told him to his face how he felt about Eleanor, the lengths to which he had gone to protect her and the expression in his eyes when he looked at her most certainly did.

Like Tony, Sir Miles knew that it would take time for Eleanor to fully recover from all Braden had subjected her to and that attending the inquest and his funeral today, however inescapable, had only added to her distress, but upon seeing the change which came over her when Tony called later that afternoon, not the first transformation he had seen, he had the very strong feeling that his daughter's recovery would not take as long as he had at first thought.

Eleanor could not deny that her marriage to Braden had been very far removed from the happy harmony shared by her parents, nor could she deny that her father's momentary lapse at the card table had been the first step to bringing her so much unhappiness and pain. She knew her father was a man of the utmost integrity, which is why his actions that night were all the more inexplicable, but they had also brought about that meeting with Tony, albeit inadvertently. She neither blamed nor hated her father for unintentionally catapulting her into a marriage which had been as distasteful as it had brutal, indeed she loved him very much and had no idea what she would do without him, but it was to Tony she now turned and confided, a man without whom she could not envisage the rest of her life.

"I'm sorry, my darling," Tony said regretfully when Sir Miles left them alone, "I wish I could have been with you today, but you must know I could not," holding out his hand to her.

"I know," Eleanor said a little huskily, putting her hand into his, "but I missed you so much."

"My poor darling," he said tenderly, kissing her fingers, "it must have been dreadful for you; and I was not there."

She perfectly understood the awkwardness attached to his attendance at Braden's funeral, or Beatrice and Tom for that matter, but as Tony held her in his arms all her pent-up emotions, something she seemed unable to control at the moment, came flooding out, made infinitely worse as the horrendous thought of returning to the house where she had been kept guard over and spied upon hovered at the back of her mind. Tony realised that stepping foot inside twenty-nine Cavendish Square tomorrow to hear the reading of Braden's will with its all too vivid and unhappy memories was going to be quite an ordeal for her and, once again, he could not be with her, but after soothing her fears by telling her softly that her father would be there with her she nodded, then, gently easing herself out of his arms, walked away from him.

Tony watched her walk over to the fireplace and stand with her back to him, wiping her nose on the handkerchief she retrieved from her pocket before turning to face him, whereupon she immediately changed the subject by telling him how glad she was that the reporters were no longer hovering outside, but from the look on his face she knew that he was by no means fooled by her determined attempt to hide what was on her mind.

"I can imagine," Tony sympathised, "but it's no good, Ellie," he shook his head, "you will have to do much better than that if you want to convince me nothing is worrying you."

She supposed she should have known Tony was far too astute not to notice when something was troubling her, and although she had not told him that she wanted nothing from Braden she instinctively knew he had already assumed as much. Despite her father's feelings towards his recently deceased son-in-law, the thought had occurred to her that he may feel Braden's financial bequest, because it was useless to suppose he had not made provision for her, could well be put to no better use than as a dowry upon her marriage to Tony, after all it was a time-honoured custom. Knowing her father as well as she did it could well be that he would regard this as recompense for the way Braden had treated her, and since her father was an old-fashioned man at heart who believed in honouring all the traditions she would by no means put this idea beyond him or that he believed Tony would be expecting her to take something into the marriage. She did not think so, but over the past few days it was something which had increasingly taken possession of her mind, even though her common sense as well as her knowledge of Tony told her that, far from expecting a financial endowment of some kind, no such thought had ever so much as crossed his mind.

Collett may have been blessed with his fair share of faults, but Tony doubted very much whether these included a callous desire to leave his widow penniless, but the disjointed explanation he gently coaxed out of her to account for her sudden awkwardness came as no surprise to him, and even though he could well understand her feelings of revulsion in not wanting to benefit in any way from the man who had treated her abominably, as she falteringly tried to further explain herself he strenuously had to fight the urge to take her in his arms and kiss away her absurdities. "My father would do more for me if he c-could, but although I… I have a little money of m-my own," she faltered, "it's not much, in fact," she sniffed, "it's what my m-mother left me, but I am afraid," she shrugged helplessly, "you may well look upon it as quite p-paltry and…"

"Are you by any chance thinking that I shall change my mind about marrying you now that you have told me all this?" Tony broke in gently. After nodding her head she quickly turned away from him, her colour considerably heightened. "Ellie, look at me," he encouraged, his voice a nice mix of tenderness and amusement. When she made no immediate move to do so, he was at her side in a couple of strides and, turning her round to face him, cupped her burning cheeks in his hands, saying earnestly, "I'm not hanging out for a rich wife; I'm rich enough, but even if I weren't I don't want Collett's money, *that,*" he told her firmly, "is yours to do with as you will. You can keep it, give it all to charity or burn it even," he nodded, "it's all one to me. All I know," he stressed, "is that I want no part of it. As for a marriage settlement from your father, I neither expect nor want one, and as for the money your mother left you, you may use that as you will. All I want from you," he told her in a deepening voice, "is your love. As for me," taking her in his arms, "I want to marry you because I love you and can't live without you and for no other reason!" Then, lowering his head, said against her parted lips, "When you are my wife, what's mine is yours, in fact it's yours now, to do with as you will," giving her no opportunity to answer by unreservedly kissing her.

"Y-you have never kissed me like that before!" she faltered a little breathlessly when he finally released her.

"No, I know," Tony sighed a little unsteadily, "not that I haven't wanted to," he admitted, "but since you seem determined on harbouring such foolish notions about me marrying you for your money I thought it was about time I did, *and,*" drawing her closer to him, "if you have no objections, I am going to kiss you like that again." Without giving her time to finish telling him that she had no objections whatsoever and that she would love him even if he was a pauper living in a hovel he happily picked up where he had left off.

The following morning, having resolutely clamped down on the overwhelming urge not to attend the reading of Braden's will, Eleanor braced herself to enter the house which held so many painful memories for her, comforted by Tony's reassuring words of encouragement and the supportive presence of her father. Jeremiah Craythorne, the only surviving son of the founder member of Craythorne, Miley and Craythorne, solicitors of Fenchurch Street, entered the portals of twenty-nine Cavendish Square feeling very ill at ease. It had come as a tremendous shock to discover the truth about Sir Braden Collett, a highly valued client whose affairs as well as those of his family his firm had handled for many years and, for the first time in his sixty-nine years, he found himself quite at a loss as to the best way of approaching the widow of a deceased client. Jeremiah Craythorne had never met Lady Collett before today, which unfortunately did not make things any easier, although he did know that she was considerably younger than her late husband, but thanks to her ready appreciation as to the awkwardness of his position he was able to say all that was proper without committing any social solecism or causing her any distress.

Mr. Jeremiah Craythorne, having drawn up Sir Braden Collett's will some years previously, had not been at all surprised when, a little more than a month before his marriage, he received instructions that it was to be revised. His client may have been in his mid-forties, but there was no reason whatsoever to suppose that he would not father children and to bequeath the bulk of his estate to his cousin and heir should he die without issue of his own was perfectly natural, as was the generous annuity to his widow. Mr. Craythorne may not entirely agree with the proviso Sir Braden had attached to this bequest stipulating that should she marry again it would cease with immediate effect, but it was certainly not an unusual stipulation for a man to make, but for himself Mr. Craythorne had always looked upon it as being just a little miserly. However, apart from the fact that his late client would have brooked neither argument nor advice, from what he could see of it Lady Collett was by no means disturbed by such a disclosure. Had he have known that she was far more disturbed by being in the very house where she had spent the worst twelve months of her life, being watched over and guarded and brutally treated rather than finding herself at risk of losing several thousand pounds a year should she decide to marry again, he would have been somewhat surprised.

The rest of his late client's will held no real surprises. Sir Braden had left the sum of three thousand pounds to be shared equally between certain charitable foundations and the sum of two thousand pounds to be donated towards the upkeep of Covent Garden Opera House of which he had been a patron for many years, but apart from Mrs. Timms, who had been cook in his father's time and to whom he left the sum of five hundred pounds as a token of services rendered, the rest of the servants were not even mentioned. Had Eleanor given any thought to it at all, it would have struck her as just a little odd that a man like Braden with his impressive connections to several prominent families, had not left any one of them so much as a memento and, apart from his intimate cronies with whom he had often visited Eliza Boon's establishment in Periton Place, he had not what one could call close friends to bequeath even a token of remembrance.

Sir Miles's acquaintanceship with Tony may be of short duration, but he believed he had summed up his character fairly accurately, and was not at all surprised to learn that not only did he want no part of any money Collett would naturally bequeath to Eleanor but neither did he want, much less expect, a marriage settlement. Sir Miles could not but applaud Tony's sentiments, indeed he thought the better of him for not wanting to benefit by so much as a penny from Collett, but for himself he was quite disgusted at the proviso his deceased son-in-law had attached to the bequest.

So too was Beatrice when Tony told her of Collett's stipulation upon his return to Mount Street later that evening having visited Bruton Street following his meeting with Bill. She could not blame Eleanor for not wanting anything from the man who had made her life nothing but a sheer misery, but that he should attach a condition to the bequest, even though it was by no means unheard of for a man to make such a condition, only went to prove, she nodded firmly, how callous Collett actually was. Tom, after echoing his wife's sentiments, went on to add that whilst he fully understood Eleanor's feelings about not wanting to touch a penny of Collett's money, such a proviso had taken away with one hand what had been given with other.

Eleanor may have had a weight taken off her mind to know that never again would she have to set foot inside Cavendish Square and that she would not benefit long from Braden's will, not that she intended to keep a penny of it, but there was still the trial of Eliza Boon and Peterson looming ominously ahead to worry her. In view of the harrowing time she had had at the inquest, the very thought of giving evidence in a murder trial caused her more than one sleepless night. She was not overly familiar with legal procedures and had no idea how long it would take for the case to come to court, but she had certainly not expected it to be almost immediately.

Unlike Eleanor, Tony had a pretty shrewd idea that it would be weeks rather than months, and upon having this confirmed by Superintendent Dawson several days after the reading of Collett's will, having tracked him down to his newspaper offices in Fleet Street, Tony knew that the news would come as something of a shock to her. Superintendent Dawson, welcoming Tony's suggestion that he be the one to tell Lady Collett, nevertheless felt it behoved him to point out that Eliza Boon, who was still vehemently maintaining her innocence, had engaged Geoffrey Dewer to act on her behalf, one of the leading solicitors of the day and one, moreover, who often secured the services of no less a person than Sir Douglas Dinsdale-Carr QC.

Even for someone like Tony who divided his time between London and New York, it was impossible not to have heard of the man who, over his long and successful career at the bar, had been aptly named

'The Champion of Lost Causes'. Even when the evidence against the defendant had been overwhelming, Sir Douglas Dinsdale-Carr's brilliant oratory together with his unparalleled skill in the art of semantics, had time and again seen him win the case for the defence. Whilst Tony accepted that everyone was unquestionably entitled to the best defence possible, he could not help but wonder whether this consummate and articulate man ever experienced any qualms in seeing a criminal escape the penalty of the law, but if nothing else Eliza Boon had certainly provided herself with a more than odds on chance of being exonerated of all charges except those of keeping a house of ill repute and living off immoral earnings, but unless Tony had read this woman all wrong he felt certain that this would be a triumph for her.

As for Peterson, who did not have the financial luxury of being able to secure the legal services of men like Geoffrey Dewer and Dinsdale-Carr but had instead to manage as best he could with one appointed by the court, was, fortunately, still singing the same tune as he had when arrested. Eliza Boon may have totally severed any connection with Peterson and certainly as far as being a party to any wrongdoing was concerned, but, and this was the best Tony and the Superintendent could hope for, was that if Peterson flung the mud hard enough it could well stick, leaving the jury with little choice but to bring in a guilty verdict for Eliza Boon. If, as could well be the case, Dinsdale-Carr adroitly parried such allegations against his client, then not only would Eleanor have to give evidence to substantiate Peterson's testimony, but there was the very real chance of Eliza Boon being acquitted of conspiring to commit murder. Realistically, Peterson, who, despite his physical appearance, which was at all times rather menacing, was mentally no match for a man like Dinsdale-Carr who would have no difficulty in either twisting his words or placing quite a different interpretation upon them, ending up totally confusing him. Eleanor too would no doubt find herself easily intimidated by a man who was a past master at his craft, especially now when she was extremely vulnerable, and if Peterson's appointed counsel was as committed to defending his client as Dinsdale-Carr would be to defending his, then she would have an extremely distressing time in the witness-box. Tony may miss Eleanor's presence in Mount Street, but he certainly had no regrets in doing all he could to protect her reputation because should it ever become known that they had lived under his sister's roof at the same time then not only would she be subjected to embarrassing questions about this in the witness-box, but he too would find it difficult to convince the court of the actual purity of his motives in bringing cold-blooded murderers to justice. Whatever the outcome of the cross-examination by either defence barrister, it was extremely doubtful whether any other verdict but guilty would be brought in for Peterson but, regrettably, the same could not be said for Eliza Boon, especially in view of Dinsdale-Carr's past successes. Like Bill and Superintendent Dawson, Tony was by no means certain that Eliza Boon would be found guilty of conspiring to commit murder, but of one thing they were certain and that was should it turn out she in did in fact walk away free from such serious charges, then it would be nothing less than a gross miscarriage of justice.

Chapter Thirty-Three

Beatrice, who had never before attended a court case let alone a murder trial at such a distinguished venue as Old Bailey, was not at all sure what to expect, but for all that she was rather surprised to discover that the case of *Regina -v- Boon and Peterson* lasted for no more than five days. Considering the charges Eliza Boon and Peterson were having to answer she would have thought that the trial would last far longer and, also, Eleanor would have been one of the first witnesses called upon to give her evidence, but much to Beatrice's astonishment Eleanor was not called until the fourth day, unlike Tony and Superintendent Dawson who were among the first to be called.

But in spite of her concerns for Eleanor, who had to sit outside with Tony and her father as well as the Superintendent together with the other witnesses who had received warning that their attendance would be required, Beatrice could not quite prevent the little frisson of excitement coursing through her as she looked around with wide-eyed interest on the very first day. Peering over the balcony she could see Eliza Boon and Peterson sitting down with their backs to her and police constables flanked on either side, her pretty mouth pursing as she considered the reign of terror they had perpetrated against Eleanor. It was just as Beatrice was about to whisper something into Tom's ear when the sound of three taps on the floor caught her attention and, turning her gaze to the front, saw the judge, wigged and gowned, entering the courtroom, followed by the authoritative voice of the usher who, holding his tipstaff, pronounced, "*Silence!*" startling her a little. "*Be upstanding in court,*" rising hurriedly to her feet. "*All persons who have anything to do before My Lords the Queen's Justices of oyer and terminer and general gaol delivery of the jurisdiction of the Central Criminal Court, draw near and give your attendance. God Save the Queen.*"

Although one of the most abiding memories Beatrice would take away with her from the five-day trial was the many occasions Mr. Justice Sheldon had found it necessary to interpose, but also the horror she felt when among the list of charges being read out was that of Eliza Boon's attempt to shoot Tony in Hertford Street, a circumstance which caused her to glance quickly up at Tom whose face reflected his feelings, but after shaking his head a little he smiled reassuringly at her and gave her hand a comforting squeeze.

Over the next three days the prosecution and both defence counsels made their opening speeches then called their witnesses, all of whom had found their answers continually interrupted or forestalled by Mr. Justice Sheldon.

"I'm obliged, m'lud," came the polite response from Mr. Myatt the prosecuting counsel with a slight inclination of his head.

"Sir Douglas, the witness has already answered this question."

"M'lud," Sir Douglas inclined his head.

"Gentlemen of the jury," Mr. Justice Sheldon cautioned, leaning forward on his elbows as he eyed the jury over the rim of his spectacles, "you will disregard the point Mr. Smilie, counsel for the accused James Peterson, has just made regarding the fingerprints on the Derringer pistol which was found beside the body of Dennis Dunscumbe as being those of the deceased and not the accused. Despite the findings of Edward Henry in his 1894 textbook 'Clarification and Use of Fingerprints', fingerprinting is not as yet deemed a precise method of identification and therefore unreliable, it is impossible to say who the fingerprints belonged to and, for this reason, cannot be admitted into evidence or form part of your deliberations."

Having heard evidence from Superintendent Dawson it was then that Mr. Myatt called Tony into the witness-box, whereupon Beatrice drew in her breath and gripped Tom's arm. As with the inquest he gave his answers in the same precise and confident way; his tall figure as imposing as his voice was firm and authoritative.

"One moment, Sir Douglas," Mr. Justice Sheldon intervened during his cross-examination, turning to Tony. "Lord Childon, are you telling this court that you personally investigated these matters for your newspapers?"

"Yes, my lord," Tony replied unequivocally.

"Is that usual?" he queried, looking down at Tony from the bench.

"Quite usual, my lord," Tony told him calmly.

"I see," Mr. Justice Sheldon sighed. "You may continue, Sir Douglas," he nodded.

"I'm obliged, my lud," Sir Douglas inclined his head. "Lord Childon, would it be true to say that you have a personal interest in this case?"

"Yes, it would," Tony told him quite unperturbed, "the same as I have a personal interest in every case that I or my reporters investigate."

"I'm sure," Sir Douglas dismissed dryly, "but is it not true that in this instance you had an added incentive in Lady Collett?"

"My lud, I *object* to such an improper question!" Mr. Myatt protested, rising to his feet.

"I quite agree, Mr. Myatt," Mr. Justice Sheldon frowned. "Sir Douglas," he reprimanded, "you know better than to put such an improper question. Lord Childon is not on trial here, and as for Lady Collett, I will not allow her reputation to be deliberately sullied in this court!"

"My apologies, my lud," Sir Douglas bowed. "Now, Lord Childon, you say you have the same interest in every case that you and your reporters investigate, but can you deny that if it had not been for Lady Collett you would not have…?"

"Sir Douglas," Mr. Justice Sheldon said sternly, "I shall not warn you again about this improper line of questioning."

Bill looked meaningfully at Tom sitting beside him, relieved to have this very delicate hurdle cleared so easily, and Jerry, sitting next to Beatrice, let out a profound sigh of relief.

"M'lud," Sir Douglas bowed. "Now, Lord Childon, about…"

"Sir Douglas," Mr. Justice Sheldon intervened some little time after, "the witness has already answered this question."

"I'm obliged m'lud," Sir Douglas bowed his head. "Now, Lord Childon, let us turn to this alleged incident of my client attempting to shoot you in Hertford Street. Is it not the case that at the moment my client was supposedly attempting to fire at you your attention was momentarily diverted?"

"Yes," Tony said truthfully, "it was."

"That being so," Sir Douglas put to him, "you could not swear to it that my client deliberately took aim?"

"No," Tony said firmly, "I could not."

"So you only have Police Constable Moore's word for it that she tried to shoot you?"

"Yes," Tony nodded.

"So," Sir Douglas cocked an eyebrow, "you admit that the gun going off could so easily have been precisely what my client has already stated to the police in that it accidentally went off as she was attempting to retrieve it from her person to hand it over to Police Constable Moore?"

"Yes," Tony nodded, "but…"

"Thank you, Lord Childon," Sir Douglas cut him short. "Now about…"

Ten minutes later Police Constable Moore, who would not forget Eliza Boon's attempt to shoot Tony in a hurry, was called to give evidence. Having answered Mr. Myatt's questions calmly and professionally he soon found himself somewhat overawed by Sir Douglas's long experience and unparalleled skill in twisting and turning words into whatever shape he wanted. "Police Constable Moore, you told my learned friend," nodding his head to where Mr. Myatt was sitting, "that you did not know my client had a gun on her person."

"No, sir, I mean yes, sir, that is what I said and no, I did not know she had a gun."

"You also said that it was only through catching the light from the chandelier glinting on the barrel that drew your attention to the fact that my client had a gun, enabling you to not only cry out but also to knock her arm thereby deflecting her aim."

"Yes, sir," he nodded.

"You said that my client was taking deliberate aim?"

"Yes, sir."

"Did it not occur to you, Constable Moore," Sir Douglas said a little sarcastically, "that my client was merely trying to hand the gun over to you?"

"No, sir," Constable Moore shook his head, "she wasn't…"

"I put it to you Constable Moore," Sir Douglas pressed, "that my client, far from taking aim at Lord Childon, was merely trying to hand it over when, through your own miscalculation," he said meaningfully, looking eloquently around the courtroom, "your pushing her off balance was the reason for the gun going off."

"No, sir," Constable Moore shook his head.

And so the questioning of witnesses went on until Mr. Myatt called Mrs. Timms into the witness-box, whose pugnacious responses to the questions put to her by Sir Douglas and Mr. Smilie brought a rebuke from Mr. Justice Sheldon. "Your loyalty to Lady Collett is not in dispute, but please refrain from offering your opinion but simply confine your comments to answering the questions." Mrs. Timms sniffed and, after casting a resentful glance at Sir Douglas, did as he recommended. Sir Douglas, impervious to reactions such as this, merely continued his cross-examination of Mrs. Timms, at the end of which he dismissed her from the witness-box, whereupon Mr. Justice Sheldon adjourned the proceedings until tomorrow morning.

Mr. Myatt, after three long days of doggedly presenting the case for the prosecution, realised that he had no option but to put Lady Collett into the witness-box as Sir Douglas was putting up a brilliant defence on behalf of his client and when, after the formal preliminaries next morning Mr. Justice Sheldon asked him if he had any more witnesses before Sir Douglas opened his case for the defence, Mr. Myatt rose to his feet, saying, "I call Lady Eleanor Collett, m'lud."

Having spent the past three days sitting outside the courtroom with Tony and her father, hoping against hope that she would not be called, Eleanor no sooner heard her name being announced by the Police Constable who had emerged from the courtroom than her fingers convulsively gripped Tony's arm. After looking anxiously from Tony to her father, she slowly rose to her feet on legs which felt in imminent danger of collapsing under her, but if either she or Tony held out the slightest hope that he would be allowed inside the courtroom with her, it was soon dashed when he was politely barred entrance, being told that as he was a witness and may well be called again, he would have to wait outside.

Mr. Myatt treated Eleanor sensitively and with consideration and careful not to distress her unnecessarily, as did Peterson's defence counsel Mr. Smilie, both of whom were polite, courteous and genuinely sympathetic, but Sir Douglas Dinsdale-Carr, sparing no effort his attempts to defend his client, soon found himself being rebuked by Mr. Justice Sheldon for badgering the witness, to which he bowed an apology.

"Lady Collett," Sir Douglas resumed, "you say you saw your husband murder Sir Philip Dunscumbe, and yet according to the testimony of Superintendent Dawson you told him you never actually saw your husband strike him. You say also that he was a party to the tragedy of Annie Myers, a young woman who, on your own admission, you had no idea existed until Lord Childon apprised you of her any more than you did of the death of George Edward Mitchell until he told you. As for Dennis Dunscumbe, whilst I admit you could not fail to be aware of his death considering it was in all the newspapers, you had no more idea than anyone else that his brutal end was something other than suicide until Lord Childon drew your attention to it. Is it not the truth, Lady Collett," he pressed ruthlessly, "that at no time did you ever witness any kind of collaboration between your late husband and the defendants? Is it not also the truth that you have allowed your feelings for Lord Childon to persuade you into believing something merely to further…?"

"Sir Douglas," Mr. Justice Sheldon intervened sharply, "I shall not remind you again that I will not permit you to badger the witness or to put questions of such an improper nature!"

"My apologies m'lud," he bowed. "Now, Lady Collett, can you deny that at no time had you ever heard my client incite James Peterson to commit murder?"

"No," Eleanor said faintly.

And so it went on. "Lady Collett," Sir Douglas pressed, "you say your husband kept you a prisoner in your own home to prevent you from telling anyone about what you," he paused, "*allegedly* say," he emphasised, bowing his head mockingly, "was witnessing him striking Sir Philip Dunscumbe to death with a poker and that my client assisted him in his aim to keep you silent."

"Yes," Eleanor managed.

"And by what means were you prevented from venturing out?" Sir Douglas cocked his head. "Did my client restrain you by manacling you? Did my client tie you up or secrete you in the cellar or the attic? Did my client, at any time, strike you or inflict any bodily harm on you?"

"No," he was faintly told.

"No," he said firmly, "she did not."

"No, but she…" Eleanor began feebly.

"Is it not the case, Lady Collett," Sir Douglas forestalled her, "that in your distressed state of mind you misinterpreted my client's presence in Cavendish Square as well as her natural concerns for your health and wellbeing for no other reason than you took her in dislike because you discovered her past association with your husband, so you determined to get your own back for the humiliation her inclusion in your household must have caused you by deliberately trying to malign her to exact revenge?"

"No," Eleanor said faintly, "that's not true!"

Beatrice, looking anxiously from Tom's taut features to Eleanor's pale and strained face as she tried to combat Dinsdale-Carr's persistent questions and suggestions as to an ulterior motive being the cause of her allegations towards his client, wondered how much longer she would have to endure such an ordeal, but just when Beatrice thought that Eleanor could bear no more she heard Dinsdale-Carr say, "I have no further questions for this witness, m'lud."

Mr. Smilie, doing his best to defend Peterson, who had not only entered a plea of guilty but from the very beginning had, by his own admission, confessed to murdering Sir Braden Collett and, also, on Eliza Boon's incitement, Mitchell and Dennis Dunscumbe, decided that the only course open to him was to get Eleanor to paint as worse a picture as possible of Eliza Boon as well as trying to get her to affirm his client's lack of mental agility.

Sir Douglas, rising to his feet with his hands gripping the edges of his black gown, his voice a nice mix of scorn and incredulity, said, as his sharp eagle eyes scanned the court, "M'lud, is my learned friend seriously trying to tell this court that his client is of diminished responsibility and did not know what he was doing?"

"M'lud," Mr. Smilie bowed, "I am merely trying to establish…"

"My lud," Sir Douglas once again rose to his feet, "if my learned friend intended to base his defence on his client's mental processes, then why has he not produced one medical expert to testify to the same?"

"M'lud," Mr. Smilie bowed, "I am merely…"

"Mr. Smilie," Mr. Justice Sheldon intervened, "Sir Douglas has raised a most valid point. Are you now telling this court that you have decided to change the basis of your defence and that you wish for an adjournment in order for medical experts to be called?"

"No, m'lud," Mr. Smilie bowed.

"In that case," Mr. Justice Sheldon nodded, "I suggest you continue with the witness."

"I have no more questions for Lady Collett, m'lud," Mr. Smilie told him resignedly.

Unfortunately for Eleanor Mr. Myatt did, but despite his sensitively expressed though persistent questions during his re-cross-examination, she could tell him no more than she had before, but it was clear that by the time she was eventually dismissed from the witness-box she looked quite exhausted. Following Eleanor's departure from the courtroom, Mr. Justice Sheldon deemed it time to adjourn the proceedings until two o'clock when Sir Douglas would open his case for the defence, but if Eleanor thought her part in this was over she soon realised her mistake when, like Tony, she was instructed to return at two o'clock in case she was re-called.

Even before Beatrice had joined them and told Tony in a quiet aside that Eleanor had had a pretty harrowing time, just one look at her had sufficed to confirm his worst fears. He had hoped it would not be necessary for Eleanor to give evidence, but according to Tom Sir Douglas had put up a brilliant defence leaving Mr. Myatt with little choice other than to call her to give the case for the prosecution some extra support and, in so doing, assist Mr. Smilie in his courageous but failing attempts to defend Peterson and prove Eliza Boon's guilt. Considering the offences he and Eliza Boon were having to answer, it had been really quite inevitable they would call Eleanor to give evidence as well as bombarding her with questions which were as distressing as they were necessary. Tony had no doubt at all that if it had not been for Mr. Myatt's objection to Sir Douglas's scarcely veiled suggestion regarding his motives for involving himself in this case, he too would have found himself faced with some rather pertinent questions. Even though Tony was by nature honest and forthright and one who held lies and dissimulation in abhorrence, when he had told Bill that he was more than prepared to go to any lengths to protect Eleanor and shield her from gossip and innuendo, he had meant every word of it.

Tony had no qualms about the prospect of being re-called, but he had hoped Eleanor would not be required again as she was in no condition to face another session of being bombarded with questions, and yet to make herself unavailable would be deemed as nothing short of contempt of court. Not surprisingly, the luncheon basket which Beatrice had had the forethought to have prepared and was waiting for them in their carriage parked just a few streets away, was hardly touched, but Tony, who wanted nothing more than to take Eleanor in his arms and comfort her, did manage to coax her into eating a small piece of chicken and to swallowing a little brandy from Tom's flask which he was holding out to her, but although she pulled a face as it slid down her throat, it did have the effect of putting new life into her. Unfortunately, this new life did not last for very long.

Sir Douglas Dinsdale-Carr, having given his opening speech in his usual expressive and inimitable style and which Mr. Myatt and Mr. Smilie thought masterly, told Mr. Justice Sheldon that he had only one witness, "I call Eliza Boon, m'lud."

Not surprisingly a buzz went around the courtroom as she left the dock to take her place in the witness-box with two police women standing behind her, but Mr. Justice Sheldon, after sharply calling for order, told Sir Douglas to continue.

"Is your name Eliza Boon?" he asked.

"Yes," she nodded.

"And is it true that up until twelve months ago you resided at fifty-one Periton Place, Bloomsbury?"

"Yes," she replied.

"And this establishment," Sir Douglas asked, "was it your home as well as your place of business?"

"Yes," she nodded.

"And this business," Dinsdale-Carr cocked his head, "was it to provide a certain kind of entertainment for gentlemen?"

"Yes," she replied. A response which sent another buzz around the courtroom.

"And were you better known as *'Mother Discipline?'* he asked.

"Yes, I was," she told him calmly, ignoring a further buzz from the spectators.

"Was Sir Braden Collett a regular visitor?"

"Yes," she replied.

"And Dennis Dunscumbe?"

"Yes," she replied again.

"Did a young woman of the name Annie Myers work for you?"

"Yes, she did," Eliza Boon confirmed.

"Miss Boon," Sir Douglas cocked his head, "it has been argued by the prosecution that Dennis Dunscumbe was responsible for the accidental death of Annie Myers, a young woman you admit plied her trade in your establishment, by violently striking her which caused her to fall backwards and hit her head on the bedstead which unfortunately killed her and that Sir Braden Collett, together with yourself and James Peterson, covered up her death and disposed of her body by throwing it into a derelict house in Heron Street. Is that true?"

"No," she said firmly. "Neither Sir Braden Collett nor Dennis Dunscumbe were there the night Annie Myers died."

"How did she die?" Sir Douglas asked.

"She had had a little too much to drink, more so than usual, and somehow or other she slipped and fell backwards causing her to strike her head on the bestead."

"Are you saying that Annie Myers often drank to excess?" Dinsdale-Carr enquired.

"Sometimes she did, yes," Eliza Boon told him.

"Why did you not report her death?" Dinsdale-Carr pressed.

"Because I knew if I did the police would arrest me for presiding over an illegal establishment."

"So you asked James Peterson to dispose of her body?"

"Yes," she nodded.

"So you are saying, Miss Boon," Sir Douglas raised an eyebrow, "that the death of Annie Myers and the disposal of her body had nothing whatsoever to do with Sir Braden Collett and Dennis Dunscumbe?"

"Nothing at all," she shook her head. "As I said, they were not present that night."

"So the prosecution's argument that you and Sir Braden Collett engineered Dennis Dunscumbe's death to ensure his silence about what happened to Annie Myers by instructing James Peterson to shoot him and make it look like suicide is untrue?"

"Yes," Eliza Boon said firmly, "quite untrue. Why should I want to kill him?" she shrugged. "Dennis Dunscumbe was a regular customer who paid well."

Beatrice, who had listened to this in wide-eyed astonishment, was to gasp her shock some fifteen minutes later, when Sir Douglas asked Eliza Boon the reason for her leaving Periton Place.

"Sir Braden had confided his concerns to me about Lady Collett's mental state of health. He told me that she had for some little time been afflicted with nervous disorders and was becoming increasingly delusional. It was during these delusions when she would hurt herself because she did not know what she was doing?"

"Are you saying that Sir Braden Collett asked you to look after his wife?" Sir Douglas asked.

"Yes," Eliza Boon nodded. "It so happened that I was considering retiring from business and Sir Braden wondered if I would help him with Lady Collett. I asked him if he had brought a doctor in to tend her and he said no because Lady Collett refused to believe she was ill, and Sir Braden, believing that the attentions of a doctor would only distress her further, asked me if I would look after her for him."

"Sir Braden Collett asked you this even though he knew you had neither nursing certificates nor experience?" Sir Douglas cocked his head.

"Yes," she nodded.

"So, it is true to say," Sir Douglas offered, "that Sir Braden Collett knew you were a woman who could be trusted."

"Yes," Eliza Boon nodded.

Sir Douglas, whose examination of Eliza Boon lasted for another hour, throughout the course of which he not only questioned her about attempting to shoot Lord Childon, which she categorically denied, but he was constantly interrupted by either Mr. Myatt or Mr. Smilie and even, on one occasion, by Mr. Justice Sheldon, finally sat confidently back in his seat while Mr. Myatt cross-examined her and Mr. Smilie, picking up on several points during his own questioning of Eliza Boon, deemed it necessary to call his client into the witness-box to refute some of her testimony. As Tony had rightly surmised Peterson was no match for Sir Douglas Dinsdale-Carr who, with no effort whatsoever, totally confused him; twisting and turning his answers to suit the interests of his client. Mr. Smilie, trying his best to counteract the impression Sir Douglas's questioning of Peterson had on the court struggled to put up even a fragile defence, so much so that he knew he was fighting a losing battle and soon found himself with no choice but to say, "I have no more questions for this witness, m'lud."

Sir Douglas, rising somewhat majestically to his feet, said, in answer to Mr. Justice Sheldon's enquiry if that was the case for the defence or if he had anything further, "I would like to re-call Lady Collett, m'lud."

Any hopes Eleanor may have had of being released as a witness were instantly dashed upon seeing the door to the court open and the Police Constable step out and call her name. With the aid of her father's arm on her elbow and Tony's steadying hand on her own trembling one she somehow managed to walk into the courtroom, but Tom and Beatrice, looking down at her as she made her way to the witness-box, pale faced and vulnerable, could only pray that she would not be questioned for too long as she was in no condition to endure a repeat performance of this morning.

"Lady Collett," Mr. Justice Sheldon said quietly as he looked down at her from the bench, "I must remind you that you are still under oath."

A barely audible, "Yes," left her lips.

"Lady Collett," Sir Douglas began without preamble, "you testified earlier that…"

"Lady Collett, I once again put it to you that…"

"Can you deny, Lady Collett, that…"

"Sir Douglas," Mr. Justice Sheldon intervened, "the witness has already answered this question."

"M'lud," he bowed. "Lady Collett, do you still say that my client…?"

"Yes," she managed, casting an involuntary glance at Eliza Boon sitting in the dock.

"I put it to you, Lady Collett," Sir Douglas pressed, "that your whole testimony, based on revenge, is nothing but a lie!"

"No," she said faintly.

"M'lud!" Mr. Myatt rose to his feet, "I must protest at my learned friend's badgering of the witness!"

"Sir Douglas…" Mr. Justice Sheldon began.

"I have no more questions for this witness, m'lud," Sir Douglas dismissed.

Mr. Justice Sheldon, after ascertaining that Mr. Myatt and Mr. Smilie had no more questions for Lady Collett or any further witnesses they wished to call looked at Sir Douglas who rose to his feet, saying, "That, m'lud, concludes the case for the defence."

By the time Eleanor was finally dismissed from the witness-box after three-quarters of an hour of further questioning she looked almost on the point of collapse, and following her departure from the courtroom Mr. Justice Sheldon, saying that he would hear the summing up of all three barristers tomorrow, deemed it time to adjourn the proceedings until the next morning when he would make his own summing up and instruct the jury. Beatrice, not waiting for Tom, hurriedly made her way to the area where Eleanor waited with her father and Tony, both of whom were taking a firm grip on either arm to prevent her from collapsing where she stood.

Totally oblivious to the brief conversation taking place over her head between her father and Tony and the decision they arrived at, wholeheartedly endorsed by Tom and Beatrice, Eleanor's only conscious thought as she leaned gratefully against Tony was an earnest desire to get away from this place as quickly as possible. She had no idea how he and Tom between them managed to forge a path to their waiting carriage through the throng of onlookers and reporters congregating outside, but to her relief she soon found herself safely inside before being driven hurriedly away.

Sir Miles had fully agreed with Tony when he said that as there was every likelihood there could well be reporters camped outside his front door in Bruton Street it would be far better to return to Mount Street in order to give them time to disperse to save Eleanor any further distress. However, no sooner did Sir Miles see the true extent of the devastating effects the trial had clearly had on his daughter in the full glare of the light in the hall than he readily agreed with Beatrice's suggestion that it would be far better for her to remain in Mount Street tonight. Tony had not needed Beatrice or Tom to tell him of the traumatic time Eleanor had in the witness-box, just seeing her almost on the state of collapse when she had left the courtroom was more than enough to tell him just how rough a time she really had, and when Beatrice had told him in a quiet aside that she had no intention of allowing her to leave Mount Street tonight, he had replied unequivocally, "Too right she's not!"

Eleanor may have been a little surprised to find herself being set down in Mount Street, but in spite of the fact that she was by far too distraught to give the reason for it very much thought, she was nevertheless conscious of feeling very safe. Somewhere on the periphery of her consciousness she heard a low-voiced conversation taking place behind her while Beatrice's soft voice coaxed and soothed as she helped her remove her hat and coat before propelling her towards the small sitting room, saying in her irresistible way as she eased her gently down onto a sofa, "Now, you just sit there quietly. I shall not be long." Eleanor, looking a little bemusedly up at her, was given no time to say anything as Beatrice, after bestowing a kiss on her cheek, was gone on the words, leaving the sitting room's sole occupant to reflect on the day's events.

Unfortunately, Eleanor's reflections were not very elevating. She had answered all the questions put to her honestly and truthfully and yet, for all that, she felt they had conveniently been twisted and turned to suit whichever barrister had put them to her. Then, if all this was not bad enough, she had been very conscious of Peterson sitting in the dock staring straight ahead of him at nothing in particular as though the proceedings had nothing whatsoever to do with him. But it was Eliza Boon who had disturbed her, silent and accusing as she continually glanced in her direction, making her feel as though she was the one on trial for some heinous crime instead of the other way round. There had been a moment when, during her account of the captive-like existence she had endured in Cavendish Square; what she had suffered at her husband's hands, Eliza Boon constantly keeping guard over her as well as the threat of being confined if she told anyone what she had seen, Eleanor caught the chilling look thrown at her out of those cold hard eyes and all her fears returned. For one awful moment, she had genuinely believed she was going to faint, but managing to overcome it resumed her explanation of all that had happened as well as answering further questions put to her, unutterable relief flooding through her when she was eventually released from what had seemed like an eternity of torment in the witness-box.

Eleanor felt sure that these traumatic and harrowing recollections would fade away in time, but now, as she sat in Beatrice's warm and cosy sitting room, leaning forward with her head bent and her elbows resting on her knees with her face buried in her hands, they were all too raw and painful, and by the time Tony came to her just minutes afterwards distraught tears were running freely down her cheeks. Upon hearing the door quietly open and close she removed her hands from her face to look up from under wet lashes to see who had come in, thinking it was Beatrice returning or her father, but upon seeing Tony's tall and reassuring figure approach her something between a sob and a cry left her lips. "It's all right, my darling," he told her gently as he sat down beside her, "I have you quite safe," then, deeming no further words were in the least necessary, he took her in his arms, content to just hold her as she poured an incoherent torrent of words into his shoulder, but eventually the warm strength of his body as he held her close against him permeated her cold and shivering one, comforting and soothing her until this perfectly natural emotional outlet gradually subsided. But the day's proceedings had taken quite a toll leaving her feeling utterly worn out, too worn out in fact to try to grapple with why she and her father had been brought to Mount Street instead of returning home. There was so much she wanted to say to Tony and just as many questions she needed to ask, but for the moment nothing mattered except his comforting presence and the feel of his arms around her as he tenderly soothed her, his deep voice acting like a balm to her battered emotions, so much so that, despite all her efforts, her eyelids began to close of their own volition until she fell into exhausted sleep cradled against him.

For some few minutes Tony was happy to simply sit and hold her, his strong fingers gently running through her slightly dishevelled hair, then, after kissing the top of her head, he laid her back against the sofa and, rising to his feet, he picked her effortlessly up in his arms, but although she turned her face comfortably into his shoulder, which, through the layers of sleep engulfing her, somehow felt strangely familiar and comforting, and laid the palm of her hand against his chest, she did not waken. Only when he laid her gently down onto the bed did she briefly open her eyes, her fingers instinctively clutching his arm as she recognised the face looking warmly down at her, his name leaving her lips on a contented sigh before sleep reclaimed her, whereupon he reluctantly left her in Sarah's care.

Since Sir Miles had remained in the waiting area throughout the trial as well as during Eleanor's time in the courtroom, he had no idea just how difficult a time she had actually had in the witness-box until informed of it by Tom. He could only express his relief that, as her attendance in court tomorrow for the judge's summing up would not be required, it was now thankfully all over for her, but announced his intention of accompanying Tony and Tom if for no other reason than to see two of the people who had caused his daughter so much suffering receive their just deserts. Although Sir Miles had accepted Beatrice's invitation to stay to dine with them not all her entreaties could persuade him to remain in Mount Street until the morning, not even when she assured him in her own inimitable way that it would be no imposition, he resisted her tempting. She was sorry, but did not press him further, merely assuring him that Eleanor would be quite safe here until he returned from court tomorrow when he could accompany her home because it would not do for her to be in Bruton Street on her own.

Tony, who was in full agreement with this, smiled down at his sister sometime later as he kissed her goodnight, "You really are a treasure, Bea!"

"Yes, I know," she twinkled mischievously up at him, "but only think what a fix you would be in if I were not!" Then, as if suddenly remembering something which she had lost sight of in the wake of what had happened over the past few days at Old Bailey, she looked worriedly up at her brother and questioned him about Eliza Boon's attempt to kill him, telling him that whilst she perfectly understood his reasons for not telling her anything about it, she could not help saying, "But you must surely have known it would be mentioned in court?"

He looked a little rueful. "The truth, Bea," he shook his head, "I never gave it much thought."

Even though she accepted this she nevertheless took some convincing that he had sustained no injury, but upon him swearing he had not as well as having this confirmed by Tom, she sighed and said, not a little unsteadily, that if this was the kind of thing that happened when he covered a story then she for one would not be sorry if he left it to his reporters in the future. Tony merely nodded and kissed her cheek, then, after assuring her one more time that he was perfectly all right as well as asking her to promise him she would not tell Eleanor, she kissed her brother and husband affectionately before leaving the two men alone.

They may not have lingered long over their whisky and soda, but it was only to be expected that the day's proceedings would be commented upon and Tony, after animadverting on Dinsdale-Carr's questioning of Eleanor, Tom was not in the least surprised to hear Tony shrug dismissively in response to his comment that he had not exactly let him off the hook, "Damn it, Tom! Do you think I care about myself?"

"No," Tom shook his head, patting him on the shoulder, "I know you better than that."

"God damn, Tom!" Tony ground out, raking a hand through his hair. "I should have been in there with her not sitting outside!"

"Well," Tom pointed out practically, "considering you were a witness yourself there was very little else you *could* have done."

"Other than force my way into the courtroom you mean?" Tony grinned. "That would have quite something, huh!" finishing off his whisky.

"It certainly would," Tom agreed, "and only think," he smiled, "you would have the best barrister in the country in Dinsdale-Carr to defend you on whatever indictment the Judge may have thought fit to charge you with; disrupting legal proceedings or something like that!" Tom shrugged. "Only think though," he grinned, "of the extenuating circumstances he would be able to put forward on your behalf!" He nodded.

"Okay, Tom," Tony laughed, slapping him on the shoulder, "I get the picture."

"Do not think for one moment that I don't understand your feelings, I do," Tom told him sympathetically, "I would feel exactly the same in your shoes, but there was nothing you *could* have done, Tony."

"I know," Tony sighed.

"At least now," Tom nodded, "it's all over for her."

"Yes," Tony acknowledged with relief, "thank God!"

"I'll drink to that!" Tom grinned, raising his glass.

Sarah, in response to Tony's concerned enquiry when he presently joined her upstairs, told him that apart from Eleanor opening her eyes for just long enough to allow her to prepare her for bed she had not stirred, although there was no denying she was very restless. Considering Eleanor's ordeal today, Tony was not at all surprised, and nor, for that matter, was Sarah when he told her that there was no need for her to stay with Eleanor because he was going to remain with her tonight, in fact she was glad of it, because if anyone were to ask her she would have to say that he did Eleanor far more good than she ever could. Medicine and rest were all very well so too was a fond and loving father, but at a time like this it was the man who loved and adored her she needed most, and it was with the utmost conviction that Sarah left her charge in good hands that she wished him goodnight.

Eleanor may not have roused from the sleep which claimed her, but it was clear from the fretful way she moved her head from side to side on the pillow and the barely stifled cries which left her lips that her dreams were very far from elevating. As Tony stood looking anxiously down at her with his hands thrust deep into his dressing gown pockets and a frown furrowing his forehead, he knew Tom was absolutely right in that there was nothing he could have done to shield her from the onslaught in court today, yet this did nothing to make him feel any better. No more than Beatrice did he have any regrets about bringing her here after what had been a most distressing day for her and, like his sister, he could not bear to see her like this but, unlike Beatrice, his feelings for Eleanor were such that her very nearness did nothing to lessen either his need or his love for her, but he could no more leave her than he could stop breathing. But his own feelings apart as well as those whose sensibilities would be greatly offended if they could see him now, her comfort and happiness were all that mattered and certainly rose far above the narrow-minded prejudice of the censorious, and it was therefore without a twinge of conscience that he sat down beside her and gently gathered her in his arms and held her comfortably against him. As if sensing his nearness, Eleanor, although she did not stir, calmed down considerably, in fact it was not for at least another two hours before she drowsily opened her eyes.

Upon turning her head slightly to see Tony sitting in the chair beside the bed with one long leg crossed over the other reading a newspaper she knew she had not imagined any of it. She was naturally curious to know what she was doing in Mount Street and if her father was also a guest for the night, but for now she was content to just lie back against the pillows and watch him, neither moving nor calling out to him.

It was just as Tony was about to turn a page that he became aware Eleanor was watching him, and switching his gaze from the newspaper towards the bed he saw her looking sideways at him when a smile lit his eyes. Folding the newspaper, he dropped it onto his vacated chair and sitting down on the bed in front of her he took her hands in his and asked softly, "How long have you been awake?"

"Only a few minutes," she smiled, returning the clasp of his fingers.

"How do you feel?" he asked gently, bending his head to kiss her fingers. "You had a bad dream, remember?"

Yes, she did, and could not help shuddering when she recalled the vivid images which had danced mockingly in front of her; brought about as a direct result of the harrowing time she had in the witness-box, leaving her emotionally vulnerable and exhausted. But now, as Tony folded her in his arms and she rested her head comfortably against his shoulder, she disjointedly recounted the events of the day ending by telling him that she had been so very glad to see him enter the sitting room, but unfortunately had no memory of him carrying her upstairs and only a vague one of Sarah helping put her to bed, but even though she could clearly remember arriving in Mount Street she was a little at a loss to know why.

"As there was every chance that there would be a horde of reporters waiting to pounce on you when you returned home this evening," Tony explained, "your father and I thought it would be better if you came here as well as staying the night; Bea and Tom agreed, especially after what you went through in the witness-box. The last thing you needed was to find yourself faced with yet another barrage of questions. In fact," he nodded, "I would say that by the time your father returned home, having dined here first, they would have given up the wait."

"Oh, Tony, I could not have borne that!" she cried, turning her face deeper into his shoulder. "Truly I could not!"

He had no need to hear her tearful and incoherent description of today's events to know how she must have felt in trying to answer the questions put to her only to have them turned and twisted until they resembled anything but the truth. It was a daunting task for anyone to stand in the witness-box, but for someone as vulnerable as Eleanor, being subjected to months of despicable tyranny, it was a most intimidating experience and one which would stay with her for some time as would the memory of having to face two of those who had been responsible for her persecution.

"It was horrible!" she shuddered. "Everyone watching and…" she swallowed a sob. "You may think I am a dreadful coward, but I can't bear the thought of having to go again tomorrow!"

"You know I don't think that," Tony said vehemently, holding her tighter against him. "I know you to be a very brave and courageous woman, were it otherwise you would never have risked your life by escaping from Cavendish Square, but you have been through an awful lot and it is perfectly natural that it has left you anxious and fearful." He knew that months of ill treatment and virtual imprisonment had left their scars and only time would heal the wounds inflicted over the last twelve months, but as he held her and soothed her fears by assuring her that her attendance tomorrow for the judge's summing up and his instructions to the jury would not be required, he felt the relief run through her. "As far as you are concerned my darling, it's all over," he assured her gently, "all over. There's nothing whatever for you to be afraid of any more, I promise."

"I am not afraid of anything when I am with you," she said huskily, laying the palm of her hand against his chest. "It's just…"

Lifting her chin with his forefinger he smiled lovingly down at her, saying tenderly as he wiped away a stray tear, "I want you to forget everything that has gone before, in fact I want you to forget everything except how much I love you and can't wait to make you my own. When you go to sleep," he told her in a deep voice, "I want you to dream of nothing and no one but me – promise?"

She nodded. "I promise."

"I shall be right there in that chair," he told her soothingly, "so there is no need to be afraid."

"I shan't be," she shook her head, her fingers moving in his, "but…"

"But what?" he urged gently.

"Well," she said a little huskily, "I can't help wondering how much sleep you have lost because of me."

"Oh, *days* of it I shouldn't wonder!" He pulled a face. "In fact," the gravity in his voice belied by the laughter in his eyes, "I've kept a daily note of all the nights I have lost sleep because of you."

A little choke of laughter escaped her lips at this, but she managed with credible surprise, "You have?"

"Too right I have!" he nodded. "And you may be sure I shall hand it over to you at the proper time for settlement."

Her own sense of humour got the better of her and, after seeming to give this due consideration, looked mischievously up at him, asking, "Does it total very much?"

"Let us just say," Tony told her, "that it's surprising how one's debts mount up."

"Oh, dear," she bit her bottom lip, "as much as that?" to which he nodded. "In that case," she sighed, "I only hope you will give me enough time to discharge them."

"Oh," Tony pulled a face, his eyes smiling warmly down into hers, "I'm sure we can come to a mutually agreeable arrangement. In fact," he pointed out, "I'm prepared to offer you very generous repayment terms."

"You are?" she said unsteadily.

"Mm," he nodded, kissing the top of her head.

"How long were you thinking of exactly?" Eleanor asked a little huskily, making no protest when he gently drew her further into him.

"A whole lifetime," he told her warmly, adding, "but I think it only fair to tell you that it is not open to negotiation. I take it that is acceptable to you?"

"*Most* acceptable," she replied on a contented sigh.

"As a businessman," Tony told her, his voice deepening as he lowered his head, "I should really be asking you for a promissory note, but as the man who loves you," he smiled, "I am quite willing to forgo such a formality and accept your kisses in lieu, providing that is," he caressed against her lips, "you have no objection." The look on her face confirmed she had not, whereupon he proceeded to kiss her, but although his kisses left her in no doubt that waiting to make her his own was going to seem like an eternity, they were remarkably restrained for all that.

If Eleanor thought that she would spend what was left of the night dreaming of the pleasurable havoc wreaked on her senses by Tony's kisses, she was sadly doomed to disappointment, in fact she had no recollection of having dreamed anything at all; sleeping soundly until Sarah came in with a cup of tea about ten o'clock with the news that Sir Thomas and Mr. Tony had left half an hour ago. "But not before he had taken a look in on you," she told her, plumping up the pillows. Upon seeing the colour flood Eleanor's cheeks Sarah turned and picked up the newspaper Tony had left saying indulgently, "However, upon seeing you were still asleep he decided against waking you, asking me not to disturb you as you had been awake for some time before falling asleep." Eleanor could think of nothing to say in answer to this which was perhaps just as well since it appeared that Sarah did not expect one, merely saying that she would come and help her get dressed in a few minutes when she had drunk her tea.

As Eleanor had no more understanding of court procedure than Beatrice they were left with nothing but speculation about how long it would take before the case was actually finalised, but Beatrice, shocked at the iniquities of Eliza Boon and Peterson, told Eleanor as she shared a cup of tea with her whilst she picked her way through breakfast that the jury would have to be totally stupid not to find the pair of them guilty. "Because if they don't," she nodded, putting her cup down with some force, "it will be the biggest miscarriage of justice I ever heard!"

For one of Eleanor's gentle nature it was impossible to understand how anyone could cold-bloodedly take the life of another; but even though she knew that one had to be punished for one's crimes, the very thought of the hangman's noose was something she could not contemplate without a shudder. All the same, she only had to think of those who had suffered at the hands of Braden and the others, particularly Mitchell, a man who had not only proved himself very much her friend, but had done nothing to deserve such a brutal death, to make it impossible for her to do anything other than agree.

Even though both ladies found more than enough to keep them occupied during the course of the day, including being given an engaging if frequently corrected recital by Alice, under the watchful eye of Nanny Susan, to see how well she was learning her alphabet and numbers as well as her nursery rhymes, it could not be denied that their minds continually turned to events at Old Bailey. Quite when the horrifying thought assailed Eleanor that she might be summoned to attend court after all she did not know, but once the seed had been sown she lived in hourly dread of an imperious ringing of the bell demanding she accompany whoever it was who carried out these duties, but as the day wore on with no official representation arriving on the doorstep, she was able to breathe more easily. But whatever peace of mind she may have been able to salvage was unfortunately killed at a stroke upon hearing Tony's watered down account of the day's events upon his return to Mount Street in company with Tom and her father a little after four o'clock.

Mr. Justice Sheldon, immediately before his summing up, reminded the jury that Sir Braden Collett was not the one on trial here. He then went on to say that they would do well to bear in mind that whilst certain testimony given under oath by this or that witness, although compelling, was not sufficient evidence to prove guilt or innocence. A witness's assumption, he told them firmly, was no more fact than hearsay, and they must take this into account when deliberating their verdict. He further pointed out that the defendant James Peterson, by his own admission, had not only murdered Sir Braden Collett, George Edward Mitchell and Dennis Dunscumbe, but had assisted Sir Braden Collett in disposing of Sir Philip Dunscumbe's body by throwing it into the Thames in the same callous and dispassionate way he had dealt with Annie Myers, and they must return a guilty verdict.

As for the defendant Eliza Boon, who had maintained her innocence throughout, no evidence had been put forward to corroborate Peterson's testimony in that she was a party to his crimes together with Sir Braden Collett much less that she incited them, and so must treat Peterson's claim of her involvement with circumspection. "As Sir Douglas has capably argued," Mr. Justice Sheldon told the jury, "the defendant has never denied accompanying James Peterson to Hertford Street, but it is for you to decide whether it was from an urgent desire to retrieve previously overlooked evidence which could tie them both to the murder of Dennis Dunscumbe, or whether it was in fact from pressure brought to bear on her by James Peterson who had threatened to reveal not only her past profession and thus damage her reputation, but to implicate her in a crime of which she is totally innocent. It is also for you to decide whether Eliza Boon deliberately meant to shoot Lord Childon as Police Constable Moore has testified, he being the only witness to the event or, as Sir Douglas has plausibly stated, merely a case of the pistol going off accidentally as she was about to hand it over; a pistol she carried on her person purely for her own protection. As for the charges of keeping a certain type of establishment and living off immoral earnings, Sir Douglas has never denied that his client had made her living in this way, on the contrary he made this perfectly clear from the beginning as well as disclosing that Eliza Boon willingly confessed at the earliest opportunity to having played a part in helping cover up the accidental death of Annie Myers. As for Sir Braden Collett's death, I would remind the jury that Eliza Boon, as James Peterson himself has testified, tried to prevent such a dreadful incident…" Mr. Justice Sheldon continued in this vein for another fifteen minutes, after which he drew attention to the police investigation and that of Lord Childon on behalf of his newspapers which had ultimately resulted in their collaboration, but although their coalition achieved its purpose in so far as bringing James Peterson to account it had not produced one shred of proof which either placed Eliza Boon at the scene of any of the crimes or proved beyond doubt her complicity and incitement much less that the pistol found beside the body of Dennis Dunscumbe belonged to her.

With regards to Lady Collett's harrowing, but unsubstantiated testimony, whose injuries he hastened to add were not in dispute, being fully verified by Mrs. Timms, he told the jury that it was for them to decide whether, in her distressed state of mind, Lady Collett could so easily have misinterpreted the reason for Eliza Boon's presence in the house or if it was as Sir Douglas had argued that Lady Collett, although she had categorically denied knowing anything of her husband's regular visits to Eliza Boon's establishment, she had known all along of Sir Braden's visits to Periton Place and so in an act of revenge had tried to incriminate Eliza Boon by claiming false imprisonment. It was also for the jury to decide whether Eliza Boon, who had testified under oath that she had no idea that Sir Braden Collett had murdered Sir Philip Dunscumbe or engineered his brother Dennis's death and that he had led her to believe he had dismissed Mitchell for stealing as well as deceiving her as to the true state of his wife's mental wellbeing, but also that at no time had she offered Lady Collett physical harm or laid a hand on her in anyway, and as for keeping her a prisoner, she has totally denied such a charge. As for James Peterson, Eliza Boon also admitted under oath that she had absolutely no idea that Sir Braden Collett had included him into the household to either act as gaoler to Lady Collett or for any criminal purpose. She totally denies any knowledge of their criminal colluding stating categorically that Sir Braden Collett had told her that upon leaving her establishment he felt the least he could do was find Peterson employment, particularly after the dismissal of Mitchell. "Gentlemen of the jury," Mr. Justice Sheldon counselled, "Lady Collett's distress is to be regretted, but it is my duty to remind you that it is *your* duty to try this case on the evidence heard in this court and not sentiment, and Lady Collett's testimony, however moving, must be treated with extreme caution given the distraught state of her mind. I would also remind you to treat with extreme caution Mrs. Timms's evidence who, it must be remembered, is sincerely attached to her mistress, but also that, by her own admission, had taken Eliza Boon in dislike and her evidence must therefore be considered as unreliable. Gentlemen of the jury, I now call upon you to retire and consider your verdict."

Taking less than two hours to arrive at a decision, the foreman of the jury informed the clerk of the court in answer to his question as to whether they had reached a unanimous verdict, announced, "Yes." Upon being asked whether they found James Peterson guilty or not guilty of the wilful murder of Sir Braden Collett, George Edward Mitchell and Dennis Dunscumbe the foreman replied, "Guilty."

Upon being asked if they found Eliza Boon guilty or not guilty of conspiring in or inciting the deaths of Sir Philip Dunscumbe, Sir Braden Collett, George Edward Mitchell and Dennis Dunscumbe, he replied, "Not guilty."

Upon being asked if they found Eliza Boon guilty or not guilty of the attempted murder of Lord Childon, he replied, "Not guilty."

Upon being asked if they found Eliza Boon guilty or not guilty of conspiring in the death of Annie Myers, he replied, "Not guilty."

Upon being asked if they found Eliza Boon guilty or not guilty of keeping a house of ill repute, of living off immoral earnings and possessing an illegal firearm, he replied, "Guilty."

A hushed silence hung over the courtroom as Mr. Justice Sheldon passed sentence of death upon James Peterson and, after being escorted from the dock, Mr. Justice Sheldon, his black cap having been removed, faced Eliza Boon, saying, "Eliza Boon, you have been found guilty of keeping a house of ill repute, of living off immoral earnings and possessing an illegal firearm. I sentence you to the maximum term the law allows for these offences of two years' imprisonment. Take her down."

Tony may have deliberately kept the information about the attempt on his life from Eleanor to save her any further pain, but Beatrice, no less than her husband and brother, was appalled at the verdict in relation to Eliza Boon, and Sir Miles, who was neither a vindictive nor a vengeful man, was totally at a loss, but the effect on Eleanor was profound. As Beatrice gave vent to her shocked disbelief, demanding of her husband and brother if the members of the jury were totally stupid, Eleanor could do no more than stare helplessly from one to the other, her eyes reflecting her shock and bewilderment, but gradually she somehow managed to find the strength to choke out a barely audible, "Excuse me," before hurrying out of the drawing-room.

Sir Miles immediately made a move to follow her, but Tony's restraining hand on his arm forestalled him, nodding his head when Tony said quietly, "No, let me."

Having fled to the sanctuary of Beatrice's sitting room Eleanor stood in front of the fire and buried her face in her hands, the events of the past few days, culminating in the not guilty verdict for Eliza Boon, taking their toll. Shock, bemusement and the horrifying thought that no one had believed anything she had said, proved too much and by the time Tony joined her in the sitting room she was giving full vent to her emotions, putting up no resistance as he took her in his arms. "They didn't believe me," she sobbed at length into his shoulder. "They thought I was lying and worse, they… oh Tony," she cried, looking helplessly up at him, "they even thought I was not in my right mind!"

"No," he shook his head, "I promise you they did not."

"Yes," Eleanor sniffed, "they did."

"Ellie, my darling," he urged, "you must not think that. It's not true."

"Then why…?" she pleaded, her eyes searching his face.

"Because Dinsdale-Carr put up an outstandingly good defence," wiping away her tears with a gentle finger, "and also because Eliza Boon was shrewd enough to know that by confessing to her part in covering up the death of Annie Myers at the earliest opportunity could only work in her favour."

"You mean he believed her?" Eleanor asked incredulously.

"As to that," Tony sighed, "I really couldn't say, but then," he grimaced, "I guess he doesn't have to. A barrister's sole aim is to defend his client by any means at his disposal whether he believes them guilty or not. However much we may dislike it," he told her, "it's his job to turn and twist the testimony of the witnesses in favour of his client the same as it is the prosecution's job to do all he can to convict them. I don't like to think that Eliza Boon has got off scot-free of murder any more than you do, but…"

"But two years!" Eleanor cried, aghast. "After all she has done!" She shuddered as a thought suddenly occurred to her. "Oh, Tony," easing herself a little away from him, "in two years she will be free and…"

"By which time," Tony pointed out, knowing perfectly well what she was thinking, "you will be my wife. My darling," he said softly, stroking her flushed and damp cheek with the back of his forefinger, "do you honestly believe that I would allow Eliza Boon or anyone to hurt you? Huh huh," he shook his head, "no way. She can't hurt you ever again. As far as *you* are concerned," he smiled, drawing her closer to him, "it's all over. All you need think about from now on is how much I love you and our future together," whereupon he spent the next few minutes agreeably laying the remainder of her fears to rest as well as leaving her in no doubt as to just how happy their future together would be.

When Eleanor eventually left Mount Street several hours later with her father she was certainly feeling more calm, but even though it was such an easy matter to think of her life with Tony and what lay ahead of them, the fact remained that she knew it would take time before Eliza Boon, a woman who had made her life such a misery, would fade from her memory. Sir Miles, apart from lightly touching upon the unprecedented events of the day, decided that turning his daughter's mind into more pleasurable channels was the only way to try to eradicate the last twelve months from her mind, and upon seeing the looks which passed between her and Tony over the dinner table, not the first he had witnessed by a good way, he knew there was no more sure way of achieving this than to promote the relationship of which he heartily approved.

Tony was no more a vindictive man than Tom or Sir Miles, but the not guilty verdict arrived at by the jury was something he could not contemplate without anger and disgust, especially when he thought of the effect it had on Eleanor. He knew that in spite of his assurances it would take time before she would be able to put all this behind her, but as he told Tom later when they were alone he could not blame Beatrice for condemning the jury. "God damn, Tom!" he bit out. "They saw Eliza Boon for themselves. Did they really think she cared a damn about her reputation or allow herself to be coerced? What the hell did they think she was doing in Hertford Street if not to search for possible evidence?"

"I can understand your being angry," Tom nodded, handing him a glass of whisky, "I am myself, particularly when I think how she explained away the death of Annie Myers."

"A shrewd move or what?" Tony demanded. "Once Peterson opened up and told the police about disposing of Annie Myers's body she knew how damaging it could be to her, so she decided to be up front about it! By saying that Annie Myers's death was her own fault because she had too much to drink and that Dennis Dunscumbe and Collett had played no part in it, making it perfectly clear they were not there that night, it could only give credence to her denials of any involvement in all that followed. Like I said," he nodded, "she sure is one tough cookie who knows her way around."

"She certainly knew her way around enough to get off with as light a sentence as possible!" Tom supplied, making himself comfortable in the armchair.

"By lying through her teeth you mean? You'd better believe it!" Tony derided. "But what sticks in my throat is that Annie Myers has not received the justice she deserves!"

Tom a thought a moment as he eyed Tony, asking at length, "Are you saying you feel as though you have let her down?"

"Damn right I am!" Tony said firmly. "Just because she earned her living in the way she did does not mean her life was any less important than Sir Philip's or the others!"

"Well," Tom sighed, "I can understand why you feel that way, but really, Tony," he shook his head, "I fail to see what more you could have done. Eliza Boon, whether we like it or not, played her cards well and, with Dinsdale-Carr behind her…"

"She sure did play them well!" Tony broke in. "So much so that the jury was left to decide whether Eleanor had known all along about her husband's regular visits to Periton Place and decided on revenge by claiming false imprisonment or if she had simply misinterpreted the reason for Eliza Boon being installed in Cavendish Square because of her distressed state of mind! What the hell do they think Collett brought her in for if not to keep a watch over his wife? And how the jury could have swallowed the tale that Collett brought in Peterson merely to give him employment beats me!"

"Yes," Tom nodded, "I must admit that has *me* at a loss! Then there's Mrs. Timms." He pulled a disgusted face.

"Unreliable evidence you mean?" Tony said ironically, leaning his arm along the mantelshelf. "The only unreliable thing about it was that she told a few home truths!"

"Well," Tom sighed, "at least it's something to know that Peterson has finally received his just desserts, but as for Eliza Boon you have to admit that Dinsdale-Carr did his work well. He's certainly a persuasive advocate and more than earned the epithet of being 'The Champion of Lost Causes."

"That's for sure!" Tony grimaced, taking a much-needed drink. "And lost causes don't come any closer to the wire than Eliza Boon's!" pointing his glass at him.

"The thing that gets me though, Tony," Tom told him, "is the way the attempt on your life was shrugged aside."

"You know something, Tom," Tony raised an eyebrow, "I can live with that, but not with knowing what it's all done to Eleanor." He looked thoughtfully down into the fire as he inhaled on his cigarette, then, raising his head a little, looked at Tom saying in a hard voice, "You know what sticks in my throat more than all the rest, Tom?" to which his brother-in-law shook his head, "leaving Eleanor to believe that the jury discounted her evidence because she was not in her right mind."

"Good God!" Tom cried, sitting bolt upright. "You don't mean it?"

"I'm afraid I do," Tony sighed, straightening up. "That's what upset her the most, in fact," he frowned, "I think that hurt her as much as knowing that Eliza Boon was found not guilty and being sentenced only for her lesser offences. Already Eleanor's afraid that she will exact revenge when she's released."

Tom thought a moment, asking at length, "Do you think she will?"

"No." Tony shook his head, sinking into the armchair opposite Tom. "She may be hard-boiled but she's not stupid. She knows that should she ever make the attempt to settle scores it could only condemn her. Unless I miss my guess," he told him, "I'd say that right now she counting herself very fortunate that things went as well as they did for her."

"Well," Tom inclined his head, "it's certainly more than she deserves, but about when she's released, I'd say there's every likelihood she'll either resume her past career or quietly disappear."

"You know something, Tom," Tony raised an eyebrow, "as long as I never have to set eyes on her again I really don't care!"

"I'll drink to that," Tom grinned, suiting the action to the words. "So," he smiled, "about you and Eleanor; what are your plans?"

"To get married, of course!" Tony grinned.

"Of course," Tom smiled, refilling their empty glasses, "but that won't be for another twelve months."

"Thanks for reminding me," Tony smiled ruefully.

Tom laughed. "I know you would much rather it be sooner than later," he acknowledged handing him his glass, "for reasons which I perfectly understand, but a year will soon pass."

"You think so?" Tony raised an eyebrow. "Then why do I get the feeling it will seem like a lifetime?" An empathetic pat on the shoulder being the only response he received to this.

Chapter Thirty-Four

As it turned out Tom's prophesy proved true, although he doubted whether Tony regarded an unexpected trip to New York, unlike the several visits he had made to Childon Manor in Kent to check on the progress of the renovations, as being conducive to helping him take his mind off Eleanor. But however much Tony hated being parted from her, he was too much the professional to ignore the demands of business and had set out for his birthplace on the RMS *Empress Elisabeth* from Southampton in response to the cable he had received from his American lawyers.

Unlike Beatrice, who had accompanied him to Southampton and waved him a tearful farewell, Eleanor, not only because of her state of mourning but also because Tony could not bear to see her disappear from view on the quayside as he sailed further and further away from her, said goodbye to him in Bruton Street. Sailing back and forth across the Atlantic over the years had become second nature to him, but even though it was always a wrench to say goodbye to Beatrice and Tom and the children, he had accepted the obligations which brought it about without question or regret, and although now was no exception saying goodbye to Eleanor, the woman without whom his life would be entirely meaningless, was the hardest thing he had ever done.

Tony's trip to New York came as no real surprise to Eleanor, in fact she had a feeling he would have to return at some point before they got married, but even though she made no attempt to dissuade him from going, fully understanding the need for him to transact business there, the very thought of being parted from him for several weeks was more than she could bear, taking little comfort from Beatrice's smiling assurance, "Would you believe it, my dear? It takes less than a week to cross the Atlantic! I find it truly astonishing the speed with which people travel nowadays!"

So too did Eleanor, but it did nothing to ease the pain around her heart at the thought of saying goodbye to Tony, and even though she tried so hard not to let him see it, at the last moment her resolve crumbled. "I shall be back before you know it," he told her unsteadily, holding her tight against him, "six weeks at most." She nodded and sniffed, but giving her no time to say anything he thoroughly kissed her before turning on his heel and leaving her without a backward glance.

If anyone had asked her what the difference was between Tony visiting Childon Manor for several days at a time and his visit to America she could not have told them except that this was the first time he had been so far away from her, leaving her feeling quite bereft without him. Beatrice, whose separations from Tom on the occasions she had visited Tony and her mother and step-father in New York, made it easy for her to understand Eleanor's feelings, and did her best to make her separation from Tony a little more bearable. It was perhaps a little unfortunate that Eleanor's period of mourning rather narrowed the scope of her taking part in certain activities, not that she wanted to attend balls or parties, and it was certainly not because she was sullen or petulant or difficult to please, on the contrary she was her usual gentle and shy self who happily lent herself to whatever idea Beatrice came up with, but it could not be denied that without Tony she had definitely lost some of her sparkle.

A few weeks in Suffolk with her father did much to restore Eleanor's spirits which had been considerably low, not only because of being separated from the man she loved but also the recent execution of Peterson. She may have feared him and abhorred everything he had done, but far from feeling elated upon reading of his lawful punishment in the newspapers it had, for some inexplicable reason, left her rather saddened. But thanks to her father calmly pointing out that a far from happy chapter in her life had finally been closed as well as what she had to look forward to, coupled with pleasurable walks in the summer sunshine through such charming and picturesque villages as Dunwich and Thorpeness and gentle strolls along the windswept sand dune beaches, soon had a most beneficial effect on her spirits.

Eleanor could not undo the past no matter how painful, but one good thing at least had come out of it and that was meeting Tony, a man who was not only the very antithesis of Braden, but one she could not live without. He had brought love and tenderness into her life when she had least expected it as well as an affectionate teasing which was as irresistible as it was indispensable to her contentment; so very different to what Braden had subjected her to or expected of her. She had never known such emotions existed, but in spite of her innate shyness she had, from the very beginning, responded easily to Tony's lovemaking indeed it was the most natural thing in the world, so much so that she felt as though some magnetic force stronger than either of them drew them irrevocably together. It was not only because she loved Tony and he returned it with equal passion and commitment which excited her or that he would be her lover as well as her husband, but that he was her friend; a friend whose sense of humour was akin to her own, a friend with whom she could be herself, talk to and share her innermost thoughts and secrets with, confidences she would never divulge to another living soul.

But Tony's love as well as his attentiveness to her happiness and wellbeing incorporated a thoughtfulness which Braden had sadly lacked; this thoughtfulness clearly demonstrated a few weeks before he left for America by arriving in Bruton Street one afternoon with Mary, having travelled into Essex to bring her to her. But it had not taken this for Eleanor to know that without him she would be utterly desolate.

Her stay in Suffolk had certainly put the colour back into her cheeks, but if the sparkle in her eyes was not so pronounced or quite so vibrant as when she was with Tony, it certainly flickered, a circumstance which was not lost on Beatrice when she called in Bruton Street the day after Eleanor's return to town with Sir Miles, two days before her twenty-first birthday. Beatrice, whose sweet smile and kind and generous nature, as her husband and brother knew very well, were utterly irresistible, and Eleanor, who enjoyed visiting in Mount Street, received her invitation for her and her father to dine with them on the evening of her birthday with genuine pleasure. "I know you are in mourning," Beatrice said gently, "but it isn't every day one has a twenty-first birthday, and although you cannot celebrate in the usual way by throwing a party or going to the theatre or something like that, I thought you and your father could do so in Mount Street. There will only be me and Tom," she assured her, laying a hand on Eleanor's arm, "so it will be a very quiet affair. Please say you will come."

It had been a little over seven weeks since Eleanor had said goodbye to Tony, his last letter conveying the news that his business was taking longer to transact than he had thought, but as she walked the short distance from Bruton Street across Berkeley Square into Mount Street on her father's arm to quietly celebrate her birthday, no one looking at her would have had the least guess of how she was pining for the sight of a tall, loose-limbed man who had come to mean more to her than life itself. For the first time she failed to appreciate how beautiful London could be on an early evening in late September, especially with the leaves on the trees beginning to turn into a deep warm gold which seemed to catch the last rays of the fading sun before it disappeared over the horizon.

Their reception in Mount Street was as warm and welcoming as the last remnants of sunshine outside, with Tom following Beatrice into the hall and warmly embracing her and kissing her cheek and wishing her many happy returns of the day, immediately dispelling the sharp edges of sadness she felt at missing Tony. Bennett, having taken their hats and coats, disappeared as quietly as he had entered the hall, entering the drawing-room some minutes later carrying a tray with a bottle of champagne and five glasses, a circumstance that totally escaped Eleanor's notice, but which brought a knowing look in to Sir Miles's eyes as he exchanged significant glances with his host and hostess.

"You know, Bea," Tom said ingenuously, looking innocently at his wife, "I've just thought, might it not be better if we gave Eleanor her present before we drink a toast to her."

Apart from her husband and Sir Miles, no one looking at Beatrice as she opened her beautiful blue eyes to their fullest extent as though marvelling at such a brilliant suggestion, could possibly have accused her of dissimulation, Eleanor most certainly did not. "I think that's a wonderful idea. Why didn't *I* think of that? Now," she pondered, pursing her pretty lips in thought, looking questioningly up at her husband, "where did I put it? Do you remember? Oh, yes," she smiled turning back to Eleanor, who had not expected a present, "I recall putting it in the sitting room."

"Oh, Beatrice," Eleanor laughed, giving her a hug, "you should not; really you should not."

"Nonsense!" Beatrice smiled, returning her hug. "As I told you, it is not every day one is twenty-one!"

Missing the smiling looks exchanged over her head, Eleanor made her way to the small sitting room at the rear of the house which, on a beautiful evening such as this, housed no fire, the fireplace being filled with a flower display whose blooms gave off the most delicious scent. Through the half open door she could see that the room was in darkness so pushing it further open she stepped inside and turned the switch on the wall, whereupon a voice as familiar to her as her own said a little unsteadily, "If you're looking for me, and I sure hope you are, I'm right here."

Spinning round, Eleanor stared incredulously at the man she had yearned to see for seven long weeks as though she could not believe her eyes. "Tony!" she cried, feeling as though she had taken root to the spot. "Oh Tony!" She shook her head. "Is… is it really you?" she managed between tears and laughter, taking several faltering steps towards him on legs which seemed in imminent danger of giving way under her.

"Too right it's me!" he smiled, his voice a deep caress, taking hold of her outstretched hand and drawing her towards him.

"But I…" She got no further.

She would never be entirely certain whether she walked into his arms or he drew her into them, all she knew was that she was where she wanted to be and, not surprisingly, every consideration was forgotten as she welcomed his kisses, kisses she had so desperately missed. As the minutes slipped gratifyingly by questions and explanations were quite unnecessary, but eventually, and very gradually, Tony released her lips for just long enough to groan achingly against them, "*Ellie, my darling!*"

"Oh, Tony!" she cried huskily. "I have missed you so much; I have been utterly miserable without you!"

"Then that makes two of us because I've sure missed you!" he told her in a ragged voice. "Although if you want the truth," he admitted against her lips, "this past seven weeks I've been like a bear with a sore head!" giving her no time to say anything more, in fact for the next few minutes she was totally preoccupied in a way which prevented even the remotest resemblance of rational thought.

But when she at last found herself sitting beside him on the sofa with his arm wrapped round her waist and her head resting comfortably on his shoulder, he told her, "I cabled Bea a couple of days ago to tell her that I would be arriving today and I would get here late this afternoon and that she was to get you and your father to come here tonight to celebrate your birthday." He smiled warmly down at her. "I asked her not to mention me because I wanted to surprise you. I *hope,"* he pulled a face, "you are suitably impressed with our stratagems?"

"*Very* impressed," Eleanor said softly, resting a loving hand on the lapel of his dinner jacket. "Oh Tony, I am so glad you are here!"

"I'm sorry it took longer than I thought to deal with matters back in the States," he apologised, covering her hand with his, "but even if I had not settled them do you really believe that I would miss this very special day in your life?" Easing himself a little away from her, he inserted a hand into the inside pocket of his dinner jacket and pulled out a small flat square box, saying, "This belonged to my mother. My father gave it to her as a wedding present. She left it to me to give my wife the day I married, but since you will be Lady Childon in a little under six months, I don't think she would mind me giving it to you now. Happy twenty-first birthday, my darling," he said lovingly, placing the box in her hand as he kissed her.

Looking from Tony's smiling face down at the box, Eleanor lifted the lid with trembling fingers, gasping her surprise at the diamond and sapphire brooch nestling on a bed of white satin and, after gently removing it and resting it in the palm of her hand, she raised misty eyes to his, saying, hardly above a whisper, "It's beautiful. I shall treasure it always!"

"It's okay," he assured her, when she mentioned Beatrice, "Bea knows that it's always been meant for my wife. I promise you," he said softly, "she's very happy about it."

And so indeed it proved. Beatrice, who had not seen the brooch in a long time due to it being stored in the vaults of Tony's bankers in New York, remembered her mother wearing it on several occasions, and was neither envious nor resentful, on the contrary she was genuinely pleased and insisted Eleanor wear it, if only for tonight, saying truthfully when she had a few minutes alone with her, "I know you cannot wear it publicly yet, but please, my dear," she insisted, "it becomes you beautifully. Tony would like it and," she said softly, "so would my mother."

Had anyone asked Eleanor if she had ever had a more wonderful and enjoyable birthday she would have said no, definitely not, but it was not solely the beautiful gift which had made it special, but spending it with the man she loved. As she sat opposite Tony at the dinner table, their eyes often meeting across the laden space which separated them and conveying the most intimate of messages, Beatrice, silently applauding such a brilliant strategy, was already making wedding plans.

But Tony and Eleanor were not the only ones to plan a wedding; Jerry and Mrs. Timms, whose relationship had blossomed, had also decided to tie the knot and Bill, upon receiving his invitation, told Tony that it couldn't have happened to a nicer guy. "Present company excepted, of course!" he grinned.

"Oh, of course!" Tony replied, pulling a face, his eyes alight with amusement.

Having by now become firm friends, Jerry asked Tony in a quiet aside as he emerged from the church with the second Mrs. Taylor on his arm, "You don't think, do you, that Janie is lookin' down on me?" jerking his head upwards.

"If she is," Tony smiled, "I'm sure she is very happy for you; as I am."

Despite Eleanor's feelings for Braden and the sense of hypocrisy she felt in mourning a man who had instilled so much fear into her, she nevertheless observed all the etiquette her period of mourning demanded, but for all that she could not prevent her mind from drifting to her forthcoming wedding to Tony. Her marriage to Braden, however reluctantly entered into as well as being utterly distasteful to her, had nevertheless been one of the major events on the social calendar. A ceremony in St. George's Hanover Square followed by a three-week honeymoon in Paris, with the intolerable exception of the remainder of what passed as her marriage, had been the most unpleasant experience of her life, but as she contemplated her wedding to Tony and their future together she was conscious of no such aversion and horror, on the contrary she was joyfully filled with an exhilaration and expectancy which, had anyone been privileged to read her thoughts, would have utterly condemned.

It had been Tony's intention to invite Sir Miles and Eleanor, together with Tom and Beatrice and the children, down to Childon Manor for Christmas, but due to one or two minor renovations still in progress, he had instead accepted his future father-in-law's invitation for them all to spend the festive season at his home in Suffolk. Sir Miles may be a private and reserved man, but for the privileged few whom he regarded as close friends, they knew him to be an excellent host who knew precisely how to entertain his guests and therefore the yuletide party eventually returned to London, having stayed to welcome in not only the new year but the dawn of a new century, with nothing but favourable observations.

Tony may want to make love to Eleanor with every fibre of his being, but apart from the fact that he wanted this special moment in their lives to be when his ring was on her finger as well as under his own roof he had come to like and respect Sir Miles, and had no intention of abusing either his trust or faith in him by taking advantage of being constantly in Eleanor's company for a whole week. It may have put something of a strain on his self-control, but no one looking at Tony would have had the least guess that he was counting down the hours before he could marry Eleanor and make love to her with a clear conscience.

As Tom's opinion ran parallel to his wife's in that it was monstrous Eleanor should find herself forced to publicly mourn a man who had committed such vile crimes as well as treating her in a way he could only describe as despicable, he had no difficulty in understanding the hypocrisy Eleanor must obviously be feeling in having to feed society's idea of convention and propriety. He easily understood the needs of two people who were not only very dear to him but clearly meant to be together and who were finding the enforced waiting unbearable. Naturally, Eleanor did not confide in him as she did with Beatrice, but having observed her despondency during Tony's absence in New York Tom knew that she was as eager for her wedding to take place just as much as Tony. Tom knew that Beatrice had always enjoyed a loving and comfortable relationship with her brother, but it was only to be expected that there were certain things Tony would not confide to her as he did to himself, such as how he was finding the waiting to make Eleanor his own in every sense as being almost unbearable. Having fallen in love with Beatrice at first sight and suffered the same desires and longings which Tony was now striving hard to curb for Eleanor, Tom truly empathised with his brother-in-law over his inner torment. Tony's regular visits to Bruton Street in addition to his daily meetings with Bill, certainly helped make the waiting more tolerable, but as January gave way to February, which saw Eleanor entering the last phase of her period of mourning, Tom was not in the least surprised when his brother-in-law confessed to him that the past eleven months had seemed like an eternity.

Eleanor, having shyly confided much the same thing to Beatrice, was at least able to find some outlet by making certain plans for her wedding, which not only included what she had in mind for her wedding dress but also where she wanted the ceremony to take place as well as where she wanted to go on honeymoon, a decision which came as some surprise to Beatrice.

"Well," she nodded, "now that Childon Manor is habitable again, I know that Tony fully intends to take you there immediately after the wedding for a week, but I thought that afterwards you may like to go to Paris or…"

Eleanor shook her head, explaining to Beatrice on a barely suppressed shudder that the very thought of Paris for a honeymoon was quite repugnant to her, a circumstance her future sister-in-law had not previously considered, but now, after only a moment's thought, agreed how distasteful it would be with all those unpleasant memories of Braden. "I have discussed this with Tony," Eleanor smiled, "and although he had every intention of taking me somewhere following a week spent at Childon Manor, I really do prefer to stay there for the three weeks of our honeymoon before we leave for New York."

Over time, Beatrice had become accustomed to her brother ferrying back and forth across the Atlantic, but now he had come into his grandfather's title, like Tom, she had wondered how Tony intended to deal with his dual interests when he married Eleanor. Although he had remarked once that it was not practical to juggle two inheritances in the air at the same time, made worse by the thousands of miles which separated them, Tony was not the type of man to shelve his obligations any more than he was to turn his back on something for any reason whatsoever. He had had responsibilities laid upon him by his father and grandfather and he was therefore determined to honour not only the legacy of the latter but the love and trust of the former, and so had decided that the only sensible arrangement as far as he could see would be for him and Eleanor to spend six months of the year at Childon Manor and six months in the penthouse apartment in New York.

When Tony had put this proposition to Eleanor and asked how she felt about it, she had looked lovingly up at him, her hands cupping his face, saying softly, "I told you once that it wouldn't matter if you were a pauper living in a hovel, I would still love you and want to marry you and, as for where we live, oh my darling," she said huskily, "you must know that I don't care as long as we are together!"

This response may have helped him resolve a situation which had occupied his mind, but it did nothing to help him contain his need of her, but since he could not think of words fitting enough to convey his feelings, he merely took her in his arms and kissed her, this pleasurable way of sealing their future being entirely satisfactory to both parties.

Eleanor's eventual emergence from her period of mourning merely served to represent nothing more than the shedding of the last remnant of a most painful and unhappy period of her past, and Tony's subsequent proposal of marriage conclusively symbolised the beginning of a future she never thought she would have with the man she unquestionably knew she could not live without. It was all so very different to that other proposal of marriage; a marriage she had never wanted and which had made her so very unhappy, but when Tony, within minutes of leaving Sir Miles's study having been given his permission as well as his blessing, took her hands in his and looked lovingly if not just a little hopefully down at her, asking, "Ellie, will you do me the very…" then, helplessly shrugging his shoulders, said, on a heartfelt sigh, "Ellie, my darling, will you *marry* me?" all thoughts of what had gone before he entered her life disappearing.

Her fingers moved in his and, smiling mistily up at him, asked, "Do you really need me to answer that?"

"No," Tony told her in a deep voice, slowly shaking his head, "but I sure would like to hear you say you will!"

"Oh, Tony!" she said huskily, removing her hands from his and folding her arms around his neck. "Of course I will marry you. It is what I want more than anything else in life!" Not surprisingly, it was some little time before he released her for long enough for him to slide his engagement ring onto her finger, replacing the narrow band of gold she unhesitatingly removed without guilt or regret.

If there were those who shook their heads or whispered snide comments to their friends and acquaintances behind the smiles that they knew all along how it would be, they were but few. For the most part, the news of Eleanor's engagement to Tony was well received, even by those who did not personally know her but had taken to the distraught young woman over the course of the inquest and the trial, their hearts going out to one who had suffered terribly at the hands of a man they would never have thought capable of such infamies.

As neither the prospective bride nor groom wanted a long engagement, the marriage of Anthony Ambrose Mortimer Mawdsley-Dart, seventh Viscount Childon, to Eleanor Amelia Collett née Tatton, was therefore arranged to take place at two o'clock on Monday 2nd April in the ancient church at Childon Magna where every member of the Mawdsley family had not only been married and christened but worshipped for generations. The day dawned bright and dry with not a cloud in the sky to suggest a shower or heavy downpour was likely to mar the day's proceedings which, declared Beatrice, entering Eleanor's room with her breakfast tray just after ten o'clock, was just the right weather for a wedding.

'The Mawdsley Arms Hotel', situated a mile outside the market town of Childon Magna, which had been a significant trading centre for

centuries, had not only the privilege of accommodating Eleanor and Beatrice as well as Toby and Patrick and Alice, who was the only bridesmaid, and Sir Miles, father of the bride in addition to a very emotional Sarah and Mary for the past two days, but also for preparing the wedding reception. Beatrice, who was just a little superstitious, had adamantly forbidden Tony to ride over to the hotel from Childon Manor where he was staying with Tom to see Eleanor, telling him firmly after he had seen them all safely installed on the afternoon of their arrival that it was bad luck for the groom to see the bride the day before the wedding and he would have to manage with Tom's sole company for the next thirty-six hours or so, to which her husband cocked a laughing eye at his brother-in-law. Not all Tony's persuasions would move Beatrice because although she was really quite romantic at heart her fear of breaking with superstition, even for two people who were very dear to her, was such that she remained steadfast.

"Are you superstitious too?" Tony smiled at Eleanor before taking his leave of her, clasping her hands in his and holding her a little at arm's length.

"Well, I suppose I am a little," she confessed, smiling mischievously up at him, "but not to *that* extent."

He laughed and, drawing her to him, groaned agonisingly before he kissed her goodbye, "You know, I get the very strong feeling that the next thirty-six hours are going to be the longest I have ever lived through!"

Eleanor had the feeling they would be for her too, but as she followed him out of the private sitting room set aside for their use some minutes later, upon hearing him laugh, "Okay, Bea, you don't have to say it, I'm going!" as he came upon her in the hall with her hand tucked in Tom's arm, brought a smile to her face, a smile which told her future sister-in-law that if ever two people were clearly made for one another it was her brother and Eleanor.

Tony's strong feeling proved true. Despite the relaxed atmosphere at Childon Manor and the enjoyable company of Tom, the next thirty-six hours were most definitely the longest he had ever lived through. On the eve of his wedding Tom engaged him in a game of snooker in the billiard room after dinner, but although Tony appeared perfectly relaxed as he walked around the table and struck the balls, his dinner jacket discarded and white bow tie and top buttons of his shirt and waistcoat unfastened, it was noticeable to his brother-in-law that he was not fully concentrating, and when he saw Tony later strike the balls with his cue signifying defeat, he was sure of it.

A rueful smile twisted Tony's lips. "Yes, I know, I should not have lost that frame. Sorry Tom," he shook his head, "I guess my mind's not on the game."

"I would never have guessed," Tom grinned, returning his cue to the rack. "Of course," he sighed, "as your best man it is not only my duty to get you to the church on time tomorrow as well as making sure one or the other of us does not forget the ring, but to try to keep you reasonably well entertained in the meantime. I don't seem to be doing a very good job."

"You're doing a great job, Tom," Tony smiled, laying his cue on the table, "it's just that…"

"You're preaching to the converted, remember?" Tom reminded him.

"Sure, I know," Tony smiled, picking up his jacket from where he had left it over the back of a chair and slinging it over one shoulder.

"It is also my duty as best man to make sure you remain sober," Tom grinned, patting him on the back, "but what do you say to a whisky and soda? You look as though you could do with one, and so could I if it comes to that!"

For two men happy in each other's company, established in comfortable leather chairs on either side of the fireplace in the study; Tony, with his long legs stretched out in front him with his whisky glass in one hand and a cigarette in the other, and Tom, reclining at his ease watching the smoke from his cigar curl up into the atmosphere in between savouring his whisky and soda, the next few hours passed very agreeably. Not until the clock struck two o'clock and the last embers of the fire flickered and died did they make their way upstairs to bed, Tom pausing before opening the door to his room to say, "I wonder if Bea and Eleanor have had a heart-to- heart?"

Tony smiled. "I'd say it stands a pretty good chance."

"Yes," Tom nodded, "so do I."

"Although," Tony grinned, "I doubt they're up this late."

"Sorry, Tony," Tom said ruefully, "I'm not doing a very good job of best man keeping you up until this time of the morning."

"Forget it," Tony dismissed, "I've never felt less like sleeping."

"I can understand that," Tom nodded, "but if you don't want Bea and Eleanor to guess how we've spent most of the night I suggest you try to close your eyes for a while," to which Tony nodded. Tom paused a moment, then, raising an eyebrow, asked, not that he really needed to, "No regrets, Tony?"

"Sure I have," Tony laughed, "but none at all about Eleanor! Nor doubts either!" Then, slapping him on the shoulder, said, 'Night Tom."

If Eleanor thought the next thirty-six hours would be the longest she had ever lived through as Tony believed they would for him, she was mistaken. With so much to do and last-minute arrangements to take care of, not to mention being kept thoroughly entertained by her future niece and nephews, they flew by. She had enjoyed her heart-to-heart with Beatrice, although as Tony had rightly pointed out to Tom they did not sit up until the early hours, but when she finally opened her eyes the next morning she could not help feeling that she had waited a whole lifetime for this moment, so much so that she could only toy with the breakfast Beatrice put in front of her, the fluttering of excitement in her stomach taking away her appetite, but upon being told that going to church on an empty stomach was not at all the thing, she did at least manage to eat some of it.

But that fluttering of excitement refused to go away, in fact it unfurled deliciously inside her as the morning wore on, making it almost impossible for her to be still in order for Mary to help her dress and thread the delicate strand of small diamanté stars through her hair, which she had elected to wear loose to cascade down her back like the photograph she had seen of the Empress Elisabeth of Austria when she had worn that famous Worth 'star' dress. Beatrice, entering Eleanor's room to take a look at her, declared that nothing could complement the delicious confection of ivory-coloured satin and gauze of her dress better than her hair or the diamond and sapphire brooch Tony had given her pinned just beneath her left shoulder. Beatrice had a fairly good idea what Tony would think when he saw Eleanor, but deciding to keep this to herself she sailed away to see how Nanny Susan was progressing with the children before placing herself in the hands of Sarah.

Eventually though, Eleanor was left alone with her father, who told her that he was extremely pleased with this marriage and that he was very proud of her. "So too would your mother if she could see you now," whereupon he fondly embraced her. "I love you very much, my dear," he said softly.

"Yes," Eleanor smiled, laying her hand against his cheek, "I know, and I love you very much too." There was no time for more as the carriage drew up outside to take them to the church.

Unlike her marriage to Braden this was no big society affair, just a happy and unpretentious ceremony comprising family and friends to celebrate the joining together of a man and a woman in matrimony who had met and fallen in love. The look in Tony's eyes as he watched Eleanor walk down the aisle towards him on her father's arm more than adequately proved Beatrice's conjectures right about what he thought at the sight of such an exquisite vision and Tom, that his brother-in-law most definitely had no regrets or doubts whatsoever.

Sir Miles, a far happier man than he had been at Eleanor's previous wedding, had neither doubts nor qualms about handing her into the safekeeping of a man who, unless he was very much mistaken, would take the greatest care of his daughter. Bill, having arrived in Childon Magna only a couple of hours ago due to a previously arranged commitment he could not get out of, was conscious of a lump forming in his throat as he watched the man he had a deep and genuine affection for firmly and unequivocally commit himself to the woman he had been perfectly ready to shield to the point of damaging his own reputation; wishing that his father and mother could have lived to see this day. Mrs. Timms, sitting next to her new husband who was comfortingly patting her hand as she sniffed into her handkerchief, watched the happy couple with joy tinged with relief, thanking Providence for delivering that dear sweet creature from the claws of Sir Braden Collett and 'that woman', who, she had told Jerry on more than occasion, had got off extremely lightly.

But for the two people standing at the altar the church may as well have been empty, conscious of no one but each other, and when Tony slid his ring onto her finger and uttered the words, "*With this ring I thee wed,*" in a deep and moving voice, Eleanor raised misty eyes to his, a stray tear of pure joy falling down her cheek. Upon seeing her brother gently wipe it away with his forefinger Beatrice's emotions overcame her and found it necessary to hurriedly search for her handkerchief, but when Tony was at last told by a smiling Reverend Thomas that he may now kiss the bride, she was quite unable to stifle the sob which formed in her throat.

Had anyone asked Eleanor what she remembered of her wedding day she would have been able to say all of it, particularly the moment when she had come up to stand beside Tony at the altar and how he had lowered his head to tell her in an intimate whisper, "You look so beautiful," with such a look in his eyes that her breath stilled in her lungs. It was a look she would see countless times in his eyes throughout their life together and it was there when he handed her up into the carriage after the reception, having divested themselves of their wedding clothes and waved goodbye to the group standing on the pavement, he turned, asking tenderly, "Happy?"

"*Very*," she said contentedly, resting her head against his shoulder as his arm slid around her waist.

"No regrets?" He shook his head questioningly.

"No regrets," she confirmed huskily, bringing her hand to rest against his cheek. "And you?"

"Huh huh," he confided softly, kissing the palm of her hand, "none; in fact," he smiled, "I can't wait to prove to you that not only do I have no regrets but just how happy I am," taking a moment to kiss her. "Unfortunately though," he sighed, "the inside of a carriage is hardly the place, besides which, it only takes a few minutes to reach Childon Manor. In fact," he told her quietly, glancing over his shoulder through the carriage window, "we're here."

Easing herself a little away from him Eleanor leaned forward and saw the red brick castellated walls of the gatehouse, a sharp intake of breath leaving her lips, "Oh, Tony, it's beautiful!"

"I think so," he said quietly, his eyes following her gaze. "I'll show you all round the place over the next few weeks."

Neither of them spoke as the carriage rumbled slowly through the gatehouse archway before gradually picking up speed to cover the three-quarters of a mile sweep of the drive to the house, a three-storey red-bricked building comprising a central edifice with two graduated wings either side that glowed warm in the late afternoon sun and whose doors were flung wide open with every member of his household standing outside waiting to greet them. Alighting from the carriage Tony then helped Eleanor to descend the steps, but even before she realised what was happening he picked her effortlessly up in his arms, surprising not only herself but Carter the butler, two footmen, four maids, the housekeeper and the cook. Having talked of little else but the wedding since their return from the church the sight of His Lordship carrying his bride across the threshold was quite unexpected, but it made the maids lower their eyes and giggle behind their hands, the footmen to look straight ahead of them at nothing in particular and the cook and housekeeper to smile indulgently.

Carter, who had been butler in His Lordship's grandfather's time, was not at all sure whether to condemn such a display or not, but whilst he may be in no position to take His Lordship to task for whatever he may choose to do he could certainly rebuke his staff, which he instantly did by giving each of them frowning looks from out of his sharp blue eyes. The maids were instantly called to order, bobbing curtsies as Tony briefly introduced them to his wife as he passed them with her still in his arms, a word of thanks and a smile to the cook and housekeeper and a nod to the footmen before entering the house, leaving the maids to giggle and shake their heads as they followed in their wake with Carter directly behind them, the cook and housekeeper to enter the house at their leisure and the footmen bringing up the rear carrying the luggage.

The late Viscount Childon, as Carter knew very well, had been one of the old school who would never even have considered carrying Her late Ladyship over the threshold and, as for publicly displaying his feelings or emotions, he would rather have died than so demeaned himself. Of course, it could be that being half American accounted for his grandson's behaviour, not that Carter held that against him, not for a moment, in fact he liked His Lordship, had done in fact from the very moment he had met him when he first came here all those years ago, but even though his grandfather would have strongly deprecated such free and easy manners as His Lordship was now displaying, there was no denying that the seventh viscount, although there was no starch to him and being very approachable, nevertheless had an air of authority about him, doing credit to the title as well as being every inch a Mawdsley.

"The small sitting has been prepared as you requested, my lord," Carter told him as he followed him into the house.

"Thank you, Carter."

"Is there anything I can get Your Lordship?"

"No thanks, Carter," Tony threw over his shoulder, "don't need anything."

"Very good, my lord." Carter bowed. "And what time would Your Lordship like dinner served?"

"Whenever it's ready," Tony told him, disappearing into the sitting room still carrying his precious burden.

"Very good, my lord," Carter said faintly, quickly suppressing a grin from one of the footmen who had come up behind him in time to hear this exchange.

Eleanor, blushing and laughing into Tony's shoulder, raised her eyes to his brimming ones, exclaiming, "Oh Tony, they must think we have run quite mad!"

"Let them," Tony smiled, "although," he confessed a little ruefully, "I must admit I did not expect a welcoming committee, but having promised myself the pleasure of carrying you across the threshold I was firmly determined to do so come what may. You think I'm old-fashioned?"

"No," she said lovingly, resting her hand against his cheek, "I think you're really rather wonderful!"

"Sure I am!" he smiled.

For the next few minutes she was given no opportunity to say anything further, but when she was eventually set down onto her own two feet she was able to look around her, her eyes alighting on two photographs standing side by side on an occasional table set against the far wall. "This must be your father?" she said quietly, picking up the silver framed photograph.

"Yes," he nodded, coming to stand beside her.

"You're so very like him!" she said, not quite able to keep the wonder out of her voice for the likeness was truly pronounced.

"Yes," he nodded again, "very much so."

"And this is your mother? Ah, Beatrice!" she cried.

"She's the image of her," Tony smiled, "Alice too."

"Yes, they are," Eleanor said quietly. "Oh, Tony!" She shook her head, laying a hand on his arm. "How I wish I had known them!"

"So do I," he said softly. "I know you would have liked them as much as they would have liked you. In fact," he told her, hardly giving her time to put the photograph down onto the table before taking her in his arms, "they would have loved and adored you, just as I do."

"I like being loved and adored by you," she told him huskily, folding her arms around his neck.

Something between a groan and a deep throated laugh escaped his lips at this, then, after searching her face for a moment or two, spent some considerable time proving just how much he liked loving and adoring her, as much to her satisfaction as his own, in fact he had only just released her when Carter, following his discreet tap on the sitting room door, announced dinner would be served in three-quarters of an hour.

Thanks to Mrs. Barker, who had been the cook at Childon Manor for longer than she cared to remember and Mrs. English the housekeeper, whose sense of what was due to Lord Childon far exceeded his own, dinner was a rather sumptuous affair served in the main dining room, usually only used on formal occasions, which neither Tony nor Eleanor could do full justice to. As both these formidable women, indulgently overlooking the newlyweds' social solecism by failing to dress for dinner, remembered his mother very well and were always glad to welcome Beatrice whenever she came to visit as well as always having had a soft spot for His Lordship, they were fully prepared to do all they could to make Lady Childon welcome and feel at home and love her for his sake. This was not difficult because even if they had not been aware of the details regarding her late husband's goings-on and the despicable way he treated her, she being just as much a victim as all the others, and His Lordship's involvement in exposing the truth, it was impossible not to take to her for her own sake, so young and lovely as she was as well as clearly loving His Lordship as much as he loved her.

Unlike Mrs. Barker, Emily English's married title was a courtesy one as befitted her position, but although she had never been in love as the saying went, she recognised the signs in those who were and, unless she was very much mistaken, His Lordship and Lady Childon were very much in love. As with Carter, Mrs. English remembered His late Lordship very well and nothing would have induced him to so much as bestow a chaste salute upon his wife's cheek in public, unlike his grandson, who knew no embarrassment or qualms in openly showing the love he had for his wife, even going so far as to lightly kiss her on the lips before handing her into her own charge to show her the way to the impressive master bedroom. It could be that Carter was right in that it was most probably because His Lordship was half American that accounted for his ways being somewhat different to his grandfather's; he certainly had his father's easy way with him, a man she had liked the instant he had first been introduced to the family as His Lordship's late mother's second husband, but whatever the truth of it there was no disguising the fact that, kiss his wife in public though he may as well as wiping away a tear during the marriage ceremony, the seventh viscount was most truly the gentleman and, more to the point, a kind and caring one.

Having assured Eleanor that if there was anything she wanted she only had to say and that she would wait on her tomorrow for her instructions at whatever time to suit her convenience, Mrs. English eventually handed Her Ladyship over to Mary, nodding her approval at this young woman's ability to care for one such as Lady Childon. Mary, who found Mrs. English a little intimidating, was extremely relieved when she showed no signs of lingering as she prepared her mistress for bed because despite that nod of approval Mary would not put it past her to either comment or offer advice on how she could do something better. Since Eleanor had handed over all the jewellery Braden had bought her to his solicitor for him to give to Sir Hubert Collett, not wanting anything from the man who had made her life such a misery, the only jewellery she had was the pearl drops in her ears – a wedding gift from her father, the diamond necklace Tony had bestowed on her to celebrate their wedding, and the diamond and sapphire brooch which he had presented her with on her birthday. Mary, having relieved her of these and putting them safely away, then began to help her undress and comb out her hair, all the time chatting happily away about the wedding and how adorable Alice had looked and a hundred other things without pausing for breath, but as Eleanor looked upon her more as a friend than a personal attendant, she merely laughed and agreed where necessary. Mary, who had always been afraid of Sir Braden Collett and did not envy her mistress being married to him, would never forget the way he had dismissed her or the shock she had received upon discovering the truth, but she would always be grateful to Lord Childon for restoring her to her mistress's charge. However, deeming it prudent not to mention Sir Braden to her mistress, she enquired if there was anything else she could do for her and upon being told that there was nothing more tonight and she would ring for her when she was ready in the morning, she bobbed a curtsey, smiled, said goodnight and left.

So far Eleanor had seen only a tiny part of the interior of Childon Manor and it was certainly impressive, yet despite its stateliness and grandeur, especially the dining room and entrance hall, there pervaded throughout a distinct feeling of homely comfort and welcome, particularly so in the small sitting room, having the immediate effect of filling her with a sense of having come home. Tony had told her he would show her all over the place during the next few weeks, but unless she was mistaken she had the very strong feeling that Mrs. English would regard it as her duty to take on the role of guide to the new mistress of the house, and whilst Eleanor would never offend her by refusing her company she would much rather see it all with Tony.

But there was no denying that Mrs. English kept everything in excellent order, yet for all that nothing was perfectly placed or positioned precisely spot on, making Eleanor feel afraid to move something even slightly out of position for fear that someone noticed and disapproved of it. From the moment Mrs. English had accompanied Eleanor upstairs it soon became evident that she was not going to have a separate bedroom to Tony as had been the case when she had lived in Cavendish Square, otherwise Mrs. English would certainly have wished her goodnight in the recently decorated and refurbished apartment designated for the mistress of the house she had briefly shown her, instead of escorting her into the master bedroom through the dressing room which separated the two. Even if Eleanor had not known that this was the master bedroom used by the head of the Mawdsley family for centuries, the various masculine items scattered all around would certainly have done so, but since she had no fault to find with this arrangement, in fact so thrilled at the thought was she that a little sigh of contentment left her lips. She took it for granted that Tony would go directly to the dressing room where he would change before joining her, the thought bringing a tinge of colour to her cheeks and a spiral of anticipation to unfurl deliciously in the pit of her stomach, unable to prevent herself from glancing expectantly across at that mahogany door as she pulled back the covers and slid into bed.

Tony had told her before she accompanied Mrs. English upstairs that he would not be long, and even though it had only been a little over three-quarters of an hour ago when she had left him, the waiting seemed unbearable. But just as she rested her head contentedly back against the pillows to blissfully close her eyes, wondering how long he would be, she heard the sound of the other bedroom door opening and closing and knew it was Tony. As she heard him moving about in the dressing room her fingers instantly clutched the soft coverlet, not from fear or trepidation as when she had sat rigidly upright in bed in Cavendish Square waiting for Braden; tense and fearful and praying to God to let her die, but in breathless anticipation. After what seemed like an eternity but was in fact only a little over fifteen minutes, the door opened and Tony walked in wearing the dark blue dressing gown she had seen him wear over his pyjamas when he had stayed with her in Mount Street, but it was not the memories this stirred inside her that brought a tinge of colour to her cheeks but that warm and loving look in his eyes which never failed to make her heart somersault.

"I wasn't certain whether you would be ready or not," he told her gently as he sat down on the edge of the bed, taking her hands in his, "but the truth is, I couldn't wait any longer."

"You couldn't?" Eleanor breathed, hardly above a whisper.

"No," Tony said softly, slowly shaking his head, "not loving you the way I do." Something like a sob left her throat at this, her fingers trembling in his. "I love you, Ellie," he said simply, "that's all I know; *that,*" he emphasised, his voice deepening, "and how empty and meaningless my life would be without you."

"Oh, Tony, I do love you so *very much*!" she said wholeheartedly, putting up no resistance when he gathered her in his arms.

"You'd better," he told her a little unsteadily, "because I sure love you!" His kisses more than adequately confirming this. "Do you have any idea how I've ached to make love to you; to spend the whole night with you and to wake up in the morning with you there beside me in my arms?" he asked her somewhat hoarsely a few minutes later.

"Yes, I do," she confessed, smiling shyly up at him, "ever since I was in Mount Street and you used to carry me up to bed and stayed with me throughout the night." She felt his arms tighten around her and the quickening beat of his heart as she snuggled her cheek against his chest. "That one time when I woke up to find you stretched out in the chair beside the bed with your hand holding mine was the most beautiful moment of my whole life," she told him huskily. "I wanted you to make love to me so desperately; I have gone on wanting you to make love to me."

"God knows I wanted to!" he groaned. "But even though I was going insane with wanting to make love to you, I couldn't do it. It was not just because it would have been unpardonable of me to abuse Tom and Bea's trust in such a way as well as taking an unforgivable advantage of *you*, but I wanted to make love to you when *my* ring was on your finger and not Collett's and I had you safely under my own roof." He brushed her lips with his own, admitting unsteadily, "You see, my darling, I wanted a clear conscience when I did so."

"Yes," she nodded, a little mischievous smile hovering at the corner of her mouth and her eyes looking playfully up at him, "it is always best to have a clear conscience, but now that I *do* have your ring on my finger and I *am* safely under your roof," her trembling fingers sliding slowly beneath the lapels of his dressing gown, "that is precisely what you *do* have."

An agonised groan left his throat at this and Eleanor, who had often wondered what it would be like to have Tony make love to her, was soon brought to realise that not all her imaginings had prepared her for the beautiful reality of it. Where Braden had virtually ripped off her nightdress in his impatience, Tony's gentle fingers leisurely and pleasurably removed it; where Braden's lips had disgusted her, Tony's lovingly caressed her; where Braden had viciously dug his teeth painfully into her soft skin and his hands repulsively roamed her body, Tony's unhurriedly and provocatively aroused and excited her to the point where she thought she would die from the sheer joy and pleasure of it. But the worst thing of all had been when Braden had forcefully and repugnantly imposed the final degradation upon her with sickening revulsion, so very different to the sensitive, almost reverent way Tony ultimately honoured their love for one another, the humble cry of her name against her lips stifling any words of hers, but as she blissfully melted into him and gave herself up to him in unconditional surrender, words were really quite beside the point.

He had told her once that he was just an ordinary guy doing everything he could to protect the woman he loved, disclaiming any pretension to being a knight-errant or anything so perfect. But this ordinary guy who had placed his ring on her finger today; who loved and needed her and who was now making glorious love to her, had proved not only by his actions but his own personal code of conduct that he did not need impressive ancestry or claims to knight-errantry to make him precisely what he was; a man of impeccable credentials.

Printed in Great Britain
by Amazon

55739330R00395